# RUSSIAN ROULETTE

## SAPPHIRE KNIGHT

# SECRETS

# SECRETS

# WARNING

This content contains material that may be offensive to some readers, including graphic language, dangerous and adult situations.
Some situations may be hotspots for some readers.

Any reproductions of this work not deemed by the author, Sapphire Knight, is Copyright Infringement and against the law.

Dedicated to

# my sons

**Jr-** For thinking I'm some famous Author. When in reality, I'm just another little fish, swimming in a great big ocean.

**Jay-** For always getting Momma her laptop and another soda. You have no idea just how important your job really is.

# Russian words
## utilized throughout Secrets

**Красивая** (kraaseevee) - Beautiful

**Красота** (Krasaaveetsa) - Beauty

**Большой босс** *(Balshoy Shef)* - Big Boss

**Босс** *(Shef)* - Boss

**Брат** *(Braat)* - Brother

**Пончик** *(Пончик)* - Donut

**Отец** *(Atyets)* - Father

**Ебать** *(Poshyol )* – Fuck

**Маленькая** (mallenkee) - Little

**Бог, я хотел ебать Вы так плохо красоты** *(Bawg,ya khatyets poshyol Vee так plawkha* Krasaaveetsa) - God, I want to fuck you so bad beauty

**Я утверждаю, вы как шахта красоты навсегда** *(YA praava vee как maya* Krasaaveetsa, *nafsegDA)* - I claim you as mine beauty forever

**Шахта** *(Maya)* - Mine

**Мой брат** *(Moy braat)* - My Brother

**Жаркое** *(zazhaareets)* - Roast

**Russkaya Mafiya**- Russian Mafia

**Торт** - Type of Russian dessert

**Сестра** *(Saystraa)* - Sister

**Она является шахта** *(Anaa maya)* - She is mine

**Сын** *(sin)* - Son

**Корзина** *(moosar)*- Trash

**Да** *(Da)* – Yes

Three sources were checked for the Russian Language. If it's not to your liking, I apologize. It's meant to help with the setting, to draw you in and help you connect with the characters.

# ONE

## EMILY

**D**EEP BREATHS, DEEP BREATHS, MMMM AHHHHHH, mmm ahhhh.

Geez, I gotta relax before I give myself a panic attack. I can't believe I'm stuck starting at a new school and had to skip a semester of my sophomore year. Definitely is not what I had imagined looking into the future for myself.

University of Tennessee; I look around and can't help but feel some excitement. The scent of the freshly-cut campus lawns, bees buzzing happily, and big bushes of Knock Out roses adorn some of the corners along the sidewalks. The buildings are huge, making the many groups of people appear small. All this orange reminds me of home and makes me love it more.

No one knows who I am or anything about me and that gives me a sense of safety, finally. Not that I'll be out when it's dark, walk by any shadows or leave my windows open. I'm not completely stupid or oblivious to my own safety, even if I am far away. I have been known to be slightly naive, but do my best not to be.

I glance at the pink carbon copy of my schedule again. Ugh.

I'm taking all my classes early in the morning. This way I don't have to be out in the evenings and it sucks, royally. I'm so not a morning person and to say I'm a little paranoid is extremely accurate.

First on the agenda is Government II. This should be interesting, or not. I'm definitely going to have to take major notes. I've always been pretty smart, but come on, History and Government? No way. Too boring for even the intelligent people.

I can seriously see this lecture going in one ear and out the other. Thank God for my Route 44 soda. One thing I love about the south is our many options for huge beverages.

Naturally, I make my way to sit in the back of the lecture hall. I really hope I can blend in unnoticed, and perhaps get an occasional nap in if needed. The room is huge with rows of plain, brown tables and standard chairs. There's a solid, black podium at the front of the room for the professor and an oversized whiteboard placed behind it, for easy use.

I'm sure my massive Styrofoam cup is like a white beacon in front of me, amongst these Starbucks drinkers. All this coffee-smelling air is making me miss my best friend, London. Missing London makes me miss home.

God, I wish I could be in Texas.

Hopefully one day I can go back to my granddaddy's land. I better call London's brother, Elliot, to make sure everything's going okay with him taking care of the house and land. I keep forgetting with everything going on. I never expected moving a few states would be so draining and stressful.

I'm brought out of my thoughts by a bright smile and chipper voice, "Hi! Boy, I hope this class doesn't suck, you know? It's so hard having a class this early that requires me to think. I'm Avery, nice to meet you," she babbles as she slides into the chair next to me.

I guess I'm no longer alone back here in my hermit-like world. I should have known potential nap time was too good to be true. I don't enjoy early conversation, but this pretty girl looks like she may talk my ear off regardless.

"Hi, I'm Emily." I shoot her a small smile. "Nice to meet you too, Avery." I normally love meeting new people, I'm just sleepy and it kind of makes me a grouch.

"Have you had Mr. Pottsmooth before?" She slides into the chair next to me, dumping her bag on top of the desk. "I haven't but I heard he can be tough if you don't study hard. But I sooo need this class, so what can you do, right?" Avery pulls out a hot pink notebook and a bright blue pen to go with it. "Oooh! I know—we can be study partners, maybe it'll make this class a little fun?" She gazes at me with a hopeful look and I attempt to return it with a friendly expression.

I really don't know what to respond to at this moment. She just asked me like ten questions and I'm not even halfway through my soda yet. She seems really sweet though, maybe just nervous. Unless, perhaps Avery talks this much all of the time?

"No, I haven't had him before, either," I mumble and chew on my lip.

Saved! In walks Professor Humpty Dumpty by the looks of it. I can't help but snort a little to myself. He and his big belly are stuffed in a terry cloth track suit. I didn't even know they made those for men. Are they even allowed to wear that to work? I know this is college, but there has to be some type of dress code for instructors, surely.

Once that disaster of a lecture is over with, I'm cornered once again by Avery.

A cheeky smile graces her face as she talks way quicker than your average southerner, "Wow, definitely didn't see that one coming!" She gestures, talking with her hands, "Did you see what that man was wearing? And he totally talked monotone the whole class. I mean, who does that? Not raise your voice a decibel and talk through your nose the whole time." She starts giggling, thoroughly amused, and I have to chuckle along with her. Avery just has such a cheery bubble around her that pulls you in and she's kind of a silly mess.

"So Emily, I work at this great little coffee shop a few blocks away. It's called 'A Sip of Heaven,' cheesy, I know. Anyhow, wanna go have a cup and talk about all these stupid requirements for this class?"

"Sorry Avery, but I have to get to my other class. Maybe some other time we can meet for some ice cream or something?"

That's if she's even really serious about us being friends. A few people to hang out with here might make it more bearable with the amount of homework it seems I'm going to have. I need to surround myself with at least a few female friends.

"OH MY GAWD! I love ice cream! Okay, that sounds great!" She grabs my phone quickly and my eyes go wide. Geez, I thought I was going to drop it and that's the last thing I need.

Avery calls her phone before I even realize what she's up to and hands it back when hers rings with some rock song. "Okay, friend, program my number since you have it now and I'll text you later so we can meet up."

Just as quickly as she swooped in, she's off, bouncing down the hallway. I think I might really end up liking this girl a lot. If only we met after ten in the morning, I would have had much better conversation skills. Avery grins, waving happily as she makes her way down the large beige hallway and I wave back.

Thankfully, the rest of my day breezes through swiftly and with no drama. The lectures dragged a little, but that's pretty standard for the first classes. So far, Avery's the only person I've said more than a few words to. I didn't realize how lonely this would be, moving out here all alone, with no one knowing where I am. Well, minus London and her family.

I had to do it though. I had very little choice left if I wanted to be safe in the future. I'm going to keep on trekking through and just try to be grateful I have a chance to start fresh. I have to remind myself that I almost wasn't this lucky. I nearly wasn't able to get out. I thank my lucky stars daily for my momma watching over me and good people that helped me.

I wasn't expecting Avery to text me right away, but she did. She invited me out to eat and I have to say I'm pretty excited to meet her for dinner. I can handle being on my own the majority of the time but there is nothing worse than eating by yourself.

I hadn't even made it in the door of my apartment after classes without having three new text messages from her. Maybe I won't end up being too lonely after all, at least I hope not. Her cheery persona seems to just rub off and makes you want to surround yourself with that type of person. On top of that I didn't have much to remember from my first set of classes either. I'd say it was a good morning.

I don't have very much money to splurge on going out, but because of Granddaddy's life insurance he set up before he was taken from me, I'm able to eat out and not completely penny-pinch. Once I turned eighteen, I was able to access my momma's life insurance policy. My granddad never spent a cent, always saying it should be for when I was starting my own life without him. Thank God for his stubbornness and future planning or I wouldn't be here in Tennessee right now.

Avery invited me to a bar and grill called 'The Flamingo Grill.' I had never heard of it but promised to meet her. Wherever doesn't matter as long as it's close to my apartment. I'm not looking to get lost just yet. This city is overwhelming as it is.

My granddaddy's teal, 1965 Ford F100 pickup truck he left me when he passed doesn't have GPS. She drives like a dream and I couldn't imagine driving something other than this beauty. This girl might be a classic, but thankfully, in this heat, her air conditioner works like she's brand new.

I didn't realize Tennessee was going to be more humid than Texas when I packed up and moved out here. Hello muggy afternoon. I know it could be plenty worse; at least I have the right clothes. I could be stuck up north, freezing my tush off.

I take extra care sorting through my tiny closet, picking out which sundress and boots I'm planning on wearing this evening. For my usual attire, I'll just throw on the first one I come across. I really want to look nice today; I have no idea what the dress code is for this place. Shoot, in Texas a sundress and boots works wherever you go, so that is pretty much what my closet is full of.

Sifting through the many colors, I pick a pale yellow that's one of my favorites. It falls over me perfectly and it still looks new enough to wear out to eat in. The dress stops above my knees tastefully and my brown cowboy boots that have a pretty 'choker' on each, completes my outfit nicely.

I throw on some Clinique Lash Doubling mascara in black. Then twist a few curls in my long, dirty blonde hair with my curling iron, and boom! I'm all set. I may not be runway ready, but this will definitely work for dinner.

As it turns out, The Flamingo is not that hard to find with its giant pink fake bird on the roof. Avery's sweet face is out front waiting for me when I pull into the lot. I park away from other vehicles. I can't have my baby girl getting scratched up from other people's negligence. Granddaddy would be turning in his grave if he saw me park too close.

"Hey, girl!" I holler and wave at Avery as soon as I open my door.

I give her a big smile as I walk toward her, weaving in between cars. There are two other rows of cars parked in front of my truck in the large parking lot. The place looks pretty busy as most of the spots are filled. Hopefully a lot of the vehicles belong to employees; I would hate it if there's a wait to be seated.

Avery meets me as soon as I step on the sidewalk near the front entrance. "Hey, Emily! Geez, you look so cute! I love your dress!" She grabs my hand while talking superfast, all excited like.

We make our way closer to the entrance and she leans in to talk lower for my ears only, "I hope you don't mind, but I ran into a couple of guys from one of my classes and they asked if we wanted to sit together. They are totally hot so of course I told them yes. I hope you don't mind. Girl, you are gonna be happy when you see these fine men!" She flashes me a brilliant smile after and I roll my eyes.

"Okay, Avery, but I'm not really looking to meet any guys. I'm just here to concentrate on school."

I am so not ready for another relationship. My life is way too complicated right now as it is. I know college guys are going to be after one thing anyhow and I'm for sure not looking for a hook up.

"Emily, you have to relax a little or you'll get burned out and we have barely bitten into this semester." She chastises me as we head towards two really good-looking guys, waiting inside by the hostess station. "Okay, here we arrrrrre! Miss Emily, this is Cameron Wentworth and Luka Masterson." She gestures towards them with her hand as if she's presenting some sort of prize.

I flash them a nervous little grin and wave my hand like a dork. Cameron is cute in that rich preppy jock style.

Clearing my throat, I mumble, "Hi, Cameron, nice to meet you."

"Hey, Emily, you too." He shoots me his bright white smile that I'm sure gets all the girls excited. I've seen his kind before and avoid them like the plague. I remember the jock types in high school, always floating around messing with as many girls as possible.

I look over to Luka and it's like a punch to the gut. He's freaking beautiful, like should be posing in a magazine type of good-looking. "Umm... Hi, Luka," I choke out.

Thank fuck I didn't stutter, sweet Jesus. I hope to God my mouth is shut right now and I'm not gawking like an idiot. I'm met with the most striking hazel eyes when I look up and I have to look up, this man is definitely pushing six foot-two or six foot-three.

"Hey, Emily, please call me Tate." His voice is smooth and rich like honey. The kind of voice that vibrates through your bones and wraps you up to make you feel warm inside. I love his name. You don't hear 'Tate' often. It suits him.

He reaches for my hand and when he touches me, I feel squiggles in my belly. I gasp in an almost silent breath. I hope he doesn't notice my reaction to him. This is the type of man that could steal me, own me and eventually break me. I'm already too broken as it is.

The tall, thin hostess leads us to our booth after a few brief moments of her collecting menus and wrapped silverware for us. I happily follow her through the main entry and around the bar. We got lucky not having to really wait. I know some restaurants around colleges have an hour or so wait time. I almost want to slip her a five for breaking up the awkward first impression, I'm sure I gave. However I doubt she noticed, since she was busy gawking at the guys.

We each slide in and she passes the menus to us, giving a spiel about our server and daily specials. The booth isn't too large, but we aren't exactly crammed in either. We have just enough room to feel the warmth of the person next to us. The tables are a shiny oak surrounded by rich, red leather covered booths.

Once we all settle in, I feel like a big nerd just staring. I can't help it though. Men shouldn't be allowed to be this good looking. It's not fair to the female population; we already have to grow up realizing we can't all be princesses, and  then life throws genes like this at us.

Tate is nicely built. He doesn't have that steroid bulk build like some of the men around campus I saw today, but he's in great shape. He has really short, dark brown hair. I could easily run my fingers through it. You know if I was looking to do that sort of thing, but I'm not. I can still daydream though. *Gosh, I bet it's really soft.*

Cameron is pretty cute himself. He's a few inches shorter than Tate but still easily towers over Avery and me. He's blessed with sandy blond hair, longer than Tate's and each time he grins, his chocolate brown eyes sparkle. The two of them together probably have to push the girls off each other with a stick.

Glancing at Tate, I attempt for some easy conversation, "Hey Tate, it sounds like you have a little bit of an accent. What is it?"

His eyes shine playfully as he gazes at me, "That's rich, coming from a sweet southern thing. You've got quite the twang yourself, sweetie."

I don't know if he is being a condescending dick to me or just taking the attention from my question to his comment. Regardless, I huff and keep quiet. I generally keep to myself until I know someone well anyhow. I just can't help myself from talking to him, it's like he sucks up all of the attention. This is good though, if I'm angry at him at least I won't be picturing his abs every time he speaks to me.

Thankfully, the server approaches to take our orders. Avery and Cameron dominate most of the conversation, so I can just sit back and watch Tate. It feels like I'm in a fuzzy dream, as my body hums with nerves. I don't want to stick my foot in my mouth and I don't really want to reveal much. I have to lie low and keep to myself. I need to be careful about too many people getting to know me. I hate having to make all new friends.

"Excuse me for a moment," I mumble, sliding out of the booth and heading for the bathroom. It'll give me a few moments to catch my bearings and pull myself together.

I come back from the restroom feeling a little more confident from the sporadic pep talk I gave myself in the women's stall to see Tate laughing. *God, he is handsome.* His laugh is deep and his eyes flicker with humor, it's like a vacuum pulling me to him. I can't help but wonder if I could make him smile and laugh that way.

I concentrate on eating my oversized baked potato that's loaded to the brim with butter, sour cream, cheese and bacon. It's delicious and I shovel it down quickly. With Granddad you learned to eat swiftly or you went hungry. He was in the military when he was young and has always been a fast eater.

I'm brought out of my brain freeze from my virgin Pina Colada I was busily sucking down by Avery's chipper voice, "Hey Emily, you ready to go?" She leans into me and bumps me with her elbow lightly, "These two kind gentlemen refuse to let us pay for our meals. Isn't that sweet?"

Avery is looking way too happy about this. Personally, I don't want to owe anybody anything, but this time I'm just going to act like it doesn't bother me. I leave the cool, sweet trance I was in with my beverage and smirk at the guys.

"Yep, I'm ready. And thank you, this is so kind of you to treat us to dinner. We owe you guys." I regret the words instantly. *Dumb ass.* I scold myself and shake my head a little. Just great, these guys probably think I'm a nut job.

"Well, speaking of owing, how about you give me your number? I might have trouble in a few of my classes and need your help someday." Tate's eyes gleam mischievously and I have to bite back my groan. Geez, did I not just say I didn't want to owe anybody anything? I guess this is better than a date or him wanting me to wash his car or something. Plus, I can always block his number if I need to.

Shrugging I say irritably, "Sure, if it's for help, then no problem, but I'm definitely no booty call," I say in my snarkiest voice possible. Maybe he'll change his mind.

Cameron laughs and chortles out, ribbing Tate, "Ohhhh, boom! Man, she put you in your place!"

Cameron looks like he just won the lottery and I'm his new best friend. I roll my eyes and turn my head away. Why do men have to act like jackasses sometimes?

"Shut your face Cameron, and no Emily, I am very aware you are not the type of girl to be just a random booty call. Trust me, I have plenty of females for just that purpose. Babe, you would know if you were going to be my booty call." He appears sincere and I don't know if that's a compliment or not, but at least we're on the same page.

We all trade numbers; Avery and Cameron way more enthusiastic than Tate and I. I think he may finally be getting it that I am not interested in him. It's probably a shock to his system, but I've had my fill of men to last awhile.

Avery and I thank the boys again for dinner. My southern manners drilled into me, almost makes it impossible for me to be mean to people. They insist on walking us to our vehicles. I agree grouchily. I may appear bitchy to them but it's on purpose. I don't want to give anyone the wrong impression and some men just don't get it when things are spelled out plain as day.

Avery doesn't have a vehicle so Cameron offers to give her a ride in his little Porsche. If I would have known that before I would have offered for us to ride here together. It would be nice to have someone who knows where exactly they are going. Judging by the look radiating on her face, I know I am going to hear all about it later. She is practically glowing.

"Thanks for inviting me, Avery; I'll see you in class," I hug

Avery and then high-five Cameron. "Bye, Cameron."

"Anytime, sweet cheeks, text me later!" She calls as they walk off. Avery is probably going to bounce out of her shoes; she's vibrating with so much excitement. *Yep, definitely going to hear about that!*

I quickly head to my truck parked all by its lonesome. It's a little spooky out here at nighttime, even with the night air whispering with the songs playing from the restaurant's outdoor speakers.

The air has cooled slightly but still feels thick. The bugs make crazy sounds, providing the illusion of the country, when in fact it's a busy city.

We make it to my truck and sense of comfort washes over me, just from being near something so familiar. "Thank you for walking me to my truck, Tate," I murmur gratefully.

I look around and take in my surroundings. The parking lot isn't packed, but there are quite a few cars. I'm always scanning for a certain face. I'm glad I don't have to walk to the truck by myself, I'd probably freak myself out and drop my keys.

"Hey, no problem. Wow! Nice ride, never pictured you in something like this."

"It was my granddad's. He built it all himself and gave it to me."

I smile fondly at her blue-green shimmer from the street lamps. I would trade this truck in a heartbeat, just to have him back. I miss him every single day. My chest always gets tight when I think of him, the man who took care of me for so long. Now I'm left without him, to make it on my own.

"Lucky girl. Hey, I meant what I said back there. I know you're not a booty call. You are way too sweet and beautiful to be mistaken as trashy." He gazes at me seriously. "Would you mind if I text you later though?" I stare at him for a beat and I think he looks like he's being pretty sincere, so why not.

"Okay you can text me," I reply without hesitation. "Good night, Tate." I smile slightly and look up into his hazel eyes.

I'm such a wimp. I put up no fight whatsoever. At this point he could ask for a back rub and I'd probably ask if he wanted lotion too. I'm sure this is how he starts with all females. He comes off as just wanting to be friends and then swoops in when they're least expecting it.

"Good night, *Krasaaveetsa*. (Beauty)"

He leans in to me and gives me a small hug. He smells so good; crisp and clean. His body is warm, and even in the small amount of contact we make I can feel him. He presses his full lips softly to my forehead and I melt.

For the first time in forever I feel safe.

# EMILY

I'M ROUSED OUT OF MY SLEEP BY THE DING OF AN incoming text. I sent London's brother, Elliot, a text last night, asking how the house was doing. He never replied back, but that's probably him now.

I poke my arm out of my comforter, flailing my hand around on my nightstand. I blindly search for my phone; I could open my eyes and actually look for it, but that would be too easy. It's nippy in here so I'm going to try to stay as covered up as possible.

My eyes bug out when I see it's in fact from Tate and not Elliot Traverson.

**Tate Masterson:** Good morning, Красота

Wow, I wasn't expecting him to text me. It's been two days since we had dinner. I thought guys were supposed to wait like three days to a week so they don't seem eager?

Okay, I have to break down and ask him what this name means. I have literally been thinking of it nonstop the past few days since I heard him say it. I wasn't sure exactly how I heard it pronounced or how it's spelled, or else I would have Googled it already.

Me: Hi, what does that mean?

Tate Masterson: What does what mean?

Me: You know! Красота?

Tate Masterson: It means pop tart.

Giggling, I flap the covers down to poke my head out. He has my heart racing excitedly and I know I won't be able to drift off to sleep again. I blink rapidly a couple times to clear my eyes and quickly type back.

Me: Pop tart! Seriously?

Tate Masterson: LOL! Have a good day, sweet Emily...

Me: I will figure it out! You too!

I can't help the beaming smile I have after our short conversation. It's been a really long time since someone has kind of flirted with me. Wait was that flirting? I think it was. My stomach flips, feeling a little giddy that he texted me after all.

Now I need soda, some clothes and then I'm off to class again. This early morning crap is for the birds. I reach under my small bed to find my twenty-four pack of Coca-Cola and pop one open. I take the first refreshing drink before my feet even hit the floor. The little zip of caffeine always helps me prepare for the day.

I brush my hair and blow-dry it slightly to get some creases out. Every time I sleep with it wet, I wake up looking like some crazed maniac. I go with a cute pink sundress, since I'm already in a happy mood. Pairing the dress with some tan wedges, since I'm barely pushing five foot-three inches, my look is complete. The shoes are the perfect help I need in the height department!

I grab my drink and backpack on my way out the door. I hope I didn't forget anything. I know my notes and stuff are in my bag, but I still get nervous. The college I came from was a little more laid back, so I'm trying to stay on my toes.

I make my way to building 119 for my Biology course with no issues, thankfully. I really enjoy the walk over even if I am slightly paranoid. I'm still a little scatterbrained with this new school. I had printed out the school map before I started and studied it countless times.

The green lawns of the university are so plush looking, I bet it would be comfortable to lie on and read a good book. I love how the sidewalks are lined with trees. They provide the perfect canopy of shade to escape some of the heat. Now if only there was a cool breeze to compliment it all.

I get into the stuffy Biology classroom and make my way down the aisle between the desks. I weave through until I find the perfect spot. I hate sitting with people to my back, but I know I have to be able to hear in order to pass this class. I just pray I don't end up having to dissect any creatures. That will be my breaking point.

A deep voice attempts to catch my attention but I stare straight ahead, attempting to ignore him, "Pssst... Hey... Pssst... Hey, Hey!"

OMG, it is way too early for any idiot to try to talk to me. After a few times, I glance back out of the corner of my eye. I don't want to give them my full attention and egg them on.

I'm met with blond hair and a sweet smirk. *Oh! It's Cameron!* He's sitting behind me, leaning his chair back on two legs.

"Hey, Cameron. You're going to hurt yourself!" I shake my head, chastising him. "I didn't see you when I came in or I would have said hello."

He's wearing his signature polo shirt; however, today it's in a different shade of grey. His white ball cap is pulled down low over his blood shot eyes and he looks exhausted. I bet if he stood up he'd be in khaki shorts.

He smirks, murmuring, "Hey, Goldilocks! It's cool, come sit by me."

*He didn't seem so bad at dinner, so what the hell, why not.* I pack my belongings back into my backpack and move beside him, attempting to quickly get resituated for this lecture. Surely this man won't talk as much as Avery does this early. He looks way too tuckered out for any meaningful conversation.

I scan the lecture hall and take in each of my classmates. I gaze at each face carefully, cataloging their features. *He's not here, you're safe.*

"Gosh, I hope I do okay in this class." I turn to him and smile a fake smile. No need for everyone to figure out I'm paranoid.

"Yeah, no kidding. Why do you think I asked you to sit by me?"

I start snickering a little until I hear a throat clear. A shadow falls over my desk and I look up. I stare straight into Luka 'Tate' Masterson's pissed-off hazel glare. God, he's even hotter when he looks mad. His cheeks flush slightly and he screams alpha.

"Well, good morning, sunshine!" I croon in the cheeriest voice I can, smiling brightly.

Tate looks fantastic today in a pair of nice-fitting jeans leading past his muscular thighs to some black Polo boots. He has the top of his black button-up shirt unbuttoned with the sleeves rolled up. *Look at those tattoos.* I didn't see them the other night at dinner. Who would have guessed this rich boy could pull off tattoo sleeves. I can't really make out what they are, but holy hotness, they make him look even sexier. He has that 'I'm a bad boy, don't fuck with me' look, going today.

Ugh, we all know I like them bad, too. With that thought, I cringe a little.

"Enjoying yourself with Wentworth, I see," he grumbles out. "Can I join you or is this a private party?" he huffs. Yep, definitely has the asshole gene. Geez, did he just growl at Cameron?

"Of course, you are welcome to sit here. You're also welcome to get some coffee or whatever you need before you come next time."

"Oh, baby, I don't need coffee to come. Your sweet smile will do just fine," he replies cockily and licks his lips.

"Seriously, Tate? I'm just going to move."

I glare at him, disgusted. I know I must be tomato red right now. I don't have time for this shit. Who does he think he is, talking to me like that?

"I'm really sorry *Krasaaveetsa* (Beauty). Forget I just said that. Stay, I'll behave, promise."

I roll my eyes and nod, irritated. Cameron scoots his chair over so Tate can sit in between us. I don't know why he didn't just sit on the other side of Cameron. I don't plan on talking to him, especially after that loser line. I was so excited about that text earlier, too.

Tate fist bumps Cameron, and then he puffs his yummy plump bottom lip out towards me. He tries to look sorry and innocent, but it just annoys me further. *I just want to bite that lip.* Holy shit, did I really just think that? No. No biting for me, focus. Think Biology, not man hunk with an accent. Is that Russian? I think that just raised his hotness factor even more. I am such a freaking goner.

I turn away from him and do my best to pay attention to the professor. Tate keeps brushing his arm against me, causing little goosebumps to erupt on my skin. I know he's doing it on purpose and I just want to kick him for it. I refuse to give in and look at him. This is going to be the longest class of my life.

I keep going back to the accent. Fuck, that's hot! Not only do I have to sit next to this absolutely gorgeous guy, but I have to smell him, too. He smells as good as he did last night at dinner. I think he's wearing Hugo Boss cologne. It's one of my favorites on a guy and it kind of makes me want to sit on his lap and sniff him everywhere. Maybe even lick his cheek at this point; I bet he tastes like a fine chocolate caramel candy. *Asshole.*

I didn't hear a word the professor said during that lecture. I stuff my things back into my bag quickly, pretending I'm in a super big hurry to get to my next class. After the longest two hours ever, I skirt out of class quickly and I give a quick "See ya," to no one in general.

I wave on my way out the door and practically run down the long hallway. I'm so glad my next class is pretty close by. I kind of expected Tate to follow me, but he didn't.

Neither Tate nor Cameron is in my next class so I can keep to myself like a hermit. I tuck back towards the rear of the room and pull my phone out. I may as well relax a little now that my body doesn't feel like it's vibrating any longer.

I sign onto London's Facebook page to troll around some. I don't have one really, so I share hers. What are best friends for, right? No one has posted anything about any jail release so I can take a deep calming breath. Another day, I don't have to worry about him finding me.

I definitely need a cool shower when I get out of class and a new pair of panties after that run in with Tate. My Facebook disappears when my phone flashes a new text from Avery. Still nothing from Elliot; I wonder if that punk got a new girlfriend or something. He's normally pretty quick to text me back.

**Avery:** Hey, chick! You should stop by the shop when you're done with class and visit me.

**Me:** Hi Avery! Do you have anything besides coffee and tea there?

**Avery:** Yes ma'am, hot chocolate.

**Me:** Oh! I LOVE hot chocolate! Okay, sounds like a plan. See you in about 20.

**Avery:** Awesomesauce!

I huff out a small laugh to myself. I know she's jumping up and down right now. That girl has so much energy all the time. Like a big happy bubble. I'm so lucky to have met someone like her so quickly.

I have to keep reminding myself to be careful. I wish I could just be happy and free like Avery. I don't know if I'll ever get to live without looking over my shoulder. I gaze at the girls hanging around campus—all so carefree—on the way to my truck. These chicks have no idea how easy they have it. Never having to worry about who could be following them, finding them, or hurting them.

That reminds me, I need to call London and see if she's heard anything about *him*. I know she said she would text but I have to make sure he's still in jail. London's been my best friend since we were five years old and started kindergarten. I know I can trust her but I just have this weird feeling. I'm probably over reacting but I can't let him find me. I can't go through that again.

God, I miss home. I wish I could feel the sweet Texas air on my granddaddy's land, softly kissing my skin. I love to just lie in the grass and look up at the beautiful stars. I want to be able to stroke my horse Thunder's soft mane and tell him everything that I'm thinking of. Just like I always have in the past.

*I want to go home.* No, this is home now. I have to learn to love Tennessee. I don't know if I'll ever get to go back to Texas again.

With that sad thought, I pull open the door to A Sip of Heaven. Drawing in a deep breath, I paste a big, fat, fake smile on my face. My mask.

Standing behind the dark green counter, Avery beams a cheerful, bright smile in my direction as I come in the door. "Hey, pretty little Emily! How's it going?" I think Avery must be the most content person I know. She is literally happy and smiling every single time I see her. I envy her so much.

"Hi, it's going okay, glad to be out of that boring-ass class, that's for sure! How's work?"

Avery has on her cute little apron and matching green polo shirt. She's the picture-perfect coffee shop employee today. She has her pretty, wavy, brownish hair tied up in a high ponytail. Adorable little silver coffee cup earrings dangle from her ears and bright pink painted nails.

Shrugging, she eyes me curiously, "Eeegh, its fine, kind of boring. Although I did see a hot man hunk, by the name of Cameron Wentworth and his dark haired god of a best friend, Luka Masterson. They mentioned something about a saucy little blonde yelling at Luka, that he needed coffee," she giggles uncontrollably and I wince. "Know anything about that?"

"Oh My God, shoot me now!" I place my head in my hands and prepare to defend myself, "I did not yell at him! He was being a total grouch when I was talking to Cameron in class today. That was like right after he sent me a sweet text this morning, too. Men are so confusing."

Ugh, I know my face is red. What a bum, telling on me! I'm so going to give him a hard time when I see him again. That tattletale!

Avery gasps excitedly, "He texted you? Spill it!" I swear her smile just doubled in size and she has this mischievous look in her eyes. I bet the faker already knows everything. She and Cameron probably spent the afternoon gossiping like a group of high school girls.

"Umm, yeah, he might have just said good morning." I shrug the question off and go sit at a table as quick as I can. I know she's up to something just by one look.

"Oh no, you don't get to escape!" She follows, eyebrows raised, "Tell me about this text."

I smirk and check my phone. There's still no text from Elliot.

I chuckle and roll my eyes, "It was nothing. He just said good morning and told me I look like a pop tart."

"He actually said, by the way you look like a pop tart?" She's studying me like I've lost my mind.

"Well, no, he calls me this name in a weird language. I asked what it meant and he told me pop tart. I think he was just being silly though."

"Holy shit! Tate totally likes you! I freaking knew it when I saw him watch you walk to the bathroom at dinner. He was staring at you like you were a piece of cake he wanted to eat!" Hmm, he's the one who looks as good as a big piece of chocolate cake.

"No way, I think you were imagining things, he was kind of an ass to me at dinner. Especially about the whole accent thing. I mean, deflect much?"

I'm over this conversation. Yes, he's hot. No, I don't need to get anyone else involved with my drama and issues. God forbid if the *Monster* ever finds me, what he'll do to me if I'm with another guy. I shudder and then rub my arms to play it off like I just got a chill.

"Okay girly, you think what you want to!" Avery calls out in a singsong voice while she walks to the counter to serve customers.

I guess it's time for me to finish this hot chocolate and get out of here. I have a ton of work to do, thanks to having to go full-time to maintain my scholarship. I do love the school though, the buildings and the surroundings, it's all so charming. The humidity is great on my skin and hair, too.

I head up to the counter, gesturing to Avery. She meets me by the register. "Emily, would you like a snack or anything, too?"

I shake my head and send her a small smile. "No. Thanks for the drink, Avery. I have to head out to work on some homework. I'll text you soon though. Have fun working!"

She throws her arm up and waves behind her as she hurries to help another customer. "Okay, bye, chickadee!" Avery responds busily, concentrating on making some kind of coffee creation so she doesn't see me return her wave.

Picking my head up off my folded arms on my desk, I blink a few times trying to wake up. *Shit, what time is it?* I must have fallen asleep reading my book. I glance around groggily and notice my phone blinking.

I rub my hands over my face a few times. Oh man, I forgot to call London, too. I probably look like a loon. I have every single light on in my little apartment, all the drapes and blinds closed and a chair propped up against my front door. *Straight nut job,* I think, and then shake my head. I push the button to illuminate my screen and see it's a text from Avery with a picture attached showing a man's butt in jeans.

Avery: Look who I saw again!

This girl is crazy. I check the clock on my phone. Ten p.m. Holy cow, I slept for hours! Great, I won't be able to go back to bed now.

I close my textbooks and neatly stack them on the corner of my little black desk I got at Walmart. I place each notebook and folder next to its matching textbook. *There, nice and organized.*

> **Me:** You are so silly, Avery, who on earth is the poor man you took pictures of?

I chuckle as I text her back. What a goofball. I wouldn't be surprised if she got the guy to let her take it willingly either.

> **Avery:** Your future ex-boyfriend! Luka Masterson!

> **Me:** You dork! And he said to call him Tate. I can't believe you took a picture of his butt! Did he see you?

This man obviously works out. I will definitely be saving this picture to my phone so I can look at it again in the future. I may not want to hook up with the guy, but I can definitely appreciate looking at him sometimes. Maybe she'll get one with his shirt off that I can keep, too.

> **Avery:** He knows I took it. He said I had to send it to you if I wanted to keep it. Told you Tate likes you!

> **Me:** OMG! You are fired!

> **Avery:** LOL! Get dressed I'm coming to get you

> **Me:** No way, you don't even know where I live! :D

> **Avery:** 1900 Adams Apt 13. I'll be there in 20, get something sexy on, cause we are going out.

Me: WHAT? How do you know where I live?

Avery: 19 minutes and I'm dragging your butt out for some fun.

*Shit! She's serious.* Okay, I am so not wearing anything sexy, I don't want any extra attention drawn to me and I know Avery will get plenty of attention by herself. What to wear?

Cute little black dress and some hot pink stilettos? Yes, please. It's fast, easy and I love my pink shoes.

I'm going to put on a little darker makeup than my norm, and wear my hair down. Hopefully, I'll just blend in with the background behind Avery. I've got to remember to not let her post any Facebook pictures of us. That could turn into a train wreck. I have to be careful and any pictures online is way too much of a risk.

He's found me before when I've tried to leave. I can't let him find me again. With that thought, I top my look off with some pin-up girl red lipstick and open my door.

Right into Tate Masterson's waiting smile. Ahhh! What's he doing here?

# THREE

## EMILY

**T**ATE'S EYES WIDEN AND HIS IRISES GROW DARK, AS HE looks me up and down. My heart speeds up as soon as I catch his scent. I draw in a deep breath, my mind going a million miles an hour.

I can't help but to feel completely blindsided. I'm going to strangle Avery! I can't believe she didn't tell me that Tate was coming. I would have pretended I was still asleep had I known.

Tate's changed his clothes since class. Now he has on a fitted white V-neck that clearly outlines his muscles and his tattoos are on full display. Light wash blue jeans hang deliciously from his hips, and I know from that picture they look amazing from the backside also. *God, he looks amazing.*

Tate leans in close, overtaking my space. His nearness startles me and forces me to back up against my door. I can't let Tate get any closer or else I will more than likely drag him inside my apartment.

I sputter out, breathless, "Tate? What are you doing here? I was just about to leave with Avery."

He grunts, leaning slightly closer to my face, "Yeah, she's with us, I came up to get you. Do you have a coat or something to cover up with?"

Tate keeps glancing at my shoulders and legs disconcerted. I know he's talking to me, but all I can think of is, God the stubble on his cheeks makes him look fantastic. Luckily he can't read my mind.

"To cover up with? Did it get cold outside?" I'm confused, it was so hot earlier.

"It's decent out, but you're showing a lot of skin with that dress on. Maybe you should wear some pants?" He suggests while raising his eyebrow.

Tate crosses his arms across his chest, causing his shirt to stretch as his muscles bulge. I don't know if it's supposed to intimidate me to change or what. It's definitely not going to work. I can't believe the nerve of this man and his caveman tactics. First, it was the growling and now he's telling me what to wear. If I wanted to be controlled, I would have stayed with my psycho ex.

"You are so not telling me what to wear. I'm dressed already and this is what I'm wearing." I declare sternly, "I'm meeting Avery, not you. Even if it was you, I still would not go and change!" I place my hand on his chest to give him a little shove away from me. When I make contact with his pecs, his nostrils flare. He glares heatedly down at me, as if I'm dinner.

"Let's just go. Avery and Cameron are waiting in the car." He growls out suddenly, looking pissed when he turns away and stomps down the hall.

Geez, is this man always so broody? I thought I was too serious all the time; clearly Tate has me beat. What on Earth could possibly be so bad in his life? Tate's beyond gorgeous, has money out the yin yang and appears to be somewhat intelligent. I swear I'll never understand men.

I trail behind him and when we get outside, I see a blacked

out, lifted Tahoe with beefy tires parked at the curb. I wouldn't have guessed in a million years that Tate would drive something like this. He just earned some cool points with his choice of vehicle. Most of the guys from where I'm from have lifted trucks on big tires.

"What happened to your Mercedes you were in the other night?"

I've been told by London that I'm a very inquisitive person. I, however, tell her I have special snooping privileges with her since she's my best friend. Maybe she's right, I am nosey. I'll never admit it to her, though.

Tate glances back at me with a huff and opens the passenger door for me to get in. "I drove the SUV because I wanted you to be comfortable with the extra room."

I get in and his comment floors me. Tate was thinking about me when he picked out which vehicle to drive? That means he had already planned to see me tonight. If he was thinking about me though, then why did he have to go and be an ass to me about my damn clothes? Ugh, God this man is so confusing!

Avery leans forward, tapping me playfully on my shoulder, "Emily! Damn girl, you look hot! I see Tate found your place without any problems." She looks entirely too pleased with herself and it makes me want to throw something at her.

I smirk, "Glad someone appreciates my outfit, Tate wanted me to go back and change." I shoot him a smug look. Take that, big boy!

Cameron starts chuckling until Tate glares at him in the rearview mirror. He starts driving and doesn't say anything for a while. I can hear Avery and Cameron talking low with Avery fake giggling at random things. *Yeah, they are so going to fuck, if they haven't already.*

I'll admit I'm a little jealous. I wish I could get with a guy and not worry about all the complications. Perhaps I should have a one-night stand? It's okay to scratch the itch, and then send them home, right? Guys do it all the time, so why can't I? I think that would be a safer option for me. No possible crazy boyfriend or posting photos of us, that sort of thing.

Maybe that's what I'll do tonight. I'll see if there's anybody worth having a one-night stand with. The idea sounds ludicrous really, since I've never done that sort of thing before. I know Tate will be pre-occupied, most likely with multiple women. I can't blame them though, he is so handsome. Obviously, Cameron and Avery are getting close, so I'm going to try to have some fun tonight.

"So where exactly are we going anyhow?"

I've been pretty much nowhere since I moved here. The most I've seen of Tennessee so far was the highway, the rest stops I made to get here and the surrounding lakes. The drive was beautiful, lots of trees and grassy hills. The road through Arkansas was absolutely horrible, all the bumps and dips. Thank God it was a quick drive through it or I would have gone nuts.

Avery leans forward between the seats, right when I turn to look into the back seat. She gets so close we almost butt foreheads and I jerk back. She laughs and I grumble. Crazy girl scared the shit out of me!

"We, my friend, are going to 007. It's my favorite club in the whole wide world! We are going to get our drink on, dance on and our freak on!" She smiles manically and I grin back.

"What is this, are we stepping into a James Bond flick?" I inquire, curiously. They all chuckle around me, and I peer at everyone inquisitively for some answers.

Avery happily chortles out, "Oh no! I want to see your reaction when we walk in. You will just have to wait and see. Geez, their martinis are out of this world! We are going to shake our booties until our feet feel like they want to fall off!" She seems to always know exactly what to say to bring a smile to my face.

"Girl, you are such a dork! I'll dance, but no drinking for me."

I never know when I might need all my senses intact. I know one day he's going to be waiting for me in a dark parking lot. Keeping alert could save my life if I'm ever in that position.

"What?! We have two good-looking men who are more than capable to carry our asses out of there if needed. You are getting toasted, Emily!"

I've learned the hard way not to rely on men, I'm not about to start now. I shake my head minutely, "I'll dance, but no drinks for me."

"We will seeeeeeee!" Avery sings, and plops back. She is pretty much sitting on top of Cameron. He looks thrilled about it though, so whatever, none of my business.

Tate glances over at me and does that one-arm extended thing, men do when they drive. God, he's absolutely delectable right now, all serious. His forehead does this little crinkle thing like he's thinking about something really hard, then he shakes his head and faces forward again.

"Huh? What was that just now?"

"Nothing," he mumbles.

Nothing my ass! "Umm, no! You just did a little head shake thingy."

"Just stay close in the club, okay? There will be a lot of people there you don't know, and I don't want you getting lost."

*Christ, this man.* "Seriously? I'm twenty years old, Tate, and believe it or not, I am a grown woman. This is not the first time I've been to a club." Perhaps I just tie a rope to his belt buckle at this point?

"I'm very aware you are a grown woman, *Krasaaveetsa* (beauty). Just trust me, please," Tate grumbles. After a moment he relaxes his features and stares at me wearily.

"Okay stud, since you asked nicely. I guess I'll stick close. But if you start getting overly bossy, I'm gone."

Turning, I watch out of my window as we drive. There is only so much Luka 'Tate' Masterson I can take. He's so handsome, and then he opens his mouth and ruins it.

I think I'm going to call the bossy ass side 'Luka' and the sweet man hunk side 'Tate'. That makes it's easier to break up the two personalities. Shit, what if he's a narcissist or something? That would be my luck, entice yet another psycho. Well, if I did appeal to him. I don't think he's that interested though. He's made it clear he doesn't see me in the booty call picture, so maybe he's not attracted to me?

I burst out, quickly before I have a chance to think it through, "Do you have a personality disorder?" I gaze at him curiously. The people with personality disorders will admit it, right?

Tate glares, fuming for a few beats before he growls, "Fuck! I'm just going to drive, okay?"

Man, he looks pissed. Yep, he could totally have a personality issue. The back of the SUV got dead silent, too. I wonder if they think the same thing.

I stay silent. I know he didn't really mean it as a question, it's best if I just keep to myself.

"Christ! No, Emily, no personality disorder, okay. Fuck! Did you ever think maybe you're a little naïve and I'm just looking out for you?"

Tate's cheeks are flushed angrily and he looks like steam could come out of his ears at my little question. That was completely uncalled for. He didn't have to get so heated, it was an honest query.

I feel my blood start to boil, embarrassed by his outburst insinuating that I'm naïve. He has nerve. *How dare he talk down to me in front of our friends!*

"Naïve? Naïve?" Swinging my head back towards him, angrily, "Fuck you, Luka!" I shriek, riled up. "I'm sure I've been through way more shit than you could ever imagine!"

Huffing, I turn back to my window. "Just forget I said anything, okay? Just be broody and drive and I'll keep my naïve thoughts to myself." Crossing my arms angrily I stew in my thoughts. Tate grunts and turns up the radio to a newer song I've never heard before.

*Asshole. Dick. Motherfucker.* He has no idea. None! He has balls to call me naïve. We just freaking met! No wonder he's single. Wait, is he single? He probably is if he makes comments like that to women.

We head through Knoxville to get to the club area. The lights and traffic make my heart beat faster with excitement. It feels big to me, but then I came from a small town. We don't have all the people and busyness unless you head to one of the cities.

Everyone is so supportive of the Tennessee Vols. It reminds me of home and all the football fans around Austin with the Longhorns. I can't wait until I have some free time to check out the museums and the farmer's market right by the college.

We end up at an area that has a bunch of shoebox-sized clubs and stop in front of the largest. The building is a dark grey color, and has a large silver sign that says '007' with lights illuminating it.

Wrapped from the front entrance to around the building is a long line of people. Everyone waiting is dressed to the nines, with the majority focused on their phones.

After circling the lot a few times, we eventually park. Tate hops out, rounding the vehicle quickly to open my door for me.

I hesitate only a moment when he reaches for me, and then I grasp his hand to let him help me climb down from the raised SUV. *At least he has some manners.*

Avery happily loops her arm through mine and we practically run to keep up with Cameron and Tate's long-legged pace. Avery hobbles like she may break her ankle in her gorgeous, high shoes. I love her outfit but I would probably kill myself in those shoes.

She leans in, eyes lit up with mischief and starts whispering in my ear. Her nose bumps into me a few times; she's so close it makes me chuckle.

"My God, Emily, I about died when you asked him if he has a personality disorder!" Avery whisper-yells, "Cameron's face was so red from holding his laugh in, he looked like a fat tomato! I thought Tate was going to explode." She flails her arms with mine in tow, "He looked like he wanted to rip someone's head off! You are freaking crazy and the sexual tension between you guys is insane!" She giggles, but I don't like what she's implying. I am so not going there with Tate Masterson!

Rolling my eyes, I grumble, "Ha, sexual tension my ass, he's a jerk face that needs to relax a little. I would not let that man have sex with me, no matter how hot I think he is. He's infuriating!"

She grins big and then squeals, "I knew you thought he was hot!"

"Shhh!" I quickly check to make sure the guys didn't hear her, but they are walking ahead, deep in their own conversation. "That's all you heard out of that?"

Shrugging, she smiles and gestures for me to look forward. We finally make it to the entrance after our trek through the parking lot. Avery and I step up on the curb, me helping her so she doesn't fall over and I glance up at the building again. The sign appears huge and almost magnetizing up close.

I'm guessing that apparently Tate knows the guys up front because he's heading right for them. Maybe we'll get lucky and get to bypass this long line.

There are three tall, largely built men dressed in black, whom I'm assuming are the bodyguards or door guys. One normal-sized guy in the middle is dressed in a sharp black suit with a strong nose and short black scruff on his face. He oozes money and self-confidence. The suit guy turns to Tate and nods at him.

"Luka, moy braat (my brother)."

*Whoa! What is that?* That sounded so sexy!

"Viktor," Tate rolls out in his deep, raspy voice and nods back.

He doesn't stop, just walks right in. We all shuffle in, close behind Tate. As we get through the door, I hear the men start talking in a language I don't understand. With the music, it's hard for me to really catch any piece of it.

Making our way into 007, I'm instantly hit with trance-like music. It's like I've entered a different realm or something. The lights are dim and flashing to the beat of the music.

It's busy but not so crowded that you have to bump into every person you walk past. There are beautiful, exotic-looking females dressed in red or black fitted dresses. They must be the servers, because they carry around trays full of different colored martinis and pass them out to whoever asks for one.

Do you have to prepay or something in order to get drinks? This is awesome, but looks so ridiculously expensive. I didn't even get asked for an ID. I'm only twenty; I hope I'm allowed to even be in here right now. No one said anything about specific age requirements.

I feel like I just fell down the rabbit hole in 'Alice in Wonderland' as I take in everything. In the middle of the club is a two story dance floor surrounded by glass walls. It almost appears as if they are in a giant glass elevator.

Well, obviously this is why the club doesn't seem too busy inside. The majority of people are dancing. I glance to Avery and she nods her head upward.

Looking up toward the ceiling, I expect to see ceiling beams or maybe dancers or something. I never expected to see a silver Aston Martin, suspended from grey metal cables above us.

# SECRETS

This place is insane! It's like walking onto the set of a James Bond movie. No wonder Avery loves this place so much!

Avery yells, "Let's get a table," trying to make up for the loud, thrumming music. Both of the guys nod at her and I give her a thumbs up.

Tate leads us to the VIP section. Even though the club is posh enough as it is, they still have a section sanctioned off. I walk up a few stairs, lined with rope lighting, to the raised section. The smaller area holds about ten different sized, round booths.

As soon as our butts hit our booth, a server is waiting with a friendly smile on her face. I bet these women make a ton in tips; they are all so gorgeous.

"I want a Cosmo, please!" Avery perks up, eagerly.

"Courvoisier on the rocks," Cameron rumbles.

"We will both have bottled water," Tate orders, gesturing to him and me, before I have a chance to say anything.

"Thanks, but you can have a drink if you want to, Tate," I turn toward him and offer loudly.

"Nah, I don't drink a lot. I like to be aware of my surroundings and stay in control of my body."

Hmmm... Something else we have in common. I'm sure it's for entirely opposite reasons, but at least he's out of dick mode from earlier.

Avery grabs my hand and starts tugging to get me out of the booth. "Come on, Emily, let's go hit the dance floor, I freaking love this song!"

'Cracks' remix by Belle Humble is vibrating off the walls. I love this song too. It's perfect to move to and get lost in.

Avery downs half her drink and jumps up out of the booth, pulling me in tow. The guys stand up with us and I pull back on Avery, peering up at Tate, confused.

"What about our drinks? Shouldn't we finish them first? It's not safe to leave them and come back."

I'm not about to take unnecessary risks just because a couple of guys are with us. I feel a little safer that we are in a group but I have to try and think about stuff safely.

"Don't worry about the drinks, everything will be okay. The server is actually called a Table Assistant." He nods at our lady handling our table. "It's her job to watch our drinks, jackets, purses and anything else we leave behind. She will even walk you to the restroom for safety, in case you feel unwell or need a cool towel or whatever. There is a girl assigned to each table."

I'm impressed; what a great idea for a club to keep people safe! So many women have gotten taken advantage of by date rape drugs or being out alone.

"Wow! That is such an awesome idea!"

I smile at him and we make our way to the dance floors. There are a few and we head straight for the large one in the middle. Avery and Cameron automatically start dancing together.

*Well, this is a little awkward.* I look to Tate, unsure, to see if he feels the same as me. He meets my eyes wearing this sexy little smirk on his face. His lips kind of go up on one side and he has some hot-ass dimples. *Sweet Jesus, I could seriously lick his dimples.* He's so yummy when he finally starts to relax.

He reaches out and lightly pulls me toward him. Tate leans in closely. He's so warm; it feels like his whole body is wrapped around me. I guess I didn't realize just how big he is compared to me. I always see him and Cameron next to each other so he doesn't appear that big.

He draws me in more and lowers his lips right next to my ear. I can feel his breath flutter against my neck and it's giving me goose bumps. His body molds to mine as we dip and move to 'Cracks.'

The beat is insane on these speakers. Mixing the music with his firm body and warm breath, it turns me on. *Maybe he's not so bad after all.*

"So, little one, why did you decide to go to college here?" Tate's voice has a deep, rich timbre and it makes me want to snuggle even closer to him. If I could crawl into his pocket right now, I think I would.

Shrugging, I go with a basic answer, "I just thought it was a good school. Good place to start my life, you know? What about you?" I don't really want to delve into my personal life with him.

"Pretty much the same for me." He returns my same answer and it makes me a little suspicious.

I take in the servers and all the drinks being handed out so freely.

Turning back to Tate, puzzled, "I don't understand, I keep seeing people take drinks off the server's trays. Did they prepay or something? I don't remember seeing you pay for anything either." I scan the floor again to see if anyone goes to the bar, but they don't.

He shakes his head, "There's a door fee when they come in. A hundred dollars per person if they drink. They can drink as much as they want from the server's trays. It's all good quality liquors, so it's a more than fair price." He gestures to the bar and I glance back at the long, oak bar top, running almost in a large circle.

"If anyone wants certain premium liquors, champagne, et cetera, then they can order it from the bar and pay the bartenders. If they don't drink, then they only pay twenty-five dollars for a glow band." Tate nods towards a young girl dancing next to us with a lit up bracelet. "When they are ready to go, a door guard will remove their glow band so they can leave."

He pulls me back to him as we sway to the beat, "The glow bands have sensors in them, in case someone under twenty-one tries to take them off while in the club, to drink. As you can see though, how everyone is dressed, this place attracts a certain older wealthy clientele with younger women."

I huff a small laugh, this guy could work here if he wanted. His scent surrounds me the entire time we dance, pulling me into craving more of his touch.

"Geez, you must come here a lot, you know everything." Probably where he gets his booty calls he was talking about the other day.

"Eh, I stop in once or twice a month to check out things." He shrugs.

We dance for four more songs until I decide it's time to sit for a few minutes and get a drink. I'm a little out of breath and my feet are hurting already. I wave for Avery to follow but she just shoos me to go on without her.

Avery attends college on a volleyball scholarship, and playing the game keeps her body in great shape. She looks like she's not even a little winded, whereas I probably look like a wet cat at this point.

After a quick break, we head back to dance some more, and Tate pulls me close into him again. It seems more familiar and we start to really get into it.

I rest my hands on his solid chest and I swear I can feel something by his nipples. *Holy shit!* He has barbells in his nipples. That is so freaking hot.

I start to rub over his nipples, being brave for the first time in so long. It's erotic and we are already grinding to the sensual beat. I feel like I'm in a drunken haze, yet I've only had water tonight.

Tate moves his hands down my back until he's closer to my ass. I softly rub over his chest and arms. His arms are flexed tight and I can't stop picturing him holding me, while pushing inside of me.

I close my eyes tightly, breathing deeply to get myself back under control. Tate smells fucking edible, making my mouth water in anticipation each time I feel his breath while he talks. I keep craving to be able to suck on his nipple rings.

My eyes shoot open when all of a sudden he's gone, and I almost fall forward.

He grumbles, "That's enough, I'm done."

Tate starts walking back toward our table and Avery sends me a confused look, questioning what just happened. I shrug, because hell if I know what I did.

She quickly makes her way to me, "What happened, Emily?"

Cameron's already caught up to Tate so we head back to the table behind them.

I shrug, "I have no idea. He just said it was enough and he was done. I know he's probably a little pissed he hasn't gotten to dance with other females by now, but it's not like I'm making him dance with just me. I would be more than happy to go find someone who wants to dance if that would make him happy."

She bursts out laughing, flashing a bright smile, "Are you insane, woman? You can't possibly think that with what he's been doing!"

I scrunch my nose, "What do you mean 'with what he's been doing'?"

"Holy shit, dude, I think you might actually be blind! We need to get you some glasses, like, yesterday. While you guys were dancing, anytime a guy starts to come near you, Tate snaps his fingers and points at the guy." Avery snaps her fingers and makes a circle motion then points with her right finger, demonstrating, "then a bouncer comes, grabs the guy and drags him off." She giggles again, "Trust me, Emily, there were probably five guys trying to come dance with you, but Tate isn't having it."

My vision clouds with anger upon hearing this. I'm so mad right now at his nerve, I could burst. *How dare he?*

"Are you kidding me?"

"Ha! No way, dude, he isn't letting anyone near you." She points at me and shakes her head, thoroughly amused.

"You know what, Avery?" I huff, "Go sit with them. I'm so fucking over that man, and I'm the one who's done! Not him. I'm not dealing with anymore of his attitude tonight. I'm going outside."

# TATE

I HAD TO WALK AWAY. I HAVE NEVER WANTED TO FUCK someone so badly in the middle of a dance floor before. When she started rubbing on my nipple rings, I was at my limit.

It took everything I had inside, to keep my hands from just grabbing her ass and pulling her legs around my hips, taking her there in front of everyone.

Then there were all those douche bags thinking they were going to come and take her out of my arms. Yeah right, I would have slit their throats if they touched her perfect body. I know Gavin and Niko, my guards, will teach their ignorant asses a lesson for me.

I peer over at Avery and Emily talking. She is so damn beautiful, like a little blonde angel. I will have her, even if it takes me a little while to make it happen. I've wanted Emily from the moment I set eyes on her but I keep screwing it up. She makes me over-think and not-think, all at the same time when she's around.

Emily storms off quickly, looking slightly pissed. *Great, she has that little attitude again.*

Some steroid induced tool steps in front of her and looks like he's attempting to be charming. I don't think so. This Bratva piece of trash will not talk to my little pet. Did he not just see her dancing with me?

I make my way to them speedily and put my arm around Emily, pulling her in close. She gazes up to me and glares. Jesus, I bet she is fun in bed when she's all wound up like this. She's got a little fire inside of her.

The guy clears his throat, peeved. Leaving Emily's gorgeous face, I glare straight into this Bratva thug's eyes.

"Maya (mine)" I practically snarl in Russian.

"Huh?" He looks at me as if he just realized I'm speaking.

"Апаая́вляется maya. (She is mine)"

He stares at me confused, taking me in as if he doesn't know exactly who I am to stand up to him, "Mine. As in, she belongs to me, you idiot," I repeat, but in English this time.

He blinks a few times and nods, "I apologize, Shef (Boss)." He looks at his feet as he calls me Boss.

I'm glad he realized his place. I have no time to waste on him, as Emily is silently fuming beside me. At least he knew well enough to call me boss in Russian. I don't need my little pet hearing that.

She huffs, clearing her throat loudly. I know she's about to lay into me. I have to quit pissing her off, if I plan on keeping her someday. She's going to keep me on my toes, that's for sure.

"Mine?" Emily shrieks. "I'm not yours! You are infuriating. Stop being a cock block! If I want to talk to a man and even possibly go home with him, it's not your damn business!" She points, bumping her finger into my chest, as she finishes laying into me. I puff my chest a little, making sure she feels muscle; I know she enjoyed it before.

"I'm finished talking to you tonight, Luka Masterson!" Emily finishes loudly over the music. She throws her hands up, exasperated, and storms out of the club.

*Fuck!* Why do women always insist on busting out the full name when they get angry? She doesn't need to be outside by herself.

I rush off after Emily. She's almost to the SUV when I catch up to her.

My brother Viktor, and the guards Nikoli, Brent and Ivan are all nosily peering at us. I'm sure we make quite the spectacle. Nikoli's definitely going to give me shit about this, I just know it.

"Beauty, wait, please?" I call after her. Emily's swinging her arms hurriedly to help her walk fast, but my legs are a lot longer so I catch up to her quickly.

I reach out to grab her arm, spinning her around to face me.

# EMILY

I feel a warm, large hand grasp my wrist, yanking and spinning me around.

I automatically raise my arms to protect myself. If Tate's anything like that *monster*, I know this could hurt. Tightly squeezing my eyes closed, I wait for the hit to come.

He drops my wrist as if it were on fire, "What are you doing, Emily? For Heaven's sake, you can't come out here by yourself! Who would protect you?" Tate grumbles, "And put your arms down! I'm not some goon who will hurt you. I might be a dick sometimes, but give me a little fucking credit. I'm out here to protect you." His expression looks a little wounded but also angry.

Dropping my arms, my own temper flares up, "Ugh! Why are you so stubborn?" I gaze at him curiously. Why can't he get it, that I want to be left alone?

I cross my arms across my body, "I told you I was done talking to you today and I meant it!"

"Please calm down, Krasaaveetsa."

"Krasaaveetsa, huh? I've heard it several times now, what does that even mean? Huh? And what is that language?" I pepper him with questions. Maybe he will just get annoyed and leave me be.

"It's Russian, okay? I'm stubborn because I want you. If I want something, I take it. I don't waste time and screw around." He drops his eyes, casually running them over my body.

Stubbornly, he meets my gaze again, "I want you to be mine and I'm willing to lay claim if someone comes sniffing around."

"And Krasaaveetsa?" He says intensely, grabbing both of my wrists and putting them above my head against the cool vehicle.

Tate leans his large body, pressing against me. I can feel his solid muscles molded through his shirt. He's hard in all the right places. It makes me excited and anxious all at once—I've never enjoyed being controlled before.

Tate screams 'dominate' to me and it almost pulls me to him, versus pushing me away as one would think. It's like my body craves someone who can take away all of my worries for once. This is a man who brings out something primal, from deep inside of me.

He leans in so close, our lips are almost touching. His breath coming out in short little pants, washing over my lips. With each warm breath, my pussy clenches. I inhale deeply and can taste the mint from his breath. No matter how hard I seem to fight against wanting to like him, my body calls to his. It's never reacted like this with anyone before, like it's found its match.

In a softer voice he says, "Baby, Krasaaveetsa means 'beauty'." Tate's lips graze mine as he speaks, "I find you so fucking beautiful, you don't even realize." The last words come out as a whisper.

After he says it I nip at his bottom lip a little. That does it. Next thing I know he is kissing me softly, almost testing my lips out. It's like he's memorizing the flavor, the texture, the wetness.

Tate's mouth is cool and fresh and his lips are so soft. I let out a little moan, as his tongue tangles with mine. I can't help it—he has me so wound up.

He pulls back and looks into my eyes, he nudges my nose softly with his, then slams his mouth onto mine. This is it. This is where he owns me.

I pull myself up his body as he kisses me feverishly, wrapping my legs around his waist and threading my hands in his hair. It's just long enough for me to wind my fingers in for a grip and pull it.

He lets out a growl and puts one arm under my ass to hold me up, even closer to him. His other hand has a firm—but not painful—grip on the nape of my neck. Tate lets me know that he is in control of this kiss. I'm just the lucky participant to be receiving a kiss like this. And fuck, do I feel lucky right now, my body burns for his.

We're rudely interrupted by a cheery Avery, "Hey, love birds! We figured the night was probably done when y'all took off outside."

At Avery's mischievous sounding voice, Tate pulls away from me and slowly sets me back on the ground. He gazes at me, eyes lit up full of need with each movement I make. We don't break eye contact the entire time, almost as if we're in our own little bubble and everything else is just static. I don't think either one of us expected that kiss to be so charged.

Thank God Avery interrupted us when she did. We would probably be missing some clothes right now if she hadn't. I know I wanted to try out a one-night stand tonight, but not with Tate. Things could get way too messy with him.

After everything I just went through and having to start over,

I wouldn't survive if I let Tate have me and then he decided he was done with me. I know that would happen; he'd get bored and move on. In return, I'd be left broken in a whole new way.

Avery and Cameron hop in the SUV while Tate opens my door for me. He nods at the guys in front of the door and they wave back. Geez, I bet they got an eye full, I had completely forgotten they were even over there.

The ride home is pretty quiet. Tate and I both seem to be lost in our own thoughts. We arrive at my apartment first.

"I'll walk you up?" Tate turns to me.

"No, it's fine; I'll make it in okay. Thank you for dropping me off." I shoot him a small smile and turn to the back, "Bye, Cameron. Avery, babe, I'll text you. Night y'all."

I jump out and close the door before Tate can even undo his seatbelt. I don't have the energy to battle with him about that kiss.

I leisurely make my way up to my tiny apartment, playing the night over in my head. I never would have guessed Tate and I would have that kind of chemistry. The sex—well, the sex—would be insane.

As I get closer to the blue front door, there's a chess piece. It looks like a king that's been laid on its side. There's some writing on it; carved into it lengthways is 'Check mate'. *That's weird.*

Someone must have dropped the piece while walking down the hall. I've never played chess before, but my ex did. I don't know why, but I snatch it up, ignoring the queasy feeling I get with it and chalking it up to coincidence.

It was such a crazy night, full of fun and drama. Kind of makes me miss London's craziness. She was always so much fun to go out with. We would dance the night away until she found her next hot guy.

Glancing at my phone, I scroll through my messages looking

for anything from Elliot. I've been patient long enough for him to reply. I'm texting him again tomorrow to check in on everything.

I'm tired and ready for my pajamas. I take my Prozac and attempt to get some sleep because I want to check out the farmer's market in the morning.

## EMILY

**T**HE NEXT TWO WEEKS FLY BY. I'M KEPT BUSY WITH MY
school work. Being at a new place, I slowly explore the city,
taking in everything at my own pace. I don't love it yet, but I'm
definitely starting to enjoy it.

I've learned that Knoxville is surrounded by seven lakes:
Cherokee, Douglas, Ft. Loudon, Melton Hill, Norris, Watts Bar,
and Tellico Lake. I've always enjoyed going swimming. London
and I spent many summer days at the lake near Austin. I can't
wait until our next long weekend. I'm going to drag Avery out to
one of the lakes so we can get a tan and relax.

For now, I'm going to buckle down for the test this week. I
never took school as seriously as I do now. I want to know that if
my family were alive they would be proud of me. I can't help but
wonder what my life would be like, if Momma were still here.
That day my life took a huge change, likes to play in my head
like a twisted joke, popping up to ruin happy memories.

# SECRETS

## Twelve-year-old Emily...

Principal Kegal pops his head in our classroom, peeking around the door opening and everyone is frozen at the sight of him.

He looks over at me with a sad expression, then turns to our teacher, "Hi, Miss Swanson. I need to speak to Emily Harper please. She needs to grab her things to leave for the day also, thanks." He nods giving Miss Swanson another sad look, which is strange. He usually looks at her as if he's seeing the sun for the first time. I think he has a little crush on her.

Principal Kegal must want to see me about our student council project. It's going to be awesome planting all those new trees at the retirement center. Kind of weird I have to grab my things though, maybe Momma or Granddaddy is here or somethin'.

Glancing over at my best friend, London, I stick my tongue out at her. She's so great; after school we are going to hang out and paint our nails with some new polish she got for her birthday. I get to see her cute older brother, Elliot, and his friends too, so it's an added bonus.

I quickly pack up the books in my bag and my new makeup compact my momma had just let me get when I told her London was allowed to have one.

"Hi, Mr. Kegal, how are you today?" I smile and ask as soon as we are in the hall.

Mr. Kegal is always wearing a polo style shirt with one of our town's sports team's logo and khaki pants. I think he even has hats to match, I've seen a few. He looks more like he should be a coach than the principal of the middle school.

There are two stern looking police officers waiting out in the hallway for us. *Oh no.* I hope Mr. Kegal's not asking questions about someone smoking behind the school again. He's way stricter being principal at the middle school than he used to be

49

in elementary. I think this place stresses him out more. I wish everyone would stop being so mean to him when they get into trouble.

He gives me a kind smile, "I'm good, sweetheart, thanks. Listen, this is Sergeant Rodderick and Detective Saint. They have some very sad news to share with you. I'll stay right here with you as long as you need me to, okay?"

I look over at the officers; Sergeant Rodderick looks a little older than Momma. He has really short, brown hair that's cut like a soldier. Kind of like the guys in the commercials I see on TV. He's tall and skinny, with a bushy, brown mustache.

Detective Saint looks a bit older, closer to my granddaddy's age. He has short black and white hair and warm, friendly brown eyes with lines like he laughs a lot. He's also kind of chubby like he enjoys his coffee and pie a little too much.

"Okay." I gaze curiously at Principal Kegal, "Where's my granddaddy?"

Mr. Kegal exchanges a strange look with the officers, and then turns back to me. *What's going on?*

"We haven't been able to reach him yet. I think he's out on old Mr. Mills' ranch somewhere. An officer went to see if he could find him, so he can come get you after we talk."

Mr. Mills' ranch is huge so I understand. He and Granddaddy are always doing something on that old ranch.

I nod at the principal and turn toward the police officers.

"Hi, what can I help with?" I'm in the student council, so it's my job to help any way I can with school problems.

The younger officer starts, "Well, Miss Harper, I'm afraid we have some terrible news. Your momma is Susan Harper, correct?"

I gasp, surprised, "Oh my God, Momma? Yes, that's her, is she in trouble or something?" I glance between both the officers, "My momma's a real good person, so whatever it is, I'm sure you have the wrong person!"

I'll have to go to the office at lunchtime and ask if I can give Momma a call. I know she'll wanna hear all about this.

The older guy cuts in, softly saying, "No, dear, your momma's not in any trouble. She was in an accident today when she was driving. I'm so sorry to tell you, but your momma didn't survive. She's with the angels now, honey. If we can do anything, we are here to help."

The officers look really sorry to be telling me this and it just makes me angry. They have the wrong person, I'm sure of it. I would feel it in my heart, in my soul if something happened to my momma.

I glare angrily at all three men, "I'll tell you what you can do. You can quit lying about my momma! My momma's just fine. You go see, she's at work, at the diner." I place my hands on my hips, scowling, "You are not very good officers by getting it wrong. You should be ashamed of yourselves, talking about my momma that way! My granddaddy's gonna fix this and show you all that my momma's just fine." I wince because my yelling echoes down the hallway.

They have this all wrong. I need to get back to Miss Swanson's room so I can finish my work. I know I'm gonna have to ask for help on this math assignment now.

Mr. Kegal looks at me as tears shine in his eyes, "No sweet-heart, I'm afraid it's true. It really is your momma, and she's gone. She died, and I am so completely sorry this is happening to you." He touches my arm tenderly as he says this.

I stare into his sad blue eyes and know he's telling me the truth. He and Momma went to school together when they were kids and I've known Mr. Kegal since he became principal when I started second grade. I know he wouldn't lie to me like this; he's always been a nice person.

I really don't know what to do. It's like someone just kicked me in my stomach, it feels like someone has a pillow over my face and is sucking all the air from my lungs. I gasp loudly, as my chest tightens. Hot tears stream down my cheeks and the world goes insanely loud with silence. I see people's mouths moving, but I can't hear a word anyone is saying to me.

They are all looking at me worriedly and I drop to the floor. I have my hands sprawled out in front of me on the cold white tiles. I don't know how to survive without my momma. I let out a gut wrenching wail as I feel like my heart is exploding inside.

Mr. Kegal scoops me up in his arms, where I sob loudly. Mr. Kegal is openly crying now, and I hear Miss Swanson come into the hallway. I know the officer tells her what happened because she comes to me and hugs me to her chest.

Everyone, all of my classmates are in the hallway staring at me as Mr. Kegal carries me to the office. I look to London and see Brandon Meeks holding her in the middle of the hallway while she cries. She looks so grief stricken; it hurts my heart even more. Momma was her other momma, and I know it hurts her heart, too.

# EMILY

A tear rolls down my cheek as I remember that awful day. God, I miss my Momma every single day. I have to remind myself I was lucky enough to get her for twelve years of my life. Even though I don't think it's fair she was taken from me, it could have been worse—I could have had her for even less time.

I wipe my cheek, as a text alert sounds from my phone. Fumbling, I dig through my bag until I find it, turning it on to see Tate's name pop up.

# SECRETS

**Tate**: Kpacota, I miss you. Have lunch with me?

It's been two weeks since we've really talked. We say hi to each other, sit next to each other in class. We even talk about the classwork we have together a little bit, but that's about it. Frankly, that night at the club has me a little scared. I wasn't expecting to have that kind of reaction to him.

I'm not ready for a relationship or to open myself up that much to someone this soon. At the same time though, when I'm around him, I never want to leave. I want him to touch me. When we talk about our school stuff, I find myself wanting to open up to him about everything. We actually have a lot in common and when he's not being bossy or territorial, my wall crumbles a little more.

Have lunch with him or not? I guess I could. Things have seemed to cool off for him around me. I'm still completely taken with him, but I can keep it to myself.

This is good; maybe we will become friends instead of whatever we've been. I don't even know how to categorize us. I am yet to really make any friends with fellow classmates. I have Avery, Tate and Cameron. I know I need to keep to myself, but it's lonely.

I wasn't super popular growing up, but I did have a few regular friends I talked to frequently. Well, up until I started dating *him*, then I was only allowed to talk to London and he *hated* that, too. I wasn't giving up London though; I had already given up everything else. I'm so not going to think of that awful stuff right now.

On to Luka 'Tate' Masterson and hopefully my new real friend.

**Me**: Sounds good, where and when?

**Tate:** Are you free today in 30 min?

**Me:** I can make that work

**Tate:** Good. I'll come get you. See you in 30 ;)

**Me:** Okay.

I pull on some cute little jean shorts from Rue 21, my hot pink, Cartel Ink shirt that has a picture of Alice in Wonderland. I love it because she's tattooed and pierced in it. It's one of my favorite shirts that I own. I might not have any tattoos, but I still love them.

I think this outfit will work, it's only lunch. I seriously doubt Tate would bring me anywhere fancy like the club to grab a bite to eat. I pair it with my low, black Converse shoes and make my way downstairs to wait for Tate.

I step onto the sidewalk in front of my apartment building and get a weird tingly sensation in my stomach, like someone is watching me. I need to give London a call and make sure *he's* still in jail.

Before I have a chance to have a good look around, a grey sports car pulls up in front of me. The car is a gunmetal grey, the grill is dark like the paint, it has 21-inch rims and the suspension is low enough the tires take up the entire wheel well. The car is full of clean, smooth lines; it's insanely beautiful.

Tate quickly exits and hurries around the car to open my door. "Damn, little pet, you look smokin' today!" I smile at him and then look at the ground. I always feel shy around him.

"Hi. Thanks for picking me up."

He smirks as he looks me up and down with his gorgeous hazel eyes. Tate's in all his glory, hotness incarnate. Relaxed, dark, straight, distressed jeans, plain black T-shirt that hugs his muscles perfectly and black leather Polo boots. He has a little product in his dark brown hair and his eyes sparkle like he's excited.

He's wearing a grin and has his dimples on full display as he notices me checking him out. He shuts the car door for me.

Watching him run around the front of the car to his side, I can see his Russian features. High cheekbones and straight, strong nose; he always walks around with his head up, as if he is in charge of everything.

Tate climbs in and it looks as if this car was made specifically for him, the way the black and red leather seat molds against his shoulders. He fills up the space nicely with his size. If the seats weren't so low, he'd probably be too big.

I run my hand against the smooth leather, "Gosh, Tate, what kind of car is this? I've never seen anything like it! The seats are soft as butter."

I actually sit down toward the ground. It feels as if you could put your feet down and touch it. The inside is all black leather with blood red accents. There is a big screen on the dash and it all looks super high tech.

When he hears my question, he looks at me and it's like looking at a little kid, he's so excited. Oh, Tate definitely likes his cars, and I just gave him an in to talk about them.

"This, Krasaaveetsa, is a Bentley Continental GT Speed. I figure I need something beautiful to drive, because you deserve to be surrounded by as much beauty as I am right now."

I smile brightly, because that is seriously sweet. I know my cheeks are red, I can feel them burning. I buckle my seat belt and look out the window. I have no idea what to say back, I'm a little twitter-pated right now.

Tate turns up the radio. 'Out of the Black' by Royal Blood is playing. I have this on my playlist for when I run at the gym. He smirks, laying down on the gas and I'm pulled back into my seat. This stunning car also has tons of power. I could totally get addicted to driving this thing.

After a short drive, we arrive at a place on the river called Calhoun's. It looks like a giant metal building with a big glowing orange sign that says 'Calhoun's'.

It's close to the UT Campus, and on the way we drove by Neyland Stadium. It feels as if we flew here, I know there is no way he was doing the speed limit. His sexy factor just went up two more notches after that ride.

The sweet hostess greets us and we decide to sit on the deck. It's early enough that it's not too humid. They have an outside deck as well as an enclosed deck with a panoramic view of the Tennessee River. The weather's actually really beautiful today. It's pretty cool because Calhoun's is accessible by boat and has its own dock.

It smells wonderfully of BBQ. I'm a true Texas gal, I love my BBQ.

The deck has its own special menu. I order the BBQ chicken sandwich with a Dr. Pepper and Tate has the Calhoun's Trio with a glass of water. He also orders us the Ale steak skewers as an appetizer. Everything sounds so delicious, I didn't realize how hungry I was until the BBQ smell hit me.

This is the kind of place I know London will love when she visits. I can see her in a bikini top and short-shorts doing shots on the deck. I'm sure she'll have, five different guys offering her boat rides, too. She's always been fun and a party girl. I bet she and Avery would be double trouble together.

Tate cuts in as I'm checking out the awesome deck set up. "Thanks for coming to lunch. I wasn't sure if you'd agree." He gives me his best sexy smirk.

"Oh yeah, no problem, thanks for the invite. I didn't realize how hungry I was until we walked in. I've never even heard of this place, thanks for bringing me."

"The food's good. My brother and I have been here a few

times before."

Tate has sunglasses on. It's a bummer they hide his eyes. I think his eyes are my favorite feature on him, or his plump lips, or his nipple rings, or, well, never mind.

"Oh, you have a brother?"

"Yes, my brother is Viktor."

"Is he in school, too?"

"No, he does some business for my father. He was at the club when we went. Viktor was the one outside at the door, dressed like he was going to a meeting instead of a nightclub."

"You mean the thinner guy who called you Luka when we were going inside?"

"Yep, that's Viktor."

"Cool, wait, does he manage 007? Is that your father's place?" The pieces start to click together about why we were able to just walk in, the free drinks, all of it.

"Eh, you could say he kind of watches the place, but no, 007 is mine, not my father's." He shrugs, nonchalant. He says it like it's no big deal, like everyone owns a posh nightclub. "Viktor likes to be sort of an accountant and see things get taken care of. He doesn't want to be the one to run the businesses."

I gape as I take in what this means, "Holy shit, Tate! You own a freaking night club?" My eyes probably look like they're going to pop out of my head at this point.

He offers me his grin and the server brings our food. We dig in right away. The aroma makes my stomach growl loudly and Tate chuckles when he hears it.

Our lunch was delicious, and I feel like I need to be rolled out of here. 'Sweet Home Alabama' by Lynyrd Skynyrd starts playing as we sit on the patio and it brings a big, happy smile to my face.

"What is it, beautiful?" Tate happily inquires.

"This song, it makes me so happy." He tilts his head briefly to listen to it, then nods slightly. "My granddaddy taught me how to drive when I was growing up. I'd make him play this song over and over. I was around thirteen years old." His eyebrows raise, and I giggle a little as I remember the pleasant memory. "We have a lot of land so we took his old tan Chevy out to a dirt patch and he let me drive donuts over and over until I learned how to drive a stick shift. I had so much fun that day and Granddaddy called me Donut ever since."

"Пончик (donut), yes, you are very sweet, not so fluffy though, huh?" He murmurs deeply in Russian, making me swoon a little.

His laugh that follows is rich and it vibrates through me. I did it; I made him smile and laugh that laugh. It's like light in a dark room. God, I could fall asleep to his voice at night.

"I'm glad I was with you when you had a happy memory; that look on your face was gorgeous."

His phone begins to ring and he looks down at the caller ID, peeved, "Just a second, Пончик (donut)." He chuckles slightly when he calls me Donut again and it brings another large smile to my face.

"Sure, no problem."

He huffs angrily as he answers his phone, "What? No. I am out. What! Call the Balshoy Shef (big boss), now!" He looks pissed and hangs up without saying anything else.

Whatever the other person said sure did make him mad. I wonder what he said in Russian. It's so sexy when he speaks Russian, like mini ear orgasms.

Tate looks at me and gives me a little smile that seems kind of forced. "Ready, Emily? I have some things I have to take care of."

He gets up from his seat and reaches his hand out for me.

"Yes, of course. I hope everything's okay."

I take his hand without hesitation. I know I need to guard my heart, but he has shown me a kind side to him and it makes me want to open up a little more to him. I can't help but feel closer to him each time I'm around him. He's turned out to be pretty sweet and thoughtful these past few weeks. He listens to me blabber and just a moment ago when I saw that smile; it brought the other feelings to the very top.

Tate swiftly drives me back to my apartment. When we arrive, he gets out also and offers to walk me to my door again but I decline. He seems a little distracted, so I want to let him take care of whatever needs to be done.

He leans over and gives me a soft, sweet kiss on my cheek while we stand on the sidewalk. I scan the parking lot, paranoid, per my usual routine. Everything appears clear, thankfully.

"Have a good day, Krasaaveetsa (beauty). I can't wait until we can do this again." He stares straight into my eyes as he says this. I wish he would just lean in and really kiss me again.

"You too, Tate, and thank you again. I'll see you later." He nods and climbs back into his amazing car. I watch him leave the parking lot, before heading into my building.

I skip up to my apartment because I just had a really great lunch. I'm so distracted with thoughts of Tate Masterson, I don't notice the long stemmed white rose laying in the hallway.

## Five days later...

I'm walking out of the Science building with Avery when I notice the back of someone in the distance. *It can't be, no way.* My heart starts beating fast, stomach fluttering with nerves.

This person does have long black hair, tattoos all over and is pretty tall. They turn around and I freak out. I start jumping up and down like a lunatic then take off running.

"Whoa! Emily! Calm down, girl!" I hear Avery call out and

start trekking after me. She sounds a little panicked and I probably freaked her out, but she doesn't see who I see.

"Holy fuckballs! That's one hot ass chick!" London hollers loudly across the courtyard when she sees me, then runs toward me, too.

I start laughing loudly, excited. I can't believe she's freaking here, in Tennessee! She surprised me. I absolutely have the best friend in the whole world!

"Not as hot as you!" I bellow back and leap at her.

London is five foot-eight and about 160 pounds so she catches me easily. She's built like a muscular pinup model. Her black hair reaches mid back. She has striking cool blue eyes that are almond shaped and legs that seem to go on for miles. Her legs are insane because she always does lunges and leg presses. She has huge boobs and a small waist, she reminds me of a tattooed Coke bottle.

London always dresses kind of slutty and is a big partier, but she's actually one of the smartest people I know. She had to do a lot of her college courses online to save money, but she's studying to be an engineer. London could probably even be a doctor if she wanted to.

We finally quit hugging, pulling away, but I keep hold of her hand. If anything so I know she's real.

"I can't believe it's actually you, you're really here!" I shake her hand excitedly, "God, I didn't realize how much I missed you until I saw your face right now." I whisper and a tear leaks down my cheek.

I feel so emotional all of a sudden. It's like I've been running a race and my relief just grabbed my baton to make it to the finish line for me. I take a deep breath, loving it that I can really breathe now, with her next to me.

London leans in, grinning happily and gives me another small hug. She's always been great at reading me, so she probably knows I'm a mess inside right now.

"I was missing you and we haven't gotten to talk much, and yeah, I just needed to make sure you were safe and okay." She looks a little uneasy when she says this and I'm instantly on alert.

Elliot didn't say anything in the last text message, though it's been a few weeks now. I think she's not telling me something and it makes me freak out a little inside. Now that I take a closer look, even her clothes are appearing a little frazzled, which is not her style. She's always dressed to impress.

"Of course I'm okay!" I send her a tense smile that she sees right through, "Why, do I have a reason to be worried?" Right as I'm saying this, Avery, Tate and Cameron walk up to us.

I glance to Avery and give her a sheepish grin, "I'm sorry if I scared you, chick, but I caught sight of London and couldn't control my excitement!" I nod toward London. "London, these are my friends: Avery, Cameron and this is Tate. Guys, this is my best friend, London Layla Traverson." I beam at London as I say her full name.

"Oh, bitch! You had to bust out the middle name?" She glares at me briefly, then turns a charming smile on everyone else. "Hi everyone and don't listen to this loser, my name's just London."

I start giggling loudly because this reminds me of third grade when I got all the boys to sing 'Layla' to her. She was so furious she didn't talk to me for two whole days. After those two days I gave in and apologized. She admitted that she couldn't hold out any longer either.

Now after all these years I still enjoy teasing her any chance I get. London is loud and has a bad mouth, but I wouldn't change her for the world. She's been there for me when I needed her my entire life and has never left my side.

That is until I had to leave hers; but I had to run away from that psycho.

Avery turns to me and smiles mischievously back at me. "Actually this is perfect. Tate and Cameron her, were just asking me if we all wanted to do something tonight. I was saying food, but now that Miss London is here, maybe she'd like to go out tonight?"

Avery turns her playful smile at London and London returns a playful smile of her own.. Oh great, tonight is going to be crazy, I already know.

"Of course, we would love to go out! Do you boys have a hot friend that can come too, so I have a dance partner? If not, I'll have to steal these two ladies to dance with me all night."

Of course she just agrees without asking me. London has dragged me to so much stuff over the years. It's miraculous we didn't end up in jail half the time.

Tate gazes at me while he answers London, "Of course we have someone, tell me your type and we will pick you girls up tonight at 9:30."

# EMILY

**W**E MAKE IT BACK TO MY APARTMENT AND A FEW hours later, London has finally woken up from a nap.

I turn to her, "So, don't take this the wrong way. I'm super happy you're here and I love seeing your lovely face, but why exactly are you here?"

I feel bad for asking, but it's driving me crazy. I keep picturing worst-case scenarios in my head over and over. I need a little bit of reassurance that I'm being irrational.

We continued getting dressed for our night out with the boys. Of course London and Avery dressed me up like a hooker after London saw Tate staring at me. It was pretty much cemented in her head to hook me up. They keep telling me the dress is hot, and I look great but I think I appear almost naked in it.

I guess we were supposed to check out some club called 'Tainted' tonight, but Avery won London over with the 007 theme. Now it's back to 007 for us. I swear Avery would go to 007 every time she's off, if we were up for it. That girl loves to dance and have some fun.

I hope it's not another drama-filled night. I don't know if I can handle Tate on an Alpha kick again. I'm not going to hold my breath, knowing London's shenanigans.

London mumbles, "Look, Emily, let's have a little fun tonight. I just got here and want to have a good time with you guys. We can talk about all the serious stuff tomorrow, okay?"

She has looked pretty stressed out since I first saw her at the university. It looks like she could use some more sleep too, which is weird for my friend. At least she got in a short nap today.

I nod and smile; it's fake but I want to reassure her, "Okay, that sounds like a plan, and don't forget we are checking out one of the lakes this weekend. I don't care if both of you are rocking hangovers or not! It'll be even more fun now that you are going with Avery and me."

I'm so happy London and Avery have hit it off and have become fast friends.

She chuckles, "Us hungover? Oh no, girly, I'm in town, you can relax for a night or two or three. It will be perfectly fine to have some drinks and cut loose with all of us around you."

London's shooting me her annoyed look where she scrunches up her eyebrows and has a line down the center of her forehead. Speaking of lines, I know how to distract her from talking me into making bad decisions and getting plowed with them.

"Wow, when you make that face it shows a big line in your forehead. Are you getting wrinkles, London?   It looks like you might be getting too much sun." Avery busts out laughing at me. Damn it, she caught on to my distraction.

"Don't listen to her, London; she's trying to get you off topic." She gives me a big shit-eating grin.

"You suck, Avery! You're fired!"

Avery giggles, "Nope. You already fired me at the coffee shop, so technically you can't fire me anymore!"

I think about lunging at her and tackling her to the ground. I know once I get her there London will at least help me tickle her. Right as I go to make my move, there's a knock on my apartment door.

Avery jumps up really fast and practically runs to the door to answer it. She must be a little excited to see Cameron. *Or not.*

She completely ignores Cameron as he walks in. Avery hurriedly gives the big guy they brought with them an excited hug. I'll have to ask her about that later.

Cam puts on a wide smile, "Ladies, ladies, ladies, are we ready to have some fun?" Cam's voice booms through my tiny apartment.

London eats up the loudness and gravitates toward Cameron as soon as she sees her. They both eye-fuck each other while Avery talks to the new hot, blond guy. Wow, never would have predicted this one.

Tate gives me a soft smile and walks toward me. He leans down and sweetly kisses me on my cheek. My heart melts a little at the touch of his lips.

"Hey, little pet, you look breathtaking. I love this dress on you. I'm going to have to break some guy's knees tonight, huh?"

Break some knees? Who says that? I look at him like he's lost his mind and it makes him chuckle. Yeah, definitely no personality disorder here! *Riiiiight.*

"Relax, Krasaaveetsa, I'm only joking. I'd have Nikoli here do it for me." He smirks towards the other guy that came with them.

Nikoli is a beast. He's huge, full of muscles, probably 6'5" and covered in tribal tattoos. He's still really good looking for being so big; he has short blond hair and dark blue eyes. He looks like the ultimate Russian fighter.

Nikoli grins down at me and I look at Tate. I have to admit, a man that big really does frighten me inside. He looks so friendly, but I'm still shaky towards men in general. Not so much with Tate, but everyone else.

Tate squeezes my bicep softly, "Emily, this is Nikoli, he was a bouncer at 007 when we went last time." He nods toward him and looks back at me, "Nikoli, this is my Krasaaveetsa, Emily." He looks really excited to be introducing me. I think he may have told Nikoli about me already.

"Nice to meet you, Nikoli."

I stick my hand out being courteous and Nikoli grabs me with both of his big, meaty paw-like hands. He brings me in for a hug and I think I squeak.

"Preevyetstvavats Shef dyevooshka (Welcome Bosses lady)." Tate beams a smile after Nikoli speaks.

I glance between both of them, puzzled. "Huh?"

Nikoli looks at me sheepishly and grins so his dimples pop out. Such a cutie.

"I apologize. I speak Russian so much, that sometimes it automatically comes out. I said Welcome..." Tate shakes his head minutely but I still catch it. "Umm, lady," he finishes, nodding.

Hmm, I wonder what he really said. I won't ask Tate right now, but I am curious. Hopefully I can remember some of it to Google later.

Everyone's heading toward the door, so I guess it's that time. I grab my small purse and shuffle out the door behind them. I lock up and follow them outside.

Tate has his large, black Tahoe again, so we can all ride together and have a designated driver. I get little flutters inside, thinking about how thoughtful he really is. He's always looking out for my comfort level and I don't know if he even realizes he does it.

Tate starts to bark orders as soon as we reach the vehicle, "You girls will have to sit on Cam and Nikoli's laps. Emily, you will sit in the front with me." Everyone jumps into action and I just stand there. *Yeah, I don't think so.* I don't take orders from men anymore.

This reminds me, I need to check out the parking lot. I start scanning all the vehicles and my surroundings. There are lights outside but there are too many dark spots for me to see everything.

At least I'm surrounded by three big men. I don't have to completely freak out right now, about being outside in the dark. I still feel like I'm being watched everywhere I go and I have to make myself stop this madness. I'm going to get an ulcer with the worrying all the time.

Turning to Tate, I argue, "Umm, why, Tate, that doesn't make sense. Let Nikoli sit up front, because we will all fit better in the back."

"Come, Krasaaveetsa, get in the front." Tate replies with a stern look and I just roll my eyes at him.

"No, Tate, I'm not jumping because you say so. This doesn't make sense and I know I'm right. You need to give in on this one."

This man is always making me feel like a teenager around him. I mean technically twenty is very young, but he makes me feel fifteen. I'm always angry, turned on, arguing or feeling like I'm falling head over heels for him. I thought this was what happened when you were young, not in college.

He grumbles, "I didn't ask you to jump, I asked you to sit down."

Tate must realize this is going to be a battle because before I can get a response out, he picks me up. Nikoli opens the front door and Tate shoves me in the front seat. Nikoli smiles really big at me and shuts the door quickly.

I'm so shocked it doesn't even register what they just did for a few seconds. I feel my mouth gaping and physically reach up to cover it. The balls on these men are uncanny.

Tate gets in the SUV and gazes at me; I can only stare at him with my mouth open. I cannot believe that just happened. I don't know whether to be pissed off or turned on right now.

Avery sits in the back giggling like it's the greatest thing ever and London's looking at Tate like he hung the moon. Freaks, damn freaks, I'm surrounded by crazies.

## The next morning...

"Oh My God, my head! What time is it? What happened last night?"

Is that Avery's scratchy-ass voice I hear pounding into my head? Why is she yelling?"Duuuude, shut up! And go back to sleep." That sleepy voice is definitely London's, so she really is here after all.

Avery chokes out, "Fuck, I'm going to be sick!" She runs to the bathroom but trips over me and goes flying onto another body under a comforter. I want to laugh at her because it was hilarious, but my head and stomach hurt too badly.

She mumbles, scrambling to get up, "Ooof. Shit! Sorry!" She takes off running again. I hear her slam the bathroom door and we all let out a collective groan.

Tate peeks his head up out of the blanket that Avery just tripped on and looks over at me. He looks absolutely adorable, like a sleepy puppy. Only hot, and male, with bed head, and wow, yep, no shirt on.

He leans up so the blanket falls to his stomach and I can't look away from his gorgeous body. Tattoos cover his pecs and little barbells adorn each nipple. He is ripped, way more so than I had thought from dancing with him. He has a little happy trail of brown hair that leads over his six pack. *He has a freaking six pack! Of course he does.*

Tate slowly leans toward me and kisses my forehead and whispers softly, "Morning, baby." I melt a little inside when he says it so naturally, like it happens daily. I give him a small smile because he just made this horrible hangover a little better by being here when I first woke up.

"Good morning, Tate."

I start to lean up also, but freak when the blanket falls down. I scramble to pull the blanket back over my chest swiftly. Damn it, Tate just got an eye full!

"Holy fuck! Why am I naked?"

Tate gives me his grin and the dimples come out to play. Oh no, here it comes.

"Well, last night all of you ladies decided to sleep naked." Tate chuckles, gesturing to me, "You all decided it would be one less thing you had to worry about in the morning. I tried to get you to keep at least your panties and bra on, but you wouldn't hear of it." I feel my face start to burn and know it's probably red as a cherry.

"I got you to lie down under the blanket, but you made me promise I'd stay right beside you or you would take the blanket off. You said something about being scared and needing me to protect you. I stayed because I swear if either one of these fuckers looked at you, I'd be throwing blows. I told you to relax, that I'll always keep you safe. You kissed me pretty sloppily and told me you like me way too much. Then you snuggled into me and passed right out." He finishes, flashing that adoring stare in my direction.

Good lord, I'm mortified at this moment. There is a reason I don't drink. I tend to binge drink when I do, and then I can't remember anything the next day.

"Oh my gosh! I'm so sorry I put you through that. That's just awful, I'm so embarrassed!"

Cameron starts chuckling and lifts his head up to look over at me. *Oh God, what now?*

"Are you kidding, Emily? Tate was in heaven. You were naked, and you're bangin', by the way. Not only were you showing your boy the goods, but he got to take care of you and boss you around last night. I think you just fulfilled one of his secret fantasies!" Cam starts laughing some more at the face I make; I guess you can call it disgruntled. Yep, I'm disgruntled.

He groans, "Ow. Shit. My head is killing me." Cameron winces and puts the blanket over his head again. Thank God, no more stories out of him!

"Good, that's what you deserve for making Emily embarrassed." Tate is looking over toward where Cam is lying like he wants to strangle him.

"Shhhhhh! Please, Boss!" That was Nikoli.

Geez, did everyone stay here last night? I guess so, if Tate is here, considering he was the one who drove everyone. I can't believe I even had enough blankets. Looking around I see there are actually only three blankets out. Guess I'm not the only one who was snuggled up to someone last night. I see the spot is empty next to Nikoli, so that means Avery must have slept beside him.

She comes out of the bathroom sluggishly and looking a little green. Avery has a bright peach towel wrapped tightly around her.

I mutter, "Surprise! I see you discovered you're naked also?!" I don't say it too loudly because my head is pounding but I do say it full of sarcasm. I need to find my Excedrin at this point.

"Huh? Oh, yeah. No biggie, Nikoli is naked, too. We had fun being naked together." She grins elatedly and crawls back under the blanket with Nikoli. Well that answers some of my questions for her.

Groaning, I lean over, "Ugh, this is why I don't drink. I'm never drinking like that again." I scoop up my shirt and lie back down. I know I can get it back on underneath the covers.

London huffs, "Yes, you are. We are going to the lake later and probably that river restaurant place y'all told me about." She perks up a little and I just want to throw something at her. I look around and spot one of my flip flops.

"Ooof!" says a deep voice. Shit, that was Cam, not London. I pick up my other flip flop and chuck it a little harder.

"Fuck!" Yep, that's London. Well that just put a smile on my face.

Tate pulls my back in close to his chest and wraps his arms around me tight. I feel his nose and lips close to my neck and his breaths tickle the back of my neck. My nipples get hard from it and I squeeze my legs together to try to relieve some of the ache he has put there. I swear I feel his teeth graze my neck and it turns me on like crazy.

Tate whispers "Sleep, my Krasaaveetsa, I have you."

And I do, I sleep the best that I have in months.

I slowly start to wake up and look around the living room. Tate and Nikoli are missing. I see London and Cameron spooning on the couch watching a movie and I hear the shower going. I'm guessing Avery is in the shower since she brought clothes with her to stay the night.

I check out the clock and see it's already noon. Wow. I can't believe the girls are up and moving around already. I was expecting to have to drag them out of the blankets and yell loudly to get them awake.

I rasp, "Mornin', where is everyone?" I ask the room in general.

Cameron pops his head up and looks at me. He's so tall his feet hang over the arm of the couch. I can't believe they can both fit on that couch together, with his size and London's butt. He has the cute lazy look going on. His hair has a bad case of bed head, going every which way like Tate's earlier. His eyes are the color of Hershey's chocolate and he has long, pretty eyelashes. He's always so put together and all preppy looking when I see him. Seeing him relaxed and lounging around actually makes him look so much cuter. He kind of reminds me of a muscular pretty-boy.

Cameron and London look absolutely beautiful together; I bet they would have little babies that would look like models. Ha! That's silly, London and Cameron are both hardcore players, there's no point me even going there.

"Tate and Nikoli left to shower, change, get me some clothes and pick up one of the boats. Avery's feeling better so she's in the shower right now. I think she's trying to be ready before Nikoli gets back. She was rushing around all crazy as soon as he left."

I look at Cameron like he's speaking Chinese. Did he just say one of the boats? Freaking spoiled boys!

"Umm, boat?" I repeat like I don't know how to use my words.

"Yeah, you said you wanted to go to the lake or river, right? Tate's family has a few boats so he went to go get one. He wants you to be pleased, so he was going to pick up a chest of drinks and everything we would need."

He uses his hands to make quote marks and tries to sound like Tate when he talks, "Tate said he wants everyone to be ready to go whenever you want to leave." Cameron huffs then goes back to talking normally, "They should be back anytime; they've been gone for a while."

I just stare at Cam, because...I mean...shit. I really don't know what to even say. Tate is thinking of me yet again. He's even going out of his way to make me happy, just like he did that first night and like last night.

I leisurely trek into the kitchen to get some caffeine. I need to wake up. On the counter there is a white, long stemmed calla lily.

"Hey, who got the flower?" I ask no one in general again. I'm still stuck in zombie mode.

"Oh, Tate brought it in and set it on the counter." London opens her pretty little mouth for the first time. Cameron must be doing something right, to keep that one so quiet. It's like he has her tamed or something right now.

Tate is so sweet. I don't remember him buying me a flower, but then I don't even remember coming home, so yeah.

Avery comes breezing out of the shower looking all brand new. You'd never guess she was blowing chunks this morning. She has on a hot pink bikini top, white jean shorts and white flip flops. She looks adorable. Avery has her hair down and brushed straight, with just a little mascara on her face. She actually looks younger than usual with her makeup missing.

"Geez, sweets, you are rocking some serious abs! Playing volleyball sure does agree with you."

I'm not a fan of abs on chicks; I think it's not really a feminine look. I have always believed women are meant to look a little softer and men are supposed to be hard and full of muscle. She sure can pull it off though; she looks hot.

She grins, "Thanks, Em. I quit the team though."

"What? I thought you were on scholarship?"

"I was but I ended up getting an academic scholarship because of my grades. It's not as good as the other, but I'm able to switch over to Accounting as my major. Now I won't have to train as much either. It was just getting old."

"As long as you're happy, Avery," I reply, giving her a worried look. She doesn't like to really be tied down to anything and I'm concerned about her not completing her degree. It's not really my business though.

I hop in the shower long enough to do a quick upkeep and

wash my hair. I have a new red bikini I'm going to try out today.

Tate seems to like it when I'm wearing red, pink or black the most. He's been going out of his way for me, so I'm going to wear a color he likes. Plus, I want his attention on me and with Avery and London's hot bodies, he might get distracted.

I put lots of lotion on since I'm going to be in the sun, some mascara, and lip gloss. That's as good as it's going to get. I hurry, knowing London and Cameron need to get in here, too.

I step out of the bathroom and am instantly assaulted with the delicious smell of cheeseburgers. *Yum.* I feel like I could eat a horse right now and drink about a gallon of water. That smells amazing.

London turns towards me when she hears me open the bathroom door. "There she is! Girl, this guy is out here trying to get us all to hurry up! Please tell your man to calm down, that you're not ready to leave yet either."

She is smiling brightly at me from teasing Tate. When I glance at Tate, he's looking at the ground a little bashful. I just roll my eyes at her. She's never going to stop picking on Tate if he lets her get away with it.

Ignoring her, I ask Tate, "Is that burgers I smell? God, it smells really good!"

"Yes, I stopped and got Freddy's. I figured the greasy food might help everyone feel a little better." He gives me a shy smile.

Oh my, Tate Masterson bashful and shy?! Where did the stubborn alpha go that I'm used to seeing? I really like it that he's showing me this side of him.

I nod, "That sounds wonderful, Tate, thanks for being so thoughtful."

I go up on my tippy toes and give him a quick chaste kiss on the lips. He briefly hugs me to him and kisses my forehead. I get rewarded with his handsome smile afterwards.

London and Cameron shower together. That's an experience

alone, with all the noise he has her making in there. That bitch is totally cleaning my shower before she goes back home. It definitely sounds like Cam knows what he's doing in there.

Afterwards, she walks out in a black bikini, full of cheesy smiles.

I just shake my head at her, amused, "Okay can we please go now? Everyone's had plenty of time to get ready." I glance at each of them, "Hey, where's Nikoli?" I ask, scanning the apartment.

"He's checking out all the stuff on the boat. I told him to make sure we had plenty of life jackets, towels, that kind of stuff," Tate responds and gestures toward the window that faces the parking lot.

"Awesome! Thank you so much for getting your boat, Tate, you've made me even more excited than I already was!" I gaze at him gratefully. He keeps stealing little pieces of me that I'm trying not to give away.

I ask the first thing that pops into my head, "Which lake are we going to, anyhow?" I want him to know I appreciate everything he's done and I'm really thrilled about it. I've never had any man be so thoughtful toward me before.

"We, my little pet, are going to Tellico Lake." He grasps my hand, wrapping it in both of his larger palms.

He brings it to his face and kisses the top of it before continuing. "It's about thirty miles southwest from here. There's a retirement community, a private gated, wealthy community and lots of warehouses with loading docks available."

"Oh that sounds cool."

"Yeah, my parents actually have a house on one of the hills, I'll show it to you when we pass by it in the boat. There are also lots of restaurants and a Calhoun's really close that we can eat at when we dock, if you would like. You should have fun."

Tate has definitely put some thought into this and planned an outing that sounds like so much fun. I swear he just made me swoon. I love a man who can take something I enjoy and plan a fun day of it. He actually looks excited to experience it all with me.

Tate looks edible in black board shorts with little white skulls in a line down each leg. He has on a white tank top with a little black Hollister logo on the left side and black leather flip flops. Ultimate beach boy but still looks manly. I can't wait to see that shirt come off again. I hope I get to rub sunscreen all over that yummy body.

I love it that he dresses so differently than my ex. Tate always has a relaxed, rich look to him. He's extremely well groomed and he appears stern, but he can also be friendly when he feels like it.

"You look really good in your boat clothes. I like that I can see your tattoos displayed, they are so sexy!" The sexy slips out and I shut my mouth quickly.

I'm supposed to be moving slow or not at all, but I find us moving a million miles a minute instead. I know I have issues and I'm messed up about some things. Tate makes me forget about any of it when I'm near him. It's like I just exist and everything bad washes itself away.

He growls, pulling me closer, "Sexy, hmm? No, Krasaaveetsa, you look fucking sexy. I would love to kiss your neck all over and untie that top with my teeth. I bet you taste delectable, all that creamy skin, begging to be bitten." He inhales deeply, and then moves himself further away from me. "Let's get going before I push you too far." I gape at what he says. I was not expecting to hear him talk like that at all.

Now that's all I can picture: His teeth undoing my top and then his teeth and tongue on my nipples, sucking, swirling and biting. That sounded so erotic the way he said it and has me turned on.

I squeeze my legs together for a minute and imagine what it would be like to have him there; his hands, his face, his cock. It's been years since anyone has been near my pussy. It's been long enough. I take a deep cleansing breath and reel in my thoughts.

Everyone is finally ready to leave. We snatch up all our beach bags, heading out of the apartment.

We all file out of the apartment building to find Tate has a huge teal boat hooked up to his Tahoe in the parking lot. I get so excited inside when I see it. The boat is stunning.

"Ayyyyyy!" Nikoli hollers 'Hey' at us but it comes out sounding kind of like 'A'.

He's standing in the middle of the boat with a straw cowboy hat that has a big blue band around it advertising a brand of vodka. Leave it to the Russian to be advertising vodka.

Nikoli's missing a shirt and has on some neon green and black board shorts. He looks like his body was made specifically to be without clothes on. His chest muscles and abs appear as if they are carved out of stone; they are so perfect and pro-nounced. He definitely spends many hours in the gym, honing in a perfect body.

"Niiiice! We are going to have a boat full of hot chicks! Hey, girls! Sun's out, gun's out!" He beams a huge smile at us and flexes his muscular arms.

We all burst out laughing. He chuckles, pleased he made us all smile and laugh. Nikoli has such a great, friendly personality you almost have to like him.

He jumps off the boat and gives me a mini heart attack, he's up so high. He walks straight to Avery, kisses her hard and then picks her up and twirls her in circles while she screams. She might be yelling and complaining, but I know she loves it.

We start our drive to the lake, with me riding up front again. *Go figure.* Tate sure is stubborn. I remember how excited he got when I asked about his car, so I'm going to ask him about his boat this time.

"Your boat is really nice. What kind is it?"

Tate smirks, flashing a small smile at me then turns back to watch as he drives.

"Thanks, babe. It's a Chris Craft Corsair 36 Cruiser. Are you familiar with boats?" I get a tingly feeling all over when he calls me babe. I'm totally falling for him and it's only been a little over a month since I first met him. Is it really possible to fall for someone that fast?

I think back to the boat. The boat is huge enough to fit probably ten people up top. I had to get a tour before we all loaded into the SUV. It has all wood grain detail and a cabin. The cabin has a table that converts to a queen size bed, a small kitchen counter with water faucet and fridge. It even has a bathroom with a shower, sink and toilet. The boat itself is a rich teal color but the inside is all creams and grey leather.

"Nope, we usually would just swim at a little lake with friends at Travis County. Not much boating experience so I'm extra excited today!"

"Where was this? What's Travis County?" He looks intrigued. Shit, I should have kept my mouth shut. I don't want to talk about home.

"Oh, umm, just a place near where I used to live," I answer vaguely and hope he drops it.

"And where exactly did you used to live, Krasaaveetsa? You haven't told me much about where you came from and your friends there. I'm sure you must miss it; I know I miss my home."

It's Tate though, so of course he asks me more questions. After the past month of being together in class and for lunch, I've done a pretty decent job avoiding talking about my life. I've given him bits and pieces about my family, but nothing about the real reason why I'm in Tennessee in the first place. Now though, he is strictly able to concentrate on me and I should give him a little bit, considering how much closer we've become.

I stammer, "I just, umm, lived by a city called Austin, but in a smaller town, in Texas. Same as London and the only other people I really speak to there are London's family. She has a brother who takes care of my granddaddy's land for me." I shrug.

Speaking of, that idiot Elliot, hasn't returned my text messages or my voicemails. I'm talking to London about that ASAP when we get back to the apartment.

"Where is it you're from, Tate? I'm assuming Russia?"

"Yes, I'm from the neighborhood called Andel, Prague, but stayed a lot in Moscow." He smiles fondly, "Your family has land in Texas? I would love to see the state you came from. Would you want to visit? We could make a road trip or I could fly us?"

I feel myself pale at his words. There is absolutely no way I can go back there right now, if ever. I have been having crazy paranoid feelings already and then London showed up. I'm definitely going to find out what's going on today, why she decided to visit, no more 'relax and have fun.' I know she's procrastinating but if that *monster* is out then I have to do everything I can to prepare myself and to hide.

Maybe even take off running again if I have to.

"That's so sweet of you, Tate, but I have no reason to visit, maybe someday though." I close the conversation and try not to think of my past that is always haunting me.

After a short drive, we arrive at the stunning, glistening lake. It's a lot larger than I was expecting and I can't wait to get out on the water. I've heard a lot of these lakes around here are pretty dangerous for swimmers so you have to be careful. This is supposed to be the nicest lake around.

Tate peels his shirt off, reaching with one hand and ripping it over his head. His muscles clench and flex with each movement.

He throws his shirt in the SUV before preparing the boat for launching. He looks magnificent with his shirt off; my mouth waters at the striking sight of him.

"Hey, girly, shut your mouth." Avery comes up beside me and starts laughing when she sees my expression, staring at Tate.

"Yeah, no kidding. Thanks for stating the obvious, chickadee!" I chuckle, "I can't help it, that man is unbelievable."

His nipple rings glint in the sunshine and he has amazing hazel eyes that I know are sparkling, hidden behind his shades. Tate's body is completely lickable. He has cuts and dips all over like he has spent serious time on some gym equipment.

He almost looks like he could be a brawler when he's wearing one of his broody expressions. I wonder if he was a troublemaker as a kid. I bet he was a handful with his stubbornness.

He has a light tan going on. Nothing too dark, but it is noticeable especially since Tate is Russian. Nikoli for example is very white; I bet that man burns his tush off today.

I'm going to have to study Tate's tattoos later and find out what they all are. I've had so many chances but I kind of go brain dead when I'm around him. Whatever they are, they are awesome. It looks like some Russian writing on his arm with swirls and shading, some bionic looking gears on his left pec, maybe the Russian flag on his other arm? I don't know. It's all together in sleeves so it's really hard to pick it all apart when I'm not right next to him.

I'm watching him on the boat as he turns around. *Oh My God.* He has a tattoo spanning his whole back; wow that looks like it was painful. It's stunning, like a painting on skin.

"Hey, hot stuff, what's the tatt on your back?" I holler up at him from the dock.

"Huh? Oh, my back? It's Ares, God of War," he says and smiles big enough I see his bright white teeth.

Holy fuck, he's hot. God of War? Yeah, I can see Tate causing a whole bunch of chaos.

We spend the day sun bathing, swimming, boating and just being goofy. Afterwards we take London to Calhoun's so she can check out the deck and have some yummy food. There are lots of shots passed around, but none of us get hammered again. I am definitely exhausted from spending the day in the sun. I had so much fun and really hope we get to spend another day like this soon.

Tate was so thoughtful; he kept coming and rubbing sunscreen on me every hour and kept offering me drinks. He even stopped at the marina to run in and buy me a twelve-pack of sodas and M&M's. Tate basically doted on me all day and I feel very cherished by him.

I've never really had that before when dating a man. I met the *monster* when I was fifteen and he was seventeen. I thought he was everything and continued to think that for a few years.

The changes in him started to show after a while though. I don't know if they were changes or if he had been good at hiding from everyone and had been that way his whole life. I like to refer to him as 'The Monster' rather than his name, because that's exactly what he is – a fucking monster.

After such an awesome day and a great dinner we make our way back to my apartment. Avery is staying with London and me for the whole weekend so the three of us unload and grab up all our stuff.

Avery and Nikoli look like they might suck each other's faces off when they say goodbye and London gazes kind of bashfully at Cam. I wonder what that shit's all about. My London never acts like that around a guy; she's always calling the shots and I mean always.

Tate comes to me and pulls me into his arms in a warm, tight embrace. Even after being in the sun and water all day, Tate still smells divine. His face and body have a nice tan going on and his nose looks as if it got kissed by the sun a little too much. We had slowly gravitated toward each other all day and spent a lot more time getting to know each other.

"Good night my mallenkee Krasaaveetsa, I will see you tomorrow?" His lips graze my cheek delicately as he says this. I love hearing him speak Russian, it's a total aphrodisiac.

Nodding, I agree, "Yes, you can see me tomorrow, as long as I can bring the girls. What was that you just said? It sounded so alluring; I love when you speak Russian to me." I peer up into his eyes and our lips align but he's much taller than me, so they don't touch.

"I called you my little beauty: mallenkee Krasaaveetsa." I beam at him because he is turning out to be pretty perfect.

"Oh, before I forget again, thank you for the flower this morning, it is beautiful!" I squeeze him to me as I say this.

"You're welcome, little pet. I think someone dropped it in the hall this morning so I thought you might enjoy it." He dips his head toward mine and places his lips on mine before I can respond. Tate takes his time and kisses me slowly, softly and deeply. I feel like I'm tasting him for the first time, like he is showing me a piece of himself. I wrap my hands around his firm waist and pull him closer to me. He has my face cradled in between his hands as he controls our kiss.

When he pulls back, I suck on his bottom lip and make him groan. Tate presses a chaste kiss to my forehead and gives me a little smack on the ass as he starts to walk to his SUV.

"Night, girls, keep an eye on my Krasaaveetsa for me!" he chortles loudly as he walks around the large vehicle.

Tate hops in the driver's side and pulls out of the parking lot. As they start to drive away, Nikoli leans out of his window and wolf whistles at us. I chuckle at his silliness. We all wave and head inside.

# SEVEN

## EMILY

THE GIRLS ARE TALKING QUICKLY AND EXCITEDLY about the day when we get to the apartment. I open the door and choke out a loud gasp as it hits me. Blinking frantically, I take in the entire area.

Every surface in the apartment is covered in white rose petals. *The smell.* The smell hits me and I lean over, resting my hands on my thighs as I gag. I knew my life was too good to be true today. The apartment smells strongly of the monsters body spray I used to love him wearing.

I feel a tear burn as it runs down my cheek but I'm unable to speak, it's like I blank out. I glare over at London and see she's gone ashy and has tears streaming down her face. She knows what this is, she knows what this means. London knew. She had to. This means *he* is here. This means he has found me.

I whisper brokenly to London, "You knew."

Avery looks really confused but comes up and hugs me. "What's going on, girl, what's with the flowers and why are you guys so upset?" She looks confused. She may be my friend, but this is no one's business. She needs to go home where it's safe for her.

"It's nothing, Avery." I try to avoid her question, sucking in some of my emotions that are dying to break free and allow me to freak out.

London shrieks, heatedly, "Bullshit! It's not nothing! It's everything! You can't keep dealing with this alone. You can't keep hiding from this. Tell her or I will, people need to know."

I glare at London as she yells this in my face; she knows this is my fucking secret. No one needs to know what I went through, what I continue to go through. He doesn't deserve to be talked about or cried over.

I look at Avery and nod my head. Fine, they want to hear some of the details of how fucked up I let my life get, fine.

"Fuck it, whatever. But don't you dare fucking cry about it. He doesn't deserve the tears; he doesn't even deserve my words." I mumble out, defeated.

I walk to my bedroom and get my pistol. I'll be damned if he does that to me again. I want Tate, so I have to fight this time.

Muttering angrily as I enter the room again, "I'm not telling her everything. I can't deal with talking about it all. I'll tell you a few highlights about the monster, Avery. First off, this is the monster's work, we don't say his name; he doesn't get that privilege."

I look from London's grief-stricken face to Avery's curious but cautious one and begin.

# EMILY

### Two years ago...

I still can't get over the fact that I'm pregnant. *I'm going to be a mommy!* I can't wait to tell London all about this.

Maybe this is just the sort of thing that Jeremy needs to start treating me better, like he used to. This could be exactly what we need and it's all because of you, M. I'm going to call you M, because you're my tiny miracle. I promise I'm going to be the best momma ever.

Let's see, Jeremy will be home in about two hours. I'm going to shower and get all freshened up. After I'm done, I'll cook a nice dinner. I hope he didn't get upset at work today. I know the factory stresses him out. Maybe now he will understand that it's good I take all those college courses online. I'll be able to get a job after the baby's born and he will have less stress to deal with.

I prepare one of his favorite chicken dishes and place it into the oven to cook. It should be ready right before he gets home.

I take a deep, anxious breath and promise myself that everything will be fine. Jeremy will stop being so mean to me all of the time. He's even started slapping me a couple times when he says I screw up. Now that I'm pregnant though I know he will stop. It's not good for our little M.

Jeremy will be so happy to have someone else to love him and show him attention. He's obsessive about having all of my focus. I'll call London with the good news after I let Jeremy know.

I stuff my cheap phone into my back jeans pocket, that way it's ready after I get done celebrating the good news. I wonder what Granddaddy will say when I get to tell him. He will probably be excited to have a little one around, as long as I'm happy.

The oven timer dings and I grab my mitts to pull the chicken out of the oven. I place the large casserole dish on our little table I have set up for us and grab the bread. I pour a tall glass of milk for myself and straighten out the silverware for the third time.

I can hear the rumble of Jeremy's truck as he pulls up. I'm

actually excited for him to be home. Lately I have been dreading it, but today is a joyful day.

The front door slams open and it makes my heart speed up. I've developed a little bit of anxiety. The doctor calls them mini panic attacks, but that can't be right because I have no real reason to be stressed.

I have flutters in my belly when Jeremy steps inside. Not butterflies, but I almost feel as if I want to puke. It's probably the baby. Oh no, I forgot about the morning sickness. I hope it's after Jeremy goes to work, because he won't like it cutting into his time.

I smile, it may look a little fake but hopefully he will be too distracted with dinner on the table to notice. He looks grouchy and worn out. The factory and stress has been ageing him.

He has grey eyes and long black hair that he tucks behind his ears. Girls in high school thought he was hot but Jeremy's very shy. I was one of the only girls to talk to him regularly, so he asked me to be his girlfriend after a while.

Jeremy has a long, muscular body like a swimmer. He's always dressed in a pair of jeans and plain t-shirt. He has always reminded me more of a musician. He looks like he could be some depressed rock singer on stage.

I look into his eyes and smile for real this time, thinking about M. I'm excited to tell him our news. I know it will cheer him up.

He looks at me surprised, "You cooked Ritz Chicken, boo?"

"Yes, Jeremy, I know it's one of your favorites."

"And it's done when I get home? Maybe you're finally learning, boo, but where's my tea? Gotta put some more effort into it, Emily."

"Right, sorry. I'll get it. I have some great news to share with you."

"Oh yeah? Tell me this greeeeeat news you have." He

86

grumbles out.

I'm not going to let it dampen my spirits. Today is about M and our future.

"I went to Dr. Anderson's office this morning."

"How did you get there?" he asks as he sits at our ugly little table and begins to cut into his chicken.

"Oh, I took a cab, I was unwell." I give him my most innocent look, hoping he won't get angry.

"Great, Emily. You're wasting more fucking money, just like those bullshit college courses." He shakes his head at me as if he's disappointed and I cringe.

Suddenly he slams his hand down on the table so forcefully the glass holding my milk shatters. Milk spills, flooding the table. *Oh no.* Where's a towel so I can hurry and clean this up? Jeremy hates messes and I need to get it cleaned up as fast as possible.

I leap up quickly to grab a towel. Once I clean up the mess and he starts to chew his food, I sit and try again.

"Dr. Anderson did a test and found out I'm pregnant; I'm about six weeks she thinks." I grin, because this is it, I know he will jump up and hug me.

"What did you just say?" He growls out lowly.

Oh no, he doesn't look too excited. Fuck! This was supposed to go a whole lot better than this.

"Umm, I said I'm pregnant. Isn't that wonderful?" I ask timidly.

Jeremy jumps up suddenly and stuff goes flying off the table when he hits it with his thighs. I leap up and out of the way at the crash and immediately attempt to hide my face with my hands.

He storms toward me swiftly and punches me straight in the face. The impact is so solid and painful, I stumble. Jeremy comes at me again; he hits me so hard, that this time I fall. On my way down I hit my head on the wall next to the kitchen table.

## Ten minutes later...

I must have blacked out. I wake to Jeremy screaming, "You will not be some filthy, fucking, pregnant teenage slut in this house. You think I'll let everyone talk about me and my knocked up whore of a girlfriend."

He repeatedly kicks me brutally in my stomach. My head is pounding something fierce and I'm in pain like I've never experienced before. My vision is hazy, like I'm stuck in a horrifying nightmare, only I know I won't wake up to happiness.

My body is screaming in pain at me with each blow he deals. It hurts so horribly, I start to puke everywhere and I pee my pants. I can't help it. I sob, as I wrap my hands around my stomach as much as I can.

He starts laughing maniacally, "You think you can protect yourself from me? You stupid bitch, I'll fix your problem."

Jeremy kicks me one last time really, really hard and I gasp. The air is knocked from my lungs and I feel as if I'm suffocating. There's this huge weight on my chest and I think I may pass out again.

The only other time I've felt this feeling is when I lost my mother. That agonizing pain in your chest as a piece of you breaks.

He grits out, disgusted, "Now, you clean yourself up and get rid of that fucking problem you have. Don't ever tell me any dumb shit like that again. I can't believe you made me hit you again. I fucking swear, Emily, get your act together. I'll be back; I can't deal with your shit right now."

Once the door slams I try my best to get my phone out. London can help me. I feel like I'm dying.

# SECRETS

## Two weeks later...

I spend two weeks in the hospital. I guess I'm 'fortunate' there is no internal bleeding. They have no idea what fortunate means.

Little M is gone. My precious, innocent little baby was stolen from me. He was condemned to his father's wrath and I was unable to save him.

I know this is not the life I want. I know I have to get away and although I'm too broken and sick inside to do anything right now, I will do it. One day he will come home and I will be gone, just like my little M.

## Three weeks later...

It's been a total of five weeks now, since I lost my precious baby and discovered the true monster I'm living with. That is what he is, a monster. I hate him and it makes me sick when he touches me. I wish that he would just die. Each day I imagine him getting crushed when he goes to work at the factory. I want him to suffer.

Thankfully the doctors told him to not be intimate with me for a few weeks or I'd have to go back to the hospital. He doesn't like to draw attention so that helped me out some. Jeremy stayed away for three weeks, but after that he said I'd just have to "get over my shit."

Things have slowly gone back to our 'normal.' Jeremy works, comes home to dinner made, he complains, treats me like crap and has slapped me twice this week. He's no longer worried about breaking my nose, since he broke it when he punched me.

Jeremy says he has to keep me on my toes, to teach me how to be a good wife to him someday. I will never be his wife. *I hate him.* This hate inside me grows with each insult, each slap, and each rough fuck he makes me endure.

It's Thursday now, I know I have one day left of him to go to work before he's off for the weekend. I can't handle being home with him for two full days; he will probably end up killing me. I have to do this, I have to get out.

Once Granddaddy finds out what Jeremy's been doing, he will shoot his ass with his favorite twelve gauge shot gun. I can't believe London has kept my secret for this long. She said I have till Saturday to tell Granddaddy then she's doing it. I hope I can get it out and tell him by then. I know she cares about me, but she has no idea how hard it is.

I'm essentially trapped. I know inside that if I leave he will hurt me if he gets ahold of me again. It will hurt me more at this point to stay though, than it would to leave and him come after me.

I can't get ahold of London. I think she's still at work. I have to go now, if I'm going to make it to Granddaddy's before it's time for Jeremy to get off work.

I pull on my black and pink Converse sneakers. I sling my backpack onto my shoulders as I leave my bedroom. Trekking to the living room, I grab up my duffle bag, and then start walking to Granddad's house.

I'm about a mile down the dirt road we live on, when I see it. Jeremy's old blue pick-up truck is flying down the dirt road in front of me. I know he sees me, I hope he just drives past and leaves me alone.

*Damn it!* He never comes home early. I wonder if he found out somehow. But how? I have only told London about it over the phone, when he was at work. He's never really told me I can't leave; he just implies that I'll be his wife one day.

The truck skids to a stop in front of me and I start to shake. Don't puke, don't puke, please don't puke.

He climbs out, "Where ya' goin', cupcake?" He gazes at the backpack on my back and the duffle bag in my hand.

I chuckle nervously. "Oh, I was just going to visit Granddaddy for a few hours."

I can't look him in the eyes. He knows I'm lying through my teeth right now. I don't know why I do it. Maybe to see how far he will let me go with it or maybe to try to buy myself some time.

"That right?" He replies in a curious tone, raising his eyebrows. "Going for a few hours and taking all your clothes, huh? You know what I think? I think you're trying to leave me, cupcake. However, I don't remember giving you permission to go anywhere."

His fist comes flying at me and hits my left eye. *Fuck! The face again?* The hit makes me stumble back into the side of the truck. He uses my stumble to get closer and hits me in the face again.

Jeremy throws my bags in the back of the truck and picks me up around my waist. He puts me in his truck and slams the door. I don't dare move, because I know it will only make things worse. At this point I still have a chance of London magically knocking on the door at the house.

I'm sobbing hysterically; my face feels like I was just hit with a brick. My head rings as if I have a huge headache, pressing down behind my eyes. I feel like I'm going to puke, but I hold it down. I know he would hurt me more if I get sick in his truck. I feel my face bleeding and it's hot, like it's on fire. I hope Jeremy doesn't hurt me because of the blood making a mess.

He glances at me and snarls, "That's okay, you fucking teenage whore, we will go home and fix this. You think I'll let you go?" He huffs, "You stupid, stupid fucking girl. I will fucking bury your ass in the backyard if I have to, before I let you go." He shakes his head, wagging his pointer finger at me. "I've been too nice, too easy on you. I will teach you though, just wait. You will fucking learn, even if I have to beat it into your fucking piece-of-shit skull." Jeremy rambles the same thing over and over, the entire way home.

He lifts me out of the truck, throws me over his shoulder and starts trudging through the small house to our bedroom. I watch the carpet and wood wall paneling fly by me as we walk down the hallway. I can only see out of my right eye; my left is swollen shut already. I watch the tan carpet and all I can think of is how Jeremy's going to kill me this time.

We enter our room and he tosses me on the bed. Jeremy heads to the dresser, grabbing the rope out of the top drawer. The scratchy, blue rope is left over from when he forcibly ties me up. Sometimes he wants complete control when he fucks me and the ropes stop me from fighting him.

I have the scars on my arms and legs to prove to myself that I'm a fighter. With his menacing expression, I know that this one is really going to hurt. I can't go through this again.

Jeremy starts walking toward me and I shake my head, starting to blubber false promises. I have tears streaming down my face; I know I'm snotty and have blood all over me. I think he cut my forehead when he punched me the second time.

I swallow, clearing my throat, attempting to plead with him, "No, no, no, please, Jeremy, I'll be good, I promise." I swallow down my next sob, "I promise to be good, please don't tie me up, please," I beg.

Jeremy glares down at me like he's disgusted with me, "Don't worry, I'm not going to touch your ugly ass right away, but I'm fucking tying you up, since you seem to think you're free to roam wherever you want to. I bet that kid wasn't even mine!" He shakes the rope in front of my face angrily, "You fucking whore, you were out roaming, weren't you?"

I shake my head rapidly and can feel my lips start to tremble with my anxiety. I choke out, "Never." I know he will really hurt me if he starts thinking this way.

Luckily he only ties one of my hands to the bedpost and leaves the other one free. Jeremy turns around and slams the bedroom door shut as he walks out. Thank God he's cocky and makes this mistake.

Since the last time he put me in the hospital, I have learned to hide phones. I have two cheap prepaid phones hidden, both set on silent. I have one under the bed, tucked into the bedframe and the other phone is taped under the kitchen sink. I figured it would be smart to put one on each side of the house in case of an emergency.

I wiggle my way to reach over the side of the bed. I feel around for a few rushed seconds until I'm able to fight with the tape enough to get the phone out. I power the cell up, breathing deeply to keep myself from expelling my stomach contents everywhere.

I ring London before I even untie my hand, just in case he comes back. I want him to believe everything is the way he left it, if that happens. Thank God London knows this is an emergency number and answers after the first ring.

I whisper the best I can, "London, park where your car's hidden and walk to my bedroom window. He can't see you; I think he's going to kill me."

"I'm almost there, already. Your granddaddy said you never showed up when I stopped by a few minutes ago." That's all she says and she hangs up. When London gets freaked out she doesn't talk very much.

I start working on my bound wrist. The rope cuts into my wrist because Jeremy wrapped it so tightly. I have tears running uncontrollably down my face but I make myself stay quiet. I'm thanking my lucky stars right now he wasn't a boy scout and I'm able to get the rope untied.

As soon as I'm free, I tuck the cell into my back pocket. I

shuffle to the window and open it as quietly as possible. I can hear the sound of Jeremy's beloved TV in the living room so it gives me some cover noise. I also have to listen extra carefully because I can't hear him if he walks down the hall.

As soon as the window is open I stick my feet through first to crawl out. The house is an older ranch style with two bedrooms, and one bathroom. The outside has the tan paint peeling off of it everywhere. Our yard has large dirt patches all over because Jeremy refuses to spend the money to water it.

The window to our room is in the back of the house and there's no fence on this side, so I just have to make it to the road. The distance isn't much, but being beaten and hurting, makes it seems like three times farther than it normally is.

Hobbling forward, I start to run on shaky legs, toward the road. I see London ahead in the distance, she's half way between me and her car. I start to run the fastest I've ever run in my life.

It's hard and I feel so dizzy and nauseous from the hits to my face. I can't hear anything. It feels like a bunch of white noise in my head. I can feel the dirt and tiny rocks under my sneakers as my feet pound the ground as I run. London starts waving her hands like hurry up.

Doesn't she know I'm running as fast as I can? I see London has the driver's side and passenger side doors already open, waiting for us to jump in. I pump my arms at my sides, attempting to gain more speed. My life is in jeopardy and it's time for me to fight back again, even if that means escaping.

All of a sudden the noise hits me like a blast of hot air and it's nothing but screaming. I hear Jeremy behind me. *OH MY GOD, RUN!* I can hear him running so I know he must be close. I focus all of my energy to run as fast as possible.

London's screaming for me to hurry. I make it to her and she grabs my arm and helps pull me to the car. Maybe I was running slower than I thought?

We pull harshly, slamming the doors and London locks them. Jeremy reaches her car right after we get the doors shut. He tries to pull on my door handle but London takes off just in time.

London presses completely down on the gas and peels the tires out in our rush. He slams both hands on the rear of the car and screams. I don't know what he screams and I don't ever want to find out. I've never seen him look so irate before.

I face London, and brokenly mutter, "Take me to Granddaddy's, please."

"Fuck that! Granddaddy's meeting us at the police station. I already called him when I hung up on you. That sick bastard back there is going to jail this time."

"I couldn't agree more with you."

## Now...

I blink, shuddering and it's like coming out of a dream. I hate to go there. I hate to relive those memories. Those were some of the worst days of my life.

I will never forget my little M. My one piece of happiness out of it all and he didn't even make it. I can't imagine going through everything while being pregnant. I have to keep reminding myself that everything happens for a reason, even if it hurts and I don't understand that reason.

I gaze over at Avery and London; they are both weeping quietly and look heartbroken. I wipe my face, attempting to pull myself together and to leave those horrid thoughts in the past, where they belong.

Avery comes to me and hugs me tight, "I'm s-so sor-sorry about little M. My God, you poor woman, I had no idea you had been through so much hurt. I always figured you had a story, but I never imagined it would be like that." She looks at me with sadness and compassion. It makes me feel a little better to have opened up to her, keeping secrets is so draining.

London walks over to us, staring at Avery, "It was horrible, Avery. It was completely awful seeing your best friend like that and not being able to make her leave. I love her so much, I always have, and I just want her to be safe and ha-happy."

I hug London as she says this and kiss her cheek. I'm so fortunate to have her. I probably wouldn't be here now if it wasn't for London.

"So what happened after; where has he been?" Avery wipes her face with her hands.

Sighing, I rub my temples, remembering more of it. "The police took pictures and documented my side of everything. I pressed charges against Jeremy and I gave the hospital consent to release my information. The hospital sent over all of my information from when he put me in there and what the doctor had believed happened in his notes. I guess when we left the house and went to the station, Jeremy went to London's house to try to find me." London huffs irritably, shaking her head in exasperation. "Jeremy got into it really bad with London's older brother, Elliot. They got into a big fist fight and then Elliot pressed charges against Jeremy. It still wasn't going to be enough in court, so London called a few nights later and made a false report. She told the cops Jeremy had broken into her parents' house and threatened to kill her, Elliot and me."

I shrug, winding my fingers together, nervously. "I wasn't even there, but Elliot and I lied and told them the same story London had."

"That's really smart, you guys." Avery inserts and we both nod at her.

"When we went to court, the judge ended up being a lady my grandmamma had babysat. Once she realized who I was, she pulled me into her chambers. The judge asked me to tell her everything, so I did. She said that if my grandmamma was alive she would've protected me. I guess my grandmamma had protected the judge from something really bad happening to her. She wouldn't say what it was, but that she owed it to my grandmamma to make sure she returned the favor and protected me." A warm tear trickles down my cheek as I think of how different things could have been if my family were alive at that time.

Sniffling, I continue, "A few days later, the judge ruled. She said Jeremy showed signs of Narcissistic Personality Disorder with signs of detachment, he has stalker like tendencies, anger problems, shows obsessive qualities and may be a danger to himself. He was denied bail. While he was in jail he got into a few fights. He ended up having to do some more jail time. I was expecting two years but it looks like he has gotten out early."

"Holy shit, all that and only two years!" Avery looks amazed and like it's unbelievable.

"Yes, he had never been in trouble with the law before and in order for the cops to really do anything there has to be several 'documented' occurrences where I pressed charges against him. I was the dumb one and only pressed charges against him once. It was really all the fights after, which got him the actual jail time. Welcome to the justice system."

"Geez, that's crazy. So you came to Tennessee to start over? Weren't you scared he would know?"

"Well, London and I had always talked about this being one of the colleges we wanted to go to together. I never could come to school here because Jeremy controlled every part of my life." I gesture to London, "and London couldn't afford it either. My granddaddy passed right around the same time all this stuff happened. I got left with our house, his pickups, and some insurance money. He had also saved all the insurance money from my momma's death, so I got everything. When Jeremy went to jail, London's mom rented me this apartment under her name. London and I applied for a million scholarships and with the insurance money I was able to move here. London's brother, Elliot, lives and takes care of my granddad's old house and land for me. London's actually been living with her parents, taking online classes for engineering and saving any money she makes. She's supposed to move here next semester to finish her degree."

London sends me a small, sad smile and I return it. "I knew he would eventually find me, I just wasn't expecting it to be this fast."

"Look, Emily, you seriously need to tell Tate about this." I shake my head at Avery. *Not happening.*

I've completely stopped crying now and I'm able to start to think clearer. I have to make up a plan before he comes back again. He could be in the building for all I know. I should have listened to my gut on the bad feelings I was periodically getting.

"No, Avery. This is my problem to deal with. I didn't want to tell you in the first place."

"He can help."

"How? By getting hurt? You don't get it. The *monster* is crazy; he will *kill* me. You have no idea how psycho he is. I only gave you little bits and pieces of my story. This is the main reason why I've tried to keep to myself here; I can't handle it if he was to come after any of you."

I shake my head, crestfallen, "I'm just glad I haven't gotten any closer to Tate or it would really break my heart, having to give him up. I refuse to get you involved and possibly get you guys injured. No way. I just need to clean up this mess and file a report. I have to get every little thing documented this time."

I refuse to let him hurt me like that again. I will kill him before he gets that chance. The harassment has to all be plain as day, documented for the cops, although jail time may be worth it in the end if I'm free.

Avery grumbles, arguing stubbornly, "Girl, you are crazy if you think I'm letting you go through this alone. I'll stick to you like glue. I don't want you to be alone with him, and if he appears or tries anything you will at least have a witness to coincide with your story."

Avery's forehead is crinkled like she's thinking too hard, her eyes burning full of fury. Her anger isn't directed toward me, but him. She's definitely hatching a plan.

London nods her head at Avery, agreeing with the purposed strategy, "Exactly. Good idea, Avery. We need to make sure at least one of us, if not both, is with Emily at all times. I'm talking like basically being her shadow." She turns to me, "But, Emily, I think Avery is also right about telling Tate about this. He seems to know some big guys he could call if we ever desired them. I know Tate would drop everything and come running if you needed him, he's shown everyone just how much he cares for you."

These women are so infuriating. I know they want to help, but they could end up getting seriously hurt. I wouldn't put it past Jeremy if he were to even end up killing them if it came down to it. I wouldn't be able to live with myself if something were to happen to any of them.

I know Tate cares for me a lot, he's told me just this past week that he likes me more than he should at this point. I don't want to take advantage of him and use him, just because it will help keep me safe. If anything it will make the monster even angrier to see me with another man.

I remember when I was a senior in high school and Jeremy saw me talking to one of the baseball players. The guy and I had known each other our whole lives. In fact, we used to even play together as little kids.

The conversation was harmless; we were just talking about the projects we made in Art class. I made a papier-mâché cow and everyone thought it was adorable. Justin, the baseball player, had shown up with metal art and he had drawn a cow on a field. Everyone thought it was fate so we had to hang our projects next to each other. Justin and I thought it was hilarious because we were both country enough to make cows for a project.

Jeremy didn't exactly find it so funny; in fact, it was the opposite. When he discovered what my classmates were saying, he got extremely pissed. Then when he saw Justin talking to me, it was his bursting point.

Jeremy walked up to us, pissed, carrying his binder in front of him. He stepped directly in front of me, blocking me from Justin, glaring crossly at him. At that time, both boys were about the same height and build.

Justin had short dirty blond hair and some cute little freckles on his face. He was normally very friendly with pretty much everyone. I remember him being so surprised when he saw Jeremy pissed.

Jeremy told Justin to "back the fuck up off his chick." He then swung his binder out and clocked Justin right across the face. I thought he and Justin were going to kill each other that day.

The fight got broken up and everyone let it go since the school year was almost finished. Justin didn't want it to affect his baseball playing (he would have been benched) so he just went on like it didn't happen. Jeremy would still gaze at him like he wanted to strangle him each time they passed each other at school, but thankfully nothing else happened.

I thought Jeremy had fought Justin because he cared so much; it made him jealous and showed how much he loved me. Not so. In reality, Jeremy was just an obsessive, controlling psycho. I wish I had realized it back then; maybe I wouldn't have gone through everything else.

The girls sit with me as I call the police and ask to file a report about what happened. I also learn that I need to get a new restraining order through the state of Tennessee, not just in Texas. I wish they would have told me this a long time ago so I could have already taken care of it.

The officers that came to the apartment were nice and understanding about everything. They each gave me their personal cards in case I need to call or if anything else suspicious shows up outside my door. I let them know about the chess piece and calla lily. I now know they were a sick, twisted, sign from Jeremy. He was basically mocking me and I had no idea.

The officers even gave me the number to a friend of theirs, who would submit the paperwork for me to get a restraining order placed on Jeremy. London and Avery also tried to get one placed but when we called and asked, the lawyer said the judge probably won't be willing to approve it.

I guess since it happened in my apartment, it's not a reason they should fear for their safety, just mine. What a load of shit. Unfortunately, that's how the court system works sometimes.

I set to work at cleaning my once-safe haven, which has now been invaded by the person I hate the most.

# EIGHT

## TATE
### The next day

IT'S FAIRLY EARLY SATURDAY MORNING WHEN MY phone starts ringing. I check the screen, hoping it's my little Krasaaveetsa calling to wish me a good morning. I haven't stopped thinking of her since I dropped her off.

I'm disappointed and puzzled when I see it's, in fact, Avery calling and not Emily. I didn't imagine Avery would actually ever use my number when we all traded numbers that first night at dinner. I really only wanted Emily's but thought it sounded better if we all traded, plus Cam got Avery's number, too. Not that he cares anymore.

Cameron's hung up on London right now. That probably won't last long, though, it never does with him. Most people think that I'm the player, but in reality, I only date a select few. I might get my dick sucked occasionally, but that doesn't count.

"Avery?" I murmur, I usually just say "what" but it's Emily's friend, so I'll try to be nicer. I swear, if this is about Cam, I'm hanging up. I don't do any kind of drama. I deal with enough shit from Konstantin, my father.

She hurriedly rambles, "Oh thank God you answered, Tate. I wasn't sure if I'd get a hold of you before you guys came over." She starts whispering, sounding rushed and a little anxious.

"Okay, what's going on? Tell me Emily's alright."

Of course Emily is my main concern. I don't know what it is about her, but I can't seem to see her enough. She pulls something beastly out of me when she's near. Emily's tiny, like a little lamb and just as stubborn as one too. I don't tell her that's the reason I call her little pet, though.

God, when she was sleeping next to me naked, it was almost painful to lie next to her. My dick was so fucking hard it could have chipped granite. My balls were floating so full, it's like they were screaming at me to just fill her up.

My dick just wants to own her sweet cunt, while I want to claim her as mine forever. I can't wait until I can finally take her the way I want to. Or when she's so turned on, she begs for me to take her to bed.

I clear those images as Avery starts talking again, "Emily's okay right now. Shit, she's probably going to kill me when she finds out I called you about this." She groans, frustrated, "I told her to tell you what's going on with her ex."

I growl, "Her ex? Who the hell is it and what's happening?"

"He's been leaving stuff in her hall, that calla lily you found? That was from him, I guess he left a chess piece at her door too and had 'Check mate' carved into it. She calls him *Monster*, Tate."

Scoffing loudly, "Monster, huh? Has the fuck done anything else?"

"Yes, last night after you dropped us off, we went into her apartment. It was covered everywhere with white rose petals and smelled strongly of men's cologne. It was so strong it made me gag." She sighs, taking in a deep breath and continuing, "I thought she had gone catatonic. Emily just zoned out like she was the only one in the room and London was bawling."

Avery clears her throat, then speaks lowly again, "At first I thought you had set it up as a surprise and I couldn't understand why everyone was so upset. Then London yelled at her and made Emily tell me what was going on. It's bad, Tate, like really, really bad. Emily needs to let you help her. I told her you would help, I know you care about her a lot, and even London sees it. Anyhow, I know about you and your family. You can easily handle this problem with your connections. I haven't said anything, that's your secret to tell Emily about when you're ready."

"Thank you for not saying anything yet. I prefer it if no one knows about that side of me and my family."

"Trust me; it's not a goal in my life to piss off the Russian Mafia. So, I told Emily that you could help, but she doesn't want to feel like she's using you or for you to get hurt. That girl has such a good heart and doesn't deserve the crap she's had to deal with." Avery speaks so rushed I'm barely able to catch it all and understand everything she says.

I'm not too surprised that Avery figured out my private life since we've gone to my club a few times. I'm glad she hasn't told Emily though. I don't think Emily could handle it to hear I'm a Boss. She thinks Nikoli's my close friend, which he is, but he's also my closest guard.

Especially if she's already dealing with issues from an ex, she's not going to want to handle all the crazy shit I go through on the regular. It's quiet right now, but it never stays quiet for long. It's also very dangerous for her if anyone finds out I care about her, she could be used to get to me.

It makes me feel so good inside she doesn't want to use me and she wants to keep me safe. It tells me she really cares about me, that she plans to keep this from me. However, she needs to confide in me so I can help her. I can take care of this without getting it too involved with the Odessa hearing much about it. I really don't want my father involved or he will be requesting an engagement announced by me; because 'the next Big Boss needs to have a little wife at home.' Yeah, that shit will never fly with Emily. I'm going to wait until we are ready to take that step and not be forced into it.

I refuse to let Emily push me away, though. I have to get her to tell me about this. She can be ornery all she wants; I'm going to take care of her.

"Don't worry, Avery, the Russkaya Mafiya isn't after you. Thank you. You did the right thing by telling me. If anything else happens before Emily tells me about it, I need you to inform me right away. I'll have one of my men tasked to keep an eye out over by Emily's place. Make sure you girls keep the doors and windows locked when you're in the apartment."

I yawn, rubbing my hand over my face and grumbling, "I wish she had an alarm or the building had restricted access to guests. Try to get me as many details on this piece of trash as you can. I need to have descriptions in order for my men to be able to keep an eye out. Does he have a Facebook account or something my tech guy can get his picture from?"

My mind's already spinning a million miles a minute, thinking of everything I need to do in order to get this guy. At least Avery's starting to calm down after confiding in me. My poor Krasaaveetsa, I bet she was a mess and I wasn't there to comfort her. Dammit!

"I don't think so; he's been in jail, and I guess he got out early. Emily pulled out a pistol last night and said she refuses to let him hurt her again. I can't believe she has a freaking gun! I know he has hurt Emily really badly physically as well as emotionally and you know how small Emily is in the first place. She thinks that he's going to kill her this time. In fact, she's pretty sure of it. Plus all these creepy messages point straight to death. He's so fucking weird leaving these cryptic messages in the hallway. I'm really freaked out for her. I don't want anything to happen to Emily."

"Alright," I respond calmly, even though I'm blistering mad inside, "just try to stay with her so she's not alone. I'll pick up Nikoli and I'll head over there with him and Cam. That fuck head won't be touching my girl."

I hang up and feel like my stomach may explode, just the thought of Emily hurt, makes me want to make this trash feel my wrath. I didn't become a Boss by being innocent. I became a Boss by hurting people.

I don't get it how some fuck can harm Emily. She's so sweet and cares about everyone. Hell, I was a total ass to her several times in the past, she gives me her attitude back, but she always forgives me so easily, each time. You would be a fool to hurt someone like that. And to hear he physically hurt her? It makes me want to gut him.

I'll catch that fucker and I'll break his knees first. I'll teach him to not touch my Krasaaveetsa, and then I'll gut him, like the piece of shit, filthy pig he is. I'll do this all on my own with just a few guys.

If I have to, though, I'll have every single member of the Odessa Mafia and Solntsevskaya Bratva looking for him if need be. He won't get far, and then I'll play with him. He's a fucking mouse being hunted; he just doesn't know it yet.

I get dressed quickly, updating the guys what's going on and driving over to her place.

We decide to circle around Emily's apartment building a few times to see if anyone looks suspicious. After a few slow laps around, we don't find anything. However, that would have been too easy with Nikoli right there, to help me bag this filth up.

I wonder how Emily would feel about maybe coming and staying with Cam and me, until I take care of this problem. I'll have to talk to her about it. Cam might be a trust fund kid, but he trains with me. He can hold his own and is a pretty tough fucker. I know he would never let Emily get hurt if I weren't around.

That's another thing to think about, though if Emily does stay with us, she's bound to find out about me. I've been able to brush off some of the mafia responsibility, but not all of it. I try to keep my personal life away from business, but we definitely talk about things that have to do with the business at my house, too.

The guys and I make our way to the apartment and we can hear the girls from outside in the hall. It sounds like they are giggling about something in there. I'm happy to hear a little bit of happiness after the shit they've just dealt with. "...and then he put his tongue..."

I glance at the guys, "That's London; let's go inside before I hear details I don't want to hear!"

I knock on the door loudly. I wouldn't mind listening if it was Emily talking about me, but I'm not wanting to hear about Cam's tongue skills. If it's even Cam she's talking about, who knows.

The door opens with Emily answering it, and they all appear beside her. *Good.* I'm glad to see London and Avery are staying close to Emily.

I push through the group, heading inside, chastising, "Tsk, tsk, tsk, Emily. You should always ask who it is before you answer the door. What if I was some psycho?" I ask this on purpose because I want to catch her reaction.

It works; she sucks in her breath and turns pale when she processes what I say. God, I'm such a dick, but I have my reasons. I gaze at her tenderly, begging her with my eyes and body to open up to me.

Emily only has one couch and a chair since her place is so compact. Nikoli sits next to Avery on the black couch and starts kissing all over her neck. They remind me of two teenagers. I'm glad Niko is getting a little down time though, that guy is always following me around, on alert. I do pay him pretty well to be my guard, but he must get bored sometimes.

London sits on the chair and Cam sits on her lap and squishes her. She yelps, giggling and he finally lets her up. He pulls her to sit on his lap.

Both my boys seem to be a little taken with Emily's friends. I'm glad, but if it doesn't work out, shit could get awkward. They better not fuck up my chances with Emily.

I step closer to her, "What is it, baby, what's wrong? You look upset."

Emily turns, shaking her head a little and walks away.

I follow her into the kitchen. She's trying to look busy, but she's shaking. Emily tries to hide her body's reaction to my questions, but I can definitely tell that she's anxious.

*I will protect you little pet.* I wish I could just hold her and tell her not to worry, that I will take care of it all, but instead I have to pretend to be ignorant. *Please talk to me, Krasaaveetsa, just let me in.*

"Hey, hey, my Krasaaveetsa, tell me what this is? Why do you look upset? What can I do?" I grab her wrists and pull her into me so I can wrap my arms around her. I didn't mean to scare her that badly, but I need her to open up to me.

I love how her body fits to mine; it's like we're two wires syncing together and creating an explosive charge. Emily fits to my chest as if she belongs there. I hope she sees it also. I know she feels something when we touch, she has to. I have never been so aware of a female in my life; it's like she consumes me.

She mumbles, looking at the floor, "It's nothing, Tate, just a stressful morning. I can deal with it, though."

Do not lie to me or withhold information. It's one of my biggest pet peeves. She will learn though with time that I'm here for her, not against her. Emily runs her hands around my sides until she feels my back. Her hands freeze and she peers at me questioningly.

I know what she feels; it's the tops of my 45 calibers. They aren't too noticeable if you aren't paying attention or looking for them. Emily only found them because she felt them. I always have two strapped on me. They are if I need to handle some business, and I plan to handle this trash if he comes back around. He will learn that I didn't become a Boss by being a pussy and that I take all threats seriously.

Emily gasps, "What on earth is this, Tate? Are you packin'?" She gazes at me with wide, curious eyes and I smirk down at her. I love how short she is, she fits under my chin perfectly.

"Yeah, baby, I had this weird feeling like someone was watching us so I brought a few of my favorite things with me today. Know anything about that?" I hate to lie to her, but I'm not going to sell Avery out for doing the right thing and telling me. Now if only Emily will get that little extra nudge to open up. Maybe if she knows I'm carrying, she will feel safer.

"I don't know, Tate, I'm just surprised you have weapons on you. You don't really strike me as the violent type."

I chuckle lowly. If she only knew.

"No, Emily, I'm not violent to the people I care about, I cherish them and give them my heart." I murmur, bending close to her lips.

I shouldn't have gone there. I know it's too soon, but I couldn't help it. I care about her a lot and she has to know it. Hell, everyone else can see it. I bend my head the remaining distance and kiss her as passionately as I can, sucking on her lips and playing with her tongue. I love how she lets me control our kisses, she doesn't try to overpower my tongue or take control. I wonder if she will let me take control in everything or if she will fight me for it occasionally.

I can't ever get enough of her flavor. Her mouth is always

cool and tastes of soda. I wish I could just set her on this counter and savor all the other parts of her also. I could guarantee she tastes sweet all over. I bet I could have her writhing and wet by just using my tongue on her pert, silver dollar size nipples. I can't wait to lick and nibble on her perfect tits.

Emily grabs my hand and starts to pull me down her tiny hallway, to her room. Her voice all raspy, ordering me to follow her, "Tate, let's go to my room okay?" Swallowing, I nod eagerly.

I check out the hall as I follow. I think Nikoli's apartment is even bigger than this place and he never stays there. He's always at my house with Cameron and me.

We arrive at her room and I take in all of the little details. Emily has light blue, sheer curtains, and a blue and grey comforter on the plain bed. No bedroom set, just a plain metal bed frame and a small night stand, no soft touches throughout. I see we share the same likes in colors for our things. There's no other furniture; it's a small room, but I'm assuming she hangs all her clothes in her closet. It appears like she doesn't even sleep in here.

Being in the bedroom is not helping the thoughts that were just charging through my mind; in fact, it's feeding all my fantasies. All I can imagine is having her hold onto that black metal frame while I take her from behind, occasionally giving her cute little ass a smack. I wonder if Emily would be the type to moan softly or if she would scream out my name.

She clears her throat, "Please come here, Tate." She sits on the edge of her mattress.

I'm getting a damn chubby already; I can't help it, we are in her bedroom and she's on the bed for Christ's sake. My dick is screaming at me to fuck her, over and over until she gives in and realizes she's all mine. As much as I would love to take her here, I won't.

I plan to have her when we don't have any company. I'm

going to make her choke out my name repeatedly; full of pleasure, each time I make her come. I'm not small in that department and I know she would be embarrassed if there were people around for our first time, and I want her to enjoy every single minute of it.

I swagger over from the doorway, to the bed and sit next to her. I put one arm around her, turning her body into mine more and cradle Emily's face with my other hand.

"Yes, Krasaaveetsa? I am here. What can I do?"

I peer at her cute little mouth. Her top lip is a little bigger than her bottom lip. I could kiss her lips all day and be a happy man. She has little freckles on her nose and forehead. I place my hand on her cheek; it makes her look even more feminine to see her face cradled in my large hand. Her skin is soft and fair. I love touching her face. When I pull my hands away afterward it always feels as if she makes my skin softer.

Emily mumbles out, worriedly, "I care about you, Tate, more than I probably should. I have so much chaos in my life and I don't want to involve you, but I don't want to let you go yet, either. I'm just not ready to."

I hope I can make it so she never lets me go. I lean in and kiss her. I've always taken control of what I want and she is no different. I try to hold myself back from her all the time just so I don't move too fast for her, but I'm tired of holding back the affectionate kisses and touches. I don't think I can keep myself away anymore. Emily just completely draws me in and makes me want her more and more with each passing day. I find myself thinking about her constantly.

I push her backward, tenderly and thread one of my hands in her soft, shiny, blonde hair. I love how her hair feels in my fingers, like silk. I begin to kiss down her throat. It's such an erotic place on a woman and it never gets enough credit. I nibble slightly on the base of her throat, but I hold myself back still.

I want to bite and suck and mark her as mine. That will come in time; right now I have to show her I will worship her as she deserves. Emily drives me backward, with her palms on my pecs. *Did I do something wrong?*

She flashes me a timid smile, taking her shirt off. That's even better for me.

I draw her bottom lip in between my lips, sucking, playing and she starts to pant. I breathe her in, I can smell her essence. She's turned on and I'm going to make sure she feels good.

That's it, baby, open yourself up to me. Let me inside.

"Bawg, Ya khatyets poshyol Vee так plawkha Krasaaveetsa (God, I want to fuck you so bad, beauty)." I start to murmur in Russian what I want to do to her. Emily thinks it's hot, so I plan to tell her how bad I wish to fuck her. If she only knew how badly that ache really is inside me.

I continue to kiss down her throat until I get to her cleavage. Leaving her bra on, I shove it aside with my lips, that way I can get a taste of those perfect fucking nipples. *God, her tits are so fucking gorgeous.* Emily's not small chested but has just enough to fill my hands comfortably.

She fits like she was made specifically for me. Her body lines up exactly where I want it to against mine. I thrust my cock against her, she feels so fucking good and I want to be deep inside her so bad.

Emily lets out a little moan and that's my cue. It makes my dick so fucking hard and my balls feel over full, so that I leak precum. I run my hand down her abdomen, making my way toward her core. I draw her left, pert nipple into my mouth and bite down lightly. She's pulling my hair harshly, writhing under me, so she must enjoy it.

I run my fingers down through her swollen little pussy lips and feel she's soaked, it makes me wetter myself, to feel her so turned on. She puts her petite hand inside of my pants and grabs my cock, gripping onto it tightly. My insides vibrate with need, I feel like I'm going to erupt all over her fingers.

I yank her yoga pants and purple thong down her thighs and calves, until they're completely free, tossing them across the room. *I've got to taste her glistening sex.* I'm going to eat this delicious cunt so much, I make her squirm and come all over my tongue.

I trail down her tummy, placing sensual kisses as I make my way to her clit. I suck on it and gently nibble on the delectable little morsel. Emily squirms, trying to close her legs but I grab the back of her thighs and hold them wide open to me. She's not going anywhere right now.

She lets go of my cock and grips on to one of my forearms while the other hand yanks the shit out of my hair some more. She can pull it hard, I like it. It makes me want to throw her up against a wall and fuck her roughly. I lick up and down her pussy lips, circling in on her clit.

Emily mewls out breathily, "Oh Tate, yes, like that!"

Her little sounds are turning me on like crazy. I stick one digit then another in her to the hilt.

"Ride my fingers, baby, let me feel those sweet pussy juices."

She's so tight; her little pussy grips onto my fingers, sucking them deep inside her. Emily rotates her hips, moving with my hands, as I pump my fingers in and out of her steadily. *She's getting wetter, so fucking sexy.* I know she's almost ready. I pull my fingers out and use the wetness to rub on her clit.

She's making little gasping sounds, panting, "Tate, oh God, Tate." I can't help but growl as I feel her clenching. If she doesn't come soon, I'm going to fucking explode inside my pants.

I stick my tongue in her core and move it around as I play with her clit. She's so sweet, tastes just like honey and it drives me to want to keep eating more of her. I feel famished. I keep my tongue as deep as possible inside her. When she comes I want it all in my mouth, I'm fucking greedy and want every drop.

Emily calls out, thrusting her hips, I feel her muscles contract several times and she gives me what I want. When she's done, I thoroughly lick around her pussy to make sure I get all of her cream..

Wiping over my face to get the remaining off, I groan in pleasure. I know I probably look like a mess, but fuck! She's so incredible and responsive to me. *Man...the shit I'm going to do to her.*

"You good, baby?" I adjust my cock, pushing it down roughly to get a little relief and grin down at her. She's so fucking cute. Emily's lying sprawled out on the bed, looking like she just ran a marathon.

She beams a smile towards me, "God, Tate that felt beyond amazing!" It makes me chuckle, she says this like she's surprised. Did she not think I would please her? Ahh, just wait, little pet, you will be pleased often.

"I'm glad you enjoyed it. Emily, I will make you feel even better when the time is right."

"What are you talking about, when the time is right? I just need a minute then we can continue. I get to taste your cock now, right?" She looks at me with a hopeful expression and it makes me fall a little more. A woman asking to please me? Yeah, sexy as fuck.

"No, Krasaaveetsa, we are going to discuss what is going on, what's bothering you." She doesn't appear too thrilled about this, but it needs to happen and I won't stop until she gives in.

## NINE

### EMILY

I RELENT. TATE JUST DEVOURED MY PUSSY AND IT pretty much drained the fight out of me.

I eventually break down and confide in him, sharing my secret about my sordid ex, Jeremy. I tell Tate the secret I live with every day, about my baby M. He looks so troubled to hear about my baby. I recognize it then in my heart, that Tate would never hurt me or my child like my ex did.

When I weep, Tate holds me close, comforting me as he murmurs promises that he will always protect me. I know I'm falling for him. It's too fast, and it frightens me. I know it's way too soon for this to happen after all the shit I went through in my last relationship, but I can't help how I feel about him.

"I'm scared, Tate. Jeremy's crazy..." I attempt not to cry again, but my anxiety level is getting too out of control.

"No, Krasaaveetsa, I will take care of him," Tate grumbles, retribution blazing in his eyes, once he's informed about some of the stuff the monster had put me through. *You have no idea, Tate.*

"What-what are you going t-to do to him, Tate?" I stammer, overwhelmed with memories haunting me.

I can't help but wonder about Tate's plan; I don't want him to get injured in any possible way. Jeremy can be very dangerous and there's no telling if he has gotten worse in jail. I glance at Tate, taking stock, he's pretty ripped, but still, I care way too much for him.

"I'm going to make sure that piece of trash never touches you, ever again. I told you pet, you are mine. Threats to myself and those I care about, I take very seriously. I do need some information on him though, so I can have my men find him."

His men? What in the hell is he talking about? Despite my confusion, I love the fact that he thinks of me as his.

"Please just leave it, Tate. I don't want you to get hurt. I think Jeremy would end up killing you and I wouldn't be able to live with myself if something were to happen to you." He doesn't realize just how much of a psycho Jeremy really is.

Tate chuckles, shaking his head as if I amuse him. I gaze at him, confused, because this shit is not funny in the least. I'm being serious about his safety. I've lost enough people in my lifetime. "I'm sorry," Tate backtracks when he sees me get annoyed, "Krasaaveetsa, it is not funny, and it's just so cute you worry about me, but don't." I notice his Russian becomes more pronounced when he attempts to placate me or when he's angry about something. It almost purrs out of him when he becomes tender with me, it draws me deeper, making me tumble towards him more with each Russian word.

"Look, Emily, understand that I am worried and want to help you also. Don't take this the wrong way, but there is just a lot you don't really know about me."

I'm glad he's taking this seriously. I know there is a lot I may not know about him. It doesn't matter to me what that is, though. He's accepting me with my freaking drama, so what could he possibly have that I can't handle?

I sigh, "No, I get that, and I love that you want to protect me and hopefully I'll get to learn more stuff about you, soon?"

"Yes, pet, soon. The first thing I'd like is for you to come and stay with Cameron and me just until this is all handled. We have a good-sized place and you will get to meet Muffin. I'll feel better if you always have one of us around to help keep you safe."

Stay with him, in his house? Who the hell is Muffin?

Hesitating, I attempt to imagine what it would be like staying with them. "I don't know, Tate, I feel horrible enough involving you, but to involve Cameron too? And invade his space? That's not very fair of me to ask him, he may like my best friend, but I don't think that's enough of an incentive. And who's Muffin? Please tell me you don't have like a live-in stripper or something." I take a breath and continue, "Also, what about London? Her classes are online and I don't know how long she's staying. I can't just leave her here alone." When I ask about Muffin he starts laughing and his irises sparkle with humor. I'm so glad to see that murderous look gone from his eyes and the happiness return. I grin when he laughs; it always makes me feel as if a coat of warmth blankets me, all over.

"Okay, look, Cam will feel better if you are there, too. We have plenty of room for London also. The place has four bedrooms and three bathrooms; trust me it has plenty of space. Cameron will be happy to have London whenever he wants her. I have a security system and high grade locks installed, plus Niko is always there, too. And Muffin is not a stripper," Tate chortles at this, "he's my dog!" I start to giggle when he tells me it's his dog.

I bet he's a cute little dog. Aww, I love little dogs! Maybe I could. I bet we would have some fun if all of us got to hang out for a few nights, anyhow.

"Sorry, but Muffin? Really, that's the dog's real name? And is

Niko, Nikoli?" I love the name Niko! I wonder why Tate doesn't go by Luka? It sounds so Russian and mysterious.

"Yes, his name is Muffin. Wait 'til he hears you laughing at him," he teases. "And yes, it's Nikoli, we call him Niko for short usually. Why don't you get a bag together and we can all go to my place and then grill out?" God, he's so tempting... But I'm still not one hundred percent convinced, maybe like ninety six and a half percent.

Shyly, I inquire, "Are we going to be sleeping in the same bed, if I stay with you?" I don't want to admit it, but I could get used to snuggling up to him at night. I bet he snores and cuddles with his little dog. I chuckle to myself, that's a cute thought. Ohhh, I wonder if he sleeps naked.

"Krasaaveetsa, you are my girl, staying in my home. Yes, you are in my bed. I won't pressure you about anything physical, but you will be at least sleeping in my bed, next to me."

I can definitely handle that. I love when he does that Alpha-growl thing. Does that mean I can't pressure him? I would not mind hopping on him in the middle of the night.

I smirk at him and nod, "Okay, but I'm not staying for very long. Thank you, Tate. I promise I will keep out of your hair and clean up. I'll be the best guest, I promise."

"I hope you don't stay out of my way, and we have a house-keeper that comes once a week to do the deep cleaning, so you don't have to worry about that either. Just come, stay and relax, concentrate on school work and we will have fun while you're visiting at the house."

I jump up, rushing to pack a bag. I grab enough stuff for five days, along with my toiletries.

"Umm, is there a place for me to lie out and tan with Avery?"

"Yeah, babe, you can lie in the backyard or bed, whatever," he responds, winking at me, cheekily.

I stuff my bikini in my bag, throwing it over my shoulder to leave, "Okay, I'm all set. Let's go tell everyone else what's going on." Tate stands, coming to me, removing the bag from my shoulder and carries it for me. I swiftly make myself presentable, pulling on fresh panties and shorts, then follow him back out to see the others.

I can't forget I need to grab some of my snacks and sodas, that way I don't eat up all of Tate's food. I like junky stuff and judging by his physique, he's more than likely a health food nut. When we get to the living room, we notice everyone crowded around my little table from the kitchen. *Please help yourself and move my furniture around.* I think and roll my eyes to myself.

Clearing my throat, I cut in, "Hey, what are y'all doing in here?"

Nikoli turns, beaming a striking smile and stands up. He has gorgeous, bright white, straight teeth. Niko spreads his arms out widely, and chortles loudly, "Winning man!"

I start to belly laugh, being followed by a few of the others. Man, I love this guy.

He smirks after everyone quiets down, "No, Luka's Krasaaveetsa, I am kidding, this Texan girl is teaching us how to play Texas Hold'em!" he declares proudly, all excited as if it's the coolest thing in the whole world. Poor guy has no idea that London cheats her ass off at this game.

"Ahh! The game of champions! Be careful with London though, she will rob you of every penny. That girl is very sneaky." I shoot her a smug smile. Busted!

"Oh! Shut your face, woman. I do not rob anyone. I win fair and square!"

"Yeah, right! You win because you play with people who have never played before." Her brother taught us that trick when he was a teenager and kept taking all of our quarters.

She huffs, crossing her arms and grinning, "Okay, bitch, get over here and show me how it's done then!"

"Actually, we're going over to Tate's house to grill out and hang over there for a few days. We should take some games though and have the boys play with us."

"I'll play with you, Krasaaveetsa," Tate mumbles quietly, but everyone still hears him anyway.

"Hell yeah, I'll play with all three of you," Cameron says cheekily and Niko nods frantically in agreement. Those shit heads! Tate is going to bust their balls.

Tate scowls, growling, "Cameron." I knew he'd get pissed. Tate seems to be a pretty territorial man.

Cameron just shrugs good naturedly and then bellows excitedly, "Woohooo! No offense, Emily, your pad is nice and all, but I miss my bed." Cameron jumps up in a hurry, putting all the stuff they had out, away. I guess he's excited to go home. Or he's probably just excited to get London all alone with an actual bed and some privacy.

Avery collects her few belongings and London walks around the living room, compiling enough stuff to last her for a few days. London may as well bring all her luggage since she always needs so much stuff. Her suitcases are dark purple with leopard print. Even the items holding her clothes have to be stylish like her.

We all step into the hall as a group and everyone suddenly halts, going silent. *What's going on?*

I shuffle into the hall, passing everyone and see there's something written on the wall. It's in huge, dark, crimson letters about three feet tall. Oh My God. Fuck! It reads-

'THE WHORE IS MINE'

My faces heats, I'm so fucking irate inside right now. *How dare he!* How dare Jeremy do this to me in front of so many people, in front of my friends, the people I care about now? I swear I fucking hate him so much.

I peer over at Tate, I know my face is red and it feels as if it's

on fire. Emotions and anxiety well up choking me inside, it's too much. It's all just way too much, I can't deal with this. I wish that *monster* would just fucking leave me alone already! I begin to sob and it's Tate's breaking point.

Before I even register what he's doing, he nods angrily to Cam. Cam stands beside me, then Tate and Niko take off outside. Tate's practically running, he's so livid, I think he's going to rip off someone's head.

I quietly slip past Cam and take off running outside, behind him. I watch them go out of the apartment building's entry doors. I'm so close behind them, but Tate doesn't recognize it.

Flinging my arms in front of me, I hit the glass doors hard, bursting out of the main doors. I make it just in time to see Tate lose it.

He bellows in an angry, gut wrenching voice, "She's fucking mine, motherfucker! Come out and face me!" He reaches behind him, pulling out one of his .45's from his back holster and shoots three times toward the sky.

I drop to the hard ground, rocks scraping roughly on my palms as I land on my tummy and cover my head as soon as the shots begin to fire. I slam my eyes closed and grit my teeth harshly, attempting not to call out to him, scared.

Tate yells out loudly, "Do you have any idea who you are fucking with? I'm the Russkaya Mafiya's Balshoy Shef (Big Boss)! I will gut you!"

I have never witnessed Tate so torn up or out of control. He always appears calm, collected and in control of every situation. I open my eyes, glancing at him now and he looks almost helpless like he doesn't know what to do to fix things right now.

Tate looks every bit his young age of twenty-two right now and lost. My heart hurts, seeing him like this. He is dealing with this massive mess, all for me.

Suddenly he turns to Niko and snarls, "Fucking find him and

bring him to me. I want him alive, he's mine to hurt. He was just here Nikoli while we were inside. Fucking find him!" Tate's voice gets louder as he clenches his free fist, "I'll make that piece of trash bleed. I will get everyone in the fucking Mafiya after him if I have to!"

Tate glances back behind him and does a double take, "Shit, my little lamb, come over here." He holds his hand out to me, "I am very sorry you are witnessing me so upset. I will take care of this issue and you will be safe, I promise." He rasps, his accent coming out really heavily.

Cameron, London and Avery have all come out of the building; they stand behind me and each one remains silent. I think I can hear London crying again. I'm so sick of all the crying, of being scared, of running. For once in my life I have friends who are standing up and helping me. It is no longer my secret, but something all of us are going to get through. I don't know what I would do right now if it weren't for them, just keeping me sane and working to keep me safe. I may not know them as well as I know London, but this group of people have become very important to me and I will cherish them forever.

Tate picks up my bag and holds tightly onto my hand, he then leads me to the passenger side of his lifted Tahoe. His cheeks are still flushed with anger, as he breathes deeply. He keeps scanning the parking lot on alert, as do I.

He opens my door, bending down and lovingly kisses my forehead. Tate then helps me climb inside and shuts my door for me. He sends me a look that I have no clue on how to read, he's so serious, but it's not really a cross look toward me. *I hope he's okay.* Walking around the back, he opens the hatch and loads my stuff in. Tate politely waits for everyone else's bags to get loaded and then climbs in the driver's side.

Tate turns to me and grasps onto one of my hands as he says, "Everything will be okay, Emily. Will you please trust me?" Can I trust him? Yes, I think I can. Do I already trust him? It's strange, but I actually do.

"Yes, Tate, with my life," I murmur. I give him a small smile and squeeze his hand in reassurance. He returns my smile, nods a little, and then drives us all to his and Cam's house.

When we arrive, my mouth has to be gaping. I know London and Avery, who are sitting in the back, probably have the same expression as I do. I was expecting Tate's house to be nice, but this is absolutely beautiful!

He wasn't kidding about having enough room; this place is huge. First off, it's not some college house like I was expecting to see. No, it's a freaking gated, wealthy community. I guess I should have expected it though with the type of cars he and Cam drive. I never see Niko drive, but I'm guessing the dark blue, brand new Chevrolet Silverado parked out front is his. Unless Tate picked him up from his apartment, but I remember he said Niko is always at his house. The house is made of stone and there is a four-car garage attached to the house. Tate does love his cars, so this is not very surprising.

Tate parks in the driveway, closest to the front door and when we get out of the vehicle, I hear barking. There is a large privacy fence, running the length of the house; it looks like his yard is huge. I can't see the dog, but I can hear him, and he definitely doesn't sound like a 'little' Muffin. No, this dog sounds big and very excited. Muffin must know what his dad's truck sounds like.

Tate interrupts the barking, "Come on, ladies, let's get you all settled in and then we can take you on a tour. Last but not least, you all can meet Muffin. Avery, you are going to stay here too, right? Niko practically lives here." Tate glances at Avery as we all walk inside and I see Niko nod at her. She looks a little unsure so I try to help out Nikoli.

"Please, Avery? It would make me feel better to know that

you and London are here with me and safe. Plus, we will have so much fun being here all together." I smile big and give her my version of puppy dog eyes.

"Okay, if you guys really don't mind, then I'll stay a few nights. I need to wash my clothes though or else go by my place."

Cam speaks up and smirks at her. "Of course we don't mind! The house is too quiet. It'll be really nice having people around making some noise. The poor dog is probably lonely, too. We have a washer you can use, just as long as you wash my clothes while you're at it."

"Yeah right, Cam! I'm not washing your undies, London can do it!" Avery snickers at them.

"I don't mind, Cam, I can wash them for you," London says quietly and looks at him sweetly.

"Oh my God! Are you serious? Where did my BFF go? London, where did you go?" I start looking around all crazy and calling her name loudly. She shoves me while laughing then sticks her tongue out at me.

The inside of their house is really nice. There is no way they decorated this place by themselves. It actually looks like a home you see in a magazine and not a bachelor pad. The couches are extra big, with really fluffy pillows and throws that all coordinate together laid on the back of each couch. The living room's large enough that they have three couches and two big recliners. The walls are this cool white color with a hint of blue in it and the floors through the whole house are a rich, dark brown wood. The kitchen is a cook's playground. Beautiful granite counters spread throughout and stainless steel appliances compliment the colors.

I gaze around at the brown wood cabinets, the cool tiled floor and can't help but imagine cooking in here. The bedrooms are spacious with huge walk in closets. I don't have enough clothes to even fill up half of one of their closets. The bathroom in Tate's room has big, plush towels and a beautiful claw foot tub. I really hope I get to try it out. Out of the entire house, the kitchen is my absolute favorite.

"What are you doing, baby?" Tate asks when he walks into the kitchen. He stands beside me and pulls me into his arms.

Tate looks so handsome right now. He's relaxed, being home and now changed into comfy clothes. He has on a pair of thin, grey sweatpants and a white, fitted tank top. His shoulders look like they bulge out of the shirt and his colored arms stand out beautifully. He looks hot and buff and I really just want to jump him right now.

"Not much, just daydreaming about cooking in this beautiful kitchen." I grin and lift up on my tippy toes, to press a chaste kiss to his sexy, stubble-covered chin.

I wrap my arms around his firm waist and rest my hands right above his plump ass. His butt looks like it's perfect to bite, just firm enough to bounce a quarter off of.

"Ahh, you like to cook?" I nod, kissing his chin again.

"Well then, Krasaaveetsa, you must cook in it while you are here. I would love to have you cook for me, it would be an honor."

"Okay, I would love to."

"Now, let's go outside so I can start the grill. You can check out the pool and meet Muffin. I'm sure he's tired of waiting patiently outside, even if the weather's been really nice. He's probably eager to come in and check everyone out." Tate tugs on my hand and starts walking toward the back door.

"Oh, my gawd! You have a pool too? Geez, Tate, you are going to turn me into a spoiled brat!" I get so excited, I start to giggle. I love swimming in pools, rather than dirty old lake water.

"Good, Emily, you deserve to be spoiled and I plan to make you very happy."

I swoon; I swear this man is perfect.

We make our way outside and I love it. Tate has numerous garden beds that line the whole yard around the fence. The back porch patio is covered and is adorned with the same stone that's on the house.

Tate has one of those outdoor, covered, man kitchens that have a TV hanging in eyesight, a built-in, stainless grill, and mini fridge combo, with the bar completely covered in stone.

There's a big glass table on the patio that seats eight; off to the side are a few outdoor couches and chairs with fluffy, bright teal cushions. The pool is a large square, with sparkling dark sapphire colored water. It has a built in waterfall, Jacuzzi, slide, fake rocks and plants all on the side. Around the pool are a few small tables with chairs and about ten lawn chairs you can lie on. It's absolutely perfect. Tate lives in my dream home and I actually get to stay here for a few nights.

I make my way over to Tate and suddenly this huge dog comes running at us. He looks like he probably comes up to my waist.

"Holy shit, Tate! I thought you had a little dog named Muffin, not a huge Cujo!" Okay, I admit I am scared of the dog. He's huge and full of energy. Tate chuckles at my remark and at my alarmed expression.

"This is Muffin. He's a full size Doberman Pinscher. You don't have to be scared or intimidated. Did you know Dobermans are the only dogs that were bred specifically for safety? His sole purpose in his breeding is to protect his master and his master's family. They are also one of the top three smartest dogs. He's not a Cujo. He will see how much I care about you and he will love you. Come here, baby, and meet him."

I approach them both leisurely, with my hand out. I was taught by Granddaddy that it's best to approach bigger dogs slowly, showing them respect and consistency. When I get close,

Tate pulls me against his body while Muffin sits still, watching how I treat Tate.

"Muffin, come here boy, be easy, this is Emily." Tate kisses my cheek a few times after he says this. It must work because Muffin watches his master then proceeds to smell my hand. I must pass a test because he comes and leans his body against my legs and lets me pet him.

Muffin is very large, with black and tan fur, his ears and tail are cropped and has on a neon orange collar that looks like it has something reflective on the stitching. His fur is really soft and he seems happy. He lets his tongue hang out and his little stub of a tail wags like crazy.

I coo as I scratch behind one of his ears, "Hi, Muffin, that's a good boy, it's nice to meet you." I look up to see Tate watching me with a bemused expression. "Hey, Tate, his collar's really cool, what's on the stitching? Is that a reflective?"

"Yes, Muffin usually goes on runs with me in the morning, so he has a reflective collar in case it's still dark out. I don't ever go alone and the guys like to sleep, so he's my road dog. He loves going to the lake and in the boat also. It drives my mother crazy, all the wet fur, so I usually do it on purpose."

I laugh at him; leave it to Tate to antagonize his poor mom with the dog. Muffin doesn't seem so bad; in fact, the opposite. He's really friendly and paws at me every time I quit petting him.

"That's really cool, Tate. He's a sweet boy, and I can tell you love him a lot. Would you mind if I run with you in the mornings? I usually use the treadmill in the community center at my apartment. It's so peaceful here, Tate, everything. I love it and I'm excited to stay here for a few days, thank you."

"Yeah, you can definitely go with me. Muffin has to come too, though. Also, you are very welcome; I'm excited you are here." He kisses me long and deep, it makes me melt into his firm body.

While we kiss, Muffin wiggles in between us and just stands there. I pull away from Tate and glance at the dog, he's just happy as can be. What started as an awful, stressful day has turned out to be wonderful.

Later that evening, we grill a small feast, including steaks, chicken breasts, baby potatoes, corn and pineapple slices. We all sit outside on the patio, sipping sweet tea mixed with vodka and enjoy the beautiful Tennessee night. The season's changing, so evenings and mornings are perfect times to enjoy being outside right now.

We all talk and make plans to have crab legs for dinner tomorrow as a group again. I can't wait; I am so excited to cook with Tate. Surprisingly, Muffin lies on the outdoor couch and doesn't beg from anyone during dinner. I remember the Golden Retriever Granddaddy had. She was named Goldie and when I was little, she always begged for anything she could get.

London, Avery and I clean up afterwards and make our way into the living room to watch a movie. Muffin snuggles up to me so he's on one side and Tate's on the other. Not only is Tate stealing my heart but so is this giant, sweet Dobie. I'm so glad we have a four-day weekend. I can't imagine a better way to spend it, than with people I care the most about.

I'm roused out of my sleep by Tate picking me up and carrying me bridal style to his bedroom, "Shhh, Krasaaveetsa, you fell asleep during the movie. I'm taking you to bed, so go back to sleep, baby."

I lean my head against Tate's chest and relish in the feel of his strong arms wrapped around me. He carefully sets me down on the edge of the bed, and then strips to his tight, black Abercrombie boxer briefs. Tate pulls my shorts and shirt off. At this point I'm game for whatever he wants to do. He surprises me by replacing the shirt I had on with the tank top he just took off. It's still warm from him and surrounds me in his delicious scent.

He turns the fluffy comforter back and adjusts the pillows for us, pushing them close together in the middle of the ginormous bed.

He rasps, rubbing his rippled abdomen, "There, baby, crawl under the blanket, to the middle of the bed." I comply, doing what he says. I'm too tired to ask him why.

Tate slides in behind me and tucks the covers all around us, to keep the chill from the air conditioner away. They keep their house really cold, so I snuggle back into him. He puts one arm under my pillow and the other, he wraps around my stomach, holding me tightly.

We lace our fingers together and poof, I fall asleep almost instantly. He's warm, soft and makes me feel safe. I know at this point my heart is gone...

## TATE

One week later ...

I SCOWL INTO THE PHONE, "WHAT DO YOU MEAN, YOU haven't found him yet? I don't care if he's fucking disappeared into thin air, I want him found! Do I have to get all of the Russkaya Odessa Mafiya involved to find one fucking person? Do not make me tell Gizya you have failed at this simple task." I hang up on the idiot who's been searching for Jeremy, Emily's ex.

I don't understand how they haven't found him yet. A week should be plenty of time to have already brought him to me. Hopefully, dropping my father's name will motivate the tracker to find the scummy fucker and if not I will call my brother, Viktor, to deal with the incompetent fuck.

My father is Konstantin 'Gizya' Ginzburg. Otherwise known as Balshoy Shef, or The Big Boss to Americans. He is in charge of the Odessa Mafiya which incorporates around five thousand members in America. I'm next in line to take the throne here and I've been avoiding it like the plague. It was really given to my older brother, but he wanted no part in it.

My uncle, Victor Averin, who my brother Viktor is named after, is second-in-command for the Solntsevskaya Bratva. My grandfather was the great 'Vory Vzakone'; real name, Vyacheslav Ivankov. He was impervious for his Mafiya-ish, gruesome ways and illegal dealings for many years. So, it's imperative I grow into a strong Shef, with all of my family heading up the Russkaya Mafiya and Bratva at some time.

Here, I'm Luka Tate Masterson to everyone. To my family however, I'm Luka Tatkiv 'Knees' Ginzburg. I enjoy breaking people's knees when they piss me off, call it my fetish. My family found it suitable for that to be my Boss name.

My brother, Viktor, has made it his life's mission to not be a Boss. My family finally accepted him when he became the family accountant and helps find disposal for any bodies we need dumped. My family hails from Mother Russia and The Odessa is mostly from around Moscow.

If we were in Russia right now, bodies would be dropping like flies. Here in America, it's a little trickier to stay out of the law enforcements sights. I know my father wants me to be corrupt and sinister with my position, but it's just not who I am. In this situation, however, I will have no problem dealing out torture and pain to this pathetic ant.

I was really hoping one of my men would find this sick fuck, but I may need to call a few of my uncle's crazy Bratva goons to see if they have any luck.

I need my guys concentrating on keeping the Italians and Chinese out of my clubs. I will do business with them, but not at my clubs. Many innocent people could get killed if something went down there.

I have to keep Emily a secret also, just so no one attempts to hurt her, because of me. She's my priority over everything—school, clubs, friends, family or even the Mafiya. Her safety and well-being is priority number one.

Taking a deep breath, I trudge back into the house, to check on my sweet Emily. She's been here a week and I love every second of it. I have come to the decision that I never want her to leave. I have also decided that I have been patient long enough. For a man who has never had to wait to fuck a woman, I think I've done very well.

I find my Krasaaveetsa in her kitchen. I gave it to her. She thinks I'm joking when I tell her that, but I'm not. Hell, she can have the whole house if she wants it. I'll even build her a bigger house if that's what makes her happy. I know no amount of money or things will matter to her though and it only makes me care for her even more.

I feel like I live to see my Emily smile; it's become sort of a goal for me every day. I try to see how many times I can put a bright light on her face; she deserves a piece of happiness after a life so sad. I don't think she knows it, but she takes my breath away each time she smiles like that.

# EMILY

I'm busy looking at my magazine on the counter, when Tate walks into the kitchen. He has black leather bar stools that have fast become one of my favorite seats in the house. I love how the breakfast bar is located in the middle of the kitchen, so I can watch him as he prepares and cooks different meals for us. I never knew a man in the kitchen could be so sexy, but when he cooks yummy food and is shirtless, well, it takes the cake.

I feel strong arms wrap firmly around me and I relish the feeling. I snuggle back into him, closing my eyes for a brief moment, resting my head on his shoulder. "Hey, handsome, you done with your business call?"

"I sure am, Krasaaveetsa," he croons in my ear and starts to kiss on my neck. *God that feels amazing.* I learned at my apartment that Tate is very, very talented with that mouth.

I turn in my seat so I'm facing him. I want to kiss on him, too.

"Want to play, Krasaaveetsa?"

"Depends on what exactly that means, Tate." I lick up the side of his neck and he shivers, making a rumbling sound in his throat and it's so sexy.

"It means I get to feel that sweet cunt, wrapped tightly around my cock, little pet. I want to make you feel good again." I pull him between my legs and kiss him full on the mouth. He returns my kiss, fervently. I match his tongue with mine, softly caressing.

If he is any good at reading me, he will know this is not just a yes, but a hell yes. I am so ready for him. It's been sweet torture sleeping next to him every night this past week, feeling his hard body holding me tightly. I wrap my legs around his body and lightly drag my nails down his back.

He growls, "Ahhh, that's it, Krasaaveetsa, you're mine, baby."

He nips at my neck and slides his hands around my waist. He picks me up and I keep my legs wrapped around him, while I clutch onto his shoulders. Tate easily carries me about a foot away and sets me on the counter.

He pushes me backward so I'm leaning on my elbows. He looks so gorgeous, his cheeks are stained a slight crimson from being turned on, he's slightly panting and his hair is sticking out every which way from my hands running through it. He snakes both hands up each of my thighs, pushing the material of my loose, white sundress up until he gets to my lacey thong. He looks at me, his eyes dilating as he takes me in.

Tate starts murmuring in Russian and it shoots straight to my pussy, "YA praava, vee как maya krasaaveetsa, nafsegda (I claim you as mine beauty, forever)."

I sigh, "Mmmm, whatever you're saying, keep saying it. I love how it sounds."

My panties are soaked, each time he rasps something new in Russian, I get wetter. He smirks at me, sending me a look that says 'if you only knew.' Tate leisurely pulls my thong down my legs and licks his bottom lip a little as he takes me in.

"Please, Tate, don't slow down, I want you so badly."

"Shhh, baby, I know."

He starts with his fingers, pumping steadily inside me. *Holy fuck, does that feel good.* I tug on his hair, to let him know I want more. I just want him. I need to feel all of him deep inside of me. Tate lifts my dress up over my head and starts to kiss me all over. He starts at my tummy eagerly moving up to the tops of my breasts. I'm so glad I chose to wear matching panties and bra today. I want to look perfect for him.

"Oh! That feels soooo good," I gasp out.

He's so phenomenal at eliciting these amazing feelings coursing throughout my body. I place my hands on each side of his face and start to tug him up my body more. I don't want to wait any longer.

"Tate, no more waiting, I need to feel you inside me."

He peers into my eyes for a few seconds, almost as if he's re-assuring himself that I really am ready for this. I grin encouragingly and bump his nose lightly with mine. It seems to shake him out of his thoughts and he peels off his shirt.

I run my hands down his smooth, cut body and then on the way back upward, lightly tug on his nipple rings. Sitting up, I draw his left nipple ring into my mouth. I use my tongue to play around with it, tugging with my teeth gently and flipping it back and forth with my tongue. I let it go slowly and look down the rest of his body. His cock is extremely hard, peeking out of the top of his pants. God, it's so erotic, I just want to lick it.

I whimper, "Can I lick it, Tate?" I keep my eyes on his straining dick so I don't see his expression.

"Fuck!"

He starts to shove his pants down forcefully. Good, he's going to let me take him in my mouth. I hope I do as good of a job as he does. I begin to slide off of the counter, to get onto my knees.

"Oh no, Krasaaveetsa, you can put my cock in your mouth later. Right now, I'm going to make that cunt all mine. Hold onto the side of the counter, this is going to be rough."

My pussy convulses at his words, eagerly awaiting his promise and I feel my wetness dripping down to my butt. Tate grasps my ankles, pulling me so that I slide to the edge of the counter. He kicks his pants the rest of the way off and I see him completely for the first time. Holy fuck he's big! His dick reaches up to his belly button. *That has to be at least eight inches.* No way will that fit in me. I look at him a little panicked and he answers my trepidation by grabbing the nape of my neck, kissing me passionately.

He grips my thigh in his other hand firmly, then moves the hand away from my nape, using it to pump his cock while he works it into me. Tate rubs the head in my wetness, drawing it up, all along my pussy lips. He parts my lips gently with his cock and then thrusts inside me deeply.

"Oh God!" I gasp at the fresh feel of pleasure and the pinch of pain accompanying it.

It's been awhile since I was with my ex. Two years actually and he doesn't hold a candle to Tate's size. I take a few deep breaths, relaxing my muscles. Tate won't hurt me purposefully. I trust him. I love him.

He murmurs close to my ear, comforting me, "Good girl, just relax and take me in, baby. It will fit I promise, especially with all your pussy juice leaking everywhere. You are so fucking beautiful like this, fuck, so beautiful."

It makes me burn up inside to hear him talk about my pussy juices leaking all around his cock. I hold on tight to the edge of the counter as Tate goes to town, thrusting hard into me. It feels as if it's a really tight fit, but no longer painful, just full.

Tate moves his fingers down between us and holds onto the base of his dick for a few seconds, as it goes in and out of me. He gets his fingers wet from it and then starts to rub light circles on my clit.

It feels out of this world, I'm building, I'm almost...*so close*...oh God I'm going to come.

"Oh my God, Tate, it feels fucking awesome, I'm going to fucking come, please, please, harder!"

"That's it, Emily, milk my cock. I'm going to fill you up so fucking full of my cum."

His voice vibrates through me and I explode at his words. I drag my nails down his back, digging in hard. I know it will leave marks. I lean in and bite his neck roughly, as I gasp his name out on the crest of my orgasm.

He hears my gasp "Tate" and his dick starts to pulse frantically inside of me. My pussy is so tight around him, I can feel each time his cock convulses. The warmth of each spurt of his cum, as he paints the inside of me is delicious.

After a few moments, he lays his big body over mine, resting on the kitchen counter for a few beats. His face is placed on my chest as he catches his breath. I relax, softly playing with his hair and close my eyes.

So this is what bliss feels like. I can't wait until we get to do that again, that's for sure. A chill runs over me after a minute and I shiver. The granite counter top is not made for warmth or comfort.

Tate must feel me because he stands back up, briefly bending over, placing a soft kiss on my lips and then my forehead. He lifts me up with him easily and carries me to his bedroom. I'm thinking round two, but am pleasantly surprised when he places me in the bath tub.

"Relax and get warm, baby." He smirks and winks, then turns and leaves the bathroom. Well, guess I'm taking a nice bath then. I don't mind that at all.

# ELEVEN

## EMILY

One week later ...

I NEEDED TO COME TO MY APARTMENT TO GET SOME more stuff to take to Tate's. London and I never once imagined that we would be staying there for so long. It's going on three weeks now, when we were planning for the latest being one week.

The boys are stuck in class, taking tests that I've already completed, so London offered to come home with me. One of the perks of having Tate drive everywhere is we don't have a car. I consider it a perk since Tate is nice enough to let me use his Mercedes. He told me I could just have the whole freaking car. *Crazy man.* I told him no and instead of arguing back with me, he declared that we will go pick one out that I like. *Yeah right.* I'm not letting him buy me a damn car.

I also can't fathom that London is still here. I heard her and Cam arguing about her looking for a job last night in Cameron's room. It took everything I had not to interrupt them. I hate it when they fight, London deserves better than that.

"Hey chick, so, I was thinking, maybe you should just stay here. This semester's already half way over anyhow. I mean, if you're planning on coming back to live here for next semester, it's silly to waste money on the back and forth traveling. You can still do your classes here on a computer, right?" I swiftly glance at her out of the corner of my eye as I drive. I'm a cautious driver; I always try to pay extra attention to everything around me.

"Well, um, about that—I kind of already finished all the assignments that were due for my classes and turned everything in. So now I just have to wait until the professor's grade all my work."

"Holy shit! That's great, London! You need to transfer here, you are way too freaking smart for those classes you take. You truly are the most intelligent person I know. I'm so proud of you, chickadee!" She nods, giving me her signature cocky smile.

"Thanks, you know, I am pretty great. But, so, yeah I was thinking if I liked it, I might just stay and have Mom send me some of my shit. I haven't done anything or shopped since you left, so I've saved literally every penny. I don't have a lot of money, but I have enough to pay for my first semester if I don't get picked up for a scholarship right away. I also received my acceptance letter before I came."

"That's great, I'm so happy for you! I bet Momma and Elliot are super proud of you for transferring to a university. Hey, we never did get to talk about why you showed up out of the blue with all the drama going on." Thinking of that shit brings a sick feeling to my stomach.

"Oh my God, I'm glad you brought that up. I completely got side tracked, but I wanted to tell you as soon as I got here. You just looked so happy with Tate; I didn't want to ruin it right away."

"And what's up with Elliot? I've called and texted that jerk, a few times."

"Okay, so I guess the Sheriff went to your granddad's house to let you know Jeremy was getting released early. Well, Rosa, the lady who Elliot has to come clean, answered the door and got the message. According to Elliot, he didn't see her for like a week because of their schedules, and the dumb bitch didn't think to write the freaking message down!" She huffs, irritated. "So, when he finally saw her she gave him the message. He was so pissed, he freaked out and fired her. He showed up to Mom's house spazzing out about how I had to drive up here to warn you and make sure you were okay."

"Okay so why didn't he just call me, then?"

"I guess he had tried to call you and it went to voice mail. I told him you were probably locked in your apartment doing homework with your phone on silent. That is your usual routine. He got pissed believing that Jeremy had already gotten to you; he threw his phone and busted it all up. Then he took my car to the station, filled it up with gas and checked all the fluids while I packed my stuff. He tried calling you again from my phone and it still went to voice mail, so he and Mom shoved me in the car as quickly as possible and programmed my GPS. Elliot handed me a wad of cash saying he'd get a new phone later and sent me on my way with instructions to warn you. It was like nine o'clock at freaking night, so I drove all night long. I was so tired when I got here, but I realized I could catch you after your class. I'm so glad you had given me your schedule and sent me the campus info, because I had a map and was easily able to find where to go. That's probably why you thought I looked like a zombie when you saw me."

I shake my head at what she tells me. I don't doubt it at all, shit like that always seems to happen to her or her family. "Wow, that's crazy. I wish you would have told me when you first got here, though. We could have avoided some of this possibly. Geez, I had no idea. I even kept telling myself I needed to call you both more, but I just had so much homework that week before our long weekend. Then we kept playing phone tag. Fuck! I can't believe that freaking psycho is out loose somewhere."

"I know. I can't believe it either. Did Tate tell you about what he was screaming about outside when ass fuck wrote on the wall? Did I really hear him say Jeremy is fucking with the Mafia? I mean what is that all about? I asked Cameron but he won't say anything about it, just tells me it's none of my business."

"Shit, I was so upset, I honestly forgot he'd even said that. I'm going to talk to Tate about it."

We arrive at the apartment complex and drive all around to make sure there are no stalkers hiding out, waiting for me. I'm scared to go into my apartment now, but at least London's with me.

We park, making our way through the entryway and up to my apartment. I glance at her as I sluggishly unlock and open the door. "Oh, thank god, I was so nervous it was going to be trashed or something." I let out the breath I was holding and step inside.

Once we get completely inside, I survey the apartment and it appears as if everything is where it was when we cleaned it up before leaving a few weeks ago. "I'm going to jump in the shower really quick since I have my razor here. I have trees growing on my legs." I smile sheepishly.

"Gross, Em! Why didn't you just use Tate's razor? I used Cam's. He wants to touch me? Then he can lend me his razor."

"I don't know. I guess I don't want him to feel like I'm completely taking over his whole life."

"Please, that man is making you his whole life. Wake up, darlin', and smell the rich, fine-ass flowers in front of you. Since everything's kosher, I'm gonna go downstairs to the laundry and wash the dirty clothes we have here, while you shower and pack. Give me your front door key and I'll lock the door. Is that okay? Or if you want, I'll stay until you're finished."

"No, go, I'm fine. That's actually a great idea. Way to kill two birds with one stone." I wink, grabbing my key off the counter and hand it to her.

"We need to get you a key made; remind me later, after we have lunch. My bed is big enough for both of us, so we can share it until we can move to a two bedroom in the building, okay?" She grabs the key out of my hand and smacks a big, sloppy, wet kiss on my cheek.

"Sounds like a plan, cow, now get your hairy ass in the shower!" She takes off, running and laughing. She's lucky I love her or I would throw something at her.

"Cow?! Your ass is wayyyyy bigger than mine!"

"Yeah, yeah!" she hollers and walks to the bedroom. I shake my head; she's a dork.

I head into my bathroom and take a deep breath. I haven't been taking my anxiety pills while staying at Tate's and it seems to have cleared my head up more. I'm a little excited, but I think it's because I get to use all my own stuff.

Tate's home is beautiful and he's so giving, making sure I have what I ask for, but there is nothing quite like using your own stuff. My hair has definitely gotten spoiled though, using his salon shampoo and conditioner. It even smells good, like juniper.

I undress, toss my clothes in a pile on the floor and start the shower. After a few beats, I step into the steamy area. I relax under the hot spray and massage my neck with my fingers. My extracurricular activities with Tate have me a little sore in some spots. *Yum.* Speaking of Tate, I can't wait to find out what he will do to me later. That man is phenomenal with his hands, mouth and cock. I picture him naked in the shower, rubbing his strong hands all over his soapy body...

Wait, what was that? Oh, I bet it's just London coming for more laundry. I stand extra still and quiet my thoughts to listen—just to make sure. I'm probably being paranoid. I hear an almost silent click. *Nope, not paranoid.* That was a legit noise.

"London, what are you doing?" I shout, so she can hear me.

I wonder if she's having issues with the front door lock. I do sometimes, I know it's cheap. I don't get a response, so whatever, she must have figured it out. I go back to washing my body with my favorite Bath and Body Works body wash. It smells divine and makes me feel soft everywhere.

The hair on the back of my neck stands up when I feel a little breeze of cold air. The a/c is not on because I would be able to hear it humming. I feel the cool air caress me again and my insides start to jump. You know when you get the feeling that you want to look, but you really don't want to look? That's exactly how I feel. I swear if this is London fucking with me, I will wring her neck. The thing is, I know London likes to mess with me, but she's not cruel.

Deep inside my belly I know it's not her and it makes me nauseous. *Fuck!* I should have brought my gun in here with me. What an idiot! Have I not learned anything? My fears are confirmed when I hear his dark voice.

"I know you're finished, time to get out."

That's all it takes for me to go into a full-blown panic attack. Oh my god, my chest feels so tight and I can't breathe. Fuck! I have to make myself take deep breaths—in...out...in...out... one...two...three...four...five...six...seven...eight...nine...in...out... in...out. I'm okay, I can handle this. I need to get to my room so I can get my pistol.

Jeremy rips open the shower curtain with a snarl. I see him for the first time since we were in that court room, two years ago. *He's gotten thinner.* He was already fairly thin before. Now it looks like every ounce of fat he had has melted off, and in its place is lean muscle. He must have spent his time working out the entire time he was in jail. Jeremy's hair is longer now, the midnight black locks now graze his shoulders and he has a few days' worth of scruff covering his face.

His face twists into an angry smirk and his eyes look at me with pure hatred. The little bits of softness I once saw in him are completely gone now. He reaches into the shower lightning quick and snatches my arm harshly, making me call out in fear, yanking me out of the shower so fast I stumble over the built-in bathtub.

"Ow! Please let go, Jeremy, I'll walk, please!" Fuck, my leg's killing me. I'm going to have a huge bruise from the damn tub. I hope he didn't sprain my ankle; it's on fire right now.

"You think I'm gonna be letting you go this time, bitch, so you can run again? I don't fucking think so."

His other hand grabs onto my wet hair to hold me, then he pulls his right leg back and lays into my thigh with a solid kick. *Holy fuck.* The breath is stolen from me and new tears crest in my eyes from the sharp pain. I'm not going to be able to walk. Please let London be okay, there's no telling what he did to her.

I choke, trembling. "Ouch! I-I'm so sorry. I promise I won't run, never again, okay? I promise, no running." I have to placate him with what he wants to hear, so he will calm down some. I have to get to my gun to get away from him.

"Boo, I know you won't go anywhere; you won't be leaving this fucking apartment."

Jeremy has a hold of me by my arm and my hair, dragging me forcefully toward my bedroom. It hurts so insanely bad, my scalp is screaming at me. If he doesn't let up soon he'll rip my hair out.

We finally make it to my bedroom, where he tsk, tsk, tsks at me, shaking his head. "You dumb, ignorant bitch, thinking you could leave *me* before I was done with you. Then you come here and start fucking somebody else? You always were a fucking whore, weren't you? I thought I took care of that issue, when I took care of that fucking thing in your stomach."

He throws me on my bed and I scramble as fast as I can to my nightstand. I may only have this chance to get to it.

Jeremy lets out a loud, deep belly laugh. "Oh, you thought I wouldn't search through your shit? You looking for something, boo? Go ahead and see if it's in there." He nods towards the little stand; I close my eyes and let the tears slip free. *He got my gun.* I reach into the drawer, under the book where it was hidden and feel it is definitely missing. I don't know what to do. I can't overpower him; I'm tiny and he's even stronger than before. I pray London stays downstairs. He has my gun so it wouldn't surprise me if he decided to kill her if he knows she's here; he hates her.

"Now, back to what I have planned. First off, I'm going to take what's owed to me. I'm glad you washed that fuck off you. Don't worry, I plan on killing him. He won't touch you again." I tightly clinch my eyes closed and put my head down. Please God no, not my Tate. I will do anything to save him. I can't let him get hurt. I love him too much...please God, I will do anything you want, just don't let my Tate get hurt.

I clear my throat, attempting to push down the pain that's radiating throughout my heart and body. "Forget about him, I don't want him. I will do whatever you want, Jeremy. I promise." I feel like I'm giving my soul to the devil, but I will sacrifice anything to save Tate.

The bedroom door flies open, crashing into the wall with a loud bang. I glance up quickly, stunned.

London stands in the doorway looking like a pissed off goddess. "Get the fuck away from her, you piece of shit!" she bellows, heatedly. *London! What the fuck—she has my gun?*

She waves the gun slightly. "Your stupid ass left this laying on the counter. Never were too smart, huh, J boy? Now get the fuck out," she grits. "I already called Tate, and he and his boys can't wait to get a hold of you!" London finishes with an evil looking grin and I can't help the little flutter of hope that appears in my belly.

Jeremy grabs me up, holding onto my arms and places me in front of him as a shield.

"Not smart huh, you fucking whore? You wanna shoot me; you have to shoot through her first. Now get outta my way, Emily and I are going to take a fun trip."

He starts to steer me out of the room. I can feel he's shaky. London backs up, keeping the gun trained on us, the entire trek to the living room. I'm so grateful for Granddaddy teaching us how to use different guns when we were growing up. I know London's not as good of a shot as I am, but if I can move at least half my body, I know she can clip him somewhere.

London smiles really big at him and my stomach drops. She's going to end up making him angrier and I'm not going be able to get out of his claw-like grip. This man feels like he has hands of steel with how hard he's gripping me to him.

I hear a choking sound and his grasp starts to loosen on my arms. A few moments later, Jeremy's hands fall completely away from me and I drop to the ground, finally free. I crawl to London as quickly as I can and she squats down. She tenderly pulls me into her arms and tightly hugs me to her. I peer over at where Jeremy was just holding me and I gasp.

Nikoli has his arm wrapped like a tight band around Jeremy's throat, in a choke hold. Jeremy's face is bright red and he's gasping, trying to catch any little breath. Good, that's how I felt when he touched me, like I couldn't breathe. Jeremy rakes his hands along Nikoli's strong forearm, but he is no match for the Russian beast's strength. Jeremy goes limp, his eyes closed and mouth wide open, almost as if he saw a ghost. I feel a semblance of relief inside that Jeremy looks like he's dead.

Nikoli drops Jeremy to the ground; he lands like a sack of potatoes. Niko grins down at Jeremy, "Oh man, The Boss is going to be so happy I finally caught you, you sneaky, little dude."

London escorts me to my room, helping me get a large t-shirt and some stretchy shorts on. I can't believe I was naked during that whole onslaught. I have carpet burn from Jeremy dragging me around, my scalp is extremely sore and I know my body is going to be littered with bruises.

After we finish in my room, Niko fills us in. Tate has had Nikoli show up at the apartment at random times ever since we left to stay with them, trying to catch Jeremy breaking in. Thank god for these men and their sly thinking, they probably just saved mine and London's lives. Niko has London run to his truck and get some rope out of the back to tie Jeremy up with.

He turns to me, with a sweet expression, "You okay, Tate's Krasaaveetsa?" Niko asks, while he has the gun now trained on Jeremy.

"You can just call me Emily if you want, Niko. Is he dead?" I gesture towards the lump on the floor. "Why do you have the gun still on him?" He smiles a little smile at me and then focuses back on his task.

"I call you The Boss' Krasaaveetsa, because that is what you are. You deserve respect, so I give it to you. And this moosar is not dead, just passed out."

"What is moosar?"

"It is trash, he is moosar."

"Yeah, definitely agree with you on that. Why do you call me Boss? Is Tate your boss? I thought he was your friend?"

"Yes, I do some work for him. He is my friend; he is moy braat (my brother)."

He glances away as if he is done talking, so I shut up. I really should take a Russian class so I can pick up some of these words they use. Whatever 'braat' means, Niko said it with great respect. I need to try to remember to look it up. I feel like a pest always asking them what stuff means.

London walks back in, looking tired and flustered with the rope in hand. Nikoli goes to work, tying Jeremy up in some complicated knot technique. I stand back to watch as London holds the gun for him.

Tate shows up about ten minutes later, appearing relieved when he sees me sitting on the couch.

"Krasaaveetsa, are you okay? Are you hurt? Thank God, Niko was here!" He rushes toward me and pulls me into his arms. Tate touches my arm where it's sore and I wince.

"Shit, baby! What is it?" He looks me all over, but can't see anything. Slowly, he runs his hand over the same spot, watching for my reaction to see where it hurts.

"Ouch," I draw my arm back, slightly, "you touched a spot where he grabbed me." Tate's nostrils flare angrily and he flexes his jaw.

I tell Tate everything about what happened and where I'm hurt. When I'm done, Nikoli informs him of the rest of the story from when he showed up. Tate looks furious.

Tate orders, "Load him up, Nikoli, and take him to Gizya's old storage building. Get my tools and the bleach ready, I'll be there as soon as I get Emily settled back home." Niko nods, looking excited. "I want his knees first when he wakes up, then I'm going to take him apart, piece by piece. Also get Viktor for clean-up tonight."

Nikoli nods, "Boss." He sets to doing what he's told; this is a side of Tate I'm not used to seeing. I've always known Tate was domineering and people seem to jump when he tells them to do something, but this is Tate in business mode.

# TWELVE

## EMILY
Dinner is served.

**C**AMERON SHOWS UP TOWARD THE END TO CHECK ON us. I think he was really there because he wanted to see how London was. He drives us back to the house in Tate's car, because we are way too much of a wreck right now for either London or I to drive it. I thought Cam was going to blow a gasket when he heard London had pulled a gun on Jeremy instead of waiting for help. There were lots of hushed, serious whispers going on between them.

The ride home is an uncomfortable silence; Cameron is looking angry and London just stares out the passenger window lost deep in her thoughts. I have no idea what's really going on with them, but I hope she confides in me soon. Tate said he was stopping to talk to his brother really quickly and would be right behind us. I guess Viktor has a house close to Tate's in a different posh neighborhood.

Once we arrive, we all shuffle into the house and Muffin greets me right away at the door. He brings a smile to my face, knowing he was anxiously waiting for me to return. I scratch his ears for a moment then make my way to the living room. He follows and we sit down on one of the plush couches. A few minutes of petting him relaxes me and gets my breathing back to normal finally. I never knew a dog could help with my anxiety.

A while later, I'm nudged awake. I dozed off once I finally relaxed with Muffin. I think it's just the dog, wanting me to scratch his ears again but glance up to find Tate, peering down at me with sad, worried eyes.

"Hi, moy Krasaaveetsa, how are you feeling?" he asks, his Russian undertone, thick with emotion. I blink a few times and process his question. I didn't even realize I fell asleep. This couch is so comfy; I keep sleeping on it every time I sit down. I yawn a huge yawn.

"Geez, I didn't know I was so sleepy or I would have just laid down in the bed. Umm, I'm okay, just sore all over. What's wrong handsome?" I don't like seeing him sad, I wish he would smile.

"Da, that's normal, it's from the adrenaline rush earlier. It sucks all your energy out. I brought you a chocolate bar to help get your sugar back up." He runs his hands through his hair. "What's wrong? Well, first off, I wasn't there to protect you. I promised you I would keep you safe." He shakes his head, annoyed. "I feel like such a damn failure. It breaks me to know you are hurt and I could have been there with you to help you." This man is the sweetest, most caring man I have ever met. What is he talking about, failing me? He's the reason I'm okay right now!

"Are you kidding me, Tate? If you hadn't had Nikoli checking the apartment periodically, I would probably be dead right now! Instead, I'm here next to you and I'm okay. Please, don't be upset. During this whole disaster, I realized something very important and I want to tell you." I gaze at him, slightly nervous until he nods, telling me to go on. "I realized that I'm in love with you, Tate. During all of that scary time at my apartment, I thought of how much I care about you and how I love you so much. I know it's quick and probably way too soon, I mean it's been what? Two months? But, I just can't help it."

I grip his hand tightly, hoping he can feel just a semblance of the warmth I have for him inside. "You helped me today, probably more than you realize. Tate, you helped me get through it during the ugly things he was saying to me and when he physically hurt me. Each time, I thought of you and it made my heart warm. Then you really did save me, by having Nikoli there. Trust me, things could have been so much worse. Let's just be happy that I'm sitting here—next to you—right now. Please."

He hesitates, a little unsure. "I care about you a lot, Krasaaveetsa, but there are a lot of things you don't know about me. I also have my own secrets. I don't know if you could handle everything about me." He glances away, looking at the floor for a few beats, then returns his glance to me. "I may be nice to you, but I'm not so much to others." He appears so serious when he says this and I hope in my heart things aren't so bad that I can't handle them.

"I think I can handle it, Tate. At least I hope so. You accept me with all of my problems and I want to be able to do the same for you. If it helps, I know you have the club and you're like Nikoli's boss. I know you have lots of money and your brother works in money. I heard your conversation earlier with Nikoli about what to do with Jeremy, so I know you're no Saint. Then there was when you yelled outside my apartment. Did you yell about the Mafia? Did I hear you right?"

"Let's start with what you heard me tell Niko to do. You do realize I wasn't just saying those things, right? I really do plan to do all of that to your ex. Can you live with that, Krasaaveetsa?"

I recall everything he said to Nikoli at my apartment. Those were some serious threats he implied and I know Jeremy will not come out of it alive. After all of the pain and suffering he put me through, can I live with myself or Tate knowing Jeremy is gone forever? That he will never hurt me again, never stalk me, and never take my babies away from me, ever again. *Yes, I can live with that.*

"Yes, Tate, I can deal with it. It may make me a bad person to say this, but I will actually breathe easier, knowing he's finally gone. I will finally be able to relax, knowing he can never hurt me again." I look him in the eyes and say it as sincerely as possible. Tate needs to know I'm completely serious about this.

"That's good, Krasaaveetsa, because I do indeed intend to kill him. It will be bloody and painful, and he will suffer a great deal for ever touching you." He sighs. "Now, about what I said in the parking lot at the apartments. What do you know about the Russkaya Mafiya, Krasaaveetsa, huh?"

"Ummm, well, not much. I think we studied about the Italian Mafia in school. Is it close to the same thing?"

"Eh," he shrugs a little, "I guess you could compare it to the Italians, but Russkaya work a little differently. Does the Mafiya scare you?"

"No, not really. But that's probably because I've never been around it before and I don't really know much of what they do, aside from some movies I've seen with London."

"Does it scare you to know I'm Mafiya?" He peers down at me questionably and I shrug, unsure.

"My father, Gizya, is The Big Boss here in America. It means he is in charge of everyone, the entire thing. That's around five thousand people, Krasaaveetsa. I may not be The Big Boss yet, but I am a Boss. People do answer to me, and I do a lot of business for my father and uncle." I nod, taking it all in.

"Who's your uncle? Have I met him yet?"

"No, you have not. You shouldn't meet him unless we decide to marry. He's another type of Boss." My eyes widen at the marriage part and he smirks, continuing on. "My uncle is second in command here, in the Solntsevskaya Bratva. They are like us too, but more of a criminal element. They take care of the really bad stuff. I try to keep our businesses on the cleaner side of the law."

"That's not so bad then," I cut in and he shakes his head.

"Don't mistake, I do also partake in an array of bad things. I do kill bad people and make a lot of decisions you would not agree with." I swallow a large gulp when he talks about killing people so nonchalantly. "I need to know if this scares and upsets you, baby. I will not put you through this if you are not one hundred percent up for it. I will not keep you if you are scared of me and of my business." He looks completely serious and I believe him. I also trust that he would never purposely put me in any type of danger.

"Okay, I trust you, Tate. It's pretty frightening, but I know you would never get me hurt and you would keep me safe if anything were to happen. Is umm, all of your family in the Mafia?"

How will I fit into his life if I am not like them? Will his family even like me? The thoughts of his family are more overwhelming to me, than the whole Mafia thing.

"Yes, my family is Mafiya. We've covered the basics now and we will talk more about this later, Krasaaveetsa. Right now I have business to take care of." He stands up from the couch and I sit up.

"By business, you mean Jeremy, right?" I don't know if I really want to know the answer to my question, but I ask it anyway.

"Look, I won't be informing you about my business or anything to do with my Mafiya stuff. I don't want to taint you with the gruesome details of my dealings. I will tell you right now though about this, yes, it is about Jeremy. I'm only informing you because it has to do with you directly."

"I understand part of your life has to be private, but we are definitely not done discussing this. I want to know as much as you can tell me. I'd also like to know how all this will affect me being with you."

"Agreed, Krasaaveetsa, I will tell you what I can. God, baby, you have made me a very happy man today." He kisses me roughly and I can tell he's excited. I'm so happy he's not sad anymore. I hated to see him so upset, it hurt my heart.

He didn't seem freaked out earlier when I told him how I feel either. I didn't say it to him so he would automatically say it back, but I can't help but wonder just how he really feels about me. Once he leaves, I head to his bedroom. Soaking in the tub for a while, I play the day over in my head again. Everything that happened, everything that I learned, it was pure over load.

I turn the water on hot, to help my muscles relax, eating the delicious Hershey's chocolate bar. I accompany the chocolate with a glass of sweet wine and I think of how lucky I am. When I came here a few months ago, I never would have guessed to meet such supportive people. For the first time since I arrived at Tate's house, I go to bed alone and I hate the feeling.

Tate didn't come home until after I was asleep last night. I heard the shower come on and then a while later I felt him crawl into bed. He pulled me close to him and kissed the back of my head. I fell back asleep comfortable, warm, happy and content.

The next day, we all have class with completely different schedules, so everyone misses each other at the house. Tate woke me up with a nice surprise. He had rolled me over onto my belly and worked some of his frustration out on my pussy. He wasn't the only one who enjoyed it. I came twice and was trying to jump him again, before he crawled out of bed. I hope we aren't too loud; I don't want anybody else to hear us. I never thought of it before, but anyone could have walked into the kitchen the other day when he took me on the counter. I haven't heard anyone else in the house though, so I think it's safe to say the walls are thick.

I wonder if London will want to have lunch today. I need to find out what's going on with her and Cameron. My phone beeps with a text. It's my handsome man.

> **Tate**: Baby, don't make plans for dinner. We're going to my parents' house.

> **Me**: What?! You can't just spring this on me right now! Dinner's in a few hours!

I'm going to strangle that man. He wants to have dinner with his parents and I know absolutely nothing about them, besides that they are part of the mafia. I also have nothing nice to wear. Oh my God, they will probably think I'm some hussy after Tate's money or something crazy.

> **Tate**: Yes, baby. Be ready at 7. I'll switch out cars then and we can go.

> **Me**: Okay, but you so owe me for this!

> **T**: Whatever you want, Kapacota <3

> **Me**: TTYS Sugar Dimples <3

Awww he sent me a heart! He's so sweet sometimes. I follow up with sending London a text. Hopefully she's not with Cam, so she can help me find something to wear.

> **Me**: 911 woman, I need you to help me find

something NICE, not slutty, to wear to Tate's parents for dinner tonight.

I look up from my phone when I hear her voice, "Seriously, lazy ass, you couldn't walk down the hallway to Cam's room and ask me in person?" She's wearing a cocky smirk.

London has on one of Cameron's white undershirts and a pair of his boxers. He would probably scold her if he saw her so informal walking around the house, but she totally looks hot in it. He seems to like to keep London in check. I think it's good for her, considering she's normally a total wild child. She has her hair pinned on top of her head in a messy bun and is sucking on a Blow Pop.

"I didn't know you were in his room or I would have. What are you doing?" I gesture to her comfy outfit. "You look like a total bum, are you guys staying in tonight?" She shrugs and looks a little bored.

London shrugs, pouting. "Eh, he has stuff to do so I'm just hanging out and doing laundry. I might head to that little pastry shop right outside the neighborhood and get a pastry and coffee. I don't know, it depends if I decide to get dressed or not." She looks really bummed out now. I pat the spot beside me on the bed and she comes and sits next to me.

"Is everything going okay with you and Cameron? Y'all just jumped into it. I wasn't sure if this was just a fling or if you really like him." I take her hand in mine to offer her comfort and my attention.

"I know, I thought it was going to be a one-night stand type of deal, then after that night maybe two nights. He kept right on me ever since we first met and went out that night to the club." She rolls her eyes, "I told him about you going to Tate's parents and he thought it was too soon. I mean, I know you've been seeing Tate longer than me and Cam have been, but it's like the thought of me meeting his family never once crossed his mind. That hurt my feelings so I told him I thought you guys were crazy and I prefer to do my own thing. After that he looked pissed off and told me he had shit to do. He stormed out, saying he'd be back whenever he was done. So I have no idea what's going on right now. I usually never even give guys this kind of chance, but I'm a little addicted to Cameron right now. I just don't want to be that girl who nags, you know?"

Aww, my poor London. That sucks. It sounds like Cam was being a dick but who knows, I wasn't there to see how it all went down. I won't tell London that, though.

"That's really shitty, London, I'm sorry you are dealing with that right now." I hug her and rub her back for a second.

"I'm okay, you know I'm not one to put up with any shit when it comes down to it. Now, let's find you something awesome to wow the future in-laws. I'm excited for you!"

"In-laws, yeah right, they will probably think I'm a hussy after Tate's money with my luck." I huff, getting up and walking to the closet. Tate has unpacked my bags and moved all of my belongings into it. He just randomly did it without even asking me. I was pretty amused when I discovered it.

"Oh no, I'm pretty sure they will know what this means. Tate's what, like, twenty-two years old? And Cameron was saying that Tate has never introduced a female to his parents or family, like ever. So relax, they will know you are the real deal." London smiles big at me like this is the greatest news.

"Holy shit! This is even more horrible! Now, I know they will hate me! His dad will probably have one of his guys sink me to the bottom of a lake somewhere with cement blocks around my feet!"

She bursts out laughing at my descriptive picture and I just glare at her. If my leg still wasn't so sore I'd leap at her ass. She smirks at me and shakes her head; bitch knows me too well to know exactly what I'm thinking.

An hour later and plenty of amusing quips from London and I'm dressed. I'm in my white, baby doll style sundress, that's trimmed out in lace along the breast line and the bottom. I pair it with some cute white wedge sandals that Avery had packed in with her stuff.

Thankfully, Avery has smaller feet than London so I can borrow her stuff. We figured white was the virginal color, so hopefully his mom will approve. It's also the longest sundress I own. I'm shooting for modesty and good girl look. I think we've pretty much nailed it.

I leave my hair down and put a few curls in it. Not too fancy, but at least it looks like I made an effort with my appearance. I brush on some black mascara to accent my long eyelashes, a dust of blush along my cheek bones and smooth on some lip gloss. London sprays me down with my Heavenly perfume by Victoria's Secret and I'm all set.

It all worked out with perfect timing too because it is now 6:30 and Tate just pulled up to the house. Muffin runs to the front door at full speed and is jumping around whining, waiting for his dad to get inside.

Tate steps inside and he looks absolutely gorgeous. He's wearing a light grey button up shirt and some black slacks that mold to his physique perfectly. He looks professional and sexy but not over-dressed. Muffin takes up his attention for a few minutes, wagging his butt around and nosing Tate to pet him. I love that he cares so much for his dog. Muffin is such a good boy. He has definitely stolen part of my heart, too.

Tate looks up and his sparkling hazel eyes take me in before they meet my green ones. "Damn, little lamb, you look breathtaking."

His eyes dilate as he walks toward me. He bends his head down and kisses me on my lips, soft and sweet, while he wraps his arms around me and pulls me into his solid chest. He whispers, "Fuck, I love coming home to you. I meant it this morning when I told you I want you to stay here." Wow, I thought that was just the sex haze talking when he said that earlier.

"I love being here too, Tate, but I also have London to think of. I can't just leave her when she's here for me." I wrap my arms around his neck and pepper little kisses all over his jawline leaving little traces of my lip gloss. It's okay, I know he doesn't mind it.

"Then I'll tell Cam to keep her, too." He shrugs, saying this like it's the simplest answer and that Cameron will just keep seeing London, like it's not their own relationship or anything.

"No, Tate, I will talk to London about what she wants to do first, and then we can talk more about it, okay?" He answers me with a cheeky smile, the answer pacifying him for the time being and he twirls me around.

"Alright, let's go to my parents' house, Krasaaveetsa."

I grab my small purse and head to the garage to get into Tate's grey, Bentley Continental GT Speed. I broke down and asked him what it was called. *God, I fucking love this car!*

Tate pulls out of the garage, heading for the main road. "This car is my favorite, sugar dimples. I love how it sucks me back into my seat when you go fast." I smirk at him and put my seatbelt on. He starts to laugh and it lights up his whole face. Gosh, he's handsome.

"I am glad you like her, she is a good car. Would you like to drive her later? Perhaps on the way back?" He leans over, quickly kissing the tip of my nose and I sigh. He's freaking perfect and I'm the lucky one who has him.

"Maybe sometime, but tonight I want to just sit back and watch you drive her. You look so sexy when you drive."

"Sexy, huh?" He gives me a cocky grin and I swat at his arm. I relax into the butter soft leather seat and watch the pretty scenery of Knoxville turn into the beautiful scenery of Tellico Lake, where his parents live.

Now, that was a great drive. Thirty miles of highway and his car got to really spread her wings. It felt like we flew, the drive was so comfortable and smooth. Tate's parents live in a very upscale, gated neighborhood full of mini mansions looking over the lake.

We pull up to a huge house that looks like a small castle made out of tan stone. The yard has a large circular driveway that is lit up and there is a beautiful pond off to the side, at the front of the house. On the opposite side of the house, there are trees and a beautiful wooden pergola with outdoor seating. The house is on just enough of a hill that when you look past the pond you can see a gorgeous view of the lake. I bet the view is even better on the second floor of the house or from the back yard.

Tate gets out, coming around the car and opens my car door. He takes my hand tenderly, to help me get out. While I'm climbing out and attempting to straighten my dress, the front door opens and a tall, lean man walks outside.

He chortles amused, to Tate, "I had to come see for myself if you really brought a date to dinner, moy braat Luka." When the man finally gets near us, I recognize it's his brother, Viktor, from the club.

"She's kraaseevee (beautiful), huh?" he says to Tate, gesturing towards me. Viktor turns toward me, giving me a wink. I have no idea what he called me but hopefully it wasn't fish food.

"Da, braat, she's moy Krasaaveetsa," Tate grumbles to his brother and then glances at me.

"I'm sorry to be so rude, baby. This is my brother, Viktor, the one I was telling you about."

I put my hand out to shake formally and he laughs at it. "Hi, Viktor. It's very nice to meet you." I mumble and peer at him confused; I don't know what's so funny.

"No, no, no, Luka's Krasaaveetsa." He pulls me to him and gives me a hug.

Tate smirks, so this must be good. I awkwardly pat his back a few times, and then pull away. Tate comes closer, resting his arm around me and I can feel myself start blushing.

"Oh, Krasaaveetsa, Atyets (beauty, father) will eat you up!" He grins wolfishly, "Atyets will love this, Luka. This is what he needs right now, to see you find someone. And such a Krasaa-veetsa at that! Christ, your children will be absolute angels!"

*Holy fuck!* Did he just say our children? I haven't even made it in the front door yet. Oh no, I wonder if Tate has a crazy family. I bet that is going to be where all his flaws lay. I'm kind of scared to meet this 'Atyets' person. I let Tate lead, entering into the house first. I'm scared to let go of him or they might try to start breeding me before we even sit down to dinner.

I'm instantly astounded. The inside of Tate's parents' house is like nothing I've ever seen before. It's decorated in rich colors and golds. Everything implies wealth and it almost feels as if it's never used, it's very sterile. I get the whole 'museum' vibe from it.

There is one thing that I love as soon as I see it, though. On a side table there are these little, round doll things of all different sizes. They are each beautiful, artistically painted in a variety of colors and don't appear as if they really belong in this room.

A loud voice booms with a strong Russian accent, interrupting my thoughts. "Those are called Babushka, printyessa." I jump at the sound, Tate chuckling at me quietly. He shifts us so that we're facing towards his father.

Konstantin walks to us with his arms spread wide open. I'm assuming it's his father anyhow. He's a very good looking man, with stunning features, resembling Tate quite closely. He's in his mid-fifties I'd say.

Tate walks into his father's arms and they embrace each other. "Atyets," Tate states and kisses his dad's cheek. Konstantin returns the gesture, kissing Tate's cheek and responds, "Sin(son)."

His father then turns to me and pulls me in for a hug and in a strong Russian accent says, "And you, printyessa, you call me Papa, da (yes)? His smile is dazzling and it reminds me of one of my favorite things about Tate. Once he releases me from his tight embrace, I grin and nod.

"Come, my son and his Krasaaveetsa, let us get vodka and sit for dinner. Viktor, join us!"

I follow the three men who are all well over six feet tall. They make me feel like a dwarf next to all of them. We end up in a bar area that's richly decorated in wood so dark it almost appears black. The floor is large slabs of travertine in a pale grey color. The walls are decorated with many, large paintings of deer, bears and other animals you hunt. It's like a rich man's trophy room of sorts and there is a very pretty blonde lady, who is most likely his mother, sitting on one of the cocktail chairs.

She glares at me, sniffing in my direction with distaste. She turns to Tate, raises her nose and in an entitled voice reeking full of venom asks, "What is this, Luka Tatkiv?" She shoos her hand in my direction, "Why you bring a woman here, to my house?"

Tate huffs, "Mother, she is my Krasaaveetsa. I brought Emily to meet my family and have dinner." He squeezes my hand reassuringly and gives me a small smile. I squeeze back. *I'm okay right now.*

Vivi annoyingly grunts, "Luka, if it is time for you to marry, we will send you to Mother Russia. You get good Russian girl to be your bride. They will know how to take care of you and stay out of your businesses." She glares spitefully at me the entire time she says this and Viktor laughs loudly. I feel tears burning behind my eyes, but I refuse to let my eyes fill with them.

"Enough Vivi!" Konstantin roars at her. "My son brings his Krasaaveetsa home to meet his family, you shut up, shut up, shut up! You treat printyessa as family, she is my daughter now!" He declares. We all stay silent—including Vivi—after Konstantin's little outburst.

"Now we eat zazhaareets (roast) and enjoy a good vodka. Come," he orders a few moments later and we all fall-in to follow him to the formal dining room.

I smirk to myself, I like Tate's dad even more after that. I wasn't expecting it to be easy by any means to meet his family, but for his mom to say that shit? That Tate should find someone else all because I'm not Russian, makes me boil with anger inside.

To say dinner is awkward is an understatement. We all sit at this humongous, beautifully carved wooden table in the dining room that can seat twenty-two people. Who on earth has that many people for dinner? That's what BBQ's are for. A little, old Russian woman, they call Mishka, serves us ice water and a variety of three chilled tumblers, with a different vodka in each. If they keep this up, I'm not going to be able to walk. Thank God there's food! Speaking of, whatever we are having smells amazing.

Not too much later, Mishka wheels a shiny silver cart out and puts what appears to be a giant roast on the table. There are a couple other hand painted, delicate china bowls that have a variety of sides filling them to the tops, but I have no clue what they are. It all looks and smells amazing.

"Printyessa, you like zazhaareets (roast)?" Konstantin grins as he inquires. I bet Tate's dad is a lady killer with that smile.

I nervously giggle a little. "Well sir, I'm not sure what that is exactly, but this food smells remarkable!" I beam a bright smile back and hope he was referring to the food and not my ovaries or something.

Nodding approvingly, "Yes, Mishka is a very good cook. Please eat and enjoy." I dig in hungrily and I think it's the best food I've ever tasted.

"Luka, did you tell printyessa about what it is we do?" Konstantin gazes over at Tate. I would expect Tate to shy away from this question since the Mafia is so secretive.

"Da, I did. We had a complication arise and a few things were revealed. Emily is smart and figured some of it out before I was able to explain." Tate glances at me proudly.

"I hope no business complication? Did you need assistance? Or is this the old boyfriend problem? Nikoli handled it, da?" His dad peppers him with questions and it surprises me they are openly discussing this in front of me, over dinner no less.

"Nine (no), the businesses are good. Da, it has been handled, although I handled this case personally. Da, it was the ex. You heard?" His father chuckles when Tate says he handled it personally.

"Ahh, my Luka, the infamous 'Knees'. Am I right, moy sin, you took out his knees first?"

Konstantin seems to soak up immense joy in hearing about Tate being violent. It's like he's very proud of the fact that his son is called 'Knees'. *Is that even a name?* I have to talk to Tate about this later.

Tate grins and nods in agreement. Viktor starts laughing when Tate nods.

"You see, little printyessa, it is funny to us because the whole time Luka was growing up, if he got into a fight he went for the person's legs and broke their knees. We thought the poor boy didn't know how to defend himself. Turns out, he was incapacitating his opponents. Very smart, my son is. As he got older, he got more and more creative in breaking knees and eventually was honored with the name 'Knees.' You go to Russia and everyone knows who The Boss is that is named 'Knees.' You grow up fast in the life of a Boss."

I smile at him and hold my breath. Hearing about Tate breaking people's bones growing up, is not my idea of dinner-time conversation. I just have to make it through this meal and hopefully things will get easier with his parents, with time.

Konstantin bellows suddenly, "Mishka, the торт (dessert)!" I jump in my seat and Tate looks over at me like I'm the crazy one. I shrug and check around for Mishka. She comes walking in unhurriedly, with a huge cake covered in strawberries and a creamy sauce.

"Oh God, it looks so good, and if it's anything like dinner then she needs to just put the whole cake on my plate!" I burst excitedly, not realizing I just said it all out loud.

Everyone laughs loudly and Mishka looks at me with a smile for the first time. I guess she likes the compliment. Tate's mom even giggles slightly and her expression toward me seems to begin to thaw. I don't know if it's because I made her laugh, or if it's because of Mishka's reaction.

Dessert is considerably less awkward and I find myself really enjoying the evening. Konstantin boasted about different stories of the boys growing up and what Russia is like. You can tell that he is extremely proud of the men that his sons have become.

Vivi chimed in a few times with little details. I'm just happy to see her replace the nasty glare with a smile full of fond memories. I was seriously thinking I was going to have to hide all the knives for dinner; luckily she heeded Konstantin's advice and was polite throughout.

Konstantin shared that they try to spend Christmas at their country house, close to Moscow every year. He said that if the weather permits, then I will get to come with Tate in a few months. I glance at Tate to catalog his feelings about it and he appears really excited at the prospect of me spending Christmas with him.

We eventually finish eating and visiting. I thank Vivi and Konstantin numerous times for having me as a guest. I butter up Vivi with compliments about the food and house, and it seems to break through her shell a little more with each one.

Konstantin leads us to the front door once Tate declares that we are tired and leaving. Vivi embraces me in the foyer and in a strong, feminine, Russian accent she says "Little Emily you must join me for lunch, we have much planning to do."

I smile, hugging her in return. "That sounds wonderful, Vivi, I look forward to it."

As soon as she lets me go, Konstantin squishes me in a strong hug. "Little printyessa, you must come pick a Babushka to take with you home." He beams happily and leads me toward the table.

"Oh no! I couldn't, they are so beautiful, but thank you." I look over at Tate and he nods at me, like 'yes, take one.'

"Da! I insist, please."

I stare at the Babushkas for a few beats. They are all so beautiful and appear very expensive. I reach out and run my hand over a smaller one that is painted bright blue. This one would look so pretty next to my bed.

"Good choice, printyessa! Now, go keep moy sin company and he must bring you back many times!" Tate cuts in by saying his goodbyes.

Viktor walks out with us. When we arrive at the car, Viktor opens my door for me and gives me a chaste kiss on the cheek.

"Good night, Saystraa (sister)."

I smirk back at him. "Good night, Viktor."

"Braat!" Viktor calls across the car and Tate gives him a fake salute before climbing in beside me.

My door closes and I'm left alone with Tate for the first time in three hours. I can't believe we were here for that long. The time just flew by once his dad started in on his stories.

"My family loves you, Krasaaveetsa." He looks like he's glowing, he's so happy.

"Yeah, I wouldn't go that far. I do like your family a lot though. Your mother is so lovely when she finally warms up and Mishka's cooking was out of this world!"

"Oh, no? You don't think so? My mother just invited you to a private lunch because she wants to plan a wedding for us, baby. The Babushka my father insisted you have is a fertility doll. My brother just kissed your cheek and called you 'little sister.' I'm pretty confident that they loved you tonight."

Tate chuckles, shaking his head. "My mother would have spit in your face if she didn't like you and my father would have called my Uncle Victor." Well shit. I guess I did okay after all. I'm glad to be on the Mafia king and queen's good side, that's for sure. His mother would have spit? And to think I almost cried when she said I wasn't good enough since I'm not Russian. What a crazy night, I can't wait to tell Avery and London all about this.

"Wow, that's just a tad bit overwhelming! I can't imagine your mom spitting, maybe scratching my eyes out. I'll tell you what though, if I keep eating Mishka's cooking I'll get fat! Then your dad will get his hopes up with that Babushka. That food was so fantastic!" He glances over at me, grinning as he drives.

"Yes, Mishka is a great cook. She is my grandmother and she taught me how to cook."

"What, your gram? Why didn't she sit with us then?"

"Mishka just prefers to cook, she is 'old Russian.' They did things differently back then. She cooks and she serves. She likes to take care of everyone and just observe. That lady is sneaky; she hears and witnesses everything. If anyone has a secret or some news to share, she always knows before everyone else does. When you talked about her cooking we laughed because we knew you had just won her. My mom had to give in; she'd never stand a chance if Mishka likes you."

"Oh man, that is awesome! I wonder if my gram would be like that if she were here."

I get sad inside and my heart squeezes.

"You didn't know your grandmother, Krasaaveetsa?"

"No, I don't remember her at all. She died from cancer when I was a year old. From what I've heard though, she was really protective and liked to help people in trouble. I hope I have some of that goodness in me, too."

"You are full of goodness and beauty, little pet, don't worry. She would be so proud if she were here today." I shoot Tate a small smile and squeeze his forearm. I love him. I do, so much.

Suddenly, I'm jerked roughly in my seat, my eyes grow wide and my head flies into the dash. My head bounces off the hard surface and everything goes black.

# THIRTEEN

## EMILY

### The Accident
### Two days later

**I** **AWAKE DISORIENTED, TO A POUNDING HEADACHE AND** beeping. I feel as though my body has been run over by a bus. The sheets are cold and scratchy. I have goose bumps adorning my skin everywhere and I feel miserably cold all over. Why do I feel so cold? And what is that damn beeping?

I open my eyes, fluttering them a few times as if I've been asleep for longer than usual. The florescent lights blaring down on me, seem extra bright. I rub my face a few times and something pinches my hand. Finally I can focus. I glance down and there's a needle and tube connected to my hand. I take a deep breath and look around.

I'm in the hospital. *Fuck, why am I in the hospital? Did Jeremy do this?* I check my body over and notice there aren't really any bruises or anything remarkably different that stands out. I don't think it was him. Oh God, in fact I know it wasn't him. Tate! Tate had gotten Jeremy. So why am I here?

I gaze all around, noticing that it's a private room and I'm all alone. It looks like a freaking florist in here. There are roses of all colors, in different arrangements on the little table in front of my bed. Beside my bed, there is another smaller table. It has a stuffed animal that looks a lot like Muffin. There's also a pitcher and a plastic cup. I'm assuming that it's water. *Thank God*, I feel like I could drink a gallon right now.

I attempt to reach for the cup but the movement shoots sparks of pain through my whole body, "Ouch!" I yip, and sit as still as possible.

Come on...really? I'm dying of thirst here. Ugh and my head is pounding so much. I reach up to rub it and feel I have something wrapped around my forehead. *What the fuck?*

The door to my room opens and I glance toward it. In walks Tate, he's busy looking at the ground and hasn't noticed me staring at him. A tear runs down his cheek and he wipes it away quickly.

I choke all raspy, "Baby?" Tate's head snaps up; once he sees my eyes are open, he runs to my side.

"Moy Krasaaveetsa! Oh, thank God, you have finally awoken! I've been going crazy!" Tate runs his hands through his hair grasping the ends tightly. He sits down on the side of my uncomfortable hospital bed and lightly gives me a peck on the lips.

"Water, please?" I rasp out. Geez, my throat is so sore and dry, and I sound like a chain smoker.

"Of course. How are you feeling, are you in pain?" Tate peppers off questions and hands me a paper cup, half full of water. I drink the cool, refreshing liquid quickly. This brings a small smile to his face. I barely nod at the pitcher and he fills my cup again. I drink it down swiftly again, famished.

"Ugh, thanks." I clear my throat a few times. "I hurt when I tried to move and get my own water. Why am I here?" I ask still confused and direct all of my attention to him.

He tilts his head quizzically, "You remember nothing?"

"No, I don't and what do you mean I finally woke up? How long has it been?"

"Fuck, Krasaaveetsa, it's been two really, reallllly long days you have been sleeping. The doctors said it was because your body was healing and also because of the strong painkillers, but I've been going fucking mad inside wanting you to wake."

"Wow! Two days? What happened, Tate? The last thing I can remember, is telling your brother good night. I don't understand, what's wrong with me?"

"Shhhhh, calm down, baby. Nothing's wrong, pet, you just hit your head really badly and had to get stitches on your forehead next to your hair."

He turns my palm over carefully, showing me all the cuts up and down my arm, glancing over I notice a few gashes in my other arm as well. "Then there was the glass that went everywhere; you got cut up fairly good in a few places from that also."

"My head is really foggy feeling and my body hurts." I whisper and pout a little. It hurts so badly, but I don't want to worry him even more.

"The doctor said the impact will probably give you whiplash in your neck, and your back will hurt for a few weeks. He said you are lucky to be so tiny because the car swallowed you up and protected you."

"How did it protect me if I was knocked out for a few days? I mean look at me, Tate, I'm covered in marks."

"Well, he said a bigger guy like me probably would have died in the passenger side. I was so scared. You were knocked out and un-responsive. I thought I had lost you."

"God Tate, I'm so glad it was me sitting there and not you. Thank God I refused to drive your car."

"No baby, just no. I wish none of this happened to you. I can't bear to see you hurt like this, it fucking guts me, Krasaaveetsa."

"I'll be okay Tate, we're fortunate to both be sitting here it sounds like."

"The fool who hit us in her car, is also in the hospital. She almost died because she hit us so hard. Stupid bitch," he hisses angrily. "The cops said she was drinking heavily and the alcohol helped relax her body." Tate looks so livid when he starts to talk about the other person. His eyes grow hard and his forehead gets a wrinkle in the middle.

Squeezing his hand, I attempt to distract him, so he will look at me and quit thinking whatever thoughts have him so angry. He gazes at me and a few tears begin to stream down his cheeks. It literally feels like my heart is squeezing painfully to see him like this.

"Please, Tate, I'm okay. I'm right here and you're here, and we're both going to be just fine."

"You just don't know, Krasaaveetsa," he murmurs, choked up, "I thought you were gone and I just found you. I haven't had enough time for something to happen to you. I'm a selfish man, Krasaaveetsa, and I refuse to wait."

He sits up with renewed focus. "I love you, beauty. I love you so damn much with all of me. I will give you everything of mine and anything I can in life to make you happy. Please agree that when you get better you will live with me permanently and that you will stay with me forever." I smile softly at the words I have been longing to hear ever since I confessed my feelings to him.

"Let me take care of you and cherish you. Let me marry you and give you lots of babies?" Tears continue to roll down his face, he grins slightly as he finishes, talking about babies. Happiness washes over me, filling me so full that I could burst and I fall deeper in love with him.

"Yes, of course Tate. I will stay with you, I promise. I love you so very much, too." He breaks out in a giant, pleased smile and gently peppers sweet kisses all over my face.

"My little love, you make me the happiest man in the world. I will take good care of you and love you always."

Savoring each of his words, I relish in the fantastic feelings they give me, while I rub my hand on his unshaven face. I take a really good look at him, coming out of my fog a little more with time and notice he looks a mess.

My Tate is always so well put together. This man beside me is a wreck; he looks like he's been through hell and back. His face is really scruffy; he has dark purplish bags under his eyes, and even they are red rimmed from his tears and lack of sleep. It appears as if he hasn't showered in days. Tate's in his white undershirt and a pair of dress pants; they are wrinkled and it's not something he would normally wear.

"Hey, sugar dimples, what are you wearing?" I look at him crazy and he starts to laugh. Ah, there's my Tate.

"I haven't been home since the wreck. This is my undershirt and the pants I had on at dinner with my parents." My God, my poor man.

"Oh, Tate," I shoot him a sad look. "Please go take a shower, put some clean clothes on, eat and take a nap. I'm okay now and I'm wide awake. You need to go and take care of yourself also."

"I'll call Cam and let him know to tell the girls you're okay and to bring me some clothes." He gestures around the room. "We're in a private suite, so I can just use the shower in here. Avery and London have been going nuts that you haven't been awake, also. I told them both that as soon as you woke up, I'd call them so they can come see you. They were worried sick about you." He pulls his phone out of his pocket and starts scrolling through his contacts. "I have to let my parents know also. I know Mishka will want to send you something to eat, so you aren't stuck eating hospital food."

"Okay, sweets, that sounds good. I would love some food from Mishka if she wants to make it." I whisper quietly. My head and throat are still hurting, along with every other single body part it seems. I hope London and Avery aren't really too upset. I'll never hear the end of how they were so worried about me and it'll make me feel super guilty.

"Will you please ask London or Avery to grab my iPod and Kindle so I can read and listen to music, when I feel better?"

"Of course, Krasaaveetsa, anything you want." *Wow.* That's definitely the right answer. I can't wait to jump his bones when I get out of here and no longer hurt.

## Three days later...

"Oh my God, Tate! Get me out of here! I can't stay in this freaking uncomfortable bed, any longer. It's hard and making my butt go numb. At least take me home so I can see Muffin and be surrounded by my friends." I plead, and Tate rolls his eyes at me, exasperated. I've been attempting this all day and I think he's close to his breaking point.

"Krasaaveetsa, the doctor said you need to stay a few days still, just be patient. It's for your health."

I huff, "Tate, either you bust me out of here or I'm signing myself out and calling London."

"Alright, you win. It's been a few days since he said that, so I'll tell him you are ready to go and see what he says, okay?" I roll my eyes at him and he sticks his tongue out at me.

"I don't care what he says, I'm outta here!" I call out, teasing Tate. Finally, I break through to this stubborn man. I blow him kisses as he walks out. "Hate that you're leaving, but I sure do love watching you go!" I chortle, smiling cheekily and winking at him, this time it's him who rolls his eyes at me. He's so freaking cute, I just love him.

About thirty minutes later the door to my hospital suite opens, with Tate and Dr. Hopkins coming in.

"Hello, Miss Emily. I hear you are ready to leave us?" He smirks and his old eyes twinkle.

My doctor has to be pushing sixty years old, if not older. Tate says he's the best at this hospital and that's why he's assigned to me. He has a head full of white, fluffy hair and big green eyes. Dr. Hopkins looks like he's in good shape for his age but may have eaten a few too many bowls of chocolate pudding from the cafeteria.

"Yes, sir, I'm ready to blow this popsicle stand!" He starts chuckling and Tate shakes his head in exasperation.

I guess you can say I've been quite entertaining to the staff here while on my pain medication. I had to be or I would have gone out of my mind. Now all of the nurses have started calling Tate 'Sugar Dimples' and it makes him blush profusely. If they come into the room he tries to act like he's reading a magazine so he has something to hide behind. Especially if it's Brenda; she's this older lady that totally looks like a sweet grandma. When she learned of his nickname she actually walked up to him and pinched his cheeks. I laughed so hard I thought I was going to bust a stitch. It's pretty great and entertaining to see him bashful.

Tate studies me for a moment, unsure, "Doc, ahh, wants to talk to you about something by yourself, is that okay with you? I can stay if you're more comfortable." I give him a puzzled look. What on earth does the doctor need to talk to me about?

"No, stud, it's okay. I'll talk to Dr. Hopkins and then we can finally go home." Tate nods at us and walks out of my room, closing the door behind him.

"What's up, sir?"

"Well, may I sit, Emily?" He peers over at me, uneasily.

"Yes, sir, of course." *Shit. Am I dying or something?*

"Thanks." He takes a seat in the chair next to the bed. I sit up and scoot to the end of the bed, closer to him, in my pajamas decorated with Batman symbols. Tate thought they were hilarious, but we all know Batman is hot.

Dr. Hopkins continues, "You see, I wanted to talk to you not about the accident exactly, but about the person who ran into the vehicle you were in." He steeples his fingers under his chin as he says this and I notice a shiny silver watch on his wrist I've never seen before. Doctor Hopkins has good taste in watches. Shit what did he say? This medicine makes me a little loopy. *Focus, Emily.* Oh right, the idiot that hit us.

"You are aware that she is staying in this hospital as well? I believe Mr. Masterson already informed you, correct?"

"Yes, Tate told me about it when I first woke up."

"Right, that's good. Well, you see I was also her doctor because her injuries were so severe. This is all privileged information that I wouldn't normally ever give out. It's just that the circumstances are, well, they are just unlike anything I've dealt with in the past. Putting the legalities aside, I feel I have no choice but to share a few things with you."

"I have to be frank with you, Doc. You're kind of freaking me out right now."

"I assure you Emily, that is not what I'm attempting to do here. I'll share a little amount and we will go from there, okay?" I nod, uneasily.

"The patient, I had to restructure her left arm, wrist and left foot. I was shocked when I saw her and then saw you. So I took the liberty of comparing a few things. You see, I had to take your blood to run tests to make sure you could be on certain medications, check for un-planned pregnancies, your white cell count, etc. I had to take her blood samples for the same reason and also for the police to know her blood alcohol content." *Okay, and?*

I shoot Dr. Hopkins a 'so what' kind of look. "Okay, I'm aware of all that, I mean, did you need me to sign some more paperwork or something? Do you have liability sheets or something for blood work?"

"No, no, dear." He takes a deep breath and sets his hands down.

"You see, Emily, the person who hit you is Elaina Harper." He looks so sad to deliver this news, but I have no clue who this chick is. She has the same last name as I do, but what does that mean?

"I'm sorry but you will have to fill me in, Doc, because I have no idea who that is." He looks shocked to hear me say this and closes then opens his mouth again.

"You have no knowledge of her, whatsoever?"

"No sir, I would like to believe that I would remember her. I mean it is the same last name and all."

"Oh no. I wonder if even she knows." He shakes his head, his eyes with a faraway look in them.

After a moment he continues, "Emily, Elaina Harper is your identical twin. You don't know that you're a twin?"

I burst out laughing loudly, bending over and holding onto my stomach. The laughs turn to sobs and then I'm crying all over the place.

"You mean to tell me I have a sister, an identical twin sister, and she almost died because we were in a wreck together and she's right down the hall from me?" I gasp out in between sobs.

"Yes, that's exactly what I mean."

I rush to the bathroom as fast as I can and up-chuck my lunch of chicken and dumplings Mishka had made me, only called something different in Russian. *I can't believe I have a sister!* I thought all of my family was dead and the one person I have left in the world almost died. I have to see her. I have to meet her. I hear Tate enter the room and begin yelling at the doctor.

"What the hell's going on? Why is my Krasaaveetsa upset? I hope for your sake I don't have to hurt you, Doc."

*Oh shit!* I better go get Tate before he takes out the poor old doctor's knees. I open the door and step back into the room swiftly.

"Tate, relax sugar dimples. It's not the doctor's fault. He gave me some news and it made me upset, but he didn't do anything wrong." I glance to the doctor and see he looks like he's about to piss his pants. I don't blame him. Tate is a mean cookie when he goes all 'Mafia Boss.' Tate clears his throat and looks to the doctor.

"Sorry about that, Dr. Hopkins, just looking after my Krasaaveetsa. What is it? Wait, is she pregnant or something?" He gets a hopeful expression and it fills me full of warmth.

"Of course, Mr. Masterson, I understand. And no, sir, she is not pregnant. Miss Harper can fill you in on what she wishes to share."

Dr. Hopkins then meets my eyes, "Emily, she is in room 309 and you are on her list of allowed visitors. Good luck. I'll have your discharge paperwork drawn up and Nurse Brenda will be in here to have you sign everything."

"Okay, thank you, doctor." Tate steps to the side and Dr. Hopkins scuttles out of my room a little too eagerly.

"What is it, little pet? What happened?"

"Okay, first I need to get my clean clothes on. Then I need to go to room 309. Then I will tell you what's going on, but first I have to see it with my own eyes." I shuffle toward my bag of clothes Tate had London bring for me.

"What's in room 309? Oh, you mean the person who hit us? No, Krasaaveetsa, you stay out of there." Tate demands and crosses his arms like the decision's final.

Huffing, I argue, "No way, I'm not staying out of there!"

"The hell you aren't! I've already called Uncle Victor and he's going to take care of her. No one almost kills my Krasaaveetsa and then lives to talk about it. I don't know which it was, the Chinese or the Italians or maybe even those fucking bikers, but I will make this right. I'm so sorry you went through this." I pale at his words and want to puke again.

"HOLY FUCK, TATE!" I shriek spazzing out, "Call Victor back now! That's my twin sister in that room!"

I rip my clothes out of my bag, changing as quickly as possible. It's not that fast because my body hurts so badly still. Tate turns white as a ghost when he hears what I say about it being my sister and immediately dials his uncle.

"I'm sorry, Krasaaveetsa. Fuck! I had no clue. I didn't even know you had a sister. I'm so sorry, I will fix this."

"I didn't know about it either, it was kept secret from me I guess and I don't even know why. I swear to God, Tate, if something happens to her because of your Mafia shit, I will never forgive you." I grit, furious at him. I can't even look at him right now. He better fix this quick.

"I'm going to her room to see her."

"I wish you would wait, but if you insist, then I'm coming also so I can protect you if needed. I think I know who will be taking care of it, but just in case I'm wrong, I want to be there also."

"Protect me? Are you kidding right now? You calling hits on people that turn out to be my sister is NOT fucking protecting me!" I retort, storming out of my room and down the hall as fast as possible.

I notice his brother, Viktor, down the hall a little ways from me, about to enter into one of the hospital rooms off to the right side. What is he doing? It clicks all in place with Tate's family being mafia. *Oh God, please no!*

"Viktor!" I bellow and start walking quicker. He looks up at me, gives me a brief smile, and then goes into the room and closes the door.

I call out to Tate who's trailing behind me a few paces, "Oh my God, Tate! Please! Get Viktor!"

"Okay, baby." He takes off, sprinting the rest of the way. I attempt to catch up to them both, as quickly as my sore muscles will allow me too.

I burst into the room, door flying open and crashing into the wall. I end up right behind Tate, breathing deeply and freeze at what I see.

Viktor's standing at the end of my sister's bed, staring at her almost as if he's in a trance. His face is ashen as he catalogs Elaina's features. His fingertips tap the ends of each other, almost as if he has a rhythm thrumming through his mind.

"Viktor!" I gasp out and it finally makes him blink. He turns, twisting his head to be able to see me and squints, confused.

"N-no, p-please!" I plead desperately. I don't even know her, but I'm already willing to protect her. "Viktor, she's my sister. Tate didn't know any of that before he spoke to your uncle. Please, I beg you, don't hurt her." Viktor blinks and glances at my sister again. He nods and walks to her.

I attempt to run after Viktor, ready to jump on his back if I have to, but Tate is too quick and snatches my arm to stop me. I turn practically hissing at him and he covers my mouth, murmuring almost silently, to watch.

Viktor leisurely walks to Elaina's side and does the sign of the Russkaya Mafiya on her forehead. He gazes at her briefly and then bends down, tenderly applying a chaste kiss on the middle of her forehead.

"She's Krasaaveetsa too, da?" he questions Tate.

"Da, braat, she is a beauty like moy own Krasaaveetsa."

Viktor turns to me, taking in each of my facial features with a look of wonderment on his face, "There are two of you, printyessa?"

I gasp, nodding and the tears I've been holding, spill over my cheeks and trembling lips. "Yes, Viktor, there are two of me, but I didn't know that before. I just found out about her from the doctor."

I approach her side and peer down at her face; it looks exactly like mine. It's surreal to witness her lying there, motionless. Elaina's heavily medicated and sedated to help with the pain, so I doubt she will wake anytime soon. I wonder how she would feel about me. If she knows about me? Why was I left not knowing about her?

"Please don't hurt her, Viktor," I beg him again.

He glances at me remorsefully, "I promise Emily. I won't ever hurt her, I will keep her safe. You have my word."

I approach him, hugging him tightly. "Thank you, brother." I murmur into his jacket and he squeezes me tightly so I know he heard me.

Tate cuts in, taking my hand and tugging me to him easily. "Now, Krasaaveetsa, you can calm down again. We can go home so you can get some more rest and we can come back to visit her." He peers over my head at his brother, "Viktor, please call if she wakes or anything changes."

"I will, Luka. I will take care of her and speak to you both soon."

We say goodbye. I graze my sister's unmoving hand with mine, and then Tate and I head on our way to my room to get my stuff. Time to finally go home.

# FOURTEEN

## TATE

**M**Y GOD, I CAN'T BELIEVE I ALMOST HAD HER SISTER, Elaina killed. I hope she forgives me. I can't lose her, I love her. We finally get past all the Jeremy bullshit and are now faced with yet another issue. I make another call to Uncle.

"Is my Krasaaveetsa sister still safe?"

"Da, but she should die for this."

"I don't care, Victor. Make sure everyone knows not to touch her."

"I will take care of it, nephew."

"Thank you."

"Da." He hangs up and I put my phone away.

Short and simple, just the way I like my calls to go.

Earlier, when I dropped Emily off at home, she was doing much better but was still a little upset. I really don't like her being distraught, so I'm hoping I can find out about Elaina for her. I'm going to call my boy, Hans, who works for my father and have him dig up whatever info on Elaina is possible. I'd like to get all of the secrets out into the open and not be blindsided again, literally and figuratively.

Thank fuck this semester is almost over with. I can't deal with classes and everything else. I need to be home more with my love. I have to talk to Emily about all of this and I'm not looking forward to the conversation. My poor girl has been through hell and back; the last thing I want to do is stress her out more so.

I arrive at my parents' house and one of the maids is already standing on the front porch. She's probably been standing there waiting to open the door for me since early this morning when I first called my father. He's a little obnoxious about stuff like that. Gizya is always treating people without consideration for their comfort.

I park my Mercedes on the circle drive and make my way up the grand front entryway that has four large, stone steps.

"Morning, Mr. Tatkiv," Marine murmurs politely.

"Morning Marine, how are you today?"

She opens the front door, following me in and murmuring, "I'm well, sir. Good day." She nods and quickly scuttles off to do whatever strenuous task my parents deemed necessary.

Gizya approaches, boasting a large smile.

"Atyets," I embrace my father and kiss his cheek out of respect.

I haven't always been close to my father. Growing up he was a hard man. Since Viktor and I have gotten older, we have both grown closer to our father. I think it's because we finally understand—at least partially—the stress and pressure he lives with, being The Big Boss here in America. When we lived in Russia he was always out on business. At least here he is able to be home more and is safe. I'm grateful I don't have to be the Big Boss. My father still has at least fifteen more years and then we will talk. I don't want my children growing up as I did.

"Sin." He has called me 'son' or 'Knees' my whole life and, in return, demanded I call him 'father' or 'Gizya'. Rarely have I been 'Luka' to him, unless I was being scolded or if we were surrounded by certain company.

"I came to ask for Mishka's ring."

I follow him to the bar right off the entry area. I have learned that my father is a busy man and it's best to get straight to the point. He appreciates it and it makes things easier. I take a seat on one of the black leather bar stools. Gizya rounds the bar, grabs up two chilled tumblers and tops them with a fresh bottle of Vodka.

"Ahh, I was surprised you didn't ask for it when you came for dinner. How is your little printyessa? Doing better, I hope."

I nod, taking a sip of my drink. "Emily is doing better. I just took her home before I came here. I'm assuming Viktor filled you in on the details with her sister?"

"Da, the little one hasn't woken up yet but Viktor seems quite taken with her."

"Oh, you picked up on that, too? I was wondering if I imagined it or not."

"I assure you, Viktor is thoroughly smitten. Uncle will have to pry Viktor's fingers from her, if anyone tries to get near her, let alone touch her. I am to assume you have Hans on her?"

"Da, I called Hans as soon as we left her room and I told him to find out anything he can about Elaina. Hans said to give him a few hours. I told him to call tomorrow because I plan to spend time with my Krasaaveetsa. I'm hoping she isn't too angry with me after my fuck up with the hit. Before this shit storm, she had agreed she would stay with me and let me have her forever. Then when we figured out whom Elaina is, Krasaaveetsa told me if anything happened to her saystraa (sister) that she would never forgive me. I want to give her Mishka's ring but I'm apprehensive that she will tell me no now."

"Ahh, moy sin, you have so much to learn about women yet. Emily will say yes, believe me. Do something special she will appreciate and show that you care about what she thinks is important. If you do, then she will come around." He takes a large swallow of his vodka.

"So, I should take care of her sister, Elaina? Move her to a suite? Maybe take my love her favorite ice cream? Or something extravagant, diamonds, a car she likes?" My father chuckles at how eager I am and my ideas.

"Da, move her sister so she's extra comfortable. You already have Viktor being your guard dog even though he was tasked with the actual hit in the first place. Take printyessa her favorite ice cream if that's something she loves and slip Mishka's ring on her finger. Tell her you love her and she can pick out a new ring, if she doesn't want your grandmother's." I bite my lip, pondering over what my father suggests.

"Everything will work out, sin. Make sure to update Vivi and me. I know your mother is buzzing inside to plan a wedding. I am happy for you. You have our blessing and best wishes. We love you, Luka."

That's exactly what I needed to hear. Now, let's do this!

# EMILY

## The next day...

I can't wait to meet my sister. *My sister.* Wow, that sounds so weird. I've always thought of London as my sister, but Elaina is actually the real deal. I'm filled with so much joy in my heart knowing I have a piece of family still alive in the world.

I shift in our bed and give Muffin a good scratch on his neck.

I glance back at Avery, as she chatters away, "I'm so glad you're back! We were all so worried about you. I brought you some hot chocolate back from A Sip of Heaven." Avery's planted beside me on the bed, "And I even brought you a banana nut muffin if London's fat ass hasn't eaten it already! I swear that girl has been eating everything in sight! I told her it was yours so she better leave it alone."

I lean over carefully and smooch her on her cheek. "Thank you, Avery, you are so thoughtful. With Mishka cooking for me the whole time I was in the hospital, I'm surprised I can fit in my own clothes!" Avery giggles at me and I grin. *It feels so good to be home.*

"Tate asked me to move in with him officially and he told me he loves me. It was the sweetest thing ever!"

She looks surprised but pleased and excited for me. "Wow, girl! That's so awesome, I'm happy for you! What are you going to do about your sister?" I had caught everyone up to speed when we arrived home yesterday.

"Umm, I just have to wait and see, I guess. It's so nerve racking." There's a small knock on the door and Muffin jumps up when it opens. In walks my gorgeous man carrying a small tub of my favorite ice cream—Cookies and Cream.

Avery's eyes go wide as she takes in the tub. "Yum, whatcha got there, stud?"

"Nothing for you," he chortles, teasing her. Avery huffs good naturedly, pretending to pout for a few seconds. It doesn't work so she gives me a small hug and stands up. Tate gives me a dazzling smile and walks toward the bed to set down the bag of stuff he has on the side table.

"I'll give you guys some privacy, love ya, Em! Holler if you need me, 'k?" Avery heads toward the door to leave and on the way she smacks Tate, dead center on the ass. He gawks at me as if he was just violated and I burst out in giggles. Avery smirks mischievously and winks, before she closes the door.

After the door shuts, I lean over and see that Tate has brought me a soda and ice cream. They are my two favorite guilty pleasures.

"Yum. Somebody's being sweet tonight!" I mumble as he bends down to lay next to me and gives me a chaste kiss on my forehead.

"Of course, my love. I want you happy and feeling better."

"I do feel much better. I think I just needed to be home and able to snuggle with Muffin."

"Good, Krasaaveetsa, that makes me happy." Tate huffs, "Muffin is not supposed to be on the bed."

I just shrug, 'cause the dog's on the bed and he's not going anywhere.

"I had your sister moved to a suite at the hospital and Viktor is staying with her."

I lean over and pull him to me so I can kiss him properly. "Thank you honey bun. That means more to me than you could ever imagine," I whisper, then slip my tongue between his lips and get a small kiss out of him. He pulls away and I suck on his bottom lip. God, I missed being so close to him.

Tate clears his throat. "Another thing, my Krasaaveetsa, is that I love you and I meant what I said earlier."

He takes my hand, drawing it in front of him to rest on his thigh. I watch, curious what his plans are and I'm thoroughly surprised when he pulls something out of his pocket. Tate covers my hand with both of his, as he sneakily slides a beautiful diamond ring on my finger.

I jerk my hand back to look closely at what he just put on me. I shoot my hand out in front of us, spreading my fingers wide; peering at the ring and see it's a large, round diamond. I'm guessing four carats with a wide platinum band. It's absolutely breathtaking and compliments my petite hand perfectly. People could see it fifty feet away, advertising that I'm taken, that I belong to someone, and that I'm loved.

It's so perfect it brings tears to my eyes. I look up at Tate in wonderment. I can't believe I have this great man in my life.

"Oh, Tate!" I choke, ready to start blubbering like an excited mess.

"It was Mishka's before, but if you don't like it, we can get you whatever ring you want. As long as it's my ring on your finger, I don't care what it looks like," he seriously declares, and I chuckle with a shaky smile.

"My God! This was Mishka's ring? It's even more perfect, I'm so honored to wear your grandmother's ring! Thank you, Tate, it's absolutely wonderful. I love you so much!" His smile beams brightly at my reaction and I can tell it pleases him that I love his grandmother's ring so much.

"I love you so much, Krasaaveetsa, truly," he murmurs, peppering soft kisses all over my face. "You make me so happy, Emily. Vivi is going to go through the roof with excitement when she hears that she will get the wedding she wants so badly to happen. I know she will want to help you plan all of it. Of course it will be whatever you want but she will be thrilled to just be a part of it. Mishka, too, if you don't mind their help?"

"No, of course not! I would love their help, but not too soon, okay?" Tate looks at me perplexed like he doesn't understand.

"I can wait six months, Krasaaveetsa, anything later and I will take you to Vegas to elope." I laugh at his time limit. He shoots me a look like he just solved world hunger.

"I guess I can try to pull it off in six months! But, I'm not giving up school."

"No, baby, you do whatever makes you happy. You want to go to school, go. You want to open a business, I will buy you one. You want to stay home and have my babies, let's do it. I want you to be as happy as I am, little lamb." *Ohhh, he's so freaking sweet!*

I think I've patiently waited long enough. I start to peel his clothes off of him and push him to lean backward. The pain meds the doctor gave me are freaking awesome. They make me feel pretty good, considering how badly my body hurt when I first woke up after the accident. I finish undressing Tate. Once he's naked and lying on the bed, I pause to take him in for a minute. God, he's fucking gorgeous. I want him so badly.

"Okay, big boy, we are gonna put this yummy ice cream to use." He gazes at me with wide eyes and a sexy little smirk.

I grab up the ice cream tub and spoon from the small, wooden side table. Smearing a little melted ice cream across the ridges of his abs, I bend, lapping and sucking up each drop. I make my way up and down, savoring over each firm, ice cream covered crest on his washboard stomach.

Placing a small spoonful of deliciousness on each nipple, I smear it in cold circles with the spoon. I continue licking over his barbells, then draw them each into my mouth, sucking strongly.

"Mmmmm," Tate groans at the cool sensations and then the heat from my mouth. Moving up, I bite his neck and he growls deeper, pushing my hips down, closer to his cock. I know he wants me to grind down onto him. So I stall, peppering kisses down his tummy. I eventually make my way down to his engorged cock.

I take his dick in my hand, squeezing slightly and then pump him a few times. I give Tate a mischievous smile and take a bite of ice cream. Quickly, I lean in and take his cock in my mouth. I swirl the ice cream over his tip with my tongue and he groans. *Good, he must like it.* I slurp all the ice cream off him which he seems to like the most, moaning and gripping the sheet tightly attempting not to hurt me with my injuries. I bob my head up and down his length a few times, attempting to take him in as deeply as possible. He pulls me up quickly by my shoulders and his dick comes out with a loud pop.

"Poshyol (fuck), baby! Jesus, you are going to make me come

already, that is fucking amazing." He tugs me up to him closer, turning, so he can lay me on my back.

He carefully takes off my night shirt, bra and thong, staring at me the entire time like he's a starved man.

He climbs between my legs and I protest, "No, Tate, I want to ride you!"

"Uh uh. It's my turn, Emily." Tate scoots down and grabs a big bite of ice cream. He zeros in, going straight for my clit, it's a shocking zing of cold and then a shot of warm relief once the ice cream is gone.

"Fuck, Tate!" I cry loudly.

Tate takes another bite of ice cream then goes back down. He licks through my pussy lips, lapping at them as if he can't get enough. His tongue is shockingly cold from the ice cream. *God, it feels fantastic.* He sinks a warm finger deep inside me, and I'm so close I almost shoot off.

He stops eating my pussy to suck each of my nipples into his mouth, they pop out of his mouth and he lightly twists and tugs on them with his fingers. "God, you are so fucking sexy with my ring on your finger, Emily. To know this pussy is all mine, I can eat it and fuck it whenever I want to, turns me on so fucking much. My pussy, baby, mine," he murmurs, breathily.

"Oh, Tate, it feels so good." My body is writhing against his and my pussy is soaked, wanting him inside of me.

Tate kisses up to my neck aligning his cock at the one place I want him the most. He bites my shoulder harshly, causing me to let loose a loud scream while he thrusts deep inside of me quickly. He pumps hard once, seating himself in me to the hilt and I start to come. Tate has me so worked up I can't think of anything but how good he feels, he glides in and out of me easily, the gush of wetness aiding him as my pussy convulses.

He pulls my legs up over his shoulders. "Ahhh!" I cry out, sore from the wreck but in too much pleasure to tell him to stop.

Tate's right hand grabs onto the headboard. I hear the bed creak and groan as he drives into me hard and rough. It's like he's making sure that tomorrow everyone will know where he has been. Raking my nails into his back, I suck one of his nipples into my mouth, nibbling each time he pulls away to drive into me again.

I know my body will hurt afterwards, but I can't bring myself to care through the pleasurable haze he has caused. My pussy contracts around his cock, pulling him in and it's his undoing. I feel his large cock jerk within me as his cum spurts deep inside. Each throb feels fantastic, sending shocks of pleasure through me.

Tate keeps his dick seated inside of me for a few minutes, resting and breathing deeply, until he is able to catch his breath. He rains kisses all over my face again. It's easily becoming one of my favorite things he does.

Tate mumbles, "Fucking amazing, Krasaaveetsa. I'm going to keep my cock here, so my cum stays deep inside of you. God, I fucking love you."

I grin up at him; he's sweaty and his hair is sticking out in every direction. The pleased look compliments his features very well. His magnificent body shines from the light coat of sweat glistening on his skin. I'm surrounded by the crisp scent from his body wash and it makes me feel safe and loved.

I'm finally home.

"I love you, too, sugar dimples. Now, let's hop in the shower, okay?" He nods and stands up from the bed.

Tate reaches down to pick me up tenderly and carries me bridal style to the bathroom. He turns on the massive garden tub and lets the water heat up, before he helps me into it with him. In the bath, he washes my body softly and gently massages my sore muscles, relaxing me all over.

I have never felt so cherished in my entire life. After our

relaxing bath, we snuggle in our huge bed and he takes me lovingly, making sweet love to me two more times that night.

# FIFTEEN

## EMILY

VIKTOR CALLS US FIRST THING IN THE MORNING TO inform us that Elaina is finally awake and to share the conversation they had already. Apparently, Elaina asked who he was and Viktor told her that he was a friend, asking her if she had family. He played it off like he was going to call them for her but Elaina told him no, that she was adopted and doesn't communicate with her adopted family.

Viktor asked her why she was drinking and driving so irresponsibly and Elaina just told him she has a shitty life, which she didn't want to share any of it with him. He asked if she had a sister and Elaina told him not that she knows of, but her biological family never contacted her growing up. He informed Tate she seems sincere and he believes her.

Tate, of course, had Viktor on speaker phone, so I heard the entire conversation. I can't believe she has no idea of me either. Viktor said it took him a while to get her to stop weeping after he asked her about the drinking and driving. He thinks she was genuinely sorry and horrified that she almost killed Tate and me. Personally, I really have no idea what to think about any of this with her.

Shortly after the phone conversation with Viktor, one of his men—a guy named Hans—called to let him know what all information he found on Elaina. Hans basically confirmed what Viktor said about her. According to him, Elaina is twenty years old, born on August twenty-third (same as me), works at a shitty little bar in Knoxville called Root's, drives a white 2010 Chevrolet Camaro (good choice), lives in a shitty dump of an apartment, was adopted, no prior run-ins with the law, and has no boyfriend.

*Hmm.* I'm dying inside to go and see her. I wonder if she would share more about herself with me, if she knew I was her sister. I wonder if it will freak her out seeing that we look exactly alike. It sure as fuck tripped me out.

I huff, irritated over this breakfast dish sitting in front of me. I have way too much going on to worry about food right now. I appreciate Tate going out of his way to make it for me, and I'm sure it's absolutely delicious, but I'm just not in the mood.

"We will go, Krasaaveetsa, as soon as you eat your food so you can take your pain meds," Tate chastises me, with his eyebrow raised. I can't help it if I'm excited and it's making me not hungry!

"Tate, you have been on me for like twenty minutes buddy. I'm not freaking hungry! I will take some Tylenol, but not the strong stuff, okay? I'm feeling a lot better and I don't want to be loopy at the hospital." I send him my puppy dog face and puff out my bottom lip. He'll give in, he loves me too much.

Groaning, he rubs the back of his neck. "Alright, Krasaa-veetsa, but if you start to get weak then you eat what I get for you, okay?" I grin triumphantly and nod. *I win.*

We finish getting dressed, me extra hurriedly attempting to rush Tate. He doesn't even need anything but a T-shirt and pants but he insists on hair gel, body spray, et cetera. Once I'm finally able to shuffle him out the door, he steers me to the Tahoe.

We load up, heading in the direction of the hospital. Tate's been a little paranoid driving me, so he's been driving the big ass Tahoe everywhere. I feel like we could crunch over cars with his SUV if we wanted to.

"Hey, sugar dimples; you think the Tahoe would make it over that little Honda?" I point at a silver Honda Civic, as it slowly passes us. He glances over at me as if I've lost my mind. I nod toward the car in question and then I shrug.

"What? It's a good question since we *are* in a monster truck."

"Oh my God, Emily, you are so annoying when you get hyped up. We are not in a monster truck; she's only got a three-inch lift and thirty-five inch tires. It just feels huge to you because you are bite size." He shakes his head and goes back to paying attention to the road.

"Are you sure personality disorders don't run in your family?"

"Stop, Emily. Just shut your mouth before you get me wound up." I roll my eyes at him.

"Okay, fine, I was just asking. I mean you did just get pissy again."

"Shhhhhhh."

"Oh my God! Did you just shush me? You freaking, shhhhhh!" He just rolls his eyes and ignores me. I feel kind of bad for him after a moment, but I can't help it. I'm so nervous I feel like I could blow chunks everywhere.

We arrive at the hospital and I'm still all jittery. Tate is annoyed because apparently I "bounce around and shit." I do kind of feel like I'm bouncing when I walk, but I won't openly admit that to him.

Tate and I walk through the hospital up to Dr. Hopkins wing with the private suites and finally arrive. I breathe deeply, taking in the large number '5' on the door.

## Suite 5

Tate raps lightly on the closed door. I can hear Viktor through the thin metal, shuffle around and inform Elaina that he has a surprise visitor for her. After a moment, Viktor opens the door and he looks...happy, like really happy. Tate and I smile at him and he smiles back. He even shows teeth in his smile. Well, I'll be damned, either he has a crush or she's just a really cool chick.

Viktor shuffles over so we can step inside. I gradually make my way around the entry and the corner in the suite, full of nerves.

Elaina's propped up in bed with a few pillows and is looking bruised up, but remarkably better. I check her over completely, taking note of every detail. Eventually, I meet her eyes that look exactly like mine, except where mine are a light green hers are a really deep, sapphire blue.

She looks me over as thoroughly as I had done with her and when she finally takes in my face, she lets loose a blood curdling scream.

I drop to the floor, frightened after everything I've been through and cover my head with my arms. Tate turns around swiftly to see who's behind me and Viktor rushes to pull her to his chest.

Elaina stops screaming and starts to stutter, "Vi-vi-vi-Viktor who-who the fuck was that? Oh m-my God, Viktor, she looked exactly like me!"

I can hear her start to cry and it makes me sad inside. I know on the pain killers it has to make things probably even weirder for her, as they did for me. Tate spins back around and realizes the reason Elaina screamed is because of me. Viktor is clutching her to his chest, his arms covering the side of her face so they are in their own little cocoon of safety. He's mumbling something to her that I can't hear.

Tate leans down to help me up, worried. "Are you okay, Krasaaveetsa?" I nod and stand up with his help.

I hear Elaina question Viktor if my name is Krasaaveetsa and it makes me giggle. She peaks her head around Viktor when she hears me, reminding me of a curious child.

"I'm fine, Tate, she just startled me." I pat my shirt and glance at him. "With everything that's been going on, I figured the best move was to hit the floor." I peer over at her and offer her a shy smile. Elaina returns my little smile but also looks weary.

*I should say something.*

"Umm, hi, Elaina. You ran into me with your car." *Shit.* I wince, did I really just open up with that? Fuck, I have to think before I speak!

"I did?" She chews her fingernail, nervously. "I'm so, terribly sorry if you are hurt because of me." Her voice is softer than mine and I just want to hug her.

"Can I come closer so we can talk, please?" I request quietly, I don't want to freak her out again.

"Yes, of course you can."

I smile and sit on the edge of her bed. "So I'm guessing by your reaction, you are just as shocked about this as I am?"

Elaina sighs, nodding. "Completely, I had no idea I had any biological family close to me or any family at all, for that matter." That really sucks but it makes me feel better that this is a big surprise to her as well.

I can't help but feel that I got cheated as I gaze at her. I could have known her. I could have grown up with her, shared things with her, loved her. I could have had my very own sister.

"Well, I'm actually from Texas. I grew up there my whole life. I just moved here a few months ago; I go to the college at UT.

And technically I'm the only biological family left. Everyone else has passed away," I finish, mumbling. *Calm down.* I'm rambling.

She chuckles sadly, "And what are the odds that on my very shitty night, I get smashed drunk and wreck into my identical twin? The twin that I've never personally met or even knew anything about, for that matter? That's really creepy if you think about it. I'm such a fuck up. I don't know how to make this better." Wow, she rambles too.

"Yep, very creepy, but it must have happened for a reason."

"We have a lot to talk about."

I nod, "Definitely."

I give her a kind smile, lifting her hand in mine and giving it a light squeeze. Elaina returns my smile and it's like looking into a mirror. Such a surreal feeling.

We spend the next two hours comparing our likes and dislikes. It's amazing how much we have in common with us never even knowing about the other one. She's like me, getting excited and gesturing with her hands while she talks. Or does that make it me gesturing like her? Viktor seems relaxed and in good spirits. Tate and he speak but not very much, he mostly just sits, watching Elaina like he's oblivious to everything else in the world.

Tate and I take our leave but exchange phone numbers prior, promising to call if we thought of something new we were curious about. I also swore to her that I will be back at dinner-time and bring her some homemade soup. Elaina has to stay in the hospital for a while for her body to heal. During that time I'm going to get to know my sister.

## Three weeks later...

It's been three weeks since I first met my sister and I love her to pieces. It's like I've found a clone, discovering all the things she does, eats, likes, et cetera. She's pretty much become an instant best friend. We've even introduced her to all of our other friends.

London and Avery seem a little on edge, unsure about her, but I know they will come around the more they get to know her. They've actually been hanging out more with each other, since I've been spending so much time getting to know Elaina. I knew those two would become good friends though; they are more alike than they realize. Ever since that first day, London showed up in the courtyard at the college and they trumped my vote to go out.

Elaina ended up losing her job from that shithole bar, Roots. Tate gave her a new, better paying job at OO7. According to Tate, Viktor prefers OO7 to Tainted so he told Tate to let her work at OO7, because he has to be able to keep an eye on her.

I personally think it's way too soon for her to be working and so does Dr. Hopkins. She barely got released two days ago. Elaina was stubborn and declared that she would lose her apartment if she didn't go to work, and refused any of Viktor's help.

She enlightened me that for the past week, Viktor was trying to get her to stay with him at his house. I think it's a great idea since it's a lot closer to Tate's house and I can see her more, but that's not my business. If Viktor is at all as persistent as Tate, Elaina won't stand a chance fighting against him. With some of the shit she told me she's been through, though, she definitely deserves a little piece of happiness.

It's a Friday night and London called earlier, wanting us to all go out. I'm feeling way better, almost completely healed up. Most of the cuts that I received from the accident that will leave marks will disappear in a few years, since they weren't too deep. I still have a few marks from the deeper bruises left but they have faded so much, that they are barely visible. After Dr. Hopkins ran all the tests, he informed me that I have something that causes me to bruise more than average and stay bruised up longer. I can't remember what he called it, but it sucks.

My body has looked like I was beaten up for weeks now. I'm sick of people glaring at Tate when we go shopping or to eat. They have no idea just how much of a good man he truly is.

London and Cameron are still up and down since I got into the wreck. I can't believe they've even lasted this long. London must really care for him. Normally, she would have kicked him to the curb by now. She's too smart for her own good, though; she ends up getting bored easily.

Avery and Nikoli still date occasionally but are not serious. I guess they're both satisfied with their friends with benefits situation and I'm happy for them both. I think they're both lonely and will end up moving forward when someone new comes into the picture. I don't know though, I could be wrong.

Viktor and my sister are adorable. Viktor is constantly chasing her and trying to woo her. I kind of hope she eventually gives him a chance; I think he could make her really happy.

I peek out of the kitchen looking for Tate.

"Honey bun!" I holler for Tate.

I think he's in the living room watching ESPN. I was so happy to find out he likes sports because I love football and baseball. I don't like to watch a lot of games but if one's on, then I will certainly take the time and check it out.

"Yeah, Krasaaveetsa?" he bellows back. I was right. I find him in the living room with ESPN muted and texting on his phone.

"Hey, stud, London texted me and asked if we all wanted to go to 007 tonight. I know my sister's off and Avery already said she wants to go, too. Are you up for it or should I just plan a girl's night out?"

He grabs my arm and tugs me onto his lap. I love being on his lap, it's so comfy. "Yes, little lamb, we will go. Is Cam going, do you know? I'll text Viktor and Niko, I'm sure they will want to tag along."

"I don't know about Cameron," I shrug, "but I would think so if London's going."

"Okay, cool, baby. Text London back and I'll text the guys." He smooches me on the lips and pats my thigh so he can stand up. Knowing Tate he's going to go scour his closet for something to wear. That man is as bad as a female when it comes to what he's going to wear somewhere.

I head back to the kitchen for my phone and excitedly text London back.

> **Me**: Yep we're in! Did you ask my sister too?
>
> **London**: Of course I did! 9:30 p.m.?
>
> **Me**: It's a date!
>
> **London**: Sounds good.
>
> **Me**: Yaay!

I finish with texting London and instantly pull up Elaina's number.

> **Me**: Hey beautiful sister, do you want a ride and a place to crash tonight since we're going out?

We didn't file any charges against her. Tate wanted to, but I refused to on my part and he followed suit. Elaina still got her license suspended for a while, since she was a dumbass and drove while drinking. The judge let up some, but not completely. Thank God for Tate's connections or it probably would have been a lot worse for her.

**Eliana:** No thanks Viktor just texted me and said he was on his way.

**Me:** Already? London told me 9:30

**Eliana:** Yes he wants to have dinner first.

**Me:** OOOHHHHH!!! Have fun. I'll see you soon!

**Eliana:** I will. Smooches. Favorite sister, ever.

**Me:** Ever, Ever!

I close out of Elaina's message box, with a large smile on my face. Pulling up Avery, I'm confident I already know her answer.

**Me:** Hey babe, you want a ride and a place to sleep after the club tonight?

**Avery:** You know this! I'll be over to your casa about 9ish?

**Me:** Awesomesauce!

**Avery:** Just like me!

**Me:** Lmao yep!

I turn the screen off, slipping the phone into my pocket. Now that I have everything as far as rides and who all is going taken care of, it's time for me to get dressed. That's always the hardest part for me. I strive to find a balance of sexy and classy.

I skip to the bedroom, excited to finally see all of my friends at once, since it's been awhile. Sure enough, Mr. GQ himself is going through his closet like a mad man. My own closet has grown considerably in size as well.

I think Tate has a shopping addiction. To him it's all normal because he grew up like this. I grew up shopping at Walmart and looking for sales. Huge difference. Once he found out the sizes of my clothes and shoes, random shit just started to show up at the house all of the time.

It all started with Victoria's Secret because he knows I love their stuff. That changed, growing into shoes and now, it has progressively gotten to him buying absolutely everything. He blames it on me, saying I don't have enough stuff, while I tell him he has too much.

I'm not really upset though, I love having him spoil me. I try to give him a hard time about it, but also make sure he knows I'm grateful. Today's delivery consisted of a silver bracelet and matching necklace, both with my initial on them, which I love! In fact I'm going to wear my new bracelet tonight.

Tate decides on a pair of dark wash regular/relaxed jeans that make his ass look fantastic. His ass is juicy enough in his boxer briefs; I always tease him that I could bounce a quarter off it. He pairs them with a white button-down shirt and rolls the sleeves up. Yum, he looks fantastic.

If he's going to be that spiffy, then I'm going to hussy it up and wear a new dress he bought me. It's a tight, short, red dress with a red lace overlay. I pick out a sexy, red lace G-string and a red lace push-up bra. Gotta help the girls out as much as possible and these push-up bras are perfect to give a little cleavage.

I snatch up a pair of leopard print heels. They have red bottoms on them that nicely match my dress. Tate said they would look sexy on me when the box showed up last week and I have to agree with him.

I slip the gorgeous shoes on to test out my walk. I get a little wobbly if they're too high. I walk from one end of the closet and back. They don't feel bad actually. Man, whatever these shoes are, they are freaking comfy for having such high heels on them.

Satisfied with my outfit, I fix my makeup in a smoky eye, black mascara and nude lipstick. There, all set and ready.

I make my way to the living room catching little whiffs of Tate's cologne. He's wearing the cologne that I love so much— Hugo Boss. I feel like I could walk behind him and just sniff him all day.

The doorbell chimes and Muffin starts barking excitedly. Awesome, that should be Avery.

As I walk to the front door, I pass the hall leading to Cameron's door and hear loud, obnoxious female moans. *Well, fuck!* That's definitely not London in there. That asshole is going to break her heart and I'm going to end up being evil for having to tell her about it. I don't know what on earth he could be thinking right now, especially doing it here where everyone will notice.

Tate, Avery, Niko and I all ride in the Tahoe to the club. Much safer to all go together and have a designated driver. Plus I love having Tate and Niko when we go out, it makes me feel safe. Tate's not huge, but he's very strong, and Nikoli, well he's huge.

We arrive at 007, get settled in and I have to admit it's way different tonight, than it was the first night we came. I love the fact that Tate owns the club. I never noticed it before, but we get treated extra well because Tate's the Boss. If we want to hear a certain song it magically gets played pretty quickly after we request that we want to hear it.

One thing I have learned about my twin is that we are opposites, when it comes to partying. I prefer to dance but I rarely drink. I can have a good time without having alcohol.

Elaina though, is the crazy one. I thought London was bad! London likes to get sloshed and take off with guys she meets or whatever. Elaina is the type where her ass is dancing on top of the bar and doing body shots. Tate takes it all in stride. He's obviously used to the party scene since he owns two clubs. Viktor, however, watches Elaina like a hawk. I think he wishes he would have become a Boss now.

Avery and Niko dance together and have fun. At least one set of our friends know how to co-exist easily.

Cameron is a no show right now, but I'm sure that's for the best. He's probably busy getting rid of his secret booty call from the house. I talked to Tate about it and I'm still not sure what to really do about it just yet.

Tate scoots closer to me in the VIP booth and kisses the tip of my nose, causing me to blink. "You doing okay, baby?" He murmurs next to my ear, so I can hear him over the thumping music.

I nod, grinning at him and drinking my water.

Avery approaches the table with Niko, huffing from dancing for a few songs, "No one else is here yet?" she questions, loudly.

"Nope, nobody except us and my sister!"

"That sucks!" Avery replies and downs her martini.

I glance over toward the entrance and London finally comes through the door. She's all dolled up, looking like the old London, before she came to Tennessee and got used to T-shirts and boxer shorts. She's got on a black 'pin-up girl' style dress, that's covered with little red cherries. London has her long, black hair down, her face all painted up with her red lipstick and she's in some sky high red shoes. She looks so freaking hot!

I stand up and wave at her, so she knows where we are. I see someone come up behind her, but can't make him out. She's already tall, throw on some really high shoes and she towers over a lot of people. The guy puts his arms through her arms, from behind her, resting them against her stomach, as they walk leisurely.

Oh My God, I'm going to kill Cameron! She reaches down and

threads her fingers through his, leading him to the VIP section.

They make it to the top of the stairs and I about fall out of the booth.

"Holy shit," I murmur, but no one hears me.

That's definitely not Cameron Wentworth! Hell no, she went to the extreme opposite. This man has a short, trimmed, black beard, black hair in a faux hawk and light grey eyes. He's probably six foot and built muscular, like a brawler. He's covered in tattoos from his neck down to his fingers.

My mouth waters as I check him over. She did damn good this time. The new guy is wearing faded, loose fit jeans, black motorcycle boots and a plain black T-shirt. Sweet Jesus, I feel like I need to high-five London right now. This new guy fits her pin-up self, like they were made for each other.

She makes it to the table, standing in front of us, smiling widely. "Hey guys, this is Cain. Cain, this is everybody!" London yells and he laughs, gazing at her like she's the best thing he's ever seen.

"Hi, Cain, nice to meet you." I do a little wave like a dork, greeting him with a friendly smile and Tate just nods at him. Ah, he's definitely in The Boss mode.

"'Sup." He nods at us both, and goes quiet.

They get settled in the booth, with Cain sitting on the outside, and London next to me, while Avery and Niko dance some more.

Tate looks away and I give London a thumbs-up and a huge smile, "Jackpot, friend!" I nod towards the hottie sitting next to her.

"Fucking right!" she hollers back and grins.

Well, looks like London's back to her normal self. Everything's going great, we're having fun at the table, screaming out the lyrics to 'American Woman' by Lenny Kravitz and generally just being silly. None of us are really drinking, I think we all just wanted to be out and about. Elaina has been doing body shots from the bar and Viktor has been silently watching the entire time, fuming.

London pulls my attention away from my sister, "So, I have a secret! Well it's not mine, it's Cain's."

"Okay, what is it?" I ask bluntly, she knows I am too nosey.

"Cain is a nickname! Do you remember a boy we went to school with named Brandon Meeks?" London leans over and whispers loudly in my ear.

"Yeah, of course! Didn't he like move in sixth or seventh grade or something?" Where's she going with this?

"Yes, exactly! That's who Cain is! He and a bunch of his friends rode into town for a few days to take care of a couple things."

"Wait, they rode in on motorcycles?"

"Yes!" She beams, excitedly. "Isn't it awesome? I have so much to tell you, this isn't the first time Cain and I have seen each other. We actually started talking again before I came out here, when I was still in Texas. I'll fill you in on everything when we have a minute and it's not so loud, okay?" She looks at me excitedly.

"Okay, sounds good!" Sounds like she has a lot she needs to tell me, besides this mess with Cameron. Since when did London stop talking to me about everything? I don't know whether to be upset or sad. I know I've been really busy spending time with Elaina and Tate, but I need to talk to her more. She's my best friend and I'm not being a very good friend to her, if I don't know what's going on. I am happy to see she's not moping around over Cam, though. London spilled a drink, so Cain headed over to the bar with her for something to clean it up with.

Well speaking of, Cameron treks up the stairs to the VIP and gazes around, looking straight for London. When he finally spots her, he looks murderous. I had told Tate about what I heard from Cameron's door and that things might get awkward between him and London.

I elbow Tate enough to get his attention, "Sugar Dimples, Cam just showed up and he looks pissed. You might have an altercation if you don't go and get him."

I point over towards Cameron and Tate's beautiful hazel eyes narrow to find Cameron storming toward London and her new beau. *Oh man.* Cain looks like he would rip Cameron apart if shit gets started. Why can't we just have one night where we can all be together and not have some kind of drama?

Tate jumps up, quickly making his way to Cameron. He intercepts Cam before he can end up getting too close to London. Cain watches everything, perked up, looking like he's ready to mop the floor with Cameron, if needed.

Elaina flops down in the booth next to me, huffing, irritated, "I just heard Viktor's freaking going around telling any guys that want to approach me, that I'm his! Can you believe this asshole?" I look at my sister and burst out laughing. She has no idea what she's into.

"Oh God, Elaina, just give in. If he's going around and claiming you to other men then you're as good as his. Trust me on this; I have already fought this battle with Tate. Viktor will drive you absolutely mad until you realize that you love the idiot too much, to let him go." If Viktor wants her, he's bound to get her eventually.

Konstantin would go nuts if both of his sons were to settle down and embrace the Russian Mafia as much as he wants them to. Tate has discussed with me that he has been moving more and more toward Mafia business only. He said it's important since it will affect my life as well. I'm not worried though, I know my man will make a great Big Boss if it comes to that.

Elaina rolls her eyes, arguing, "Whatever, he can try all he wants, but it's not happening." I just smile and nod, yes, my dear sister, it looks like it will happen.

She has no clue that this is exactly how the Ginzburg men work. They see what they want and go after it until it's theirs. Tate's momma, Vivi, told me all about Konstantin chasing her back in the day. I guess their marriage was more of an arrangement, but according to her she didn't make it easy for him at all.

I gaze over toward Tate, Cameron is yelling and gesturing with his hands. London's just smiling at Cain and acting like Cam doesn't exist. I know inside she loves it that he's so furious! After a few beats, Tate wraps his arm around Cameron's shoulders, trying to calm him down.

My sister gets torn up off a few more shots she does and Viktor has to practically carry her out of the club. He chastises her but you can see he enjoys getting the chance to take care of her. I offer to let her come home with us but he isn't letting anyone near her. I think it's adorable. I know Viktor will take good care of her and make her life easier. After seeing how hard she works and how little she has, she deserves her life to be a little easier and happier. I don't know everything but we have talked a lot about how different each of our lives were growing up, and hers was very hard. I wish I would have had the chance to have her by my side growing up. I think my life would have turned out a lot differently, as would hers. She doesn't know it yet but Tate's giving her time off so she can come with the family to Russia for Christmas. I guess Viktor had asked Tate before I even had a chance to.

Tate finally gets Cameron to leave and we all decide it's time to head home. This night was awesome, besides the altercation with London and Cam. I got to relax with the girls and my man, what's better than that?

# SIXTEEN

## EMILY

### The Wedding
### Four months later – March 27

**I** **STARE BLANKLY AT MYSELF IN THE WIDE MIRROR. WE** have the opulent Presidential suite for three blissful nights. The magnificent room is in the same hotel that has the large ballroom we rented for the wedding. I can't believe today is my wedding day. I know it was fast, but at the same time it feels as if I've been waiting forever to marry the love of my life. I blink, feeling my eyes starting to crest with tears.

London huffs, griping at me, "Girl, don't you dare cry and mess up your face. You look beautiful but I can't fix red rimmed eyes! Plus you don't want mascara dripping on that enormous dress of yours."

I gaze at my reflection once more, taking in the beautiful hand stitching and lace on my dress. This dress was designed specifically for me. I told the designers what I wanted, they drew it up and then they made it.

Tate's mother Vivi, and grandmother, Mishka, took me dress

shopping. It was the worst and best experience ever, all rolled into one. I have never tried on so many dresses in my entire life. It got to the point where eventually the boutique called in a well-known designer to just make what it was that I wanted. I was exhausted but also extremely happy. My mother and grandmother are in Heaven, or I know they would have been the ones helping me, so to have family there to support me and be a part of it all, was beyond a great experience.

I sniffle, "I can't help it, London! Everything's just so perfect. I'm so blessed to have you guys in my life, marrying the man of my dreams, I have family here to stand beside me, all these changes and I'm just so fortunate my life turned out like this." A tear leaks out of my left eye and I try to hide it.

Avery walks back into the dressing area, glances at me and shakes her head, scolding me, "Geez! Is she crying again? When will you stop, woman? Today's a good day. Be happy and quit your damn crying, you're an emotional mess today, Emily!"

"I know," I clear my throat, "I know it, I'm just so lucky and extremely happy." A few more tears trickle out and both of them roll their eyes at me. *Bitches!*

London hugs Avery and grins at me, "Thank you, I was just telling her that!"

Elaina pops in the room, "Hey, hookers, leave my sweet, little sister alone!"

This shit again. Elaina's been teasing me for the past few months that she's older but I know I have to be the older one. She won't show me her birth certificate so I know she's fibbing.

"Aghhh! You! Are the little sister! Clearly I'm bigger." She starts to laugh evilly.

"Yes, you are definitely bigger in the waist!" I start to throw everything that is surrounding me and she takes off running.

"I'm taking back all of your key cards!" I threaten and they all laugh at me.

"She's going to cry again, dammit!" London yells at my sister.

Elaina holds her hand out for me to grab, "Come on, cry baby, it's time for you to go officially belong to that hunk standing at the altar."

I can't believe London even had the energy to fix me all up like this and touch it up a few times too, since I keep crying. I shoot her a wobbly smile, full of gratitude and she smirks at me, with a teasing glint in her eyes.

I breathe deeply and let it out in a whoosh, "Okay, you girls go stand up there and keep my spot for me."

Avery starts giggling at me and hugs me, "You dork, Tate would shoot their asses if they tried to take your spot!"

I shrug, "Eh, wouldn't be the first time he shot someone for me." I wink and smile.

She probably thinks I'm being silly and fibbing. Very few people know what all Tate has done for me. I do and I'm grateful my fiancé likes to keep me safe, and by any means necessary.

The girls go ahead of me to take their places in the ballroom. Konstantin, Tate's father is patiently waiting for me in the hallway when I open the suite's large, mahogany door. He smiles widely, his face lighting up when he sees me.

"Ahhh! Little printyessa, such Krasaaveetsa! You look like a true printyessa in the big, fluffy dress!" Konstantin opens his arms wide, embracing me in a warm hug and sweetly kisses me on my cheek. He came to walk me down the aisle and give me away to Tate. I've gotten close to Tate's parents, which they love. I'm over the moon happy that he asked if it was okay for him to walk me down the aisle. I was thinking about asking Elliot to come and do it, but this way is better.

I beam a bright smile, "Yes, thanks to Vivi and Mishka! They did such a wonderful job with planning the wedding. I would have been lost without them." I loop my arm through his, grasping on his elbow as he leads me down the hallway to my beloved.

I chatter away, the entire time, nervous, "I still can't believe they planned everything for it to be here in New York. I'm so blessed to be a part of your family."

We eventually make it to the double glass doors, leading into the room full of my future. I turn towards Konstantin, overcome with emotions, "Thank you for everything, Papa!" I hug him again, squeezing him tightly. I love this man; he's been very good to me and my sister, and he doesn't even know her. I finally gave in and made him happy by calling him Papa about two months ago. He was so happy I looked to him 'like a father' he tried to send me and Tate to Fiji. I told him no way, but we'd definitely go to Fiji for our honeymoon!

# TATE

My breathing stops when I see her. I gasp, at the beauty walking toward me, on what is fast becoming the happiest day of my life. With each small step she takes, I think of how lucky I am. Emily's absolutely breathtaking, resembling an angel. I can't believe in a few short moments she will finally be my wife.

Our path was stressful but to know we made it this far and love each other so much makes it worth it. I would do it again in a heartbeat. I would do it five different times if I had to.

This woman is my heart and soul and I would do anything for her. I never believed I could find a woman who would accept me for all my flaws. I never thought I could have a great relationship while being so involved in my Russkaya Mafiya roots. Or that I would find a woman to stand beside me and look forward to our future together.

Emily steps to the altar, and while I gaze in her sparkling green eyes, all I can think of is that this woman is finally mine.

# CORRUPTED

# CORRUPTED

# WARNING

This content contains material that may be offensive to some readers, including graphic language, dangerous and adult situations.
Some situations may be hotspots for some readers.

Dedicated to

# LINDSAY and ABBEY

You ladies mean so much to me.

You've dealt with me happy, excited, mad, and crying.

Yet you're still here.

Love you big.

# PROLOGUE

## Viktor

**WARM, SYRUPY LIQUID COATS MY FINGERS,** bleeding onto my hands and drips to the cold cement below. The sky is black, the stars and moon hiding, helping me complete my task. The calming *swoosh* of the waves mask my noises as I drop the lifeless body to the ground to finish securing weights to his limbs.

The small pier is deserted and the men on the docks know to mind their own business. No one wants to be involved with the Bratva, especially when its leader is dumping bodies. They keep their concerns to themselves, knowing they would be next on my list.

I relish the power.

I was the smart one, the one strictly handling the money of the business. Then my uncle gave me my first taste of disposal. I don't necessarily enjoy the kill itself, but I love watching them sink into the deep, murky waters of the lakes surrounding us.

# ONE

## Elaina

"JUST A MINUTE!" I GRUMBLE AT THE DRUNK ASS-hole waiting for me at the end of the bar. Geez, my feet are killing me. I sling another vodka-seven and set it in front of Tate's big brother, Viktor. Rushing to the other end of the bar, I address said drunk.

"Yes, sir?"

"Yeah! Umm, gimme ahhh beer! Yeah, beer!" he chortles, lazily lying the top half of his body across the bar. Ugh, men like this make me sick.

"Sorry but you've had a bit much to drink and I can't serve you any more alcohol." I try to keep it polite, when in reality I want to get the soda gun and spray this idiot with the nappy hair.

"I'm the paying customer here! This is bullshit. Give me a beer!"

"Look, you can have a glass of water or I can make up a pot of coffee, but no more beer. I'm sorry," I yell over the pulsing music. His rancid breath washes over me and I gag slightly.

"You're sorry, huh? Good for nothin' fucking cunt." He spits the words out angrily and it takes every bone in my body to stay professional. Being a bartender I know I will deal with assholes but I'm no one's door mat.

"When you calm down, then I will get you some water."

He reaches over the bar, grabbing onto my mid-length, blonde hair, "Calm? Get over here, I'll show you calm!" My head snaps back, and with the pain I'm immediately thrown into another time of my life.

# Elaina

### ten years old...

"Where are you going, baby girl? Daddy wants to talk to you for a second."

"I'm sorry, but I have to go to bed. I have to get up early for school," I reply, trying to make a decent excuse to escape his clutches.

"I only need you for a few minutes there, baby girl. Come here."

I squirm uncomfortably. "Ummm, please, I'm really tired." Brent likes to get close and touch me. It makes me feel weird and I don't like it.

"I said NOW, Elaina." His voice is menacing as he reaches his large fingers towards his belt and dutifully releases the clasp. Brent wraps his hand around the thick leather, pulling it free from the charcoal grey suit pants. Looking at me longingly, he reaches out and grasps my blonde hair roughly. The action forces my head back and my eyes crest with tears. *Ouch, please, no.*

At a creak in the floor, he glances up quickly, taken by surprise.

"Brent, what's going on? Was she bad again?"

My eyes rapidly scan the room until they fall on my foster mom, Paige. Thank God, she came at just the right time. She's standing in the doorway with her hand on her hip, glaring at me spitefully. She always looks at me like that.

He speaks through gritted teeth, "She was talking back again." He sits up to adjust himself.

Brent releases my hair at the same time as he propels me forward, dropping the belt to the floor. I stumble, splaying my arms out wildly to catch myself. I tend to be a little bit of a klutz sometimes and I've gotten pretty used to grabbing for anything within reach when I start to go down.

Paige grabs my shoulder and I cringe at the pain. Tightening my tummy, I hold my breath.

"Come along, Elaina. Such a pretty little girl. It's a shame you are so ugly inside and can't behave properly. We certainly won't be keeping you."

Paige walks me quickly down the long hall to a small room I'm staying in. I shuffle my feet hastily along the plain, tan carpet to keep up with her pace. "Now, go to bed and don't make a sound," she tells me sternly and shoves my small frame inside the shoebox-sized bedroom.

The door swings closed and I jump out of the way before it hits me. There's a loud *click* as she locks the door. She doesn't realize it, but I enjoy that sound. As long as that door is locked, I know I won't have to submit myself to being uncomfortable around them. I know as long as Paige has the key, the lock will keep *him* out.

I shed my jean shorts for my pajama bottoms. I swear it always feels like someone is watching me; I wonder if there are ghosts in this house or something? Sighing loudly, I lie in the single-sized bed provided to me with the bright yellow comforter. The blanket is the only happy thing about this room. Is this what it's like for normal kids? Do their parents treat them like these people treat me?

•••

As I snap out of it, wheezing with shock, I see Viktor crushing the drunk onto the bar top, whispering something in the man's ear. The drunk man shakes his head rapidly, sending his shaggy hair in every direction.

"No, no pleeeease. I swear it, I swear never again. I won't even look her way, man, I swear it!" he sputters, sounding surprisingly sober and Viktor says something in Russian, nodding at the man beside him in black. Viktor straightens up, adjusting the jacket of his suit and steps out of the way.

The guy next to Viktor bends swiftly and grasps the drunk harshly, forcing him from the bar stool and carts him off towards the back of the club. The drunk drags his feet, begging the guard to reconsider.

Viktor brushes off his suit jacket, annoyed, and shrugs so the sleeves drop back in place. As he comes around the bar, he has completely returned to his ever professional façade. He's always so well put together, so handsome and stern. The word *dashing* suits him perfectly as if he could step straight into a movie and fit right in. He'd easily take on the lead role.

He steps carefully across the slippery floor behind the bar, not scuffing the expensive shoes decorating his feet, until he is a mere twelve inches away from me. He gazes at me, wiith an expression full of concern.

Viktor's eyes can be filled with menace at times, though he's shown me nothing but kindness since I first woke up out of my hospital haze over a year ago. Another horrible memory to add to my list; unfortunately that one was my own doing.

"Are you...?" he starts to ask. Puzzled, I tilt my head. He brushes his hand tenderly down the side of my arm and peers into my eyes, trying to gauge how I am.

I clear my throat loudly. "Uh, yeah, I'm okay." It comes out a tad gruff for me but I'm still a bit overwhelmed.

He nods minutely and bites the side of his lip. He regards each crevice of my face, watching, reading my features for any clues. He won't find anything, I've been hiding my feelings about many things, those for him included, for far too long. I do care about him as a friend and of course he *is* devastatingly good looking with his strong Russian features.

I blink rapidly a few times and step back, "Sorry, that guy just caught me off-guard."

He can't be touching me like that. I don't know what to think when he touches me so I shuffle backwards more and try to collect my bearings. I turn away from him, effectively putting up my protective wall.

He simply nods, clenches his fist and makes his way back to his seat at the end of the bar.

I quickly walk to the opposite side of the bar to tend to the other customers. 007 is a very busy club, but thankfully only special orders come to the bartender. With the unlimited drinks here, included in the huge door fee, there is always a drunken guy being a dick at some point.

After growing up in foster homes it really doesn't bother me. I have met my fair share of assholes trying to take advantage of me. I guess I feel like there is this barrier, like they can't get to me because of the large bar between us. It's probably naïve of me to feel that way but I do.

At least here there's some sort of monitoring; Viktor

always takes care of any issues I may have. He doesn't know just how grateful I am for that. I try to keep those things to myself though.

I don't want to appear weak to any man. I've definitely gone through my fair share and I have learned  a man will take full advantage of any sign of weakness. Viktor doesn't know just how scared I get when someone crosses that line.

I glimpse over at him nonchalantly while refilling the four napkin stations placed randomly on top of the bar. He's beautiful. My sister is so lucky to have married someone who looks like Viktor. He is tall, and strong; not the beefed up strong, but solid enough to easily carry me out of the bar over his shoulder. I know that much for sure, since he's done it a few times.

Vik is dressed in a crisp suit each time I see him. His clothes fit as if they were made specifically for him. With his money though, I wouldn't be surprised if they were custom made. We could be running an errand and yet he still dresses so formally, I tend to look like a bum next to him.

Personally, as long as I'm wearing clean clothes and they are comfortable, I'm good. He says appearances are important. However, when you are deep in mafia territory I doubt it really matters. He could be wearing a tank top and board shorts, but if they see Viktor, they know he is the king ding-a-ling around here besides Tate.

His hair is short, complimented by a proud nose, almost as if he was bred to be stuck up. He's not though. Viktor's just observant and quiet.

His eyes are the same as Tate's. They're a gorgeous hazel, except a little more on the green side. Viktor's also older at twenty-seven, and acts every bit of it. I rarely see him smile unless I pop off and say something amusing.

I swallow as I take in his five o'clock shadow. He shouldn't be allowed to look so good; it's not fair to other men.

I'm caught blatantly staring as he looks over at me and our irises meet—his hazel to my sparkly blues. I blush and turn away. No more gawking, it's time to finish up my shift.

# Viktor

I sit observing her, every single shift. Each time she's here, she wears a tight little skirt that hugs her hips. It's glued to her like a second skin. I feel as if the skirt has a leash on me, taunting me every time she passes me to serve someone else. Then there are the times she bends over cleaning or digging out more supplies and I'm met with the smooth skin on the backs of her thighs. I would insist she wear pants but I fear they would outline her ass perfectly and be just as taxing on my libido.

Her sweet little smiles I get on occasion are payment enough for sitting here, putting up with obnoxious drunks. I don't mind a few drinks. However, when you are in here all the time and act abhorrent, I have no patience.

Every week I corner the manager for her schedule, so I can be here with her. I threaten him each time with being fired. I know he secretly looks at her, wants her, and fantasizes about her. He's lucky I do not kill him for it. If she were mine, I would hurt him.

She may be stubborn and believe I am bothersome, but I have to be. Ever since that day I was sent to dispose of her, it was like something in me demanded to protect her. I've never looked at a woman before and felt as if I was literally pulled toward her.

I cherish that day in the hospital, her lying there helpless and sweet. The taste of her skin, her scent, even tainted with the after smell of alcohol made me want her desperately. I promised Emily I wouldn't let anyone harm her sister and I meant it. Now that she is Tate's wife, she is also like a little sister to me.

In the past I have hinted to Elaina about my feelings, but she hasn't taken me seriously. I feel as if I'm a desperate fool, constantly lusting after her. Not once has Elaina made a move to show she wants to be more than just friends. It's crushing, but I still hold out for her with each shift she works.

She zigzags behind the bar, working in haste. I love how her cheeks flush with a fine mist of perspiration. I can picture her beautifully, riding me, covered in that same pink blush. Perhaps her ass is pink too, with a few of my hand prints. She looks like the type of sweet girl who could use a few spankings.

She is a hard worker and I admire how well she handles customers. 007 is lucky to have her as an employee. The men here should be paying me just to watch her work the bar.

I offered once to take care of her. She brushed it off as if the idea were ludicrous. Taking in her loveliness, it's far from ridiculous.

In Russia when I was a small boy, we were taught to look for splendor, so it's natural for me to gravitate towards her. She is all beauty. She encompasses the all-American, girl-next-door look.

She's perfect with her freckles and blue eyes. With her corn-colored blonde hair she screams American, but if it were a few shades lighter, she could definitely pass as a Russian girl.

At least I know that if Mother were to ever meet her there would not be any issues, since she adores Emily. God, that dinner prior to Tate and Emily's wreck was hilarious. I thought our mother was going to pull her hair out and then spit on Emily. I couldn't stop chuckling at the little comments she kept making. I knew Tate was a goner as soon as I saw them get out of the car. He had an almost feral look when I greeted Emily. Frankly, I'm surprised he let Mother get away with as much as she did.

Mishka is the one I would really want Elaina to meet if I had a choice. She was always more of a mother to Tate and me growing up. She cooked for us, got us ready for our private school and even slapped us on occasion if we were out of control. Mother didn't dare touch us or my father would have gone ballistic, but Mishka would have busted Papa's knees. Tate had to get his knee fetish from somewhere.

I know my father would call Elaina a princess, as she resembles such. However, that trash will never meet her, I'll make sure of it. He may be my father, but he died to me when he double crossed me and my brother. He is fortunate we let him live this long.

Have you ever met someone and just known there was something about them? That's exactly how I felt the first time I heard her speak to me from that hospital bed.

I was already drawn to her, to her beauty and sweet smell. Then her soft, sweet voice sounded like a melody and it was like my eyes were opened for the first time to this love at first sight notion. Now each time she talks to me, I hear that harmony and it brings a little bit of bliss into my stressful life.

None of it matters though, as she couldn't care less if I sat here. She has told me many times she is a grown up and can take care of herself. She may be independent, but deep inside she needs me, I know it.

When she wrecked her car into my brother's she was extremely drunk. She tried to get crazy the last time

London, Avery and Emily all came to OO7. Luckily, I'd brought her and was able to take her home safely. She is careless and it drives me mad. How can such a perfect creature not take better care of herself?

I turn away from her as Alexei, my guard, approaches me. I'm still sipping on my vodka-seven Elaina prepared for me. She's passable at making drinks, not great, but okay. I won't be drinking her martinis anytime soon, though.

"Boss," he says quietly, scanning our surroundings.

"What is it, Alexei?"

"I dumped him out back. Are you sure?" he double checks. He really is a diligent employee and I enjoy him working for me, but I have to keep them all on their toes.

"You question me?" I stare him down crazily. "He touched her. Yes. Take care of it, or I will," I snap, annoyed.

"Very good, sir. Consider it done," he replies and stands to his full height. He isn't a big man, maybe six foot or so like I am. He may have me beat muscle wise, but I've been training for most of my life in killing methods.

I gesture with my hand, indifferent. "Take him to the docks. Feed him to the rats."

"Yes, Boss," he replies, unfazed, and strides toward the back entrance.

The punishment may appear harsh, but everyone in here who watched what happened with her needs to see. They will witness Alexei leave through the back and know that the drunk will never return.

They will learn she belongs to the Solntsvskaya Bratva. To the boss, to me. Even if she's unaware of it, they won't be.

Hawk, the manager of Taint is here filling in. He's a decent employee, but I prefer it when Elaina works with another female. I take special notice each time Elaina talks to Hawk, trying to work out what exactly they are saying.

Unfortunately for me though, I can't read lips very well.

I can't stand it when he leans in close, or touches her. I want to fire him each time he lays his hand on her sun-kissed arm. I hold myself back though. I know she wouldn't forgive me for acting so petty.

I tend to take stock when she speaks to any male who isn't just there for a quick bar transaction. Hawk's here to fill in for one of the other bartenders who was meant to relieve Elaina, but called in sick. Of course I already know this from the manager informing me earlier, but act oblivious to it.

She gives him a small side-hug and a smile, then grabs her purse. She's getting ready to leave, throwing the sling of her purse carelessly over her shoulder as she comes to me. Sitting up straight, I wipe my features clean of any dark thoughts and concentrate on her lightness.

She flashes me a small smile and a little wave as she shouts over the noise, "Goodbye, Viktor. Thank you for earlier."

I can't help but stare into her eyes. I may seem like a stalker but it's like getting lost in a sea of blue and I can't help myself.

"Have a good evening, Elaina." I keep it formal, not acknowledging her thanks. She should just forget what happened. I run the Bratva. That was peas compared to what I normally deal with. She doesn't seem to realize I would do so much more for her if she were to ask.

She gives me a shaky smile and heads toward the door to the club. I gesture to Spartak who's been watching me closely, waiting for the signal. I nod toward her and he quickly follows.

Spartak will trail her home to her crappy little apartment and make sure she is safe. It'll be his job to park outside her building and keep watch. Spar's her unofficial guard. I know it's not a practical thing to have my men do, but it's a new requirement of them and no one ever said I was reasonable.

I leave to go home too because if she's not at the club then I don't want to be there either. I live close to Tate, in the same gated community. My house is tan with decorative landscaping.

When I bought my home, Mishka came over right away with a list of plants she wanted. The guards went and picked up everything she asked for. That crazy, old woman came and worked in the yard for a week straight. It looks beautiful, but I'm just thankful I only have to worry about the sprinkler being on and nothing else.

Tate's backyard is absurd. Mishka and Emily are always changing it up and planting new flowers everywhere. I wouldn't be surprised if my little brother fattens up with all the cooking Mishka is teaching Emily.

On the plus side, I can visit now and eat a good dinner. My brother and I can cook fairly well, but we always just grill at night. Mishka will make delicious old Russian recipes.

Thankfully the trip is short. My house is only about ten minutes from the club. I love my sporty James Bond type cars parked in the garage, but I'm too exhausted to really enjoy them today.

Running a bunch of criminals makes you age inside quickly and my uncle has always told me to drive a car you love. He says we have too many things to worry about, that we need to have something we can enjoy in the small amount of free time we have.

I pull my black Mercedes-AMG GT S into my three car garage, next to my Jaguar. My Mercedes purrs like a pleased kitten, enjoying the attention, but god do I love my Jaguar. My Jag doesn't purr, no, she growls when I give her gas.

Maybe I'll take her for a drive after I rest for a while.

I'm greeted by a silent house and it's refreshing. Leaning my head back, I close my eyes tightly for a moment and breathe in the clean air. *Ahh.* That's nice after the noisy club for the past five hours.

As I strut leisurely to my office I shuck my jacket and shoes, diligently unbuttoning my shirt. One thing I thoroughly enjoy about being home is the lack of clothes.

I sit in my comfortable, overly plush leather desk chair and fill a tumbler with Grey Goose. Growing up around my uncle, I learned to drink vodka as if it was water. Now it's second nature to have it at home when I'm relaxing.

Taking a deep breath, I'm met with the vibration of my personal cell phone ringing. This better be important. If it were the ringtone to the business phone I would let it keep ringing. I glance at the flashing screen to see it's Tate.

"Braat," I answer 'brother' in Russian on the second ring.

The majority of our conversations are in Russian, even though Tate hates when I call any attention to our native language. I am proud to be Russian and use it to my advantage when I talk business.

"Viktor. What went on at the club today?"

"I'm well, brother, thank you for inquiring."

"Save it, Viktor, what happened?" he asks, frustration coating his voice.

"Nothing happened."

"Bullshit! I heard you took a man out the back door, is this true?"

"Yes, and? What is it to you, Luka? I had business, it was handled."

"Business! Are you joking? You carried a man out the back door in front of customers! That is reckless, Viktor. You are being too bold."

"Bold, Luka? No. You forget that I was the one handed the Mafiya, but gave it to you. You may be the Big Boss now, but I run the rest. The only thing *bold*, is you speaking out of place. Mind your business, Luka. I will handle things as I please."

"Viktor, you will go to jail if the wrong person sees this. I know you stepped down, but at the same time I stepped up into a position you so desperately ran from. Don't you lecture me about giving up your spot. I took it for you so you could have freedom, yet you embrace the Bratva for Uncle."

"Yes, someone has to embrace the dirty deeds of our family. I clean up messes, Luka, it's what I do. The trash put his hands on Elaina at the bar and I was fixing the issue, little brother."

"Why didn't you tell me that in the first place, instead of fighting with me? We have to stick together, Vik. With father out, it's you and me, now."

"I know this, it will be fine, Luka. Don't stress, I am doing my part."

"Thank you, and if you need anything, call."

"I will, if it comes to that."

I hang up and pound my fist on my desk, shaking the glass of vodka. My little brother has some nerve, getting angry with me. He has no idea what he's talking about. I wonder which little rat called him.

Truth? I didn't take over the Mafiya because I knew my father really wanted Tate to have it. He always favored Tate over myself and that was fine, I had my uncle. I stepped down to make my father happy. Had I known what he was doing to Tate and me, then I would have taken it over and not had the burden placed on my little brother. Should have known he wouldn't think twice to lie to his sons. He's a slimy two-faced fish and doesn't deserve the air he breathes.

Tate went ballistic when he found out about our father being even more crooked than he had suspected. He knows I had worked very hard to make all the books appear legit. They weren't legit but I altered them in good faith that I was helping my father change his ways.

Tate doesn't mind being in guns, but he loathes the drug and sex trade. I don't mind the drugs and my men make plenty of money from them. I do not dabble in the sex trade however; that stopped when I took charge. I know my uncle was very supportive of it, but I can't fathom selling another human being.

Drugs are another thing entirely. I feel the person has the choice. If they choose to be a user, that's on them. The same with gambling; we have many circuits of gambling that we support and profit from, also the occasional gambling debt one might incur. I have no problem lending and having my men collect my interest due.

I still handle some disposal. I know I don't have to, that I have men for it, but I enjoy it. I guess it's just another mess for me to clean up.

I take a large drink of my vodka and call my guard, to check on Elaina.

"Spartak?"

"She's good, Boss, just stopped by a little store on the way and got a few things."

"Alcohol?"

"No, sir, just snacks."

"Very good. Pay attention."

"Yes, of course, sir,"he replies diligently and I hang up. I pull up her number to send her the nightly text I've sent since I first took her home.

**Me:** Good Night, Принцесса (Princess)

I'm met with the only response I have ever gotten from her at night. One evening I hope she will add an endearment to it, but I won't hold my breath.

**Принцесса**: Night.

# Elaina

two days later...

I WAKE WITH A START. *FUCK.* ANOTHER BAD DREAM. The dreams have never stopped. I had to live through everything with Brent and now I'm stuck dreaming about it. I don't want to remember.

God, that dream was so vivid. It felt like he really was touching me again and my skin crawls with the after effects. Gagging, I take a few deep breaths to try and calm my nerves.

It always felt wrong each time. I didn't really know it was immoral until I got older and saw how my friends' parents interacted with them. Their parents treated them completely differently than what I was used to. I think back to when I started to question things.

I was thirteen and staying the night at my girlfriend's house. I had never been allowed to stay away but Brent and

Paige went out of town. I got to stay with Stephanie for three days.

Stephanie's house was a two story, warmly decorated home and her family was the kindest I had ever met. Each night I lay beside her in her big bed with its fluffy pink comforter. I was always waiting, scared for her father to come in, but he never did.

Finally, I worked up the nerve and asked Stephanie if he came to lie beside her when I wasn't there. I thought perhaps it was my fault, disturbing what fathers do with their daughters.

I remember she had looked at me like I had lost my mind. Stephanie then drilled it into my head that fathers don't normally lie with their daughters, especially when they are older.

She never told anyone about that, but we did start to grow apart. I didn't understand at the time why she drifted away, but I did once I got older. I didn't blame Stephanie, I was dirty and no one wanted to be around that. I never spoke of it to anyone again. I couldn't stand the thought of my case worker finding out.

Brent and Paige were small worries compared to what some foster parents put kids through. I could handle Paige being mean and saying hateful things. I could even deal with Brent and his touching, I had to.

As soon as I was old enough to leave without the cops picking me up, I split. I had been working a part time job after school and on the weekends at the Dollar Store close by. I was saving every penny and delighted in the time spent away from that house. I got my crappy apartment after some time and eventually was able to get my car. It was rough, but I refused to sink.

Shaking off those ominous feelings, I head into the

shower. I scrub extra hard, attempting to remove the feeling I have crawling all over my skin. Turning the faucet to hot, the water heats quickly and I get a tingle from the burning. The pain helps clear my mind of some of the details. My skin turns bright pink, but it's better than the creepy crawlies I had before. I'll take the pain over memories of that sick fuck any day.

Raiding my small closet, I throw on my short jean skirt, one of the few nice tank tops Emily gave me and the boots I borrowed from her. Not my usual style but the guys at the bar seem to eat it up. Any extra tips I can make by wearing a skirt or borrowing boots, I'm going to take full advantage of.

Thank God I have Emily now. I had no idea how much a sister could truly impact my life and make things better. I'm even more excited about the fact of becoming an aunty.

My car is almost paid off, thankfully. It seems like all I do is work and pay my bills. I'll occasionally go on a drinking binge or party but that's about all. I can't afford much more even if I wanted to. It's okay, this life is way better than the one I had growing up. I just have to keep my ducks in a row and keep my eyes on the prize—being car payment free.

I'm usually too afraid of getting close to any guys and them touching me, unless I drink. If I'm toasted, I'll let them kiss me or grab my breast, but that's as far as I've ever let it go. I get creeped out and reminded of how it felt when Brent would mess with me.

People don't understand that sexual assault of any kind can affect the victim for the rest of their lives. I may not have been raped or anything that serious but this still impacts my daily life, no matter how strong I feel I've become. I've read online that it's a form of PTSD. I don't think I really have it, but I do have my triggers. Not like I'm going to visit a doctor anytime soon and discuss it with them.

I'm fortunate working at the club and having Viktor there. He has no idea just how much I appreciate him looking out for me all the time. Not only do I feel safer but I'm able to work at a high end club. It helps dramatically with me meeting my goal of paying off my debts. I never want to be that vulnerable again, of being in a position I can't escape if I need to.

Tate is drastically protective of my sister, Emily, and with Viktor doing little things for me, I figure it's probably a family trait. I know very little about his family besides the stuff Emily has told me. She's not very forthcoming about them though. I know they both have a group of scary-looking guards. For what reason, who knows? My guess is because they are rich and because of all the Mafia-ish people in this area.

I grab a banana on my way to my white Camaro. It's all I can afford right now, so I make do. It's not the fancy version of the Camaro and it's not even that new, but I love her. She's good to me and I do my best to take care of her. I'm thankful I can park my car close to my apartment and right under a light every night as I get a little spooked in the dark around here.

I take a large bite, stuffing my mouth with a third of the banana. I'm hungrier than I first thought. I wipe the banana off my fingers onto the towel next to me after I climb into the car. I start her up, loving the little rumble she makes; it's almost as if she thinks she's fast.

Glancing in my rearview mirror, I drop my banana and shriek in surprise. *What the fuck?* One of Viktor's thugs is standing directly behind my car. I shut the engine off and climb out quickly. *What a waste of a good banana, damn it!*

I snap rudely, "Umm, can I help you?"

This is it, Viktor has overstepped the boundary this

time. We formed a small friendship when I was in the hospital. I've tried pulling away but he just keeps pushing me. This time he's out of line and I plan to give him a thorough piece of my mind. I place my hands on my hips and cock them to the side, tapping my foot. This better be good.

"Forgive me, ma'am," he says with a slight Russian accent. "I am Spartak." He smiles warmly and my anger melts slightly.

"Okay, Spartak, what's going on? You're in my way."

"Ma'am, please, your tire is bad, may I fix?" he asks, gesturing to my back tire on the passenger side. I walk around the rear end and look at him skeptically at the same time. I glance at the tire.

"Shit! What am I supposed to do with this?" I flail my arms toward the very flat tire and cringe.

I have to get to work soon or I will be late. There's no way I have time to get a new tire and I definitely shouldn't drive it like this. I'll have to call a cab and that's going to be so expensive.

"I fix it for you." His Russian gets a little stronger and I'm immediately reminded of my sister's good friend, Nikoli.

"You can fix it? How?"

He walks to the trunk and gestures for me to open it. I press the trunk release button on my key fob and he proceeds to show me where the spare is. He also shows me how to remove it from the trunk, what the jack is, and how to jack my car up. Then he takes the old tire off, puts my spare on and loads the flat back into the trunk for me.

I'm in awe that this man just offered to help me and do all of this work. It took him about twenty minutes total. He did it efficiently and never once made me feel guilty for his help.

I never could have changed it that fast, once I figured

out what to do. I cataloged each maneuver so I have it for future reference. I like being able to do stuff and not having to depend on someone else all the time.

I clap my hands happily and smile. "Wow, thank you so much! Do you want some money, for umm, fixing this?"

"No, no, ma'am. Please just go to work, I don't want you to be late." He gestures with his hands for me to get in the car. I nod and climb inside.

The flat tire sucks, I'll have to pay for that eventually. At least I'm not out a cab fare and since I leave early, I should be right on time.

That was so nice! What a friendly guy; I wish there were more people out there willing to jump in and help someone else. I have to tell Viktor his guy was so polite and helpful. Wait, why was his man here anyhow?

There's no telling with Viktor, and I plan to ask as soon as I see him.

After a short non-eventful drive, I arrive and it's my favorite time in the club. There isn't anyone here besides the manager and Viktor's guy who changed my tire. He ended up following me here and opened the door for me. It's kind of neat feeling like I have my own personal assistant, but creepy at the same time.

I check the place over, then turn on lights and fans for the main room, storage and the bathrooms. I enjoy opening the club up, makes me feel really useful.

I wonder where Viktor is today. He's normally here eating his dinner or lunch from some random restaurant. It's amazing he's in such great shape with always eating out. I wonder... could Vik not know how to cook? I really want to ask his guy here about him, but at the same time I don't want to seem too eager.

An hour passes with me busily chopping up lemons, limes, oranges and refilling the maraschino cherries. I usually have opening shift and do the prep. I get paid fifteen dollars an hour for doing prep, which is amazing. Every place I've worked at required you to do it, while paying you a measly two dollars an hour. The only thing I hate about opening is filling the ice bin. Lugging the ice bucket back and forth gets heavy after a few trips. The later shifts all have a bar back that does that kind of stuff.

The other bartenders and floor guys start arriving and the music gets cranked loud while everyone sets up their own stations.

I've been doing everything I can in the past hour to stay busy, but it's driving me crazy! Viktor is never late and he never misses a shift that I work. It's like he's a part of the whole shift. We barely speak to each other but we exchange glances about a million times a night. I have to at least make sure he's okay. Yep, that's my excuse, and I'm going to use it.

I throw my towel down on the beer cooler and quickly round the large bar. I go searching through the club to find Viktor's guy. Spartak, I think he said his name was.

Busily looking everywhere but in front of me, I run straight into something solid.

"Ooof," I yelp.

Large hands grab my arms to steady me and I look up, glancing over a leather vest that says in bold letters *Enforcer* on one side and *Ares* on the other side. It's followed by massive shoulders, a thick neck and finally a stern but friendly face.

"Uhhhhh?"

"Careful, doll, you ran straight into me. Say, do you know where I can find the owner?" he asks in a gruff voice. I stare like a deer trapped in the headlights. He looks at me curiously, slowly peeling his hands off my arms and steps back, cocking his eyebrow, "Doll?"

"Yes! No, I mean sorry. I don't see him much."

He nods and smiles slightly. Wow, scary to gorgeous with just a small smile. How do men do that so easily?

"Alright, bet." He walks past me and I have to stop to catch my breath for a second.

I watch him walk down the hall; his beefy back has a large symbol reading 'Oath Keepers MC'. I've got to remember to tell Tate if I see him, and what on earth does 'bet' mean?

I continue on my journey until I spot Spartak propped up against the wall near the office, "Ma'am?" he queries when he sees me approach.

"Hi, Spartak. I was just wondering, can I ask you a question?"

"Yes."

"Okay, umm. Where's Viktor?"

"Why, is there something you need? I can help or fix it."

"No, it's not that. He's just normally here. I was wondering if he was coming."

He smirks a little when I ask if Viktor's coming. No doubt he's going to tell him about it. "He couldn't be here, so I'm here to watch over you."

"To watch over me? You have got to be joking!"

"No, ma'am, I'm not. I'm here in case you need anything."

"Well, Viktor always sits at the bar," I reply tartly and spin on my boot heels. I storm back to the bar in a huff.

That man has some serious nerve, planting someone to monitor me. So Viktor really is here each shift to watch me! I knew it. I have no idea how to deal with this whole stalking situation.

I grab the towel back up and wipe the bar top thoroughly trying to scrub some of my frustration out. A few minutes pass and I hear a stool scrape. I look over to see Spartak posted at the end of the bar where Viktor usually sits. I hate to admit, but seeing him sitting there does bring me some comfort. It's not as much as Viktor, but it'll do.

# Viktor

Tapping my fingers on my desk to a beat in my head, I sit bored at one of my warehouses down by Tellico Lake. We have a front set up as if we store boat and lake supplies. However the crates in here are not filled with anything remotely close to skis or life preservers. Actually, quite the opposite; I house guns, knives, drugs, any of that sort in my storage buildings. I have them spread all over this area of Tennessee. I simply look like a productive business man with a lot of merchandise for the different lakes.

My uncle came up with the idea years ago. We've had great success with it. Not to mention, Tate and I combined own many cops in the state as a back-up plan. We still get the occasional new curious face popping in though.

The door leading to my office slams. It has to be Alexei coming to report to me. I have a main reinforced metal door you have to get through before you can get to my real office door. You can never be too careful when dealing with criminals.

Alexei's one of the few with the access code to get back here. I've known him for many years and he helps me a lot. I trust him more than I should, but I never let anyone else know that.

"Boss?" he calls out and knocks on the door, staying in the hall.

He's trained well. I have very little tolerance for

foolishness. I'm in charge of this organization, I expect respect. This isn't some after school boys club I run around here.

"Yes, Alexei, come in."

My brother worries that I keep things so formal, and that I have no friends. He doesn't realize I deal with a different crowd in my businesses. Keeping things formal keeps my eyes open and my heart beating.

Alexei enters and I gesture to the chair seated in front of my desk. He adjusts his suit and sits. Being around me frequently, he is required to dress the part and is usually in a suit or occasionally black military style cargo pants and black fitted tank top. It all depends on what job he's performing.

He's a very valuable asset to me but every chance I get I have to make it known he can be replaced. My uncle taught me it will make people work harder trying to please you and so far that has held true. Of course I do reward them with a few perks when acknowledgment is due.

"Boss, the specialty weapons you were waiting on from Russia arrived."

"Very good, any issues arise with it?"

"No, sir, it went smoothly."

"Good, I love when a plan is executed correctly and it comes together as intended. Those weapons will bring in a large profit. Make sure you call the Columbians that were interested in them and let them know it's now an option. Tell me, how did it go with the man from the bar?"

"The drunk was no problem either. I shot him up with heroin and fed him to the rats as you asked. He screamed for a while and I made sure the big body pieces left over were dumped. I'll call the Columbians today and get the weapons taken care of."

I nod my approval. I'm pretty impressed he hasn't called

me for instructions or anything. He's just taken initiative and completed everything that needed doing. It's such a relief to be able to at least rely on one person around here now that my uncle is out of the business.

"Very good. I am pleased, Alexei. What's next?"

"Thank you, Boss. I do have a guy here waiting to talk to you."

"Who's here?"

"The gambling guy I told you about a few days ago. He's just like the rest, acting like he doesn't need the money when he wants it really bad."

"All right, search him then escort him back," I say and he jumps up quickly to get the customer.

After a few seconds he arrives with an older, average-sized man. The guy's sporting neatly trimmed brown hair, a big nose, khaki pleated pants and a pale blue Ralph Lauren polo shirt. He looks the part of your typical business man douche.

He stands in front of my desk appearing rather intimidated. "Mr. Masterson, thank you for meeting with me," he states graciously and I gesture to the chair. Alexei stands between the door and the man.

"No problem, Mr...?

"Yes, sir, I'm Brent Tollfree, nice to meet you," he utters nervously in a strong southern accent.

Brent reminds me of some of the older southern films my mother liked to watch when we first moved to the States. She believed it would help her understand people better when they spoke, I just thought it was a waste of time.

"Okay, what exactly can I do for you?"

"Well, I would like to take out a personal loan."

Refraining from rolling my eyes and scoffing, I nod. "All right, how much were you looking to borrow and what do you have as collateral?" I probe and he fidgets a little in his chair.

I love watching grown men squirm when they realize they are about to make a deal with the Bratva. They might as well be signing a contract with the Devil. We don't pride ourselves in being good and kind but in being strong and ruthless.

"Can I borrow sixty thousand?" he queries quietly, cocking his head and Alexei whistles at the amount. Alexei's quite the business man and knows how to play the game well.

"Well, let me see, you got referred to me by your colleague who has had a loan with me, correct?" I inquire and he nods. "What can you provide as collateral?"

"I have a Cadillac Escalade I can give you if it comes to that."

"Oh, Mr. Tollfree, I will be taking a lot more than your car if it gets to that point." I steeple my fingers and wait for him to decide his fate. It only takes a few seconds, but then that's normal for everyone coming to borrow money.

"I understand, Mr. Masterson. It won't come to that. Thank you, thanks so much," he declares graciously and I give in, rolling my eyes. I deal with these types of people all the time and they are all the same. I wave my hand toward him and Alexei signals to the guy to get up.

"Alexei can get you that money, since it's not much."

"Okay, thank you so much, Mr. Masterson, I really appreciate it." I nod, already aggravated and Alexei rushes him out of my office. He's lucky he quit talking or I may have just cut his tongue out. *Annoying little piss ant.*

I'll probably have to make my men pay him a visit in about three months when he conveniently forgets to repay that loan he wanted so badly. I remember his buddy well. I thought I was going to have a new body to dump when his father came to his rescue.

Gamblers are the worst, always looking for that quick buck. It usually ends up costing them everything.

I wonder how the beautiful princess is doing today. I loathe the fact I'm missing her shift. This is the first that I've missed and it's all I can think about. I have to take care of my businesses though. I hope one day she allows me to make her my priority above everything else.

Alexei comes rushing back into my office interrupting my pleasant thoughts of Elaina. My stomach drops at the sight of him. I'm stunned, gaping; he never enters unannounced and yelling loudly.

"Boss! Boss!" He is bending over, panting, and resting his hands on his knees.

"What is it?" I inquire, concerned, jumping into defensive mode. I scan his frazzled features, taking in his rumpled clothing and sweaty forehead.

"One of the fucking men was just caught taking product!" Breathing deeply he hurries on, "I got to him before he could steal any more, but he was able to get out of the building. He ran and escaped out of the east side door. The alarm is off, but we must hurry!"

"Christ, Alexei! You were just in here not even twenty minutes ago! Damn it, find him, Lexei! Now, and return him to me!"

I can't believe these idiots let him get out of the building. I jump up quickly, shoving my chair back and grab my piece out of my desk drawer. You steal from me, the Bratva, it's going to end one way.

I follow Alexei down the hall to the main building. The men are all standing, waiting for orders and gazing at each other as if it's vodka time. They may as well have their thumbs up their asses.

"Quit standing around and find him!" I roar angrily and

they all scatter toward the door.

"You five!" I point toward a group to the left, "Stay and guard the product." I gesture toward the crates wildly and move to the entrance.

Alexei steps close to me, "Boss, please stay and let me handle it."

Turning, I scoff, "You handle it, Alexei?" I snarl, "You were just out here and let him go! You want me to trust you? Then go bring him back!"

I bustle out the door in a fit of irritation. *Just what I wanted to deal with today.* I need to be monitoring the new inventory and making deals, but instead I'm faced with foolishness. Why weren't the doors being watched? Simple tasks yet they can't be done.

Slamming the door behind me, I run outside and around the back of the warehouse to where I hear my men making the most noise. This idiot better hope he can run and find some place to go. There are all types of wildlife out here and I wouldn't be surprised if he didn't survive. He could always go steal a boat off the docks, but I'll be sure to have my guys down there.

There are close to five thousand in the Solntsevskaya Bratva organization together and about thirty who work with me on a regular basis. The majority of the others are delegated through different channels from myself or others I have assigned to certain tasks.

I fly around the corner, ready for just about anything and find four of my guys lugging the thieving idiot roughly back to me. The bum pulls, pushes and fights back trying to get free. Bastard doesn't make it far as they hit him in the stomach and kidneys several times.

It's in his best interest to fight, he knows what's about to come of him. I have a zero tolerance policy for stealing. Watching for a few moments as my men beat him, I smirk.

It's the least of his worries.

Approaching them carefully, I attempt to stay out of the way of swinging fists and elbows.

Taking in the surroundings, I cautiously scan for anyone who could be watching. I'm pleased to find that we are indeed alone, as we should be. I picked this location as my main supply building for a reason.

I sneer at him, getting angrier with each step as I approach. "Where was it you planned on going? There is nothing but trees and water, you imbecile! Did you seriously think you would get away with it?"

He shakes his head and spits in my direction.

"Do you have any clue just who I am?" I ask curiously.

This man seriously has a death wish by spitting toward me. That is such a disgraceful sign of disrespect. My uncle would have chopped him into little bits, starting with that nasty tongue of his.

"Nyet," he replies in Russian and shakes his head.

"Ah." I click my tongue. "Shame. I am Viktor Masterson, head of the organization you were working for and are stupid enough to spit at," I reply snidely, glaring at him.

He turns his face away from me and looks in the other direction. This trash has lost his mind if he thinks I will tolerate this behavior in front of my men. I remove my suit jacket and hand it to Sergei, one of my guards. He follows me pretty much everywhere so he's accustomed to being my coat rack when needed.

I unbutton my cuff links and roll up my sleeves leisurely, taking a nice deep breath to clear my lungs. Moving my head side to side to pop my neck muscles and loosen up. I draw my arm back and punch the jackass square in the jaw.

His head flies backwards with the momentum and there's an audible crack that echoes in the trees. "Ugh!" he moans loudly. I'm sure he has a tooth floating around in there now.

Swiftly, I pull out my weapon. Cocking it, I smile and aim it straight in the middle of his forehead. His eyes widen, surprised. I pull the trigger without a moment of hesitation.

He drops like a sack of potatoes and the men stand there holding him. They're all silent, staring at me and waiting. I guess I surprised everyone with that one.

"Let it be known that this was me being gentle on someone who steals from me. I will not show the same compassion to the next person who is caught."

"Boss," Alexei answers and nods, motioning at the other men. The group follow suit and nod as well. I turn on my heel and head back inside to my office.

"Take care of it!" I call out loudly as I walk away and hear them scurry to follow orders.

A few moments later I receive a message from Spartak and it makes the entire evening better.

> **Spartak:** She asks for you
>
> **Me:** Everything okay?
>
> **Spartak:** Yes, sir

I can't even fathom the fact that she has finally asked about me. My stomach feels as if it wants to implode. I don't know if that feeling is a blessing or a curse. Spartak will have to update me when she's not working. I can't wait to hear what she said.

I grab the keys to my Jaguar; my heart is beating quickly, excited. It's time for me to head home. Clearly I've had enough excitement for today. I nod to Sergei so he knows I'm leaving.

We make it down the hallway before getting caught by Alexei, "Boss?" He gazes at me, questioning.

"I'm leaving. I have to check on the other warehouse tomorrow, so I will expect you at my house at ten in the morning."

"No problem, sir, I will be there."

"Good, you will stay and look over things?"

"Of course, sir. I'm sorry about earlier."

"Until tomorrow," I say and take my leave.

Sergei and I make our way to the cars. He gets in my Jaguar and starts it while I stay about twenty feet away. He always starts my vehicles for me. You never know when someone may try to get back at the Bratva.

# THREE

## Elaina

**T**HIS IS THE THIRD SHIFT OF MINE HE'S MISSED. IT means an additional day with Spartak following me around like he's a puppy. He's pleasant; I'm just finding myself speculating about Vik.

I know Viktor and Tate aren't the greatest of guys, but it makes me wonder what they really do if Vik feels I need someone around me constantly. As each day passes, my curiosity and speculations grow. I'm sure I'm imagining something way more sinister than what it really is, but at this point I'm ready to give Viktor a piece of my mind.

I stroll behind the bar in 007. Another day, another dollar, I suppose.

Hawk is filling in for the other bartender again. He must be exhausted, poor guy is already the manager at Club Taint. He's one of the best bartenders I've ever worked with. He will make my night a cake walk, thankfully. After the scuffle with the drunk, I haven't been too keen on coming in to work. At least I have some eye candy to look forward to. He's sporting his signature blue mohawk, sexy grin and Chucks. I don't mind being around Hawk; he's friendly and has always been respectful toward me. He's one of the few I don't mind with the pet names. Viktor and my sister are the others I've gotten used to.

"Hey, beautiful," he murmurs in his killer raspy voice.

"Hey, you, how's life?"

"It's good, just having woman issues."

"Uh oh, anything I can help with?" I lean my hip against the beer cooler and cross my arms.

"Well, I met this chick, total babe, bright red hair, killer smile and body. She brings food to my shifts a lot but every time I think we are going somewhere, a groupie comes up and fucks it all up. Now Dillian, that's her name, is pissed and is backing off again."

Hawk is a drummer in a rock band when he has spare time. He has some great arms to prove it too. His brother is the singer of the group; I can only imagine his voice with how great Hawk's is. I wonder what the rest of the band looks like.

"That sucks! Have you told the groupies to back off and explained to Dillian that you aren't interested in them?"

A stool scrapes loudly and I glance back to see what Spartak is doing, only I'm met with annoyed green-hazel eyes and a scowl to match.

Viktor looks at Hawk angrily. "Correct me if I'm wrong, but you're supposed to be doing inventory, yes?" It's not really a question, just formed like one. It's more like an annoyed growl.

Hawk nods. "Yeah, I was just on my way to do that."

"Very good," Viktor replies shortly and Hawk walks quickly to the storage room. I put my hand on my hip and spin to face Viktor fully.

"Well, hello, grouchy pants. Why aren't you friendly with

Hawk? He's a nice guy."

"He's not my friend, he's my employee. I pay him to work." He shrugs indifferently.

"Well, you also pay me to work, but yet you never seem to have an issue with me talking to you."

"That's entirely different, Elaina," he murmurs, running his hands through his hair.

"Reeeeally? How so?" I lean on my elbows against the bar, closer to him. He copies me and leans in closer.

"He's a single man."

"Annnd you're not?"

He grasps my wrists tightly in each of his hands and I draw in a startled gasp. He leans in close and his breath washes over me. I clench, turned on at the sensation.

"No, Printsyessa (Princess), last time I checked, I was all about you."

I tear my hands away and step back. "Uh, Viktor, you're wrong," I reply quietly.

I pace toward the end of the bar and busy myself. I bow down and start shifting glasses around into straight rows. I get nervous and it causes me to act as if I have ADD.

Regardless of feeling a presence behind me, I stay bent over. It's one of those moments where you clench your tummy tightly and lie, telling yourself nothing's behind you when in fact you know there really is something there.

I'm startled when a strong hand grasps my bicep, pulling me up and backward. I spin, ready to fight and let loose a piece of my mind. I'm met with Viktor's serious expression about four inches from my face and it makes me pause, forgetting every word that had been wanting to come out.

"NO. You are wrong. I have been chasing you for *months*. Open your eyes." He steps closer so I can feel his warm, sweet breath whisper over my face each time he speaks.

"Printsyessa," he whispers and tenderly takes my bottom lip between his. My pussy throbs wantonly at his touch.

Freezing up, I open my eyes wide, chanting inside not to freak out. He pulls back, releasing my lip from his. His hand brushes my cheek gently and I feel his breath as he pants close to my lips. I can taste each breath of his I breathe in. I open my lips slightly, my mouth watering at the idea of his being so close to mine.

"Viktor," I choke and he dives in roughly, ravaging my mouth as if he is starving and I can quench his hunger. One hand grasps my cheek and the other rests on the bar behind me as he forcefully pushes my body against it with his.

His body is hard, demanding, and wanting. I tightly grasp his shirt as I let him take my mouth. His tongue caresses mine, teaching me how to please him.

His hand leaves my face and trails up my thigh under my skirt. It's like a splash of cold water and I push him away forcefully.

Panting, I step to the side and press my hand to my swollen lips. "I'm sorry, but I just can't," I say, ashamed. Why does there have to be something wrong with me? Why can't I just be like everyone else?

"You can't now, but you will," he says sternly and walks away from me.

I stand still holding my mouth and shake my head. My skin is sensitive to the touch from his five o'clock shadow. God, I wish I could give him what he wants, but it will never happen. I watch him walk down the hall and to the office. *Just great, what am I going to do now?*

I attempt to make the night pass quickly by being diligent and extra friendly to the customers I get. It just doesn't work, Hawk asks me like twenty times to tell him what is eating at me, but I'm not someone who opens up. I learned many years ago to hold it all inside.

I guess my sister and I have more in common than I realized. I like to keep stuff to myself and she is stubborn, always trying to do everything by herself. We are twins, so I guess we are bound to have things in common.

I know one thing; I will never forgive myself for hitting her with my car, but I'm torn, Had I not been drinking and driving I never would have found her in the first place since I had no clue she even existed. Yet I always end up beating myself up because I could have killed my only family member. I could have killed her before I ever had the chance to know about her.

Thank God she ended up being okay without serious injuries. Now she's giving me more family with her baby. She's had nothing but struggle in her life. I deserve every ounce of pain I received from that damn wreck.

Viktor eventually makes his way back out sometime during my shift. I am busy making another tray of martinis and when I turn around, notice him sitting in his usual spot. He doesn't say anything; he's being his normal quiet self and glaring at any guy who looks at me for too long. I never would have pegged him for the jealous type. After the endless refills of martinis I've made this shift, I could do with never making one again.

The club is brimming with thug-like guys tonight for some reason. I don't know what is going on, but Viktor chewed out his guard, Alexei, earlier. He looked so angry I thought he was going to strangle him. I don't like seeing his guard getting in trouble, but have to admit seeing Viktor with so much power draws me to him.

I'm busy finishing up my closing duties. I always have the early shift doing the prep work, so I get to leave earlier than the others. Grabbing my things, I notice a chick approach Viktor. She's all skanked up in a short dress and a pound of make-up. I suppose men probably find her pretty, whereas I like a more natural look. Viktor watches me as she whispers in his ear, giggling like a hyena.

Whatever, I don't have time for that. I roll my eyes and grab my soda in my Styrofoam to-go cup. I walk from behind the bar and he stands up, brushing off the girl and quickly makes his way to me.

The woman glares spitefully when she sees him come to my side. I'm not a hateful person but I can't help the smirk that appears on my face as we pass her by. My stomach flutters with excitement at the prospect of someone believing he's my man.

She steps in front of me with her hands on her hips, wearing a snotty expression. She obviously thinks she has something important to say.

Stopping abruptly, I look at her like she's lost her mind. She's crazy to just pop in front of people as they are walking, we could have run right into her. I have a feeling I'm not going to want to hear whatever she plans to say.

Viktor places his arm in front of me, pushing me back slightly and I shoot him a peeved look. He ignores it and commands the female's full attention just by his strong presence. His back muscles stiffen under his suit jacket as he stands in front of me.

"Get out of the way, Kendall," he says sternly, looking at her in irritation and demanding her immediate compliance.

She continues to poke her head around him and glare at me hatefully. My blood boils as I realize something; she has no valid reason to act this way toward me. I've had my fill of the ugly looks I get from people.

I push against his arm and get up close to her, right in her face. I may not like a man touching me, but after growing up in a few foster facilities, I've learned how to hold my own with a female. This is no exception; you put chicks in their place right away or you'll have issues with them forever.

"Can I help you?" I inquire, staring her down and flaring my nostrils.

Scrunching up her pointy nose, she sneers, "Uh yeah, I wasn't done talking to Viktor." I swear, I could just grab her nose and give it a good twist. I can't stand women who act like this. They think they're so entitled, when in reality, no one owes them shit. She's got a bad case of too many handouts.

I splay my hand beside me dramatically like I'm introducing the President or something. "Have at it then, sweetie pie."

I turn to Viktor and he shakes his head.

I glance back at her, wide eyed. "Well, Kendaall, guess you have your answer, huh."

I tend to draw my words out when I'm being sarcastic. It's a bad habit, but I can't seem to shake it plus it drives people crazy when I do it. I'm betting it will grate on her nerves also.

"Ugh!" She yells and shoves me backwards.

*Yeah, I don't think so, bitch.* I shove her back and she comes at me. Grabbing her shoulders, I head butt her in her pointy nose without hesitation. *That will definitely need surgery to look perfect again.* I'm not about to let her get a hit in, I've learned about that the hard way. Blood sprays from the gash and her nose bleeds heavily.

She shrieks and I can't help but snicker a little. Call it payback from some of us less entitled folks. People start pointing and surrounding us, ready to watch a fight. They're too late though, I know she won't bounce back from a hit like that.

Viktor gapes at me, surprised and maybe even a little impressed. He yanks me forcefully toward the back door, shouting for Sergei to grab the other girl. I'm sucked into the chaos and shouting; it feels like we're leaving the club. Everyone's voices melt together and I start to feel a little dizzy from the adrenaline rush.

I glance down to make sure I still have my stuff and notice I have blood sprayed all over the front of me. I have little drops all over my arm and shirt. Well, Emily's shirt. *Shit.* This is another reason why I don't buy nice clothes, well, besides not really being able to afford them.

"Come on, you little trouble maker," Viktor says loudly, threading our fingers together and pulling me through the throng of people.

We head out the back door toward the alley where he always keeps his vehicle parked. Sure enough, his car is there waiting with Spartak driving. How convenient.

"Wait, I have to get my car." I pull back from his grasp, slightly resisting but he holds on.

"No, Elaina, come on, just get in. I'll bring you back to get your car later. Curious people will start coming out that door, and we need to be gone. Things could turn very ugly and I refuse to submit you to that."

Spartak jumps out of the driver's seat quickly to open the back door and Viktor rushes me inside. I slide to the rear passenger side and he scoots in beside me.

"Go, Spar," Viktor orders and Spartak speeds away efficiently.

"Why are you in such a hurry? It was just a little blood." I glance at him curiously. From the way he acts in the bar I thought he was a bad ass.

"Yeah, it was just a little bit of blood you took from an important man's daughter. Christ, I'm pretty confident you broke her nose back there."

I open my mouth to respond and defend myself but he holds his hand up, signaling that he needs one minute. He pulls his phone out and quickly dials a number. I eaves drop the best I can.

"Alexei, have you left?"

"Okay, when you leave, call her father and schedule a meeting, offer my apologies."

He presses end and places his phone in his inside jacket pocket. The whole inside is lined in what appears to be silk or some other delicate material.

I sit still, staring at him and he turns to me, giving me his attention again. I wish I could have heard what Alexei was saying on the other end. It's the club's fault with all the loud music, my ears are still ringing.

"You may finish now," he says and reaches across me to grab my seatbelt. My heart quickens as he stretches it across me and buckles it. "Just like your sister," he murmurs and sends me a chastising look. "Tate always tells me that he has to buckle her in." He shakes his head again and smirks at me. I roll my eyes in defiance.

"I'm honored to be like my sister, she's a good person."

"I know she is. That poor girl has been through a lot. She will make a fantastic, strong mother."

"I know! I can't wait to be an aunty!" I grin excitedly. "I'm going to have the baby call me Tanta."

"I did not know you were German, you strike me closer to Russian."

"I don't know if I'm German or not, I just think it sounds cool. I haven't talked to Emily much about that part of our lives. Is that why you like me, because I look Russian?"

He shrugs and sits back in his seat a little. The smooth leather seats are out-of-this-world comfortable. I hope he doesn't just like me for my looks. That Kendall chick was pretty in her own face-painted-like-a-clown way.

"Who says I like you at all, Printsyessa (Princess)?"

"Well, the stalking factor sort of clues me in."

He chuckles loudly. "Stalking, huh? Is that what you call

it? I call it looking out for you. Kind of like a guardian angel. Yes, think of me as an angel."

"An angel? Yeaaaah right." I smile cheekily and wink.

"I know. I am not a very good man, maybe a dark angel. Nonetheless, I will care for you."

"But why, Viktor? I don't get it. Why you would care about me in the first place? It's been so long and you've gotten nothing from me. A failed date and some not so interesting family dinners with my sister, Tate and myself. I don't understand why you would still be giving me the time of day and not moving onto someone else by now."

I swallow deeply as he lightly runs his pointer finger along my skirt hem next to my thigh. He scoots back in; close enough to me that I can see the stress lines next to his eyes. My tummy flips over and over as I try to concentrate on not moving my leg away from him.

"You are wrong, you give me everything."

"What could I possibly give you?" I mutter in a disbelieving voice, studying his beautiful eyes.

"I'll settle for your heart," he purrs and smiles devilishly.

"Good luck with that one, bud." I chortle, raising my eyebrows and he laughs again. I always see him stressed and serious, it's nice that when he's around me he can relax and laugh. In fact, he always laughs and smiles a lot when we are together for lunch or whatever. I get all warm inside knowing that, I love it.

"Are you hungry?"

"No, not really, but I do need to go to my car."

"All right, if you insist. Spartak, please take us to her car."

"Yes, sir."

Spartak turns the car around and makes the short, uneventful drive to the employee area where my car is. I love being around Viktor but I don't think I can handle it if

265

he keeps playing with my skirt. My nerves are bouncing all over the place.

I start to reach for the door handle, ready to jump out as soon as we stop.

"Wait." Viktor voice is husky as he gently grabs my wrist. I glance down at his hand and he follows suit. I snatch my wrist out of his grasp and he looks at me, puzzled. Spartak opens my door and I quickly unbuckle, moving to get out.

Viktor grabs me again. I turn quickly to correct him, only I'm met with his mouth on mine before I even have a chance to process what's happening. I'm pulled to him so my shoulder and part of my breast are firmly resting against his strong chest.

Grasping my face, he keeps it turned to him so he can ravish me as he pleases. Returning his kiss fervently, I pour out all of my pent up frustration and aggression into the kiss. My stomach melts inside as his tongue thoroughly caresses mine.

Viktor gradually pulls away, kissing my top and bottom lips softly, chastely. I remain still, unmoving, relishing in the feeling of being touched and kissed and actually enjoying it.

He tenderly places his forehead on the side of mine, holding my face in place, and I keep my eyes closed. *Just enjoy this feeling a little longer.*

He whispers gruffly, "Now that – that is how our kiss should have been."

Vik places a tender kiss in my hair and I pull back. I look him in the eyes and nod minutely, staying silent. He literally took my breath away just now. My mind is reeling trying to process this feeling of wanting to do more right now instead of being scared as I normally would be.

Grasping my purse, I scramble out of the vehicle quickly and he lets me go. I was almost expecting him to hold me back. Maybe pull me in and kiss me again. Perhaps that's just what I wish would happen.

Turning to face him, I stand beside the car, peering at him dazedly. I take in his dilated eyes, chest rising rapidly and clenched fists making him appear even more delicious. I lean in, kindly saying, "Thank you for caring about me, Viktor."

"Good night, my lovely," he responds and grins as Spartak closes the car door and leads me to my vehicle. Minus the scuffle in the club, I'd say it was a very good night.

# FOUR

## Viktor

### one week later...

**I**'M STANDING IN THE CLUB CHATTING WITH ALEXEI about business when he immediately moves in front of me to intercept Nikoli. Niko's my brother's pet, the blond gorilla, who is storming toward me at full speed.

He would probably smash Alexei up quite easily, but my guards are loyal. They will take it as much as possible in order to protect me. I can't imagine what could possibly have Niko wound up in a tizzy, to come at me like this.

"It's okay, Alexei, he's Tate's man." I tap him lightly on the shoulder and he moves back to my side.

Niko yells loudly, his Russian accent stronger than mine, as he shoves in to me "You fuck!"

Backing up, I place my hands up in a placating gesture and breathe deeply, attempting to cool my rising temper before I do something to upset my little brother. Niko obviously has a death wish, pushing me like that.

"Nikoli! Touch me again and I will put you in a lake!" I growl sternly and he huffs angrily in return. "Did you jump Tate's leash? He would have your head if he were to witness your behavior right now."

"I am on no leash, ass face. Tate is my best friend, he would show me support." His outburst is defensive.

"No, you are his guard, Nikoli, and you are messing with business and family right now. Tell me, why are you wasting my time and why am I not drowning you right now?"

"Do you have any clue who Kendall is?"

"Of course I do, I have had business with her father in the past."

"Well, I hear from her sister you bust her nose. Bina not happy so I come to fix."

"I did not bust that troll's face. She was interfering with Elaina and me leaving the club. She started it and Elaina finished it. I spoke to her father the other day and everything is settled."

"How is it settled? I have not heard of this."

"He asked me to take her to lunch and apologize. I agreed. Not that it's your business. Who is Bina?"

"Sabrina Cheslokov, Kendall's younger sister."

"Ahh, I see, and you fancy her?"

He looks at me skeptically. "She is good friend."

"Very well. I understand. Is that all?"

"Yes, my apologies, sir, I didn't know it was fixed."

"I understand that." He starts to turn around. "Oh and Nikoli?" I call out calmly and he turns back to me.

"The next time you want to inquire, have my brother call. You approach me in such a manner again, and I will not hesitate to teach you manners. You forget my brother is not the only powerful man around here."

He looks taken aback for a moment then nods in

269

resignation. "Sir," he says and when I nod back he takes his leave.

"You okay, Boss?" Alexei turns to me, concerned.

He scans me from head to toe once Niko is out of the club. I pull on my jacket to straighten it out again, brushing the small creases with my hands. I can't stand not looking professional when I'm out in public.

"I'm fine," I grunt. "I'll let that one go." I rub my temples, trying to soothe my irritation, and continue, "I know what it feels like to be taken with someone and wanting vengeance when they are hurt."

"Are you planning on letting Knees know about what happened?"

"No, I know if I call my brother he will put Niko down and I don't want to take his close friend from him. Don't call him that in public either. That name is for our ears only and I don't want the wrong person getting wind of it. There are many Feds out there trying to figure out who matches up with that name."

"Yes, sir, of course. It won't happen again," he responds and goes back to watching the club.

"Would you like anything, Viktor?" my Printsyessa asks, distracting me from my anger.

Smiling slightly at the light she ignites inside me each time I hear her voice, I gaze at her, entranced by her stunning blue eyes. "No, lovely, I'm fine. I need to go handle a few things. Are you okay? I will leave Spartak for you."

"I understand you can't always be here, Viktor, and it's okay. Thank you for always hanging out, but go. I'll be okay and you don't have to leave Spartak if you need him."

"No, Elaina, I will leave him. I like knowing someone is here to help if you need anything. It gives me peace of mind and calms me."

"Okay, if you insist. I'm going to pretend he's my

personal assistant though, less of a stalker feeling. I have to go sit in on a meeting, so I'll see you later?"

"Of course, you can see me anytime you wish." She blushes and I grin in response. "Shall we have dinner?"

"I guess that would be fine, but nothing crazy. Just something simple, please."

"I promise I'll keep it tame." I had tried to wow her in the past and it was the opposite, she left and went home prior to even eating. I was embarrassed to say the least and haven't had the nerve to ask her for another chance until now.

"Okay, great," she replies with a beautiful bright smile.

Finally she agrees to dinner with me again. It's been months and this time I'm not screwing my chance up. Now I just have to figure out something she will like. I wish I didn't have to leave her right now.

It's Saturday morning, around eleven, and Elaina has to go to that boring staff meeting she mentioned. Then she'll be stuck here doing the weekend prep for the staff. She's off but comes in to get paid for a few hours of prep and stocking.

I came up with it so she would have an easy way to make the extra money I know she needs. She isn't aware that it's not a normal position and I prefer it that way. I wanted to pay her even more but the manager said it would be too obvious. The other bartenders were happy to give up some of their required side work. They are lazy goons wanting to slack off, nothing like my sweet Elaina.

Unfortunately I have to meet with Kendall today for our 'lunch date'. I don't want to, but I am keen on keeping the peace between our families. The best part about today will be getting to have dinner with Elaina. It will completely make up for having to subject myself to Kendall for an hour or so.

# Elaina

I'm sitting through this mind-numbing meeting listening to the manager basically telling us all how we are doing a shitty job and to quit slacking off. I work my butt off here so I'm pretty much ignoring him. As if dealing with the drunk assholes isn't enough, the manager has to be one too.

I stare, bored, at his bald little head and beady gaze. I don't understand how he even has this position. I wonder if he's related to the Masterson's and they just gave him the spot. I could do a better job with this place than he does. Aren't managers supposed to interact with customers and motivate their employees? Because we get none of that with him.

My phone beeps loudly with an alert in the quiet room and everyone in the meeting turns to me. *Shit!* I forgot to turn it on silent. I always do that and hate when this happens! Todd, the asshole manager, grunts and stares at me, irritated.

"Umm, sorry," I stammer. *Fuck!*

He shakes his head and turns back to resume talking. I roll my eyes defiantly; that idiot just makes me want to throat punch him, he's such a jerk. I'd bet your sweet ass his phone isn't on silent either.

Might as well check it out since everyone knows it went off anyhow. I swipe my finger across the screen and a new message pops up from an unknown number. I click on the message to download the attachment.

A few beats later after it finishes loading I'm staring at an image of Viktor and that snotty bitch from the other night.

Kendall's dressed to the nines. All slutted up in a snake skin print dress that dips so low down her chest her breasts would be showing in a strong gust of wind. She probably weighs an extra ten pounds with her obnoxious jewelry. Her painted on face is bright with laughter, and Viktor's smirking. They're seated in what appears to be a fancy restaurant and Kendall's arm is stretched across the table, resting on his wrist.

My anger swells up into my throat. I study Kendall's features closely, I'm glad to see her nose still looks bruised. *Ugh! Stupid bitch!* I know Viktor's not mine, but he's here for me almost every shift! Does this mean he sees her during the day? Then shows up here in the evening? I tell him nothing fancy, so he takes her to a nice place instead. Viktor has nerve to spew that shit about caring for me and then take Kendall to lunch.

He can go fuck a duck. I'm not meeting his ass for dinner. Fuck that shit. I look at the number again. I don't recognize it; I'm going to text it back.

> **Me**: Who is this?

> **Unknown**: No one

> **Me**: Why did you send this?

> **Unknown**: You should know the Devil you spend time with

> **Me**: Devil?

> **Me**: Why is he a Devil?

> **Me**: Hello?

I get no response and I feel my throat wanting to close up on me as if I've just been stung by a thousand bees. I stand abruptly in the middle of the meeting, "Fuck this." I choke the words out loudly and walk out.

Todd stands there with his mouth open, gaping at me. I don't care, won't be the first time I walked out of a place and probably won't be the last. I'm sick of these Russians.

I hurry to my car in the employee parking area. Slamming the door and revving the engine, I peel out through the gravel parking lot, spewing rocks all over Viktor's car that the guard uses and grinning manically as it happens.

Good, fuck that dude. I start to pass the liquor barn and flip a U-turn to go through the drive-thru. It dings loudly when I pull up to the window.

"Can I help you, ma'am?" I start to reply *vodka* and gag on my words.

No vodka and no Russians.

"Tequila. Give me a pint of José Silver, a pint of cheap rum and a two liter of Coke."

The dorky kid sniffs and nods. "Sure, just a sec." I wait impatiently, drumming my fingers on the steering wheel. "That'll be twenty-four dollars and fifty-one cents please."

I hand the guy twenty-five dollars. "Keep the change." I gesture to him, indifferent. He beams, showing off his acne-decorated cheeks and hands me my paper bag full of liquid pain killers.

I pull up in the parking lot and pour about a quarter of the Coke out my window onto the ground, then dump the pint of rum in it. Screwing the lid on tightly, I turn it upside down carefully, then back upright and rest the bottle between my legs for when I'm ready. I twist open the cap on the tequila and place it next to me in the cup holder, perfect for easy access.

Rolling my window back up, I take a large swig of tequila, swiftly chasing the tequila shot with my soda/rum mixture. It burns my throat and chest, but I delight in the feeling, knowing it will steal away my thoughts from me soon.

Hammering down on the gas, I head to my apartment. My poor Camaro's taking a beating today but I don't want to have a repeat of when I crashed my car. It's amazing that I'm even allowed to drive.

If it wasn't for Tate's lawyers I would have spent time in jail, paid a hefty fee and lost my license. I almost killed them. Tate got me off with a lot of cash. It's just something else to beat myself up about while I drink myself into a stupor.

I take another large gulp of my rum, swerving as I hold the big bottle. Pulling swiftly into my parking spot I'm surprised when hear a screech of tires. Glancing in the rear view mirror, I see Spartak's black car parked behind me, effectively blocking me in.

He jumps out in haste as soon as he slams the car in park, rushing to my window. Spartak beats angrily on the glass with his fist, glaring at me. I unlock the door and stagger out leisurely.

Spartak bellows, "Have you lost your mind?! Viktor will KILL me if something happens to you! What was that back there?" He's too close so I shove against him to back off some.

"Yeah right! Viktor doesn't give a shit!" I shout back at Spar and round the car to get my purse and bottles.

"You've completely lost it, woman, he follows you around like a love sick fool. You're the only person he cares for besides his family, the only one he's even remotely nice to."

"Is that so? Then why would he be seeing *her*?" I ask, the liquor starting to thrum through me.

He peers at me, bewildered, as if he doesn't have a clue what I'm talking about. "Pshh, whatever, it's not even worth it." I shoo him with my hand. Snatching up my things angrily, I take a swig of tequila and head to my apartment. Spartak stands next to my car, staring at me, worried.

I make it into my apartment, slam the door and lock the crappy locks. Screw them all, I'm going to forget about all men, about all of my problems.

I chug my soda mixture and love the dizziness that starts to show up to overtake my mind.

# Viktor

My phone vibrates and I check it immediately. Deep inside I hope it's Elaina. She's the only one I ever want it to be.

> **Spartak:** I don't know what happened, Boss. She's drinking and upset. She almost wrecked driving crazy. I'm at her apartment but locked out.

My heart speeds erratically as I read the message. What on earth happened? Elaina was just fine. God, I hope she's okay. I can't listen to this twat for a second longer, my princess needs me.

Clearing my throat loudly, I lean forward. "Please excuse me, Kendall, an emergency has come up. Sergei will finish out lunch with you, I am truly sorry." She shoots me a look mixed between worry and pouty.

"Oh no, okay, Viktor, I understand. Go, baby, and we can finish up another time. You will be missed badly," she replies in her whiny voice. God, Kendall disgusts me. She's so pretentious; I could never care for her no matter how much her father wants me to.

"Thank you for understanding," I answer and nod at Sergei. I'm just not interested in being here. I speedily make my way to the valet and give him my ticket. I slip him a hundred.

"Quickly, please."

He nods. "My pleasure, sir."

The valet rushes off and a few seconds later my Mercedes approaches. I get in swiftly and lay on the gas. She screeches on the smooth surface and I'm off like a rocket. I turn up the radar detector volume and get to Elaina's hole-in-the-wall as quickly as I can.

As I park next to Elaina's car and my sedan, I see Spar standing outside. He's leaning against her wall next to the door looking pale. Music is pouring out from her place.

I hustle out, slamming my door. "What's that?" I gesture to Elaina's door.

"I think it's called 'Superman' by an artist called Eminem. She's had it on repeat, so I Googled it."

"No, not the song, idiot, what's going on with her? What's the mess?"

"I don't know, sir. When she arrived she was drinking and talking about you not caring for her. I knocked after she went in, but she won't answer."

He looks distraught. It appears he has also come to care for her, probably from me having him always watching her. I'm glad; it means he will protect her better. On the downside, if he gets too close to her, I will have him put down.

I look up at the sky, exasperated. "Of course I care for Elaina, have you tried the door?"

"Yes, Boss, it's locked."

I nod and pound on her door a few times. I get no answer so I remove my jacket, hand it to Spartak and roll up my sleeves. I pull my pants legs up slightly and kick forcefully next to the locks.

The door splinters next to the lock, from the crappy quality. I kick once more and the door goes flying open. The music loudly thrums around me as I scan the living area. *God, I can only imagine what she's thinking while listening to this song, over and over.*

I find her in the kitchen, sitting at her table. She has her arms resting on the plastic surface with her head in her hands, gripping her hair tightly. Her shoulders shake; she appears so fragile, almost broken.

"Have you gone mad?" I boom.

She's surrounded by an empty rum bottle, a large soda and a tequila bottle that's about a quarter gone. Elaina freezes in her trembling and slowly glances up at me as if she doesn't believe she heard my voice.

"Well?" I bellow and gesture around me at her trashed apartment.

She glares crossly at me, spearing me with her gaze. Her face is swollen and she has hot tears running down her cheeks.

"What do you care, Viktor? Go back to your priorities," Elaina responds heatedly.

She's not fragile after all, broken maybe, but she's definitely ready for a fight.

"You are my priority, Printsyessa"

"LIAR!" she screams and throws the empty rum bottle at me. I duck to the side. She would have clipped me with the bottle had I not moved so quickly. This is new; I've seen her upset, but she's ready to castrate me.

"I do not lie! Stop this nonsense and talk to me!"

Elaina jumps up quickly, roars and charges at me. She goes ballistic, beating on my chest, and I let her. "Ugh! I hate you!" she screams.

Rearing back she punches me violently in my chin. My

temper ignites and I slap her. Not hard but enough to get her attention. I clench my hands into fists, trying to reel in my anger. The last thing I want to do is cause her any harm, but I won't stand for her hitting me like that.

"You hit me as a man, Printsyessa, I will hit you back! Now pull yourself together, Elaina! Enough of this. You want to talk, then tell me what this craziness is about and I will fix it."

She drops her hands and buries her face into my chest, sobbing. She's had way too much to drink and it's amplifying her anger.

"Please, lovely, tell me what is hurting you?" I ask, burying my nose into her hair.

The music stops and I glance over to see Spartak. He looks at me anxiously and leaves, closing the broken front door behind him.

"PaZHAALoosta, moy lyooBOF, gavaREETS, (Please, my love, speak)" I murmur in Russian.

She gasps, choking out, "You were with her and I just couldn't take it anymore. All men do is hurt me, and I just couldn't take it."

"With who?" I clasp her chin gently, tilting her face up to mine.

"The bitch from last week who I hit."

"Ahh, Kendall. I was at lunch trying to apologize. Her father is a powerful man and I was trying to keep peace, that's all. You thought I was seeing her?"

"Yea-yes, I mean the picture looked like it was more."

"Picture? You got a picture? Show me."

Elaina pulls her phone from her back pocket and hands it to me. I turn on the screen and the first thing that appears is a photo of me about an hour ago. Elaina's right, it does look like an intimate date between lovers.

"No, no, no, you are wrong. It really isn't how it looks. I

am so sorry. I was telling her about my brother's friend coming to her defense and she was laughing. Kendall's fake, she is absolutely nothing to me. Elaina, if there is anyone, it is only you. I swear it." After this conversation is over, I'm finding out who the hell took that photograph.

She leans back, looking at me for the first time like I'm not some evil creature set out to destroy her.

"You really care about me?"

"Of course I do, I've only been telling you this for months. However, I'm curious as to what you meant by men hurting you. Please elaborate."

Elaina's expression shutters and she shakes her head. "It's nothing. I was just upset. God, I can't believe I punched you. I'm so sorry."

"It's not a big deal; after seeing the picture I can understand why you were so angry." She nods, chewing on her lip.

Murmuring close to her ear, I ask, "Is it sick of me to think you look absolutely beautiful right now?"

She shakes her head and looks at the ground. I tip her face back up toward mine. After that fight, I'm spinning with need.

Bending slightly, I grab the outsides of her thighs, picking her up, and I wrap her strong legs around me. Elaina peers at me, taken aback for a moment before she leans in and kisses me passionately.

Eagerly I return her kiss, as I carry her to the couch. After stooping down and laying her gently on the squeaky furniture, I rest on top of her, trying not to squish her, and kiss her fervently.

I weave my hand in her silky blonde locks, clutching them tightly and pull her head back, exposing her neck. I lick and kiss, sucking, nibbling on her throat, getting lost a little more with each one.

Elaina squirms underneath and I thrust my hardness against her. Each little movement sends a powerful stroke of pleasure surging through my anatomy. It envelops me with need, causing my body to vibrate with hunger.

"Oh, Viktor, I want, I want," Elaina pants, breathless.

"Yes, Princess," I mumble and thrust against her again.

I grind my cock in a circle motion and she calls out loudly. I use my other hand to grasp onto her breast, lightly pinching her pebbled peak through her thin shirt and bra.

"Oh please," she begs and I push her shirt up quickly. I pull her breasts out of her bra, exposing sweet little peach nipples.

I grind my hardness into her again and she gazes at me with flames in her eyes. Elaina's so turned on she looks as if she would burn up. The only thing separating us are her little panties and my pants. I push her skirt up higher so I can get to the top of her cotton panties.

"Sweet, sweet, Princess." I groan as I rub her clit tenderly. She throws her head back, face and neck flushing. She looks astounding.

"Oh, Viktor, that feels so, so good."

I use my free hand to pull my cock out while rubbing her. She has her eyes closed so she doesn't notice. I slide her panties to the side. Her bare sex glistens with wetness and my cock throbs with want. *Yes.*

I place my tip to her opening and her eyes snap wide open, staring at me as I thrust forcefully into her extremely tight little hole.

"Ahhh, OH!" she yells and clutches onto my shoulders tightly.

Wow, she may be the tightest woman I've ever been with. I push in again slowly as her tender pussy squeezes me snugly, burying myself to the hilt. She gasps and a tear escapes.

I kiss it away and purr, "Shh, Princess, it's okay. This is how it's supposed to be, just you and me. You feel amazing."

"Viktor, I...I haven't." I interrupt her and kiss her soundly. I don't want to hear excuses or anything else. I just want to lose myself in her.

After a few beats Elaina relents, relaxing her muscles. She's still extremely tight but at least it's not painful to move anymore. She gets a little wetter and I bend her knee up, driving deeply. I feel each little squeeze her pussy makes and in return I pant, attempting to hold back from pounding her too roughly.

"Yes," she groans quietly and stares into my eyes with each full plunge.

I use my free hand to capture hers and pin them on the arm of the couch behind her head. Gripping her wrists tightly, I drive my dick in quicker, thoroughly lubricating it in her juices. *I'm going to make sure every piece of her remembers this moment.*

"You're so perfect," I whisper against her mouth, kissing her lips.

She makes little moans as her pussy drips, her wetness coating my cock and testicles. I move my hips in circles spreading her essence, grinding into her and stimulating her clit.

"Oh! It's feeling even better!" Elaina pants, gasping in pleasure and I feel the first strong pulses of her pussy starting to orgasm.

I suck strongly on her round peach peak, making it stiffen further. Her cunt spasms erratically, her walls clutch me fiercely and push me over the edge. I can't help myself; I drive into her forcefully a few times, gripping Elaina's thigh tightly. I know there will be bruises left but I can't stop, she feels too good. My dick throbs, pouring my cum so completely inside her.

"Oh, moy lyooBOF . (Oh, my love)" I grunt in bliss, completely sated, kissing her neck and cheek.

It takes a minute until I realize she's stiff as a board underneath me. Glancing down at her, Elaina appears as if she's seen a ghost. "What is it?" I ask kindly.

"Please, move," she whispers, lip trembling and her eyes pooling with water again. *What did I do now?*

"Alright, am I too heavy?" I grin at her, trying to lighten the mood. It just went from great to awful. She shakes her head and I climb off, puzzled.

Elaina glances at my cock and I stand proudly for her to admire my length. I know I'm not a small man and I'm proud of that fact. Her lip trembles again when she looks at it.

She scrambles up and walks to her room. I glance down at my cock, confused. He didn't do anything wrong, in fact Elaina seemed to really enjoy him for a while.

I don't understand why she's upset now. I thought we were past it. Only my cock isn't just coated in wetness and cum, but a little blood as well. *No way.*

Glancing up after her, I call down her small hallway, "Come here, Elaina."

"Please just leave. I don't want to talk anymore." Her declaration is shaky.

"Oh no, Princess, we are talking about this."

"I said just go, damn it! You got what you wanted, now leave."

I make my way down the hallway and stand in the doorway. Elaina's in her shoebox-sized bathroom, turning on the shower. I push my pants the rest of the way off and unbutton my shirt.

She's not going to get in that shower and wash me off her completely. I'll get in there with her so she can't try to forget what just happened. Elaina climbs in and after my shirt's off, I climb in with her.

She shrieks a little when she sees me. I guess she wasn't expecting me to climb in here. She's mad if she thinks I would just up and disappear.

"What are you doing in here? I told you to leave!"

"I'm not leaving you, I just took you, and it means you're mine now. You're mistaken if you think I would leave after something so important happening. I may be cruel but I will never treat you that way."

"Important? What's important?" she asks stubbornly, snatching up her loofah and dumping Caress soap all over it. It's a tan color and smells sweet like her skin did earlier.

"Elaina, I am not ignorant. I know I just took your virginity."

Tears start to rain down her cheeks. They mingle with the shower spray and she turns away from me. She scrubs harshly at her arms with her pink poof.

"Please, you will harm yourself," I say and clutch her arm softly, attempting to stop her. I take the loofah from her and begin to run it over her back delicately, cleaning her while she silently cries. It hurts me inside to see her so upset and all I can think about is how to fix what's eating at her.

"Please open up to me, I promise I will try to help with whatever is going through your mind right now." I put soap in my hands and gently massage her tense shoulders. I rub deep circles into the muscles, then up and down lightly.

Elaina leans her forehead against the white tile shower wall as she sobs. "You would never understand, Viktor."

"I might understand more than you can fathom; try me."

"I just have a thing with touching," she utters quietly and my hands stiffen. I spin her around carefully to face me and study her face closely.

"What do you mean, with touching, exactly? Please

elaborate a little."

She picks at her purple nail polish and stammers, "I don't-don't normally like to be touched. Now when you touch me, I crave it and I don't understand why. I have never wanted a man to touch me like I do you."

"Tell me, why were you never touched? Why was such a beauty as yourself, still a virgin?" I hold her shoulders tightly and look at her with genuine concern. She looks to the ground, tapping her fingers against her thighs and shakes her head.

After a short pause she chokes brokenly, "I'm dirty, Viktor," and I catch my breath.

She winces then brings her blue irises to meet mine. "I was touched too much before. I know you would never want someone who's so fucked up and I don't blame you," she murmurs. "I'm just so glad it was you and not him." She starts to sob again.

I remove my hands and tip her chin up to me.

"There is nothing dirty about you. You, sweet princess, are pure. You're kind, helpful, caring and beautiful. There is nothing sullied about you. You're telling me someone touched you wrongly?" Anger clouds my gaze.

Elaina nods slightly, bringing her fingers to her lips, upset and I lose it, punching the shower wall wildly. "Give me a name!" I roar.

"It was nobody. Please just forget I told you, I try to forget."

"A name, NOW!" I am furious.

She nods slightly, looking at the floor again, and whispers, "My foster father, Brent Tollfree. It was years ago, I'm okay now."

"Okay? This is not okay! Tollfree? Brent Tollfree – he has short brown hair and is about this tall?" I hold my hand up and she looks at me, perplexed.

She nods. "Yes. You know him?" she hisses, eyes widening in horror.

"Oh, don't you worry about Tollfree ever again. I will take care of this immediately."

"No! Viktor, you can't! You will get in trouble, please, he's a mean man. Just leave it, I've moved forward."

"Elaina, do you know who I am?"

She tilts her head, confused, "Of course, you're Viktor, you own businesses with your brother, including the club I work at."

"Princess, I am the goddamn king of the Solntsvskaya Bratva and it just so happens that scum, Tollfree, owes me a debt. Not only does he owe me money but your innocence. It's time I collect." I step out of the shower quickly and grab her blue towel to dry off with.

Elaina jumps out and swiftly grasps onto my bicep. She uses both hands as one of her hands can only hold onto about half of my bicep.

"Please, Viktor, don't get in trouble. This is my problem, not yours."

"Elaina, an hour ago you became mine, that means your problems became mine. I take care of dirty deeds, it's what I do. I hope you see I'm the one who's truly fucked up." I grab my cell phone out of my pocket to ring Spartak.

"Spartak, you need to stay with Elaina. Call Alexei and Sergei. Tell them to get here and bring the SUV."

"Yes, sir, consider it done."

I hang up and pull my white undershirt on. No point in putting my button up shirt, tie and jacket on. They'd just get dirty with the plans I have.

"Viktor, don't go. He's disrupted my life enough; please don't let him do this to us. Please tell me about the solinska thing."

"The Bratva. You don't know what that is?" I ask, baffled.

286

I thought everyone knew.

"No, I have no idea."

"Are you familiar with Mafia?" She nods her head. "Good, I'm basically the criminal version of the Russkaya Mafiya. It's called the Bratva."

"I see, and you're the leader?"

"Yes, is this an issue?" I retort gruffly.

"It could be. I don't want to live a life hurting people or worrying about you going to jail for the rest of our lives."

"You will hurt no one and you will not know anything about my business, it's not like you think. We can talk about this when I have time. I must go."

"You're making a mistake," she pleads, sadly.

"One thing you will learn, Elaina, is my business is *mine*. Someone has to be willing to make those types of mistakes, just so happens that person is me. You need to accept me for the type of man I am, because I will not change." I kiss her chastely and head out the door.

# Elaina

**M**Y MIND WON'T STOP REELING. THE ALCOHOL has pretty much worn off. I don't think I would've let Viktor go that far if I had been completely sober. I wouldn't change it for anything though. It was time and I'm glad out of everyone, it was him. I feel myself falling a little more for Viktor each time I see him. Now this happens and I know I'm going to be completely infatuated with him. Isn't that what normal girls do with the guy they lose their virginity to?

I can't believe I told him about Brent. I've never admitted that to anyone but with everything happening it just came pouring out. Surprisingly, I feel better now that I've got it out. It seems like any barrier I believed I held, eventually comes crashing down with him. Does it make me a horrible person that I don't feel an ounce of remorse for whatever Viktor's going to do to Brent?

I need to call Emily about this Mafia stuff. Surely she must know about Tate. I grab my phone and quickly close the photo that started this mess of a day. I bet Viktor forgot about it or he'd be looking for two people right now.

"Hello? Little sister?"

"Haha, shut it, Emily! You're the younger one."

"Nope. I'm waaay wiser, so that means I win."

"Whatever!"

"So how are you today?"

"Oh my gawd, today was crazy!"

"Why, what happened? Ouch! Baby pains, this kid is a kicker."

"Aww, I love feeling the little one kick. So yeah, crazy day. With Viktor, no less."

She gasps and lets out a little squeal. My sister's been pushing for Viktor and me to get together for months. She's totally on his side and I've been fighting every step of the way. I should have just given in.

"Tell me!"

"Okay, so what's this Mafia business?"

"He told you?!"

"He said it's the Bratva, like Mafia."

"Yeah, not just Bratva, Elaina, he's in charge of all of it. He took over for his uncle. It's kind of a huge thing, you'll learn over time. This life can get crazy but it's also a tight group. Tate and Viktor watch each other's backs and they have a ton of men to protect them."

"So you did know about all of this. Why didn't you say anything about it, ever? I really don't know what to think about it. I don't know if I can handle it like you do."

"I couldn't tell you, I'm sorry but I had to respect Tate's discretion. Of course you can do it. You're as awesome as I am, so you will be fine."

"Haha, thanks. Pretty sure I already know I'm full of awesome though. Anyhoo, I love your face, can we eat together soon?"

"Of course, I would love that! I love your face too."

"Bye, Em."

"Bye, little sister."

I hang up and sit in the middle of my bed. I'm glad she has faith in me being able to live that life, because I'm not so sure. Me and the Mafia? What kind of things does Viktor even do? I stare at my phone, hoping for it to ring with his number or for his nightly text, only it doesn't come.

# Viktor

I'm so angry inside after what she told me, I feel like I have lava coursing through my veins and I can't stop shaking. I had Spartak call my guys because I know I'm too mad to drive. I will probably wreck or kill someone if they cut me off.

My guards show up in the black SUV. I don't think I've ever been so pleased to see them. The windows are so heavily tinted I can't see inside the vehicle. Black is better when transporting bodies, fewer people will see it or pay attention to it at night.

"Stay with her," I bark at Spar and gesture toward Elaina's apartment.

"Yes, sir." He nods and immediately walks toward her door as I quickly jump into the SUV.

Scooting into the middle, I glare at both of my guards. "Alexei! Get Brent Tollfree."

He stares at me in the rearview mirror for a beat, then nods. "You're coming with us, Boss?"

"Of course not, drop me at the warehouse and bring him to me. Make sure he is alive."

"Certainly, sir."

We drive the twenty minutes out of town to one of my

warehouses and stop at the one with barely anything inside. It's always deserted unless I pay a visit and it's easier to clean up messes when there isn't much there. The whole place is pretty run down, but it gets the job done for what I use it for.

They drop me off and I give my men their orders to get back as quickly as possible. It's going to feel like ages until they get back. Hopefully Tollfree isn't too messed up, I will thoroughly enjoy being the one inflicting the pain.

Frustrated, I plop down in the single metal chair in the building and drink my vodka straight from the bottle. I'm angry. So fucking mad right now, I don't trust myself to not kill him too quickly if I'm sober. I know the alcohol will slow me down a little and I want to drag this out for a while. I'm going to make him hurt.

I swipe through pictures and stare at the beautiful photos I have of Elaina on my phone. I want her face fresh as I rip this idiot apart. She doesn't know it, but I have many photos of her. Each time she was busy not paying attention and the light would hit her just right I would snap a new one.

I had to have something each night to keep me sane while she was ignoring my advances. Now, she seems to finally realize I'm serious. I wonder if she knows that I'm invested enough I plan to keep her forever? If not, she'll figure it out.

One thing that runs in my family is stubbornness. My father, Tate and I all have it. If we want something bad enough we will usually make it happen. The only reason my father was stopped, was because Tate and I teamed up to squash him.

Taking in her gorgeous blonde hair, I stroke the photo like a stalker might. I guess in a sense I am a stalker since I follow her around like a fool. The long, pretty locks remind me of that scum at the bar. I wonder if he reminded her of Tollfree and that's why she freaked out.

My rage grows all over again and I impatiently check my watch. Storming angrily over to the square sterile table we use for information extraction, I lay out my preferred tools. I glance over, pleasantly surprised when I'm interrupted by Alexei and Sergei dragging Tollfree in by his ankles.

"He's out?"

"Yes, sir."

"Good, strap him to the table," I order, nodding to the metal brackets and cuffs attached to the table. I enjoy using cuffs so that way if they squirm, it cuts their wrists and ankles. In the end it inflicts even more pain on them.

Alexei and Sergei drag him over and drop him roughly on the table. I walk over and supervise as they clip him in.

"Salts, Sergei."

"Sir." He complies and hands them to me.

I open the small container carefully, placing it under Tollfree's nose. It only takes a second for him to jerk awake, eyes wide, ready to plead.

"Save it." I grab a rag and stuff it in his mouth.

"I want to hear you scream, not your words. Your muffled whimpers will suit me just fine." He shakes his head rapidly at me and tries to plead through the rag.

"I told you when we met that I collect what is owed to me. You hurt someone I love, and that's the biggest debt you can ever owe me."

"Na! Na!" he shouts through the rag.

"No?" I question and he shakes his head. "Ah, but you are mistaken. The answer is yes. You see, I love a sweet little blonde. She reminds me of a fairy, with her long, wispy hair and short legs." He gazes at me, confusion clouding his features.

"I heard you like to touch young girls," I growl and his

eyes widen again but this time with a sense of recognition.

"First off, we're going to remove any sense of manhood you may possess, and then I'm going to remove most of your blood. To finish you off... well, I'm going to let you drown. All the way until you sink to the bottom of the lake out back." I nod behind me, toward where the lake is.

By the time I finish with the details, he has tears openly flowing down his face. Good, I hope this trash is terrified. He should be because this is going to hurt, that much I can promise.

I nod to Alexei and he cuts strips in Tollfree's pants so we can easily remove them. "Gloves," I snap and Sergei rushes to get me a pair.

Grasping my tongs tightly, I approach Tollfree's midsection and his shriveled penis. I snap the tongs together a few good times, causing Tollfree to shriek loudly and attempt to move away.

"Aghhhhhh!" he cries out, quickly learning that the cuffs will slice into his wrists, and I chuckle for the first time in hours.

I snatch his penis up in my tongs and he goes deathly still. I have to breathe deeply in order to stop myself from squeezing them too forcibly and snap his penis off. I nod to Alexei and he approaches with a small blow torch.

"Hold the tongs; I want to do the burning."

Alexei grabs the tongs in one hand, squeezing Tollfree's penis and making him cry out again. I grin maniacally as I get close to him with the torch. It's going to smell horrible and look disgusting, but my princess deserves to be avenged with every ounce of pain I can cause him.

Carefully aiming the flame at his penis, I watch as the skin burns off it until Alexei drops the tongs. My ears ring with the soul shattering shrieks of a tortured man.

"Shit, Boss, sorry, but they got too hot," Alexei confesses

sheepishly.

"It's okay, it was time. He's shit himself, and I want to let him sit in pain for a little while before I continue."

I'm amazed he didn't pass out. Anytime I do penis torture and the meat begins to bubble, the person usually passes out, well, eventually. This is working to my advantage nicely.

I step outside and take a few swigs of my vodka. I need some fresh air. The burnt skin smell is disgusting and makes me nauseous.

"Boss, do you want to tell us what this is about?" Alexei approaches me timidly. He can read my moods pretty well, so he knows I'm in the mood to slaughter someone if they get in my way.

"Not particularly, but I will. He hurt Elaina when she was a little girl." They both look surprised. Sergei then immediately looks angry once he processes what I mean.

"Nooo! That sick fuck!" Alexei, my more emotional guard, whispers, astonished.

I nod in agreement. "Yes. Now do you two understand fully why I must do this?"

They both agree solemnly. Good. I don't care what they say about it anyway. I have already made my mind up.

I head back inside with them both close on my heels. Sending Tollfree an evil smile as he lies there in his own shit, sobbing. I have no sympathy for him, he deserves so much more.

"Now, you have heard of the Bratva bleeding people, yes?" I stare at him as he shakes his head. "No? Okay, well let me enlighten you. It is a signature of Bratva, bloodletting the idiots who cross them. It makes you weak. Only I don't do it the old fashioned way with a little straw. No, I do mine a little differently."

I pull out a large steak knife. I grasp his arm and saw a

few large cuts in it, and then I repeat it with each leg and his other arm. When I'm done he has eight large, sawed in cuts on his limbs and his blood trickles out.

"There! Much better," I chortle, throwing my knife in a five gallon bucket full of bleach.

"The dick burning was for my princess, the blood for the Bratva and next, the drowning. That's for my own anger you have caused by making my love doubt her purity."

I sit back in my chair, relaxing, and watch him bleed.

I have no concept of time. I just wait until he is weak, but alive enough that he will still suffer when drowning. I nod to my men and they get him up, tying his legs and wrists with brown rope. Alexei hoses the shit off him with the portable pressure washer, that way he doesn't stink up the SUV. Afterwards, they load him up in the back of the vehicle.

We gradually head down to the docks. My men are very cautious, completely checking out our surroundings on the way. Sergei parks deep in the shadow of one of the buildings.

"Boss?" Alexei questions.

"No, I want to do it alone."

He nods, understanding what this means to me. I climb out using the lit running board step. Alexei opens the hatch, illuminating the back trunk area.

I pull all of the concrete weights out. Their heaviness forces me to take my time. I place the weights and rope down on the dock for later.

Rushing, I return excitedly for the body. This will probably end up being the kill I appreciate the most out of any other. Hauling him over my shoulder, fireman style, I carry him closer to the water.

Warm, syrupy liquid coats my fingers, bleeding onto my

hands and drips to the cold cement below. The sky is black, the stars and moon hiding, helping me complete my task. The calming *swoosh* of the waves mask my noises as I drop the lifeless body to the ground to finish securing weights to his limbs.

He's almost dead, but not quite. I can't help the elation I feel in the pit of my stomach. I've gotten used to this part over time and it's now become my absolute favorite.

The small pier is deserted and the men on the docks know to mind their own business. There aren't many around here at this time of night. No one wants to be involved with the Bratva, especially when its leader is dumping bodies. They keep their concerns to themselves, knowing they would be next on my list.

I relish the feeling of such power. I never said I was a good man, I said I clean up messes. I'm the dark angel, waiting to take care of the dirty deeds of the Mafiya.

I was the smart one, the one strictly handling the money of the business. I didn't want anything to do with this life, and then my uncle gave me my first taste of disposal. I don't necessarily enjoy the kill itself, but I love watching them sink into the deep, murky waters of the lakes surrounding us. This kill though – this one I will enjoy every single moment of.

He stares at me in a daze and I can't help but smile.

"You asked for this when you touched that innocent little girl. She couldn't defend herself, so now I come for you, and here you are, helpless. I hope you experience this feeling up until the moment death comes to collect you." I end my speech by spitting on the trash.

I stand up and kick him, rolling the weights along until he eventually tumbles into the deep, dark water. I want every last minute leading up to his death to be miserable.

# Elaina

### three days later...

I CAN'T BELIEVE IT, I STILL HAVEN'T HEARD FROM him. I fucking knew he wouldn't want me once he found out about me and my baggage. It's just like Stephanie all over again, except this hurts worse. I've been sitting in my apartment moping and waiting for him for three days. It's time I got up and looked for a new job.

I grab my purse and make my way outside. Spartak is in his car, reading a book. I walk over and peer in at the book. *Pride and Prejudice.* Hmmm, I never would have guessed. When I knock on his window lightly he jumps, startled, and turns to me. Cocking his eyebrow, he rolls down the window and grins.

"Time for work?"

"No, what are you doing out here?"

He looks at me, puzzled. "The same as always." He shrugs "Reading new books."

"Viktor didn't call you off?"

"No. Mr. Viktor would kill me if I left."

"How long have you been here?"

"For three days."

"Three days?!" I gasp, astonished. "Where have you gone to the bathroom, and what about eating?"

"I used the bushes and I have food in the trunk."

"You haven't left at all?"

"Nope."

"Holy shit! Come on."

"Where?"

"You're taking a shower at my place."

"No, thank you. The boss would get upset and a shower is not worth risking my life over."

"What on earth could he get angry about?"

"About me being inside your apartment."

"Oh! Gotcha! Okay, well then you stay alive and stinky and I will drive around looking for a new job." I smile and shrug.

"What's wrong with your old job?"

"I walked out in the middle of it the other day."

"Doesn't matter, Tate owns it and Viktor runs it for him. You could go in there and sit on the bar stool and you'd still get paid."

I look at him, stunned. "Are you serious?"

"Yes, ma'am, I'm serious."

"Well, then I'm going to work and I'm wearing my shorts," I respond tartly. He beams a smile and nods.

So Viktor hasn't called me, but he keeps his guy on me and I still have my job. I really don't understand him at all and I ponder this as I head toward my car.

I arrive to work and everyone acts normal, like I just had a day off or something. It feels like I'm walking around in the Twilight Zone. Maybe I really could do whatever I want and not get in trouble. Nice.

I clock in and start my regular set up. Might as well; I have nothing else to do, but worry about *him* and I will lose my head if I sit and dwell on it all day. I feel sort of guilty. I bet Hawk was dragged over here to cover the shifts I've missed. I'll have to apologize the next time I see him.

An hour or so goes by and I hear keys clink on the bar. Turning, I'm faced with Viktor sitting in his normal spot, grinning at me as if he hasn't been absent from my life for half the week. I don't know whether to be excited or angry right now.

"Can I have my usual?" he murmurs and my pussy clenches when I hear his voice. I swallow and nod.

I go through the motions of making his vodka-seven with lime wedge. I place it before him on top of a bar napkin and he smiles sweetly at me. Bastard has some nerve popping up like everything's just dandy.

"Ugh." I huff, irritated, and turn to finish my shift duties. The more I do now, the less I'll have to worry about later.

"You are displeased with me?"

Rolling my eyes, I sigh and look at his gorgeous face. "I'm upset that once you found out about me you left." I shrug as I reply bluntly.

He looks taken aback for a moment before he adopts a serious expression. "I didn't leave you. I told you I was taking care of the problem. I would never just leave you without a purpose. I had a very big issue needing to be handled, so I took care of it."

"You took care of it? How exactly do you take care of something like that?" I ask, exasperated.

"You will never be faced with him again for the rest of your life," Viktor says proudly.

"Well, that's a relief I suppose, but I hadn't seen him in a long time anyhow. I told you I just want to forget that stuff."

"Well, now it's forever. You won't ever see him again." Just the way he says it makes me suspect something entirely different than what I had originally imagined, like him moving away or something.

"Tell me what you did." I am beginning to get scared for Viktor's safety and freedom.

"My business, Elaina, is not yours about that kind of stuff. It's my job to protect you and know that I am protecting you as much as I can." I nod and bite my lip.

"So you didn't leave me then, you're still around for me?"

"I'm right here, watching you, wanting you, as I have since I first laid eyes on you." He states all this in a raspy voice as he runs his eyes all over my body, pausing on my breasts and hips.

"Okay, good."

"Good, as in I can stop chasing you?"

I shrug. "Maybe, but only if you like me."

He laughs loudly. "Ah, Princess! Of course I like you." I give him a large smile, recalling our conversation in his car when he kissed me.

"I kind of like you, too."

"Oh, so finally you concede, and admit it." He chuckles and I smile back at him.

"Hey, bar wench!" We're interrupted by a whiny voice. I swear I shoot daggers as I face Kendall.

"Yes, whore?" I retort in a nice, chipper voice. I want to test this theory that I can do what I want and Viktor will let me keep my job.

"Whore?" she screeches and I wince. "You have some nerve! Viktor, you see how this trash speaks to me?"

He rolls his eyes, grunts and looks over at me. I shrug.

"Look, Mob Candy, get your painted ass out of here." I sneer back at her.

"Ugh! Viktor, Daddy will hear about this!"

He stands and faces her. "Kendall, get out of my club. You just insulted my bar manager who happens to also be my princess. You can leave or I will have my men remove you."

Viktor nods at Sergei who comes to intercept her and get her to leave. She pouts at Sergei, but he still escorts her to the door. Viktor turns back to me and I could maul him right now. I can't believe he stuck up for me and said that stuff to her.

"You're pretty awesome," I state and smirk at him.

"Oh, you think so?" He smirks back, showing off his sexy dimple.

"So I'm your manager and princess, huh?"

"If you want the position, it's yours."

"To be your princess?"

"Yes, and the club manager, since you won't let me fully take care of you."

"You're serious?"

"I am completely serious. Now, what will your answer be?"

"Of course it's yes!" I yell, leaning over the counter and planting a kiss on his lips.

He freezes, surprised, then pulls me over further on the counter and takes my mouth in a toe-curling kiss.

# Viktor

"But what about Todd?" she asks after kissing me soundly and completely surprising me.

"Don't worry about him, if you want the job then I can send him to my father's club with Hans."

Hell, I will even buy Elaina a club if she would like one. I know she would never go for it, but I really would. I want to make her life easier any way I can.

"Yaaay! Okay, thank you so much!" she says excitedly and jumps up and down a few times. I chuckle at her enthusiasm. She works very hard and deserves it.

"Now, can we go to dinner since you are the boss here?"

"I think we can celebrate!"

Elaina lets the other bartender know she's leaving, grabs her things and meets me at my stool.

"Mind if I?"

I gesture with my hand and wrap my arm around her waist to pull her close as I stand up. She freezes up for a moment, her body going still like a statue. I grasp her face and turn it up to mine, gazing tenderly in her eyes. I wish she could see it in the way I look at her. She needs to realize I would never hurt her or touch her in any unwanted way.

Elaina studies me for a minute and I feel her muscles start to relax. She smiles and kisses me softly. To see her so happy makes my heart feel so full, as if it could burst. I hold her closely and nod to Alexei so he knows we are leaving.

We make our way out the back door to my car. Elaina lets loose a blood-curdling scream, making chills crawl up my spine. She covers her face with her hands, ducking behind me.

I scan the area but notice nothing amiss at first. I look to the driver's seat because Sergei should have the door open for us, only I don't see him. I diligently look over everything again.

Elaina whimpers softly behind me and I reach back, squeezing her hand, attempting to comfort her. The bright light glints off the Mercedes and for the first time I notice the front of the vehicle. Sergei is laid out on the hood, throat slit, covered in dark blood.

I walk toward him, noticing something on the windshield. The club door bangs as it slams closed. I jump a little, ready to protect Elaina with my life if necessary. Twisting, I find Alexei, looking at me, perplexed.

"Shit! Boss?" He moves to do an area search.

"No. Stay with Elaina." I growl at him and remove my gun, screwing on my silencer. I'm going to kill any of them that I find still here. They have nerve, coming at *me*, the king of the Bratva. I will feed each one to the fish if necessary. Whoever did this deserves to hurt. They will pay; I will make sure of it.

I carefully walk around the car and scan the surroundings but I find no one. I return to the front of the vehicle, and move closer to check on Sergei. He is very much dead and across the windshield in his blood, is smeared WAR.

It's sloppy, so I know they were in a hurry to get out of here, as they should have been. This club is crawling with my men. I can't believe there wasn't any other guards back here with him.

Just when things start to look up with Elaina, I am faced with this. I can't let her get hurt in any of this nonsense. I pull my phone out and call Spartak.

"Sir?"

"Spar, bring the car around back quickly!"

"Yes, sir!"

I hang up, watching our surroundings the best I can. I make my way back to Elaina. I keep her behind me against the club wall just in case someone comes at us, I can protect her better this way.

"Poor, poor Sergei!" She sniffles, grasping onto the back of my suit jacket with one hand.

"I know. We need to call his family. I will make sure they are taken care of, it's the least I can do."

"He has a family?" she enquires gloomily. "God! This is all my fault." She starts to sob.

"No, lovely, this is some demented little girl stirring the pot to something she has no idea about. You did nothing wrong and I can assure you, this will be handled."

I can't believe this is happening. I have to call Tate and get everything prepared just in case this really is war. If so, none of us are safe.

"Alexei, put Sergei in the trunk for now and transport him to the warehouse until we can arrange a proper burial for him. Get the car cleaned up and trade it in for a new one." I'm not a big enough bastard to make him continue to drive the same car around. It's bad enough he's stuck cleaning it up.

"Okay, Boss." He glowers at the car, furious, upset that his workmate was murdered.

"I apologize, I know he was your friend."

"He was a good man, Boss."

"I know. You both are," I answer solemnly as Spartak arrives with the other car.

Elaina and I climb in, hastily shutting the door and Spartak drives off immediately.

"Duck down, Elaina." I push her head down as we exit the alleyway.

You can never be too careful. I want her safe and I wouldn't be surprised if someone is waiting for us to leave. Spar shoots me a wary look in the rearview mirror.

"Spartak, take us to my house, then go back with one of the guys to sweep Elaina's car. Use caution, I wouldn't doubt it if they did something to it."

Elaina gasps and turns to me, surprised, "My car! I can't lose my vehicle, Viktor!"

"You won't lose it, Elaina, that's why Spartak will check on it. He can even drive it elsewhere if you would like."

Nodding somberly, she leans on me, worried.

I tap his shoulder lightly, murmuring quietly, "Pick her car up and park it in my garage."

"No problem, sir." Agreeing, he faces forward and I clutch Elaina tightly to my chest.

What on earth am I getting this beautiful creature into? I promise I will do everything in my power to make sure she doesn't witness that sort of thing again. She has had enough negativity in her life. I don't need to add to it.

The car ride is eerily silent. It feels like we drive for forever. I busy myself by concentrating on what needs to be done. I'm sure Elaina's playing that scene repeatedly in her head while Spartak gives his full attention to our surroundings. He's on high alert because you never know who or what could be coming next when you're in a war.

# SEVEN

# Viktor

**I** **OPEN THE GARAGE WITH MY CELL PHONE APP AND** we pull in. After the club incident, I can't help but glance all around, scanning everything for a potential threat. I want every corner and bush checked; I'm paranoid and it makes me even more irritated. I've gone through a mini war before with my uncle, years back. Many people died pretty gruesome deaths.

Leaning closer to Spartak I say sternly, "I will rearm the system. You take the guard room." I can't help my tone, I'm tense and angry. I need to release this pent up energy before I shoot someone.

"Thank you, sir," he replies, unfazed, and heads inside first to do a sweep.

My home is very secure but we take every precaution when something like this pops off. You can never be too careful. I'm fortunate to have good men on my side, even if I am hard to work for sometimes.

I mumble quietly, "Come, lovely," and grasp Elaina's hand.

Swiftly, I lead her down the plain hallway toward my office. There are no pictures or little decorations, just light grey walls and dark hardwood floors. It's simple and tidy, just the way I prefer.

Undoing my shirt buttons and cuff links the best I can with one hand, I prepare. There's only one thing I can think of right now to get me to calm down, and that's Elaina. The only decision I want to have to make right now is whether to feast on her cunt or spank it.

"Your office?" she inquires curiously and I smirk.

"Yes, Princess." I growl, focused and eager, removing my jacket and shirt.

Her eyes widen and she takes a step backward. "But, I—"

Interrupting her, I reach out and bring her close to me, taking her mouth with mine. Her hands land on my chest and I pull her tight against my body. I know she has to feel my hard cock resting against her tummy. Now's not the time to move sluggishly. I needed her twenty minutes ago, and I need her even more so now.

I walk backwards, pulling her along. Eventually I bump into my desk and stop, perching on the edge. Releasing her mouth, I loosen my belt buckle and unbutton my pants.

Elaina leans back, lips red and glistening, her eyes lit up with fire. "What do you want, Viktor?" she asks me boldly and my cock strains against my boxers.

Leaning up slightly, I push them off my hips so they pool at my feet. She licks her lips and I weave my hands through her smooth, Cinderella-like locks. I push her down easily until she rests on her knees, staring up at me with her bright blue, curious irises.

I grin at her as if she's my prey. "Kiss it," I purr and she gulps, staring at my dick, intimidated.

Releasing her hair, I tip her chin up and press my thumb between her soft lips. She sucks automatically so I pull her chin closer. She leisurely releases my finger, coated in her sugary lip gloss. I bring it to my own mouth, copying her and sucking the sweetness off.

Elaina gasps slightly, nose flaring and leans in, taking my throbbing member into her mouth. "Yes, like that," I mutter huskily, pleased.

I curl my toes inside my shoes, attempting to stop the craving to grab her hair roughly and thrust until she chokes on my cock. I can just imagine her shocked expression and the tears that would float down her cheeks afterwards. *Mmmmmm.*

I know I have to be vigilant with her needs and not give her too much time to think. If she thinks, bad memories will creep in, and I want to steal every negative thought away from her. I snatch her up swiftly by her chin. She squeaks as she stands, surprise clouding her features.

I huff, "It was perfect, love," and turn her hastily so she's now perched on the desk, with me standing instead.

Her skirt hikes up, offering the perfect little glimpse of her white panties. Taking two fingers I slide them over.

"Viktor!" She gasps against my mouth when I check how wet she is.

Rubbing softly in circles, I prime her pussy, coating it in wetness. Her body trembles with need each time I apply pressure to her clit. Gazing into her eyes, I stop, pulling my hand back slightly to spank her plump little pussy lips three times.

"Huhhh!" Elaina mewls, crinkling her eyes in pleasurable pain, and I grin.

I dip my finger in her nectar, covering her clit in it. Once it's nice and saturated, I pull my hand back, spanking her pussy two more times, then grind my palm back and forth into her clit, relentlessly at the end. She leans forward suddenly, resting her head on my chest as she cries out. Her cunt soaks my fingers in her cum.

I draw back, thoroughly turned on, pumping my dick with her juices a few times. Her cheeks flush as she stares at me hungrily.

Gripping her hip in one hand, I line myself up and shove my cock forcefully in her tight pussy.

"Oh shit!" Elaina moans loudly, spurring me on and I thrust in deeper.

"Just lean back, love, and let me take that cunt like I want to."

She relaxes her body, lying down and I shove her shirt up so her breasts are free. I don't want sweet right now, I want to fuck. Hard.

Placing my large hand in the middle of Elaina's chest, I hold her down securely on the hefty cherry desk. Her breasts sway with each hard pump. Her nipples are stiff and begging for my touch.

"Oh my!" she mewls loudly.

I'm sure Spartak can hear each little noise from her, but I don't mind. Pulling her fingers back to my mouth, I suck strongly on each digit making her pussy pulse snugly over and over. Each time she clenches, my cock screams with want.

I pound into her savagely, moving my hips in an up and down motion, trying to reach her perfect place, her sweet spot. With each up motion I shake the desk and make the wood creak. Her mouth gapes as she watches me suck and release each of her fingers.

Snarling, I attempt to hold myself back. She just feels too good and I want her so badly. Her body sings when I touch it. It's like her skin is waiting to be pressed against mine and when it finally happens we both ignite.

"If your pussy doesn't behave, I'm going to end up finishing a lot quicker than I want to," I tell her. As soon as the words leave my lips she calls out my name, her chest heaving as she regains the breath stolen by the strong orgasm.

Thoroughly spent, she stares at me in a daze as I grip her breast and spill myself deep inside her.

"Perfection," I utter, replete.

Elaina blinks as if coming out of a daze and moves to get up.

"Stay." I shove her back down and she huffs as she shoots me an irritated look. She doesn't like it when I boss her around.

I gently pull myself out of her, shivering at the aftershock zing of sensations. I grin and quickly make my way to the bathroom that's connected to my office and get a warm, wet wash cloth. It's my cum dripping out of her, so the least I can do is clean it up for her.

"What are you doing, Viktor?"

"I'm cleaning you. Would you prefer to take a bath?"

"No, thank you, but I can do that."

"Nonsense, Princess," I grumble and start wiping her skin softly with the white fluffy towel.

She scrambles away slightly "No, please stop." She covers her breasts.

"What's going on? I was absent not even two minutes. What changed between then and now?" I gesture to the bathroom, confused.

"I just like a little privacy. I would like to do that on my own. You're watching me and cleaning me."

"Yes, I want to take care of you. Why is this a problem? Of course I'm watching you, you're stunning."

"Please. The watching and touching," Elaina replies

softly, bowing her head.

I let loose a growl, getting exceptionally angry. "The touching!" I yell, "Fuck!" Throwing the towel down beside her I storm a few steps away. "That *thing* will never touch you again! You want to know why?" I step closer, clenching my fists. I feel as if I could rip apart my office right now. "You know why? I'll tell you why! Because I watched that pathetic *thing*, sink to the bottom of the lake after I burned his tiny penis off with a fucking blow torch! So don't you cringe from me! I am NOTHING like him! I have waited, *months* for you! Months! I will never harm you." I rip my hands through my hair, pulling harshly, and I cringe, angry, defeated.

I rush back to the bathroom for a large towel, thrust it at her and turn away. Not because I am upset with her, but because I am so irate at the thought of someone causing her any type of harm. I will make it my life's mission to keep her safe. To an extent I already have been protecting her. But now, *now* she is mine. I have had every piece of her and I don't intend to ever give that up to anyone else. If I need to have five men on her at all times to make sure nothing ever happens to her, I will. I will flatten whomever crosses her in life if I need to.

She will learn that she is stronger now. She not only has me beside her, but behind her as well. I will always come for her when needed and she needs to realize that no one will ever hurt her as long as I have breath.

Hearing sniffling, I turn to quickly glance at her. She has a tear tumbling down her cheek and it makes my gut clench. "Lovely, please talk to me, please tell me what I can do to fix it?" I say softly, gently.

She looks at me with heartbreak in her eyes, "That's just it, Viktor. You can't fix it. I'll always be broken."

"No, Elaina, you are strong, you know why?"

She bites her bottom lip and shakes her head.

"You, my love, are strong, because not only did you survive, but you escaped. Instead of staying and succumbing to that life, you worked and left as soon as possible. You, Princess, you are an inspiration. I am proud to have you." I say this genuinely, staring at her in awe, full of love and respect. *How can she not know how wonderful she is?*

She sits silent, processing everything I said and I leave to my bedroom. She really does need some privacy to pull herself together. I know she will, she's stubborn and that stubbornness has kept her strong over the years.

I'm standing in the middle of my bedroom in my boxer briefs after my shower when Spartak calls me through the intercom system.

"Mr. Masterson?"

"It's okay, Spartak, I'm alone."

"Right, well, boss, we had an issue come up."

"Go on."

"We found a note and some pictures of you with Kendall at lunch on Miss Elaina's car and a mini starter bomb was wired."

"Spartak, what did I tell you about calling her by her first name?"

"I apologize, sir, but she told me to go by first names."

"If that's what she wants then. Everyone was okay handling her car?"

"Yes, we just loaded it on a trailer to take it to the old warehouse out of the way."

"Good idea. Hold on to the note and pictures, I want to see if they are like the one Elaina had on her phone."

"Yes, Boss. Sir, umm I think you two should head to the cabin. This is looking like it could turn serious."

"I'll get Elaina. Tell the housekeeper to pack what we need."

"Of course, sir."

# Elaina

I step out of Viktor's enormous office shower and grab a fluffy white towel. People often don't put much thought into towels, but geez what a difference it makes. My towels at home feel like rough carpet compared to these.

I'm so grateful he gave me some privacy and a little time to cool down. Twenty minutes can have a huge impact when you're on the verge of a meltdown. I was awash with too many emotions all at once, I felt as if I was drowning trying to express how I was feeling.

I'm interrupted mid-drying and mid-thought, by an agitated Viktor. Christ, this man needs to drink a vodka-seven and take a breather.

"Yes? I wasn't drying off or anything."

Viktor hears my sarcasm and raises an eyebrow, slowly scanning my body. He starts at the foot propped up on the side of the tub. He follows my calf to my thigh, pausing for a beat. He gazes between my thighs taking in a deep breath as he catalogs my pussy.

I watch, amused, as he licks his lips while looking at my breasts until he makes his way to my eyes. I shoot him a peeved look, raising my eyebrows and flaring my nostrils, all though I'm fairly entertained after that long glance he just gave me.

Vik grunts and says sternly, "Stop fooling around, Elaina. I'm here because we need to head to another one of my places."

Snorting, I playfully reply, "Really? I was under the

impression you were in here to stare at me. Surely you can't be hungry for more already?"

He studies my eyes for a moment as he grits his teeth, then he practically growls, "You have no clue what my appetite can be like." Viktor quickly scans my body again, "Get dressed and get to the Jag." With that he turns, slamming the bathroom door behind him.

That went well. He's normally so sweet to me and helpful all the time; this moody shit has my head spinning. I know he's stressed out about everything going on, but this sucks. I feel like he wants to put me over his knee and spank me for being bad or something.

I pull my skirt and shirt on from before since I don't have the luxury of a change of clothes here. I refuse to wear dirty underwear though, and Viktor got them soaked earlier. *Hmm, where can I put these?* I snatch a fluffy wash cloth to roll them up in and toss them into my ginormous purse.

I venture out of his office in search of the garage door from earlier. I know we pretty much just walked straight but his house is huge; like fit-ten-of-my-apartment–inside-his-house type huge. I should have asked him if he turned that alarm thing off. *Ugh! Where is that man?*

I glance into a sitting area as I walk down the hall, another bathroom and what looks to be the entry to the kitchen, but no Viktor. Stubborn man will just have to get over his temper tantrum if I trip the alarm. At least I'll know where he is if I do.

After the lengthy hallway I end up at the giant metal door we came in from. I make it through and thankfully there are no lights or sirens and no metal blinds coming down over everything. I release my pent up breath that I hadn't realized I had been holding since I walked in the door, and head toward Viktor's beautiful Jaguar.

I lightly graze my fingertips along the smooth lines. I wonder if he would let me drive this bad boy. I know she's a whole lot faster than my little white Camaro. I love my car but come on, this is a Jaguar! Surely he won't have it unlocked, being Mr. Security. Screw it, if the alarm goes off, oh well. I seem to be a little risk taker today anyhow.

I lightly pull the door handle and sure enough it comes open silently and smoothly. I slide right in. I'm already this far, so I'm going to sit here and soak up the brilliant feel of the leather and imagine myself making this beauty jet down the highway.

I feel something cold press against my temple and my lungs seize up immediately. *Oh my gawd.*

"Click-Clack, *bitch*. Guess who's going to be bleeding now?"

No. Fucking. Way. I know that voice. I don't know if I can speak though as my stomach churns crazily. Bile starts to climb my esophagus and I clench my throat closed tightly. I'm pretty sure I just want to puke all over everything. I've never had a gun held to my head and I'm not sure what the fuck to do. This bitch is just plain stupid.

"Kendall, are you crazy? This is Viktor's house! When he finds you, he will slaughter you!" I wheeze, breathing deeply to try to keep from expelling my stomach contents all over Viktor's butter-smooth interior. "How on earth did you even get in here?"

Kendall laughs shrilly and I clench my eyes closed at the noise. "You dumb piece of filth. You really think I would come alone? I'm not stupid. You thought you could humiliate me in that club? I don't think so, bitch. Viktor is supposed to be mine. He doesn't need to be wasting time on you!"

"If Viktor sees you in here doing this then any chance you think you may have had of having him, will be gone.

Think about this for a minute."

Kendall shoves the gun against my temple harshly and I wince.

"Shut up!" she screeches in her nasally voice.

There's a loud crash to the side of us. Kendall turns to watch Alexei tackle her man and I use the distraction to try to get the gun away. I will probably end up being shot regardless, but it's better than point blank range in the side of the head.

I grip onto her wrists tightly, growling and thrusting her arms away from me. Kendall fights back, desperately trying to aim the gun at me. I struggle, screaming at her angrily, fighting for my life.

She shrilly yells, "Let go, you cunt!"

"No way, you psycho! Give it to me!" I scream, leaning over to bite a chunk out of her boney little arm. I move her arms back and forth as much as I can, attempting to free the weapon from her.

Suddenly I'm hit with a blinding pain on the side of my head; it momentarily dazes me and I lose focus of what I'm doing. I release my teeth and let go of her arms, trying to blink and shake away the pain. *Ouch.*

I feel like I've been hit with a Mack truck, and I realize I'd let go of the gun. Turning rapidly I see the gun pointed at me for a split second. I gasp in a deep breath and close my eyes. This is it, I'm dead. I wait for a beat then hear Kendall scream savagely.

I open my eyes and see the back door open, with Viktor bent inside the car. Viktor has Kendall in a tight choke hold with one arm and has his other arm pointing her hand with the gun toward the ceiling.

I swear it's like a rush of adrenaline hits me as I leap through the two front seats. I grab her tit in one hand and squeeze as hard as I can. She starts stomping her feet and I get kneed in the face as I lean over to take a large bite of her exposed thigh.

Kendall wails and lets go of the gun, flailing her arms crazily. My hair is ripped upward for a second before she is dragged out of the vehicle. Alexei is there waiting and grabs Kendall forcefully from behind.

She glares spitefully at me. "You stupid bitch! I will kill you, I promise you that. And if I don't, then my daddy will kill all of you!" Alexei yanks her arms back even further and I swear they could pop out at any time. He mutters something in her ear and she shakes her head angrily.

Suddenly a hand pops in front of me. Blinking rapidly, following it, I meet Viktor's worried gaze. I grab it tightly and let him pull me out of his beautiful, mistreated car.

"Princess?" he inquires quietly.

I shake my head. "No, you got here in time. I'm alright."

"You're sure?"

"Yes, I'm okay." I nod and attempt to fix my screwed up clothes. It looks like I just took a roll through some prickly bushes. I can only imagine what my hair looks like after that spaz got ahold of it.

Viktor takes a step back and in doing so, reveals the man Kendall had brought with her. Only now, the guy is on the floor. He's perched on his knees, badly beaten and in handcuffs.

"You realize, Kendall, that I get retribution now, right? I know you have heard the stories, probably from your own father about me. Is that why you've become so infatuated with me?"

She adopts her naïve, innocent expression and attempts to appear coy with him. "Retribution for what, Viktor? Daddy said we were meant for each other, so I was only taking care of this pest for you."

Viktor's eyes widen. "Meant for each other? That's

positively ludicrous. You don't have a chance; you're not even on my radar, Kendall." He turns toward her man and raises Kendall's gun—"You took a very close guard from me"—and shoots her guard right center in his forehead.

The guard drops to the ground and I swallow forcefully. Kendall starts laughing like a hyena and looks at me happily. She really is insane.

She nods to me, grinning. "Look at her, Viktor! She can't even handle a kill! I'm not worried about it, he was just a guard. I will easily get another."

Viktor glares at her as if he wants to kill her. "Consider this is your only warning. Tell your father that next time I will not hesitate to kill you." Viktor nods to Alexei and he starts to drag her toward the door, she giggles as he does and it shoots chills down my body.

That chick is a complete Looney Tunes. I'm now sure that she wouldn't have hesitated to shoot me. She gave off that impression when we were fighting in the car, but one can always hope that the other person is not as bad as they appear. I don't know how Viktor does it. He looked completely blank when he pulled that trigger. I know he said he ran the Bratva, but it feels like that title is really hitting me full force right now. I like to think he would never hurt me like that, but he looked completely zoned out. It didn't affect him at all to pull that trigger. I may be on the tougher side, but I could never kill anyone like that. What on earth have I gotten myself into?

I notice the guard's blood and cough, rushing to the side of the vehicle. I regurgitate everything left in my stomach all over Viktor's shiny grey, speckled garage floor. After blowing chunks for a few minutes I feel a hand on my back.

I can't help but cringe away. I can't be touched right now, especially by a hand that brought someone pain. The guy was bad, here to hurt me, but it still screws with my head.

Viktor murmurs and it brings tears to my eyes. "Moy lyooBOF, paZHAALoosta?" (My love, please)

I have no clue what it means, but the Russian sounds so beautiful, it flows out of his mouth like water flows down a stream. Hiccupping, I take in his features. Even after committing murder, he's beautiful. His hazel eyes stare longingly at me, worried and sad. Why? I have no idea, but I'm curious.

"What, Viktor?" I tremble and the first tear makes its way down my flushed cheeks.

He reaches his hand toward me slowly, cautiously, gazing at me fearfully. "Please, don't fear me, Elaina," he replies softly.

Nodding, I reach out and accept his hand. I know I should be more cautious, but he promised long ago to never hurt me. Viktor promised my sister and Tate, I know this, Emily told me. I have to trust that, right? My gut tells me he will protect me and to go to him. My gut usually tells the truth, I'm not sure yet about my heart, and lord knows my mind is torn on what to do.

He pulls me toward him. I hop over the puke and let him clutch me tightly to his chest. He whispers something into my hair but I can't hear him over my sobs. It's surreal, like I have no idea I'm even crying this hard. I didn't pull the trigger, so why is it affecting me so strongly?

"Shhh, shhhh, it's okay, Princess. Calm down, it's over with now," he says as he delicately pets my hair. It's soothing and after a few moments, I'm able to slow the flow of tears and catch my breath. I hate being a mess and not being able to pull myself together right away. I'm usually pretty decent at hiding my emotions. I guess murder is my breaking point. God. Murder.

We're all going to go to jail now. Fuck. I can't believe

this, I wonder if the cops are on their way right now. Did anyone hear that gun shot? The neighbors aren't that close, but still the garage had to have echoed. Damn, I wish I could hear if there are sirens coming. What can I do? Run? Yeah right.

No, this is Viktor, he said he cleans stuff up and takes care of things. The way he looked, surely he knows what to do. He'll know how to clean this up and, knowing his stubbornness, he will take care of everything. I need to chill out and see if he will tell me his plan.

"What's going to happen?" I ask foggily, gazing past him to the ceiling. I can't focus on him right now, I'm scared what I may find in his eyes if I look at them right now.

"Lovely, this is Bratva business. I will fix it and keep you safe." I blink, cataloging his scruffy jaw while he speaks then stare off solemnly for a few moments. Right, this is his business.

"I just don't know what to think right now," I utter and he nods understandingly at me.

"I know, and we will discuss it more later. For now we need to get into the car. Alexei and Spartak are coming with us. My house has obviously been compromised. I had the alarm off for ten minutes and that loophole was utilized by my enemies. I will not take any more chances with your safety. I would never forgive myself if anything were to happen to you," he says kindly and helps me back into his Jaguar.

The guys load up and next thing I know we are driving along through hills full of trees. I have no clue how long we drive, but it feels like I stare out of the window for hours.

# EIGHT

## Elaina

I MUST HAVE FALLEN ASLEEP DURING THE RIDE, because I awake drowsy and confused. I take in my strange surroundings. We're parked in front of a beautiful little log cabin, and it appears to be surrounded by forest.

There's a small private gravel drive that ends in front of the charming little porch. It has four steps leading up to the door and a hanging bench swing off to the side. I bet it would be amazing to sit out here on the swing in the morning, sipping a sweet coffee or hot chocolate.

It feels like we are enclosed into our own little bubble. The trees and bushes make a natural curtain around us. There's a detached garage or shop building off to the side, and a little toward the back of the cabin, all along the side is lined with rows upon rows of chopped wood.

"Miss Elaina?" I'm brought out of my thoughts by Spartak.

"Yes, Spartak? Where are we?"

"Come inside please, ma'am. The boss had me wait out

here until you awoke, but wants you inside as soon as possible."

"He made you wait for me? That's crazy! Where are we exactly?"

"We are at Mr. Masterson's cabin."

"You don't say? Clearly I can see we're at his cabin! I meant as in *here* here. Where are we? Are we even in Tennessee still?" I ask dramatically and he blushes a little.

"Oh. Yes. We are just in the mountains, didn't leave the state or anything. You actually weren't asleep for that long."

"Hmm, it feels like it. I thought we drove for forever." I slide across the leather seat and make my way out of the car.

Poor guy has been stuck on babysitting duty for me again. Ugh, my neck is stiff and my jaw is sore. It must be from Kendall. I have no idea what to do about her and I don't want to even think about it right now. I need to find Viktor and figure out what he plans on us doing.

I glance over at Spartak as I make my way to the porch stairs. "Say, Spartak?"

"Yes, ma'am?" He looks over at me curiously and follows me up the stairs.

"Where is Viktor anyhow?"

"He's inside handling business."

I step to the side for Spartak to enter first. "What is his business, anyhow?"

"He has a storage business."

"Sure, if that's what you call it."

He smirks a little at me then shakes his head, locking the thick wood door securely behind me.

The inside of the cabin is just as fairytalesque as the outside. I wouldn't have believed in a thousand years this was Viktor's had I not driven here with him. His house seemed very plain and sterile; whereas here it's quaint and homey feeling.

There's a giant fireplace as the focal point with a large square rug in front of it. The tan couches look more worn than new, but the kind of worn where you know they are really comfortable. A few wooden side tables with lamps and coasters resting on them are placed conveniently around the couches. There are family photos all along the decorative mantle, many of Viktor and Tate. They seem to be so different, yet so alike at the same time.

The living area is open and leads into a cozy kitchen. The kitchen is decorated in a wine theme, with matching pictures and hand towels to coordinate. I can't make out much more besides a wooden staircase and a hallway. I'm guessing the bedrooms are upstairs.

"Does he come here a lot?" I gesture around the living room, taking in all the small details.

"When he gets some time off he does, especially in the summer. This is Mishka's favorite place."

"Oh! That's his gran, right? I think that's the name Emily had told me was hers."

"Yep, she comes sometimes and will cook for us, good Russian meals. I haven't eaten like that since I was last in Russia with my family."

"Wow, Russia! When were you in Russia last?" I hear Viktor on the phone as he comes closer to the living room, he tells whomever he's speaking to that they need to hold on for just a second.

"Elaina, that's enough. Spartak, go do a perimeter check," Viktor barks and I scowl at him in return.

"We were having a conversation," I bite back and Spar looks like a deer trapped in headlights. I see his Adam's apple bob quickly as he gulps and rushes toward the door. I don't know what that was all about but whatever. He may boss Spartak around all the time, but he's lost his marbles if he thinks I'm okay with him talking to me that way.

"Yes, I will get back to you," Viktor says in a monotone voice to the caller and hits end, pocketing the cell phone.

He looks at me, amused, then steps closer, adopting the look of a hunter stalking his prey. He circles around me and I stand stock still, waiting for the yelling or anger to come. Whatever I did, Spartak sure was quick to bolt. Thanks, friend. If it ever comes down to it, I guess I know who my allies are.

I feel warm breath close to my ear, caressing my skin, giving me goose bumps, and my stomach flip flops crazily. I draw in a deep silent gasp of air, holding it, trying to be as still as possible. I don't have a clue why I'm still trying to not move, but it just seems like the right thing to do. Like when you're faced with a powerful beast and you're told to stand still so as to not provoke it. This man makes my body go wild for him, stirring up emotions and feelings I've never encountered before.

In a raspy rumble close to my ear he says, "You don't need to be nosing in his business. You are here for me, not him." He licks up the outer shell of my ear and I squeak slightly, licking my lips in return. It's like a conditioned response, picturing him licking me in *other* places.

"Now, be a good girl and go wash up for dinner. Bathroom's through there." He brushes along my arm to point and I shudder in response to his nearness.

I nod silently and rush to the restroom. Holy shit, that man completely throws me off balance. I can't even remember what I was saying to him before he licked my ear. Damn it!

# Viktor

I practically hung up on Tate when I saw Elaina all wispy-eyed talking to Spartak. I'm glad she appreciates his company but if I see them getting too close I will assign him to another detail and put my next best man with her. I know I should trust her, but it's in my blood not to trust anyone entirely.

Thankfully my little trick at the bar worked. Since I made her a manager she should mainly be in the office and won't have to bartend unless someone doesn't show up. For me that means no more watching pathetic idiots checking her out on a daily basis. There have been plenty of times when I have wanted to sink one of those fools in the lake.

Enough of that, I need to prepare my love some dinner. I think she has it in her head that I don't know how to cook. Is it wrong of me that I almost want to pretend like I don't know how? That way she will make me a nice meal. I know she would, too. I probably wouldn't even have to ask her for it.

Opening the stainless steel refrigerator, I scan the contents. This may be a cabin, decorated to Mishka's standards, but I refuse to not have top of the line appliances. I have some stew meat and veggies, whipping cream, strawberries; I can definitely make something up with this.

Mishka must have sent some fresh foods up this week. I usually have a groundskeeper that helps maintain the place while I'm away. Luckily Mishka is sweet on him so she sends up fresh foods frequently. He'll enjoy having the next few days off and I'll have peace of mind knowing Elaina is safe with me.

I'm preparing a nice stew for the main dish with fresh baked bread my grandmother made recently. The strawberries and fresh whipping cream will go splendid afterwards. I hope Elaina enjoys it.

I didn't even stop to think about asking what foods she likes to eat. I see her sneak a cherry or orange at the club occasionally, and I've seen her eat at my brother's a few times, but she just picked at her food.

I grab the bottle of vodka from the freezer, pouring half a tumbler full and gulping down a good portion of it. I can't even fathom the fact that I'm nervous right now. Since when does Viktor Masterson get nervous over anything? Well, other than making sure Elaina is protected. There was the time I was at lunch and also when she freaked out at her apartment. Christ, maybe she really does make me nervous.

"Viktor?" Elaina calls hesitantly and I spin around to face her.

"Yes, Printsyessa?" (Princess)

"Are you cooking right now or is someone here?" She walks into the kitchen glancing over everything nosily. She's never been much of a curious cat, more standoffish than anything. This new side she's showing me is quite amusing.

"Of course it's me, why is it so strange to believe the idea of me cooking? Surely you must know that men cook."

Rolling her eyes, she huffs, "Of course I know that men cook! You on the other hand, not so much. You bring food to eat, like, every single shift I work. Naturally I would think you don't cook."

"Well for you, Elaina, I cook," I rasp and she blushes slightly.

"What are you making anyhow? It smells fantastic."

"I'm making a beef stew, is that alright with you?"

"Oh yes, I love it!"

I nod and she peeks over my shoulder as I take the chilled bowl and beaters out of the freezer.

"What are you making now?"

"Whipping cream. Hand me the sugar." I gesture to the canister and she quickly complies.

She bumps her elbow into mine several times while I'm mixing, sending heat through my body with each small caress. She does it again for probably the ninth time and I feel like slamming her into a wall.

I growl, frustrated, and toss the beaters into the sink, then grasp her arm, pulling her close. Elaina jumps as I grab her and I chuckle. "Oh, little lamb, you have no clue how much of a wolf I really am," I rasp, completely turned on by her soft touch, her sweet smile and flowery scent.

Trapping her between myself and the counter I reach past her while she stares at me, shocked and intrigued. Swiping up a dollop of whipped cream, I smear it down the side of her throat.

I bend down, following my finger with my tongue to clean up the fluffy, white sweetness. The sugary goodness melts in my mouth with each swipe of my warm, wet tongue. Elaina shivers as I get to the sensitive spot on her neck. Grinning, I take a small nip, just enough to make her jump a little and grasp tightly onto my shirt. I pull back slightly and she gazes at me, lost in a daze, I lean in and lightly nip at her bottom lip.

She stares at me longingly and whispers, "God, Viktor, the things you make me feel."

Turning slightly, she gets her own fluff of cream on her finger. She looks so sexy, I want to take her here on the counter. I study her as she returns the favor of smearing me with whipped cream, painting my lips and coating the tip of my pointer finger.

"Well, what's your plan, Princess?" I ask and swallow in anticipation.

She smiles and draws me down closer, sucking the

cream off my lips. "Ummm, Elaina," I growl. Picking up my hand, she sucks my finger deep into her mouth making me instantly picture my dick in there instead.

I quickly yank my finger out.

Shocked, she pants, "What? What did I do?"

"Just, let's just eat dinner, okay?" I mumble and she nods reluctantly.

I watch her swinging her little ass as she walks toward the table and it's the last straw.

"Fuck it." I throw my kitchen towel on the counter and stalk toward her, spinning her quickly, then I lift her slightly and place her on the dining table. "I'm hungry, lovely, but for pussy, not fucking stew."

"What!" She gasps, taken by surprise and I push her back on the table, lifting her skirt.

"What happened to your panties?" I'm staring at her pussy lips, they're just waiting for me to suck on them.

"I-I didn't have clean ones, and the wet ones are in my purse. Geez, you just startled me." She giggles, resting her hand on her chest.

"Startled, huh? Hold on to the table."

"Huh?" I spin her over so her belly is resting on the table, her bare ass on display in front of me.

"Nothing, just hold still," I reply and land the first rough smack on her butt cheek.

"Agh! Viktor!"

"Louder!" I say and land another smack to her backside.

"Ouch! Are you crazy?"

*Smack!*

"You've lost your marbles, mister!"

*Smack!*

Her ass is nice and cherry so I rub it soothingly for a minute and then quickly insert my pointer finger that she was busy sucking on, deep inside her little cunt. Elaina inhales loudly and I'm elated to find her sopping wet, ready and wanting me.

Taking my finger out, I suck her juices off my finger and wrench her legs apart.

"You're here for me. This pussy is all mine." I dip my head and take her tiny clit between my lips, sucking lightly. She squirms and I brace her legs tightly.

"Oh my gawd! That feels good!"

"Yeah? This is the best tasting cunt I've ever eaten out. You keep creaming like that and I'm going to burst in my pants."

I reach over to grab the white taper candle from the glass candle holder. Rolling the larger, rounded portion of it on her hungry pussy, I coat it in her wetness and insert it slowly into her opening.

"Oh my God! Viktor!"

"I'm not God, Printsyessa, even if you do feel like heaven." I play with her little kitty until she starts to tremble slightly with the pleasure. "You ready for my cock?"

"Yes, please," she pleads as I remove the candle. I unzip my trousers and push them down enough to pull my large, hard cock free.

"Are you sure you're ready this time?" I rub the head of my dick in her wetness, dipping my tip into her hole and pulling it away each time she pushes backwards to get more.

"Damn it, Viktor! Give it to me!" she demands. I grip her hip tight and drive swiftly inside, making her call out loudly.

"I thought you were ready? And now this tiny cunt grips me so tight, pulsing."

"I am, I was, just please, God, that feels so good." Elaina clutches the sides of the table as I push deep into her.

"Oh you sweet, sweet girl, this is one greedy little pussy

you have here, lovely. I want to feel this cunt come all over me," I murmur and smack her ass sharply.

"Ouch! Fuuuuck!" she chokes and her center begins to spasm around me. This is proof that she loves it rough. She's going to be so much fun to break in.

I lean over her, clutching a handful of hair and wrench her head back toward me. Leaning in closely to her ear, I growl, "Make this fucking cunt come, NOW," and thrust harshly into her multiple times.

Her legs spread as her pussy grips harder me with each ringing spasm flowing through her body. Her legs go crazy as she attempts to scale the table to take me deeper but I grip her hair tightly, holding her in place. She will move when I'm ready for her to move. Each little squirm makes my cock throb, antagonizing it to finish deep inside her.

"What did I say when we started this? Who are you here for?" I ask, my voice gravelly.

"Ahhh, you, Viktor, I'm here for you. Oh!" Elaina moans as I pick up my pace, rapidly slamming into her.

"That's right. Me. This. Is. MINE," I say harshly, emphasizing the words with each hot spurt of cum I squirt deep inside her. Her pussy gets really slick from our combined juices and I pump into her a few more times, making sure my cum gets as far in as possible.

I free my hand from gripping her hip to rub all around my cock that's still resting inside her. I collect our combined essence and lightly brush it all over her swollen kitty lips and clit. She squirms slightly, sending little zaps of pleasure through my body.

I need to make sure she's covered before I'm done. I want every inch of her to smell of me. Next time my cum will be painting those plump tits and slender neck. I pull back from the table, bringing her with me.

"Woah, that was awesome!" She smiles happily,

standing in front of me.

"Good. Now get on your knees and clean me up."

"Excuse me?"

"Get on your knees, Elaina."

"Okay, geez, quit being so damn bossy." She grumbles about it but she complies.

"I want you to lick all of your cunt juice and cum off my cock." She nods and looks at me timidly.

I caress the smooth skin on her cheek and smile slightly. She looks so beautiful, perched on her knees with my cum dripping down her legs. I nudge her slightly and she takes me deep, licking all over my head and shaft. I clench my eyes closed at the amazing emotions she elicits inside me. Her delicate hand grips me tight, pumping as she cleans me off thoroughly.

"Good, lovely, now clean my nuts."

She sucks them into her warm, wet mouth one at a time, swirling her eager tongue around them repeatedly.

"Elaina, my princess. You are amazingly talented with that succulent tongue and mouth of yours. I'm going to spill again any minute if you keep it up like that."

She releases my nuts and starts to bob her head on my cock quickly, causing me to curl my toes. My ass cheeks flex, and I reach out to grip the table so I don't fall over. *Christ, she's amazing at this.* She gets a good rhythm going but I'm brought out of my reverie by a quick smack on my behind. I gape at her, flaring my nostrils as she repeats the action and I feel the first signs of my impending orgasm.

"Christ, *again!*" I groan.

Elaina tightly grips my ass cheek and lightly bites onto my cock as she bobs. I surrender to the need and pull back quickly, pumping my cock rapidly with my fist, causing my dick to shoot hot jets all over her pretty breasts.

Leaning in, I softly rub my cock in my cum, spreading it

over her neck the best I can. "Absolutely breathtaking," I murmur and she blushes, looking to the ground from my praise.

"Can we clean up and then maybe lie down? Or at least I need to. I'm actually pretty worn out from all the drama."

"I apologize, truly, I wish it didn't happen. Yes, of course. You're not hungry? I promise it is edible." I reach down for her and help her stand. She grips my hands tight, getting her balance and smiling gratefully.

"No, not really, perhaps later?"

"I'll just turn the heat down to low and it'll stay warm for when your appetite appears."

"Sounds good, thank you."

Hurrying, I put everything away that's decorating the counters from my meal prep and grab her hand gently to guide her to the large suite with master bathroom. This may be a small cabin but I had to have a larger area to sleep and a nice sized bathroom. This cabin is meant to be for relaxing as well as a safe house. I refuse to not be comfortable while I'm staying.

She looks around in wonder and I use the extra time to gaze at her gorgeous features. "Viktor, this bedroom is gorgeous! In fact, this whole cabin is, but this room is amazing!" Elaina turns to me excitedly and I grin at her in return.

"I'm happy you approve. Later I need to show you where the safe rooms are located."

"Safe rooms? As in, plural?"

"Yes, Printsyessa, there is one in the kitchen and another that goes completely underneath the cabin. There are three secret doors, I'll show you after you rest up."

"That is so freaking awesome!" Her eyes light up with excitement and I chuckle. "I don't know if I'll be able to sleep now, I'll be busy trying to figure out where they are!"

She makes her way to the bathroom and turns on the multi head shower.

"Ah lyooBOF, ya VAWLya paKAAZeevats vee meeraVOY vee poost ya (Ah love, I'll show you the world if you let me)" I mumble under my breath. "Tomorrow, lovely," I call out and she glances at me with a smile. She's full of mischief; I'll probably catch her checking out the house later while I'm trying to sleep.

# Elaina

### two hours later

I try to get comfy next to Viktor in his extremely comfortable bed, but continue to toss and turn, staring at everything in the room through the shadows. The fan spins quietly, I miss my fan in my apartment. It's old and loose so it makes a ton of noise, blanketing the late night silence. It's so irritating, I hate not falling right to sleep when I'm drained. When this happens at home I will get up and vacuum or something, but I'm sure Viktor and his men would not appreciate the gesture.

I keep wondering if someone will find us here. The events from earlier keep playing through my head, like a CD on repeat. Kendall was pretty pissed when she left and I would not put it past that ugly psycho to come creeping. I would never wish ill on anyone normally, but that bitch puts the *cray* in crazy.

Those safe rooms have continuously been on my mind since he brought them up. Is his life really so dangerous that he has to have not one but multiple safe rooms? I wonder what they look like. I've never seen one in real life before. I remember that movie *Panic Room*. I wonder if his are the same way and where they are. I want to get up and search for them *so* bad, but I don't know whether one of his guards will shoot me if they see me.

I carefully scoot out of bed, trying not to shake it or rouse Viktor. That man is knocked out, sleeping like the dead. I don't know how on earth he can sleep well with so much drama going on.

My feet hit the floor and relish the feel of the plush carpet. The rest of the house has hardwood floors, but in here it's creamy white, thick carpet. Perfect, it'll make it easier for me to creep out unnoticed.

I snatch up his grey button down business shirt and slip it on, fastening it up to the crest of my breasts. At least if he wakes up I can try to distract him with a little cleavage. I've barely given up my virginity and already I'm thinking like a pro.

I'll just head to the kitchen and check things out. He said there was one in there. This way I can at least pretend I'm hungry or something, but I mean really, who can eat at a time like this. I want chocolate and that's about it, anything else is just a waste of time. I'm shooting for pure carbs and sugar overload. I could use a good sugar coma to help me cope.

I slowly open the door just enough for me to sneak through it.

*Thunk!*

*Ouch! Fuck!* I stubbed my toe on the damn door trim. *Stupid cabin full of wood, ugh!* I can probably turn on a light but want to get past the hallway first. I silently make my way to the living room and click on one of the lamps resting on a sofa table.

I'm met with Alexei's cold, tired gaze. "Eeeeek!" I let out a noisy screech and clutch my chest. "Shit, you gave me a heart attack!"

"Hmm." He grunts, unimpressed.

A door crashes open and footsteps come pounding down the hall. Viktor appears, disheveled, pointing his gun equipped with a fancy silencer, ready to shoot someone.

"Alexei, report," he gripes irritably.

"Yes, sir. Miss Harper here was sneaking through the living room, when she saw me and let out a yell." He glances at me harshly, and then looks back to Viktor.

I huff angrily going on the defense. "Oh bullshit! I wasn't sneaking, I turned on the light in the living room for heaven's sake! If I was sneaking, do you think I would have turned on a light?"

Viktor glares at Alexei like he's going to scalp him. "Seriously, Alexei? Give her a break, with the day she's had, of course my princess would get frightened easily."

I smirk at Viktor, practically ready to purr at his kind words. "Yes, I was simply out to get a glass of water," I reply snottily to Alexei.

Alexei turns away hastily and Viktor looks at me, perplexed. "Lovely, you have water on the bedside table."

He says it like a statement but I know it's really a question. It's a stupid test to see if I will tell him the truth. It irks me even more to know that he knows I'm lying.

"Ugh! Fine! Yes, I was sneaking, damn it. You told me about the safe rooms and that's all I can think about now! Technically that makes it your fault. I wasn't expecting Rambo here to be waiting in the shadows and cause me to stroke out in the middle of the living room!"

Alexei just shakes his head and Viktor gives a low chuckle. "Printsyessa, really? All this because you're a curious kitten? Come on and I'll show you, so we can put this nonsense behind us and go to sleep."

I pout, bastard just called me a freaking kitten in front of Alexei. Obviously I am too tired to be dealing with these two if all I can think of is throwing a lamp at them.

"Nope, I'm over it. I'll just wait until tomorrow. Good night, gentlemen!" I grumble and stomp down the hallway.

*Stupid comfortable bed.* I huff as I fluff my pillow and straighten the blanket over me up to my chin. They have it freezing in here with the air conditioning running non-stop.

I mumble to myself, griping about men as I quickly fall into a deep sleep, not even feeling Viktor crawl into bed and pull me close.

# NINE

## Elaina
### three days later...

FOR THE THIRD DAY NOW, I'M AWOKEN BY THE smell of bacon in the air. I never would have thought Viktor could cook like a boss. His grandmother surely taught him well. I think he knows that I was doubtful of his capabilities, so now he's going to the extreme and making me food every chance he gets. It's sweet really; helps make up for me getting annoyed by Alexei being a permanent fixture in the living room. I know he's just here for my safety, but it feels a little extreme at this point.

It's the third day I've been holed up in this cabin. It's not some vacation either. None of the guys will even let me go outside. I really would enjoy just walking down to the lake and taking a nice long dip.

This sweet little place is nestled right between a lake and a mountain. I still haven't found out where we are exactly. Every time I ask, I get the same reply, "We're in the mountains." If they say it one more time, I swear I will scream.

The door kicks open and Viktor approaches, complete with a tray full of my breakfast and a sweet smile.

"Wow, you didn't have to bring it. I could have come and sat at the table."

"I know but I didn't want to wake you, I was just going to leave it if you were still sleeping."

"Puhlease, you are going to spoil me and fatten me up. I've done nothing but sleep late and eat for the past few days."

"There is nothing wrong with that. You work hard all the time. I've told you many times before that I'll take care of you. You're a princess and deserve to be treated as such."

"That's kind of you, Viktor, but we've discussed this. I can't just do nothing. I have to work and stay busy."

"Then discover what your passion is and do that instead."

"I have to figure out what it is first and even then, I won't just roll over and let you take care of me without pitching in."

"Christ, woman, why do you have to be so stubborn. I know you are independent and can take care of yourself. I'm the man, damn it. Let me do my job and give you what makes you happy."

"Fine, you want to make me happy? Then take me swimming in that beautiful, giant lake I can see from the back window."

Viktor rolls his eyes and clenches his jaw. "You know I can't do that."

"See, then it's settled. You can't give me a simple thing to make me happy, so don't expect me to change everything just because we slept together."

His eyes widen in anger and he throws the tray against

the wall, scattering the food and dishes all over the wood and white carpet. "You are infuriating sometimes! Stubbornness will get you nowhere but killed!" He's growling as he storms out of the room, slamming the door behind him.

That jerk didn't even give me a chance to reply.

Tossing the thick comforter and soft sheet aside, I hastily climb out of bed and head for the bathroom. I better not go out there right now, or God knows I will throw something back at him. I know throwing stuff is not the way to a healthy relationship, but I have to keep him on his toes. Relationship. Hmmm, I guess that's what this is after all. It's been a little while now since we first met, since we started being more intimate and we seem to be getting closer. Oh and there's the part where I was there when he killed someone.

I turn the water to scalding hot; I need a good scrubbing and it's been a little while since I scrubbed off my past. Now is a great time to do it too, since I'm angry. I don't know if scouring one's self is really the way to go about this, but it's something I've always done and it seems to help me cope.

Climbing under the hot water I grit my teeth at the high temperature and influx of steam surrounding me. I scrub as fast as I can stopping only to wash my hair. I thoroughly rinse my hair and body off and then get back out. My skin burns bright red. It coats me in a false sense of comfort, as it is pain I feel and not creepy crawlies.

Even after so many years I still catch myself feeling finger tips running over me, sickly, unwanted. *I'm not that girl anymore.* He can't touch me anymore and I have to get it through my head. After witnessing Viktor pull that trigger, I really should trust him that Brent won't get me again.

Enough of this shit, it's too early to pour over these

thoughts and feelings right now. I'll save it for later to worry about. I have a bone to pick with a spoiled Bratva king, I don't have time to be wasting in the shower or on my bullshit past.

I pull on a pair of comfy sweat pant material shorts, one of Viktor's plain undershirts and a pair of ankle socks. Might as well, all I've been doing is lounging around. I took some scissors to a few of Viktor's things and made them little person approved. He towers over my short self, but I refuse to not wear clean clothes the entire time I'm here.

Viktor's clothes are very formal and boring, but when he puts them on, he looks edible. I never thought I could be so attracted to a man in a suit, but he wears it with finesse. It's not just me who notices him, everyone does.

Thank goodness I was able to bring my giant purse with me. It holds my basic necessities like deodorant, mascara, an extra razor, mace in case someone makes me really angry, those types of things.

I dig through it until I find what I'm looking for at the very bottom. I put on a swipe of deodorant and a spritz of my body spray, I'm good to go. I should learn to keep a spare bra in here as well.

Maybe I'll get lucky and there will be bacon left. With Alexei and Viktor though, it usually goes really quickly. Perhaps I should bring my mace and try it out on Alexei? That could be entertaining and possibly open up the opportunity for me to swim. Definitely an option to consider and I chuckle as I make my way down the hallway.

Arriving in the kitchen, I'm met with Viktor on his phone at the dining table and Alexei MIA. Thank God, some alone time without the puppy, Alexei, following us around. Don't get me wrong, he's a good protector, can be nice sometimes, it's just weird constantly having him sitting here up my butt when I'm so used to being alone at my apartment all the time. It was hard enough getting accustomed to Spartak following me around constantly, and that was nowhere near as serious as this is. I do think I would be happier and more accepting if it was Spartak in here constantly though. I should ask Viktor to switch them when I'm done being mad at him.

Glancing around, I notice the squeaky clean kitchen. What the hell! I can't believe he cleaned this kitchen so fast and there's no food. He's been stuffing me full of it and now that I'm actually hungry, it's gone! Definitely not helping his chances, I'm even crankier now. I'm going to turn into a hungry plus angry person; they call it a hangry person. *Yep, I'm hangry all right.*

Perching against the fridge I glare at Viktor with my arms crossed. This is his fault for treating me like a spoiled princess. Before, I wouldn't think twice about there not being breakfast. I'd just go ahead and make my own.

In fact, that's exactly what I'll do. I'll show him that I am perfectly capable of making my own and I've never needed to rely on a man before. Slamming each cabinet as I go, I search for everything I need to make myself a yummy breakfast.

After a few moments Viktor mumbles to the caller that he needs to get back to him and hangs up. I giggle inside because obviously my antics are working to distract him. That's what the ass gets for throwing food around. You don't mess with a woman's bacon, it's just wrong.

I start whistling an Andy Griffith tune cheerfully to add to his punishment as I whisk some eggs. I can't stand whistling, so hopefully he has the same pet peeve and it drives him a little crazy. Geez, I guess we are in a real relationship. I always read about couples annoying their partners and I'm definitely trying to get on his nerves.

"zabiVAATS, moy lyooBOF (Enough, my love)" he says

pleasantly and it pisses me off that he sounds so freaking delicious when he speaks Russian.

I wish he would say more things in Russian to me. He could have called me an angry bird for all I know, but I don't care. His language is beautiful and it makes me want to climb him like a tree.

I bang the pans around in the cabinet causing him to wince. "*Elaina*," he chastises and I smirk.

Alexei comes tumbling in through the back door, breathing erratically. "Boss! The alarm was tripped, get in the safe room. Hurry!"

"Nonsense! I'm not going to hide away."

"Please, sir, take Miss Elaina and go. We need to see who is coming and I want you two safe."

"I don't like this one bit, but I'll go because I want her secure." Viktor jumps up, rushing toward me. Alexei nods at him and shoves me toward Viktor.

"Hey, asshole! I can walk myself, don't touch me," I yell angrily, snatching my arm away from him.

Viktor puts his arm around my back and brings me close to his chest, kissing the top of my head and corralling me to the tall pantry cabinet.

"We're getting snacks?" He shakes his head, moving a few cracker boxes around. Suddenly the pantry shelves suck backwards and a doorway appears. "Holy shit, that's so cool!" I chortle excitedly and he pulls me in with him.

It's dark just long enough to creep me out, then a dim light magically turns on. Confused, I glance around until I see the light switch next to Viktor. "I feel like we are in a spy movie right now. Why are you being so quiet, you're making me freaking nervous."

The safe room we're in is a box about four feet by four feet with plain concrete walls, plush carpet, vents and bottled water. We are already really close, and with Viktor's size the room instantly feels smaller. Definitely not *Panic Room* level like I was expecting. I really hope I don't have to go to the bathroom. That would be a whole new level of embarrassment in front of him.

"Relax, Princess, I'm just thinking. When I have a lot running through my mind, I tend to get quiet."

"Well, you're quiet all the time, so you must have too much air up there." I gesture to his head and he smirks back at me.

"Christ, you're feisty when you get wound up. Are you always going to be like this? Even when we are old and grey? Will you be whistling and throwing items at me?"

I smile widely. "Last time I checked, you were throwing food at me, and who says we will be together when you're a rotten old man?"

He laughs softly, stepping in front of me. I look up, meeting his gorgeous hazel eyes that shine with amusement. He's so close I can smell his rich, clean scent enveloping me in warmth that gives my stomach happy flutters.

He leans in a little more and I gulp, he's so close I can feel his body heat. "Umm, what are you doing?" I question, tapping my fingers nervously on the sides of my thighs.

"Oh, Elaina, I'm settling this little temper tantrum you've been throwing all morning."

"We can't talk about this right now. Alexei was just in the kitchen and I really don't feel like having your guards jump in when it's convenient."

"Don't worry, they can't hear us. The room's completely soundproof to the kitchen. We are handling this now. I'm amused with your banging around the kitchen, but not with the sarcastic attitude. I won't tolerate others speaking to me like that." He places his hands on each side of my body against the wall, leaning in and effectively trapping me in front of him.

"I don't care what you will or will not tolerate, that's your problem, not mine. And just what exactly are you planning on doing to handle this?"

Viktor comes even closer, so his mouth is next to my ear. His warm, sweet breath brushes over me as he whispers, "I'm planning on fucking you *so* hard, that's how I'll handle you."

I draw in a quick breath. Viktor rarely swears and when he does it stands out even more so. His words make my pussy contract and I clasp my legs together tightly, imagining him fucking me savagely.

I've turned into quite the wanton hussy since he first had me. He's been 'breaking me in'—his words—ever since we arrived at the cabin. Frankly, I can't seem to get enough of it. He has my body responding to him as if it's his own.

"Hard fucking, huh? I wasn't aware you knew how to do that," I mutter in return, taunting him. He has fucked me very hard, but I'm going to poke the bear as much as possible in this sense, I know I will be the one benefitting from it. That's one thing about Vik, he's very satisfying.

Viktor lets loose a ferocious growl and drops to his haunches, ripping my shorts down my legs. Standing stock still, I watch him.

He rises up, hurriedly stripping his belt off and unbuttoning his pants.

"I should spank you for that mouth. I won't though, only because you know how to suck my cock so well. Shall I make you suck my cock until I cum all over that pretty face of yours?"

Reaching into his pants he frees his swollen member, pumping and squeezing it a few times until pre-cum gathers at the tip.

I roll my eyes, still playing the part to wind him up

further; this is going to feel so good. "I'm not sucking your dick, you're lucky if I ever suck it again," I retort stubbornly.

His eyes widen in disbelief and he huffs. Moving close to me again, he grasps onto each thigh, effectively picking me up against the cold concrete wall. He lines his thick cock up to my little hole and pushes in wildly.

"Ahhh, Viktor!" I let loose a scream as he pumps into me roughly.

My back scrapes against the ridges in the concrete and I rip my nails down his shoulder blades. He wants it rough; I can give it back to him as well. He knows exactly what I need and I know just how to push him to get it.

"Good girl, I'm going to fuck this pussy so hard, every time I touch it afterwards it'll ache. You'll learn not to push me, Princess, or you'll deal with the consequences." He forces the words between gritted teeth and I squeeze my pussy as tight as I can around him. He glares at me, then slams his eyes closed as he pushes into me harshly, grinding himself against my clit.

I moan quietly as he brings his nose against mine, his lips lightly brushing over mine as he murmurs, "And if you want a diamond on that finger, then you will suck my cock and love every minute of it." Drawing my lip into his mouth he sucks and gently bites down.

It takes a few moments for his words to register, my eyes flashing to his in surprise. "Vik?" I start to question, but I'm cut off by him thrusting his tongue into my mouth, taking me for a rollercoaster ride with his earth shattering kiss.

He pulls back from my mouth leisurely, and pumps into my cunt with passion. "Shhh, Princess," he murmurs, grasping my ass cheeks tightly to keep his rhythm. He squeezes them forcefully making me moan louder and I swear I feel his dick throb inside me.

"You feel so good, please don't stop, I promise I'll suck your cock," I gasp between thrusts.

"I know that, love, and I'm going to fuck this little ass sometime too. I will own every single part of you, as you own me. Bawg, ya lyooBOF vee (God, I love you)."

"Oh, keep talking like that, shit, I'm going to come."

"Good, Elaina, you come all over my big cock and I'll fill you up with my own cum. I want to watch it drip out of your cunt when I'm finished."

I call out loudly, climaxing at his words. My pussy squeezes him over and over and with each compression Viktor breaths out heavily.

"Please come, come in me, please," I beg and feel his cock start to pump his seed into me. He leans his forehead on my shoulder and breaths heavily while he shoots his cum deep.

I start to relax my body after a minute, sliding down so my feet are resting on the carpet once more. Viktor pulls back and I smile sweetly at him. He clenches his jaw then drops to his knees, pushing my legs apart.

Glancing down, confused, I see him studying my cum-covered pussy with pure lust. I feel it drip and try to clench my legs closed but he holds them steady. Meeting my irises, he quickly goes back to watching my pussy.

When I least expect it, he leans in, feasting on my cunt. He sucks and licks at the combined juices like a starved man. Shoving my hand into his wild hair I yank forcefully, attempting to hold on while I'm on this amazing ride known as his mouth.

"Holy shit, Viktor! My God, you're going to kill me!"

He thrusts two fingers into me deeply, curving them towards my belly. I bear down with the feeling of having to pee. "No, stop! I feel like I'm going to pee my pants!" I plead but he ignores me, sucking strongly on my clit.

Out of nowhere a mind-numbing orgasm hits me. I swear rockets and fireworks explode in the sky when it happens. I grasp onto him tight, attempting not to fall as I ride out the amazingly strong orgasm.

When the feelings finally subside and I feel as if I can once again open my eyes without a blinding light being there, I gasp, "What in the ever loving fuck was that?" I grasp my chest dramatically. "I've never in my life felt something like that!"

He shrugs nonchalantly and stands up, adjusting himself back to his perfect façade. I stand here, probably looking like I was just run over. Viktor on the other hand, with a few buttons and a tuck, returns to his normal orderly self. I don't understand how he can pull that off so flawlessly and have to admit I may be a little jealous.

"Well, that was new! Geez, we can definitely do that again," I chortle, grinning cheekily. "Can we head out there though, because I'm really hungry now."

"You should have eaten this morning," he chastises and I'm too satisfied at the moment to argue with him. If this is his plan for the future arguments we have, then I'm in for some incredible orgasms. I smirk and he shakes his head at me, exasperated.

I hear a weird snap noise and pause to concentrate. Viktor does the same and then shuffles over to the wall, putting his ear against it.

"What was that noise?"

"Shhh!" he whispers harshly and glares at me.

I swear, with his moods today, he needs to eat a freaking Snickers bar or something. I stick my tongue out at him and he turns away, focusing on the wall in front of him. The strange noise rings out several times. I can't figure out what it could possibly be, but Viktor appears stressed. His eyes crinkle in the corners and he wears a grim expression.

"Oh for heaven's sake! Just tell me what that noise is!" I whisper-yell, glaring back at him.

"It's gun shots okay. Now hush."

"Gun shots?! Holy shit! It sounds like there have been a lot. Are they going to find us?" I inquire on the cusp of freaking out.

"No, Elaina, we are in a safe room and I'm the only person who has the code to get in here. There are only two of my men who know where this room is anyhow. I believe the gun fire is probably coming from my men. They will shoot or be shot before they allow anyone in the house."

"I don't understand why anyone would want to shoot at each other anyhow," I gripe, picking the nail polish off my nails. I guess now would be a good time to get dressed.

I slip my shorts back on and pull the T-shirt over my head. Geez, when did I lose my shirt? I don't even remember him taking it off me. Good thing my head is attached or I would probably lose that too.

"SpeSHEETS (Hurry)," Viktor says to the wall.

"What conversation are you having with that concrete wall exactly?"

He turns to face me, not looking amused and cocks his left brow.

"I was saying to hurry up. I'm hoping whatever is happening out there is over quickly. It's been quiet now for," Viktor glances at his shiny silver watch on his left wrist, "ten minutes. I'm thinking I can go and see what's going on."

"You mean we."

"I'm sorry?"

"You said for *you* to go and check it out, but you meant to say *we* can check it out."

"No, I'm fairly certain I said it correctly. It's simple. I go check it out, and you stay in here, secure." His response is stern.

"I'm not staying trapped in this tiny box! You can take me willingly or as soon as you leave, I will leave on my own."

"Absolutely not! You don't have any kind of a weapon. You need to quit being stubborn and realize we are at war here. I won't have you out there getting injured, or even worse, killed!"

"Oh no? And what if there's a fire? You're so sure I'll be safe in here and all."

"A fire? What are you talking about? They are shooting, not starting fires."

"I'm aware of them shooting. But what if they kill everyone and then torch the cabin? My butt will not be locked in this box while the rest of the place goes up in flames!"

"Clearly you watch way too many movies."

"I'm going, Viktor," I huff at him, standing my ground.

"You know, I could lock you in here."

"And I could kill you in your sleep, looks like we both have decisions to make."

Viktor turns away, angrily grumbling to himself, pulling out his gun from his leg holster and meticulously screws on the silencer. That's one mean-looking weapon he totes around.

He glances at me shortly. "Coming?"

I smile and nod.

# TEN

## Viktor

**THIS WOMAN IS INFURIATING. I NEVER CATER TO** anyone else, but I need to make some adjustments if she's going to stay in my life. I don't know if she realizes just how serious I am about us being together. Ever since I first saw her, I knew she was made for me. Tate has his Emily and I have my Elaina.

I'm brought out of my thoughts as she bumps into my back. "Shhh!"

Elaina nods hurriedly and looks around the kitchen. I follow, taking stock of the broken glass and bullet holes everywhere. It looks like someone just stood outside the cabin and shot the place up.

The wind blows in, swaying the pale yellow curtains.

I gesture toward it all. "Be careful with the glass, I don't want you to cut your feet."

She stares at the glass riddled counters, lost in thought. Tears spill from her eyes and track down her cheeks.

"It's okay, Princess, come here," I utter softly, pulling her to me. She grasps my shirt and buries her head in my chest, crying silently. My poor love has been through enough this week as it is.

I have to figure out a way for this craziness to stop. She will break from it eventually and I will never move past that. I'm torn from my thoughts as a sharp pain slices from my head down through my body.

I drop my gun in shock and melt to the ground, staring in horror at Elaina. She gasps and scrambles backwards. Mouth gaping and wide eyed, she points behind me.

I feel wetness drip down over my forehead creeping towards my nose, and I touch it lightly. Pulling my hand away, I'm met with red fingers coated in my own blood. I stare at Elaina in a trance as she screams bloody murder.

In a fit of rage she dashes for my gun, raising it up in front of her, aiming it behind me. *What on earth is she aiming at?* Blinking a little of the fogginess away I watch as she yells, body jerking as she empties the clip into something behind me.

I turn slowly due to the wobbly feeling I have in my head. Lying face up on the ground behind me is a very dead Kendall, along with a large, bloody butcher knife. Confused and foggy, I consider Elaina again, and then everything goes black.

# Elaina

"Alexeeeeeeeeei!" I wail as loud as possible. Rocking back and forth, weeping uncontrollably, I clasp Viktor to me tightly. The glass crinkles and stabs into my bare skin with each movement but I feel none of it. "Spartaaaaaaaaaaaak!" I scream between sobs and hiccups.

As soon as I saw Viktor close his eyes, I ran to him as quickly as possible. I shook and shook him, but he never opened his eyes. I can see and feel him breathing, but there's no telling just how bad the damage is to his head. *God, the blood. There's just so much blood.*

I glare, angrily yelling at Kendall's motionless body, "You evil, stupid bitch! I HATE you! How could you hurt him? He was mine! How could you?"

Coughing, I lean over and lay Viktor's head in my lap. "I'm sorry, my love, so fucking sorry, my God," I gasp to his unmoving body, tenderly running my hand over his soft, bloody hair.

"Alexeeeeei! Pleeeease help him!" I call frantically, my crying hysterical. I wait, holding my heart in my hands and pray to any possible being out there that can help me.

After what feels like hours, Spartak rushes in the kitchen door. He scans the entire room until his eyes fall on us in the middle of the floor.

"Miss Elaina! Are you hurt?" he asks, rushing toward me only to stop abruptly when I raise my head, pointing the gun straight for him.

"Don't touch him," I growl savagely.

He raises his hands up in a placating gesture and takes a step backwards. "Woah! It's okay, it's just me, Spar. I'm here now, so you are safe. Let me check the boss."

"Where's Alexei?" I sniffle and keep the gun trained on him.

"He's outside doing perimeter and building checks. We weren't prepared for so many people to show up."

"Go get Alexei," I croak, my throat raw from screaming.

"Ma'am, please. I can take over and help now if you would let me."

"I SAID, go fucking get Alexei! I will not leave Viktor, end of discussion! Now!"

"Yes, of course, ma'am," He nods worriedly, quickly jumping up and rushing out the back door.

I'm so sad and angry inside I feel like I could shoot ten other people right now. Not that I can. I emptied the entire clip into that bitch, but no one else knows my weapon is spent.

Seconds later I hear Alexei shouting frantically, "Viktor is hurt? Where is he? What happened to him?"

I clear my throat, and then call out hoarsely, "In here, Alexei!"

I don't even get to finish with his name and he's already charging through the door. He turns white as a ghost when he sees Viktor lying on the ground, frozen.

"Put the fucking gun down, Miss, now." He grumbles and hastily makes his way to me, not even flinching as he passes my outstretched weapon. His accent is more pronounced, I'm assuming because he's stressed out. "Tell me what happened to him, damn it."

I draw in a deep breath and calm my tears, having to concentrate on explaining everything. "We came out of the safe room, there," I point towards the pantry door a few feet away.

"He was warning me about the glass everywhere, you know how he is." Alexei nods and I continue, "then out of nowhere blood pours down his forehead. When he fell to the ground I saw Kendall had that huge knife. I realized she had stabbed him in his head and when she went to stab him with the butcher knife again I shot her."

"You shot her? But why didn't the boss shoot her?"

"Because he was bleeding like crazy and on the ground! Look around you, there is blood all over the place!" I flail my arms violently in the direction towards the bloody mess. When he fell, his blood splattered and smeared everywhere around us. "Anyhow it doesn't matter who shot her, what matters is Viktor is hurt. You need to help him, please!"

He crouches down next to us feeling Viktor's pulse. "I understand your upset, but did you check his pulse?"

"Well no, he was unmoving and unresponsive, I just figured he needs to go to the hospital or he'll die from all this blood loss. I know he was breathing, I saw his chest rise, but he passed out and hit the floor. It has to be bad, right."

"Head wounds bleed a lot regardless. It looks like he needs some stitches. I'm calling one of the guys in who used to be a medic in the Russian military. Try to calm down a little, you will help him out more that way." I nod and stroke Viktor's cheek lovingly, not paying attention to anything he says passed the word medic.

I hope he will be okay. I have come to care for Viktor so much. Do I love him? Yes, absolutely. There's no doubt in my mind that I do, after the events that occurred today. Alexei pulls out his phone and I stare at him questioningly. I don't know who he would be calling at a time like this. It's hardly the time, and he needs to be concentrating on helping Viktor right now.

"I'm calling Dmitry. He's the one who can help."

I nod, wiping at my tears. Shit. I have blood all over my hands, I'm sure I just rubbed it all over my cheeks. I probably look the part of a psycho killer now. Zoning out, I don't pay any attention to what is said on the phone. I have Viktor's gun and as I stare at him, I vow to shoot anyone who hurts him. I lightly kiss his bloody forehead and whisper to him, promising, "You'll be okay, love."

"Oh shit! Boss?"

I'm pulled out of my reverie by an unfamiliar voice.

"Relax, мышь (mouse), it's Dmitry. He will help as much as he can."

"What's going on?" Dmitry inquires, coming to squat beside myself, Viktor and Alexei.

Spartak stands in the doorway, concerned, but also ready to protect us in case something else goes wrong.

Glancing up, I mutter, "He won't wake up and his head is bleeding all over the place."

He shoots me a worried look with his whisky-colored eyes and nods, bending his head to look at Viktor. He reaches for him and I raise the gun.

"Easy, Miss. I'm just going to have a look. I have to see what's going on, so I can attempt to fix, yes?"

I look him over from top to bottom. He looks older than us, probably around forty and in great shape. He has very short brown hair to match his sparkly, intelligent eyes and has a pleasant nature about him. He doesn't strike me as a threat so I lower the weapon and he scoots in to get a better look.

"Well, it appears as if the blood flow has had some time to slow down and start clotting. Head wounds bleed more than most anyhow, that's why it looks as if you butchered someone."

As soon as the word 'butcher' comes out of his mouth, I start to weep miserably again.

"You fucking idiot! The nutso over there used a fucking butcher knife on the boss. Meesh peeLAA desyiVAW (Mouse saw everything)," Alexei growls angrily and Dmitry pales.

"I'm so sorry. I didn't mean it like that," he says to me, remorseful.

I choke up. "Please just fix him."

He goes straight to work gathering everything he needs and cleaning the area. I sit stationary and watch every move Dmitry makes. Thank God the blood has slowed down some. It's still bleeding but it's not pouring out like before.

My skin feels stiff and gross from the blood drying. My nails are grimy and caked with it but I refuse to leave him like this. Even if Vik has someone here to help, I'm staying next to him every single minute. A harsh scrubbing can wait.

Meeting my eyes Dmitry kindly says, "Hold him still. I have to put in a lot of little stitches and don't let his head fall backwards, keep it elevated so the blood will flow downward."

"Okay. Do you know if he will he wake up?"

"He will wake up after some rest. I think his body went into shock when he saw his own blood. It went into protection mode and had him pass out. It's actually fairly common when people see a larger amount of their own blood. The wound's not deep enough to do permanent damage to the brain area. Luckily this was right over the skull, so it acted like a protective barrier. Now, if he wakes up and after a while doesn't seem to be himself, then we should take him to the Emergency Room. I'm confident this will suffice."

"Thank you." I show my appreciation and Alexei grunts in agreement.

"Please don't thank me yet. Wait until we see if it works. And Alexei, we need to get him on the couch or to a bed and put a pillow under his head."

"Okay, now?"

"Yes, now. He is all stitched up and the only other thing I can do is put ointment on the cut. I'll do that after we move him though."

"Okay, Doc, sounds good." Alexei gestures to Spartak to come help lift Viktor.

"You're a doctor?" I quiz Dmitry.

Alexei interrupts, "Yes, he's a great doctor. He went overseas to help tend to the soldiers over there with the war."

My eyes widen marginally. "Seriously? That is so kind of you."

He shakes his head sadly. "No, Miss, they are the ones who truly sacrifice. I just sew people up."

I squeeze his arm gently and follow Alexei and Spartak to Viktor's bedroom.

I race ahead of them to fix his pillow perfectly. They get him all settled and the doctor puts a thick coat of clear ointment on Victor's wound.

"Thank you all so much for helping him," I say as they start to leave the room.

"Are you going to watch him?" Alexei inquires, peering at me curiously.

"Yes, I will not leave him," I state, making a silent promise to myself and glancing back at Viktor for a brief second.

"Good, take a shower and wash up while you wait. If he wakes and you look like that, then we will have World War Three on our hands."

"I would rather just sit beside him."

Spartak grumbles at me. "No, Miss Elaina, please listen to Alexei about this."

Rolling my eyes, I turn away from them. "Okay, geez, but I'm shutting this door because I'm leaving the bathroom door open for him."

They all leave the room and I'm met with a loud silence when I shut the bedroom door.

I'm not sure exactly how I should do this. I can see a large portion of the room from the shower, but not the bed, which is where Viktor's lying. I'll set the gun on the counter, beside the shower. That way just in case I don't hear something and he needs me to protect him, I'll be able to jump out quickly and take care of it. I know the cabin is empty besides the guards and the area is supposed to be secure, but I can't help to be paranoid. We were just attacked for heaven's sake.

I strip him of his filthy shoes and unbutton his pale blue, blood-saturated shirt, attempting to make him comfortable without moving his body or head too much.

Using a wet wash cloth, I do what I can to clean off his face for him.

Once I complete that task, I cover Viktor up with the soft, light sheet. Dipping down and gently kissing his cheek, I make my way to the bathroom to start the shower. God knows I need a strong scrubbing. Today's a completely new kind of dirty.

## Viktor

### five hours later

I'M AWOKEN BY MOVEMENT NEXT TO ME AND A
sharp pain  shooting through my skull. Everything's a
little fuzzy but from the sweet brown sugar smell I know
it's her beside me.

Taking a deep breath, I open my eyes tiredly and glance
at my princess. Elaina sleeps on her side curled into my
body, with her hands clasped together tightly next to her
chin. She's breathtakingly beautiful. She has no clue just
how much I worship her. The gun rests beside her with the
safety on. *Good girl.*

Reaching over to lightly touch her silk-like skin makes
my head throb and I hiss through my teeth. I've got to see
what's going on back there. I remember the pain, but I don't
remember getting hit with anything. It was instant pain,
sharp and stabbing. And blood. I remember lots of blood.

Bit by bit, I attempt to sit up, holding onto the bed as I

fight the dizziness. Christ, what did I miss? *Oh no, the kitchen!* I have to check out the cabin. I don't know if we're secure and if everyone is okay. At least Elaina is here so I know she's okay.

Okay, let's try this again. I rise gradually, until finally I'm standing at my full height. *That only took ten minutes to accomplish.*

I arrive at the bathroom mirror and I have to admit, I'm not impressed. There is still quite a bit of dried blood on my face and my hair looks disgusting. I can't look like this, call me vain, but I pride myself on always looking my best. I can't believe she saw me looking so terrible.

I flip on the shower and strip the rest of my clothes. It appears Elaina was nice enough to undo all of my buttons and to remove my shoes for me. That's fortunate, because at this moment I don't know if I can bend over without falling or puking. I can't get over the fact that I didn't protect her. What kind of man am I, to not be able to keep her safe?

Stepping into the steam, and under the hot spray, I grit my teeth to keep from yelling at the pain on my head when the water hits it. My appearance will obviously have to wait, there is no way I can run my fingers through my hair with soap to wash whatever's going on back there. I'm going to look for a small mirror once I catch my bearings a little better and see what hurts so badly.

Clambering out of the large shower, I'm unamused at how ungraceful every action of mine seems to be. I feel like I'm an inexperienced toddler, banging around everywhere. I don't know if I'll even be able to get my clothes on successfully.

Leaning over the sink to brush my teeth, I catch a brief glimpse at a pile of clothes on the floor and do a double take. They are covered in blood. Not soaked, but it looks as if blood was smeared all over them. Surely that can't all be from me? If so, that would explain why I was so dizzy on waking up and especially after showering.

I didn't see any injuries on my lovely girl, though a lot of her was covered up in my t-shirt. I love that she steals my clothes to wear. I told Elaina to cut them all up or do whatever she wants to anything. I only care about a few suits, but even then I can always replace them.

Leaving the bathroom, I'm met with a sleepy Elaina sitting on the end of the bed. Her blonde hair is a complete mess, as if she fell asleep with it wet, and she looks absolutely adorable in her rumpled shirt. She rubs her eyes tiredly, not realizing I'm watching her.

"Princess, are you okay?" I rasp, standing in the doorway.

She gasps, head shooting up to look at me eagerly. "Me? Are you nuts? How are you feeling? I can't believe you took a shower already! You need to rest." She's rambling and I smirk. I adore the fact that she cares enough to chastise me and want to take care of me.

"Why is my pillow case black and not the others?" I ask, puzzled.

"Oh, well, because of your head of course. I didn't want it to stain the light one with blood, so I changed it before the guys laid you down."

"Who laid me down? What exactly did I miss and what happened to my head?"

"Alexei and Spartak are the ones who laid you down with the doctor guy who works for you."

"Okay and what happened to my head? Why does it hurt so badly? The last thing I remember was a sharp pain, but it didn't feel like I was struck with something. I remember seeing you yell and that's about it."

Elaina's pretty blue eyes tear up and she stands, walking

toward me timidly. "You were stabbed." She chokes brokenly, irises so full of sadness and fear. A tear trickles down her face and she glances away. "You lost a lot of blood and passed out. The doc sewed your head up and put cream on it."

"I see. So what happened? Who did it and are my men holding them?" Reaching out, I grab onto her hand, squeezing it to bring her some comfort. She seems so distraught. I know it was probably scary, but we're both okay.

Glancing up at me, more tears rain down over her cheeks.

"Princess, please. We are both alright. Stop crying and tell me, baby," I murmur.

"O-kay," she says brokenly. "K-k-ken-dall got in and sta-stabbed you with a big knife. You're lucky you're so tall compared to her or she could have seriously injured you. She was going to do it again, I swear. I saw her try to-to do it. I saw her rear back with the knife, aiming for your back, so I had to shoot her. I'm so sorry, Vik-Viktor. I promise I had to or Kendall would have hurt you more." She sobs and my insides mash together seeing her so torn.

Standing up straighter, I pull her to my chest, wrapping my arms around her tightly and whispering, "It's okay, lovely, you did the right thing."

Rearing back, Elaina glares at me, incredulous. "The right thing? I killed someone! You can't just wash that off, Viktor! Trust me, I tried. I scrubbed so hard I bled in some places and yet it didn't help with the demons screaming at me inside."

She pulls away from me and perches on the edge of the bed.

"I can't believe I killed Kendall. I thought you were fucking dying. You wouldn't wake up and there was blood everywhere. You wouldn't open your eyes and I just wanted to kill her all over again for taking you away from me."

She buries her face in her palms and weeps. I'm lost. I've never felt remorse for a kill before. I've always just taken care of the job. I clean up messes and take care of the bad things my father or brother never wanted to touch.

I step close to her. "Then why, Princess? Why on earth would you do such a thing if you are to feel so guilty afterwards?"

Glancing up at me through her fingers. "Why, Viktor?" She stands abruptly, putting her hands to her sides, face swollen from her weeping. "Because I love you. I would kill a hundred people to protect you, even if it makes me a completely horrible person. If it comes down to you or someone else, I will always kill for you." She sniffles and wipes her face, looking at the ground, obviously ashamed for admitting that she would kill again.

Placing my hand on her cheek, I tip her head to meet my eyes. "I love you, so much. Vee oo moy dooSHAA (you have my soul)," I whisper and bend to delicately touch my lips to hers. The kiss evolves from sweet to possessive where I own her mouth. Elaina submits, grasping my sides and returning the kiss with pure love.

Leisurely I pull away, resting my forehead on hers. My heart sings inside knowing that finally she loves me as well. I lightly run my pointer finger over her bottom lip. I wish I could make love to her right now, but I can't. I'm so wobbly and I have to take care of the pressing issues.

She mumbles sadly, "I killed someone."

"Elaina, I'm so sorry this is upsetting you so much, but to be frank with you, I've killed many bad people. You did it to protect me and out of self-defense. I'm positive after she killed me, Kendall would have come after you next. She never would have let us happily be together, or let me be with anyone for that matter," I say sternly, determined to get her to let some of the guilt go.

She nods, but I don't fully believe her. I pray she can move past this and find some peace. I'm not even going to blink twice at it.

"Come, little love, I need to touch base with my men. I've been indisposed for too long."

I eventually locate my cell and send a mass text so everyone can meet us in the living room. I'm too worn out to hunt everyone down. Elaina puts more clothes on, as do I with her help and we head out there to speak with everyone.

"Boss, glad you are doing better, sir." Alexei greets me as we sit down on one of the comfortable sofas. He sends Elaina a concerned look. I squeeze her hand tightly to help ease her discomfort and show her support.

"Thank you. Now where is everyone?" I scan the room, missing two of my men that I had sent messages to.

"Anatoli and Mikahel didn't make it, sir." Alexei delivers this news solemnly.

"Christ!" I snatch up the lamp from the sofa table beside us and throw it hard, shattering it against the wall. Elaina jumps but my men don't even glance at it. They are so used to my temper that the little outburst doesn't affect them.

"Calm, lovely," I murmur afterwards and she clasps my other hand tightly. Surprisingly, her touch soothes me and I sit back, cataloging all the thoughts racing around inside my head.

"Okay, first off, where is Kendall?"

"Boss, the Missus is in here." Spartak speaks up and gestures toward Elaina.

"I am fully aware of who is in this room. I'm the one who called you here, in fact. Elaina is mine. You shall treat her as boss, as you do me. Is that understood?" I say sternly and everyone nods their acceptance, looking at Elaina with a higher form of respect.

"Now, I'm sorry to hear about our men. I will take care of their families accordingly. That being said, where is Kendall?"

Spartak glances at Elaina nervously then toward me. "I had a few of the guys put her in the barn. I thought you may return her to her father as a show of good faith."

Surprised, I nod, pleased at Spartak. "Yes, that's very good. I will contact her father and see if there is any way we can talk and reach an agreement. How many of our men were killed here?"

Alexei leans forward in his seat. "Fifteen. They came in with guns out and ready to shoot. We weren't ready."

"Someone round up the bodies and take them to Minska Funeral Home, while you're there check on how Sergei is doing. We may have one large funeral for all the families to pay their respects at once since there are so many. Clean this place up and get it secure again."

"Sir, I took care of that already. I wasn't sure how long you were going to be unavailable."

"Good work. I'll call Kendall's father and get back to you about how we're going to move forward." I attempt to stand up but have to sit back down.

Alexei reaches to help me stand and I swat him away. "I can do it!" I grumble and stand by myself. Slowly, but I do it.

"Come on, Princess," I say and hold my hand out for Elaina. She stands and eagerly accepts it again.

"Are you okay? Do you want anything while we are out here?"

"No, lovely, just to lie down, my head is bothering me."

Alexei steps forward with a tube, handing it to Elaina. "For the boss's wound. Doc said to apply it to the stitches and try to keep them soft for a few days. He also said not to wash the area, just rinse it for a few days."

She nods and eagerly takes the ointment. "Thanks, Alexei."

We take our leave and leisurely make our way back to the room. I can't walk too quickly or I get dizzy. I refuse to have my guys help me to my room when I am still able to do it myself. It doesn't matter how long it takes us, I'm too stubborn to give in.

I'm moody and exhausted when we get back to the bedroom. That's the first time my men have seen me look so unprofessional and I don't want to make it a habit. I should have had Elaina help me dress in my suit prior, instead of being so stubborn.

She squeezes my shoulder as I sit on the side of the bed. "You sure you don't want anything to eat or drink?"

"Not now, I still feel too nauseous. Perhaps later if my stomach settles some."

"You should just get some more rest then. I want you all better and you never get to just relax. You always have something going on or some kind of drama it seems. You must feel like you're going to explode inside with the copious amount of stress."

"I can't relax just yet, I have to call Kendall's father, Kristof Cheslokov."

"I understand, Viktor. Geez, I feel bad for him having to learn to spell that growing up."

I chuckle and dig through my pocket for my personal phone.

"Da (yes)."

"Kristof? This is Viktor Masterson."

"Mr. Masterson, what can I do for you?"

"I was hoping to meet to talk peaceful terms."

"That sounds like a wonderful idea."

"I have something that belongs to you."

"Is it well?"

"No, it has gone bad and perished."

"I see. Then perhaps you should bring very good terms with you."

"I have an offer I believe you will be pleased with."

"Very well."

"Three days at the dock?"

"Da."

I hang up and plug my phone into the charger.

"Well, lovely, that went surprisingly well and he took the news fairly easily."

"How in the world could he not care that his daughter is dead? I couldn't even imagine talking about it just now like you did."

"Kendall has given him many problems for a number of years now. She was always stirring up trouble with men, she was the type who enjoyed them fighting over her. Kendall even got her sister suspended from her boarding school because she was sending random guys there, saying it was time her sister became a woman. Kristof will probably miss her since it's his daughter, but I'm sure he is also relieved. He didn't have to be the one to kill her and now he will get a piece of my stuff like he has always wanted. If anyone has an issue it would be his wife, but if we meet terms then he will handle her."

"How do you know so much about Kendall?"

"Are you being jealous right now?" I smirk and she rolls her eyes at me.

"No, just wondering, you're like an encyclopedia on her life choices."

"Her father has always wanted me to marry her. He believed I could make Kendall settle down. She'd have money and of course he wanted an *in* at some of my territory."

"Ugh, sounds like that whole family has lost their marbles."

"Pretty much." I make a disgusted face and she smiles. I'm so thrilled to finally see her send me a genuine smile again.

"I had Kendall watched for a long period of time and had extensive background work completed on her. I've never wanted any part of that mess."

She yawns and quietly says, "Can we go back to bed? Now that you are okay, I feel drained. I had just fallen asleep when you woke up. After all of the chaos today I would like to just put this gooey stuff on your head, go to bed, then eat something when I wake up."

"Yes of course, Elaina, whatever makes you happy, though I'm not looking forward to you touching my head. It burns horribly."

"Dmitry left you a few Vicodin tablets in case you were too uncomfortable. I can get them for you, if you would like."

"No thank you, I will deal with it and just take a few Tylenol. I want to be alert not loopy just in case anything else pops off."

"You believe something else will happen?" Elaina utters, worried.

"Princess, I think we will be perfectly fine, it's just a precaution."

"Okay sounds good," she rushes to the bathroom and brings me two pills along with a glass of water.

"Thank you lovely. You're going to end up spoiling me, you know."

She skims over my face, looking at me compassionately, "you deserve it Viktor. Not only because of what happened, but also because of before. For months you have taken care of me, watching out, offering if I ever needed anything, I was blind. I'm sorry it took me so long to realize how wonderful you are."

"You think I'm wonderful, huh?"

"Really, that's all you heard?" She giggles and I pull her down onto the bed with me.

"I want to make love to you so badly," I rasp.

"I know, but you need to get better first. Please just rest. We have plenty of time to make up for lost time in the future."

"That sounds perfect."

She cuddles into me and I wrap my arm around her, holding her warm body securely next to mine.

Tipping her face up and meeting my eyes, she says quietly, almost bashfully, "I love you Viktor."

"Ah, baby, I love you too." I respond happily and Elaina gives me a chaste kiss on the mouth.

God, I can't wait to make love to her, to fuck her, to marry her, all of it. I love her more now than I ever have before. I can't believe she finally gave in and admitted to me that she loves me back. Hmm, I wonder if she will even want to marry me.

We have to discuss this work thing also if I'm not able to reach terms with Kristof. I swear if anyone tries to hurt her again, I won't hesitate, I will kill them in a moment's notice. Elaina deserves so much; I hope I can give it to her, while running the Bratva. I wonder what she thinks of it all.

"Princess, how do you feel about my life with it being so involved with the Bratva? Can you live with it?" I pry and get no response. "Princess?" I question louder.

"Hmmm?" she mumbles sleepily.

"Never mind, Elaina, get some rest, god knows you have worked for it."

"Love you, Vik."

"Love you, too."

No one's ever called me Vik before and I think I like it. My stomach clenches firmly with excitement each time she says it and I just want to squeeze her tight.

I hope she's lucky enough to sleep without her horrible dreams haunting her. I won't hold my breath though. Every night Elaina screams in her sleep; I shake her gently, hold her and do what I can to comfort her. There are even nights when she cries out and claws at her skin.

I don't believe she's aware of it as she never acts like any of it happened in the morning. Some days she looks so exhausted. In the past when she appeared tired and worn out, I always believed it was from her working late hours and partying. However, now I see the real reason is that she has this monster coming after her in the dark.

I wish I could go back and torture that scum, Tollfree, all over again for her. I would hurt him in many other excruciating ways. I know it's him Elaina dreams about. I know he still haunts her even long after he's dead.

Now she has this truck load of guilt dogging her as well. I can only imagine what horrific things she will dream of now. My poor love. I will continue to love her and hold her tight. I will do everything I can to protect her, even if it is only from her dreams. It's my job now to make sure she's okay.

# TWELVE

## Elaina

### three days later

I PERCH MY HIP AGAINST THE TAN GRANITE kitchen counter and cross my arms. "I'm pretty sure I'm going with you," I argue stubbornly. He's not going to get away with bribing me with bacon. I love it, but it doesn't help his case in any way right now.

"Why would I take you with me when I'm attempting to reach an agreement with the man whose daughter you killed?" He glares at me, irritated. Big bad Viktor isn't used to anyone arguing with him, well, news flash! I won't just lie down and take orders.

He sighs loudly and continues, "Not smart, Elaina. I want you here and kept out of sight. I won't be able to think clearly if you are there and can get hurt."

"I appreciate your concern, but I need to go."

"What do you mean you *need* to go? This is men's business."

"Oh, you pig. You seriously just went there?"

"I didn't mean it like that, Princess. I'm Russian, we just handle things differently. You Americans think everything has to be a discussion."

"Us Americans? My God, you just keep sounding worse today! Please, dig yourself a deeper hole."

"Look, you're not thinking about this rationally. There will be many angry men there with plenty of weapons. You could be shot at any moment."

"Viktor, I need to be able to look at her father and tell him I'm sorry. It may not mean much to him or you, but it's something I have to do."

"So I'm supposed to chance losing you completely, just because you have the need to apologize?" He looks at me incredulously.

Exasperated, I huff, "You won't lose me, geez!"

"Oh, you're damn right I won't lose you. I'm a very selfish man, Elaina. If something were to happen to you, I'd blow through that whole goddamn family to get my justice. Now is that a chance you really want to take? Because you know it's true. I will slaughter that entire family as if they were cattle."

I can't imagine the devastation it would bring to those who don't deserve it if that were to happen. I don't doubt Viktor's word at all, especially when he looks so determined. I refuse to be the cause of more pain like that for any family, so I relent.

"Fine, Viktor, I'll stay put. *But* you have to keep me updated. It can just be a text message with a smiley face or something. I just need to know you are okay as well. Every hour, you better send me something."

"Consider it done, lovely." He nods and steps closer to me.

"There are so many things I could do to you on this

counter," he murmurs close to my ear.

Shoving bananas and spices over eagerly, he easily lifts me so my butt is resting on the counter and I'm almost the same height as he is. Leaning toward him, I nibble on his lip for a moment, causing him to groan in pleasure before I pull away. His breath is rich with coffee and a touch of mint.

Viktor's pupils dilate and bore into mine as he trails his fingers into the leg of my shorts. They were his sweats that I cut so there's plenty of room. His eyes widen when he finds me without my panties and he softly runs his fingers over my pussy lips. Each inch he gets closer to my opening I clench it, shuddering with need.

Grinning at me, he inserts a finger in me to his knuckle. It goes in smoothly as I'm soaked and ready for him. I tighten my pussy around it and Viktor purrs something in Russian.

He pushes my shorts over more, creating a larger opening. I salivate in anticipation of him shoving into me with his cock. I love when he's in a frenzy like this.

Viktor kisses sweetly down my jawline until he reaches my lips. Softly whispering over them, "You want my cock, Princess? This is one wet little pussy you have here." As soon as the word 'cock' leaves his mouth I moan breathlessly.

We are rudely interrupted by a throat clearing. "Um, excuse me, sir. It's time."

Viktor swiftly makes sure he's completely in front of me even though his guy is looking in the opposite direction.

"I'm coming," he rasps to the guard and I can't help but giggle with my mind resting in the gutter at the moment. When I start to laugh, he pushes his finger into me roughly and I gasp, instantly quieting.

"I apologize, Boss," the guy says and walks out of the room.

Viktor is practically hissing as turns to me. "I have to finish this later. I'm not happy about it, but I have no choice."

"Ugh, I wish you didn't have to go," I pout at him.

"I know, Printsyessa, me too." He slowly pulls his finger out of my cunt, sending lightning bolts of pleasure throughout my body. Grinning, he sucks on his finger then kisses me chastely before walking off.

After I've had a few minutes to catch my breath, Spartak comes into the kitchen with a whole new set of plans.

"Hey, Miss Elaina."

"Hi, Spartak, what's going on?"

"The boss set a temporary code to the safe room under the house, so we get to hang out down there while they're gone."

"Okaaay, and why do you seem happy about that prospect? I've seen the other panic room, and trust me it's nothing to get excited about. Take it from me when I say you're not missing out." I make a crazy face and he chuckles.

"I've actually seen this one already. I got the tour, and it's really cool."

"What do you mean the tour?"

"It's under the cabin, and huge I might add. It's bigger than this place. The boss told me it runs the length of the cabin, all the way underground to the barn. It even has another secret door we can use if we ever need to escape that way."

"You're joking, right?" I'm a tad skeptical.

"No, I don't joke. I thought I was going to get shot the last time I tried to joke with Alexei." Shaking his head at that, he continues, "The boss is in charge though, so he has to have a few secure areas. This one just so happens to have a movie room."

374

"A freaking movie room?"

"Yep, I asked why and he said if he was trapped down there for days he would want to be comfortable."

"At this point, I shouldn't even be surprised." I shake my head and eat a piece of toast topped with butter and strawberry jelly.

"Do you want to take some snacks with us?" Spar questions and stares longingly at my toast.

"Why, did you not eat?" I mumble with my mouth full.

"No, ma'am, not since yesterday."

"Okay, we can definitely take some snacks and sodas." I grab up a few things and follow Spartak to this mysterious panic room.

# Viktor

"Alexei, give me some specifics about the other day in the cabin. I know you've told me a few important details, but I want to go over everything so I have my facts straight. I spoke to my brother yesterday and informed him of what I was planning to do. Tate's not thrilled, but he said if we need any help to give him a call."

I shift more toward Alexei in the backseat, giving him my full attention as we speed in the Mercedes sedan toward the dock to meet Kristof. *Sail* by Awolnation thrums low from the Harman Kardon speakers.

"That's good, Boss. I believe I gave you the most important parts. Miss Elaina would be able to fill you in more about the actual act, if that's what you're wondering. I told you, we were all out in the yard and she was in the cabin, screaming hysterically until we came to help you. I thought she was going to end up killing us all when we tried to get near you." I grin at hearing my girl was protecting me fiercely and gesture for him to continue.

"I was wondering if Knees would be meeting us there, since Nikoli is close with Kendall's sister."

"No, Tate will stay out of it as much as he can. I knew Nikoli had a soft spot for her, but I didn't know it was that serious. Are they exclusive? And how do you know all of this?"

"I speak to him occasionally, and no, they aren't really serious yet, not that I know of."

"That could turn into an issue if Nikoli decides to get involved with the sister and becomes devoted. The last time he stormed into the club, it was because of Kendall running to her family and crying over Elaina fighting with her. I think he may want Sabrina more than you believe and he needs to be aligned with Tate's organization, not a female."

We're interrupted by Miesha, my driver. "Twenty minutes out, sir."

I meet his eyes in the rearview mirror and nod. Turning back to Alexei I have to refrain from rolling my eyes. I know how long it will take us, I own the damn buildings. I miss having Sergei here to drive me. All of this is Kendall's fault, she deserved to die.

Alexei clears his throat. "Let me speak to Niko before you talk it over with Knees please. I would like to make sure you have the correct facts about it all. I know Niko will tell me. If he's excited about a female, he likes to talk her up."

"I'll give you twenty-four hours," I murmur.

"Yes, sir."

The car stops and Miesha jumps out to scan the area prior to opening my door. He knocks on the window with his knuckles. Lev, my guard up front, gets out, performing another scan.

After a moment Alexei's door is opened and he gets out.

376

They all walk around the vehicle to my door, that way they can surround me when I get out. It's the best way to protect myself from getting shot. They would have to hit a guard first and I would have a better chance at diving back inside the car or elsewhere for cover.

The docks over here are always dark and filled with filth. The air reeks of fish and old gas fumes from the boats. I'm fairly used to it, frequenting this area. Part of that dead fish smell is probably stink from all of the dead bodies I've watched sink around here.

"Watch your step, the rats are bad in this area."

Miesha looks at me with a horrified expression. "Rats, Boss?"

I huff at him, irritated. "Yes, rats, do you need Alexei to hold your hand or will you ask your balls to drop."

The men chuckle and Miesha turns away, embarrassed.

Alexei leans in closer. "Umm, Boss, did you pick a meet point? I would like a heads up."

"Yes, I discussed this with a few of the men yesterday. They've been checking the area since then and reporting to me regularly."

I hear Alexei grumble under his breath and shoot him a glare. He shuts up but keeps the bitter look on his face. We stick to the formation and carefully make our way to the meet point.

Kristof is patiently waiting, sitting in a black, standard folding metal chair. Three of his men surround him, and continuously scan the area, looking paranoid. When he sees us approach, he stands, extending his hand out of respect.

I shake it and one of his guys pushes a second metal chair forward. What a dirty place to have this sort of meeting. I glance around the battered building beside us and the trash on the ground.

"I'll stand." Kristof crosses his arms across his chest. He

also stands, looking the part of an old man with his full head of silver hair. He's not as tall as I am, perhaps a few inches shorter. I'm more of a cut guy, not quite muscular but not small enough to be considered lean. Whereas he's slim, like he could use a few good meals in him to fill his clothes out properly.

I glance over at Kristof's men, scanning them from head to toe. He obviously doesn't care too much about what they wear. I firmly believe they are a direct link to the boss himself.

I always have my men dress decently. They may not all wear suits, but they're always in clean clothes that don't have rips and such in them. I don't pay quite as much attention to the street rats, but the guys I surround myself with, well, it's important and a requirement of the job.

Kristof's men look like hoodlums he found in an alley full of thugs. I wonder if he even provides them with any type of training. All of my men around me have been trained in hand-to-hand combat and weapons. I refuse to be surrounded by some waste of space who has no idea how to do his job.

"So how would you like to begin the negotiations?"

"Just like that, huh? You're not even going to pretend to be distraught over losing your daughter? You did receive her body?"

He nods, irritated. "Of course I received her body, you know this as well as I do. Why ask and have pleasantries? Let us get straight to business and leave Kendall out of this. Do I want revenge? Yes, of course, but I am aware that you did not want any of this. She started a war with the Russian Bratva who also happens to be the braat (brother) of the Big Boss of the Russkaya Mafiya. I'm not so blind and cocky as to think that there will not be consequences."

I'm pleasantly surprised at his rational thinking but not

quite sure if I buy into it all.

"Kendall had one of my best men's throat slit, she put a bomb on my beloved's car, she had my cabin shot up, killing an additional two of my best men and last but not least, she stabbed me in the back of my head in an attempt to kill me. I'd say you and your family are getting off extremely light. I'm prepared to negotiate a very small amount. Mind you, remember this is not compensation for her life, but a mutual agreement to keep peace once terms are reached."

He hisses angrily. "You don't think I deserve some sort of compensation?"

I chuckle menacingly. "You? Deserve compensation? You're joking, surely." He glares but shuts his mouth. "I'm the king of Bratva in America, perhaps I should demand more of what measly territory I allow you to have."

I snap my fingers and my other guards take a step out of the shadows. They stand like towers compared to the grease buckets here to protect Kristof. I had an additional ten men here waiting in case I needed assistance. All part of the plan I had discussed with them yesterday that Alexei threw a fit over. He may be my right-hand guy, but I don't run everything past him, it's the other way around. They all have to run things past me.

"What exactly is it you want, Mr. Masterson?" Kristof sighs and I know he's relenting.

"Well, how badly are you wanting to expand?"

"Very much so. I'm willing to do almost anything."

I rest my chin in my hand, thinking of what deal I can cook up that will benefit me. I had a plan in place but he seems to realize he's stuck and needs to be begging my forgiveness with this situation. This is exactly why I didn't want Elaina to come. He would have used her as leverage. Perhaps he would have played on her guilt, but it's not going to happen with me. My uncle taught me to be lethal when it comes to business.

"Kristof, I believe I have the perfect plan." I grin wolfishly. I know my ideas will frazzle him further.

"Okay, what is it you would like? Hopefully we can come to an agreement, I am a very reasonable man."

"I want a few things actually. First off, I want you to declare peace and call your goons off."

"Consider it done," he replies immediately, almost too eager.

I nod, pleased. "Secondly, your family and associates will stay out of all the clubs my family owns."

He blinks, confused for a moment, he doesn't know it, but it's to keep them far away from Elaina if she's at one of the clubs.

"Very well, is that it?"

"Not quite."

He looks at me questioningly. "Number three?"

"You always wished for Kendall to marry me, yes?"

"You were my top choice, you know this. I offered her many times to you. Perhaps all of this could have been avoided if you had taken me up on my offer in the first place."

"Good, then this should please you. And I wasn't ready for marriage at that time. Kendall would have been nothing but trouble for me. You were simply trying to push your burden off onto someone else. Anyhow, now I need your younger daughter."

His eyes widen and he chokes. "What do you mean you *need* her?"

"Exactly that. You send her to me and she doesn't ever go home. She will belong to me from here on out. Maybe after time if she does well, then she can visit you."

"So, let me get this straight, you're basically asking me to sell my daughter to you?"

"She's not for me. One of the men wants her. And yes, you will be trading her for your precious new territories."

"NeekaagDAA (never)!"

As soon as he spits the word out, I draw my weapon and swiftly put a bullet through the head of the thug closest to him. It makes little noise with my high grade silencer attached, but enough that Kristof stands gaping as his guard drops to the ground, motionless.

I gesture to one of my guys, Lev, to clean it up. My guard grabs him under the arm and drags him to the dock, smearing a little trail of blood as he goes.

Lev checks his surroundings, finally settling on a little bench. He secures the body to the small concrete bench then two more of my guys walk over to help him lift the bench and toss it into the water off the dock. Kristof's thug goes with it while Kristof gapes comically at the whole process.

Shrugging, I turn back to a shocked Kristof. "That's no problem, Kristof. If we can't reach an agreement then perhaps I should just start killing off people." I smirk and he cringes.

"No. No. No, now don't get hasty," he sputters and I'm pleased he can see I'm serious. "What do you want my daughter for? You won't be selling her to anyone else, right?"

"I won't sell her. I imagine she will be kept to be married."

"You don't plan to hurt her? No rape or torture, that sort of thing?"

"Christ. No. I don't get my rocks off by torturing young, helpless women. I got the Bratva here out of the sex trade for a reason. A person who works for my brother wants her. This will give you each a little of what you want. You can have warehouse E, which will expand your territory and the Russkaya Mafiya will get something that they want. The other terms are for me personally."

He eventually nods after a few moments. "I think that can be done."

"No, it's either done for sure, or not. You pack her up and send her over. You have a week. Then you will get the warehouse and I won't kill everyone you know."

He nods. "That should be feasible. I'll make it happen. Does that mean we will be at peace again?"

"It means we will be at peace when I have your daughter and I know you won't attempt to kidnap her back or anything. I'm warning you—and this is the only one you will get—do not cross myself or my family again."

"Yes, you have my word. If anyone attempts to cause trouble for your organization, I will personally see to it being handled in a manner you approve of."

"Then we have come to terms and have an agreement. This war ends." I am relieved, even though I hide it well. He nods and we shake hands again.

"Thank you."

I don't acknowledge his thanks, he's pathetic. We head for the car promptly, with my guards keeping watch the entire time.

We all load up and start on our journey back to the cabin. I forgot to text Elaina and I'm going to hear about that I'm sure. I'll have to come up with a creative way to make it up to her. I'm contemplating taking a nap when Alexei barges in right away about the deal I made.

"Boss, I thought I was going to talk to Nikoli first before you did anything with the girl."

"You can still discuss things with Niko. If he wants her then it will help keep her close. Then Nikoli gets a present that really cost me nothing; and I have an incentive for Kristof to stay on his toes. He doesn't know it but that warehouse is garbage and the State Troopers have been poking around it a lot lately."

"I understand that part, but what if Nikoli decides he doesn't want her, then what?"

"Then I will find another of my men to take her or she can become my house maid for all I care."

Lev speaks up. "Yeah, I've seen her. I'd take her if needed."

"There, see, she already has a contingency plan," I murmur and grin.

Alexei kicks the back of Lev's seat, "No. I will take her if Nikoli doesn't want her. I would get the first pick, right?"

Lev turns around and scowls. "You sound like whiny brat, Lexei. You probably wouldn't know what to do with that type of pussy."

"Enough!" I say sternly. "Look, Alexei, if he isn't happy with her then you may have her. I don't particularly care what happens as long as she is taken care of. No beating her or anything."

He grumbles and looks angry. "Of course I would never beat her or hurt her in any way."

"I'm not implying you would, I'm strictly putting it out there. Many men have it in their heads that when a woman is bought or sold that it's okay to treat her savagely. That is not the case; most women are actually sold to repay some sort of debt in the beginning. They should be treated decently, not inhumanly by a group of pigs."

He folds his arms over his chest grumpily and stares out his window. I guess that conversation is over with. I raise my eyebrow at Lev and he turns back around in his seat, watching the road.

Pulling out my cell I quickly type out a small message to my beautiful Elaina.

**Me**: I miss you.

**Принцесса**: You are in trouble!

**Me**: We will talk soon.

**Принцесса**: XXX

I watch the scenery as we make the trip back. It's so beautiful around this area. I hope Elaina will want to stay here or somewhere close. I love the warmth. Russia was always too cold for me, it made my bones feel brittle.

## Viktor

**L**EV OPENS MY DOOR WHEN WE ARRIVE, EAGER TO speak to me. "So, Boss, does this mean you will get each of us a wife?"

I give him a look that says 'you have to be joking' and shake my head.

"I'm sure you could find some girls cheap," he says stupidly and I have to restrain myself from punching him.

"No, if you remember, I got out of that business. The deal today was done for a completely different reason than to just buy and sell women. Regardless, that's none of your business. You want a wife, then find one when you have some time off."

"Yes, Boss." He sounds irritated and Alexei gives him a Cheshire grin.

I don't know what it is with them, but every time they are around each other they egg the other one on. Unfortunately it's quite a bit. There is no way I'm going to make a habit of buying wives for my men. This is all so I can keep Elaina safe, not some free for all. I despised it when I watched my uncle sell off women to be maids, wives, sex slaves or target practice. I had to sit by and watch for so long, but now that I'm in charge, I refuse to do the same.

Alexei comes up beside me, clearly thinking seriously about something. "Boss."

"Yes, Alexei, talk while we walk, I want to see my girl."

He nods and follows. "Umm, when are we getting Kristof's daughter?"

"You heard the same conversation I had with him. She will be here within a week."

"I was thinking that maybe you would like for me to stay with her here at the cabin for a while to see if her father tries to take her back. You have the safe rooms and everything, so we would be able to hide her pretty well."

"That's not a bad idea. But Alexei?"

"Yes, Boss?"

"What is it with you and this girl? Nikoli already stormed my club for her once. I need to know if you have a vested interest in her as well."

"No, sir. I would just like to keep things within your best interest."

"So you don't want her then?"

"No, sir. Well, yes I do, but not if Niko speaks for her prior." His cheeks tinge slightly and I wave the other guards off to the shop.

"I'll keep you informed on what is to happen with her."

"Okay, thanks, Boss," he says as he plops down on one of the sofas.

I continue walking and make my way down a small set of basement stairs off the hallway by my bedroom. It's dark and steep. The stairs are lined with rope lighting in case of an emergency. I would hate to end up falling down the stairs or breaking my ankle when I'm trying to get to safety.

They lead me to the larger safe room where Elaina is supposed to be. I can't help but feel excited at the prospect of seeing her, with each step I take bringing me closer to her. We haven't been apart much since everything happened at my house.

I can't wait to take her back there and have her belongings waiting. She doesn't know it but I had a few guards clear out her crappy little apartment and move her stuff to the house. Elaina will probably be a little upset that I did it without asking her, but she'll get over it eventually. I can't help it if I want to surround myself with her all the time.

I get through all the security features and eventually find her in the movie room. She and Spartak are in the movie chairs, wearing 3-D glasses while staring at the one hundred sixty inch screen and eating snacks. They are so caught up in the new Transformers movie they don't even notice me standing beside them.

I speak loudly and they jump. "How's it going?"

They both turn to me, Spartak a little pale and Elaina clasping her chest.

"Viktor! You scared the crap out of me! Spar, pause the movie please."

"Yes, ma'am." He pauses it, nods to me and then heads for the bathroom.

"Having fun, lovely?"

"Yes, this movie is insane in 3-D."

Shrugging, I take Spartak's seat. "Eh, it wasn't as good as I thought it would be. I wanted more with the dinosaurs."

"Don't say anything! No spoilers allowed," she chastises me and I chuckle.

"So what's this I hear about being in trouble? Are you

planning on punishing me?"

"Maybe, depends on how you are planning on making it up to me."

"Well, I was able to reach an agreement with Kendall's father. We still have to be careful for a little while, but I do have an idea I think you will like."

She smiles widely and raises her eyebrows. I had no idea she enjoyed surprises so much, I'll have to keep this in mind for the future.

"I was thinking that you keep mentioning that lake outside—" She squeals excitely midway and jumps up. She starts to leave the room, but I interrupt her. "Elaina, what are you doing?"

She grins. "I was going to look for something to wear while we swim."

"Right now?"

"Yes, right now! I've been cooped up here and I'm ready to do some exploring."

I grumble, trying not to appear as if I'm pouting. "I have a feeling you're not talking about exploring my body."

She rolls her eyes and laughs a little. "Come on, *please*."

"All right, you win." I huff at her and head for the door to enter the code. "Come on, Spartak!"

He rushes out quickly, his hair flat on one side. Surely he wasn't eavesdropping. I need to give him some time off.

We all shuffle out and head to the kitchen.

Elaina squeezes my hand and I realize I haven't kissed her since I've been home. As soon as we hit the water I'm getting a nice long kiss from her.

"So what should I wear?" she asks while chewing on her nail and looking up at me happily.

"Wear your black bra and a pair of my boxer shorts, it should cover enough." I will probably want to strangle each of my guards if they so much as glance at her, but I'll attempt to restrain myself. No promises however.

# Elaina

I'm so glad Viktor's back and taking me swimming. It's about damn time, I feel like I'm ready to go insane from being stuck inside. I'm not much of an outdoor kind of person, but the woods surrounding this place are gorgeous and I really want to check it out. Hopefully we can come back some time to enjoy this place when we aren't trying to hide out from the world.

Once I'm dressed I head back to the kitchen with a bundle of towels for us. I don't like to dry off with the same towel I sit on. It may be a weird quirk or something but I feel like I'm wiping dirt all over me when I try to dry off.

It's bad enough my toenail polish is shot to shit. I didn't have any remover to fix them and when I tried to paint over the old, it made it look like I have some sort of toenail growth.

Viktor's on his phone as usual, but beside him are some sodas and sandwiches. I swear I'm going to gain twenty pounds by the time we leave here. I had thought I needed to feed this poor man when it's been the other way around. I've never had a man cook for me so much in my life.

He trails off telling someone to 'take care of it,' and I can't help but be nosey.

"What are you taking care of?" I inquire as soon as he hangs up.

"Would you like the truth or shall I make something up?"

"What? The truth of course! Always the truth!"

"Okay, I was having some of my men move your things over to the house."

"My things. As in, the stuff from my apartment? A few items or all of it?"

"Umm, yeah, that would be all of it." He's sheepish when he replies.

Viktor's normally so sure and goes for what he wants, not worrying about other's opinions. It's pretty amusing to see him a little uneasy about going behind my back and doing something that he knows could get him in hot water.

I pace around the kitchen, tapping my fingers against my thigh, looking him over closely. He clears his throat and stands up straighter. I almost giggle when he does it, but am able to hold myself back. This is nice, making him stress a little. I can't believe the fool didn't ask me.

"I guess I'll have to think about it, now let's go swimming." Viktor nods, swallowing and scooping up all the supplies he gathered. "Aren't you going to change?"

"No, I wasn't planning on it, why?"

"You're going to swim in your suit, seriously?

"No, I swim naked," he declares quietly and I catch my breath.

"Oh! Okay then!" I quickly head out the back door but come to an abrupt stop when a giant man steps in front of me, making me gasp. "Eeek! Shit, you scared me!"

"Vat are you doing?" he asks in a really deep voice, laced with a heavy Russian accent.

"Ummm," I mumble. I don't finish as Viktor's body presses against my back and he casually wraps his arm around my waist.

He barks loudly at the guy, "Lev! Back up."

"Yes, Boss." Lev nods and steps to the side. I don't know what that was all about but I don't want to wait and find out.

Swiftly walking down to the beautiful lake, I take in the fresh air. It's muggy being in Tennessee but as you get closer to the lake it's like the air seems fresher, perhaps because of the mountains. I know it definitely feels cooler than normal, surrounded by so many trees and being right next to the water. This would be a beautiful spot to camp if there weren't a cabin so close by. I wonder if I would be able to swim here every day when it's warm once things have calmed down.

The water is cool and refreshing as I dip my toes into it and walk a few steps in. Turning, I take in Viktor. He peels off his under shirt and I'm met with his glorious stomach. He's not over built like some men, more lean. He has the magnificent 'V' going on, leading straight to one of my favorite large places.

"Water's not too bad." I twirl my foot to create mini waves around me. I didn't swim much when I was growing up. I did everything I could to keep my clothes on, at all times.

"Good, I'll join you shortly." He sends me a grin and I answer him with a little smirk.

Shedding the undershirt I had worn down, I toss it next to him, drawing his attention again.

"I'm glad you're not naked, or I'd have to shoot someone, I'm sure of it," he grumbles and I laugh.

I head more into the water, relishing the coolness enveloping me. It's peaceful and relaxing.

"Come here, my lovely," I open my eyes and find Vik close by.

"Jesus, you're like a cat! I didn't even feel the water move!"

"That's because you're like a wet chicken, flapping around out here."

I glare at him and walk straight into his arms. "I'm not a damn wet chicken," I grumble and he chuckles.

"Are you warm enough, Elaina?"

"Yes, I'm good. I love it out here."

"Yes, so do I. It makes all the daily things go silent."

"We should swim more." I kiss his stubbly jaw line.

"I agree. So have you thought about staying with me? Well, it would be our place but you understand what I'm saying?"

"Why are you babbling? Is this making you nervous? Is it us living together? You know we don't have to. I'm perfectly fine going back to my apartment."

"It's not that. I'm not nervous. Ugh. I'm just... Well, I'm excited. I've never had a woman live with me, and now you are here. You are my love and I may have the chance to spend my life with you, to share a home, and it just makes me a very happy man. I guess in a way I am nervous, because you could always say no."

"Oh, Viktor, I love you, too. I would love for us to live together. After this week, I wasn't looking forward to us being separated anyway."

"Good, it is settled. Thank you."

"Wait, I do have a request though."

"What is it?"

"Is it possible for us to stay here?"

"Yes, we can stay longer and visit whenever you wish." He smiles and I shake my head. It's not what I meant.

"No, Viktor, can we stay here, as in move here?"

"Here at the cabin? But it's so small. We could make it bigger if you would like, or change it?"

"It's not small to me. It's perfect. I don't want to change any of it, well, except having the guards leave. This place feels like home to me. At least what I imagine a home would be like."

"Ah, it is Mishka. I wonder if that old lady did this so one day I would have love."

"Your grandmother? How would she know?"

"She always tells me my house is too sterile, that no woman wants to be cold. I never knew what she meant, but I think I get it now. Yes, Princess, we can stay wherever you want. I'm just happy you want to stay in the area."

"Yay! Thank you! And yes, this area is beautiful."

"Now kiss me, Moy lyooBOF (my love)."

So I do; I kiss him with every feeling of love I have inside me. I long for him to have all of me so I pour as much of my soul into it as possible. Viktor answers me with the same meaningful kiss. It's a kiss full of promises, of devotion, of happiness.

Viktor's sweet kiss turns more rushed as he relieves me of my clothes, tossing them toward the shore. He holds me tight, his skin setting mine on fire as he touches me. I dig my nails into his shoulders, silently asking him for more.

"Please, Viktor, I need you."

"I know, lovely, I want you too, so bad."

His sharp teeth nibble where my neck and shoulder meet as he gently pumps two digits into me. I clench my pussy tightly around them but then he moves them slightly, frustrating me so much that I grind myself on them, wanting more.

Running my hands over his smooth skin allows me to feel each dip and groove of muscle, his pebbled nipples and his rippled abs until I reach his large cock. I grip it tight and pump quickly, trying to get him worked up enough to take me.

After a few minutes it works and he pulls my legs around his hips. After sliding swiftly inside me he moves, unhurried, making each pump delightful. God, he feels like heaven.

Viktor leans me back and feasts on my breasts, pulling each hard peak into his mouth and ruthlessly sucking on them. He holds my hip firmly with one hand and lightly bites all around each nipple. With each nibble I clench snugly around his dick, making myself moan.

Tightening my grip on his shoulders, I pull myself up against him. His pecs brush deliciously over my nipples with each thrust.

Moaning "Harder!" into his ear makes him grip my side to the point of bruising.

"I've been too rough on you. You were a virgin and I have been tearing you up for the past week. I'm a selfish man. I should be being gentle; loving you, and not hurting you."

"No, please, I love it hard, I don't want you to stop," I plead while each drive of his dick sends my head into a whirlwind of pleasure. *Please don't change it up.* I love how rough he is.

"You will enjoy it soft, I promise."

Frustrated, I argue, "I love it when my pussy is sore all week long. I don't know if that's wrong of me, but each little twinge or pain I get, I remember you being there. I get these reminders all day of how well you loved me, of how much you wanted me."

He pushes into me slow and deep. I cry out quietly, enjoying the feeling of being completely filled.

"I always want you, Elaina, never doubt that. I love you and this body. Now shhh, I'm making love to you." I bite my lip at his stern reprimand.

Sweetly, he kisses up and down my neck, murmuring in Russian, pausing only for little bites. He feels incredible. I'm just impatient and get so eager when we're like this.

Viktor's hands run tenderly over my body as I hold onto his neck. "I'll make sure you still feel me, love." He growls and pumps into me fully over and over. The water splashes in between us causing pleasurable little sensations all over my clit and anus, highlighting his movements.

I clutch him, my nails biting into his skin. All I can manage is to gasp, "God do I feel you"

"You feel me now, Princess?" He murmurs, repeating me.

"Yessss." I moan loudly as he drives in to the hilt, gritting his teeth as he tries to prolong our pleasure.

Right when I start to feel my orgasm coming on I jerk him to me tighter and ravish his mouth with a crazy kiss. He grasps my hair tight, slowing me to control the kiss.

"Thank God you are mine," he whispers as my pussy clamps down on his large cock, milking him for everything he has.

He wraps me in a hug, burying his head in my neck and releasing his seed. My pussy spasms greedily, pulling each drop of it as far inside me as possible.

# FOURTEEN

## Viktor

### two weeks later

"**P**LEASE EXPLAIN THIS TO ME MORE. WHAT DO you mean we have to go to the house? We just got our things moved here to the cabin. We finally get everything calmed down and settled; now you want to change it up? What aren't you telling me here, Viktor?" Elaina asks. Her hand is propped on her hip and I groan inside. I know this isn't going to go over well.

When explaining things to Elaina, I *may* have left out everything with Kristof's daughter. I should have told her all about the trade but it didn't seem important at the time. We've had such a wonderful time together while moving into the cabin. We did change a few things around, but not too much.

Kristof ended up needing another week after his wife threatened to call the police. I guess his daughter—the one everybody is going so mad over—was supposedly betrothed to a member of some other Russian family. It's caused a big uproar on the wife's side of the family. I don't know the whole story and frankly I don't care.

I do know his extra week worked to my advantage with my princess, but it's also going to hurt me for not telling her sooner. She's probably going to go ballistic, so I need to figure out the right way to tell her how I traded a girl's life for a warehouse. However I spin it, she's going to have my balls.

Ever since I made love to her that day in the lake, she's pretty much ruled the roost. Elaina says we eat at a certain time or we have a certain color curtains, I've learned to step back and just nod my head. I want her happy and if these little things make her happy then that's the least I can do.

This however, I will probably be cast out to the barn for.

"Viktor?"

"Well, I didn't tell you absolutely everything that happened at the meeting with Kristof."

"I assumed you left some out, but what's so important that we have to move to another house for?"

"We have a guest coming to stay with us."

"Oh, cool is it someone from Russia? Or maybe your grandmother?"

"No, it's Kristof's younger daughter."

"Are you fucking kidding me right now? Her sister almost killed us!" she screeches, making me wince. "Why does she need to stay here? They don't have somewhere else for her to go?"

"It's not so simple." I close my eyes and take a deep breath. *When did I turn into a pansy?*

"So make it simple," she hisses.

"I kind of own her and she's coming because her father traded her." I swear I hear her growl when she hears my answer.

"You can't *own* another human being, Viktor. This isn't the eighteen hundreds or anything. Things don't work that way!"

"Yes, lovely, when you are in this lifestyle, they *do* work that way. Don't act so blind to my dealings, Elaina, you know what my family is, what I am."

"I can't do this, Viktor. I know all about you, but trading people? I have to draw a line somewhere. I just can't live with that. Does her mother know? My God, how could you do this?"

She sends me a heartbroken look and it makes me sick to my stomach. I walk to her to comfort her, but she backs away, and I bite my tongue to keep from getting angry. She shouldn't pull away from me, she has no reason to, and I'm not some atrocity she should fear.

"Please calm down, my love," I say quietly and reach for her again. Elaina turns away from me, disappointed, and I choke up as tears try to fill my eyes. It's the worst feeling; to have the person you adore and love the most be disappointed in you.

I can't possibly lose her, not now that I finally have her after all this time. I have to make her believe it's not my fault. Christ, I'm such a fool for making that deal. I should have known she wouldn't be able to handle that. The only way I can handle it, is knowing nothing bad will ever happen to the poor girl.

"Let me explain this further." I lean against the wall and place my head in my hands. I have to clarify this so I can dig my way out of this mess with her. "Kristof wanted to expand his territory and he is willing to do practically anything. The warehouse I have in a certain location has been being scoped by the Troopers and possibly the Feds so I needed to get out of it anyway. Kristof is a slime ball so this will kill two birds with one stone. As for his daughter—

" She makes a noise and my eyes shoot to her just in time to see a tear trickle down the side of her face. "Love, please," I plead but she shakes her head so I continue. "On the way there to make the deal I was speaking with Alexei. I remembered that Nikoli was crazy about this girl. He was so over the moon with her that he stormed the club and tried to attack me for what happened between you and Kendall. I know that if I'm enemies with Kristof, then Tate will never let Nikoli and this girl be together; and it will be all because of me." I glance at her beautiful face again to see her watching me with curiosity, and I'm thankful her tears have dried up.

"So I told Alexei about it and he said he would talk to Niko and see what he could find out. When Kristof told me he would do anything, I knew if it wasn't to me, then he would eventually sell his daughter off to someone else. This way she will be kept safe, and have the things she will need. Kristof will have a reason to back off from myself and my family, and Nikoli gets a chance to have the woman he wants."

"So you will just give her to him? Just like that? What if she hates him?"

"Well, that's why we are going to the bigger house so I can see how she really feels around him. I'm not just going to throw her at him if she hates him. I would never do that to a woman."

"Okay," Elaina says quietly.

"Okay? Princess?"

"Yes, Viktor. Okay, she can come and stay. I'll forgive you for this. Just...don't trade people, Viktor, it's not something I can handle."

"Ah, thank you so much, my love!" I pull her to me finally and hold her tight. I breath in the sweet scent of her shampoo and relish the warmth from her body. I thank the stars for bringing her to me and allowing me to keep her.

"But if she tries to hurt us, I'll kill her too."

I try to refrain from chuckling, but can't help it. She's gone from protester to protector in a matter of minutes.

"Okay, but I'll kill her instead. You can't go through that load of grief again. I can take care of it."

I can't bear the thought of Elaina hurting inside from some ignorant person making a stupid decision. I don't know if she could even handle killing someone else, unless it were life or death situation. Elaina is the warm to my cool; it gives us a nice, even balance.

"I have an idea, can I make a suggestion?"

"Of course, you are always welcome to."

"Okay, what if you bring them both here? There's practically another house in the barn. You could have them stay there to test things. Both would have everything they need, and you would be here to make sure she doesn't run off. It's a win-win for all of us. Have you spoken to Nikoli about any of it?"

"No, I haven't. Alexei is supposed to be handling that end of it and I was going to see how she felt once she came. I think your idea is really good, but what about my guards? Where would they sleep and eat?"

"You always tell me that expanding is not a problem. Why not get a few small campers or something. Plus they're portable if you ever need them somewhere else and they have AC/Heat/Stove/ bed, that kind of thing. Plus you have that big shop out there if you need more room."

I lean down and pepper kisses all over her face, causing her to giggle. "You, lovely, are a genius! I never would have thought of all of that. I think it sounds perfect. I'll send a few men out and see what they can come up with."

"Awesome! And now I don't have to pack up our gorgeous cabin. Thank you, baby Jesus!"

"Elaina, you finally said it," I reply happily.

"What are you talking about?" she inquires quizzically.

"You called the cabin 'ours'." I smile wolfishly and she rolls her eyes.

"Oh my gawd, you're so silly about somethings. I have embraced that this is our home, happy?"

"Yes, I am, one hundred percent. I love you so much," I mumble against her mouth and she closes her eyes.

"I love you, Vik, with everything that I am," she answers and I kiss her tenderly.

Pulling back leisurely, she gets a panicked look on her features. "When is she coming?"

"Today, that's why I've been rushing you."

"Crap!" She jumps up and runs around.

"What? Why are you freaking out?"

"Because, Viktor! We aren't ready!"

"Of course we're ready. There's nothing to prepare for, she's just a girl coming to stay."

"Shit! Men never understand this kind of thing! Tell whoever does the cleaning around here to get to washing the sheets for her bed!"

"My love, you've been the one zipping around cleaning stuff."

"Oh. Right." She scrunches up her nose, "Well then, I need to go clear out that barn and get it situated."

"Why don't I call the housekeeper who visits weekly? I'm sure she would enjoy the extra work time. Mishka will probably be up here again when she hears of another female staying."

"I can't wait, I love that mean old woman." She smiles fondly then gets that determined look on her face again, "Yes, the maid is a good idea. I'll go get started and you call her." She bolts right out the back door like a woman on a mission and I can't help but think about how amazing, and a

401

little crazy, she is.

As soon as she leaves I slip my hand into my pocket. The box I pull out keeps feeling like it's burning a hole there. Flipping the lid open eagerly, I'm just glancing down at it when the screen door crashes open. I slam the lid closed, hiding the box behind my back.

Elaina peeks her head around and looks at me suspiciously. "What were you doing?"

"Nothing, I was just getting ready to make that call," I reply as nonchalantly as possible, my heart beating a million miles per minute.

She nods slowly. "Right, well, I was just going to ask you to ask your men to pick up some more sweet tea. We need tea if we are having company."

"We usually drink vodka." I shrug as I shove the box in my pocket as if it's my phone.

"Please get some tea."

"You got it, lovely."

"Thank you," Elaina croons, blowing me a kiss. She runs off to finish doing welcoming stuff and I breathe normally again.

I think she just gave me a miniature stroke by coming back early. *Let's try this again.*

I pull out the nondescript white box and flip it open. A stunning three carat, Princess cut diamond, shines brightly back at me. The plain Platinum band accents the nearly flawless diamond even more. Pulling it out carefully, I flip it over to read the inscription. Engraved in beautiful lettering is 'Прекрасная принцесса' (Lovely Princess). This ring was made just for her and it deserves to have her name in it always.

Elaina seems to favor more simplistic things. I have to come up with a good way to ask her. I don't want to be over the top and scare her, but I want her to remember it. I think

I'll ask her tonight. She'll be so distracted with the company coming, she won't even realize what is happening until it occurs.

It's only been a month since we've been official, but I can't hold off any longer. It seems like I've wanted her for ages. We can have a long engagement if she would like, but this needs to happen sooner rather than later.

# Elaina

I'm busy cleaning up the barn and trying to make it as presentable as possible when the maid comes in to relieve me. She thanked me graciously like I was the one who called her, so no telling what Viktor told her. He gives me way too much credit for things. I just give my input or complain about something and he acts like I hung the moon.

When I first met him I never could have imagined this would be my life, or that I could love him so much. I was so incredibly blind to not see what was waiting very patiently right in front of me. I could kick myself for holding out on him for so long.

I still have some setbacks with my touching issue. I've tried to let him know what triggers things and he has backed off a remarkable amount. He still shows me a huge amount of love and affection, he's just more aware of how he does it. I'm so lucky to have found someone so understanding of it all.

I used to think Emily was a little nutty with how she always acted with Tate, but I get it now. Emily's growing with Tate and I'm so proud of the woman she has become given all the stuff she has dealt with. Having a baby on the way has made her grow up so much and it seems like it's really good for her.

Now, onto seeing about Nikoli and this new chick coming to stay. Viktor calls it a visit, but I seriously doubt it will be short. I'm pretty wary about having someone from that family around here, and especially around Viktor. He doesn't believe I would kill her, but he doesn't realize how much Kendall changed me. I would never cause harm to anyone for pleasure, but best believe I would shoot this one in a heartbeat if it came down to it.

I hit up the shower to scrub this grime off and find something appropriate to wear.

I throw on some jeans, t-shirt and combat boots. Nothing fancy, I want to be prepared if this new girl gets wild and crazy. She's lucky I don't have a gun or I'd tuck it in my pants to look really bad ass.

I wonder if Viktor is aware what exactly he's getting into with me. I'm probably going to drive him to drink more than a normal Russian drinks vodka, and that's a lot.

Chatter comes from the living room so I silently make my way to see what's going on. Peeking around the corner ninja-like, I'm met with a gorgeous blond giant, also known as Nikoli, and a small sprite of a girl. She's dressed in skinny jeans, a plain tank top, flip flops and has short, brown hair in a pixie cut.

She comes up to Niko's chest—granted the man is like six foot four or something crazy—but I think this chick may be shorter than me and I'm short. They main thing that stands out though, is she is the exact opposite of Kendall.

We lock eyes and stare at each other for a few moments. She doesn't seem scared nor overly brave. I wish Vik would have told me her damn name.

Nikoli turns, catching a glimpse of me for the first time and beams a bright smile at me. He's freaking beautiful in a completely different way than Viktor.

"Elaina!" He gestures for me to come to him, holding his arms wide open. Of course he would be happy to see me, he loves my sister dearly and I look exactly like Emily. Well, besides the eye color. I don't think I've ever met a man so protective over females who don't belong to him.

Making my way leisurely into the living room and attempting to keep my features blank, I step to Viktor's side. I feel a large, warm hand grab onto mine and it's like instant relief. I have real live proof that he's right beside me and he's okay. Nothing like the last time will happen. I'll make sure of it.

His breath tickles my neck as he leans close enough to whisper, "Relax, lovely. Everything is going to be okay. You appear as if you've swallowed something sour. Please show them your sweet smile and be happy. I love you."

I briefly check him over then nod. "I love you, too," I murmur quietly. Inhaling a deep breath and attempting to look friendlier, I bend in to give Nikoli a brief hug. "Hi, Niko."

"Hi, little sister!"

"Geez, I'm not the little one! It's Emily, she's so stubborn sometimes. I'm going to look it up on our birth certificates; just so I can rub it in her face that I know I'm for sure older than her."

He chuckles and pulls the female in front of him slightly bringing her much closer to me. He nods to her proudly then introduces her, "This pixie girl is Sabrina." He grasps her shoulders, dwarfing her like a football player would. "Sabrina, this is Em's sister, Elaina. I told you about them all, yes?"

"Da, blondie," she answers half in Russian and I cock a brow. I'm not amused, she better bust out with the English.

Snotty attitude firmly in place, I prop my hand on my

hip. "Excuse me?"

"I'm sorry, Niko likes to speak to me in Russian and it's become habit to just automatically answer him that way." Her voice is small and pleasant. She speaks kindly and it makes me feel like a tool for being bitchy, but her family doesn't like the man I love. It should be expected that I act wary around her.

Niko jumps in, razzing Viktor, "Never thought you would settle. This one must come with whip."

I giggle and Viktor shakes his head. "She doesn't need the whip, although I wouldn't exactly write the idea off completely." Niko busts out laughing and Sabrina smiles.

How on earth can she be so calm about all of this? She was just traded for a warehouse and she's acting like this is no big deal. I would be flipping my shit right now if I were in her shoes.

Hmmm, at least Sabrina is a better name than Kendall. I just met the chick five minutes ago so it'll take some time to warm up to her. I'll back off a little but she better not walk behind Viktor or I may go psycho. I do kind of feel bad for her besides the resentment I feel for her family. I can relate; I grew up with a family that didn't want me either.

# FIFTEEN

## Elaina

"**COME ON, PRINCESS, LET'S SHOW THEM WHERE** they will be staying. I'm sure Sabrina would like to get settled." Viktor carts me out the back door, Nikoli follows and Sabrina trails last. I sneak little looks back behind us a dozen times, paranoid there will be a blade in her hand at any moment.

I have to stop thinking that way. I just can't help my feelings; it's in my nature not to trust people. It's not a switch you can simply turn off and on when it's inconvenient.

I catch up quickly, whisper shouting, "Viktor! She's behind us! Let her go first!"

Viktor stops abruptly and catches me off guard. He shoots me an irritated look and then speaks over my head to Niko.

"You both head to the door and give me just a second with Elaina, please." It's not a real question, even though he makes it appear so. They smile and walk to the barn, waiting next to the door for us like this is totally natural.

He grumbles at me. "You need to stop this nonsense."

Glaring, I practically hiss back, "Nonsense? Have you lost your marbles? Her sister stabbed you in the back of the damn head! Your wound isn't even fully healed up yet and you want me to calm down? Not just no, but *hell no!*"

"Ugh, you're so infuriating sometimes! I know who she is! I was the one who was stabbed for Christ's sake!"

I know he's irritated but he just sends a friendly smile to Niko, like we're having a normal conversation about dinner or somthing. "If you give me two minutes I could tell you that she apologized profusely as soon as she came in the door and explained her sister had terrorized her. She's grateful because she thinks you helped her out but feels guilty because it was her sister. Her father has already told her that if she so much as screws this up with any of us that he will kill her himself. They are *not* a very caring family. I would assume you have a touch of compassion to share, being you were her advocate not too long ago when you found out about the trade."

"I'm not sure I buy it just yet. I just met her. You can't expect me to be buddies with her when I know nothing about her. And I gave you two minutes; in fact you had two goddamn weeks." I finish my reprimand and stomp the rest of the way to the barn, painting a smile on my face.

I open the barn door so we can all go in and get our new 'guests' settled in comfortably. We will definitely be talking more about this crap.

Viktor catches up quickly, acting as if he didn't just get put in the dog house. We show them around the ginormous building. If it wasn't for the safe room under the house, then this place would be bigger than the cabin. The barn actually resembles the cabin slightly, being that it's all wood. It's missing the porch, and the windows in here are fewer but much bigger.

The barn has been converted into more of a loft type space. Up the ladder there is a landing large enough to fit three full size beds for the guards. I had them take the stinky mattresses with them when they left though and asked Alexei to bring up a new large bed the same size as ours. It's a king size, which I'm now patting myself on the back for because otherwise Niko would have been hanging off the bed from the knees down.

I hung the old light blue curtains we had in the kitchen and used one of the new packaged comforters from the safe room downstairs. Being broke the majority of the time meant I never really had many options when it came to decorating. I may have gotten a little overexcited at the chance of sprucing up the barn.

Looking pleasantly surprised, Viktor's eyes shine with approval. It warms me inside to know he is proud of something I did, no matter how small.

The bathroom was a disaster. Thankfully, the cleaning lady gave it a good scrubbing and I brought new cream colored towels over from the cabin's guest bathroom. I love the huge fluffy towels we have.

The kitchen is a tiny space. It's adorned with a two-seater wooden table and was hard to do anything with, so it's still dreary. I did pick some pretty purple and orange wildflowers for the table though.

I can't believe I went to all this trouble to make them comfortable and it hadn't even registered until now. It didn't seem like I was preparing for an enemy, but for a guest instead. I guess because of Nikoli I have been treating this whole 'stay with us' issue as if they really are our guests.

At least Sabrina will be sleeping out here and we will be locked securely in the cabin, with Alexei as a watch dog.

Hopefully Niko will keep her in check, so I won't have to worry about it too much.

"Well, I hope you will be comfortable staying here," I direct to Niko.

"I will be very comfortable," he smirks cheekily towards Sabrina.

She glances at me a little unsure. "So, where's the other bed?"

"What do you mean? We showed you the bed up in the loft."

"I know that but there has to be another bed, right? I mean there's only one bed but there are two of us."

Niko jumps in. "No problem, I sleep on the floor. Unless you would want me to keep you warm at night."

I look around at the wooden floors crazily, then back at him. "Um, no. The floor's way too hard to sleep on! I thought you would be sharing or I would have had another bed set up. I'm so sorry. I just figured you know, since you are staying together and everything…"

Niko squeezes my arm gently causing Sabrina's eyes to shoot straight to the place he touched me.

"It's no problem. We will figure it all out."

"Are you sure, Nikoli?"

We can probably get another bed in here, maybe not tonight, but probably tomorrow.

Grabbing my hand, Viktor responds for him, "My love, they will figure it out. Come on, let's give them some time." Giving in, I nod. Screw it, why not; I've already gone out of my way when I don't even know the chick.

"All right. Well, the fridge is well stocked so help yourself." I head to the door and Sabrina follows.

"Look, Elaina, I just wanted to say thank you so much. You have no idea what you and Viktor have done for me. I don't know how to possibly repay you for it, but someday I hope I can."

Swallowing a large gulp, all I can do is nod with the sudden blockage in my throat. She clutches my hands in hers and gives them a firm squeeze before walking back over to Niko. He smiles at her as if she's the best glass of sweet tea he's ever had.

Score one for Sabrina. She completely blind-sided me with that one. Vik and Nikoli do a small hand shake and say their goodnights. Sabrina squeezes Viktor's hands the same way as she had mine and looks at him gratefully.

# Viktor

The barn situation was strange, and yet a success, I believe. Sabrina did the right thing to reach out to Elaina. I have to admit it took guts and it earned her a pinch of respect from me in that moment.

I already know where Nikoli stands with Sabrina without even speaking to him about it. One look at him and I can see it in his eyes. He has that same determined look I had when I first saw Elaina. I wish Sabrina good luck in fighting him.

I should let Alexei know his chance of having Sabrina is a lost cause. Nikoli is bull headed and very intelligent; he won't let her slip through his grasp. Alexei won't have a fighting chance if she even feels a smidge of that toward Niko in return.

We arrive back in the cabin and I try to think up stuff for Elaina to do so I can plan my surprise. I already informed the guys earlier of what my plans are and they are doing their tasks on that end. I called Mishka and she was sending stuff up as soon as possible. I've been thinking about this a little for a few days now, but I can't wait any longer for it. The rest is on me.

"Princess, go to the safe room please. We need a nice blanket, a few candles in jars and a lighter or matches."

"Oh, sounds fun! Okay, I'm game. I'll go see what I can come up with and bring it up here okay? Oh and can you think of what to do for dinner? I'm starting to get hungry."

"Sure, thanks love." Landing a chaste peck on her soft lips, I open the refrigerator to appear as if I'm looking for dinner.

She flashes me a soft smile and heads downstairs. As soon as the door leading downstairs closes I race around digging through the kitchen cabinets. Once I find a note pad and pen, I scribble 'Meet me at our swim spot. Love, Vik.'

Thank God my men already took everything down there to be set up. That's why it was so important to show Niko and Sabrina around the barn. Normally I wouldn't have done that but the guys needed time to get everything I need without Miss Nosey seeing it.

Quickly, I drop my pants, slip my shoes off, and deftly undo my zillion shirt buttons. I yank out the pair of swim shorts I had hidden in the kitchen cabinet with the pans while Elaina was in the shower. I tug them up speedily and slide my house shoes on that I also stuffed in the cabinet. Elaina would kill me if she knew they were in with the clean dishes.

I need to put the note somewhere she will see it. *Hmm*, I'll leave it on the stove and put her soft drink next to it. Hopefully she notices it right away and doesn't go looking all over for me. That could be a disaster.

Dropping the note, I quietly sneak out the back door. The door makes a rather loud noise and I don't want her to freak out if she hears it. She'd probably run up here thinking Sabrina came over to slaughter us all.

In my excitement I practically run to the beach, making it in no time at all. I can't wait to see her expression when she arrives, and then again when it's time for dessert. She has no idea what's in store for her.

"KhaRAWshee (good)?"

Spartak stops his task to approach me. "Yes, Boss, a few touch ups and it will all be finished. I'm happy for you, sir. She's a good fit for you." I shake his hand, bouncing with energy inside.

"Thank you, she is perfect. I don't know if I will even be able to eat."

Alexei walks over and smacks me lightly on my back. "You will be fine, Boss. You deal with criminals all the time, what's one little lady, yeah?"

"For being a little lady she's given you plenty of hell." I chortle at him, grinning.

"Da, that she has!" he chuckles and they efficiently finish setting up the beautiful table and dinner I had Mishka put together.

Mishka made us her famous жаркое and sent it up. It's one of my favorite dishes. It won over Emily to the family and I'm hoping Elaina enjoys it as much as her sister did that night.

I take it all in, the wonderful spicy aroma from the meat, freshly baked loaf of bread, and the buttery goodness coming from the veggies. I have a lovely red wine and also some tea if she'd prefer. For dessert we have Swiss truffles I had Alexei order especially for this occasion a few days ago and overnighted. Then a homemade pound cake with a decadent caramel glaze.

The small table is formally dressed with white linens. The votive candles are placed tastefully around and a small beautiful arrangement of cut purple hydrangeas and pink peonies are placed to the side. I don't want anything besides the food between us.

I want to be able to reach out and caress her anytime the feeling to do so hits me. I hope she's pleased with it, as everything was planned for her. This is our special evening and I want to remember each moment I'm able to make her smile. This is only the beginning of many more days and nights that I hope to spoil her.

The guys plug in the strands of tiny twinkle lights and try to hide the extension cord. They eventually make their way back up to the campers and cabin, fixing the lights along the way.

This way she now has a path specifically leading her straight to me. The lights twinkle dimly, it's not dark enough for them to stand out just yet, but by the time dinner is over it should complement everything beautifully.

I have the ring hidden with our dessert platters. I don't plan to actually ask her over dessert, just thinking it will be a safe place until I'm ready. I can't believe I'm actually going to ask her to marry me.

"You did this for me?"

# SIXTEEN

## Viktor

**E**LAINA LOOKS STUNNING, AS SHE ALWAYS DOES IN her white bikini with navy paisleys adorning it. I could ravish her now, but I have to hold off. I have a plan and want to stick to it. This is her night, so it all needs to be about her needs. Right now she needs to see that I love her completely.

"Christ, your beautiful," I utter. "Yes, I did this for you." I hold my hand out to her so she comes to me. Tucking her into me tightly, my eyes close at the feeling of her warmth. She feels like home. "Let's sit, my love, you said you were hungry earlier and the food is ready whenever you are."

The emotion shines in her eyes as she whispers, "Viktor, this is the most thoughtful thing anyone has ever done for me. Thank you."

"You're welcome, lovely," I murmur back and kiss the top of her hair, helping her into the chair.

She sits and takes the lids of the dishes off, her eyes growing wide at the delicious foods.

"My God, this looks amazing! Did you do this? When did you have the time?"

"I didn't. Mishka sent it up for us. She knew I wanted to have a dinner for you and she planned accordingly."

"Your grandmother is so awesome! I'll have to call and thank her tomorrow."

"She would enjoy that, now please dig in."

I load her plate up with some of each and do the same for myself. The meat is tender and flavorful. The bread is moist and I inhale the divine smell with each bite I take. I even finish the vegetables in a flourish, probably eager to get through the food portion of the night.

"Viktor, slow down, you're going to choke if you eat any faster!" Elaina laughs, amused with my shoveling.

"I guess I was hungrier than I thought." Shrugging and smiling sheepishly, I clear the food away to the small side table. I need to make room for dessert.

Setting the truffles directly in front of her she groans and it makes me chuckle. I knew she would love them. As soon as her hand reaches for one, I bat it away. "Oh no, I get to feed them to you."

"Really, you think you are fast enough to stop me from grabbing one?" She teases me and I laugh loudly.

"Shall we try it out and see?"

"Maybe, but I see more dishes over there. I want to know what's in them before I decide if I should eat all these truffles. I want you to have a fighting chance and all." Winking, she gestures at the other desserts.

"You're quite bossy, you know that, right?"

"Yes, and it's one of the things you love about me," she responds cheekily.

"It is, and there are many others."

Placing the cake on the table with two dessert plates and new forks, I automatically serve her a small slice and place a few truffles on her plate.

"One rule."

"Okay, shoot."

"The first taste of truffle comes from me. Then you can have free range."

"Now who's the bossy one? Okay, I'll play."

I moan as I pop a truffle in my mouth. These are so much richer and more decadent than I was expecting. No wonder they cost me a fortune. The flavor is intense and leaves you feeling as if you just had a chocolate induced orgasm.

"Hey! How's that fair? I want a bite!"

"You'll get your taste," I murmur as I lean in, nibbling on her bottom lip until she opens her mouth. I stroke her tongue with mine, sharing the rich chocolate taste still exploding through my mouth.

"Oh God," she groans through the kiss and returns it fervently as I linger a few moments more.

Unhurried, I pull back from her tender lips and playfully tap the tip of her nose with mine. She keeps her eyes closed for an instant longer, taking in the flavors. I'm finally met with dazed blue irises and a lazy smile.

"Wow."

"Yeah?"

"Oh yeah! That has to be the best chocolate, like, ever."

"I thought you meant the kiss," I retort, disgruntled.

Laughing, she backtracks. "I was talking about the kiss, I loved it, but the chocolate made it out of this world."

"I'm corrupted, Princess, I never promised to play fair."

She rolls her eyes. "You don't play fair, you make it impossible to say no to you!"

"Good. Would you like to take a swim?"

She nods, moaning as she takes her first real bite of truffle, "Oh my gawd! We need more of these!"

"I don't eat many sweets but those could end up being a bad habit if we have them around frequently."

Grinning, I hold her hand as we walk into the refreshing water.

"You're getting quite the tan for being a pale Russian."

"Christ, you just want me to spank you today. I'll take it as a compliment. It's your fault, dragging me down here every morning for a swim. I'm getting tanner and leaner; you sure you're not trying to turn me into an Italian?"

"Haha! No, of course not. I wouldn't dream of saying the 'I' word around a macho Russian man, and I'm not opposed to spanking." She giggles happily.

I truly delight in the fact that she's in such a good mood after all the drama earlier. It makes my plan seem even better and more feasible. She loved the chocolate, I just hope she loves the ring as much.

"I love you so much, Viktor, thank you for this. I never thought I would be able to rib you. You've always been so quiet and grouchy looking. I see now that it just takes time for you to let your guard down to anyone and I respect that."

"I love you, too."

After swimming for about an hour, I spread the large quilt on the ground that Elaina brought with her. Lighting some big candles, I place them all around us since the sun has set and the only real light is the little twinkle lights leading up to the cabin.

The moon peeks over the mountain and casts a beautiful rippled reflection on the lake. It's the perfect setting. The temperature is warm but comfortable, our bellies are full and we've had so much fun spending the evening not worrying about anything else.

I pull my board shorts back on since I'm done swimming

and have had time to dry off. I should probably start wearing shorts to swim in regularly since we have a female guest here. That could be an extremely awkward situation if we ever ran into each other and I was naked from swimming.

Elaina dries off and plops down on top of the blanket. She's still in her damp bikini, skin sun-kissed, hair dripping, and relaxed. She's soul crushingly beautiful when she's like this. So natural, I can't even comprehend how she believed she wasn't good enough or that she was impure.

"Are you going to join me?" she asks sweetly.

"Of course, let me get a few things."

I grab some more chocolates so I can feed a few of them to her. I've never really done that before but it sounds like a great idea. Sneaking the ring into my pocket so she doesn't see it, I head over and lie beside her on the blanket. Her scent surrounds me and I have to bite my tongue to try to keep my dick from getting hard.

# Elaina

I can't think of a better way to end this evening than by Viktor making love to me on the beach. If he doesn't make the first move soon, I'll probably jump him and take him for myself.

Vik murmurs softly, "You know I love you with all of my soul, Printsyessa, right?"

Glancing over at him, intrigued, I nod slightly. "Yes, I like to believe that. I love you with all of me. I hope you already know that though."

He brushes my cheek fondly with the tips of his fingers and I close my eyes, delighting in the soothing sensations.

"And you also know I think of being with you forever, right?"

My eyes spring open, gazing at his hazel irises. "I know. I want that too, that's why I agreed to move in with you."

"Good, then this won't come as too much of a shock then."

I perch up on my elbows, staring at him seriously. What is he talking about now? It better not be anything new to do with stuff in that meeting.

He stares at the blanket for a beat while his cheeks pink slightly. Reaching into his pocket he brings out that last thing I was ever expecting to see today. He opens his palm.

The diamond glints in the candle light and I choke out a surprised gasp as tears gather in happiness. "Love?" I question.

"Yes," he says softly as a tear tracks down his cheek. "Please, Elaina? I don't think I can live my life without you." He bites his lip and I sniffle.

"I'm already yours, Viktor. I would be honored to be your wife as well."

He smiles brightly, his eyes shining with happiness and excitement. Crushing me in his arms, he kisses me as if his life depends on it. Eagerly I respond until he pulls away, and places the exquisite ring on my finger.

"Thank you, I love it!"

"I'm elated that you approve, and thank you for agreeing."

He takes a bite of the truffle and feeds me the other half. If this is any indication of how the future will be, then I'm going to be happy and probably overweight. He's right; I don't think I would be able to contain myself if we had these around all the time. His yummy cooking is bad enough, but in a good way.

Once I swallow it I push him down onto his back. I draw

one of his small nipples into my mouth, flicking back and forth with my tongue until it pebbles.

I run my fingers over his hard stomach, grazing my nails lightly as I go until I get to his cock. He's as stiff as a rod, ready and excited. Freeing it from his shorts, I run my fingers over it several times, following his happy trail with my tongue, I take him into my mouth as far as possible.

He threads his fingers through my hair and flexes his leg muscles. I know he's trying desperately to hold back from slamming into my mouth. He loves my mouth. I run my tongue around the little ridge at the top of his dick and suck hard.

"Arrghh! Elaina!" He groans and I bob my head a few times before coming up.

Climbing over his muscular hips, I rest my swim suit clad pussy on his bare cock. He sits up abruptly, yanking me to him and taking my mouth with his. I grind my pussy against him and he kisses me roughly.

Viktor unties the frilly bows on my hips, pulling the bottoms out of his way. My wet pussy rubs against his dick, greedily coating him from base to tip with my juices, but I'm left wanting more.

He pulls away from my mouth. "Fuck, baby, you trying to kill me tonight?"

"I just want you." I raise my eyebrow, and line him up with my hole.

I watch him swallow hard as I swivel my hips, circling my opening around the head of his cock. After a few moments of teasing, I slam down on him until he's fully seated.

"KhreesTAWS (Christ)," he calls out and clamps his eyes closed.

He grasps onto my shoulder and grinds himself against my clit. God, that feels amazing.

I bite onto his shoulder and moan, "Oh yessss," into his skin.

"That's good, love, ride my cock just like that," he rasps.

Viktor wraps his arm around my back and flips me over so I'm lying flat on the ground. I shriek in surprise and giggle.

He kisses me tenderly across my jawline while pumping into me a few times. He pops his hips and my eyes roll back.

"Yes, don't stop!" I plead as my cunt hugs his large dick hungrily, ready to come.

"Forever, Princess," he grunts into my neck as he thrusts into me over and over.

"Forever," I reply loudly as my pussy spasms, draining me of every last drop of energy as I ride out the most satisfying orgasm.

He groans, clutching me tightly as he empties himself into me, sated and spent.

After a moment he pulls back, regarding me lovingly.

"You're going to be my wife."

I smirk. "Yep."

# Viktor

### six months later

**"H**URRY UP, SLOW POKES!" ELAINA YELLS AT ME, Spartak and Alexei. "I should leave you all here and just have Sabrina come with me!"

Grumbling, I shake my head. "No way, it's my brother's baby too. I don't care that you've become such good friends with Bina, I'm taking you."

"Well, the baby was born if you haven't noticed and ya'll are standing around as if it's time for vodka or something!"

I may have taken Tate's advice and lightened up a little toward my guards. Spartak, Nikoli, Alexei and I have regular card games at the cabin and tend to end up drinking a little too much vodka occasionally. If Emily's feeling well enough, Tate even joins in. I'm still very much focused on my businesses and my way of life, but I have to admit it's a pleasant change to have people to share life with.

I grab a few snacks from the kitchen, I have a feeling this will end up being a long day.

"I was supposed to be there when she had the baby, not afterwards!" Elaina yells again and I roll my eyes. I hear the guys chuckle from the living room. They find it really amusing when she gets into a tiff like this. She usually ends up throwing some random object and I'm always the target.

"Coming, Princess! Relax, Emily will understand."

I head to the living room to find her nearly in tears, she's so upset. "Come on, lovely, I know you're mad but no one knew the baby would come so fast."

"I know, it's just...I wanted to be there for her. For once you know? I wanted to be one of the first people to see the baby; she's the newest member to our family."

"You still can be. Let's get there before everyone else, okay?"

She nods and the four of us load up into the Mercedes sedan.

When we eventually reach the hospital she jumps out and runs to the front desk, babbling a hundred miles a minute.

"Yes, ma'am, maternity is up on level four. You need to check in at the desk and they can let you see her."

"Thank you!" She glances at me excitedly and takes off for the elevator. We all trail behind her like a group of lost puppies. People probably think she's someone famous with two of us in suits, and Spar clad in all black with his combat pants and boots.

Mishka stands at the front desk, eagerly waiting to greet people and brag about her new great-grand baby. We each hug her warmly and she leads us straight to Emily's private suite. Nothing but the best for my brother's wife and baby, as expected.

I have to admit, at this moment I'm jealous. Emily rests,

tired and proud, showing off her little baby for us all to see. I hope one day I can see Elaina wrapped in her robe, carefully holding our new baby.

# Elaina

Emotion pours from me as I stare at my happy sister holding her sweet new bundle of joy. It feels as if it's taken ages for her to finally pop.

"Congratulations, little sister." I sit next to her on the hospital bed and kiss her cheek, "I'm so sorry I couldn't get here sooner, I feel terrible."

"It's not your fault, she came quickly. I thought Tate was going to break a few pairs of knees during the delivery. I can only imagine what the hospital staff would have thought if you had been here and started throwing things."

"Oh my gosh, what happened?"

"Not much, just a rude nurse who got snippy with me when I cussed. I mean, really? I was having a baby! Tate threatened to buy the hospital and have everyone fired. The doctor spazzed out and had the two head nurses on duty come in for the rest of the delivery. It was interesting to say the least," she explains.

"Wow, all that over cussing?" I look over the little bundle of blanket to see my new baby niece.

"Yeah, I don't know what her issue was, but that's what prompted it. I can't wait to just get out of here and take this little one home."

"I bet. Just ask the nurses if you need help with something though. When I had to stay here I met some really friendly, helpful people."

"I did too, just a bad experience this time. I promise I will ask for help. Would you like to hold your new niece?"

"Definitely!"

Emily places her into my arms; I gently bring her close to my chest. She's so tiny and perfect. Her hair's so light it looks white.

"Emily, she looks like a little sleeping angel! Look at that hair!" I say excitedly and glance at my sister.

"I know, Tate said the same thing. We decided to name her Mishka after his grandmother. We're going to call her Mishka Angel Masterson. Angel because she looks like one and because I know she has many watching over her."

"That's beautiful, Emily, I'm so happy for you."

"Thank you, now she just needs a little blonde haired cousin."

I glance over at Viktor and smile. "Yes, someday she will have one."

I'm cut off by loud laughing and excited voices outside the room. The door opens and sure enough London and Avery pile in. They both have windblown hair, sparkly eyes and bright smiles and are followed by big bikers.

London's excited voice carries through the room, "What's up, sexy ass bitches!"

# CORRUPTED
## *counterparts*

a

RUSSKAYA MAFIYA

happily ever after

# THE WEDDING

## Spartak

**I**F ANOTHER GUEST ASKS ME TO HOLD THEIR DRINK, I may just tie them up. I'm security; it doesn't automatically make me a waiter or man candy. My boss, the groom, is nowhere to be found at the moment and that's stressful enough.

A feminine voice from my side interrupts my perusal, "Excuse me, sir."

I shift, turning away from the latest cougar attempting to have me do something for them and spot Tate. He's standing next to an enormous white tent-like structure, set up behind the cabin. It's fairly perfect weather for the outdoor, beach wedding ceremony, and guests are fluttering around like they've never been to such an event before. *Finally someone who I can ask.*

Quickly, I make my way over to him, weaving between random people. Tate nods when he notices me approach him, "Spartak."

"Mr. Masterson." Clearing my throat, I continue, "Sir, I'm attempting to locate your brother."

Tate chuckles, "Knowing Viktor, he's probably bothering his fiancée. Those two seem glued to each other at this point."

"Right. Thank you."

He nods hurriedly, greeting the next guest approaching him.

I head toward the massive barn that's closer to the beach. The women deemed this building theirs, since it has much more room to make preparations than the cabin does. This intimate wedding is turning into way more than what was originally planned.

Knocking on the old door I wait and get nothing.

Rap.

Rap.

Rap.

I knock a little harder against the giant door. The wood scraping into my knuckles and pissing me off before the door slides open about three inches.

Elaina peeks her sweet little face between the opening. "Hi Spar, is everything okay?" She peers at me worriedly with her sapphire colored irises.

"Yes, Miss Elaina, just checking if the boss is in here."

"No, he's actually behaved and hasn't tried to lock me in any of the safe rooms yet." She grins, sliding the door open a little more, and I step closer, blocking the opening to keep others from seeing her.

"Wow ma'am, he is going to be floored when he sees you."

"You like it?"

I hear women laughing behind her; they must know how silly the question is. Elaina's beyond beautiful. I nod, not sure what to really say to her, without Viktor sinking me in the lake if he hears.

"This is that new Vera Wang dress he had you and Lexei go pick up."

I swallow roughly as I skate over her in the delicate

white lace, formfitting gown. It's understated class and Elaina knows how to pull every stitch of it off. She touches lightly to the dainty, diamond-encrusted tiara resting in her long blonde, Cinderella hair. "This, umm, this was Mishka and Vivi's, they wore it for their weddings." She gazes at me, seeking my approval.

"It's very fitting. I'm really happy for you Elaina, you and the boss deserve this."

She leans in, clutching onto my forearm and squeezes affectionately. Elaina's eyes begin to crest with tears, full of happiness, as she whispers kindly, "Thank you, Spar. You helped keep us safe so we could have this day. I'm so happy you get to be a part of it."

I close my eyes briefly, thanking the Lord that my close friend is able to have this day and that she's genuinely happy.

I shoot her a sheepish grin, "I must go. Alexei is monitoring the guests on the beach and tent area. I need to find Mr. Masterson, I don't like him alone." She smiles at me gratefully, backing up a few paces so I can slide the door closed again. At least I know Elaina's surrounded by others and is being protected.

I make my way down the small grassy path, toward the shop building. It's more of the guards' building now, but it should be empty at the moment. I believe all of the men are on assignment, either here or out handling business.

I don't quite make it to the shop when I hear Viktor arguing with someone. It sounds as if it's coming from behind the building, so I head straight back there.

Viktor glances up, a scowl adorning his flushed face when he sees me. I stay silent, standing in the shadow of the building in case he needs me.

The other gentleman has his back to me, but by the voice, I recognize it as his Uncle Victor. I'm curious as to why he's back here, considering he was not on the guest list.

His uncle places his placating hand on Viktor's shoulder and Viktor glares in return as if he may head butt the older man. "Look Viktor, I apologize for barging in on your wedding day, but Sabrina Chestkolav was already sold in a previous deal."

"She was traded to me, Uncle. I don't care which ratty family thinks they have claim to her. I've warned you about selling women. I told you to stop, you are no longer in charge, and you are forcing my hand."

"I'm not here to step on your toes, nephew, only to collect for her betrothed."

Viktor grits angrily, "She's going nowhere. Sabrina belongs to me now. Not only that, but she was obtained for Nikoli. You are aware how close Nikoli is to my brother?" Viktor's voice turns to ice as he finishes, "You warn this interested family, that they will have every element of the Mafiya and my Bratva after them if they do not back off."

The older man huffs, but keeps his words to himself.

"Now, pack up and leave. You are not going to disrupt my Printsyessa's day."

"This isn't finished, Viktor." The old man attempts to argue as Alexei appears.

Viktor glances from me to Alexei, "Lexei, you and I shall escort my uncle off of the grounds. Spartak, you may go back to the main party."

Uncle Victor stares at me angrily, unaware I was privy to the conversation and I swallow nervously. I know my boss is in charge of the Bratva now, but his uncle is still an extremely intimidating, powerful man.

"Yes sir," I answer dutifully and watch as Alexei and Viktor lead his uncle to the cars.

Before I turn around myself, someone grabs onto my

shoulder, startling me, since I'm still on alert from the threatening conversation I just witnessed. I grip onto the person's arm harshly, propelling them forward and bringing their back to my chest. I drop the knife resting in my jacket sleeve, sliding it carefully and swiftly down my wrist, digging it into their neck, just enough for them to stand still.

I have to stop myself from gasping when I discover long brunette hair cascading over the feminine shoulder, enveloping me in a sweet smell.

The woman stutters out in a whisper-soft voice, "Umm, ummm."

I drop my arms, deftly stepping back and putting a few paces between us, "Forgive me," I mumble as my heart beats franticly enough to feel as if it may pop out of my chest.

She promptly spins around, and I'm met with dark, sinful eyes, wide with excitement. Her hand clutches her neck at the area my knife was just touching, as she swallows nervously. Her chest is rapidly rising and falling with each labored breath.

"I didn't mean to startle you. I was following you, because you ignored me at the party."

Shit. I hadn't even glanced at her face back there. *Stupid Spartak.* This woman could have stepped straight out of a fantasy and yet she's chasing me around.

Clearing my throat, I tug on my jacket, attempting to fix the rumpled mess, "Yeah, I'm sorry about that. Did you need something?" I may as well go with being polite since I've already snubbed her once, and then almost impaled her with my blade.

She grins mischievously, her irises gleaming with intent as she approaches. She stops about four inches from my face and I lick my lips nervously, as I feel my throat get tight. I don't do well with people in my personal space, but her, well I want to pull even closer.

"Yes, Spartak. I do need something." My eyes widen with the way her smooth voice caresses over my name, surprised that she was behind me long enough to hear Viktor mention it.

She grasps onto my suit lapels, pulling my body against hers, molding her plump breasts against my firm chest as she takes me for a kiss so powerful I've never felt anything like it in my life. With a few twists of her skilled tongue, my cock stands to attention, seeking something it hasn't had in quite a while. I clutch tightly, onto her small biceps, probably bruising the lightly tanned skin as I kiss her back with everything I have. If this is some sort of attack plan, I'm screwed.

After a few minutes I pull back, panting, heavily turned on, "Fuck," I gasp. She nods, her eyes dilated with heat.

"I want more," she orders as she deftly undoes the button on my slacks, backing me up to the shop's back wall.

"More? What's your name?" Stupid, but it's the only thing I can think of as she wraps her petite, soft hands around my throbbing member.

"Victoria," she murmurs hastily as she finishes pulling my boxer briefs down and pumping my cock a few times.

I clear away the frog in my throat, twisting her body so that she's the one pressed against the wall and hike her mid-length, plum colored dress up, around her waist. Then sliding her pair of tiny lace panties over so I can get to her sweet spot, I slip my finger in her deeply, watching for any signs of me going too far. I've never met this woman before, yet she seems keen on getting to know me. I don't know what I've done in my previous life to deserve this sort of reward, but I'll gladly accept.

"Yessss," she lowly groans out, as her head leans against

the building, exposing the smooth skin on her neck. "Mooore."

Victoria laces her fingers behind my neck, raising her breasts a little higher and causing my gut to clench tightly with need. Slipping my fingers free from her center, I hike her leg up, lining my cock up where I want to be the most.

I peer down at Victoria, "Are you sure?"

"Damn it, do it already!" Her small hands cover my scruffy jaw as she pulls my face down, vigorously taking my mouth again.

Victoria's tongue slips in my mouth at the same time I plunge into her tight heat. I groan through the fantastic sensations, pulling out slightly and then seating my cock fully inside of her.

"Perfect, Spartak!" She moans in between kisses. Her hands skate up and down my chest, further rumpling my clothes but I can't make myself give a shit about any of that besides the delicious feeling of her wrapped snuggly around me.

"Fuck, you're amazing," I croon as I use my free hand to slip her sleeve off her shoulder, freeing her full, left breast. I hike her leg up further around my hip, grinding into her and leaning down just enough to slip her perfect pebbled, strawberry colored nipple into my mouth.

My head is wrenched backwards, my eyes meeting hers as I suck strongly. Victoria pulls my hair forcefully, gazing down at me, "Bite it," she demands.

I nip down on the morsel, treating it as if it were my favorite sweet treat, even if in reality that would be the juncture between her thighs. She yanks on my hair again and I wrench upwards quickly, her breast making a 'pop' as I let go, I grasp her hand, raising it above her head.

"Enough, unless you wish for me to pull your hair, you asked for it, and I'm giving it." I grit, winding my other arm around her waist to save her from hurting her back. I pump into her a few times, clenching my ass as the feelings course through me, begging for a quick release.

Her face flushes, and she bites her lip, grinning slightly. She uses her free hand to grasp tightly onto my shoulder, helping herself climb up and wrap her legs around my waist.

"Pull it."

"Excuse me?"

"Don't threaten me Spartak; pull my hair, because when you do, I'm going to cum all over your big cock."

"Fuuuck me." Groaning, I let go of her wrist and weave my hand into her thick hair, winding it around my large fist and pull.

Victoria's mouth gapes as she lets loose a near silent moan, her pussy pulling and clutching at my engorged cock. I thrust wildly through her orgasm, gritting my teeth as her cunt spasms around me. Little droplets of sweat gather on my hairline from concentrating so hard on not filling her up.

"Cum inside me, Spartak," she orders as she licks up the side of my neck. I shiver and growl low in my throat, attempting to hold myself back from slamming her into the wall like I want to. My inner beast claws inside my chest, pleading for me to rip her apart and bury my seed deep.

Her tender lips pepper kisses along my neck right before she sinks her teeth into my skin, sucking intensely, no doubt leaving her mark. It doesn't faze me as I know my suit will cover it for the ceremony.

"Nooow," Victoria croons against my throat, her hot breath whispering over my skin, and my dick lets loose, painting her in my essence. My balls were so full I thought they were going to fucking explode.

I lean into her heavily, against the wall as I finish

436

throbbing through my release, resting my forehead on her shoulder and breathing in her scent.

I'm startled by my boss's voice, as I catch my breath, "Spar, time for the vows."

"Yes, sir," I reply in a gruff voice, glancing back towards him, his chest rises slightly quicker as he watches us. Viktor nods, his gaze skirting over us one last time and then turns around, giving us his back.

I draw away slowly and cover her up with her lace panties. Victoria pants, silently watching my face. I can't break eye contact as I catch myself murmuring the words I never fathomed would leave my mouth, "Come with us."

"Where are you going?" She questions softly.

"Russia, for the honeymoon. I have to work, but I'll have time off."

Victoria peers off to the side briefly, then meets my gaze again, "I'm sorry, but I can't."

"Why not?"

"Because my friend and I flew in from Italy. I leave tomorrow."

"Italy? Fuck!" Grumbling I straighten my suit, as she combs her fingers through her hair. My mind races with ways for me to see her again. Viktor grunts, drawing my attention to his stern face, nodding for me to come on.

"I have to go, are you coming, too?"

"Yes, I'll be right there; I'm going to visit the ladies room first."

I bring her knuckles to my lips and kiss them softly before walking towards Viktor. Halfway to him, I turn back and glance at her, taking in her beauty once more. "How will I see you again?"

Victoria's eyes twinkle as she smiles, "If it was meant to be Spartak, then we will see each other again."

I bite my tongue and nod. I hate being unsure of things, I

like simple laid out plans. Following the boss down the short path to the lake I can't stop picturing how her face looked while I was deep inside of her.

The beach is adorned with a wooden pergola and platform, draped in some silky white material, the little lights wrapped through it, twinkling in the evening air. The guests all sit patiently on the white wooden chairs; smiles grace their excited faces to see the other Russian leader find his happiness in love. The party really isn't that large, it's overwhelming to me because of safety precautions with everything that has recently gone down.

Viktor takes his place on the platform with Tate and Alexei standing beside him. I post up a little to the side and behind them. It's the perfect spot for me to scan over everyone and keep a look out for Victoria.

Elaina glides towards us, on Nikoli's arm. They've gotten closer ever since Sabrina has come into the picture. Nikoli, decked out in his light grey suit, makes Elaina appear even more petite, dwarfing her small frame with his massive size.

A motion catches my attention off to the side and I watch as Victoria approaches, speaking to another woman sitting towards the back of the group, before she eventually takes her own seat. Her irises briefly meet mine, igniting a ball of need in the center of my stomach.

Tate and Emily's daughter squeals excitedly when she sees her Aunty Elaina approach the pergola, drawing all attention to Emily. She's standing across from Tate, waiting to be beside her sister for the nuptials and proudly holding the newest addition to the Masterson family.

Elaina kisses the baby's forehead lovingly and then takes Viktor's hands as they each say their vows, promising to love each other more than they already do. It seems pretty impossible to me, as they are hopelessly devoted to each other.

As the wedding winds down and the honeymoon time approaches, Alexei and I follow the newlyweds to Viktor's Mercedes. I hop in the driver's seat scanning for Victoria, but I haven't seen her since she was sitting next to her friend.

Alexei climbs in beside me after the boss and Elaina load into the back seat. Viktor leans forward between the seats, "Is she meeting you in Russia Spar?"

"No, she's from Italy."

"You're not going to see her again?"

"I don't know, she told me if it was meant to be that we would find each other again."

Elaina pipes up. I know Viktor clued her in, he tells her pretty much everything. "You got her information?"

"Nope."

"How will you find her?"

"I have the guest list," I grin cockily. All I need is some time off and she's mine.

# Unwanted SACRIFICES

# WARNING

This novel includes graphic language and adult situations. It may be offensive to some readers and includes situations that may be hotspots for certain individuals. This book is intended for adults 18 and older. This work is fictional. The story is meant to entertain the reader and may not always be completely accurate. Any reproduction of these works without Author Sapphire Knight's written consent is pirating and will be punished to the fullest extent.

Dedicated to

# MaryAnn Comer Christopherson

and

# Patti Novia West

You both have been there to build me up and push me through the hard times and also to experience my happiness. Thank you for the pick-me-ups and being truly wonderful women whom I've been so lucky to get to know over the past year. You bring a smile to my face and happy tears with your kindness.
You each have a special place in my heart.

Russian words utilized throughout

Thanks/Thank you  -  Spaa see ba
No  -  Nine/Nyet
Brother  -  Brat
Princess  -  Printyessa
Mine  -  Moy
Sister  -  Say straa
Young Lady  -  Dye voosh ka

# Nikoli

**A**S I GAZE INTO THE MIRROR SECURED TO THE OLD, wooden bedroom door, I concentrate on the reflection in front of me. My body is fairly large, toned to what some may think of as perfection. My blond hair is cropped short so I don't have to mess with it. I have tiny scars decorating different parts of my body; but they're small, so not bad. For the most part, I'd say I look pretty good.

My chest swells as I think of how my mother's kind eyes would look at me if she were here. I know she'd be very pleased with me—her strong boy. I'm no longer a small, scared little one, but a solid man.

Yes, she would be proud of her Nikoli.

Nodding to myself, my gaze travels lower, fixating on the dark grey weapon secured in the holster at my waist. My mother would *not* be delighted with that, however.

"Blondie?" My self-assessment is interrupted by the quiet, sweet voice coming from a little pixie of a woman, Sabrina.

We've been friends for many years, and I've always cared for her. At first, it was in a big brother, protective sort of way, but over the years as I've watched her grow into a stunning young woman, my feelings for her have changed into something much more than a sibling or boyhood crush. Now, she encompasses my every thought it seems. Well, besides the times when I'm remembering my mother and sisters—may their souls rest in peace.

Sabrina grew up in a very strict lifestyle, completely opposite of me. However, her family traveled in the same circles as mine. They've always been wealthy, too, where I wasn't; at least, not until I became a valuable asset to the Mafiya.

After years of knowing her in passing, her family packed up and brought her to America. I believed back then that I would never get to see her again and was pretty upset about it. I hadn't exactly made a move to stake my claim on her, so I just tried to get past it.

I lost sight of her for a period of time, but when my best friend, Tate, asked me to come to America with him to get away from his controlling father, I practically leapt at the chance knowing I might be able to find Sabrina again.

Before they moved away her father, Kristof, was always scouting around looking to buy up pieces of land in Russia, but Tate and his father, Gizya, along with his Uncle Victor pretty much owned all of the property around any docks there so it made sense for them to move away.

I'm assuming it would have been easier for Kristof to keep the women he sold on water versus on land. The lake kept them invisible and helplessly secured. With the winters in Russia, the women never would have survived if they escaped off the nasty boats; not to mention, they were malnourished and nearly beaten to death until they were sold.

Even though I didn't want to, I had made myself stay out of it all, always keeping my eye on the prize. I hated not helping all the women I saw being traded, raped, and beaten by the Bratva and their associates, but I had to find the person responsible for killing my mother and sisters. At least I tell myself they were killed. I still pray they were killed quickly and not subjected to what I've seen other women go through now that I'm older.

When my family was stolen away, I was only a child. I still remember the night it happened—the loud pounding as my mother's shack of a door was kicked down and the men tearing through our small place until they had my mother and the girls. I had watched as the men drug them through the doorway, my mother sobbing and pleading as my sisters screamed in fear. I held my teddy tightly as I was partially hidden under the blanket my mother had knitted for me.

My eyes were wide with fear, and I clenched my legs together tightly to not wet my pants. I had wept large alligator tears as silently as possible. I wanted to help. I wanted to yell out to save her, to rescue them all. With each scream from my sisters' mouths, I heard my mother's strong Russian voice inside my mind, "Nyet! Nikoli! You stay. Shush, Nikoli! You nyet make nyet sound, be good boy and stay put."

Those words never really left her mouth but they didn't have to. I knew in my heart she would have wanted my silence, my strength. She would always tell me it was a man's job to be strong and love their family; but I was no man, only a boy. Being terrified and confused, I had no way to really help them, and I had no idea who to turn to for guidance.

"Blondie?" Sabrina calls quietly as she climbs the stairs to the loft apartment we're staying in, compliments of my Boss' brother, Viktor.

"Yes, Bina?" My gaze shoots to her, shaking off the terrible thoughts of that cold night so long ago.

"You okay up here?"

"Yes, I was only looking," I reply and gesture to the mirror.

Sabrina meets my eyes with a playful grin. "Of course you were looking in the mirror; you're so vain," she giggles.

Rolling my eyes, I let loose a huff, pretending to be offended, but in reality I really do stare at myself in the mirror a lot. I like to look. So what? Nothing wrong with being happy with myself.

"I was preparing breakfast; are you hungry?"

"Of course. I'm like ox, always big and hungry."

She laughs again. Her bright smile warms my heart and I have to grin at the beautiful chime-like sound. She never giggled before when she was around her family, and I simply adore being able to hear the sound now.

"Okay then, I'll fix enough for you."

"Thank you, Bina." She doesn't respond, but turns around and hops back down the stairs, her short dark hair flopping with each new bounce.

I never predicted to be in this situation with her in the first place. Tate and Viktor actually made a trade with her father to bring her back and get her away from him. Sabrina's sister attempted to kill my Boss' brother, Viktor, who also happens to be the head of the Russian Bratva in America. Viktor contacted me about it, explaining that Sabrina needs protection in case her father retaliates or attempts something with her, so here I am. Only I wasn't expecting to actually be living with her.

I've always been beside Tate offering protection when I wasn't out on a job for the Mafiya. This is the first time though that I've been away from his side—for an extended time period—since I was fifteen years old. At least with Sabrina I don't have to hide myself from her. She grew up associated with our ways.

The scents float up from below and my stomach lets loose a famished growl. I smell bacon, and let's face it, bacon can get any man to move. I make my way down to the small kitchen and sit at the even smaller table.

Viktor's fiancée, Elaina, did her best to fix this place up for us. It used to be the guards' house and they were nice enough to kick them out so we could have a remote place to stay with some extra security. It's really like a giant barn-turned-loft house, but it's perfect for us.

Sabrina set the plastic plate loaded up with toast, eggs, and bacon in front of me. I could easily get used to this sort of thing. The only person who ever really waited on me was my other best friend, Avery. She always made me good coffees and snacks, but she moved away to Texas. I haven't gotten to see her in quite a while, and I need to make a trip out to visit. Maybe I could bring Bina with me; I doubt she's ever left Tennessee without her father in tow.

"Spaa see ba," I grunt my thanks and she blushes slightly. She's used to my Russian and often will reply back to me in our native language. One of the many things I enjoy about her. I don't have to worry about being correct with the words I try to say in English. I'm getting better, but I still get things mixed up sometimes or will answer people in Russian not realizing I'm doing it.

She fixes herself a plate with only a small portion of scrambled eggs and it makes me realize she was really cooking all of this food for me and not her. She always does this and it warms my belly knowing she was thinking of me being hungry.

"Why so little?" I gesture to her plate. I've never seen her eat much; she's a tiny sprite of a thing and could definitely use a little meat on her bones.

"My mother would faint if she saw me eat more than half portions."

"She is not here; she doesn't see you eat."

"Yes, but when I have to go back..."

Pushing her plate closer, I argue, "Nyet, you are done there. You will never go back; you eat as much as you wish."

I keep trying to tell her she's done with those people, but she doesn't believe me, always thinking that her father will come for her. That trash can try all he likes, but he'll never leave with her; I'll make sure of it. I've already lost too much, and I won't sacrifice her too.

She quiets, pushing her eggs around her plate. I load my toast up, shoveling as much food into my mouth that will fit. Not having my mother around and growing up on the streets taught me that you eat quickly and as much as possible.

The old neighbor lady that kept me for a few years after they took my mother wasn't too big on teaching me any manners; she just wanted to keep me in a safe and warm place in the winter. I will never forget her kindness.

"Slow down, Blondie, there's plenty more if you're still hungry."

I grunt and keep stuffing my mouth. She's called me Blondie since we first met. I'll never forget her sweet young face from that day.

••••

I had been with Tate for a year. We were both around sixteen years old. Tate had been learning the ropes from his father, while his father regularly trained me to keep his son safe.

That day we were at a birthday dinner for Tate's dad at a famous restaurant in Russia that his family owns. Tate and I were sitting at the table joking about him flirting with the waitress when I saw Sabrina's sweet face.

I turned from Tate, laughing at his next scheme to get the waitress' number and was met with doe eyes, staring at me from across the table. She was younger and looked so innocent in her soft pink, baby-doll dress. She had blushed then also, when my heated gaze met hers, turning her face away quickly from being caught.

I didn't turn away though. I licked my lips eagerly and stared, taking in every sweet inch of her. At the time she had long dark locks full of soft curls; her thick lashes had fluttered almost too quickly as if she knew I was still watching her. I couldn't look away; her looks were too captivating to the likes of a hormonal sixteen-year-old boy. Her small nose was slightly upturned and seeing her lips were almost in a pink pout gave me thoughts of

454

ravishing her mouth until it was rosy to match her cheeks.

I was forced to look away as Tate's father, Gizya, introduced me to Sabrina's father, Kristof. Gizya had spoken of how I was becoming very promising and was quickly becoming an asset to the business. That was the first time I'd seen a face to match to Kristof's name. I had heard about him on the streets and how he'd pay thugs to help out with his business ventures. I was busy with the Bratva and being paid by Gizya to train at that age, so I was never swayed to check out the rumors further. Even then, though, I could sense he was a dirty snake. He definitely didn't deserve a daughter like Sabrina.

••••

Finishing up my breakfast, I chug the glass of orange juice Sabrina was kind enough to get me and then stand.

"Would you like some more?" She peers up at me.

"No. You cooked, I clean—same as usual." Grabbing our dishes, I head over to the sink, quickly rinsing the plates and cups off and load them into the old dishwasher.

She's beautiful today, but that's nothing new. She's gorgeous every day. Her mother used to force her into wearing these stunning dresses everywhere, but she's older now and wears the complete opposite. Every time I see her, she's clad in skinny jeans and a plain tank top or short-sleeved shirt.

I remember when she cut off her long shiny hair. She had escaped one day and called me—upset. I picked her up and she went flat out crazy at a shopping mall making all these changes right before my eyes. I loved her hair but kept my mouth shut so she would be happy. Now it's in a short style that reminds me of the little psychic vampire on "Twilight." She also has like ten teeny black studs decorating each ear and wears a variety of brightly colored flip-flops.

She had called me sobbing from her private school a week

later, explaining that her mother lost it when she saw the changes Bina made without her approval. Her mom changed whatever she could and sent her right back to school. I tried to come and get her right then, but she begged me to stay away, telling me that her family would only make it worse for her if she left. I was so stupid to believe her; I should have gone and taken her away.

Her sister, Kendall, was an evil person; she tried to kill Viktor and his fiancée not long ago. Growing up she made Sabrina's life a living hell, always attempting to get her in trouble or kicked out of the private schools she attended. Kendall was such a jealous little bitch, always fantasizing after Tate's older brother. Thankfully, in the end, Viktor's soon-to-be wife, Elaina, lost it and killed Kendall.

Sabrina hasn't mentioned a word about it since we've gotten here. I wonder if it even bothers her that her older sister is dead? She was such a hateful thing; I would think Bina would be relieved in a way that Kendall is finally gone for good.

Drying my hands off on the kitchen towel, I turn toward Sabrina as she watches me—a small smile gracing her lips. "Want to swim?" I ask and nod toward the small window facing the lake that sits peacefully behind Viktor's cabin.

"You swim, I'll watch." She stands, wiping her hands on her jeans and heads over to the large barn door to wait patiently for me to change into my swim trunks.

Every time it's the same answer. I offered to get her a bathing suit and still she never agrees. I know for a fact that she can swim. We swam together as teenagers at Tate's mansion in Russia. Back then she was only permitted to because her father was trying to settle a deal with Gizya.

Kristof had brought along Kendall and Sabrina hoping to entice Gizya and sweeten the pot. If he was interested in the girls, he thought perhaps he'd be able to weasel a contract on the docks with the older man. He hadn't expected Tate's mom to

456

be right there. She was readily prepared for the younger women and gave them each swimsuits so the girls could accompany us to the pool, where we got to shamelessly flirt with them for hours. Tate's mother had already dealt with Gizya's wandering ways and was becoming better at thwarting them off onto her son's. She was a force of her own to be reckoned with.

It's weird, but I don't get why Bina won't give in and swim with me now, especially since it's just the two of us.

I grab a bottled water for her and an extra towel so she has a barrier between her and the ground to sit on. I need to get a folding chair to take so she'll be comfortable when we're out there. I don't know why I never thought of it before, she sits there sometimes for a good hour or two just watching me and drawing on the ground, sometimes she'll read or look over a magazine, but I enjoy it the most when she watches me. I'll have to ask Alexei, Viktor's right hand man, if they have one around here.

Hurrying back upstairs, I quickly get changed into my favorite shorts, grab my straw hat and flip-flops, then collect the water and towels as I head to the front door.

Sabrina and I have been here for six months now and we've gotten into a small routine. I'll admit, I've gotten used to it and I pride myself on not having any sort of set schedule. It's safer with variety in the line of work I do. This new calmness in my life has me a bit stir-crazy to be honest.

I enjoy being here—being with her—and having some time off, but I'm growing more and more restless with each passing day. I don't like to be away from Tate like this; we're too close. I know he has other people to watch out for him and he's able to protect himself, but he's more than my Boss. He's my best friend and brother. He's become a piece of me basically after being around him for so long. Not only do I love him like a brother, but I love his sweet wife, Emily, and their dog, Muffin. They've all grown to be my family and I can't wait until I can finally take

Sabrina around them. Bina and Emily have never met, but I hope to change that soon.

Pulling the heavy barn door open, I'm met with Viktor's girl—her hand up in the air ready to knock.

"Elaina?"

"Oh! Hi, Nikoli. I was just seeing if Sabrina still wanted to look at the wedding catalog with me."

"Bina?" She's waiting behind me so I scoot to the side. Both women are so short they couldn't see each other with me in the way.

Sabrina's still a little shy around Elaina, and I can't blame her after what her sister pulled on Viktor. I'm so glad that we've had dinner with Viktor and Elaina a few times since we've been here. Elaina has finally started to thaw a little towards Sabrina, and I'm hoping they become even friendlier towards one another.

"Hi, Elaina. I was about to walk to the lake with Nikoli. When did you want to look?"

"Oh cool, I'll just go with you, and we can look through them down there, if that's okay? Niko swims in shorts, right?"

I chuckle and Sabrina looks at her puzzled.

Elaina smirks, shaking her head and hints, "You've seen Vik swim with no clothes on by now, haven't you?"

Sabrina beams a bright smile, giggling, "No..."

Hell no, she hasn't. I've made sure of it, because I've seen it many times and that's plenty for the both of us. That's why we swim at a certain time so she doesn't see Viktor with his muscular swimmer's body. I'm not like that; I'm big and bulky. I don't want her comparing us and for me to fall short in any way.

"Great, then. I was scared you had been flashed by now." Elaina's eyes widen and they both laugh again. I stay silent and hold my breath to keep myself from growling.

"Ready?" I ask and start to close the door; it's more of a suggestion than a question, but they both agree.

I trek along behind them, listening to their excited babble

about Elaina's wedding as we make our way to the beautiful, shimmering lake.

# Sabrina

Elaina chatters about her wedding plans and I can't help but think that I wish she was the type of sister I'd had. She would have been perfect. Instead, I was tormented by the evil bitch who lived to make my existence hell for basically my entire life.

Here in front of me sits the one person who killed Kendall. She put an end to the abuse I had suffered at Kendall's hand, yet she has no idea how truly grateful I am. When I first arrived here, she was worried I'd harm her or her boyfriend when, in reality, all I wanted to do was kiss her and express my undying gratitude. I didn't do that, though; I just thanked them politely for having me and vowed to help in any way possible.

I've kept my distance, sticking next to Blondie's side in hopes they'd realize—in time—I wasn't any type of threat to either of them. Both of their guards even viewed me as a pariah at first. Over group dinners these past few months, Elaina has become friendlier and opened up to me and inviting me into her life. Even though we're opposite in many ways, we seem to have much in common also.

I can't remember a time I've been so happy and relaxed before. Maybe when I was a teenager, but even then my life was a constant struggle, fighting against my family. My mother was always griping at me to not eat, to look my absolute best, and do what I must to learn to be the finest wife possible.

She wanted her girls to marry someone powerful and with influence. She drove it deep and she wouldn't accept anything less. It was my duty to seek out the most prime candidate and marry him as quickly as possible. I've always believed her to be nuts.

Once my family had met Tate and Viktor, Kendall and my father had their sights set. Viktor was heir to the Bratva title and it would have benefitted my papa the most for her to marry the head of the organization.

Papa soon found out after Tate had become a Russian Boss, that he would eventually be running the Mafiya. It was perfect to keep both organizations in the families, to continue having brothers run each side as they've done for generations, and in the end working together to rule the Russian crime life. Viktor Ginzenburg-Masterson and Tatkiv "Knees" Ginzenburg-Masterson were a goddamn gold mine and powerhouse together that my father became obsessed with.

You would have thought my father had hit the lottery. He was so strung up on Gizya having two sons and him having two daughters that he believed it was fate. He decided that even if it didn't work as planned, at least one daughter was surely going to marry a Boss and give his trashy businesses the one up they needed to get ahead.

He became practically desperate, dressing us up like dolls and parading us to any function of theirs he could get an invite to. He eventually stooped to offering us both to Gizya himself, to do with whatever he pleased. My stupid mother stood right at his side through everything, claiming to do what was best for the family. It didn't matter that she was ruining the lives of her own children. My sister sucked up all the attention she received, being 'destined' to be with Viktor and played their games—sometimes better than my own parents—crying to Viktor and pretending to want to be his friend. Nothing matters to any of them except making more money and becoming as powerful as they can. Thankfully, neither of the men succumbed to their schemes.

When my father told me he had traded me to the Bratva King and that I now belonged to Viktor to pay off Kendall's debt for trying to kill him, I can't say I was even a little bit surprised.

Inside I had been expecting as much or something similar; he always did whatever he could to clean up her messes.

Papa had announced not too long ago—before trading me—how he'd found a suitable man for me to marry and he was setting it up. I didn't have any say in it whatsoever. Learning I was the payment to Viktor instead, at least I would be going to someone I knew.

I wasn't sure what he would do with me exactly, but everyone's heard the rumor that he's out of the sex trade business. We've also heard how he's been quietly torturing and killing any of the bosses he finds selling women. It could just be talk, but it's hard to say in this lifestyle.

That alone had made my stomach flip with joy. I didn't care if I would be scrubbing his floors with a toothbrush if it would get me out of my parents' house and away from my betrothed. That was payment enough for my eternal gratitude; throw in the death of my sister and it may as well have been Christmas.

I knew I would probably get to see my longtime friend Nikoli as well. My parents despised Nikoli. They wanted me to chase Tate, but I couldn't. I saw Blondie when I was a young girl, and I couldn't picture another man for me. He was so beautiful and smart. He had no trouble ever making me laugh or smile, and he was always kind to me and made me feel safe, like he wouldn't ever let anyone make me uncomfortable, especially Kendall.

I've seen him around with a few women at functions, but he never touched them—never like he did with me anyway. Under my papa's watchful eye, I didn't get much alone time with him, but he would still manage to sneak a soft graze against my palm as he stood by me or tenderly squeeze my hip as he'd pass by. It was always just enough to quicken my breath and cause my heart to flutter excitedly. Never once, however, did he approach my father to ask to take me out.

Over the years I tried to understand why he wouldn't come for me and shed many tears over it. Eventually, I realized he's just a sweet guy and wanted only to be my friend. In my mind, those small touches were no longer from his interest in me, but just as a silent hello. Too bad my heart never got the message, because it still skipped a beat every single time.

I gave up on hopes that one day he would be mine and just concentrated on being his friend. Since then, we've always managed to find each other and we've gotten along great. Imagine my surprise when I arrived here and Viktor fills me in that not only will I live with Nikoli, but that I will belong to him and not Viktor. It was like being fed sweet torture with a spoon, knowing I would be around him all the time. After all, that's what I had dreamed about for many years while growing up. The kicker was, I knew I'd be following him around like a love-sick puppy and would never receive the same affections from him.

This may all sound completely crazy to some people—the buying, selling, and trading of human beings—but it's more normal than one would think. I'd much rather belong to a man I love inside, than to be sold to a man in the sex trade or wedded to a man I've barely met before.

I surprised everyone by being so grateful, but they had no idea of the fate they'd saved me from. I belong to the Russian Bratva and Mafiya now; my father will *never* go against that. I was thrown straight into the hands of the man he hated—straight into the arms of the man I love.

Elaina speaks up, pulling me from my thoughts, "What do you think of this?" she asks, pointing out a simple, elegant gown in one of the five bridal magazines she lugged down to the beach with us. Her private guard sits not far from her, quietly reading a paperback book.

The dress she shows me is understated elegance. You'd never guess Elaina grew up poor and was bounced around foster care. She has the taste of a seasoned rich woman.

"The simple cream gown with lace overlay is stunning; you

would command everyone's attention."

She laughs a little nervously. "I don't want everyone's attention, just Viktor's."

"Then I'd say it's perfect." I smile and she turns to her guard.

"Spar? What do you think of this dress?"

He cocks his eyebrow, clearly not wanting to be in the conversation, but leans over anyhow. His eyes go a little wide for a second and he clears his throat, "Yep, he will love it." He nods his approval and Elaina beams a bright smile.

She's been complaining about the dresses all costing too much and her wedding is fast approaching. Elaina wanted simple, and the one she has finally found is simple yet gorgeous. I bet it will cost a small fortune and she has no idea. I don't know why I find it amusing, but I do. Not maliciously, and I just bet Viktor will be very pleased thinking she's embracing his wealth when she hasn't a clue just how deep his pockets really are. His family is way more influential in Russia than most people know about. I'm privy to that tidbit from my father constantly attempting to dig up something on their family to use against them.

"Do you think I can wear my flip-flops?" She glances at me a little unsure, needing some guidance.

"Elaina, love, it's *your* wedding. You can wear shorts and it won't matter. Viktor will just be happy to see you at the altar," I respond automatically and her guard looks over at me with—I don't know—a little respect, maybe? He nods briefly and goes back to reading.

She's clearly surrounded by people who love her, and I'm lucky enough to be brought into this tight group.

# Nikoli

### ACCUSATIONS AND MARRIAGE

You don't marry someone you can live with-
You marry the person who you cannot live without
-Unknown

**W**E'VE BEEN HERE FOR MONTHS NOW, AND WHEN Viktor comes down the beach to find us, it's the first time his expression makes me uneasy inside. With him it could be absolutely anything. My first thoughts go directly to Sabrina and Tate; they're my two priorities and the people I care about the most.

I had just finished swimming and gotten out of the lake, so I dry myself off quickly while he heads to Elaina. I call out in greeting, "Viktor!"

He nods, kissing Elaina as they gather up the wedding books and extra towel.

"Niko, I need to speak to you after you've gotten changed."

"You got it," I reply and he shoots me a look over Elaina and Sabrina's heads, that has my interest piqued. Clearly some-thing's up, and if it were Tate I wouldn't even wait to change my clothes. Viktor's much more formal, however, and likes to schedule meetings for practically everything.

I head back to the loft alone, get showered and changed, then meet everyone back up at Viktor's cabin.

The girls decide to prepare lunch, so while Bina's pre-occupied with Elaina, I follow Viktor and Alexei into the living area.

We all sit on his comfortable couches and the anticipation builds. I know if it had anything to do with Tate I would have gotten a phone call immediately, so this tells me that whatever Viktor has to say, it's probably about Sabrina's family.

He sits forward, fiddling with one of his cufflinks. He's a very commanding man, always sure of himself and has extremely high expectations of his men. I hold a great deal of respect for him, taking control of the Bratva and getting out of the sex trade that his uncle was into knee-deep.

When he stares at his cuff link for a few more beats, I get restless and clear my throat. His gaze meets mine and instead of the friendliness I'm used to, I see pity.

"You wanted to speak, Viktor?"

Alexei sits back, running his hands over his face as Viktor takes a deep breath and nods. He glances towards the kitchen, but Sabrina and Elaina can't hear us.

"Yes. Christ, this is hard. I found out some information that you need to hear. There are rumors floating around that someone is looking for Sabrina."

"Yes, but that is what I am for. I will protect her from such rumors."

"Right, look brat," he glances away and my hackles rise when he calls me 'brother.' He has never called me that before. We aren't that close; I'm only close to his real brother. "This person is supposed to be her husband." He finishes quietly and I swallow down the sudden rush of feelings making me want to vomit.

"Nyet, Viktor. I know Bina, I would know if she had gotten married, if she has this husband. I have known her nearly as long as Tatkiv," I grumble, using Tate's full name, the seriousness of the situation coming out to play.

"Look, Niko, I'm just passing on the information I was given. I hope you're right about her. Because *if* she's really someone else's wife, then we can't keep her from him. You know how this works; her father wouldn't be allowed to trade her, only her husband."

"There is no husband!" I end on a growl, my anger flaring inside.

Viktor nods quietly and Alexei doesn't meet my gaze. I don't care, there's no way what they say is true. I know Sabrina; we've lived together for months now. I would know if there was a fucking husband.

We're interrupted by Elaina's smiling face, "Hey guys, lunch is done, come eat." The smile falls as she takes stock in our expressions. "Vik? Everything okay?"

"Yes, Printyessa, relax. Let's eat my love." He stands, going to her and taking her hand. She leads him away as Alexei stands.

"I mean it Lexi, there is no husband."

He shrugs, his eyes shining with empathy. "None of my business."

I stay silent, huffing out a sigh and head into the kitchen myself with him trailing.

I'll figure this nonsense out. I'll have to confront Sabrina myself. I hate to get her upset with this news, but she deserves to know what's being said. Fucking wannabe Russian Bosses, can't keep their damn mouths closed when something doesn't go their way. I may be Russian and proud, but that's one thing I don't do. I restrain myself from killing everyone that pisses me off or try to ruin their happiness.

Sabrina's tender gaze meets mine as we all sit and eat a nice lunch. She watches me closely as I eat slowly, her expression curious. Food doesn't last around me; I scarf it down as soon as the plate hits the table like any good soldier is taught to do early on.

Not now.

I can't stop the thoughts crawling over my skin, attacking my mind with questions from every direction. Who would say this about her? I can't imagine her father having the guts to make such accusations if they were false. He knows I would kill him for that sort of thing; he's been privy to my feelings for Sabrina for years now.

I need to keep my faith in her; we've known each other too long for me to doubt that she would leave out something that's so vital to our arrangement. I'll ask her about it all later, acting like it's an absurd joke, to see what she thinks of this. I cannot afford the consequences of offending Bina, my affections run too deeply for her and I couldn't stand to have her upset. Not only am I in love with her, but she's a close friend to me and I'll hurt whoever is tainting her name.

With that decision, I reach over, giving Sabrina's dainty hand a light reassuring squeeze. The touch warms me and I finish my food, my appetite rejuvenated with the sweet promise of what's to come.

## that evening...

"Sabrina...Come here, I must speak with you," I order.

She's been upstairs most of the day on her laptop ordering things she and Elaina picked out for the wedding. Everything's in Elaina's name, of course, so there's no trail of Bina left anywhere.

She descends, paying attention to the steps in front of her, "Da, Blondie?" Her mouth turns up at her nickname for me.

As she gets closer, the pitter patter in my chest makes me grit my teeth. She's so goddamn stunning, I want to pull her to me, demanding she tell me the truth, and then make tender love to her after she laughs about how silly these rumors are.

"Let's sit."

We take a seat and I grab her hand, entwining our fingers, flashing a smile so she doesn't think I'm too upset about any of this. In reality, it's driving me absolutely crazy, clawing at me inside that she's going to tell me that it's actually true.

"I'm going to be frank with you; please do not get upset. I know this is stupid, but I need to hear the words come from your mouth."

"What's going on, Nikoli? You're kind of scaring me."

"No, no, don't be scared; it is fine, I promise you."

Sabrina nods and swallows nervously, giving me her complete attention.

"I was informed that someone is going around saying that you're married. I told them that it was nonsense."

Her gaze hits the floor and she scoots back more into the corner of the couch, dropping my hand. She may as well have just hit me with a ton of bricks, as it would probably have felt the same. I don't know what's going through her mind, but I wasn't expecting silence to be her response. She's always been fairly outspoken with me, quick to tell me her thoughts on things.

"I apologize, I know it's dumb of me to even mention it, but I promise I will find out who would say such false things about you."

Her head lifts as a tear escapes, leaving a sad trail down her cheek. Instantly my fists clench and my body grows taut as my mind explodes with the new possibilities floating around. It can't be fucking true. I can't have already lost her when I don't even have her yet. What am I going to do? I don't want to give her back; I don't want her to be *married*.

My heart will be broken forever. I've denied my affections for her for so long, but inside I know my feelings for her. If she has devoted herself to another man, I don't know if I will ever be able to move past her. I don't know if I can possibly forgive her for this and that's one of the most painful things. I don't want to hate her...I love her too much.

Choking down the urge to blow up and break every piece of furniture in sight, and then this husband's face afterward, I breathe deeply, and turn to her. "Please speak to me...You-you need to be honest. I will not hurt you, Bina, ever."

"I know that, Nikoli." Her lip trembles slightly. After a moment she runs her hands over her face and groans.

"Bina?" I try to speak further, but my chest aches and it comes out more like a gasp. It feels as if someone has reached in, gripping my heart in a death grip and is holding it, waiting for the words to spill from her rosy lips, so it can squeeze and finish off the job. My hand shoots to my heart, as I take another deep breath. I gaze over the floor, noticing each little spec of dirt that was missed when she quickly vacuumed over it yesterday.

I can't believe this. How could she do this? *Fuck it hurts.* This is all my fault. I left her alone with those people. They were supposed to be her family, and I was always nearby if she ever needed me. I can't believe Sabrina never told me; she could have called. I would have come for her.

Did they keep her from contacting me? Was this forced on her? She's not with him now; perhaps she was unhappy. But I can't keep her if she belongs to another man. How did we not hear of this? It must have been forced...It had to be. I know her father would have made a huge spectacle if she was marrying someone with influence; so this was one of his fucking dirty, scheming deeds.

I never should have let this happen.

Sabrina breaks through my silent self-destruction. "No, no, no... Nikoli. It's not like that. I promise you, okay?"

Blinking the red haze away, I eventually turn to her; she

scoots close to me, her shoulder touching my arm, as she adjusts so her thigh presses against mine. My body flares with awareness; it's like she calls to it and even heartbroken it awaits for her next order.

"Nikoli, I'm not married."

My fists unclench as I register her amazing words. My gaze trailing over each tan freckle on her face as I inspect for any possibility that she could be lying to me. She hasn't in the past that I know of, but growing up dealing with shady people has made me wary of everyone.

"Huh?" I manage to croak out.

"I said," she speaks louder, "I'm not married. Let me explain everything to you though."

My eyebrow raises, intrigued and impatient for this 'story.' "What is there to explain if you're not really married?"

"Well, my father had arranged a marriage for me. He ended up giving me to Viktor before it ever happened though, thankfully." She says it so matter of a fact, like I shouldn't be upset in the slightest. I understand in our ways it's normal to be married off, but I know inside that she's always been mine.

"He's fish bait," I growl and Sabrina's eyes widen. Her hand instantly clutches onto mine and I find myself breathing deeply for an entirely different reason.

"You can't."

"You know what I do, Bina. You're one of the few who know what type of man I am and the life I lead."

"I would never change any of it either, but please. That family is so dangerous; let them go after my father if they choose. I just want to stay out of it, and I would never forgive myself if anything happened to you."

Leaning in, my nose nearly touches hers as I whisper, "I'm dangerous also."

She draws in a breath, her mouth closing quickly as her gaze shoots to my mouth. Licking my lips, I edge a few inches closer.

"I won't let them touch you." I promise as my own eyes seek out her lips.

I want a little taste. Just one will hold me over. I need reassured that she really can be mine someday.

Her other hand finds my cheek and just when I think she's going to lean in the few inches to meet my lips, she stands.

"Oh I know, Blondie, and that's just one of the reasons why I'm so thankful to have your friendship. Now, I need to start on dinner," she finishes with a soft smile. Her hand releases mine and the other falls from my cheek as she makes her way into the kitchen.

Jumping up, I follow her, resting my hand on the small of her back once I'm close enough. She's so short that every time I'm in her space like this I feel as if I'm an ogre, dwarfing her elf-like stature.

"We need to discuss this more. Tell me his name."

"Geez, Nikoli, just let it go, da?"

"Nyet. You tell me his name."

"They will kill you, damn it!"

"Not if I kill them first," I finish in a huff, and she shakes her head, exasperated. She knows I won't stop until I get what I want. It's part of the reason why I'm so good at my job.

She rushes to the refrigerator removing ingredients for what looks like a chicken casserole. Sabrina's taken the liberties of making grocery lists with my favorite foods on them. I don't know if she realizes I've picked up on it over the past few months. She's always doing sweet little things like that for me though.

After a few moments of her cooking and silently stewing, she finally stops, facing me again. "His name is Kolya from the Minski family."

"The Minskis? Are you certain? What the hell would your father want with their family? What was he gaining?"

I know exactly who she's talking about. They had attempted

471

to hire me many years back, but Tate warned them that I'm not out for hired contracts. I only work for Tate. I would help Viktor if he needed it also, only because he's Tate's brother; otherwise, I don't risk an individual commissioned hit.

The Minskis have money, but as far as I know they aren't involved in the sex trade. In Russia you don't usually marry off your daughters unless it benefits you somehow. Maybe Bina's father is getting low on cash?

"Yes, I met him. I had to have dinner with his family. Well, my family and his family had dinner together anyway."

"Did you go out together alone?"

"Not publicly. We only went for a walk after the dinner through their garden. My father insisted that Kolya get some time alone with me to make sure he would want me. I mostly just listened to him talk about himself, and then when we returned, he shook hands with my father and told him that they had a deal."

"It's sickening he has no thought for your well-being. They tried to hire me a few years ago to kill off his first wife. I am loyal to the Mafiya and refused. They must have found someone if you were going to be the new replacement." *Sick bastards.* They would have ended up killing Sabrina when Kolya got tired of her as well.

Her eyes widen and she holds her stomach as if it hurts, "They-they killed her off?" she stutters and I nod. She deserves to know the truth. I don't disclose Mafiya business, but this had nothing to do with the Mafiya and I'm not going to keep it from her.

"Shhh, Bina...relax, I won't let any harm come to you." She takes a deep breath and slides the casserole into the oven. "Do you know what your father wanted from their family?"

"Ummm, no. I don't really know much, my father never spoke to me about those things, just my sister. He would plan things with Kendall, but I was never close to him like she was. There's really no telling what he had planned; he's always plotting one thing or another."

"Well what do you think it was about?"

"The only thing I could guess is if maybe they were conspiring against Viktor or for more money. I overheard Kolya's family talking about needing transport for some type of product."

Hmmm. The Minski's money comes from crank. I wonder if Kristof was going to use the Minski's drug running to transport the girls he sells off in the sex business. I could see him trading off his daughter to secure transportation that would leave him scot-free if the other family gets busted by the police. I'm not completely certain, but it makes sense to me.

"Okay, thank you for telling me about it. I'll talk it over with Viktor, but remember, you have nothing to fear."

"I can never repay you for all of your kindness, Blondie, thank you." She pops up on her tippy toes to kiss my cheek. She's still too short and only makes it to my jaw.

"Keep cooking like this and it's payment enough." I flash her a large, bright smile trying to give her some comfort and change the subject. She grins and rolls her eyes, turning back to the stove. "I'll be down shortly; I need to make a few calls." She nods, staying focused on the green beans she's warming up.

Heading upstairs, I pull my cell out. Tate and Viktor both have to know about this new information and my plans. I need to find out when Sabrina can hang out with Elaina also, because I'm going hunting.

# THREE

## Nikoli

You make my heart beat like the rain.
-Borns

### one week later...

I ADJUST THE SIGHT ON MY SNIPER RIFLE AGAIN. THE wind isn't bad; I'd say around five mph. Exhaling a deep breath, I peer through the scope again. Still no sign of Kolya.

*Fuck.*

Patiently I wait out another ten minutes and sure enough, Alexei's intel is right. He said Kolya eats at the same restaurant each week. Hard to believe that someone being accustomed to the criminal lifestyle would be so careless as to have a strict routine, and worse yet that he would let his old goons leave knowing about it, without tying up loose ends first. Drugs will get you many enemies if you piss the wrong person off, and crank? He's lucky some wigged out druggie hasn't attacked him yet. Being cocky and careless will get you killed easily. *Fool.*

A juiced up gym rat stands close to Kolya watching him as he finishes speaking with an older Italian man. Sabrina's father and another younger guy come outside as well, shaking hands and giving their ticket to the valet. They're up to something if their meeting with old Italian guys.

I often wonder if it was the Italians behind the kidnapping of my mother and little sisters. The men that came that night spoke Russian but I have always hoped my own kind would never do it. The only other clue I have is the dagger tattooed on one of the men's throats; it was dark, but I'll never forget it.

I too have a tattoo like it. Mine is done with quality while I'm positive his was done in prison. We both share the classic Russian sign of a hired killer. Only I'm not some thug on the streets; I'm contracted by the most respected branch of Mafiya in Russia. Many years of training and precise kills earned me my dagger along with the large spider tattooed on one of my shoulders.

Kolya approaches his car waiting at the curb and his head lines up perfectly in my sights. He's just far enough away, that the bodyguard isn't blocking my shot. I must do this to protect my Bina.

This will make my twenty-sixth kill with this weapon alone. That doesn't include any others that I have killed with my bare hands, let alone another type of firearm. I've grown accustomed to this choice of weapon. Call me lazy, but I like to sit back and watch the enemy come to me.

Rapidly I think over my checklist, making sure I'm not leaving anything out. I let loose a soft breath and right as my finger is about to lightly tap the trigger, my business cell that's strictly for Tate and Sabrina rings. Glancing down briefly at the cell phone resting beside me, Tate's name flashes across the screen. *I'll call him back in twenty minutes when my task is fulfilled and I'm back in my truck.*

My gaze jumps to the scope again, only Kolya is no longer there. I use the sight to scan over the whole front of the restaurant and nothing. The trash has loaded up and left as if his ass were on fire. The older Italian is still there on the curb, waiting for what, I haven't the slightest idea. Sabrina's father and the other mobster Italian have left as well.

My fingers itch to just let go and pull that small trigger back.

Cursing loudly, I snatch up my phone and dial Tate right away. I no longer have to worry about making a quick, quiet exit. "Da?" I say a little too loudly when he answers.

"Nikoli! Where are you?"

Shit, I didn't tell him that I was going to be out doing this today. We discussed Bina's issues and all the talk surrounding her about the fake marriage, but I didn't call him about this.

"I'm near a restaurant, is everything okay?"

"Yes, it's fine. Emily had a great time with Sabrina and Elaina, so I want to have you and Viktor bring the girls over for dinner tonight."

"It would be safer for you and Emily to come to the cabin."

"Niko, no one's going to hurt Sabrina. Not only does she have you protecting her, but she has Viktor, myself, and a handful of guards."

I'm grateful knowing I have such a loyal friend who would put himself in danger for a woman I care deeply for. However, Alexei told me that Sabrina's father keeps calling for her. Lexi's redirected any calls made from Kristof to not reach the landline thankfully, so Sabrina hasn't a clue about them. Hopefully it will stay that way; I'd hate to argue with her over her pathetic excuse of a father.

"Thank you. Your words mean more than you know."

"I'm serious about it; you would do the same for us. So, any updates on the douche who keeps saying he's married to her?"

Grumbling, I let the truth loose. "I'm sort of here where he eats. I was planning to eliminate the issue altogether; your call distracted me and now the trash has left."

"Fuck, Niko! Why didn't you tell me? I would have helped you more if I knew it was this serious."

"Nyet, Tate. You worry about your Emily. This was no problem, so I take care of it." My accent gets heavier as I try to talk faster without thinking out my words. Every time I get angry or flustered it comes out as well.

"It's a problem if you're there and about to shoot the dude. Does Viktor know about this?"

"He knows I was going to check out the threat and possibly acquire him if it was an option."

"Goddamn it! I can't believe you two left me out of the loop like this. I don't like it. We don't know what sort of repercussions this could have on everyone if you do take him out. You're blinded by Sabrina as you've always been to see any possible consequences."

Shit! He's completely right. I didn't even stop to think how this could possibly affect him and Emily if word was to get out that the hit came from the Mafiya.

They wouldn't bat an eye if it came from Viktor and the Bratva since he's the one who was granted permission to have Sabrina in the first place. It would almost be expected for him to take care of any loose lips. I'm quickly learning that she clouds my judgment on things. I would have thought this through much more clearly if it was another job, but instead I'm too focused on seeking revenge.

"There's a few old pasta eaters here meeting with Kolya and Kristof."

"Are you fucking with me? What do they want with them? Send me a pic."

Snapping a photo, I blue tooth the image of the remaining man to my cell and text it to Tate. Today's technology works amazing in situations like this.

Tate curses angrily; it's so loud I almost drop the phone.

"Da?"

"Eliminate him, Nikoli."

"What did the old Mobster do?"

"He's a Boss associated with the crew that recently tried torching one of the dock properties. They're trying to push me out so they can store their containers by Vik's warehouse."

"Fuck! This is why I should be with you, not being a bitch for Viktor!" I grumble angrily and drop the phone. I check the chamber again out of habit, lining up the sight, and breathe out deeply.

The gun pushes into my shoulder slightly, but not too much as I'm a big guy, and I watch through my scope as the older man drops, dead weight, a perfect shot through his skull.

*Fucking Italian Mob, always messing with us.*

Afterwards, I pack up my weapon, the extra ammo, not that I was expecting to need any extra, but I always set it beside me just in case. You never know how a hit may turn out.

Growling, I can't stop myself from picking up the cell and yelling at my Boss, "Damn it! You must keep me informed! You are my best friend!"

"I get it Niko, I'll update you, but you're in the wrong here, you should have contacted me. It sucks being out of the loop, huh?"

"I apologize, Boss; next time I will be sure to speak with you prior." Hell yes, it sucks. I can't stand not being around him, handling everything. I can't believe he didn't inform me about the fire. Looks like we've both been holding back.

"Good. I'll do some research on my side. Send a few of the guys to feel it out and if nothing major will come back to bite us in the ass then we schedule the termination on Kolya, along with any others who may impose a threat, okay? This is just a little trickier due to them being Russian and having ties with my father. It's not just random Italian mobsters we plan to kill you know."

"Da."

"Do I need to send out for a clean-up? I can call Viktor if you want."

"No, I say let it hit the papers; if anything, the FEDS will be happy to have one less pasta eater around."

"Very good, I agree with you. Get out of there and take care of yourself. I miss having you around."

"I will. Hopefully I'll be back soon and thank you."

"No problem. Later, man."

"Later."

Slipping my phone into my pocket, I shoulder the strap for the small duffle bag carrying all of my gear back to my truck. I have a special compartment built into the backseat of my truck to hold everything nicely in case I ever need it when I'm out and about. You never know when an opportunity may present itself, and it's imperative to always be prepared.

Shit, I never gave Tate an answer on dinner, but he should understand now that I've told him what I've been up to. He and Emily need to just come out to the cabin instead. I love the remote location of Viktor's place. The lake and mountains offer us just the right amount of privacy we require. When I'm not there, I live with Tate at his house so I can always protect him when needed.

If everything turns out good with Bina, I'm going to have to speak to Tate about moving out. I would love a place close to Viktor's if possible, but that's too far away I'm afraid. I wonder if Tate would consider moving out closer to Viktor also? That could end up working out in everyone's best interest actually.

After our conversation I feel like a kid who just got caught stealing cookies and I hate it. I shouldn't feel guilty about not telling my friend before coming here, but I do. I never thought it would bother him if I worked on something with his brother, but then I would get pissed sometimes also when Tate would go off with our old friend Cameron. They're friendship always had me a little uneasy. They were close for so long, but Cameron ended up being a two-faced trader and I dumped him in the lake with Viktor's assistance.

The complicated part of the hit's over with now, but it's probably best if I make a quick drive through the parking garage next to the restaurant. I need to make sure there aren't twenty Italians down there ready to shoot everyone in sight now that their Boss is dead.

The lights on my truck automatically switch on once I get in the dark parking area and it's easy to pick out where the mobsters are waiting. With the normal steroided-out, tan, Guido-looking guy standing guard at the car, he pretty much gives them away. There's a second thug trolling through the parking lot; more than likely his back up.

Creeping my truck along at a slow pace, I notice a tiny black haired lady perched down next to a Chevrolet Impala a few spaces away from the guy making his rounds. She looks scared out of her mind, hiding.

I press the button on my arm rest and roll my electric window down, attempting to talk softly, "Pssst...Miss, come here!"

She turns to me, eyes as big as saucers and shakes her head erratically.

"Yes! Come, jump in and I keep you safe."

She swallows, takes a deep breath and lunges for my truck. Once she's inside with the door slammed, not so quietly, I hightail it out of there. She's nuts to close the door so damn loudly. We'll be lucky if no one chases after us, wanting our heads for snooping around their business meetings.

"M-my goodness, thank you!"

"It is of no problem." My accent plays heavily, probably making me sound more like a vampire excited about a snack than a Russian hit man. "What is your name?"

"My name is Anna. I work for channel seven news. I got separated from my cameraman and his van; I was hiding because there was a gunshot." She rambles and digs out a small recording device from her bag, showing it to me. "Did you, sir, hear the gunshot that just rang out on Gibson Street at approximately twelve oh three p.m.?"

"Turn the device off, Anna, and put it away. You look inquisitive, not stupid."

She nods her head; eyes large again and shoves the device into her purse after turning it off.

"Did you hear those men in the garage speak of anything?"

"No, they just said to check on their Boss to another guy who left the garage before you showed up. Once I heard the shot, I dropped and was too scared to stand back up. I wanted to get the story, but I have a feeling those aren't the type of men I want to see me. There was actually a big group of guys in the garage a little while before I heard the shot—when I first parked."

I bet the guys were Kolya, Kristof, and the other Italian guards or drivers all waiting around. I should have known they wouldn't show up for lunch without a small army on standby.

"You have good instinct. You forget my face and vehicle; I will drop you a block away so you can wait for the police and be safe. There is one thing I want from you, however."

"Umm, okay, I can see what I can do within reason."

"Your story, it must be titled 'Vengeance is served with Vodka.'"

"I'm not sure I can get that approved. You're telling me, that this is a Russian job?"

"I didn't say that, I said use it as a title. I need to get a message to someone. They will know what it means. Surely you can't think I am stupid to believe you have no power to choose the title. Be smart right now."

"Fine, but can you at least give me the name of who was shot?"

"No, but I can tell you he was an old Italian Mobster."

"Holy shit...The Russians *and* the Italians?"

"This is your stop, Anna." I pull the truck to a stop and click a photo of her with my phone. "Don't make me regret this." I wave it in front of her.

"You've helped me more than you realize. No worries on my part." She sends me a shaky smile and hurries out of the truck. *I sure hope not; I'd hate to have to kill someone with such a pretty face.*

I pull away quickly so she can't get a good picture if she decides to suddenly be brave. That should work nicely to get our threat out. They need to stop fucking with the Mafiya, because we always clean up our messes.

My phone chirps with a text from my good friend Avery.

> **Avery**: Taco Tuesday big guy, wish you were here!
>
> **Me**: Tell biker bitch he sucks and I wish you were here too Bean
>
> **Avery**: Come visit, Texas misses you also.

Her text sends a small pang to my chest. I worry about her sometimes now that she's moved to Texas to be with her motorcycle club boyfriend. I know he can protect her, but Avery and I had gotten very close before she up and moved sixteen hours away.

Shaking it off, I toss my phone into the center console. Texting and driving don't mix, especially since these Americans drive on the opposite sides of the roads as we do in Russia. Total mindfuck the first time I tried driving here.

During the few hours it takes to drive back to the cabin, I'm engrossed in my thoughts about what to do about moving, Tate, and the damn Italians. I made a quick stop at the tattoo parlor I frequent—another kill means another mark for me to wear.

Twenty-six drops of blood tattooed across my abdomen make me look as if my stomach is torn open and weeping tears of blood. Those tears of blood to me are for my mother; one day

I'll find who tore my family apart.

# Sabrina

Elaina hangs up the phone with a goofy smile on her face. "That was Emily. She tried to get you out of the house, but according to Tate, Niko wasn't having it, so she and Tate are coming here. I tried to get her to bring my baby niece but she said another time. Tonight the angel is going to visit her grandma and papa."

"Awww, I'll miss the little one, but I'm glad they are coming to visit. I had a lot of fun with them."

"She is entertaining, huh? Tate has her spoiled rotten; but she's had a rough life, losing the people she was close to. She was with her own brand of psycho for a while, so I'm thrilled for her."

"The two of you together are crazy. You look the same, but you're pretty much opposites. It's like I get the best of both worlds with you guys."

"Yeah, but I'm the better half." She answers with a grin and I roll my eyes.

All day they had gone back and forth over who was older, prettier, funnier, etc. It's hilarious since they're twins and look almost the same. If you didn't know them personally, you'd never be able to tell them apart.

I feel so fortunate to not only have made one new friend by coming here, but many. I count Viktor, Alexei and Tate also. Alexei is a little grumpy, but he's thoughtful. Tate is cocky, but his love for his family shines through. Viktor is domineering, but he also takes care of everyone, probably because he's the oldest.

"So what are we doing for dinner then? Or are they coming over to play cards and drink?"

We've had a few dinners so far along with a couple of vodka nights that always end with lots of giggles from us and at least one person puking or getting carried off to bed.

"I thought we'd make a roast? The one Viktor's gram taught me to make is my favorite."

"Oh, I love that dish! Are we making the Topt for dessert also?"

"Don't get all crazy now; Emily can bring the dessert."

Laughing, I nod and pull the loaf of French bread out of the pantry so we can pair it for dinner.

"You know what? I think I'm going to go change into a cute dress for dinner. It's been a while since I wore something nice. The roast has to cook for a few hours; what do you think?"

"That sounds like a great idea! I'll text Em and let her know...All three of us can dress up."

"Okay, I'll be back then, unless you need my help some more?"

"Nope not right now, I'm going to throw this baby into the oven then get dressed myself. I have an adorable new silver colored dress that I've wanted to wear for Vik."

"Oh, I bet that's pretty! I'll be back soon."

"Okay cool, bye." Elaina smiles as I close the back door, hurrying to my and Nikoli's place.

Spartak, Elaina's private guard is out back, always on duty.

"Hello Spartak." I greet as I pass him. He shoots me a small smile and nods.

He's always so quiet unless Elaina's around. I asked her about it and she said that they became close when my sister was terrorizing her and Viktor. It's been months since I first got here, but I don't think I'll ever stop feeling guilty since it was my own sister causing their lives to be so stressful.

Once I make it up the stairs to the loft bedroom, I peel off my jeans and long sleeve t-shirt. I have just the dress in mind. It's a mint green color, baby-doll style dress that comes a few inches above my knees. I may dress plain now and live in flip-flops a lot, but I still have a stash of dresses that I actually like. With no more forced obsessions with my looks from my mother, it has opened my eyes to what styles I like.

Tapping on the alarm clock, 'Blurred Lines' by Robin Thicke starts playing. Naturally I start wiggling my butt as I dig through the closet Nikoli built for me once we got settled. He's been so sweet and helpful, always rushing to do whatever he can to make sure I'm comfortable.

I happily sing along; it's 'Blurred Lines'—you can't not sing and dance to this song. I probably look like a giant fool parading around in my plain bra and panty set, but who cares? It's fun.

The song ends and Salt 'N' Pepa's "Whatta Man" comes on next. I love this song; it reminds me of being a kid at private school. My girlfriends would play it over and over; we were *so sure* we knew what it was actually about. Our parents would have thrown a fit if they knew what all we were listening to back then.

I try to shake my booty along, singing loudly. I could never do this at my mother's house.

Spinning around and getting into the song, I let out a loud shriek. Nikoli stands at the top of the stairs, gazing into the bedroom with wide eyes and a smirk. He looks thoroughly pleased he's caught me like this.

"Umm...Hi?" Nibbling on my lip, I'm struck still by his heated gaze.

"Sorry to interrupt. I called for you but you didn't answer me, so I came looking for you."

"Oh it was probably the radio. I didn't even hear the door close downstairs or anything." I'm not embarrassed he caught me singing. When he would take me to hang out, I would constantly turn up his radio and sing loudly; he loved it and would always tell me to do it more.

"You were singing pretty loudly, and I did not mind the free dance show." He chuckles and I smile. Then I glance down, realizing I'm in my bra and panties.

I bring the dress up in front of me as a shield. "Shit, I-I was getting dressed."

He's seen me in my bathing suit before but I don't want to make him feel awkward by me being in my underwear since we're just friends. He's too important to me; I don't want him thinking I'm trying to come onto him when that's not what he wants.

"I see that." He starts to prowl towards me, making the room feel remarkably less significant with his huge size. "Let me help." His cheeks tint slightly as he gets closer.

I don't know if he's embarrassed or turned on. No, he can't be hot and bothered for me; he thinks of me as a friend only. *So much for wishful thinking.*

"Okay, great. I really appreciate it." I stammer and my stomach stirs with excitement as he gets closer. My heart beats so hard, and I wonder if he can see it.

Do I put the dress on right now? He's okay with me being in my undies in front of him? I guess there's only one way to find out. I hope he doesn't get the wrong impression from me, even though I would love to have that sort of attention from him. I'm not a virgin, but I'm not very experienced either.

Spinning around, I stop so my back is to him and lift the silky material over my head. It slides down over my body easily. I could have stepped into it, but I've always preferred putting a dress on the same way as a shirt. I'm glad he offered to help, the zipper runs all the way down to the small of my back.

"Ready?" He asks huskily, his breath feeling extremely close to my ear and neck for some reason.

I draw in a gasp as goose bumps appear all over my skin from the warm sensation. Swallowing deep I whisper, "Yes."

"Me too," is murmured against my ear and my hands make a tight fist, my short purple nails digging into my palms. There are so many different meanings to that and thinking about one in particular has me clenching my pussy muscles over and over. I should stop myself, but it feels too good.

His fingers flutter over my back lightly as he slowly closes the zipper. It feels more like an erotic caress than a helpful hand. Biting my bottom lip, I stop myself from moaning his name aloud.

"There Bina, all set," he mutters and steps away.

The spell is broken as cool air hits my upper back where the material is missing. My gaze drops to the floor, hoping I can mask the heat blazing over my cheeks, from imagining him ripping the back of my dress off.

"Thank you, Blondie."

"Of course. You look stunning as always. I'm going downstairs until you're finished, da?"

"Da," I mumble and turn towards the small dresser holding my makeup. I'm going to need to wear some tonight, because I know I won't be able to get those thoughts out of my mind and I definitely won't stop thinking about it being around Nikoli all night.

He leaves, heading back down the stairs. *God, he's flipping gorgeous.* He used to have women basically falling at his feet when we'd hang out. If we went to the mall or movies or dinner or wherever, he'd have pretty girls flirting with him like crazy.

Hmmm, I wonder if he's been with anyone since we've come here. I mean it's been months, so surely he's had to. It's not fair of me to expect him to be celibate too. I don't want to think of him being intimate with anyone else; it hurts too bad.

I fish out my shiny black flats to wear along with my dress. I'm leaving the heels since we're dining in and I'll take them off at the cabin anyhow. Viktor hates dirty carpet. Weird, but if we're staying in the house for a long time we have to take our shoes off.

Since it's getting cooler with the change of season, I grab a cardigan—just in case—and make my way downstairs. I know Nikoli would offer me his jacket if he saw me cold, but I don't want to put him out any more so than I already do.

Nikoli grabs his own light jacket and puts it on. It hides his shoulder holster and gun. I'm surprised he's taking it. I know he wears one on his leg under his pants. I've seen him unstrap it many times before he goes to shower. He must have had a busy day himself since he's carrying multiple weapons.

Niko's eyes light up when I reach the bottom and he takes my hand to escort me.

"Thank you."

"It's nothing." He shrugs and smiles kindly.

"Is everything okay?"

"Yes, why?"

I point out his other weapon and he straightens.

"I'm protecting you. Since when do my weapons bother you?"

"You know they don't. I'm just curious. Relax, Blondie."

He lifts my hand to his mouth and plants a chaste kiss on it without responding, and then he leads me towards Viktor's. Spartak's still sitting outside in the same spot. Niko ignores him like he's a piece of furniture but I turn back quickly and wave.

I know there's sort of a pecking order in these organizations and Nikoli is towards the top. His tattoos clearly state he's not to be crossed, but I still want to be friendly with everyone. My family was hateful enough when I was growing up; I don't want to live my life that way being rude to others. I swear I hear what sounds like a growl come from Nikoli... But I know that can't be right.

We knock and Elaina answers the door and lets us in. The cabin smells wonderful; the air is rich and heady with the spicy scents from the seasonings on the roast. It reminds me of the holidays. My mother would always have the servants make ham, topak, and different roasts at celebrations. The mansion would smell delicious and looked beautiful with all the decorations going up to be festive. Too bad it's the only good things I remember from those times.

"Wow, it smells divine in here! Need me to help with anything?"

She looks beautiful in an understated knee length silver-grey toned dress. Tonight she fits perfectly next to Viktor, who's always dressed up in a fancy suit. They scream power couple when you look at them.

Viktor's a ruthless Bratva leader, always taking care of things for everyone, and Elaina watches his back like a freaking fox. To most they would come off as cold and detached, but inside they're caring and fiercely devoted to their family. I've seen Viktor steal kisses from Elaina and they have a fire that crackles between them that I can only dream about.

Elaina smiles brightly, "No ma'am, we're all set. Alexei set the table for us, and you already got the bread taken care of. Emily's bringing a fruit salad that tastes amazing. She got the recipe from her friend, London, and has been making it at least once a month along with a macaroni casserole. I swear Tate's going to get plump if he ever stops working out." She laughs. Elaina has a positive energy that pulls you in, making you want to be a part of it.

"Well it all sounds wonderful; I can't wait to try it. Thank you for having us."

"You should know by now you're welcome anytime; I love when we get to have our dinners. I'll miss you a lot once you guys finally move to Niko's place."

She catches me off guard, but I reply breezily, "Oh, are we moving there soon?"

This is the first I've heard of it. I'm a little surprised...Okay I'm a lot surprised. I can't believe Niko hasn't brought it up. Plus, he lives with Tate and Emily. I don't know if I would fit in living there with them. I like Tate and Emily; I'm just used to our own space.

"Shit! I didn't mean it like that. I meant like eventually, you know, once there's not such a big threat going on with your family and you. The guys haven't said anything about it. I just assumed so for the future."

"Okay, I was scared for a moment that Nikoli hadn't told me something important." I chuckle anxiously.

She shakes her head and squeezes my hand softly.

"Speaking of, he disappeared into the living room with the guys pretty quick. Is he okay?"

"Yeah, I believe so. But just now when we were walking to the door, I swear I heard him growl at Spartak. Did you get a new guard dog that I don't know about?"

Elaina busts out laughing, "No, we haven't. That's too funny. I wonder if he caught Spar staring at you again."

"Again?"

"Girl, you are so blind. Spar stares at you every time he's in a room with you. I thought Nikoli was going to turn completely red and throat punch him the last time it happened. I don't think he's said anything to him about it yet, but I wouldn't be surprised if he did soon."

"I hope Nikoli doesn't get the wrong impression from me."

"What do you mean?"

"I don't want him thinking I'm interested in Spartak at all."

"Why would it matter? Y'all are just friends. Wait...Do you want Niko?"

"Shhh! He can't hear you! Blondie only likes me as a friend; it's always been that way."

"Shit! How did I miss this?" She starts giggling mischievously.

"I don't just like him Elaina, I love him." I mumble as a loud knock interrupts us.

"That must be Em and Tate. Let's get the door."

Luckily she doesn't bring it up again; besides, we have a wedding in two weeks to prepare for! I'm sure I can keep her busy with planning to keep her mind off of me and my personal love problems. The last thing I want right now is for Nikoli to get wind of my feelings and have it stir up any sort of drama when this time needs to be spent on her and planning the ceremony.

Another reason why I worry so much about Nikoli—or any of the other guys—finding out I have such strong feelings for him is that they may separate us. For all I know, Nikoli could feel uncomfortable enough to want to leave completely.

It's not as if I lust after him every moment of the day, but there are times I catch myself just gazing at him. He's gorgeous. Any woman would have to be blind not to notice him. I'm not ready to be apart from him yet. It would probably be better for my heart, but I'm apparently a glutton for punishment.

I've even woken up a few times in the middle of the night either holding him or finding him holding onto me. Luckily he's sleeping so he doesn't realize it. Once we started sharing the same bed a few months ago, I couldn't stop my body gravitating towards his in the middle of the night.

He keeps me warm when I get cold, and his scent surrounding me helps me to fall asleep. He's woken to me being pressed up against his body plenty of times, but he just gets out of bed quickly, pretending as if it didn't happen, or like it's not a big deal. Perhaps he's shared a bed with another woman who was just a friend? I don't want to think about that, so I push those thoughts back and concentrate on the wonderful people surrounding me.

We have an amazing evening filled with laughter and good food. Before I know it, the night is over and the next two weeks take us by storm with orders, crafts, food, fittings, and other preparations for a whimsical Russian wedding.

# FOUR

## Sabrina

### A MASTERSON WEDDING

We long for fairytales
In a world full of nightmares.
–Natalia Crow

**TIME FLIES WHEN YOU BUSY YOURSELF WITH SO MANY** tasks daily and before I know it, two weeks have passed us by in a blink. It seems like just a few days ago we were sitting at Elaina's kitchen table, talking over all of the details. Our crazy days of planning and preparing have finally come to an end.

I missed being away from Nikoli so much, but I'm glad we got a little bit of distance. When I'm with him all day—every day—I catch myself pushing the boundaries. There will be little looks here and random extra touches there. I sit closer to him. I sleep next to him. I sit with him for meals and prepare his food. It's almost as if I am his wife, only without the title and the love-making or kisses.

Today was the magical day for Elaina and Viktor, and everything went off without a hitch. I had no idea so much work and creativity would go into a smaller sized event, but I still look forward when I'm hopefully able to do it again—for my own wedding. Oh who knows if I'll even get married at this rate? I may just grow to be an old maid, lusting after a blond Russian hit man who doesn't return my feelings. Occasionally I'll catch him flashing me a weird look, but then I brush it off, not wanting to call him out on it and make him feel awkward.

The wedding was a beautiful afternoon ceremony held down near the beach in a white wooden gazebo, decorated with sheer white fabric and twinkle lights. By the time the bride and groom were finished exchanging vows and sharing a blistering kiss, the twinkle lights were more pronounced—the epitome of romantic.

Everyone looked so beautiful all dressed up, and the guests seemed to enjoy themselves. Emily and I did whatever we could to make things less stressful on the bride, and she got to relax a little.

It's truly an honor that Elaina trusted me enough to help her pull off this whole shebang. I know if Viktor had it his way, he'd have
just hired a team to take care of it all and sat back to bark orders occasionally.

I couldn't be more pleased for my newfound friends and wish them many years of happiness to come. Maybe Viktor will get lucky and Elaina will be pregnant when they return from their honeymoon. He plays it off that he isn't quite ready to share Elaina with anyone else, but I can see them very content some-day with a few children running around. I'm confident they'll both make splendid parents.

I like to think we did a great job decorating and ordering all the different foods. Viktor's grandmother baked a massive three-tiered cake that tasted like a fluffy, vanilla-caramel piece of bliss. I'm thinking I may speak to her about making mine someday—that woman has a gift!

Personally I would prefer a snowy Russian wedding, but I

could easily see how at ease Elaina and Viktor seemed being on the beach surrounded by loved ones. The setting sun and the twinkle lights were a perfect ending to the sweet vows they proclaimed to each other.

They're so lucky to have found such a true love in each other; I envy that. The afternoon seemed like one big dream and I'm sure the other guests felt the same way. I hope one day I'll get my chance to have all of that too.

The downfall, however, is the clean-up of this place. Thank God the cleaning crew we hired will be able to get majority of it. I wonder if someone put the cake topper aside for Elaina. I know she wants to keep that memento safe and sound. Lucky ducks were going to visit a few different countries. I'm sure Viktor will be spoiling her plenty on this trip. I can't wait to see what she comes back with, besides a tan and possible baby bump.

"Hey, Blondie?" I tug on his black and white pinstriped suit jacket.

We're all gathered around in the front since Viktor, Elaina, Spartak, and Alexei just left for the airport. We wanted to get our good-byes and waves in with the rest of the crowd. I didn't get a chance to speak to them, but I got a hug and kiss on the cheek from Elaina telling me she would miss me as she was pulled away by her new husband.

"Da?" He leans over so I can reach up and talk in his ear. The man is a mountain compared to my stature, and half the time he misses some of the things I say if we're in public.

"I just thought of the cake topper. I need to get it for Elaina. I would hate for something to happen to it."

You never know who might steal it or if it got mixed up in the trash and thrown out. She's become too good a friend to me, and I promised to take care of things and I meant it.

"No problem. Stay on the path so the guards can see you." He nods and I squeeze his arm to me a little. He smirks at my pathetic attempt of an arm hug and I make my way to the back.

Another downfall of having the wedding next to the lake is trekking in my heels back and forth. I hate these damn things. My feet were made for flats and flip-flops.

That's another thing Elaine and I have in common—our love for comfortable shoes. As a wedding gift I got her a pair of low top glitter chucks. She declared she was wearing them at the wedding and I thought Viktor was going to stroke out. She didn't, but it was still hilarious to watch him freak out about it. I know for a fact she packed them for their trip, so he'll be seeing them soon.

I damn near twist my ankle and it's the breaking point... *Screw this.* The important stuff is over with, so I'm taking them off. As I pass by mine and Blondie's place, instead of carrying my tan pumps with me, I throw them towards the door and head to the beach.

If I were lucky, Nikoli would follow me down here and profess his love for me, but I know that'll never happen. That would be so romantic if he would take me to the gazebo and kiss me passionately, declaring his undying love and devotion. *Clearly I read too many books.*

I finally make it down to the gazebo and tents full of chairs, tables, food, etc. I'm surprised to find it completely deserted. I must have beat the clean-up crew because everything is just how we left it before sending off the bride and groom. It looks like a tornado had blown through the place with everything in such disarray.

We picked out a variety of fresh flowers to be flown in and decorated each table in a different color and type. The tent was decorated in understated elegance, just like Elaina. The tables were adorned with thick white table cloths, flowers in rich, vibrant colors held in clear crystal vases, the cake display set up with sparkling crystal candelabras, and glass vases full of fake white pearl beads.

It felt like a celebration for a true princess and Viktor was pleased about it. He even suggested I throw Elaina's next birthday party. Could the future hold a profession of event planning for me? Hmmm—not sure I'm up for all the work that comes with it.

Well, it was gorgeous until the guests arrived and pretty much acted like it was a free-for-all Sunday buffet. Ugh, people are so damn messy—pigs, the lot of them. How hard is it to throw out your trash in a bin?

Anyhow, I'm back here for the topper. Viktor had surprised Elaina by ordering a beautiful set of Russian hand-carved and painted bride and groom figurines. The figures look remarkably like the real bride and groom and the one that looks like Elaina even has a crown atop her head, just like the real one worn in the ceremony.

A few napkins should work just fine to keep them safe until I can have one of the guards get me the case for them, I think.

I carefully place the small portion of leftover cake on one of the heavy crystal platters and place the silver cake cutter next to it, then wrap up the toppers in napkins and put them on the same platter as well.

Searching over the food tables, I eventually find some foil that I use to securely cover the platter. That should suffice until I make it to the cabin and can rewrap everything separately. I don't know how Viktor and Elaina are about their traditions, but I want to put the cake in their freezer just in case they want it for their first wedding anniversary. It will taste gross by then, but it's the meaning that counts.

I don't know if Elaina wants me to save anything else. Perhaps I'll send Vivian and Mishka down here to see what they think. Surely Viktor's grandmother and mother should know what he would want to keep or if there's anything that they would want. With that, I grab the platter and make my way to the tent exit.

I pass a striking man on my way out of the tent. I'm not

familiar with him, but he's in a navy suit so he must have just blended in with the others. The invites said black and grey suits only, but clearly he didn't get that memo.

"Excuse me." I nod politely and he steps to the side a little for me to pass through the open doorway. He barely gives me a large enough area to squeeze by without hitting him, but I make it by anyway.

"Sabrina." He nods briefly and my name spilling from his lips takes me by surprise, enough so that I pause.

"Yes?" I squint, running my eyes over his features, slower this time. "Do I know you? I apologize but I don't recognize you."

I've met many people over the years when I'd go out to dinner or wherever with my father. I can't remember three quarters of them or their faces when I think of it. I was always in my own little bubble, daydreaming about something, reading a good book or worrying about what my sister was planning for me next.

"No ma'am, you do not know me, but I know you." He shifts, partially blocking my exit. His voice is Russian with a slow southern twang to it. I'd guess he's used to being in Russia but when he comes to America, he only visits the deep south.

I raise my brows to him, my stomach tightening and go to move past, when he catches my arm tightly. The platter wobbles slightly, the cutlery inside clinking.

"Excuse me!"

He leans in close enough to my ear to growl out a threat. "You make a sound and I will have my men open fire on all these lovely guests out front. I've been waiting for you."

"Are you crazy? Now let go of my arm and you will live." I can't help the entitled rich girl coming out; I'm too used to having my father or Nikoli by my side to handle any repercussions.

It didn't happen often, but occasionally a boy would get a little too brave, and one of them would step in quickly to school the fellow on acceptable manners. *I guess I really have been sheltered more than I'd like to admit.*

The man chuckles, amused, his deep timbre causing goose bumps to rise on my arms. The hairs on the back of my neck stand as he grips me even tighter—definitely not the response I was expecting. Doesn't my voice sound serious at all? I probably sound like a pissed off squirrel.

"You're hurting me; please stop!" I whimper, tightly holding onto the platter so I won't drop it.

"Oh Sabrina...I've only just begun to hurt you," the man whispers cryptically before my head goes fuzzy. I think I hear the plate crash, but all I feel for sure is the strong pinch at my side and the immense feeling of wanting to sleep.

"Nikoli?" I desperately cry out.

"You don't belong here beauty, you belong to someone else. No more hiding from him." I'm thrown over his shoulder and everything goes black.

••••

You know those times you wish you could go back? You think why didn't I scream or kick and thrash to free myself? There was a small window of opportunity when I probably could have gotten loose. If I had dropped the platter and taken off in a sprint when he first said my name, there's a slight chance I'd have gotten away—at least far enough so I could have screamed and gotten someone to help me.

But that's the problem with getting too comfortable, especially when you're involved with the Mafiya, because when it comes down to it, no one's ever safe.

# Nikoli

"Well, shall we get the girls and have some dinner? Maybe a

drink or two? It was a great afternoon, but frankly I'm worn out. I'm ready to get my love and chill for a while." Tate suggests right before he yawns.

"I think Sabrina would enjoy that. She and Emily worked so hard on putting this together. We can go to a town over, yes?"

"Sure, I don't see any problem with that. I'll let the driver know the change of plans."

"Thanks, Boss."

He nods and walks towards his temporary guard. The temp guy is good; I know because I hand-selected him to protect Tate prior to me leaving. Sabrina is my main focus, but Tate's safety will always be one of my priorities. It's pretty much been my life's work to keep him alive and well, I won't be stopping that anytime soon.

Viktor's man he left in charge, Lev, approached me, shortly after Tate left, looking as if he's seen a ghost.

"Nikoli, a word?"

"Da?" Grumbling, I step off to the side with him, away from any remaining guests waiting on their cars to come pick them up. The wedding's over, they've been fed, Viktor and Elaina left, and now I'm ready for everything to go back to normal.

"I believe something's happened. I walked Miss Mishka down to the tent because she forgot her scarf thing. I offered to fetch it for her, but she insisted she wanted to go for a walk. Well, we get to the tent and there's cake and the little bride and groom thrown all over the entryway. A large crystal dish was a few feet away on the ground as well." He adjusts his tie nervously, then continues, "Mishka flipped out and thought someone ruined it, but then one of the men said they had seen Sabrina walk down there a few minutes prior. Please tell me you've seen her since then and she's okay?"

"I don't understand. Bina would never ruin those things and leave them there; she adores Elaina. I'll go to our place and check for her. I hope she didn't injure herself or anything, she can be clumsy sometimes, and she could have fallen and hurt herself. Maybe that is what happened."

That's a reasonable explanation, considering she was so adamant on getting the damn things in the first place. I hope she's okay. Where were the damn guards and why didn't anyone help her? Or did someone help her and she's alone with them? At least Spartak is gone with Viktor or fuck if he wouldn't be with Sabrina trying to speak to her alone. *Idiot.*

Lev shrugs, peering at me worriedly. "Mishka said its Uncle Victor, whatever that means."

I let loose an angry growl and storm towards our loft. Their Uncle Victor better pray it wasn't him bothering her. Former Bratva King or not, he will be mine if he did anything to harm her. These old men don't know how to just sit back and let the next in line take care of things. They're always meddling in their kids' business.

Arriving at the barn, I notice that Sabrina's shoes are thrown carelessly to the side of the front door. *Typical Bina.* Whenever she has too much wine she throws her shoes, and I've gotten used to it. I've even had to duck down on occasion—she has quite the aim.

In a rush to make sure she's okay, I slam through the front door, calling out, "You in here, Bina?"

I get nothing in return, not even a chirp from a cricket. Maybe she's in the shower?

"Sabrinaaaaa!" I shout and hurry up the stairs to our bedroom.

Every damn night I sleep next to her but have to keep my hands to myself. It drives me fucking insane. I swear I must be a saint to show such self-restraint and the dreams, good God if I don't have delicious dreams about her all night long. Sometimes I even wake to her cuddled up to me. Those are the days I have to hightail it downstairs, because my cock is so hard it would probably poke her eye out if she were to see the effect she has over me.

When I arrive, the room is empty and exactly as we left it: her pajamas thrown on the floor, makeup stuff scattered over her dresser top, the bed unmade. A search of the other rooms comes up empty.

*She's nowhere.*

My heart rate increases as my chest tightens at the thought of not being able to find her. *I have to get to her.* I jog down to the beach, over by the gazebo, then through each of the tents and around the back sides of the buildings.

The last place I scour is Viktor's cabin, but she's not fucking there either and I feel like I can no longer breathe.

"Nooo!" I cry out, defeated and angry, kicking the cabin's back door for good measure.

My mind can't seem to process her just disappearing on me and not knowing where she is. We've gone for months of basically being attached at the hip and now it's like half of my lung has been stolen from me and I can't catch my breath.

*Fuck. When did I start needing her?*

Tate comes barreling around the side, appearing anxious and concerned, "Hey man, are you okay?"

"Fuck!"

Am I okay? He's lost his mind asking me such a foolish question. Of course I'm not fine. Sabrina is nowhere to be found and I'm flipping the fuck out. I'll be okay when she's back in front of me where I can yell at her for scaring me like this.

"What's up? Talk to me."

"Sabrina is gone." I spew out angrily, "Lev and Mishka find mess by tent. Now I look everywhere and nothing. I do not know what to do, Tatkiv."

I can't calm myself as I replay it to Tate. Instead of assessing the situation and thinking up a plan, I go ballistic, punching Viktor's door over and over, my chest compressing more so that it feels like I'm having a heart attack.

"Stop!" Tate yells, but I ignore him, continuing in my pursuit to beat the door off the hinges. It may not solve my problems, but it feels damn good to explode on something. "Nikoli! Stop! Damn it, you won't be able to use your fucking hands if you don't calm down!"

Ignoring him, I pound on the hard surface, looking to destroy it. The pain steals away the thoughts of her being taken or harmed in any way. I hit it even harder, gritting as I feel the bones in my knuckles start to crunch and become numb.

Tate hunches down, turning so his side is faced towards me, then he drives into me with his shoulder like when we used to play football. It works, and his momentum knocks me off my balance, throwing me off my course of self-destruction and away from the door.

"Goddammit Nikoli! I said enough!" He shouts and I grow quiet, lying in a heap on the floor. "Calm down. You can't track her if you don't chill the fuck out."

"She is lost."

"No she's not, you're being dramatic. You found her before, and if needed, you'll do it again."

"What if I'm too late this time? I can't let anyone hurt her and it almost happened this last time. I don't get it; who's foolish enough to come into the Mafiya, let alone a Bratva wedding? It's like a goddamn hornet's nest here today."

Lev speaks up, "I think I may have an idea of where to start."

Tate and I both turn to him, not realizing he's been witnessing my meltdown the entire time.

"Speak," I grit out sternly, on the cusp of blaming him for this mess, since he's the one who discovered the mess in the first place.

"Yeah, so ummm, well, Viktor had an issue earlier. His uncle, the old King, Victor, showed up here. Alexei and Spartak know the details, I just had to watch the old man get shoved in a car and carted off the property."

Tate barks suddenly, "Fuck! Viktor told me he needed to speak with me after the wedding. I got so tied up in everything and the guests, and I never got to talk to him. I bet that's what he was going to say to me. Fuck! Alexei and Spartak left with them on security detail for the honeymoon too."

"What an utter fucking mess. I made sure there were no issues at your wedding, Tatkiv; the Bratva cannot do the same?"

"It wasn't the Bratva's fault, Nikoli. We will get Sabrina back. I'm going to call my brother now and I'm sure as soon as he gets off the plane in Russia, we'll hear back."

"So I sit here, twiddling thumbs until he arrives after his fifteen-hour or more flight?"

"No, you call the tech guy; tell him to start a search. You didn't have her chipped or wearing a tracking device?"

"She is no dog Tate; of course she is not fucking chipped."

"Whatever, Niko. Emily is chipped, because I love her and want her as safe as possible in this lifestyle."

Standing angrily, I answer with a grunt and pull out my business cell, ready to call into tech and find my woman.

# Sabrina

## USELESS INFORMATION

Words have no power to impress the mind
without the exquisite horror of their reality.
–Edgar Allen Poe

**W**AKING, I'M CHILLED TO THE CORE. SOMETHING'S not right; I usually wake up way too warm from Nikoli's body heat burning me up.

"Welcome, welcome!"

There's that voice again—the creepy one from my dream. Am I still in my dream? No, I'm waking up because I'm absolutly freezing. The dry, musty smell hits me and my eyes shoot open, my body finally registering that something's definitely not right.

I run my gaze around the room, taking everything in—it's dark, cold, and concrete. It stinks like wet cement, piss, and a weird rusty smell. It reminds me of how I would imagine blood to smell. I begin to ask where I am, but only a croak comes out.

The man laughs and my body locks up tight as a freezing burst of water hits my stomach.

"Aghh-hhh!" A broken whimper escapes as a million tiny ice

cold needles hit my body.

"Drink up sweetheart, you won't get anything later."

The frigid spray continues to soak my body but I manage to wet my fingers and suck the liquid off to help refresh my dry throat.

My teeth chatter and my body shakes, goose bumps taking over everywhere and ruining the nice shave job I had worked hard on for the wedding. "So-so cold!" I swear I can feel my leg hairs sticking up and it pisses me off more than the water.

More eerie laughing ensues and my head begins to throb so much that it feels like it may explode.

"Please?"

The water stops immediately. "That's a good girl. Remember your manners; it will help you in the end."

His cryptic half sentences give me no help, along with a pounding head and being frozen, my body aches like I've been run over. I'm assuming I ache so badly from sleeping on the hard concrete floor; no wonder the cold has seeped into my muscles.

"I'm so-so cold." My jaw shakes, causing my teeth to chatter harder.

A painful screech rips from me as a hard boot connects with my back harshly.

*Holy fuck that hurt! What is happening to me?*

"No one enjoys whining. It's my job to make sure you're worth keeping. Complaining will get you nowhere, now shut up."

Biting my bottom lip, it takes everything in me to not lash out as the tears begin to fall. I want to so badly just scream 'fuck you' to this fucker. How on earth can anyone be expected to not complain in conditions like this? Not only am I now a human icicle, but my back has a huge piercing pain shooting through it, and he doesn't strike me as the type of man who hands out painkillers to go along with the abuse.

*Will he kick me each time I say something he doesn't like?*

Tears trickle down my face onto the concrete as I realize that I would give anything in the entire world to be waking up too warm next to Nikoli right now.

*Nikoli, I love you.*

# Nikoli

I drive down by the docks yet again, hoping i'll catch Kolya or Kristof. So far they've pretty much disappeared, and that's difficult to do when you have a hoard of Russians on the hunt for your head. Kolya has officially broken his routine. Believe me, I checked the restaurant; I wasn't going to let the fucker get away from me now, but he was a no show. I'm practically foaming at the mouth wondering if he's the one who took my pixie.

It's been twenty-two hours, thirteen minutes and forty-nine seconds since I first discovered Sabrina missing. At this point, she could be located anywhere in the world. Her captors have had plenty of time to fly, boat, or drive many miles away from here, and I'm not even one step closer to finding her. Whoever has her better pray to their god that they don't harm even a hair on her head.

I keep playing it on repeat, over and over in my mind of her telling me she needed that stupid fucking cake topper. I know if I would have gone with her, she would be beside me right now. Tate says I can't blame myself, but I do. I feel it in my gut that she would have been safe accompanied by me. I would have died to keep her that way. It was my *only* job; I had one thing to do and I have failed.

I don't even deserve to have her at this point. Hell, who am I kidding? She's always been too good for me. Sabrina's a pure little angel of beauty, while I'm this big ogre, full of dirty blood and secrets.

I can't help but wonder what my mother would think of me

right now—may her soul rest in peace. Not only could I not protect her and my sisters, but now—even as an adult—I'm useless when it comes to protecting the women I love. Must I be forced to sacrifice everything? Am I not destined an ounce of happiness and love in my life? I will find the trash that took mother and Bina. I'll search until I take my last breath if I have to.

My cell chirps and I damn near swerve off the road trying to get it out of the truck console. I slam on the brakes and pull off on the shoulder of the road. People need to stop texting me so much and just call; at least then the voice will come over the speaker instead.

> **Tate**: Tech found Kristof
>
> **Me**: Address
>
> **Tate**: I will send guys to meet you at 407 Grape
>
> **Me**: The projects?
>
> **Tate**: No, it's a small house

Tossing the phone in the cup holder, I peel out, spraying rocks everywhere, pushing my truck's limits to get me to Kristof as soon as possible. Every second wasted is a moment too long not being with her.

I'm grateful for Tate having my back on this and sending some guys to help, but I hope I arrive before everyone else. I want to get to her father first so I can beat her location out of him. The scum deserves to hurt and I have every intention of introducing him to real pain. I've wanted to for years, but out of respect for Sabrina, I've held off. No more though; that trash is mine and if he doesn't sing like a bird, I'll float him with the fishes just like he deserves.

The drive is short, about ten minutes or so, but they feel like ten of the longest drawn-out minutes of my life. There's a slim chance of her actually being here, but I'm praying with everything in me that she's here, safe and waiting.

*Come on, Mother, if you have really moved on to another place, please help me find her.*

I bring the truck to a stop and park a few houses away. Kristof has always been a paranoid idiot and I wouldn't put it past him to have a group of wannabes outside keeping watch for me or anyone else that may drop in unannounced.

Quietly and swiftly I leave my truck and head up the small alley running behind the shack of a house. The yard is overgrown and I'm correct about him being suspicious. There are a few thuggish looking guys posted on the front porch, one guy on each side of the house and two in the back. So about six or seven total.

I can take them; hell, I could have taken them out when I was barely sixteen. Not to mention they all look like skin and bones—probably strung out on something strong. I get why some feel the need to escape and do a little recreational drugs—and it's their choice—but I prefer to stay sober. I need to be completely focused, feeling everything, and in this instant, I can't wait to feel myself steal the breath from their lungs.

Kristof owes me something and it's time to collect.

One guy in the backyard steps off to take a piss and I creep behind him like a snake, performing my flawless choke hold; I tightly grip his throat and cut his air supply. Instead of releasing him once he's passed out, I keep my hold longer, waiting precious seconds until the air has escaped him completely and his heart no longer beats.

The kill energizes me and I rush the remaining guard out back. His arms shoot up in defense, but I'm too quick for him. I immediately snap his neck, his head flying to the side with the force of my hands. I actually feel the break as it happens, and for the first time in twenty-three hours, a ghost of a smile graces my lips.

Using the pick in my wallet, I unlock the cheap door and get into the house easily. The door opens up into the kitchen, shocking another guy. I don't give him enough time to process what he should do, but rush forward, ramming my forehead into his nose.

I immediately reach for a weapon to finish him off. I don't have time to waste; this house could be full of guards for all I know. My small knife does the trick nicely as I stab his kidney repeatedly, the blood spilling everywhere making the tiled floor a slippery mess.

I know I'm coated in the man's blood and probably look like something straight from a horror story, but that's perfect. I hope to scare this fucker to death. Kristof's time is up.

I find him in the living room, laid back on an old beat-up, brown couch while a young girl's head bobs eagerly in his lap. This is rich. I'm worried sick about his kidnapped daughter's safety, and the sick old fuck is shacked up, getting his cock sucked by someone who doesn't even look to be eighteen years old yet. Probably one of his girls he plans to ship off into sex slavery.

Menacingly I let lose an angry growl, "Out, now!" and I step closer.

Kristof's eyes widen in alarm, as he scoots back into the couch, pulling the girl in front of him as a shield. "Nikoli! What the hell are you doing here?"

The young girl sits, mute, looking dazed out. Her eyes look hollow like she's on some sort of drug.

Good, at least the poor thing isn't forced to do this shit sober. She'd probably kill herself with the stuff Kristof and his men have been known to put the slaves through.

"Let her go, Kristof; I'm not even here for her."

"Get out! I'll have my men come in if you don't leave

immediately."

"Your goons are all dead. Only took me moments to kill them. Would you like to be next?"

"Nyet! Nikoli, wait a minute. I can pay you much better than whoever is doing this, please reconsider."

"Pay me better?" I lash out, kicking his leg.

"Aghhh! Stop! Who sent you? What do they want?"

I let loose a humorless laugh and fling the girl to the side before he has a chance to really hurt her. With her tiny frame, I easily toss her across the room. I hate to cause her more pain, but it's much better than what Kristof would have done to her.

"Hey! Don't touch the product! She's going to someone very powerful."

"No, you're mistaken," I wrench his arm up, twisting it to the side so the sad excuse of a man is crouched before me with my face close to his. "You have no women anymore; you're officially out of business. You've been warned over and over not to step on Tatkiv's toes. Yet you creep, like a scrawny, pathetic rat, always lapping up whatever bread crumbs you can find. Well you have taken too big of bite this time, Kristof. I've come to collect what is rightfully mine."

"Yours? My empire is not yours or that Mafiya brats!"

A chuckle escapes me as I apply enough pressure to feel the bone in his arm give out. He wails like a bitch in heat and I switch to gripping his good arm. "We do not want your pitiful diminutive business venture. In fact, Viktor will be shutting that all down soon also. You've crossed way too many lines. Not only does the most powerful Mafiya branch want you gone, but so does the criminal mastermind of the Russian Bratva. Both brothers want you to vanish, Kristof. There's only one thing that can help make this death less painful on you."

"Death?" Kristof squeaks and I nod. "Wha-what is it that you want?"

"Sabrina is mine; now where is she?"

"I never gave my daughter to you. She was only on loan to Viktor."

"You are mistaken and a fool to lie to me. Everyone knows she is my property. You fucked up and had to give her to Viktor to save your ass. In turn, Viktor gave her to me. She was due to be my wife once everything blew over with you. I was giving it time before I told her."

"Wife, eh?" He laughs evilly. "Too bad she is already betrothed to someone else."

At that remark, I can no longer hold myself back. In a fit of rage, I snap his other arm, the bone breaking and causing the tendon to dangle like an unwanted growth. Then I drive my fist into his ugly smug face—over and over.

He gasps and blood sprays everywhere, coating my face. Gritting my teeth, I force myself to stop. I know I'll kill him too soon if I don't.

Shooting him a sinister smile, I try again.

"Now, where is Sabrina?"

"Not...not...not yours," he sputters and I clench my fist, wanting to impale him.

"She's mine!" I roar savagely. "Do you know where she is?" I shout, standing.

"No," he mumbles, dipping his head to the floor. It's said with truth, so I do the next best thing to finding her. I beat him to death.

## two hours later...

"You killed off our greatest chance at finding her, Niko," Tate grumbles and I wince. There's so much truth to his statement. I know I fucked up, but I couldn't restrain myself, and Kristof needed to go.

"He didn't know where she is."

"But he knew how to get in touch with Kolya. I have a feeling if we find Kolya, then we find Sabrina."

"I was thinking the same thing."

"I left a message for Viktor. Wherever they are, they don't seem to have good service. It goes straight to voice mail when I try him, Elaina, Alexei, and Spartak."

"Fuck! Why did this have to happen the day he was going out of town?"

"That's exactly why, Niko. It was the best chance for something like this to happen. Whoever did this couldn't have picked a better time to have you distracted. Elaina wanted to see a bunch of random places and I know Viktor was excited to show her a lot of little spots in Russia where the service is shitty. As soon as one of them gets service, I know they'll call us back."

"Yeah, I just hope it's not much longer and they're able to remember something helpful. Did the tech guy find out about the car? We're very fortunate Lev remembered the license plate number."

"It was a hired service. I have them checking to see if it ties back to any names that may stand out for us."

"And what about your uncle?"

"He still won't take my calls. Whatever Viktor said to him, really did the trick. Unfortunately, it's hurting us in this situation. I doubt my uncle would be much help anyhow, but any little clue could be just the thing we need to have a break-through. I wish I knew what all he had to speak to Viktor about."

"I'm going to go check the docks again."

"Niko, you need to get some sleep. You haven't slept since she was taken and you won't be able to think straight pretty soon. You need at least four hours; you know this."

"I can't sleep, Boss. Every minute wasted is a minute she could be scared or hurting. I must do whatever I'm capable of to find her."

"I understand that and God knows I would be on a fucking rampage myself, but you have to rely on all of your training."

"So I sleep...What if I close my eyes and see her being hurt? I can already imagine horrifying things happening to her while I'm awake, but then throw her into my dreams and they can do even worse."

"I know it, man, but you have to remember we're dealing with a bunch of rich fuckers. They won't want her all messed up if Kolya is trying to force her to marry him. Even when my uncle was into the sex trade heavily he wanted the girls to look good for as long as possible."

"You have not seen the boats as I have in Russia. It's no joke. I used to go out and watch them, praying my mother would step out one day so I could rescue her and then my sisters. The way they treat those women is sickening. It's worse than the dogs; they live in filth, getting sick, catching pneumonia or syphilis, stranded out on those rotting fucking boats."

"Enough! This is not Russia and I won't let you go down that path."

"But that's the thing; she could be in Russia by now!"

"I said enough. Get some rest, and then we keep looking. I mean it, even if you lie in bed for four hours, do it. Take a shower and force yourself to eat. You'll need your strength; it's your best asset."

"Boss." I answer shortly, nodding and head back inside mine and Sabrina's loft.

*Sleep huh.* My body's depleted and sore, but even then, sleep doesn't entice me. I'd rather be searching for her, exhausting every option over and over until I'm absolutely certain that there's nothing of value to help. I'll humor Tate, lying down and breezing over strategy for a while, but I'm not making any promises of actually sleeping.

It kills me to be inside this building, because everywhere I turn, I'm reminded of her. In the bathroom her shampoo and soap smell still lingers in the air. Our room is her normal tornado of items out everywhere. She's so disorganized when it comes to herself, yet she knows where everything is located. It's torment, but at the same time, it also makes me feel close to her again.

Once I get showered, I lie in our bed naked, gripping her pillow to my chest so I can smell her. Her scent relaxes me and after a while my drained body shuts down, making me fall into a fitful sleep full of dreams of her screaming for me to help her.

# SIX

## Sabrina

### THE HUNT CONTINUES

*Toska*

## one week later...

IACHE... NOT JUST MY BODY, BUT MY HEART. MY SPIRIT feels broken, and I'm honestly surprised that I'm still alive at this point.

Where is Nikoli? Did he give up on me? Chek says Niko isn't even bothering to look for me. Chek's the name of the guy holding me hostage. It's not much of a job, because I can barely move. I just lie here starving, freezing, and hurting. I've stopped being physically able to fight, I just *be*.

Oh how I tried to stand up for myself at first, but after being hit so many times and starved, you begin to cave, to stop caring. I'm not even really cold anymore. I don't feel anything temperature wise. Just numbness. And pain. I do feel the sting each time I upset Chek and he has to punish me though.

Gazing at the door, I watch as his booted feet approach. A square piece of bread about the size of my palm is dropped in front of my face, and as much as I want to rush to grab it and eat it, I've learned. Chek likes manners, and if I don't show them along with obedience, he will take the bread.

Keeping my eyes trained on his boots, I ask eagerly, "May I eat now, Mr. Chek?"

He crouches, his body coming into my view as he runs a finger over my cheek.

"No tears today, beautiful?"

"Would you like tears, Mr. Chek?" I shoot my gaze to the floor, giving him a fake display of respect and submission.

"No. You're being very polite today. I like it. You may eat now."

I go to grab the slice and he steps on my hand lightly. Instead of calling out, I swallow deeply, collecting myself and utter, "Thank you."

Once the words leave my mouth, his foot moves and I'm able to bring the food to my mouth to take a few small nibbles. The first time I ate it too fast he told me it was unbecoming and punched my stomach until I threw it all up.

That was the last time I thought of his long dark hair worn tightly pulled back, his chiseled jaw, and stony eyes as being handsome. He grew into something else entirely. He became a sick fucking monster whom I despise with every breath in my body.

I cried, pleading with him to stop, to show kindness. Then I tried to bargain, offering whatever he wanted. Nothing worked; he laughed and then struck me again for acting like a whore.

He doesn't like to make me starve, but he told me it's his job to break me and make me acceptable for Kolya unless I want to end up dead like his last wife. I think the only thing that has kept me going for this long is thoughts of Nikoli. I imagine him storming in and rescuing me.

I've used a tiny rock to make indentions in the ground and I think I've been here for a week or longer. I'm starting to believe

Chek that Nikoli isn't coming—that he isn't looking for me. Perhaps he's right about me being too much trouble and the Bratva wanting to be rid of me.

My heart hurts; no better word can describe it than *Toska*.

I fell in love with Nikoli and all of his friends. I thought of them as my friends, as my family. Was it all fake? Was I really such a burden as Chek says? I would have gladly cleaned and cooked to try to help make up for my stay. I know I'm not the most pleasant to some, but I thought that they had opened up to me. It's even more miserable toying with the notion that no one out there cares for me. Am I so wretched that not anyone really loves me, even just a small amount?

"You become more beautiful as the days go on." He pets my skin again, this time by my shoulder. "Get rid of the filthy clothes, fix your hair, and you will make the perfect companion for Kolya. If he doesn't want you, I may even take you."

"Will I get to leave this place, Mr. Chek?"

I'm met with a swift kick to my mouth, blood and a throbbing ache burst through my gums, making my entire mouth hurt. I do my best to hold back, but can't help the depleted whimper that escapes.

Chek clicks his tongue, about to give me a new lesson of some sort. He always does it before telling me something that I need to pay attention to.

"You know better. No questions until I permit it. Now you must stay longer until your face is not fat."

"Yes, Mr. Chek," I gasp out, feeling the blood run down part of my chin. I have to make myself say something. If I don't respond I'll get reprimanded again and the pain in my mouth will be far less than if I were to keep quiet. I don't know how much longer I'll make it down here and part of me is looking forward to it finally being over.

*Nikoli, I will see you again in death my love.*

# Nikoli

I rip open the door to another huge maroon shipping container. It's the exact same as the one we found on the last boat. It's just a large metal box, and right inside the door is a clear plastic sheet with pockets hanging up. Each pocket holds a Polaroid picture of every woman in that specific container. It makes me sick to my stomach as I breeze through the sheet, over the many malnourished faces, praying I find Sabrina, and at the same time, hoping she wasn't exposed to this way of life.

I swear when I find the vile fucks responsible for torturing these women, I will gladly scalp them.

"Anything?" Tate asks coming up beside me.

"Nyet, Boss." Shaking my head in sadness, I hand him the plastic case so he can see the faces and names for himself.

"Fuck!" he shouts, frustrated and punches the metal, causing the women to huddle farther into the corner even more. "Lev," he demands loudly, "get the blankets and come help get these women loaded up for the doctor to examine."

Tate shakes his head and turns to me. "I have to call my wife and let her know to expect fifteen new girls. She needs some notice to get enough supplies for them." He runs his hands over his face, knuckles bloody, but they don't mean anything. It's the sadness in his eyes that tell me this is starting to wear on him heavily.

I nod and head back over to my laptop in my truck. I don't get it. How is the tech guy able to find the containers but no trace to who's actually responsible for shipping them and picking them up? They can't all be registered under false names. Someone has to be accountable for this shit.

It's been a fucking week for God's sake. *Where is she?*

I feel like I'm losing my mind. I've gotten shit for sleep. I can barely eat. What if she's hungry somewhere? I can't eat at the thought of her not being able to.

I'm like an angry bear. I don't want to talk to anyone and my knuckles are raw from getting pissed and punching shit. I can barely bend my fingers without cracking the scabs open. I gave in and had my tattoo guy script her name down my thigh. I needed some kind of pain, to do something for her. I couldn't sleep, the thoughts and images were killing me.

I keep playing it over and over in my mind what it'll be like to pull the responsible fucker apart, limb by limb, for taking her from me. I've never wanted to kill someone so much in my entire life. I feel like I could rip him apart with my goddamn teeth.

There's a rap on my window. Blinking, I look up to find a drained looking Tate. Her disappearance is weighing on him more each day, on all of us actually. I know he feels like a failure for not yet getting her home safely.

With the massive search going on for Sabrina, we've opened up so many gaping wounds, looking in every crevice of the criminal areas we can, including finding the shipment containers of women looking like they're on the brink of death. I can only imagine what they've been through. I don't know if they will ever be able to recoup and hold meaningful lives. Hell, I doubt many of them are even legal to be here in the first place. The last container held women from all over the world.

"Da, Boss?"

"We're headed to the club where we're keeping the other girls. Elaina and Viktor are looking for more bilingual doctors and therapists to fly in to help with rehabilitation."

"Okay, good. I'll follow."

"Stop by the house and grab a shower. You're filthy and I don't want you scaring the women any more than you do by being a male."

"Boss." I reply, and pull off after he gives me a fake half smile. I think he does it to try and reassure me, but nothing will set me at ease until I have Sabrina in my arms, safe and healthy.

I head to mine and Tate's house. I haven't been back to Viktor's for a few days. I brought Bina's pillow with me; otherwise, I don't even want to look at the place with her not there. She should be there, cooking too much food and fluttering down to the beach while I try to talk her into swimming.

Viktor and Elaina returned home immediately once they found out why we'd been calling them so much. Sabrina and Elaina have grown close and she was a mess when she found out Bina had been taken. Viktor said she threw a huge fit until they were back on his plane headed home.

I already liked her, but after I heard that, I grew a huge amount of respect for her. I know she wanted home so Viktor could help aid in the search and honestly I couldn't have asked for better friends. They've been with me through each new clue, and shared my devastation when the lead didn't take us to Sabrina.

I never imagined I could possibly love Sabrina any more. Since she was taken, my feelings have grown into a whole other level completely. I had no clue before, but now I know my heart only beats for her.

My phone pings as I'm stepping out of the shower, and these days, anytime it makes a sound, I practically leap to check it.

Tate: Get to the club.

Tate: Are you on the way yet?

Tate: Nikoli, it's important. At least call me.

Me: Was showering. I'm coming

It could be her. He could know something. I yank on a pair of basketball shorts and a t-shirt as I run out the front door. Tate likes for us to be dressed professionally at all times, but with the hours I've been holding, he's lightened up on me. Slamming down on the gas, I drive like a maniac racing to the club.

When I arrive, I don't even shut the truck off or bother to close my door. Instead, I park directly in front of the club entrance, hop out of my truck, and run inside. I'm met by Tate waiting for me in the front entry.

"Tatkiv! Where is she? Is it her?" I pant, catching my breath.

His eyes go round, realizing I was thinking Sabrina was here or that he had found her.

"Fuck! No, Nikoli. I'm so sorry, man. Fuck. It's not why I texted you."

"Aghhhh!" I let loose a gut-wrenching scream, clutching my hair and pulling. I haven't bothered to cut it so I actually have some to grip now. "No! Fucking shit! Where is she?" My eyes fill with tears of despair, because for the first time, I truly feel like there's a chance I won't actually find her.

"I don't know, Niko. I'm so fucking sorry I got your hopes up." He pulls me into a huge bear hug, holding me to him tightly as the tears trickle down my face.

*Where is she? I need her; I'm breaking.*

Emily comes in, looking worried. When she sees my face she runs to me, "Oh, Niko!" She hugs my back and even being wrapped in my two closest friends' arms, I feel empty. Hollow.

*Toska.*

After a few seconds, Emily let's go, and Tate tells her to give us a minute.

"Niko, I wanted you to come down because I think we may have found someone important."

"Da? Important huh?" I chuckle miserably, because what could possibly be more significant than the woman I've been searching for?

"Her name is Vishna, and Nikoli, she looks just like the photos of your mother. I think she's around the same age as your youngest sister, Vishna."

"Vi-Vishna?" My mouth gapes, caught off guard. No way, she and my three sisters have been gone for too long; I don't believe it.

"I could be completely wrong, but it's a good possibility."

"Where is she? I need to see." If he's screwing with me on this, I may sincerely lose my mind and strangle him. I've been searching for my family my entire life. I knew there was a good chance the men on the boats had taken them, but I've never been able to find anything about my family leading directly to them.

"Wait! I had the doctor speak to her first, once I noticed the name and saw her for myself. The doc informed me that Vishna got lucky and was a maid the majority of her life. However, that being said, she's pretty fucked up now. She also told the doctor that she was 'broken' by someone named Chek. I guess he 'taught' her to be perfect and was finally being shipped off because she was sold to someone."

"If she is my little sister, I will break whoever this was that touched her," I growl, already feeling my blood begin to boil, and I haven't even seen her with my own eyes yet.

"She, ah, she's really frightened of men. You need to tread lightly and try to keep calm. I know you're pissed—and you have every right to be—but when she's scared, she won't speak at all. Oh and you will have to ask her the questions; she doesn't really volunteer to say anything first."

"I will keep calm. This I promise."

He nods and heads into the club, and I dutifully follow. I've gotten my emotions more under control and I may appear calm, but I'm raging on the inside. This is a blow from the left; I wasn't expecting our intel to lead us to finding them. I had begun to think of my family as probably being dead.

If I'm honest with myself, I haven't been looking for the girls. I've been looking for who took them, so I can make that person pay.

We wind our way through the club's hallways into the back towards the business rooms until we get to room number three.

Tate peeks his head in, talking quietly to someone for a moment. After a few seconds, he opens the door wider and I see Emily inside holding the tall, thin woman's hand. Her face is surrounded by long stringy blonde hair, the color matching my own.

I don't think before her name tumbles out, "Na-na?"

It was a childhood name I called her. I had them for each of my sisters, but she was so small and instead of calling me Nikoli she called me Niki. In return I started calling her Na-na.

Her head shoots up, wide ice blue eyes looking at me with alarm. "Niki, moy brat?" Her mouth gapes. Her cheeks are sunken in and her face has an unhealthy yellowish tint to it.

"Da, Na-na moy say straa?" At 'my sister' she leaps at me.

"Oh, Niki! Natasha and Brenna told me so many stories of you!" She rambles excitedly, "They used to say we were princesses and when you were big you would come save us! Oy moy brat!" She finishes in a flourish, hugging me tightly.

I thought she was scared of men. Perhaps my sisters kept me in a good light for all these years and she does not fear me?

"Natasha and Brenna? Where are they and Mother?"

Vishna pulls away, her eyes filled with hurt and sadness. She stays quiet, her gaze shooting to the floor.

"Na-na, where are they?" She stays mute and I can't help but to shake her. The foolish girl needs to tell me where my family is.

"Na-na! Speak, damn it!" I shout, and she falls to the floor, covering her head with her hands.

"Fuck! I am sorry. I'm such a fool...please, forgive me? I will not hurt you, I promise you. I will never cause you harm. Your fairy tale was right; I will protect you. Now I need to know where they are so I can save them too."

She wipes away her silent tears, meeting my gaze as she sits crumpled up on the floor. I reach my huge paw-like hand out to her, offering her my help. After a beat she reaches out, slowly taking my hand and lets me pull her to me once again. This time I wrap her in my arms tightly, cocooning her frail body so she knows I love her and try whispering instead.

"Please tell me."

Her big icy eyes fill again as she murmurs, "They are no more, Niki. It's been a long time since they were with me."

"I-I see. That is okay. I will find the men who hurt you all. I have been searching my entire life, and I won't stop now."

"No, please," she chokes out. "No, I-I don't want them to hurt you too. I have waited many years to see you again."

"I promise you don't have to worry about them hurting me. I am much more respected than these men and they will never touch you again." Her face brightens as she sends me a beautiful smile, and then kisses my cheeks like my mother used to.

Her doing that seals the deal for me that she is who she says. The nickname gave me hope, but her kissing me like my mother, tells me that she was also kissed like that many times for it to be a natural habit.

"They have someone I love though, and I need to find them. If I keep you safe, will you help me?"

"I wish, but I know nothing." She shakes her head.

"You just relax and eat; I'm betting you know more than you think."

She nods. "Okay, Niki, I will try for you."

"Good." I kiss her forehead and give her hand back to Emily.

"Vishna, why is it you trust me so easily?"

"Because, I have already had everything taken from me, Nikoli. I have nothing to lose but to trust you and be happy inside. Even if you weren't my brother, just the dream of you being real is enough to give me a small piece of hope that there is more to this life."

Tears fall from me again at her words but I quickly wipe them away. The men can't see me so emotional; I have to appear unmoving at all times so no one messes with me or the Boss.

524

*Tate and I have serious shit to talk about.* I need to find out exactly where those containers came from. Never in a million years did I think intercepting that box would bring me my baby sister. I had grown to believe I would never see her again.

It's a miracle Vishna was spared to being a maid. She's beautiful; no doubt as to why they had finally sold her to someone. It grates at me imagining what this 'Chek' person has done to her. They sold her into sex slavery so I know that she has had to endure being put through some sickening acts of abuse.

The poor mouse. At least she's here now and I can finally keep her safe. I'll do everything possible to take care of her and make sure she can live out a happy life.

"Say straa, can you tell me more about this 'Chek'?" I ask quietly while she eats a slice of bread. When Emily begged her to eat she said she only wanted a slice of bread. Personally I would be asking for a horse by the looks of her tiny body, but she probably isn't used to eating like I am.

She clears her throat. "Da, umm...He is, well, he is a teacher. He takes girls and shows them how to be perfect so they get new owners."

I can't help but to scoff at the new owners bit. *Such bullshit.* I'll show this prick what it is to be owned when I gut him. "I apologize for the interruption, please continue."

"He is very mean at first but once you do the right thing, he becomes nice and rewards you. He's a very handsome man."

"He's mean? How? Please explain."

"Well he pours this cold water on you and your bones freeze, and he will keep you hungry. I was always hungry cleaning for the master, but never hungry like that. If you upset Mr. Chek he will kick you or hit you. That was okay though, but the cold is what made it bad."

"Vishna, how is it okay that he kicked you? You know I would tear his insides out if I saw him touch you like that?"

She giggles like it's silly for me to be angry. She's fucked up, and I have a new name on my hit list, only he's not getting it from a weapon, but from my bare hands.

"Can you tell me more about where this place was or did you ever hear a last name? Does the name Kolya Minski sound familiar to you at all?"

"I do not know this place. Our say straa's said we were once in Moscow, that one of the men took them to see the giant babushkas and how they were filled with colors beyond what I could imagine. I wish to go there some day." Her eyes grow excited like a child's and the pang hits my chest again. I had a rough time growing up, but she missed everything, all the little bits of good I *was* able to have, she didn't get.

Tate interrupts, smiling kindly. "I know where you're talking about, and if you wish to go, we will. I have a plane that can take us. Nikoli and Emily, along with a few of our other friends, would love to all go if it would make you happy?"

"Yes, please!"

"Okay then as soon as we get Sabrina back, we'll make it happen."

Vishna smiles broadly at him and Emily.

"You know you're in America now, right?"

"Yes, I thought so, you all sound so funny. Even you too, Niki. You can tell you are Russian man, but you sound so different."

"I sound different than the men you are normally around?"

"Well yes, Mr. Chek, he is Russian man too but his is slower, like he makes his words longer...Kind of like you and Mr. Masterson." She nods towards Tate and a light bulb goes off inside. I'm betting this guy has been to the south before—enough so, that he has gotten part of the southern drawl. "The other men sound like they are from Russia and a few speak other words entirely."

"Do you know what the other languages are?"

"No, I'm sorry, but I didn't get to take any kind of classes like you and our sisters. I was too young, and I was not of importance at the master's house. Our sisters taught me all they could before...well, just before."

"It's no problem, what about the other name I mentioned?"

"I know of a man called Kolya. I pretend like I not pay attention to him, but I did."

"Really, so if I showed you a photo, you could tell me if it was him? What was said when you saw him, do you remember?"

"Yes, I could tell you. I'm so sorry I couldn't help when Mr. Masterson showed me the photo of the pretty girl."

"Boss, you showed her Bina?"

"Yeah, man, it was one of the first things I did."

"Thank you."

He nods and I turn back to Vishna. "What did Kolya say around you?"

"He and the Master were talking about a man named Gizya's sons getting in their way and about a partner in the UK who wanted to expand their business. I wish there was more but the cook found me listening and sent me away. She threatened to tell on me and I lied, telling her I thought the man visiting was handsome. She shushed me and said he was evil."

I glance at Tate to see him wearing the same expression. Gizya's sons could mean only one thing: Tate and Viktor. "Yes, Kolya is very evil. Thank you for your help. If you think of anything, please let us know."

"I promise I will."

"Good. I have to talk to Tate and do a few things."

"Wait, you'll come back right?"

"Of course. I just found you. You're not getting rid of me that easily, but you need to get some rest. Emily will help you. I love her like a say straa. I know she will take good care of you. You're going to live with me now for as long as you like, and you will never be harmed or hungry again."

She nods, wearing a shaky smile and then Tate and I head out.

527

# SEVEN

## Sabrina

I don't need a knight in shining armor.
A stubborn Russian in a suit will do just fine.
-Sapphire Knight

**"I HAVE A TREAT FOR YOU TODAY."**

"Thank you, Mr. Chek." I say just above a whisper. I've developed a nasty cough being here and it's stolen away most of my voice. My throat is raw and in serious need of a cough drop or twenty.

He bends down to me lying on the ground and lightly pets my face. I no longer flinch at his touch; I'm just used to it. He's a smart man, putting the body through so much discomfort so that when it's offered just a smidge of tenderness, it jumps on it like a money hungry whore. His touch is the only thing I've felt besides pain in who knows how long. I've stopped keeping track. I no longer care how long I've been away.

Some might believe I'm weak to give in so easily, but they haven't been kidnapped, frozen, starved, beaten, and taunted for weeks on end either. So fuck their judgment; they don't know shit. My entire life has been centered around being perfect for someone else, being constantly judged by my family, by men, and I'm so damn sick of it.

Why is it wrong to just be me? Why can't these deranged people just leave me alone? No one cares what I want for myself.

Growing up, all I ever dreamed about was happiness, freedom, and Nikoli. I've prayed for him to be mine every single night since the first time I met him.

Now this...I'm freaking the fuck out inside over Chek's latest treat. He decided the tiny flower tattoo that surrounds one of my black diamond studs on my earlobe wasn't 'appropriate' so he kindly used a wire brush to try and scrub it off of me.

That was the day I discovered that my body was still capable of moving. Being kicked and hit is *nothing* compared to being held down while having wires ruthlessly scrubbed into your flesh to remove a permanent marking. I don't think I've ever screamed so loud in my life.

He wasn't joking when he first said he was going to hurt me. I've replayed the day of the wedding over in my mind so many times now that it feels more like a dream than reality. Kendall would have loved to see me like this. I wonder what I ever did to make them hate me so much. I'm beginning to wonder if this was my father's plans for me all along. I've always believed my father was evil and this certainly confirms it.

Not only does Chek put me through physical torture, but he loves to mess with my mind the most. I'm to the point where I'm beginning to believe him when he says no one will find me here. It's been too long. This is either a really good hiding place or no one cares enough to look hard. If they would just dig down towards hell, I'm sure they'd find this place on the way down.

I could really use that knight in shining armor I used to always read about. Too bad they don't seem to exist—at least not for helpless women who've been beaten and trapped like me.

If I'm ever getting out of this god-awful place, I have to do absolutely as he says and hope that the next place is somewhere

I can get away from. I can't be sick or starving to death either. My chances pretty much suck.

But one thing my father has always hated about me, is that I'm a fighter and it looks like I have to be the hero of my own story.

"Ready beautiful?" Chek inquires like I'm privy to have some sort of choice about it and my skin crawls. If I never hear that pet name again, it would still be too soon. How can I possibly be beautiful after being trapped here and living like this? No, not living; at this point I'm simply existing.

He cuts away what's left of the back of my thin, cami undershirt and washes an area on my back with a rough dish pad and then pats it dry. I have no idea what he plans to do; it could be a tattoo or he could be stealing my organs. Nothing would really surprise me anymore. I just know that one will hurt remarkably more than the other.

"Yes, Mr. Chek," I respond automatically and feel the tip of something sharp on my back.

"You're getting your mark Sabrina. It means that if you stay on track, once it heals you get to see Kolya. He will be very pleased with how tame you've become."

"Thank you." I gasp out as the sharp blade digs further into my flesh. The ripping sensation of skin and meat making me hold my breath to keep myself from retching what little is left in my stomach.

The tears come and I suck on my bottom lip until it hurts to keep myself from crying out. His deathly grip on my side keeps me from twitching away. Although as much as it hurts, I know he could drive that blade into my back at any time and it keeps me still.

"Ah, the mark of belonging to a Minski." He sounds almost as if he's in a lustful trance as the blood drips down my naked back. I feel something wet wipe one of the long drops off, and I'm trying hard not to believe it was just his tongue.

A tiny whimper escapes as the blade goes in a little too deep, my nose clogs and I wonder if this may be it. If I'll somehow suffocate myself.

*I'll never belong to a Minski.*

# Nikoli

"You heard my sister; she mentioned your father's name."

"Fuck! I know. I just wish I knew who it was that was saying his fucking name," Tate grumbles. Hell I do too; right now we could possibly be on our way to finding Sabrina.

I lean back in my desk chair. We're in the club office that we share. It's large enough that we each have our own big black desks, chairs, filing cabinets, etc. I thought we should just get a couple couches for in here, maybe a rug and coffee table, but apparently since it's an office, Tate thinks we need to do actual work in it. I thought it would be a great spot to take secret naps when we needed them, but he didn't quite agree.

"It's been too long; Sabrina could be dead by now."

He's my best friend so I share exactly what's been beating me up inside. I should have found her by now and I'm terrified that I won't. Tate can help me the most out of anyone and so far I'm in awe of all the resources he's put to use to try to help me find Sabrina. Given enough time, the Mafiya can usually hunt almost anyone down.

It gets tricky when it comes to women though. Men are quicker to give up another man to get ahead or to save their ass, before they'll voluntarily give up a sex trade business that makes them a massive amount of money. We've searched for years for my mother and sisters' captors, never hearing a word. I hate to admit that the same could happen with Sabrina. Unless people start finding out that she belongs to the Mafiya and

Bratva, it could help save her or hurt her further.

"You thought it was too late for your sisters also and one is sitting next to my wife a few doors down that hallway right now. I still can't get over that we found her and by accident at that."

"It doesn't feel real to me. She's not the baby face I remember anymore. My memories have become so fuzzy over the years, that it hasn't sunk in yet. I wish she would tell me what happened to the others. I'm so fortunate to have her back in my life, but I'm still missing my mother and two sisters. I wish she would tell me so I can have some type of real closure. I know they're dead, but I'd like to know that they didn't die in pain."

"I get it man; just take it one step at a time. Vishna's alive; that's the first step, you know? Your family's deaths could be too raw for her to remember. Just give it some time and hopefully she'll trust you enough to open up to you."

"Yeah, Boss, you're probably right."

"I wish I could speak to my father to see if he knows anything."

"Too late for that now."

"I know. I texted Viktor and filled him in on what all we found while you were speaking to Vishna. He's freaking out for you. You know how Viktor likes everything organized with no surprises and all. Thank God he's not as uptight as he used to be. He's going over any contacts the Bratva has done business with in the United Kingdom right now to see if he finds anyone who may be of interest to us."

"Good. I wish I knew what to do. I feel like I should be handling this like a hit. I want to do the research on the mark and the planning, but I don't have a fucking name and I'm going mad inside."

"I'm not trying to sound like a pig here, but maybe you should go to one of the topless bars? It may help clear your mind so it opens up some new thinking?"

"I can't look at damn tits right now. All I can think of is

Sabrina!"

"I know, and I don't mean to sound fucking heartless, but you used to love that place before you became obsessed with taking care of Sabrina. I just thought it may help you clear your mind some so you can step back and look at this like a job."

"She isn't some kind of a job, Tatkiv; she's my fucking life, my soul."

Sabrina's also the only woman I've seen semi-naked in months. If only I was able go back to that day she needed me to zip up her dress. I had walked up those stairs to her dancing around in nothing but a pair of black and hot pink lace panties with matching bra, and holy shit if it isn't the sexiest thing I've ever seen. I've had the pleasure of witnessing many women naked and in various outfits, but Sabrina is beyond comparison. Probably a good thing I hadn't seen her fully naked first; she would have ruined any other woman for me afterwards.

If I could go back now, things would be completely different. I wouldn't have hesitated and then done the gentlemanly thing. I would have ripped the back of that dress right down the seam, until she was completely exposed to me and let her know she was all mine. Many times I've fantasized about how her snug center would feel wrapped around me, about how her sweet strawberry colored nipples would taste as I nibbled on them.

Now all I can do is lie awake worrying about her. I can't even picture her naked right now due to what she could possibly be going through. What if some scum has her bare and is torturing her right at this moment? Anything could be happening to her and I can't do a damn thing about it.

"Sorry man, forget I mentioned it." I nod and Tate's ringer goes off alerting us of an incoming call. He checks the ID and holds up a finger to me.

"Moy brat." Tate answers his phone.

*Viktor.* He always did work fast. Once he starts thinking about something, he can't let it go until he's able to figure it out.

"No shit!" Tate utters surprised and glances up at me.

"No, no that's awesome news. Yeah, anything you can find out will be awesome; we appreciate it."

He scribbles something down on his desk calendar, "Thank you, Viktor. You may have just given us exactly what we need to find out where this guy is."

He finishes and hangs up, grinning as he looks at me.

"We have a last name for this 'Chek' guy." Tate tears the paper off and holds it up like the prize it may be.

"No fucking way."

"Put on a suit; we're going to London for a meeting."

## Nikoli

## I'M LEAVING ON A JET PLANE

"SERIOUSLY, NIKO, OUT OF ALL YOUR CHOICES, YOU had to wear Armani?"

"It's a good black suit." Shrugging, I recline my seat on Tate's jet. I needed black because I'm not sure if this will turn into a bloody trip. If I have my way though, it will.

"It's Italian and right now is not a good time to be wearing it. I don't want any type of support going to them at all at the moment. The last message we sent seems to be keeping them quiet, but who knows how long that will last. I'm sick of watching them attempt to shake us up."

"Your shoes are Italian." I counter and Tate stares at his shoes disgusted.

"When this is all over with, it's time we go shopping."

"Whatever you say, Boss, but Emily won't make it that easy for you. She once told me that she still has jeans still from high school."

"I'll let her donate all of our old clothes to a needy charity; it'll persuade her."

Shrugging, my eyes close; I'm worn out. The flight to London always takes forever. I'm not holding my breath on getting any sleep, but I really could care less to discuss clothes with Tate right now. I could be in combat pants and a T-shirt right now for all I care. As long as I can move easily in it, then I'm content. My only priority right now is finding Bina.

My phone pings. It's Avery again.

>**Avery:** Coffees hot!
>
>**Me:** I could use a gallon
>
>**Avery:** It's here waiting, anytime you want some.

If things weren't so fucked up right now, I could damn sure use a trip out to see my friend. It's about time I check up on her and make sure the biker is treating her good. I should tell her what's going on with me, but I don't want her worrying.

Tate's in good with their motorcycle club and it's been fairly quiet for him too. I'm glad though, because when the bikers call, it's never for good news.

I shove my phone in the inside jacket pocket of my suit and close my eyes again. I must be more exhausted than I realized because my eyes are barely shut before I'm out.

# Sabrina

This time I'm burning up. One minute I'm shivering and my teeth are chattering so hard they feel like they'll chip, and then it's right back to being really hot. I stopped sweating hours ago. At least it feels like hours, it could only be minutes for all I know.

My head's pounding so much that time holds no real meaning at the moment. It can't be good, if I even realize I'm no longer sweating. Doesn't that mean my body is severely dehydrated?

The only water I get is when Chek sprays me down with the freezing cold water from the hose, surely that can't be enough to keep me alive? Although I'm not really moving or anything, so I wonder if it differentiates.

This sickness all started after he cut me. I don't know if there was something on his knife and I'm suffering from an infection or if he's poisoned me. Poison could cause me to be sick and die. I bet his plan all along was to put me through hell and then poison me to death.

*Fucking coward.* He couldn't even shoot me; he had to take the pussy way out and not let me know I was dying. His biggest mind fuck of all? Making you think there's a chance to live when there was never one in the first place.

Chek better pray this kills me, because if I'm ever free and able to, I will gladly kill him. I've never felt the need to take someone's life—even Kendall's for as bad as she treated me. This man, however, has done more than my sister ever had; he took Nikoli from me when I was so close to finally having him.

There's a scraping noise from the heavy door and a brief burst of light filters into the concrete room. I've decided this must be a basement or warehouse of some sort.

My vision's blurry but I swear it's not Chek I see, but Kolya. I keep quiet, just in case he will take me out of here. My head throbs, but I'm still able to make out what he says to another man in Russian.

"He has a meeting with Knees and Nikoli. I want you to spray this room out while he's gone. Spray each of the women down and then cover them with blankets. I believe at least one is dead in the other section—could be more."

"Is there heat, sir?" the other guy asks.

"No, we don't waste any extra money on them. If they don't survive, they're weak, and the buyers won't want them. The buyers need women they don't have to worry will die if they lock them in a basement or cellar."

"Understandable," the other man answers and they both leave the room.

I want so badly to scream out for help, but it would do no good. There are other women here besides me, and according to Kolya, it isn't a big deal if we die. Maybe Chek didn't poison me after all. Could I be sick? I've been stuck down in this cold, damp area for quite a while, it would make sense that my body is protesting.

I'm pretty smart, but I can't figure out what's happening to my body. My mind is so screwed up right now, I don't know left from right, yet I'm trying to think up a diagnosis. Oh God, he's going to spray me down again and it'll probably make this worse. I don't know if I have enough of a voice to even attempt to ask him to spare me the icy spray. Maybe if I use all of my manners like Chek has taught me, the man won't spray me. And maybe a blanket too—for warmth when I'm not overheated.

Moving my tongue around, I attempt to clear my throat, but it's just too dry. I keep on and try to speak. "Haa." It comes out sounding between a hoarse bark and a gasp for air.

The ache in my head intensifies as I strain to speak and I feel like I could pass out. I wish I was able to cry, and then I would have tears that I could use to wet my mouth. Right now it's so parched it's hard to believe it will even open for me.

I have no sweat, no tears, no voice...I may as well be dead.


# Nikoli

We touch down and as the plane hits the tarmac I'm jolted awake.

"Woah man, calm down." Tate has his hands out as I frantically look around.

"Bina?" I gasp.

"No, I'm sorry. We've just landed." he mumbles—his voice

empathetic.

"Shit! Fuck, it was a dream!" My eyes water as it hits me she's still gone. "I feel like my fucking heart's ripping in two. She is a part of me, yet she is missing. We have to find her, Tate; I don't think I can live like this."

"We're one step closer, Niko. I promise you moy brat, I will do everything in my power to get her back for you."

I nod as a tear trickles down my cheek and run my hands over my face in frustration. I have to pull myself together. The man we're meeting with could be the one who hurt my sister; he could be the one who still has my Bina, and I need to be on my game.

A sleek, dark grey Mercedes sedan is waiting for us when we depart the jet. As posh as Tate's plane is—filled with rich leather seating—plush carpet and delicious snacks, I still don't care too much for flying. No amount of food can make me feel comfortable when I'm as high as the clouds.

The driver opens the back door of the car so an older gentleman can get out to great us.

"Mr. Masterson, a pleasure," he says genuinely and shakes Tate's hand.

"Mr. Tsepov, thank you for collecting us."

"Anything for an old friend." He turns to me, "Nikoli."

"Roman." I nod back. It's custom for people to call Tate by his last name as a show of respect. I'm his right hand so they all know me by my first name instead.

They get into the back seat, more than likely to make small talk over one of Tate's restaurants here in London and I climb up front. The drive feels like it takes forever to get to the office building where we're supposed to be meeting this piece of scum for our afternoon meeting. I wonder if he'll be able to tell that we literally flew all night long to get here or if Tate will play it off like we're here on a leisure trip, just popping around everywhere, vacationing.

"Would you like us to wait for you, Mr. Masterson?" Roman's driver inquires as he opens the Boss' door for him.

"No thanks, we'll be fine. I don't want to hold you up; it was more than generous of Mr. Tsepov to meet us."

I tip the driver a twenty and nod my leave to Roman. He shakes Tate's hand again and then we're making our way inside the massive glass building. I don't know what the hell Tate's thinking letting our ride take off without us.

"Can I help you, sir?" A cute little brunette with a British accent asks as we approach the vast white desk. Her eyes scream she's interested as she sends us both playful smiles. She couldn't handle three hours with either of us in this lifestyle, even if we let her.

"Mr. Masterson," Tate replies. "I have a meeting."

"Oh, you're Mr. Masterson! Yes, I have you scheduled to go in straight away. Just let me page the PA in the back." We stand silently, listening to her announce our arrival to someone else over a tiny head-set. "You're all set, sir; Kelly will show you back." She gestures towards a gorgeous red head for us to follow.

"Right this way please." Kelly's shapely legs carry her quickly down a long hallway decorated with simple paintings in blues, greens and greys, not giving us any time to get off course. She stops in front of a massive black door around fifteen feet tall with a large silver cylinder as a door handle. It reminds me of a super-sized refrigerator. "I'm the PA in charge here, so if you would like a refreshment just let me know, and I'll have someone fetch it for you."

"Thank you, Kelly, but we're both fine right now." Tate responds automatically and I almost argue. Having just woken up; I could use a bottle of water or a Gatorade. I bite my tongue and flash a fake smile to Kelly.

"Very well then, Mr. Chek will be right in. Please feel free to make yourself comfortable on one of the sofas and thank you for visiting Perfectcore."

She slides a badge over a scanner in the wall, types in a code, and then pulls on the large handle. The huge door slides open easily, revealing a massive room. I feel like I'm entering a scene from the "Hunger Games" or something with all of this. The entire building has an oversized, wasted space feel to it.

For all I know, Sabrina could be locked up somewhere here right now, but I'd never get to find her without a fucking badge and code. I'm sure the desk girls follow a certain protocol in the case of threats, so I'll have to figure out something other than that so I can give the place a search.

Tate and I each take a seat on the same white couch as a united front not to be toyed with.

"Stay quiet," Tate mumbles so only I can hear him.

"You're joking."

"No, I'm serious. I want you to stay silent and take in as many details as possible. I'll do the talking."

"Yes, Boss."

It makes me livid inside, knowing that I can't confront this loser myself. This could be the only time I get to see him up close like this and Tate is forcing me to stay quiet. I don't want to speak up and defy him since I have utterly no fucking idea what his plan is.

I guess now that I have a name and will soon find out more information on him I can always hunt him down later if nothing comes of this. The brass knuckles feel like they're burning a hole in my jacket pocket, begging me to unleash them and take my vengeance.

"Gentlemen." A voice rings out from behind us and I instantly jump to my feet on high alert. Tate rests his hand on my arm and leisurely turns around.

"Thank you for meeting us."

"It's my honor to have the great Mr. Masterson in my humble abode." Chek approaches us wearing a slimy looking grin. "And my what a feral guard dog you have with you." He chuckles and Tate flashes him an evil smile.

"You can never be too careful these days, always on alert."

"Yes, I can imagine." He comes around and sits on the couch adjacent to us. I stay standing, just staring at him, and hoping I make him feel an ounce of discomfort.

Tate chuckles, lightly tapping my forearm.

"I apologize," he directs towards the shitbag then looks me in the eyes. "Nikoli, sit!" he barks and it clicks for me.

Ahhh, I see. Tate wants me to play dumb obedient lap dog so the imbecile doesn't feel like I'll step out of line. I guess if I appear ignorant, then he may possibly let his guard down a smidge.

*I'll bite, Tatkiv.*

"Boss." Grunting, I sit back on the sofa, appearing relaxed.

The weasel looking man clears his throat, "Call me Chek."

"Very well then, Chek, call me Mr. Masterson."

Biting my tongue, I have to concentrate not to laugh. Tate's being a dick, so this will make it much more fun for me. At least he isn't attempting to be polite straight away or I probably wouldn't be able to restrain myself.

"As you wish, I'm here to serve."

"Right, well, I'm hoping you'll be able to do just that, and help me out with a problem I have."

"Oh?" Chek leans forward, clearly intrigued as to what Tate could want with him.

"Yes, it's my wife."

"Certainly she must be perfect, being married to a man of your stature."

"Actually that's the problem; she's not."

"I find it hard to believe you would have married her if she wasn't everything you wanted. Your wealth could offer you many options."

"Funny you say that, Chek. My mother actually wanted to

purchase an obedient Russian girl for me to take as a bride, but I just had to have this little American."

"Ah! They are interesting creatures, aren't they? Tell me, what is the problem you're having with her?"

"She's ill-mannered, outspoken, taking off to do whatever she pleases when it suits her, not servicing me when it's needed... She's in desperate need to be taught how to be the wife I should have: obedient and pliant. I've heard from a few *associates* that Perfectcore is just the place to go for those services. Am I being pompous or does it sound like a reasonable request to you?"

"No, of course you're not being pompous, Mr. Masterson! A man of your wealth deserves to have what he wants! We, as men, should have what we want, do you not agree?" Chek turns to me and I bite the inside of my cheek so hard I draw blood as I nod my agreeance. I've never agreed to such bullshit as this before, but if it finds me my love, then so be it. If I happen to discover this sick fuck tried to change anything about her, I'll chop his fucking legs off and drown him in the closest body of water.

"Great, when is the soonest you can fix her? Should I bring her here? She's out spending my money as we speak."

"I can start my training almost immediately. You are able to get her here willingly? I won't need to have her-ahmmm-acquired, or anything?"

"This is the best news I've heard all day! I wasn't aware of you offering pick up or I would have called sooner. So, no, actually I believe the easiest way would be to call her back to the jet. I can tell her we're flying to Paris for dresses and she will drop whatever she's doing to meet us. Do you have an SUV or something you can bring to the airport so it's easy to transport her?"

"Yes, absolutely not a problem. We can take my vehicle. I have a BMW SUV that should work out nicely."

"Great. I believe I have her Xanax on board; will that be

enough to sedate her for the transfer? Oh and have your PA give your account information to Nikoli, he'll have my accountant wire some money over."

"Actually I have something stronger that I keep in stock. It'll work a lot quicker and I can bring it along. It's in a liquid form, either I could insert it in her while you distract her or you may feel more comfortable using a syringe. Either is fine."

"I'll do it. I don't think she would expect anything if I was to just hug her and then stab her with it. I mean, once you're done with her, she'll forgive me for it, right?"

"Why, yes, of course! And don't worry about the money Mr. Masterson, let me do this for you free of charge. I think we could have a great relationship ahead of us. In fact, I believe many of my associates will be pleasantly surprised and relieved to find out your quite easy to work with."

"Thank you, Chek. Shall we?" Tate stands and Chek practically jumps up to follow him.

"Shall I have one of my associates ride along to help load the body?"

Tate laughs like it's the funniest thing he's heard. "Chek, if it will make you feel better, then sure, bring along whomever you wish, but clearly Nikoli can load her. Hell, I can as well; she's a tiny thing." Chek strikes me as the type who's too smart to go alone, self-preservation and all.

# NINE

## Nikoli

### BE THE WOLF

TATE MAKES A FAKE PHONE CALL TO EMILY OR SHIT, IT could be a real phone call for all I know. Anyway, the person he speaks to plays along and Tate makes a huge deal about meeting us at his plane immediately. If I didn't know he was screwing around, even I would have thought it was real. Kind of scary just how good an actor my Boss really is, and I guess that's why he's in charge.

Turns out I'm right, as Chek has a 'driver' take us to the airport. We're not fools either; the driver's boxy, muscular shoulder build clearly shows us that he's not accustomed to just using a steering wheel. No worries though. With the anger I'm harboring, it'll be like Christmas morning if I get to use some of it up on this thug.

As soon as I sat back in the meeting and paid attention like Tate wanted, I could hear Chek's accent. He's definitely been to the south and frequently. I'd bet he's there half of the year with how pronounced it is when he speaks.

I get it now why Tate told me to let him do the talking. Chek played right into the palm of his hand. I never would have been able to keep it together for that long without smashing his face into the coffee table and demanding a location.

I'm so damn proud of Tate getting Chek to go back to our jet. I don't exactly know his plan, but I have a good idea of it. I just hope we're on the same page like we usually are. I wonder how it's going to go down when Cheky boy discovers Emily really isn't at the plane waiting for us like an eager little gold digging wife.

She'd flip her shit if she heard how Tate just spoke about her. Maybe I should tell her after this all blows over with, just so she can torture him a little about it, keep things interesting for them

My body stays hyper alert as we drive, just in case they get brave and attempt to take us somewhere else. I'm on pins and needles with excitement knowing we have him right where we want him. But it almost seems too easy, and it turns my stomach. Tate and Chek make small talk as we go, and I can tell Chek is getting more comfortable with us as he sits back comfortably with his shoulders relaxed and his face at ease.

*Can't wait to be able to break it.*

Smug fucker, treating women as if they can be programmed and changed to a man's liking. We're the lucky ones to be given a chance from them, and yet it's assholes like him that make women hate us. They make women believe that all men want them to change.

Tate plays the part of aloof, spoiled Mafiya brat well. I guess in reality he is a wealthy Mafiya brat, but he works his ass off and he's very street smart. Most people wouldn't get that from him. He tends to come off as cocky and demanding, but through the years, I've learned that almost everything is a face when it comes to him. He only takes his mask off for me, Viktor, and Emily—no one else.

"So this wife, what else would you like taught to her? I can make her submissive, break her in for you to do with as you please sexually. If you just like to play with her, I can break her in pain, or I can do a variety. You pretty much tell me what your dream wife would be like and I'll do my best to shape her that way."

His choices make me want to puke. Did he do a variety on my sister or is he doing one of these things to Sabrina? He acts like we're ordering party supplies or something. There's no fucking variety pack when it comes to women. You love and cherish them—the end!

"Speaking of that, how exactly are you able to mold them? I really don't care what's done to her. I'm just curious about the process."

"It's very in-depth, but I can give you the gist. We have a center that the women are kept at and I have only a few trusted associates keep an eye on them when I can't personally be there with them. I work with them daily unless they're learning a particularly taxing lesson, then it's a few times a week. They are fed, but she can be thinner when she comes home if you'd like."

"A center? I wasn't expecting it to be so well organized! So will I get to visit her then and see her progress?"

"No, I apologize, but I've found that it's best if they are kept away during the entire process until I can assure they have made the transition effectively."

"Understandable. And the security of this establishment? I won't have to worry of her safety, such as break-ins or if she will throw a tantrum and take off?"

"No, sir. We are very secure; in fact, no one has escaped or been bothered."

"Fantastic!" Tate exclaims as we approach the jet. I'm glad we were able to get a little more information willingly, but if no one's escaped then they could still be holding Sabrina hostage.

"Before she notices, here's the syringe." Chek offers.

"Okay, and I use this whole thing on her? She's really quite small; it won't kill her?"

"If she's under one fifteen then use half; if she's over, then use all of it. That syringe will work up to around two hundred pounds. The effects will just vary from being completely knocked out to being tired and dizzy, depending on her size."

"I see. This could be quite useful; I may need to get more of this."

"I'm always available to help out in that department as well."

"Good to know."

The SUV comes to a stop, the driver hops out to let Chek out first, then makes his way around the vehicle to open the door for Tate. I stay sitting in the vehicle, watching him let everyone out. To save face the driver's forced to open my door as well once he figures out that I haven't budged.

It's all part of my plan, because if Tate decides to shove that syringe into Chek like I'm expecting, I need an easy way to incapacitate dumb-dumb here. My gaze remains locked between the guy and Tate, waiting for him to give me some sort of a signal.

Lev descends the plane's stairs wearing a friendly smile. "Welcome back, Mr. Masterson. Will we be having company for the flight home?" He gestures to Chek like he's excited.

Due to Lev's overly friendly demeanor, it hits me that Tate had actually called him and not Emily earlier. Lev is normally a huge prick to everyone but Viktor; I'm quite shocked he knows how to even pretend to be nice.

"No, Lev, perhaps a drink though." He turns to Chek, "If you'd be inclined, that is?"

"A drink sounds wonderful." He smiles and turns to the driver still standing beside me. "Bruno, stay with the vehicle. I'll be back shortly to have you help with the loading."

"Okay, Mr. Chek," Bruno grunts out and turns to me, clearly wanting me to go to the plane so he can sit back down in the BMW. *Lazy slug.*

"I'll keep you company," I grumble to Bruno.

"Want a fag?" He holds out a crumpled pack of cigarettes that has clearly been stuffed into his pockets for too long.

"Thanks." Grabbing one, I bring it to my lips and lightly hold it with the side of my mouth.

Tate and Chek head into the jet. Once I see Lev stand at the door with his back blocking the entrance I make my move. "Lighter?"

"Yep." Bruno replies automatically in his British accent and concentrates on digging it back out of his pocket.

With his head tilted and him distracted, I fumble through my jacket pocket until my fingers slide against the cool metal. The brass knuckles fit my fingers snuggly, making my hands even more deadly, and I expel a breath of relief. *I love having my knuckles on.*

As he pulls the red lighter free and starts to look up, my fist connects close to his temple, the brass knuckles driving in to do their share of the damage. It's enough impact to make him a little wobbly. Jumping behind him, I lock my arms around his throat. I can't risk him making any noise and Chek getting spooked before Tate's ready. I'll never be able to repay Gizya for all the different methods of training he put me through. The lessons were imperative and brutal, but at times like these, it's extremely helpful.

Bruno squirms and struggles, his hands clawing at me to get free. It's no use. I'm way too strong for him. I outweigh him by at least fifty pounds and could eat guys like him for dinner if needed.

Concentrating, I inhale and exhale a few calming breaths, counting as I do to keep focused on my timing and not let up too quickly. It doesn't matter to me whether he dies this way or not. I plan to leave a mark that will ensure his death regardless.

He gurgles a few times with his head eventually twitching randomly as his oxygen depletes.

Once he's dead weight, I toss him to the ground and step back a few feet in case I misjudged and he lashes out. He lays like a lump on the asphalt, unmoving and I do what any experienced criminal would. They leave their signature.

Bending down next to him, I tug his shirt up, exposing his side and take my blade out. Bruno's still alive so I have to make this quick if I don't want him to come too and squeal like a pig. He's not fat, so this one should be easy.

Lining my knife up directly where it needs to be, I hold it still, and then use one hand to press down and heave my weight on top. The finely sharpened blade slides in slowly, almost as if I'm cutting a thick, under cooked steak.

*Yummm steak. That sounds really good right now.*

Adjusting the angle, I reposition and slide the knife towards the ground. Once there's a large enough slit to fit my hands in, I peel the skin away and reach in until I locate his kidney. Tate's father had me do this many times during my years of training. He always told me that any respectable Mafiya man should know how to remove a man's organs.

I work quickly sawing out the man's kidney. I don't need it, but it's going to leave one hell of a calling card for the UK police to discover. He'll bleed out effortlessly and it'll keep his lips closed to the authorities or any of Chek's buddies.

Once that's finished I leave Bruno where he is since we'll be leaving shortly anyhow and climb up the steep stairs, bloody and all to discover an entirely different situation taking place. Chek is passed out, lying in the middle of the walkway between the seats, while Tate and Lev sit, having a glass of chilled vodka. I'm a bloody mess and these two are having a damn drink without me.

"You couldn't wait ten minutes?" I grumble.

"With the way you were hacking at the driver out there, I wasn't sure if it would be a few minutes or if you were planning to cut all his limbs off as well." Tate counters and Lev chuckles.

"Okay, good point." I agree but shoot a glare at Lev.

He shuts up quickly, and I make my way to the back

bathroom to wash up. As the blood mixes with the water, discoloring the sink, I stare at it in a trance. I wonder if I just killed someone who hurt Sabrina or who helped kidnap her? If he was involved, I should have made it slower, more painful. God I wish she were here right now so I could pull her body to mine. There's nothing like fucking after killing someone, only I wouldn't fuck her. Sure I'd slam myself deeply into her, but then I would take it slow, rocking in and out of her gently so she could feel every piece of me.

I'm interrupted by banging on the lavatory door.

"Niko! I'm sorry we didn't wait. Are you okay, man?"

"I am fine, Tatkiv." I mumble. My feelings are hurt a little, but fuck, I'm on an emotional roller coaster right now. Sometimes I feel like he's my little brother and he's meant to torment me.

"Do you need me to get you anything?"

"Nyet."

"Okay then," he answers and leaves me be. My stiff dick's gone now with him talking to me, so that's one good thing.

Damn it. When did my dick being limp become a good thing?

Leisurely I dry my hands and head back out to the main area, ditching my bloody jacket on the way in the onboard bedroom. Chek is still knocked out on the floor. Lev uses some zip ties to secure Chek's hands and legs in case he wakes up.

Once we touch down back at home, we can take him to the club and have my sister look at him to be certain. I had Emily bring Vishna to live at our house until Tate and I can figure out future living arrangements for all of us. When Sabrina is found we'll discuss what she wants as well.

"Any news on Kolya yet?" I question as I take a seat across from Tate, my body singing in happiness from the comfortable seats.

"No. I called Viktor while we were waiting on you, and he hasn't heard a thing about Kolya's whereabouts from anyone. It's like he's just up and disappeared, which is really hard to do with the nature of business he's in. Disappearing from the FEDS is understandable, but vanishing from other criminals as well, is strange."

"Do you think something happened to him?"

"I'm honestly not sure, but it is a possibility."

"Shit fuck! Has anyone spoken to the family?"

"Viktor said that they've had eyes on the brother and a maid inside the house, but not anyone else."

This is such dumb bullshit! I'll go to the house when we return if I must. How has no one knocked on the front door and just asked or left a message yet? I understand it's not customary to just drop in unannounced, especially with people in our type of lifestyle, but desperate times call for desperate measures.

My mother used to always tell me 'A wolf's legs feed him.' In other words, effort is necessary. It looks like I may have to do everything myself, in order for stuff to get done.

# Sabrina

I'M AWOKEN BY WARM WATER HITTING MY SKIN. NOT freezing cold and I'm no longer burning up either. My back still feels like I've been carved up for a Halloween special though. God, I hope Chek falls in a gutter and gets eaten by an alligator somewhere. *Bastard.*

"Pssst!"

I'm sprayed again—the wet droplets feeling refreshing against my tender, chapped skin, instead of miserable like sharp pricks stabbing me all over, per the usual.

"Pssst!" The sound comes again. I don't think I'm hallucinating. It's pretty dark and considering how sick I've been, I could be hearing a rat next to me for all I know.

"Hey!" It's whispered louder now and my eyes flicker around the room until they land on a shadowed figure. The surprise of warm water was enough of a distraction that I didn't even notice him.

"Mmmm." I moan out. I can't speak. My mouth is still parched and my throat feels like it's filled with shards of glass.

"Drink." The raspy voice quietly orders and water gets sprayed close enough to my face for me to bend into it without drowning myself like Chek would do.

I try to take a plentiful gulp, but it doesn't happen. In fact, nothing happens. The water's there—available for the taking—but nothing gets in my mouth.

My fingers shoot to my face. The movement sends shocks strong enough that would normally cause me to gasp...if I were able to gasp. But the sparks of pain are nowhere near as bad as being thirsty and unable to drink.

My fingertips flutter over my chin until I find my lips, but not my tongue. My mouth isn't even open. Why the fuck is my mouth not opening? I want to scream, but I can't. I want to cry tears of frustration but... I. Can't. Fucking. Cry.

I'm like a prisoner trapped inside my own mind. Not only am I stuck in this horrifying place with a man who enjoys causing me discomfort, but now I can't even use the one thing I've worked so hard in my life to find—my voice.

"Mmmmm!" I moan out again as loud as possible and wave my hand for him to come near me.

The water comes to a stop with a quick flick of his wrist and I want to wail in protest of the missing warmth, of the fact that I may have fucked up my one chance at finally having a decent drink. I don't only want that water; I fucking need that water to survive.

The figure shuffles towards me, crouching down until he can see my face and I can tell in the outline of the light that he's a medium-sized man.

"What?" He mumbles and instead of answering, I tap my mouth.

He turns the spray on lightly and puts it in front of my mouth. I do nothing but lean towards it and tap my mouth, trying to show him my lips are stuck.

"Holy fuck!" he says with more meaning behind it.

He's definitely American, that much I can tell and his hands are covered in Russian tattoos. Odd, considering he has no accent, but nothing should surprise me anymore. My eyes trail up further but I can't see anything else with his long sleeves covering his arms. If you know what to look for, you can learn a Russian man's story just by reading his tattoos; they hold such great meaning when they're criminals and they've done time. In this instance, it would be a relief to know if he's simply a burglar or a convicted rapist. I don't see anything on his palms, so probably not a seasoned thief.

"I'll be back."

"Mmmm!" I moan out in objection. *I want that damn water, please!*

"Look, I'll be right back, okay? I promise." He stares down intently at me with deep hazel eyes that hold some familiarity and I give a small nod. At that, he jumps up and quickly leaves the room, slamming the door behind him.

*What have I just done?* He could have been my only chance at a sip of water, and now he's gone. Although he did seem genuine about helping me, I'm still skeptical of any man in this place. I don't know why he doesn't throw up the usual red flags for me; perhaps I'm so desperate and depleted that I'll make an admission for anyone now.

The memory of seeing Kolya here in my room floods my mind again. This was the man he was speaking to in Russian before, but this guy sounds like he's American. Clearly my mind's too warped right now to figure out details. Hopefully, if this man really does help me, and once I get some water, I'll be able to think much more clearly.

The coldness starts to set in again now that I'm wet and unmoving on the chilly cement floor. My teeth start to chatter, but my lips still stay glued shut. Holy shit, what is wrong with me? Did Chek do something to me? If he knocked me out and sewed my lips together, that will surely be the end for me. Ultimate method of suffering right there—have your lips sewn shut so even if you can get to something, you still can't eat or drink it. The heat from my sickness seems to have thawed me out, because my body is no longer stuck in a numbness feeling, because it's back to aching in protest.

After a few moments of me shivering and trying not to move because each time I do it sends uncomfortable muscle spasms throughout my body and separates the gash in my back, the man returns with a small yellow tub of something.

"I have to touch your face," he mumbles.

I lay unmoving at first, unsure of what he may end up doing; but in the end, I nod my acceptance. He could help me, and I'd be a dumbass not to take any little ounce of help offered.

He scoops out some thick clear like goop out of the tub and globs it all over my mouth, massaging it into my lips and trying to get it in between my lips. Up and down, back and forth, round and round in circles, he's surprisingly gentle; forceful, but gentle. Still, it's almost like he actually doesn't want to hurt me as he stares at my mouth intently.

I can feel my lips separate in a few spots but not completely. It's stuck in the middle section. He pushes the oily gel into the spots that are cracked open, packing it in as much as possible.

"I'm going to let that petroleum jelly set for a second and it should help separate the skin for you. If your mouth doesn't open, I'll have to force my fingers in to part the skin for you." I nod, my eyes shining with gratitude, trying to convey just how grateful I am for his touch of kindness.

I'm not getting my hopes up with this guy. I'm just happy about the fact that he may get my mouth open so I can have a small taste of water. I can't remember the last time I had one...was it yesterday that Chek had come in? No, it must be a few days now I would think.

"Okay, let's see if it worked." He gently probes his fingers in the tiny openings of my lips again. It's still not enough though and before I know what he's up to, he forcefully shoves his fingers in my mouth, a rough moan full of pain squeezes through my swollen throat and the skin on my lips rip apart from being stuck together.

I can't speak, just pant from the stinging discomfort. My stomach feels twisted up inside like it wants me to puke, but I have nothing in there to expunge.

"I'm sorry, but I had to. They weren't coming open anytime soon. It's been too long, and you're severely dehydrated."

I huff a few more times, calming my heart rate down a little and nod my acceptance.

"The Vaseline will help your lips heal." He reaches forward and softly spreads the remainder over my torn skin to bring a little relief. "Do you want to try some water now?"

I nod my head again and he moves to get the water, turning the sprayer on low.

The water softly hits my cheek and again, it's warm. I turn my entire face into it, letting my nose thaw out slightly while the water runs in and out of my mouth, bringing some wetness back. It's like pure fucking heaven. I've never imagined in my wildest dreams that I could miss something as common as water so much that I feel like I was just given the most precious gift I've ever received.

"Try to drink some of it, if I can find an IV bag with saline, I'll bring it, but I have to be careful about helping you."

His eyes run over my face in pity. I don't care; they did this. It's their fault I look like this, why I ache like this. Keep looking at me that way and feel bad. Hopefully I'll get more water because of it.

I attempt to swallow but it's raw, even with the warm water coating the inside of my mouth.

"Can you speak now?"

I try but have to stop and clear my throat, "ErrErrmmm." I sip a few more drops of water and attempt it again. "Heiiiii" It comes out shrill and hoarse, but it's a start. "Huuurrts...throat huuurts."

"Your throat hurts you too?"

I nod and let the water run through my mouth again. The man pulls out a tiny flash light and clicks it on.

"Open your mouth and let me check it out."

I move my head a little, adjusting my sore neck, and open my mouth as much as I can.

"Goddamn it. You need antibiotics; it looks like the inside of your throat went through a fuckin' meat grinder or something."

"Huuurts." I gasp again and he tilts his head, staring at me sadly.

"Okay, I'll go look around and see what I can find around here to help. I know you're wet...do you want like a blanket or something?"

"Yes," I whisper gratefully.

He walks over to the door, opens it, and bends over into the hallway. He comes back with two thin blankets and I feel like I could weep. *A blanket.*

He covers me from my toes all the way to my chin with both blankets, tucking it snugly around me and if I could smile at him right now, I would. This has been the first smidge of kindness anyone has shown me here, and I wish I could repay it with a smile.

Once he has the blanket fixed to his standards, he leaves the room and I actually say a little prayer, hoping that he comes back again. Then I start to drift in and out of sleep like usual.

I know I must be sleeping, because this time I see the man coming back, but now he has Nikoli's face.

# Nikoli

We arrived home exhausted from such a long flight, fitting everything into such a quick trip. Even with sleeping on the plane I have a bad case of jet lag. An anxious Viktor met us at the plane. He insisted on taking care of Chek for us until we're ready to question him. We had him gagged on the plane, so he would have to wait to speak until we want him to. Personally I wanted to question him right away, but Tate told me to wait until he's set up at Viktor's warehouse. He thinks it'll get bloody, and I am fully confident that it will, especially if my sister recognizes him.

We're not even completely through the front door before Tate is bum-rushed by his wife, Emily. She leaps at him and he catches her, spinning her around, just like you'd see in a movie or something. I'm usually very happy for them and I love them both and they deserve happiness, but right now I feel like telling them to fuck off. I wish I could be doing that right now with my little pixie.

"Niki!" Vishna yells and gives me a big hug. Her cheeks have some healthy color in them now and she's dressed in one of my huge hoodies. She's tall but it swallows up her thin frame.

"Na-na! I'm happy to see you say straa!" I grip her tightly back, over the moon to have a piece of my family in my arms, alive. "Let us go to my room, I need a shower and some comfortable shorts."

"Okay moy brat. How was your trip?"

"It was educating. I think we found who we're looking for."

"Really!" She says surprised and lies across my bed on her stomach. She watches me as I go to my closet and grab a pair of basketball shorts and a plain T-shirt.

"Da, I'll show you soon. I must shower." She nods and I head into my private bathroom.

I think I removed all the blood off me on the plane, but you can never be too sure, so I give myself a good scrub over. I'll get dirty again at the warehouse, but no need to freak my little sister out now. She's been through quite enough already.

Once I'm clean and dried off, I dress quickly and head back out to my room. I don't want her sitting out here waiting on me for a long time.

"Na-na did you eat yet?" I probe and slide on my comfy house shoes.

"Da, breakfast with Emily. That bossy American has been shoving food at me every two minutes—not that I'm ungrateful."

I can't help but to let loose a belly laugh. "She is Southern. It is custom for them to feed you a lot, one of the many reasons why Tate loves her so much. They both cook religiously. Did you enjoy yourself while I was gone? You weren't too scared?" I inquire and head towards the kitchen. I'm always hungry so I love having the food around constantly.

"No, it wasn't bad. I hope you don't mind, but I slept in here instead of the room Emily gave me. I just needed to be close to you while you were away. I never want to be apart again," she murmurs and trails behind.

"Of course I don't mind. You are welcome to any of my things. I will take care of you from now on, I promise, Vishna."

She nods, her eyes swelling with tears. "It's just, we-we were practically babies when we were separated...I can only remember your eyes and white hair from when you were a child. Now you are grown man, full of accomplished markings and strong—Niki—you are so handsome, I am proud to have a brother that is you." Tears tumble down her cheeks as she stands and I can't help but hug her again. My poor sister has had too much persecution in her life.

"I'm proud of you, too, and we will never separate again. I won't lose you, either."

"Brenna was right; she would always say that you would grow to be a good man. She said you were a Phoenix inside and would overcome to prosper, never becoming one of the men that they feared."

"They feared men, but you didn't?"

"No, their lives were different than mine. We slept in the same room for a time, but then they grew faster than me and their bodies changed, but mine stayed looking like a little boy. The master put me to clean, but the others were not lucky."

What she's implying makes me fucking retch inside. If I could gut each one of those filthy pieces of trash, I would—happily.

"And Mother? Was she in the same room?" I busy myself stacking bread with turkey, ham, cheddar cheese, pickles, olives and mayo, and place it on a paper plate and grab a full bag of Doritos.

She starts to breathe faster, blanking out as we stand in the middle of the kitchen.

"Na-na? You okay?" I set my plate on the counter, stepping closer to her. I don't want to freak her out, but offer comfort if needed.

"She did not stay with us; she was taken away very quickly. Mother was so beautiful," she replies hauntingly, her gaze set on the window leading to the backyard.

"I remember," I mumble and, as if on autopilot, take a bite of the sandwich. Time to change the subject; I need her feeling well for when I show her the picture I snapped of Chek.

# Nikoli

## REVELATIONS AND WAREHOUSES

**S**O, I SHOWED VISHNA THE PICTURE OF CHEK. I PROB-ably should have waited longer, but I couldn't. I wish it went over well, but it was an arctic fucking meltdown in the kitchen after I had my lunch. First with her upset and then again afterword's with me ready to take my revenge.

Once I got her to stop hyperventilating and she was actually able to speak, she confided that Chek was indeed the man who prepared her to be sold. I felt like a total dick for putting her through it, but it was necessary. The few details she spilled were horrifying, and I know that was just a small part of it. I hated that my sister had gone through that.

What is it with men hurting and defiling the greatest gift given to us? I will never understand it. Do they not realize that a woman is like a butterfly? She can be pure and beautiful the more you encourage her and let her spread her wings. My Bina was kept closed off growing up, but once she was with me and free, she was such a wonderful person to be around. Her parents had never given her the chance to show them.

I have to find Sabrina now, and this Chek guy could be the

only link I have to her. I'm hopeful my sister will be able to heal over time with the right kind of doctors and the love and support from me. Bina, however, may be on her way to death at the moment or already dead. I need answers, and I'm tired of waiting, I've already lost too much; I won't lose Sabrina as well.

I'm honored that Vishna feels comfortable enough to open up to me a little. My sisters must have built me up over the years for her to have such trust. I'm afraid I may let her down though once she gets to know me. I'm no hero. If I was anything of the sort, I would have saved them all long ago.

Wasting no time, I leave my sister with Emily to comfort her in my absence. I text Tate that I'm headed to the warehouse. I can wait no longer; I need to do something and it has to be now.

Chek needs to pay for what he's done. Life is no bed of roses, and Chek needs to realize that goes for him as well.

The trip to the warehouse takes no time at all and I'm happy to see that Alexei is here. It's good to know that Viktor has his best man on guard duty. I watch as he sends a quick text message. No doubt, he's logging my time and alerting Viktor of my arrival. I would do the same thing if I were in his position.

I doubt either Viktor or Tate want me to kill Chek. He probably has much more information than only where Sabrina is or what he's done to my sister and countless other women. It's clear Perfectcore is no business to help women become their idea of perfect; it's a place for sick, powerful individuals to go and order their idea of perfect, then the woman gets 'broken in' until she fits their fucked up mold.

There's no such thing as perfect. I could eat right and spend countless hours in the gym and I would never achieve perfection. Who wants perfect anyhow? Perfect is boring. All these men involved need to be taught their own type of lesson. Too bad I'm on my own mission or I would be interested in taking on an extracurricular project like that.

Climbing out of my truck, I decide to leave my black leather gloves behind. I usually like to hide any type of evidence that could lead back to me but I want to feel his blood on my hands too badly.

"Niko." I'm greeted immediately.

"Lexi. You spoke to your Boss?"

"Yes. He said you're welcome to his tools, but you are to leave the prisoner alive for future questioning. He also wanted me to inform you that you're welcome to finish him after the Boss collects more information."

"Now *that* is perfect," I utter and Alexei stares at me confused. "I was just thinking about it on my way here."

He nods and knocks on the thick metal door.

"Yeah?" is called and Alexei rambles off a sequence of random Russian words. After a moment the door screeches open and I'm met with two men loaded with AK-47's ready to do damage if necessary.

"Alexei?" they question.

"Da, Nikoli." He nods over at me and the men move away.

Once I'm inside, the heavy door closes and locks, leaving Alexei outside to stand guard. I'm finally faced with the pathetic creature that tormented my sister, putting her through torture and sadness. You ever want to slice someone open and then bathe in their blood? That's me, right now.

He yells something but with the gag on, his words are too muffled to understand.

"Oh you wish to talk?" I mock and he yells rubbish again. "It must be horrible to be kept somewhere, like a prisoner with no voice. I won't speak in circles like Viktor or Tatkiv; I'll let you know exactly why I want you here. The Boss' reasons are separate though, so rejoice in knowing you have much suffering ahead."

Untying the gag, I remove the material so the 'canary has a chance to sing.'

"So, they send the dog to gather their information?" he

angrily spits.

My hand connects with his cheek in an automatic response of his disrespect. He coughs and spits. No doubt I just busted the inside of his cheek open.

Making my way over to the long surgical table Viktor has set up, I'm pleased to find he's left behind a variety of specialty tools he likes to use. He's one creative fucker when it comes to his signatures. He's not like most Bosses pawning the work off; he likes to do the torture himself.

I discover one of his favorites—the mini torch—and chuckle. This could work nicely and quickly. I tend to get overheated easily when I fuck with someone, so I lose my shirt, stretching my muscles in preparation to dole out punishment.

With the torch and lighter in hand, I approach Chek with a giddy smile.

"A-a General?" he stutters taking in my markings.

"Oh, you thought I was a mutt, yes? I am the right hand to the Mafiya, you fool."

"Please for-forgive me, I wasn't aware. I can get you a woman as well, whatever you wish, just name it, and I'll get you one also."

"A woman?" I growl angrily.

"Yes, that's why you've taken me, is it not? I never offered you a woman and was disrespectful."

"Fuck, for being a man as warped and wealthy as you are, you really don't get it, do you?"

"Excuse me, but what am I missing?"

"You *took* my woman!" It spills out in a furious roar and he blanches.

"Impossible," he mumbles and instead of igniting the torch, I take the bottle and slam it into his knee cap.

"Aghhhhhhh! Nyet!" His face bunches in pain.

"Do you work with a man by the name of Kolya Minski?"

"Nyet." He pants and I slam the bottle down on his other knee cap. He screams out again and I break a sweat, my anger boiling up inside ready to explode.

"Then let's talk about my say straa and we'll come back to my woman."

"Say straa?" he gasps and I nod. I think the severity of my hatred is finally starting to sink in.

"Da, Vishna, blonde, eyes like ice, very thin; take a good look and you will see resemblance."

He shakes his head, looking away.

"Nyet, you do not get to forget her. My family was taken and I find my last sister in a shipment—sold. Tell me her buyer."

"I-I don't know the buyers for the containers; only the Master knows."

"Who is this Master?"

"I'm not allowed to know his name. No one knows his name."

"Bullshit! Someone has it and I will get it."

"I've worked for him for many, many years and never found it."

"And Kolya?"

"He has helped us with moving the women, but he stays out of the rest."

"Where is he?"

"The last I heard, he was going to have a meeting with the master. I have heard nothing since."

"Well, the fact remains that you put your hands on my baby sister."

"They don't come to me as babies, only as women," he utters and it makes me nauseous that he thinks he can justify his actions by age.

"She was a baby the last time I fucking saw her, you idiot! She will always be that way to me, and I will take my vengeance, you wait. Your journey is not complete. After the Bosses are finished with you, you're mine." I slam the bottle down repeatedly, this time crunching it against his shoulder, until I'm sure the bones inside are in pieces.

"Aghhhh my arm!" He sobs but I don't feel an ounce of sympathy for him.

"That's for touching her! I will cut each finger from your body for laying your hands where they do not belong! Everything has a consequence!"

"Please, please...please," he whimpers and I laugh loudly.

"Not so fun when you are the one in pain, is it? Now tell me where Sabrina Cheskolav is."

"She is Sabrina Minski," he mumbles, his eyes growing wide as he realizes he spoke it aloud.

"What did you just say?"

"Nothing...I said nothing."

I charge him, his chair falling over as I straddle him, wrapping my hands around his neck, I slam his head into the ground, choking him and screaming, "She is no fucking Minski! She is Miiiiine!"

In the heat of it, I don't feel arms wrap around my chest as I work to squeeze the life out of Chek, but then suddenly I'm being pulled away in my fit of rage, noticing Chek's face an ugly blueish color.

"Nikoli! Nikoli! Niko, snap out of it! Fuck, someone make sure that guy's not dead over there!"

I get shaken enough to jostle me out of my darkness to see Alexei's face in front of me.

"Niko? You with me? Niko?"

"Da, I am here." Blinking and drawing in a few deep breaths, the room and the people all come back to me. It was like I had tunnel vision and the only thing I could see was Chek and the need to kill him.

"I've never seen you lose it like that; you need to get some sleep and get your shit straight."

"I don't need sleep; I need my fucking woman." I shake his hands off my shoulders and head to the bathroom.

Slamming through the restroom door and flipping on the cold water, I splash the cool drops over my face and chest to get my body to calm down.

He said her name, I know I heard it...only she's no goddamn Minski.

# Sabrina

I'm feeling so much better thanks to the new man that's been helping me. He found an IV and gave me two bags of saline to help hydrate me, and then he came back with a shot that he said was antibiotics for my throat.

Now I can actually swallow without feeling like nails are raking over the inside of my mouth. I've gotten more water over the past two days than I have the entire time I've been stuck here. Today I'm supposed to start eating food again. I can't remember the last time I actually ate anything; it's amazing my body has gotten me this far without completely shutting down.

The disgusting thing though, I have to pee on the floor. It's better than peeing on me with what little I have and then being hosed off like before. The creators of this place are despicable; thinking the drain in the middle of the floor will let them just wash away everything. I can't help but wonder how many other women there are, and how many have already died from such cruel treatment.

The door opens, the extra light filtering in as the friendly guy comes in. We've barely talked, keeping everything clinical, but I will never forget his generosity in helping me get better.

"Hey little one," he says quietly and shuts the door behind him. "Unfortunately there isn't much for food selection in this place. I found some crackers, bread, and dried cereal. You'd think birds were living here." He stops in front of me, squatting down so we're eye level. Today he's got on another plain black long sleeve shirt and black cargo pants to match his boots.

"Thank you; anything is better than nothing." I try to smile but my lips are still too sore. It's an amazing feeling just to be able to speak again.

"Ouch, your mouth still looks bad. Keep putting the Vaseline on that I gave you. That and lots of water should get them back to feeling better soon."

"Okay, thank you."

"You keep saying it, but you don't have to thank me for every little thing."

"Yes, I do. Mr. Chek requires it," I mumble and his eyes flash with realization.

"Then you keep doing what is expected, and I'll do what I can to make things a little easier on you, okay?"

"All right."

"I noticed you looking like it hurt each time you moved your back, is it just sore from the floor?"

Cringing as I think about it, my back involuntarily twitches and causes a sharp strike of pain to flash over me. "No. I-I have a cut."

"Can I check it out?" he asks and hands me a few slices of bread. I nod, tearing a piece off so it won't touch my lips. Chewing will hurt them enough.

He walks around me and instantly I hear him draw in a deep breath like he's surprised.

After a few moments he clears his throat then speaks quietly, "I'll see if I can find some ointment."

"Is it bad?"

"To be honest...yes. I'm sure some of your weakness is from the blood you've lost. I'll be back."

I don't reply, just concentrate on chewing small bites of food at a time. I don't want to eat too quickly. I've read that if I eat too fast I can get sick and puke it all back up. The last thing I want to do is waste what little food I have to give my body.

After what I'd say is ten minutes or so, the man comes back with a first aid kit and a new syringe.

"A shot?" I peer towards his hands once he's close to me.

"Yes, I brought you another dose of antibiotics. I wasn't aware of your back and we need to get enough in your system to fight everything off. There's really no telling what kind of infections you have going on. Did any of them touch you elsewhere?"

I know what he's insinuating and captor or not, I'm not speaking about my sexual experiences with him. "Are you a doctor or something?" His forehead scrunches and it reminds me of what happened the last time I requested information from Chek, "Oh wait! Sorry...I'm not supposed to ask questions. I know better."

"It's okay. With me, you don't have to worry about those rules. I'm not a doctor; I've just learned a few things here and there. I'm going to give you the shot and fix up your back now."

"All right."

He walks around me, poking me in my arm with the shot and inserts the burning medicine inside. I'm sure a doctor wouldn't do it like that, but he's helping me, so no complaining from me.

I hear him twist the cap off the bottled water he brought in, and then feel the coolness run down my back. It's refreshing, but when he gently pats me dry, it hurts so bad I want to cry. I hold strong, trying to be brave so he knows I'm thankful for his efforts. He sprays something cold on that stings and then quickly covers it with a bandage.

"There. I put the ointment on the gauze so I wouldn't have to touch you and it should help keep it from sticking." He crumples up his trash and comes to sit in front of me.

"Okay."

"Try not to lie on it; let it do some healing. You need stitches, but I can't do that; I'm sorry. Once the ointment has a chance to work and clean it out, I'll try some superglue."

"I'm happy with anything. You've helped me more than anyone."

"I wish I could do more." He shakes his head, dejected.

"What's your name?" I whisper, finally getting up enough nerve to ask.

"My name?" He looks at me puzzled and I shake my head. His face is scruffy from missing a few shaves and goes well with his dark hair. He's not buff, but looks like he most likely has corded, lean muscles underneath his fitted shirt. God, he reminds me of someone, but I just can't place it.

"It's Beau."

"Beau." I repeat and he nods. "I like it. Mine's Sabrina." He nods again, like he knows.

*Shit.* He's here with my captor; of course he already knows my name and everything about me. I wonder if this is part of the process. Chek puts me through hell, and then I meet this dark angel who makes me well again only for Chek to come torture me all over again.

"This is part of the game, isn't it?"

"No little one, I swear to you, I'm not a part of this." He rasps sincerely and I believe him. If he's not with them, then who the fuck is he?

## Nikoli

## MY SAVIOR

**A**FTER I COOL DOWN, I DRY OFF AND STROLL BACK OUT into the main area. Tate and Viktor are both waiting for me.

"I apologize, I got carried away." I put my hands up and explain to Tate.

"We're not here about that, Niko, relax," he answers and I breathe a sigh of relief. I don't need to deal with him pissed off right now along with all the other shit that's happening.

"Oh, then what's going on?"

"We're here to see if you've found out any new information."

I share with them both everything my sister informed me about Chek and the process, and then continue with everything I found out here. It's not much, but it's more than we were privy to this morning.

"One step closer, just keep being patient Nikoli and we'll find her." Viktor pats me on the back.

"I appreciate you keeping him here. I hope you'll get what information you need soon, so I'm able to kill him. He deserves to swim with the fish."

"I agree. Keep focused on getting the information out of him and in time we will work on him about the rest. Sabrina is the priority right now. Elaina keeps searching the property looking for clues, but she and Spartak have come up with nothing."

"She is good friend to Bina."

"She loves her a lot Nikoli."

"As do I."

"Then you will wed when we find her. No more pining and waiting for her. Tate has told me how many years you've wanted her."

"I agree."

"Then it's done! Go fuck this asshole up for Christ's sake," Viktor orders and I gladly oblige.

# Sabrina

More time passes and as it does, I get my strength back. I can finally shuffle around and eat more than one piece of bread at a time without getting a horrific stomachache. My back is still disgusting and hurting, but Beau was right, the superglue is helping it close up. God it burns like no other when he puts it on though.

Each time he helps me, he chinks away at the stones around my heart, gaining my trust. As I heal, my thoughts and memories of Nikoli come flooding back. While my body gets better, my mind is the opposite. I begin feeling even more depressed than before. I thought he would have come for me by now. I thought we had a strong love, even in friendship. I no longer feel kidnapped, but almost abandoned by my love.

Chek is yet to return and I'm still silently praying inside that I was lucky enough that he got eaten by crocodiles. It would serve him right and with his heavy Southern accent, maybe it will actually come true.

Beau interrupts my thoughts as he saunters back in. He checks on me every hour. It keeps me sane knowing he's coming back. Sometimes when he leaves I'll start counting so I know when he'll be back. The few times he's been late, I've freaked out, so now he sets an alarm on his watch.

"I brought you something mouse." His term of endearment warms me and brings a smile to my face.

"Oh? What?"

"A brush and hair tie for that bird's nest you have going on."

Bringing my hand up to the back of my head ends up shooting a pinch of pain all over, stretching the skin on my back but I ignore it and feel my hair. It's twisted and tangled in massive knots. No wonder he wants it brushed, I bet I look like a crazy person.

"I don't know if I can even brush it out," I mumble.

"It's okay. Just try your best, or, well I could help you." He hands me the small black brush and elastic band. My hair is barely long enough to be tied up, but I bet he doesn't realize that.

"All right."

"Good, now I have to go on my rounds, but I'll be back."

I nod and he's out the door again.

I do as he says, trying to work it through my hair, lightly pulling through the knots. It's no use, no matter which way I brush or try to fiddle with it in my hands, I get nowhere. My back aches, my arms are tired from the lack of movement they've had since I've been gone, and my hair probably looks worse now than it did before.

Before I know it, I'm sobbing. Finally hydrated enough and the tears come; they don't drip, they fucking pour out. Crying not only for my hair but for everything—all of it. What a big fucking mess and all I ever wanted was to be free and live my own damn life.

Through my tears I watch Beau come back to check on me.

I'm too upset to speak, so I just cry. And to my surprise, he sits, his legs surrounding me and holds me tightly to his chest as I weep brokenly into his shirt.

"Shhh, it's okay Sabrina, just take a few breaths and try to calm down," he mumbles and I concentrate on breathing him in. He smells good—strong, manly.

"I'm so-sorry."

"Don't be. Now talk to me, I thought you were feeling better."

"I can't do it. I tried to brush it, but it wouldn't work."

"You're this upset over your hair?"

"Yes...No. It's the whole point, I can't even brush my own hair out, and how do I expect to ever make it out of this place?"

"You want to leave?" He leans back, asking seriously and makes eye contact.

I stay silent but nod. Serious repercussions could come with me asking to leave. Chek made it very clear that I only go where he wants me to when he wants.

"You concentrate on getting better," Beau rasps and hugs me softly before standing and leaving.

My heart races when he shuts the door.

Did I upset him? What if he tells Chek what I said? I'm so stupid. Dumb, dumb, girl, my mother used to say, and she was right. How will I ever dig myself out of this one?

I cry myself to sleep instead of trying to save my strength, so I miss Beau coming to check on me again.

## six hours later...

I awake disoriented from hearing a noise and instantly I'm on alert. I feel like I've slept longer than usual. I'm used to waking up each time Beau checks on me, but I feel like a long time has passed.

"Shhh, it's me." At the sound of Beau's voice, I breathe deeply.

He places his hand on my forearm and I bring my sleepy eyes to his hazel gaze.

"Do you trust me yet?"

"If I say yes are you going to kill me?" I ask and he chuckles.

"No death threats or plans over here."

"Okay, then yes, although I probably shouldn't. My mother always told me I was ignorant growing up."

"She's wrong, there is absolutely nothing dumb about you," he compliments and my cheeks heat at his kind words. "Hold this, right here." He turns on a huge flashlight and positions my hand so it points at my hair.

He pulls out a small electric shaver and plugs it into the wall beside us.

"Why the shaver?" I whisper.

"They're hair clippers," he replies absently and brings them close to my hair.

He works at shaving the knotty clumps off. I watch as they fall to the floor and I can't help but giggle. At this point, losing my hair is just another thing to chalk up to this fucked up mess I'm stuck in. Maybe it will make me ugly and Kolya will be finished with me.

"What happened to Kolya?"

"You know his name?"

"Yes, I know him. I think he's the reason I was stolen from my friends and brought here." There's a chance me confiding in him could be the wrong move and it could kill me, but he's the one who asked me if I could trust him.

"He had an accident," he mutters and turns the clippers back on. My mind races with what that means exactly. Please let him be dead. But what if someone else even worse takes me? Hopefully this hair cut will repulse them.

It feels like I hold the flashlight for ages as he randomly stops to position my hand in a new direction to give him light. Once he's finished, he sits back, takes the light away, and shines it all over to inspect.

"I like it. It's different, but it looks ten times better."

"Only ten? It must look bad then."

He chuckles and shakes his head. "I didn't realize you had so little hair. I was able to cut through the knots, so you still have some length." He takes the brush and lightly combs through it all. It still hurts like hell, but nowhere near when I was trying to rip through the tangles. When he finishes, I reach up, feeling my hair in a choppy cut, coming to the bottom of my ears. It was to my shoulders before, so this isn't the huge change I was expecting, thank God. If I'm going to be stuck in here, then it'll be easier to deal with.

"Okay, now you need to change." He pulls a duffle bag next to us.

"I'm allowed a new set of clothes?" I gasp excitedly, hoping for a pair of sweats to ward off the cold that seems to be getting worse with time. Any more surprises and I may actually hug him. Though, I'm sure I smell terrible.

"Yes. It's nothing fancy, just some things I was able to get easily at the nearby store."

"I'll happily take anything!"

Beau pauses, looking at me sadly, before mumbling, "You didn't deserve to go through this." He shakes his head and digs out clothes.

He lays before me a black pair of children's sweats, black socks, black ski mask, black gloves and a pair of sneakers a size and a half too big.

"Are we going on a robbery?"

"Something like that. Now get dressed."

I pause briefly, and then peel my clothes off, too excited for the warm sweats to care that he can see me naked. He turns his face away, showing me that not only is he kind, but has manners as well. The cold air hits the rest of my skin, bringing on chills and my back protests, but I grit through it, eager for the new things.

"Thank you."

"Don't thank me yet. Put on the ski mask." I do as he says and he pulls me to my feet once I tie the sneakers and get the cheap cotton gloves on. I have no freaking clue what he's up to, but I'm game.

"Okay." I stand, watching as he puts his own mask on and loads himself down with an abundance of weapons.

"If something happens to me, you take my gun and shoot anyone who approaches you, even if he has a badge on. Don't stop until they're dead. You get to a phone and call Tatkiv, tell him you are in the UK and to pick you up. The street in front of here is Bollington. He'll know how to find you. You just have to stay alive until he does."

"O-Okay." I repeat again, floored that he's giving me a chance to escape him if something happens. But who the hell is Tatkiv? And how do I reach him? I nod my head to Beau, but inside I know if I get away, the only person I'm calling is Nikoli.

Beau leaves the big duffle bag, shoving things into his side cargo pockets and grabs my hand, pulling me to the door.

"Be as quiet as humanly possible, even if you see someone."

"Got it," I whisper and we're through the door.

We race through a long, cement hallway filled with doors on each side.

# Nikoli

Heading back into the warehouse, I pat my overstuffed stomach. Viktor sent Lev to pick us up some lunch, and now it's time to get back to work on Chek.

I have to admit, I'm impressed. I've been beating him off and on for twenty-six hours and he hasn't cracked. It's been a struggle, not punching him in the face as badly as I want to, but I know he needs to be able to speak. I've broken many bones though and that's been entertaining. I can't wait to tell Vishna that he's dead and can never harm her again.

I've gotten him to admit he knows Sabrina. He's given up information on another shipment of girls he broke at the same time as my sister. Chek has even been kind enough to let me know that yes, Kolya is a part of all the sex trading; he even went as far as telling me where we may be able to find him in the UK. I'd mark it as a success, but I'm still not any closer to finding Bina. I'm at the point I just want to kill him, but I'm starting to believe that he may really not know where she is and it's heartbreaking.

"What next, Boss?" I turn to Tate and he huffs.

"How can you still have any energy?"

"I have to. I'm what she has against all these fuckers that want to hurt her. I've already eliminated Kristof, now I'm going through Chek, once we are able to secure Kolya, he's next. I'm going to make sure that once I finally find her, she will have no one to hide from."

"I get it, this anger you have inside, but it's tearing away at you. You're no longer the happy man I'm used to. Now you're like an animal, always on the hunt. You need to take care of yourself also, Niko. You don't want her to come home to the wrong man."

Tate's grown into a wise friend. I wouldn't have thought of myself changing so much that she wouldn't recognize me. Not my looks, but the inside that she knows so well.

Being in this life, we're all a little jaded in one way or another. Me with the emptiness left behind from losing my family, and Tate has had some serious shit happen with his father betraying him. Viktor's been put through hell, damn near dying in his love's arms. Add in all of the shit the women we adore have gone through and we're one group of fucked up people. I think that's what makes us all so close though, our demons we've beat and dealt with, we always support each other if needed.

"I agree, Tate, but if me changing so much that she will no longer love me saves her, then so be it. I love her enough to let her go if it comes to that, but it won't be because I haven't done everything possible."

"Then let's see if we can get anything else out of him before you kill him."

"I'm glad we're both in agreement that I get to finish him," I grumble and follow him back over to Chek.

"Chek!" I bark and pick up the cup of lemon juice next to him, splashing the juice on his face.

He lets loose a roar of pain and a string of curses at the burn from it getting in all the little cuts I've inflicted.

"You're out of time. You must talk now, because the agony has only begun. You decide how much it will hurt."

Viktor smirks and hands me a pair of special steel cutters.

"I promised to take your fingers, and I'm a man of my word. Now where is Sabrina?"

Viktor holds Chek's hand still so I can cut his middle finger off. It takes a strong grip, the resistance from the bone not wanting to break, but once I get it to snap, Chek leans to the side, expelling his stomach contents down over his good shoulder.

"Please Nikoli, please st-stop this. I can tell you that I knew your other sisters, they were sent to me, but ba-back then, I couldn't do it. Those women were just too beautiful and innocent. It was different with the old whores that they brought to me to try and fix. It was when they brought the stolen girls I couldn't do it. Th-the Master put me through hell at the time, threatening to kill me if I didn't suck it up and break the new girls. Your oldest sister was in the first group. I failed at hurting her and they killed her for standing up to them. I-I'm so sorry." He hiccups and I feel sick myself.

"And my mother?" I grit, snatching up a hammer.

I nod to Viktor and he holds Chek's other hand still, against a small side table as I drive the hammer down onto the top of his hand.

"Aghhhhh, nyet, nyet, nyet, please," he sobs, but my hatred only grows with his pathetic tears. He's hurt probably hundreds of women and yet he can't stand the discomfort now.

"My mother?"

"Nyet, your mother, the master took her himself. I don't know what he did to her, only that your sister was left alone to clean for years, and then he brought her to me because he had a buyer.

"And Brenna?"

"Wh-wh-who?"

"The middle one of my little sisters, Brenna. What did you do to her?"

"There was no one named Brenna. I'm sorry. She either didn't come to me or they changed her name."

I nod at Viktor again, taking another of Chek's fingers from the hand I had hammered. He bellows, "I speak the truth! Only the truth! Forgive me, please, forgive m-me."

"There were three of them!"

"No, Nikoli, I only ever saw two of them, I swear it. I swear, two, one big, one little."

"Two had blonde hair; one had brownish-red hair like my mother's."

"No, I only ever saw the blondes, I promise."

"And where is Sabrina?"

"I do not know."

Viktor grabs the hammer and slams it down on Chek's junk, making the man puke again.

"Errmmm, huhhh-huhhhh-sh-she is with the master, sh-she belongs to Mamama-Minski."

"Good boy, Chek!" Viktor says jovially and I grab up the torch, slamming the bottle into Chek's head.

"Where the fuck is this master?" I bellow, but Chek stays silent, his eyes trained on nothing.

Tate turns to me, "I think you broke him, moy brat."

I can't reply, only huff out heaving breaths to keep the tears away. I just heard about my family, finally after all of these years, I have some answers and it feels like the world wants to tumble down on me.

These people are sick; I need to find my little pixie.

## Sabrina

## HOPE

I GRIP ONTO BEAU'S HAND SO TIGHTLY IT'S PROBABLY cutting off his blood supply.

"Where are we going?"

"Shh, keep quiet!" he grumbles.

The hallway's dim and cold with weak lights placed in sporadic places. As we pass the doors, I notice random supplies outside them, towels, blankets, buckets and others have cleaning supplies and mops propped against the doors. The ones with blankets each have a loaf of bread placed on top and it brings a bad feeling to me. I bet there are people in those rooms. Not just regular people, but women like me who are being tortured and held against their will.

I jerk on Beau's wrist until he stops. He turns to me in a rush, his eyes wide and mouths, "What?"

"We have to save the others!" Whisper shouting, I point at all the doors.

"We can't, come on!"

"Beau! We have too, please?"

"I'm not here for them, Sabrina; only you. Many of them can't even move. We'll send someone once we're out of here, you have my word."

At his promise I nod in agreement and he takes off running down the hall pulling me along again. Even if he doesn't alert someone, if I'm able to figure out where we are, I'll definitely be reporting this to the authorities. What these people are doing is not only illegal, it's vile.

We both hear a noise and he jumps into a little grooved out area tucked into the wall, shoving me in first and placing his body in front of mine. Pain explodes through my back from my wound but I force myself to choke it down. *I need to be brave.* Fortunately, the lighting's so bad, and with us in all black, we probably blend right in with the dark corner.

Footsteps pass by and I think I hold my breath the longest I've ever held it before.

"How do you know where to go?" I poke him and mumble when I'm confident I don't hear the steps anymore.

"I work here," he mutters back. I figured that, but it's still painful actually hearing it come from his mouth. "Come on."

He tugs me along and we sprint through another hallway. This one has better lighting, and I can almost make out the names on charts hanging beside each door. We pass an open doorway with another guard but he has his back to us and never bothers to check it out if he had heard us running.

It seems like this place goes on for miles and I start to grow tired easily from not getting any exercise or the right amount of vitamins recently. If he's really here for me like he says, then it makes sense why he kept telling me to concentrate on getting better, but who could he work for? My father perhaps or maybe a different man is trying to kidnap me now? I seriously doubt my father would go to the trouble of hiring someone to find me. I'm pretty confident he's one of the people who wanted me here in the first place.

"Psst! Which family do you work for?" I mumble and he

shakes his head.

"No one! I'm American."

"Doesn't mean you don't work for someone; I saw your markings on your hands."

He shrugs, "I like tattoos." Suddenly he whips me down another hallway, this one with a white tiled floor and white painted walls. It's so stark it burns my eyes, causing me to blink a million times taking it in.

A guard rounds the corner, walking towards us, staring at his phone. I stutter to a stop but Beau doesn't slow down, just grips my hand tighter as he uses his free hand to aim his gun and shoot the man in the head. I shuffle along behind him like a disoriented tail of some sort.

"Holy shit!" I gulp as we pass him by. "Should we just leave him there?"

"Fuck, you're right, but where would we put him?" He stalls and looks around, stopping at a door in the corner. "Over here! Grab his feet but don't hurt your back," he orders, and to my surprise, I listen, and help him as he pulls the body to a door.

He takes out a plain key card, swiping it over a piece of the wall next to the handle. To everyone else it looks like there's nothing there, but when the key hits a certain area, a blue light shines and the door unlocks.

"Holy crap, where are we?" I grunt as he scoots the guy into the closet.

"Perfectcore."

"Perfect what? What kind of name is that?"

"I'll explain it to you later once we've gotten out of here."

"But wait, why are you helping me if you work here?"

"The job was a front so I could find you; my dad got it for me when he asked for my help."

"Why would your father want me? Oh, wait, was he a buyer?" I gasp, getting upset all over again.

"God no! He's not a saint by any means, but he wants to make amends for some things he did in his old life. Now stop talking and come on!"

Beau peeks his head out the door and then motions for me to follow once the coast is clear. He doesn't grab my hand this time and I actually have a chance to get away if I wanted to, but I don't want to. I think he's really here to help me, so I plan to stay next to him like white on rice.

We make our way down another hallway. Beau tries to get me to run, but I can't, I'm too exhausted already.

"I'm so sorry; I'm going to get us caught!" I whine, almost in tears at the notion of having to stay here longer. God knows what Chek will do to me if we get caught.

"It's okay, and no, you're not spending another day in this place if I have anything to do about it. Now shush."

I swear if he shushes me one more time I might attempt to punch him. I may be tired but I'll muster up what little energy I can to get him to stop that annoying sound.

We hear two men approaching us, speaking Russian and there's nowhere for us to hide this time. Beau comes to a halt, moving me so that I'm hiding behind him and holds his gun up, ready to shoot. I'm more confident about trusting him now that I see he's literally put his life in front of me to save mine. Not many men would do that for a woman they don't know.

Two guys a little bigger than Beau stride down the hallway, but they're not distracted with their phones like the last guard and notice Beau right away, yelling at him to put his gun down in Russian.

"Nyet." Beau barks back angrily and shoots. He hits one man and the other guy gets a shot off before Beau is able to kill him as well.

"Fuck, those gunshots are probably going to alert more men; we have to hurry!" he pants, gawking at me with wide hazel eyes.

Nodding, I pull my big girl panties on and push aside the

winded feeling I'm experiencing to move my feet as hard and fast as I can to keep up with him. We leave the dead bodies in the middle of the floor where they fell and storm the rest of the way down the hallway.

We turn the corner and are forced to come to a stop. We're at the very end of the hall and faced with two nondescript white doors.

"One's an elevator; the other is stairs. We can't take the elevator. It has cameras and we'll be stopped the moment they see our masks."

"All right then, I'll do my best to follow."

He swipes his card over the wall again and the door clicks open. We're through it and barreling down flights of stairs so quickly I feel like I could sit on my butt and slide down. After three floors I have to stop, pulling on Beau.

"I-I'm so-sorry. I can't go anymore. I feel as if I will pass out, my head...it's light and dizzy." I hold my forehead with one hand and grip the railing with the other.

"Can you hold on?"

"Yeah, I believe so."

"Climb on my back then and I'll take you down, you just have to hold on, and close your eyes so you can concentrate and not get sick."

"Sure," I utter breathlessly.

He steps down a stair and I carefully climb onto his back, wrapping my hands and legs around him as tightly as possible without choking him. I lay my forehead on his strong shoulder, resting my eyes and I start to bounce as he takes the stairs two at a time now without him having to wrench me along.

It hurts as my bones are jostled all over, but it's better than the torture they put me through in this hellhole. I can tell each time he hits a new landing, as he has to take three regular steps. We get to the fourth and his body comes to a stop, him panting, "All right, climb down."

I slide over his back, opening my eyes to take in the dark alleyway before us.

"I don't get it, we were in concrete halls, then all of the stairs, and I didn't even feel us go through a door." I glance back and there is indeed a door—a very big, steel door that I should have heard and felt us go through.

"I'm pretty sure when you closed your eyes towards the end you passed out. I had to hold your hands on my neck to keep you balanced."

"You were holding me?"

"Yeah, if you don't remember that then you definitely passed out. Your body still has a lot of healing to do. We were in the very middle of that building behind us on the seventh floor." He points upward. "The owner had a complete level built of concrete to hold you securely—crazy fucker. We still have to hurry, but we should be able to walk quickly now and arrive at my flat before they realize you're missing."

"Okay, the sooner we're away from here, the better."

"I couldn't agree more."

We remove our masks and then hold hands like an excited couple hurrying home together so we don't bring any unwanted attention to us. After a swift ten minute walk we arrive at a plain, brick building with a black side door. We go through it and up a flight of stairs to get to his place. *What is it with foreigners and stairs?*

Beau and I arrive inside; the apartment's only decorations are a few very nondescript essentials. A brown suede couch, coffee table, laptop and pop-up bed.

"Charming," I slip and he chuckles.

"It served its purpose. We won't be staying here anyhow."

"We aren't?"

"Nope. You lie on the bed and get some rest. I'm going to shower and change. Oh, and whatever you do, do not go out that door. They'll be looking all over the country for you and I don't want them finding you when I've barely gotten you free.

The pop-up bed and couch look like heaven on earth compared to the concrete floor I've been sleeping on. I make myself comfortable on the fluffy couch while he heads down the small hallway.

I must drift off because when I open my eyes, Beau is busily clicking away on the computer in a fresh set of clothes. I'm finally starting to feel a little rested. I've been so exhausted and my body hasn't felt normal at all. With the extra sleep, my mind's getting quicker and I no longer feel like I have to lie down for long periods to get a little energy.

"Errerrm," I clear my throat, waking up. "What are you doing?"

"I'm getting us a jet."

"A jet? Just who are you and who sent you to find me exactly?"

"Oh yeah, my names Beau. My father, he used to be a part of the Bratva. You've probably heard his name before—Victor."

A gasp escapes me at that name, "Holy shit! Your father? You're a Masterson?"

"Yes, my father, and no, I go by a different last name."

"Oh my God! You're Tate and Viktor's cousin?" I practically scream and he nods.

At his nod, I leap off the couch and tackle him in a huge hug. "I fucking love your family! Thank you, my God, thank you so much for coming and saving me! Where is my Nikoli?" I ramble excitedly.

"Nikoli?"

"Yes, he's the one who contacted your father, right?" I ask curiously.

"I have no idea; sorry but I don't know who that is. I'm not really a part of that family. I know some stuff about most of them, but I don't speak to anyone."

"Oh. You are here to bring me back to them though, right? I

don't get it why you would help if you aren't close to them."

"Yes, I'm bringing you home. The short story is, my mother and I went to the U.S. when I was a baby. I guess my mom found out my dad was this crazy gangster after she was pregnant and made him send her back to the states so we would be safe. She had him promise to leave us alone if he really loved her to keep us alive and not take on any possible retribution directed towards him. My father and I speak occasionally, and he was nice enough to put me through private school. This last time when he called he said my cousins needed a favor, that you had been taken, and that no one knew who I was so he could get me a job and get me close to you. When it comes down to it, they're my family; so of course I agreed to help out."

"Wow!"

"Yep."

"Can I please use a phone?"

"Not yet, we need to get you to safety first."

"What about you? Aren't you worried they'll come after you?"

"Naw."

"Not even a little bit? You saw what they did to me."

"I'm a cop, mouse," he answers automatically and I damn near choke.

"You're a cop and you're Victor's son?" I burst out laughing after the words come out at how ironic that is.

"Yes, and I'd appreciate it if you didn't laugh at me. I just risked my life to save you."

"I'm not laughing at you, I promise. It's just so funny—the irony—considering you're a cop and your father is as corrupt as they come. It's like the ultimate payback."

"I wanted to prove to my mom that I'm not like him."

"Well I'd say you did a good job."

"What happened to the sweet, quiet girl I was visiting back there?"

"She started getting better and found out she's going home!"

"Fair enough," he chuckles, his smile making him even more charming.

"So what's the plan now?"

"Well I have some more clothes for you here. My father had a guess at your size. I thought he was nuts when I first got the clothes, but I discovered he was right about you being a sprite. Once you change, I have a friend of the family named Roman that I'm supposed to call and he'll give us a ride to the jet, according to my father. This is really all his stuff, well besides the laptop, I was just borrowing it." He gestures to the place.

"Okay, umm, am I allowed to take a shower alone? I haven't had one since I was taken."

"Of course. Use whatever you'd like. The clothes for you are hanging in the bedroom connected to the bathroom. You can even lock the door if you want, and I promise to give you some space."

"Oh and Beau?"

"Yeah?"

"Thank you."

"No worries, Sabrina; I'd do it all over again."

# FOURTEEN

## Nikoli

No one is too old for fairytales.
-Unknown

## the next day...

**I** **JUMP OUT OF THE SHOWER AT TATE CALLING FOR ME.** He usually knocks, and if I don't answer, leaves me alone, so this must be important. Wrapping the plush towel around my waist, I hurry to open my bedroom door.

"What is it?"

"We need to go man. Vik just called and said our uncle wants us to head to the old airport. His jet's about to land."

"Are we on security or just greeting him? I wonder if he knows anything."

"I have no clue. Vik just said to be there in twenty, and that Uncle sent a jet and then hung up. I damn sure plan on finding out if he knows something if he's there."

"All right, let me dress," I reply and he leaves my room, closing the door behind him.

Before I would've worn a suit at the prospect of seeing his

uncle, but since he's retired I just throw on some faded jeans with a plain black T-shirt. I no longer answer to him or Gizya, only to Tate and Viktor now thankfully. I slip on my running shoes at the front door and make my way as quickly as I can to Tate's black Tahoe.

Climbing into the jacked up beast, I slam the truck door and he turns to me. "You good, man?"

"I got a few hours of sleep; it'll suffice," I shrug and turn up the radio. 'Angels Fall' by Breaking Benjamin plays and it tugs at my heart, making me think of Sabrina. Hell, everything makes me worry about her.

"I'm so sorry about all of this," Tate speaks over the music.

"It's not your fault that he wouldn't tell us where she is. It doesn't matter now anyhow since I already killed him." I shrug. "Now we need to find another lead, we need this master person he kept speaking of." My sister couldn't believe it when I told her Chek was dead. I thought she would freak out over me killing someone; instead she hugged me until it was hard for me to breathe.

"Wish I knew a name or something. Fuck!"

"I know; me too." I watch the beautiful green scenery of Tennessee float by as we drive out towards the old airport we all prefer to use. "Did you hear from your brother again after you came and got me?"

"No."

I hear movement and turn to find Vishna and Emily in the back seat. I'm so distracted I didn't even notice them. This is a serious security issue when it comes to keeping Tate safe. "What are you girls doing with us? This could be dangerous!"

"Tate said we could come, that he thought it was his uncle visiting." Emily perks up.

"Fine, but you both stay in the truck until we know it's secure."

"We will." She responds quickly and my sister keeps quiet. I know they probably won't listen to me and will do whatever they want to.

"Good," I respond and we all grow quiet, listening to the radio.

The ride is over fairly quickly and we arrive just as the plane is touching down. Viktor's already there waiting for us in his Maserati. I sure love those little cars, but I'm too large to sit in them comfortably.

I jump out of the truck and greet him. "You showing off for your \uncle?" I nod to the car. His Uncle Victor practically raised him and one thing he always instilled was for Viktor to have nice cars to drive when he was able to.

"No. Uncle called briefly about the jet, but he said he wouldn't be on it. He said that he hoped this would make amends for the argument we got into at my wedding that I told you about. I can't believe he'd show up demanding things anyhow. After growing up around him, I never believed that our relationship would become so strained."

"Make up for it? How?"

He shrugs, "I haven't got a clue, we just have to wait and see what he found. Maybe it's this person we've been hearing so much about."

"The master?"

"Yes."

"Tate and I were discussing it on the way over. I hope it is him; if not, we need to find him."

"I couldn't agree more." He nods and Tate heads over to us.

"Viktor."

"Moy brat, Luka," Viktor responds, calling Tate by his Russian birth name.

I call him Tatkiv at times from his middle name, and he also answers to Tate from everyone. I know it's confusing, but being who he is, he wants people to be jumbled with his name. It makes him harder to find by possible threats, not to mention the

FEDS, if everyone knows him by a different name. Viktor, on the other hand, gets pissed when people call him 'The Cleaner.' He should take it as an honor, the name speaks of his consistency of taking care of things.

After the jet lands and comes to a stop near our vehicles and the copilot opens the door, a man about Tate and Viktor's size, quickly descends. He has dark hair and a scruffy face. I'd guess him close to our age.

As he walks towards us, I stand in front, ready to take the brunt in case he's not someone friendly.

"What the fuck! There are three of you?" Emily bursts out suddenly, glaring at Tate.

I have no clue what she's talking about so I face the man again. "Who are you?"

"I'm Beau," he grumbles as he gets close and Viktor steps forward around me to shake his hand.

"Beau, it's been years. I don't know if you remember me, but I'm Viktor."

"Right, the older one," he answers and Viktor nods.

"Tate, you didn't tell me you had another brother!" Emily whisper yells, chastising and Tate chuckles.

"He's my cousin Em, not my brother." He smiles and then shakes Beau's hand next.

"Beau, this is my beautiful wife, Emily." Emily steps forward to give him a small hug with her damn Southern manners. Then he gestures to me, "This is my best friend and right-hand man, Nikoli. Oh, and the shy girl in the truck over there is Niko's sister, Vishna."

"Nikoli?" Beau says puzzled and stares at me for a few beats. I'm confused also. I thought Gizya only had one brother, Victor. I'd not heard of Victor ever having a son.

"In the flesh," I respond, intrigued.

"Do you know Sabrina?" He asks quietly and my breathing picks up rapidly.

"Bina? You know my Bina? Where is she?" I bellow and charge at him, Tate and Viktor each grab my arms, holding me tightly to keep me from mauling their cousin. How could he possibly know that name if he hasn't seen her recently.

Beau takes a step backwards, eyeing me cautiously. "You love her?" he asks cryptically and we all go still, wondering why he'd ask that sort of question.

"With everything that I am," I growl sincerely and he lets loose a sharp, loud whistle.

I turn my gaze back to the jet expecting a hoard of guys to come out, guns blazing. I never once thought a tiny short-haired pixie would walk down those steps.

"Moy Bina?" I shout, tears gathering in my eyes.

Is my mind playing tricks on me? Is it really her face I'm seeing right now? She's alive? What happened to her hair?

Sabrina rushes closer, calling back, "Da, Blondie?" And I drop to my knees, tears raining down my cheeks as she finally reaches me close enough for me to touch her delicate body.

"It is really you? I'm not dreaming again?" I choke out and she starts to cry.

"It's me. I'm here and you're not dreaming." She takes my hand, placing it over her heart so I can feel it beat.

"Oh thank God!" I cheer as I pull her to sit on my lap and wrap her in my arms. I rain kisses all over her hair, cheeks, forehead, and nose. "I've dreamed of you, I've looked everywhere for you, I cannot believe I hold you in my arms right now." I mumble and wipe my face dry. Tears keep falling from her, so I wipe her face as well.

"I prayed for you, Nikoli. I thought of you and made any promise to God I could think of just to see your smiling face again," she chokes out between sobs of happiness.

"I am here my love, and I will carry you around forever if I have to so nothing ever happens to you again."

I take her face in my large palm and tilt her head up to meet my gaze. After a moment of staring into her beautiful, happy eyes, I drop my gaze, zoning in on her lips. I watch as she swallows and waste not a second more, as I dip my head, my lips finally meeting hers, where they've longed to be  forever it seems.

The kiss is like magic, two souls meant to be, and fusing together full of love. My tongue caresses hers lovingly and I know inside that I'll never love a woman as I love her. She's it. She's the one for me, forever.

She pulls away, tears cascading down her pale cheeks. "I've waited my whole life for you to kiss me like that, Nikoli."

"I was stupid before, keeping my distance from you, but no more. I love you, Sabrina Cheskolav, and I want you to be my wife."

"Your wife? Have you thought about this? I don't want you to make a mistake because you're excited that I've been found."

"The only mistake would be not to marry you. I should have scooped you up as soon as you turned eighteen. I wanted you to have a chance at the life of freedom you wanted, without me tying you down. Now I wish I had asked you anyway."

"I would have said yes, Blondie. God, I would have agreed in a heartbeat. I've loved you for so long."

"I've loved you as well; please agree to be with me always?"

"Da. I would be over the moon to have you as my husband," she cries, leaning forward to softly kiss my lips.

My Sabrina induced fog starts to lift as I remember where we are and that our friends are here. I listen as Viktor tells Elaina excitedly on the phone that Bina is home safe.

"She needs to see a Doctor as soon as possible. Sabrina's been severely dehydrated, malnourished, injured, and endured psychiatric trauma," I hear Beau tell Tate, and it kills me inside to listen to it spoken out loud. I can't bear to think of her going through all of that.

Pulling my head back a little more, I really take her in. Her lips look awful, they're all chewed up, like she was biting them and pulling the skin off. Her cheeks are sunken in a little and she feels boney in my arms, telling me she's lost too much weight. Her hair's chopped crooked as shit, but that's not a real issue. Her eyes don't sparkle as much as they used to; they appear happy to see me, but I can see the torment in them. Her ear has a massive scab on the tip where her tattoo belongs and she has what looks to have been a deep cut under her bottom lip at one point.

Those are the things wrong on the outside, easily noticed, but who knows if it's even everything. I can't see underneath her clothes, to tell if there are more. I wonder if she knows it yet that she's been missing for weeks?

Fuck! My poor, poor pixie. I'll do whatever I can to help her get back to her beautiful self. I need to find this fucker responsible for all of the shit he's put her through and get her the vengeance she truly deserves.

"Did he touch you?" I grumble and gesture to Beau.

"No! Not at all, h-he helped me heal, Blondie," she responds softly and I glare over at him.

"Good, he better not have; you belong to me," I growl and she stands up, pulling away.

"Stop this please! I know you're upset, but you can't treat me that way or him for that matter. I wouldn't be here right now if he hadn't risked his life to save me. You should be thanking him."

"Thanks, Beau." I pout and stand, pulling Bina over towards the truck. I know everyone wants to say hello, but I want her all to myself. They can wait, I get her first.

"Where are we going?"

"To the house. We have a lot to discuss and I want to spend time with you."

Bina stops, turning back to face everyone and sends them a quick wave. Emily comes over, hugging her for a minute and babbles on about how happy she is.

"Beau, what about you? Are you coming with us to the house also?"

I interrupt before he gets a chance to speak. "He can go to Viktor's if he wants, but we're bringing you home, to my home."

"But what about the loft at Viktor and Elaina's?"

"I do not care if Beau chooses to stay there or not." I shrug and she grows angry.

"Nyet. I want to go back there. That is my home Nikoli!"

"No, that was just temporary. I live with Tate, so we will go there."

Beau steps towards us. "Look dude, she doesn't have to go there if she doesn't feel comfortable."

"Tatkiv!" I bark and turn to Tate. He has point zero five seconds to get his cousin in order before I teach him a lesson. Beau's not a part of this crime family, so he has no say in my matters.

He clears his throat and pulls his cousin to the side, speaking to him quietly.

"Pixie, I apologize. My head is all over the place right now. I've been so fucked up without you and now you're here, and now all I can think of is locking you up in my room for me only."

She starts to pant, her hand fluttering to her chest.

"Shhh, breathe, tell me, what's wrong, what can I do to help?" I ask frantically.

"I-I can't go to your house and be locked in a room. I can't be locked in anywhere. I have to be able to leave at any time."

"Leave? Why on earth would you want to leave me when you've only just returned?"

"I don't want to leave you; I just can't handle being locked in a room," she whispers and like a smack to the face it all sets in that she's been locked up somewhere this entire time.

"It is settled then, we'll go to the loft. My say straa can come or nyet?"

"Sister?"

"Yes." I nod towards the truck and her eyes shoot to Vishna sitting alone, waiting on us.

"Oh my God, Blondie, you have a lot to share, huh?"

"Yes. We found her searching for you."

She suddenly hugs me tightly to her. "You were searching? Oh God, I'm so happy for you my love."

"Thank you, I am beyond lucky to be surrounded by women I adore. And, of course, I searched since the moment I found out you were missing. I would never let you go and not fight for you."

Sabrina smiles and we head over to the truck. She seems excited to see my sister. I'm glad; I was a little worried how they would be around each other. Sabrina has always been a little touchy when other women would speak to me, and if Vishna is anything like me, then she'll be very protective.

I open my sister's door and she gives me a shy smile.

"Vishna, this is Sabrina."

"Hi," she says quietly.

"It's so nice to meet you! Nikoli has talked a lot about his family to me over the years; it's truly an honor to get to meet one of you. I wish it were under better circumstances and you didn't have to see me such a blubbering mess. I love your brother and I have missed him terribly." Bina reaches in and squeezes Vishna's hand, making my sister relax a little. I almost can't believe my eyes right now. I finally have my love *and* my baby sister in front of me, safe.

"I understand. I was very happy and sad at same time when I see Niki too. Welcome home."

"Thank you," Bina mumbles, almost like she can't believe she's actually made it *home.*

"Vishna, we're going out to Viktor's, okay? Sabrina and I were staying in his barn before she was taken. We'll probably stay out there until we can get a house situated or something."

"Okay, Niki. Can we get my things from Emily's?"

"I'll have one of the guards get everything, don't worry."

"Thanks, brat."

"Of course." I grin and she pats the side of my cheek.

I have no idea where she's going to sleep though, maybe on the pull-out bed in the couch? I understand that Sabrina's freaking right now, but we have to figure out a comfortable living situation and fast. She and I will need our own privacy along with my sister needing hers.

It's not fair to Vishna to be stuck on a couch bed; she deserves a large comfortable bedroom and her own bathroom. Hell, she deserves her own house when she's ready. All she'll have to do is ask and I'll provide whatever she needs to have a happy life.

I wish I knew what happened to my other sister, Brenna. That piece of me inside still feels like it doesn't have closure, not knowing her story also. The man they call Master should be able to give me the answers I need on her and my mother. Then I'm going to kill him, just like the others.

# FIFTEEN

## Sabrina

### TROUBLE IN PARADISE

WE GET SETTLED BACK OUT AT VIKTOR'S PROPERTY, and it's strange—but wonderful—to be back. Nikoli goes straight into his 'fixer mode' and barks orders at five different guards. One to get groceries, another to fetch his sister's things, he sends a third to get wood so he can build a temporary closet, the fourth on a sweep of the property for safety precautions, and last but not least, he orders one to collect the doctor for me.

I make my way up the stairs, letting him do his own thing and find my belongings exactly how I had left them. My brush is still in the same spot, along with my pajamas on the floor from when I had worn them the night before the wedding.

It's like I never even left. Well, except my pillow is missing.

Why didn't Nikoli stay here while I was gone? Was he at Tate's house the entire time? I'm drawn out of my thoughts as he tops the stairs into the room and approaches me.

Gesturing to the bed I question him right away, "What happened to my pillow?"

"Are you tired?" he counters with a small smile.

"A little, but I was just wondering, did you do something with it?"

"Da." He shrugs, "I couldn't sleep so I brought it with me to my house. I wasn't able to sleep while you were gone without having your smell near me."

"My smell?"

"Yes, Pixie...I told you I have wanted you for many years. I got used to sleeping beside you for months and then poof, no more. I couldn't close my eyes without wanting to rip my hair out of my skull."

Hearing him admit he missed me so badly is such a turn on, I can't help but pull him to me. Niko's lips meet mine passionately, and his strong hands palm my ass cheeks, and pull my body up his until I'm able to wrap my legs around his waist.

My nipples harden as need explodes throughout my body. I've wanted him like this forever it seems. He's hard in all the right spots, needy for me also.

Pulling away, I mumble against his lips, "I want you so bad."

"You have me." He murmurs back, kissing down my throat and bringing one of his hands up to cup my small breast.

"Please make love to me."

"Say it."

"Say what?"

"Say it, Bina."

"Please, Nikoli?"

"Fuck yes," he grunts and pulls the thin long sleeve shirt off over my head. I'm left in the plain cotton bra and leggings Beau had for me at his flat.

Nikoli's mouth travels lower, kissing and licking over the swells of my breasts as he walks forward and gently lays me on top of our bed. Standing up again, he quickly shucks his T-shirt and flicks open the button on his jeans. He leaves them on, just parted at the hips as he bends over to strip my leggings off.

I'm laid before him completely bare, giving him my body now, as he already has my heart. Shamelessly, I part my legs, offering myself, wanting him badly.

Licking his lips in anticipation, he covers my body with his warmness and takes my mouth in a sinful kiss. His tongue twists and turns, taunting and enticing me to want even more of him. *I missed him so much.* I'm surrounded by him, his touch, his taste, his scent; it's like heaven on earth.

"This is it, Sabrina. I take you and there's no going back in our friendship, it seals the deal for me. It would already be painful turning back now, but I'd do it if you're not one hundred percent sure you want this." He presses his body into mine and I rub myself against him in return. He's everything to me.

"You're the one thing I'm sure of; the only person who I know won't ever hurt me and will always own my heart. I'm more than ready."

"Thank God," he gasps and frees himself from his pants.

He's fucking huge. I'm not talking a little above average, I'm talking oh-my-God-that-monster-won't-fit huge.

Reaching down, he lightly rubs small circles over my clit and sucks my nipples into his mouth so strongly it brings a pinch of pain with the pulses of pleasure. There's no need for any of it though, I already want him so badly I feel like I may implode. After a few moments, Niko rubs the head of his cock through my wetness before working himself inside me.

A loud moan escapes as he pushes in deeper, my back is throbbing right now but I ignore the discomfort, as he kisses me into pure bliss.

"Fuck, Bina."

"Oh God, I know!" I gasp and wrap my legs around his waist again, pulling him in even deeper.

"You can't do that; I will fucking explode," he grunts and I reach around, squeezing his muscular ass cheeks and pulling him into me.

"I love you, Nikoli." I kiss over his chest, sucking and biting in about twenty different spots. He's going to look like he got attacked by a sucker fish when I'm finished with him. I want him to look in the mirror every day and remember this for the next week or longer.

"I love you, too, my little pixie," he says on a powerful thrust causing me to moan out again. "I need a ring for you."

"Don't worry about that right now."

"I can't stop picturing you as my wife, in a big white dress, with a huge rock on that finger proclaiming you as mine."

"I'm beginning to think you're obsessed with this idea."

"It's because I am. I need you to have my last name and be in my bed every night. I need to know that anyone who looks at you will know that you belong to the General and I will take vengeance if they so much as look twice." At his proclamation I call out, relinquishing the control I was trying to hold onto and giving in to the amazing feelings racing throughout my body.

"God Nikoooo! I'm coming!"

He growls and starts to pulse inside, letting himself go as well.

"Thank fuck! I don't think I could hold off any longer, love of my life."

I grasp his hair, roughly yanking his head back, making him let loose a loud roar and drive inside of me a few hard times as he finishes. Making love is amazing, but I want him to remember the ending being just as fantastic.

"You want to kill me?" he pants, resting on his forearms to keep his weight from smashing me.

Laughing, I shake my head. "No, I just want to love you."

A throat clears and Niko's head shoots over to the stairs as his body falls on top of me, crushing me, but effectively covering me.

Vishna stares at the carpet, her cheeks red with a deep blush. "Excuse me, but they have returned with the doctor."

"Thank you Na-na, we'll be down in a moment," Niko replies and Vishna nods, keeping her eyes trained on the floor as she turns around and hops down the stairs.

I can't help but laugh and after a moment Niko joins in.

"Poor say straa, come to new place and see brother's butt."

I burst out laughing even harder. "Oh God! Blondie, get off, you're crushing me!"

"Shit! Are you okay? I didn't hurt you badly, no?" he rambles and stands up, his cock still straight up and ready for more play time. *Later.*

"No, I'm okay now." I chuckle and slowly sit up. My body is still really sore all over but I don't want to make it that obvious for Nikoli's sake. I'm afraid he would worry so much he wouldn't even let me walk by myself.

"Fuck! You're bleeding!" He climbs over the side of the bed so he can check out my back. "Motherfucker!" he grumbles when he sees my gash.

"I'm okay."

"No you're not, and thank fuck the doctor's here. Get dressed." He stands, quickly pulling his jeans on.

"Stop ordering me around!"

"No, dammit. This is bullshit!"

"How is it bullshit? I'm the one who's hurt, and I say I'm fine! Now back off!"

"It's because I should have protected you! I should have been there to keep this from happening in the first place!"

"It's not your fault; this was my father and Kolya, along with their helpers."

"It is my fault, and trust me, I know about them. We'll discuss this after you're looked over."

I have to admit I'm a little frightened about what he may already know and tell me. I'm not sure if I want to know if my father or Kolya planned to do other things with me, what I experienced was bad enough.

Nikoli holds his hand out to help me up and I gratefully accept the help. I'm glad he hasn't had a chance to really look me over and notice the fading bruises all over my back also. If it wasn't dim up here with the curtains, he'd be able to see everything like a bad game of tic tac toe.

"I killed a man by the name of Chek. Do you know who that is?" he asks suddenly and I feel my chest squeeze tight in the beginning of a panic attack at that name.

"Did you just say Ch-Chek?"

"Yes, we captured him in the UK from his business and flew him back here. I thought he knew where you were but no matter what I did to him he wouldn't admit to having you, but every once in a while he'd say something to get me suspicious."

"Oh?" It comes out as a squeak.

"He said you were a Minski and then I see that gash on your back and it's the same as the Minski's mark for their women, you want to enlighten me if you know anything about it?"

I stare at the floor and whisper, "Chek is the one who gave me that mark, said he was preparing me for Kolya."

"Bastard! I knew it!" My hands shake with fury. That mother-fucker, touching her like this. I would chew him up and spit him out if he were still here. Taking a deep breath, I attempt to speak rationally, even though it's eating at me. "We can get it fixed or covered, something. A tattoo perhaps, if you'd like or maybe laser removal? I'm not keen on the idea of you wearing the mark of that family, but I won't pressure you to be put through any more discomfort."

"I would like it to disappear. Actually as soon as it's healed enough, I want it gone."

"Good, we'll take care of it."

"You were at Perfectcore?" I question sadly as my gaze finds his.

He blinks, tilting his head and nods. "Yeah, Tate and I went, hoping to get a lead on where you were."

"I was at Perfectcore. They kept me on the seventh floor, locked in a cement dungeon and you're telling me you were right downstairs?" I start low but graduate into a yell by the time I finish.

"You were there, the whole time?"

Tears rush to my eyes and my lips begin to tremble as I shake my head at him.

"Oh Bina! Fuck, I wish I would have tried to break into that stupid keypad and come find you!"

Shaking my head, the tears flutter over my too warm cheeks. "No, there were guards all over; Beau had to kill some of them to get me out."

"Beau, where did this Beau magically appear from anyhow? Tate and Viktor didn't even know he was with you. He could be working with the enemy!"

"It's not like that!"

"Nyet? Then explain it to me, because clearly I'm not seeing it the same way!"

"Why are you being like this? Didn't you want me to come back?" I begin to sob, confused why he seems so angry at me.

"Of course I want you back! I begged for you every fucking day you were gone, but I was the one who was supposed to bring you back! You were supposed to see my face save you, not some half-blood Russian who magically fucking appears!" he roars and I sit back on the bed, my face in my hands as I cry.

I didn't think it would be so hard once I got home. I guess I was expecting everything to be exactly the same. I never took into account how me being kidnapped would affect everyone else. I was just worried about making it back here.

"I'm sorry, Nikoli. I love you and I'm so, so sorry you had to experience me being taken and feeling so helpless. Please, just be happy I'm home. You have no idea what it was like in that place, and being here, able to feel your arms around me and see your amazing smile, it's more than I imagined I would get, once I was stuck in the horrifying prison."

"God, I am stupid man. You just get here and I yell and make you cry and boss you. Please forgive me." His hand runs down my arm and I grab it, to hold onto tightly in mine.

"Always my love."

He pulls me into his arms, holding me tightly and kisses me sweetly on top of my head. We stay like that. *Frozen.* Just loving each other until we're both able to calm down and collect ourselves.

Taking a deep breath, he steps back and turns to the stairs, "Come, let's get you looked at by the doctor."

"Alright." I easily agree and slowly follow him down the steps to our kitchen where the doctor sits, patiently waiting.

"Ready?" The friendly looking older African American lady asks.

"Yes, I'm sorry for the delay."

"Oh, no need to be sorry. You've had a traumatic experience and it'll take time for things to level out again. We'll get you back there though. Let's go sit on the couch and chat. I'll check you over and write you a prescription if you need anything. After all that, we'll discuss me coming back and seeing you again to make sure you're healing correctly, all right?"

"That sounds good, thank you."

I don't want her attention, but maybe she can help with my newfound fear of locked rooms.

# SIXTEEN

## Nikoli

### TEAMWORK

### two days later...

**W**E'RE AT VIKTOR'S CABIN 'HAVING DINNER.' IT'S really an excuse so we can talk about what to do while all of our women are safe and in the next room over.

"I want this trash," I grumble out and each man shakes his head—Tate, Viktor, Beau, Alexei, and Spartak. "Chek knew about two of my sisters and my mother, and then I find out from Bina that he's the one who was keeping her."

Viktor speaks up. "Whoever this person is has to be at least the same age as Gizya and Victor or older which means he's probably in his late fifties to be able to make such orders that long ago to take Nikoli's mother and still be doing it today."

Tate nods, "Yep, we know he answers to 'Master' and he's an international man. The girls we found in the container were from all over the world. Chek gave us info to another container but it was empty with an inventory sheet of just last names. We counted fifteen again. It looks like that's the lucky number for their big transports. According to what Beau found out about level seven at Perfectcore where they keep the girls, it sounds like they're equipped to hold two sets of fifteen at a time."

Beau interrupts, "That's correct, but also, not all of the rooms were occupied and some women were...well they aren't alive anymore."

Alexei turns to him angrily. "It's been about four days since you were there, has it not? And you're saying some were already dead? Who's to say others haven't died by now as well! We should have been on this the moment you touched down!"

"Look, I told my father about it and he has some people watching the entire place in case they try to transport or bring more in. You're all lucky I'm not calling this in to my chief and telling him everything that I found out."

"Is that a threat?" Alexei jumps to his feet and I feel giddy inside that another person in this group doesn't feel so comfortable with the latest person to pop into our tight-knit organization..

Beau jumps up, facing off with Alexei and it's the first time I can easily recognize his father in him.

"You want to test me? Just because I'm not some damn kingpin, it doesn't mean you want to fuck with me bro."

A chuckle escapes at his bravery and all eyes shoot to my wide smile.

Viktor cocks his eyebrow and orders, "Enough Lexi, calm down. He's a part of my family; please show him a little respect. We all need to work together on this and Beau has sources we aren't privy to."

Alexei huffs but does as he's told. Beau sits as well, then we continue.

"Also Sabrina spoke about knowing Kolya Minski. I wanted to update you that he had an unfortunate accident and won't be returning to the states."

And Beau moves up a notch to me. "Serious?" I respond.

"Yep, he's toast...literally."

"You're definitely part of this family," I chuckle. "So what are we planning then?" I ask and Viktor turns to me.

"We're planning a cease and desist. We send in a large number of men to clear out the building and then we obtain any women still alive. Anyone deceased, we'll leave alone and alert the local authorities so their families are able to get some kind of closure. We charter a bigger plane than the jet and fly the girls here, have a few doctors on standby to help them get well, and then offer them a chance to go back to their old lives, or give them a new life if needed. I've spoken to Roman about it all on his end and everything is in the works as we speak."

"The same plan we spoke about this morning?"

"Yes, just catching everyone else up," Viktor finishes.

Beau draws in a quick breath. "My mother told me you were all bad, I wasn't expecting you guys to want to help them. If anything I was wondering if you were partially behind it and that's what started this whole mess."

Tate shakes his head. "No, Beau. Since Viktor and I took over, things have changed. Now we aren't squeaky clean or anything, but we're trying to make our family businesses legit. Viktor has abolished the sex trade from his side and I've stopped all of the money laundering and drugs running through my clubs so far. We've pushed our father and yours completely out."

He conveniently leaves out that we're heavily into weapons trading and linked to a notorious biker club. But I guess we can't be all good, or we wouldn't be criminals.

He nods and we're interrupted by Elaina, "Dinner's ready!" She beams and we all stand, ready to eat.

# Sabrina

We sit for dinner; I have blondie to my right and Spartak beside me to the left. On the other side of Nikoli sits Vishna with Beau beside her. To say things are tense for Niko would be an understatement. I'm sure his neck is going to be sore from twisting between Spartak and Beau, keeping tabs on them.

"Spartak, have you read anything good lately?" I ask quietly and he looks up at me surprised.

"Umm, no, ma'am." He shakes his head and takes a big bite of his food, effectively ending our conversation.

*Okay then.*

The guys continue their talk from the living room and it's thrilling to hear their plans to rescue all the other women we had to leave behind at Perfectcore.

After listening to them shoot ideas around for a while, I interrupt, "Will we be able to help out at the club also?"

They all quiet, turning their attention on me. It's so freaking annoying when they do that. I know it's being respectful, but it makes me really uncomfortable to have everyone focused so intently on me.

Tate's gaze meets mine and he smiles kindly, "Yeah, Sabrina, you girls can run the entire show over there. I know we'll need lots of supplies: new clothes, sanitary products, food and medical supplies. I'm sure the doctors will be grateful for your help."

"Good, I would love to be a part of this," I beam back and Nikoli reaches over, squeezing my hand to show me support. He's been nothing but a rock since I've come home. He's been building me up with his words and making me feel like a queen with his actions. "When is this happening?"

Nikoli pulls my hand to his lap and speaks up, "We've agreed for it to happen tonight. We have men from Russia flying over to handle everything. A friend in the UK is supposed to make sure all of the women get loaded onto a plane that Viktor is chartering as soon as possible. We hope to have them here by late tomorrow night if everything runs smoothly."

"Wow! So fast."

"Da, pixie." He grins. "Now onto other things, if I may have your attention please?"

I quiet along with everyone else and stare curiously as a huge smile graces his face.

"My love, Bina, has agreed to marry me when she arrived, so I hold her to it." He stands and pulls a small square box free from his inside suit pocket, his eyes meeting mine. "Moy Sabrina, you still agree to be mine, to let me love you with everything that I am?" he asks, opening the box and removing the tiny ring from inside.

"Da, Blondie." I respond, beaming a bright smile and he lifts my hand, sliding the ring securely onto my finger. He keeps ahold of it and kisses each of my knuckles sweetly. Chaos breaks out as our friends clap and cheer us on.

Nikoli mouths, "I love you," and I nod and say it back. His cheeks grow red and he sits back down, brimming with excitement.

Once everyone calms down again, Niko releases my hand so I can eat. A flash catches my eye as I bring my glass of water to my lips and I realize it's my new engagement ring. Quickly, I replace the glass to the table and bring my hand close so I can get a good look at what he's picked out for me.

"Holy shit, Nikoli!" I gasp as I take in the size and weight of the pink diamond securely resting in a platinum band on my tiny finger. The ring would make even my own mother envious if she were to see how obnoxious it really is. "It's huge!"

"I know," he answers proudly, "I told you, everyone will know you're my wife."

"Da, Blondie, no missing that!" I laugh, crazy man. The ring almost touches the knuckle on my finger!

Glancing around, Tate, Viktor, and Alexei all wear matching large grins as they stare at Niko. They must have told him the same thing, but my man obviously doesn't care in the slightest.

At this rate, I may get robbed next if the wrong person sees it, not that Niko will leave me alone long enough for that to actually happen. I don't mind it, though. If anything, I love knowing that I'm safe and no one can harm me anymore.

I never have to worry about my father ever trying anything with me either. Nikoli filled me in on what he did to him. I cried, a lot, because when it comes down to it, he was still my father. In the end though, I'm happy he can no longer hurt innocent women. I'm still curious as to what rock my mother scurried under to hide. Hopefully she stays gone, and I never hear from her again.

After dinner as we clear plates away, Elaina leans over, "And to think, it was just a month ago that you were scared of Niko finding out you loved him in that way." She gestures to my ring, "And now you're marrying the love of your life."

"I didn't think you paid attention to that conversation." I giggle and she smirks.

"Honey, I always pay attention. If there's one thing being with Viktor has taught me, it's to pay attention to details." She bumps her hip into mine and takes the dishes to the sink.

"It was nice for everyone to be here for dinner to welcome me home." I follow her to the kitchen with my own load.

"Of course, silly woman, we all love you. When you went missing, it was just horrible around here. Someone was always crying, moping around or angry and everyone was searching for you. To have you home makes us all remember why we missed you so much. But I wanted to talk to you about something I discussed with Viktor while you were gone if you don't mind?"

"Oh, definitely. If it's about us taking up the barn again, I'm sorry, I just don't feel right at Tate's house."

"Actually, it is." She laughs. "While you were gone, I started to become depressed. I had forgotten how much Viktor works when he has something important going on and I'm so used to having my close friend around all the time now. I missed you because I've grown to love you, but I also realized how much I depend on seeing you every day. Does that make sense?"

"Yes, it makes sense. You missed me because we're friends, but you also felt lonely because we spend so much time together normally?"

"Yes, that's exactly what I mean! So I brought it up to Vik that I would love to expand here. He owns so much of this land out here and there's nothing on any of it. I asked if you and Nikoli would want to, if it is okay to have a house built for you to live here permanently."

"Are you joking right now?"

"No, God, I'm so sorry for over stepping...I should have spoken to you first before I even brought it up to him."

I set the dishes down and grab her into a strong hug. "You've just made me a very happy person, thank you."

"Oh-oh, I did? Yaay! So you think it's a good plan then?"

"I love the idea! I'll ask Nikoli if it's okay with him and maybe see if we can work out a date to have it built and then talk to Viktor about where a good spot is. Honestly I wasn't looking forward to moving so this answers one of my wishes. Thank you, Elaina, and thank you so much for being such a sweet friend to me."

She squeezes me back. "Always, chick."

We let go as Nikoli, Vishna, and Viktor come into the kitchen. Viktor cocks his head, "Everything all right?"

"Yes, it's good, Vik." Elaina responds, walking over to his embrace.

"You ready, Bina?"

"Sure, we're done clearing the dishes and Vishna and Emily agreed to wash, so I'm officially free."

"No, Vishna, go with them, I'll help Emily," Elaina offers.

"Are you sure? It is no problem; I can do them all," Vishna argues quietly and Elaina shakes her head, kissing Vishna's cheek.

"All of you need to get some rest."

Nikoli shakes Viktor's hand. "I'll return in a few hours to monitor how everything's going with you guys."

Sounds good. Text first and I'll send Lev over to watch your door."

"Okay thanks." He gives Elaina a small hug. "Thank you for dinner —wonderful as always."

"You're very welcome, Niko, good-night." Elaina hugs him back and sends me a small wave as we leave and make our way to the loft.

We head down the small path, and I kick off my shoes as soon as we get through the door, making Nikoli laugh at me.

"I didn't realize I had missed that until now."

"Me kicking my shoes off? I can't help it my feet hurt."

"I know. You do it every time you drink wine."

"Nyet, seriously?"

"Da." He chuckles and Vishna joins in.

"Na-na you okay on the sofa? We'll get you a bed soon."

"I'm fine, Niki, don't worry. I'm just happy to be close to you."

"Me too, say straa. Sleep well." He kisses her forehead.

"Night, Sabrina." She calls.

"Good-night!" I wave to her and Nikoli heads up the stairs with me, shucking his jacket before we make it to the top.

"Are you hot, Blondie?"

"Only for you, gorgeous."

A smile and a blush take over at his words; he's always saying things like that, making me feel special. His phone goes off and I can tell right away it's his friend Avery. Their friendship used to bother me, but now that she's super in love with a motorcycle club guy, I no longer worry she'll end up wanting Nikoli. I never told him I was scared of her wanting him back, but it used to drive me crazy to listen to them joke around when we were together. He goes on telling her about our engagement excitedly and I can hear her yell through the phone that she's so pleased for him. *Maybe she's not so bad after all.*

Wanting his attention back on me, I start stripping my clothes off when we hit the landing. Each piece I remove, I throw at him while he watches me intently. He keeps his conversation going until I give in, approaching him, fully naked; I take his hand, placing it where I want it the most. He stays on the phone, he's quiet now, but he's doing it on purpose, making me wait.

*Too easy.*

Taking one of his fingers, I push it inside my achy center. It's enough that he stutters out a good bye and finally hangs up.

"Good talk?"

He clears his throat, breathing heavier, "Yes, great talk. What are you up to, little one?" He swallows harshly as I hold his hand to me, grinding down on it while I keep eye contact.

"Oh you know, I just thought it might be fun for you to make me come," I gasp out and lick my lips. Reaching forward, I flick the button on his suit pants free.

"Da? Like this?" He grabs my ass cheek, yanking me to him, while moving his hand, creating delicious sensations.

"Uh-huh." I give his pants a push and they fall to the floor exposing his Superman briefs. Through the pleasure I chuckle slightly. He's adorable but at the same time sexy as all get out. I didn't realize that was even possible.

"I never imagined you could be any more beautiful, but to see you naked in only your ring, makes you look absolutely amazing."

Concentrating, I unbutton his dress shirt, so it hangs open, showing me his muscular body and markings. The wine from dinner is working in his favor, giving me more courage to take control and show him what I really want.

"Why the blood on your stomach, my love?"

"You don't want to know about that, especially now. You'll think I'm fucked up."

"Are they the marks for each hit?" I groan as he continues his onslaught of pleasure to my body.

Nikoli nods and it makes me even wetter to learn he's that much more powerful, to know that my man has killed people. It makes me feel safe, like he'll protect and cherish me, never letting anyone harm me ever again. I'm the fucked up one, getting turned on by tallies marking death, by being drawn to his tainted side.

I pull his fingers free, briefly sticking them in my mouth one by one to suck them clean, causing him to moan in bliss and then I squat down to kiss and suck where each little droplet of blood is tattooed across his abdomen.

I don't know if it's the area or the significance of me loving everything about him, but his cock fully stiffens. Grasping his thick length, I pump it up and down, then around in circles. I wish my mouth was completely better so I could suck it. Not one to be deterred, I lick up and down all over his cock and then around over the tip.

He copies me, sucking the fingers that he had inside me, he loves the pleasure as he flexes his thighs tightly with each pass of my tongue over his tip.

"Enough, pixie, I need to have you," he grumbles impatiently.

"You have me already."

"I want your sweetness; I'm ready to burst already. Get up here."

Grasping my hand, he gently helps me to my feet, then walks backward, pulling me along until he hits the oversized bed.

"Lie down, sexy man," I order and he flashes his brilliant smile.

"As you wish." He winks and lies back across the comfy pillow top mattress.

Quickly I follow, climbing over him until I'm straddling his length. He wastes no time, lining himself up with my center and thrusting upwards powerfully while pulling me downward by gripping my shoulders.

"You feel so damn good, Bina,"

"Yesss!" I call out, raking my fingers over his chest.

I lean forward, holding his shoulders as I move my hips, twisting them from side to side, bringing us both enjoyment. Being with him is mesmerizing—his body and scent draw me in, making me feel as if I can never have enough of him.

Nikoli's right, riding him while witnessing that ring resting on my finger is sexy as hell. The simple fact of knowing that not only am I his, but that he belongs to me as well is simply enthralling on its own.

He tastes my nipples, taking turns between them, and I ride him harder, making him whisper my name in a quiet chant, begging me to go slower so he doesn't come already. When I don't comply, he transfers me over to my side so he can enter me from behind and be more in control of our movements.

He reaches a new place and it feels as if I could shoot off like a cannon. I whimper quietly as he murmurs in Russian about his love for me next to my ear, his breath trembling over my neck.

"You complete me, Nikoli. All these years you've been my best friend and now I finally get to have the rest of you. I think I've always been in love with you. I knew you were the one I wanted, and now I'm lucky enough to be with you like this, soon to be your wife."

"Yes, my wife," he replies as he reaches around to play with my clit while plunging deeply inside my core.

I try to fight it off, to delay it longer, but I can't stop myself as the delicious warm feelings of ecstasy and his love envelope me, making me soar through my climax.

Clutching me tightly against his body, he holds me in a strong grip, grinding into me and professes his commitment to me as he finishes himself.

I could die a happy person now, knowing how he really feels about me and knowing that even after weeks of believing that I was going to die, that I get a real chance at living. A fresh start at a life spent with him and our wonderful family of friends. I couldn't ask for anything more.

I remain lying on my side in the bed, unmoving, being a total lush after he's done. I'm exhausted and after such close, tender moments spent with him, I just want him to tuck me near him again and fall asleep in his heat.

"I may clean you?" he asks shyly and I giggle.

"Of course, Blondie; you may do as you wish, my love."

He leaves the bed briefly, returning with a warm, wet cloth which he uses to gently clean me up.

"I'm on no birth control, Nikoli. Not for weeks now."

"Good, little one." He grunts and that's all I need to know about his feelings on having children with me. There isn't a superior man I could want to raise children with.

"Elaina said her and Viktor would like for us to build a house here, on their land."

"That's very generous, have you thought of it?"

"Da, it would make me content."

"Then I'll get it set up. Would you mind if Na-na lives with us? I need to see if Tate will move out here closer as well. He's still my Boss and I'm with him a lot, you know this."

"Yes and I would love to have her. I can't wait to tell Elaina. Thank you!"

"It is nothing."

"I have money in my account still from my trust fund. I didn't spend a lot of it when I was at school."

"I don't need your money; it is yours to do with what you wish."

"It's our money, Nikoli."

"Nyet."

"Stubborn Russian."

He shrugs. "I am. Use it on new clothes or something."

I'm not blowing a million dollars on new clothes; he's nuts.

"I'll use it to help the women you find. If they need a home or something, I'll use it on that."

"If that will make you happy, Bina, then it's a great idea."

"It will. Those women are going to need all the assistance they can get. You don't know what it's like being trapped in there, caged up like an animal. I heard your sister crying last night and talking in her sleep; these things don't just disappear."

"Shhh, okay, I don't want you working yourself up. I want you to get some good sleep. I'll check on Vishna when I shower downstairs in a few minutes also."

"You're not staying in bed?"

"No, pixie, I have to go back to Viktor's to help out with everything. I'll send Lev to sit outside, da?"

"Da. I love you."

"And I love you." He kisses me sweetly on the tip of my nose, then grabs a new set of clothes and heads downstairs.

# SEVENTEEN

## Nikoli

I ARRIVE BACK TO VIKTOR'S CABIN AND FIND THE GUYS in his office, watching a large screen, full of guys clad in tactical gear running through what appears to be Perfectcore. "Hey, what's happening?"

Tate glances over, as I take a seat in the extra kitchen chair they must have brought in for this occasion. "We've been watching them take control of Perfectcore."

"When did they start?"

"About twenty minutes after you left, you know time difference and all. They wanted to get in before daybreak."

I nod, understanding the importance of being discreet, especially with something so sensitive.

Viktor shifts, taking a gulp from his tumbler of vodka. "So far it's gone well; they've secured three guards and have eliminated seven." *I could go for a liter of vodka talking about this.*

Paying special attention to Beau's reaction, I'm curious about him being on the opposite side of the law as we are. Surprisingly, he doesn't even flinch as we discuss it like it was what we ate for breakfast.

"Did they find the girls yet?"

"That's the problem right now. Someone must have been

watching—I'm assuming remotely—and locked level seven down. The men have to get through the concrete barriers without damaging the rest of the building too much. I'm hoping there isn't anyone on that floor with the women, planning to kill them while they're locked down. At this rate though, nothing would really surprise me. These people are obviously sick."

Drawing in a deep breath at his words, that notion brings a pang to my stomach. I can't help imagining it if my sister were still up there and being killed as she was trying to be rescued. Those innocent, broken women don't deserve to meet an end like that. They deserve a chance to live.

God, I hope we're able to get through it quickly. Leaning back in my chair, I settle in and watch along with the others as the leader of the group wears a small camera for us to witness everything ourselves. I wish I could help, but at the same time I'm thankful that I'm not having to experience it in person. I would probably lose my shit knowing Bina was there.

And that's how the evening plays out; for hours we sit, quietly taking in everything. The guys attempt different ways to get through the thick concrete, but eventually it takes a small bomb and heavy drilling equipment to make an entry large enough for the men to squeeze through. I can see exhaustion in their faces, having been flown in from Russia to be straight on a job requiring intense concentration and expertise. They're being shot at, killing others, looking for tools they didn't know they'd need and drilling for hours, only to uncover a horrifying sight ahead of them.

They get through the wall to find three guards in the hallways with their brains blown out all over the place. No doubt they were instructed to kill themselves so they couldn't be captured and be made to talk, and then there was the decaying bodies they discovered. I couldn't even smell it, but I still puked several times from the sight.

It looks like the bodies had been left there, no one wanting to clean up the mess. The men kept walking and gagging, stopping to puke multiple times from the stench down the back hallway where Beau says Sabrina was kept. He mumbled quietly that she would have been one of them left to die back there as well. It hurt so badly to hear it, I couldn't breathe for a moment imagining one of those deathly shadows being her.

Down the white tiled hallway, there were fifteen women discovered alive and on the mend. They were each allotted a cot and a small night gown. Clearly they were who the three guards were there to monitor.

I'm thinking since we had taken Chek the men didn't know what to do and just left things the way they were. What I wouldn't give to have that fucker alive again now that I know what he was really up to.

In the end, the women are all carefully taken to the private plane to be flown here immediately.

## a week later...

There's absolutely no trace of this Master guy anywhere. It seems like no matter what we look into, there's nothing. There are two girls in the group we rescued who think the Master may be from Italy. We put feelers out but have gotten zilch back so far. We're nowhere closer than we were when we first discovered his name. But at least we know what to look for now and we have a nickname he uses. If there's one thing the Mafiya is good at, it's finding other criminals.

I'm thinking it may be time to give Anna, down at Channel Seven News, a friendly call. She may know something that can help us out now that we have a few clues and I can ask her about other container shipments. I wonder if anyone else has found any in the past. She would probably know as that would normally be something that makes the news. Ours should have also, but we kept it under wraps.

It will probably take some time, but eventually that bastard will get what's deserved. As much as I would enjoy it, it may not be by my hand. But it'll happen. Karma always gets her man in the end.

With Sabrina safe and home, it's time for new beginnings. We'll help these women any way possible to rehabilitate into society. I'll marry the woman of my dreams and build her a beautiful house to hold all of the babies I plan on giving her. My sister will be beside me always, reminding me how truly blessed I am in this life.

My phone vibrates and I'm happy to see its Avery calling me back finally.

"Hi, Bean," I answer cheerfully.

She sobs, "Niko, I'm scared."

My best friend crying instantly sets me on edge. "What is it, Avery? I can be there in sixteen hours, sooner with Tate's jet."

"N-no it's nothing like that, but I love you for being so willing to come help me." She cries and it worries me that the biker has hurt her.

"Talk to me, tell me how to fix whatever's wrong. Do I need to kill him?"

She chuckles a little through her tears, "Niko...I'm pregnant."

"That is wonderful, bun in the oven!"

"No," she hiccups. "I do-don't know who the father is."

"What did you just say? It's not 2's baby?"

"It could be Ares'." *Holy shit, the Butcher!*

"There are two bikers now? Fuck Bean, this makes it harder for me to kill them."

"I love them both."

"Of course you do. Now, do they hate each other?"

"No, it's complicated, they love me too. Can you come visit?"

"I'll bring Sabrina and Vishna; I think they'll like Texas."

"Thank you, Niko; I can always count on you."

"Yes, always Bean."

After all, I love her and I've dealt with many unwanted sacrifices in my life, but they've taught me about what really matters in life—love.

# FAST FORWARD

## Sabrina
## five years later...

Our little brownish-red haired daughter dances around at the end of our oversized bed, waiting not so patiently for me to get up for breakfast.

"Dye voosh ka, go tell Papa to put chocolate chips in our pancakes."

Her bright blue eyes grow wide at my request. "You're not supposed to have chocolate in the morning, Momma!"

Cocking my eyebrow, I sit up and question her, "Says who?"

"You always tell me no!" she retorts sassily with her hand resting on her hip. She's like a mini version of me but full of her father's bossy attitude all stuffed into a nightgown with princesses on the front.

"That's different, Brenna. I say nyet because you like to ask every day for a month straight. Right now, Momma wants them because she has a baby in her belly."

"You don't look like you have a baby in there." She nods to my waist and I fight to hold in my giggle. No one knows about the baby yet, except me and now her and it's so exciting... Okay so Elaina knows also, but no one else!

"That's because it's a new baby."

She huffs, irritated, "Another one?"

"Da."

"But I already got a sister; I don't need two."

Chuckling, I shake my head. "What if you're wrong, it could be a boy you know."

"Puh-lease, Momma, we all know you have girls!"

"Oy, I know. Go tell Papa we're having another."

"Nuh-uh, this is your doing, you tell him."

"How is it my fault?"

Brenna taps her chin, and then reasons, "Papa said you'd have a house full of kids, so that means it's your fault."

"Ugh, get out of here little girl. Go put chocolate chips in my pancakes, if not I'll tell Auntie Na-na not to paint your nails!"

"Fine, but you better let me choose the name this time, and Auntie Na-na has say straa outside on the deck."

"Okay, thank you, my little love," I call loudly as she breezes out of our room and down the stairs to the kitchen.

She's barely five years old and already wheeling and dealing. She's been hanging around Uncle Tate and Uncle Viktor way too much when they play cards.

My brain hurts thinking of having a five-year-old, a two-year-old, and now a brand new baby. These girls are going to be the Black Death when they become teenagers. I should strangle that man down there for having me knocked up one after the other. Everyone was right when they placed bets at our wedding years ago, damn them.

A house full, huh? I'm never fitting into another cute dress that doesn't have elastic involved again. I feel like a duck always wobbling around, I muse as I climb out of bed, and wrap up in my pink polka dot robe Blondie got me for my birthday last year. I loved it and had an extra surprise when I reached in to the pocket to find a beautiful mother's necklace tucked inside.

Nikoli's a good man, a great husband, and an absolutely wonderful father to our little girls. They think he hung the moon and he treats them like they're precious diamonds, always spoiling them.

We nearly collide as he meets me in our bedroom doorway as I'm about to make my way downstairs. "Careful, Pixie," he mumbles with his sexy deep morning voice. "Brenna says you're demanding chocolate chips. Is she trying to eat chocolate for breakfast again?"

Laughing, I shake my head. "Nyet, it was really me."

"You're not one for sweets in the morning, well unless..." He glances down at my stomach, wrapping his arms around me and pulling me to his big body. "Unless you have something to share with me?"

"I sent Brenna down; I figured she would have spilled already."

"No love, she was just eager about the chocolate chips. Should I be excited about something also?"

"Maybe," I shrug and smile sweetly.

He releases me, pushing my body up against the wall while pulling the robe open.

"Let me see what you're hiding, little one," he mutters and drops to his knees to lift my long night shirt up under my breasts. There's a small pooch there, but it's hard to tell if I've just eaten too much or if it's truly a tiny baby bump.

Nikoli rains sweet tender kisses all over my stomach, taking his time to make sure he gets the entire area where a baby would be resting beneath the surface.

"It's hard to tell with so many clothes on; I may need to remove more." He works my panties to my thighs and exposes my tender part to his mouth. He attacks me like a man starved. I reach out to hold his hair, enjoying each pass of his tongue, when we're interrupted by the impatient minion, yelling that her papa is burning pancakes.

"Oh shit!" Niko hops up, adjusting himself as he practically leaps down the stairs. I hear the thumps from his heavy steps then the smoke detector alarm goes off, triggering the other two downstairs to blare loudly along with it.

My morning went from quiet and sleepy, to hot then noisy as the beeps continue and Vishna rushes in screaming if everyone's all right. The baby, Lala, starts wailing, it's pure utter chaos, but that's my life now and I wouldn't change it for the world.

I yank on a pair of shorts and throw on a bra, ditching my robe and hightail it downstairs to help calm everyone down.

# Nikoli

I make it downstairs and the smoke alarm's alert with its shrill buzz that's loud enough to give you a migraine. Brenna has the stool in front of the sink; water turned on full blast pointing the sprayer towards the smoking pancakes on the stove, doing absolutely nothing since the spray won't actually reach that far but soak the floor.

Avery's son, Kane is busy throwing handfuls of flour at the smoke, making it all an even bigger mess. The kid looks like he should be seven, not five, taking after his massive father. I'm keeping my eyes on that boy, already egging Brenna on and trying to flirt.

The dog comes in barking crazily and then my sister runs inside screaming about the smoke alarm, pissing off Lala. I could rip my fucking hair out and Bina just announced she's pregnant again. I see what this is; it's payback for me giving my mother hell when I was a boy.

Even through all the turbulence with Sabrina getting well and learning how to cope with what happened to her and then the struggles we've had discovering how to be decent parents, I've never been so happy, in love, and at peace in my lifetime. She has given me hope, family, and joy. I'll be eternally grateful and always cherish her as the prize she truly is.

I can't wait to experience the rest of my years with her and my beautiful daughters. My beautiful *single* daughters who won't marry or move away from us until they're *forty* and that's only if I approve of the dude.

It's been five years and we still haven't found the man known as 'The Master.' It haunts Sabrina some nights, but I'm always there to offer her comfort. We still search for him all the time. In fact, Beau has become his newfound tracker. Turns out he kind of likes being the Mafiya's hunter.

# AUTHOR'S NOTE

So who's next in the Russkaya Mafiya? Spartak, Beau, Alexei, The Master? Let me know who you want more of, and thank you tremendously for reading! If you would like to know about Avery, she has her own books called Relinquish and Forsaken Control.

*XOXO- Sapphire*

# ACKNOWLEDGEMENTS

**My husband** - I love you more with each book I write.

**My boys** - You are my whole world. I love you both.

**The lovely beta readers, thank you -** Abbey Neil-Clark, Kelly Emery, Sarah Rogers, Lindsay Lupher, Wendi Stacilaucki-Hunsicker and Patti Novia West. You have become my friends—a group of women I know I can count on and I love you for it. You ladies are my rocks!

**Photographer Eric Battershell** – Thank you so much for the amazing support and friendship you've been kind enough to give me. I feel very lucky to have you in my book world!

**Model Johnny Kane** – Thank you for being such a great person to work with and a good sport about being 'a mafia guy.' You capture my characters as a whole, beautifully.

**Cover Designer Clarice Tan with CT Cover Creations** – Thank you for such a gorgeous cover design. I'm grateful for your friendship and kindness you've shown me. I have never worked with someone so professional and truly delightful. Sending you many hugs!

**Editor Mitzi Carroll** – Thank you tremendously! My books wouldn't be possible without your hard work, and I appreciate it tons. Once I receive the approved seal from you, I breathe easier.

**My Formatter Max Henry** – Thank you for making my work look beautiful again and again. I couldn't imagine my paperbacks not having your touch on them!

**My gorgeous PA Abbey Neil-Clark** – I would be lost without you and I look forward to the day I can finally hug you in person!

**Sapphire's Naughty Princesses** – Thank you ladies for everything you do to help promote my work and for all of your support and encouragement.

**My blogger friends** –YOU ARE AMAZING! I LOVE YOU!

**My readers** – Thank you tons for making this possible. I'm so grateful for your continued love and support you give me with each new book! Hopefully, I'll get to meet many of you soon.

# STAY UP TO DATE WITH
## Sapphire

### EMAIL
authorsapphireknight@yahoo.com

### WEBSITE
www.authorsapphireknight.com

### FACEBOOK
www.facebook.com/AuthorSapphireKnight

Printed in Great Britain
by Amazon